Mike Malaghan has authored a story for the ages. As a Nisei, I didn't witness the horror stories of the immigrants from Japan to Hawaii, but my Issei parents had to overcome many similar situations after immigrating in the early 1900s. *Picture Bride* is a remarkable story of immigrants' courage and perseverance, creating a future for their children in their adopted land, the United States of America.

LAWSON IICHIRO SAKAI
BRONZE STAR VETERAN, 442ND REGIMENT

I am impressed with Mike Malaghan's attention to historical detail. Seeing my mom's life with the Shivers family recreated in this story made it all the more special.

MAE ISONAGA
DAUGHTER OF SUE ISONAGA (ADOPTED DAUGHTER OF ROBERT L. SHIVERS)

Picture Bride is an authentic novel of the Japanese immigrant experience in Hawaii.

TED TSUKIYAMA
MILITARY INTELLIGENCE SERVICE (MIS) VETERAN
AND 442ND-MIS HISTORIAN

Mike Malaghan takes readers through a time-tunnel via the eyes of Haru, a picture bride from a poverty-stricken village in Japan, bound for Hawaii. *Picture Bride* is not only an adventure-filled story, but a great Hawaii history book.

HIROKO FALKENSTEIN
AUTHOR OF *WAR IS NOT COOL AT ALL, FOOLS!*

Picture Bride

A NOVEL

Picture Bride

A NOVEL

Mike Malaghan

LEGACY ISLE
PUBLISHING

Cover Photos:
Picture bride portrait courtesy of Lester Kaneta
West Maui Mountains with rainbow © David Olsen / Alamy
Aloha Tower © Andrew Zarivny / Shutterstock
Bon Sho (Sacred Bell) © Leigh Anne Meeks / Shutterstock

ISBN 978-1-935690-80-1
Library of Congress Control Number: 2016940286

Production Coordination: Book Publishers Network
Editor: Julie Scandora
Cover Designer: Laura Zugzda
Interior Designer: Melissa Vail Coffman

Legacy Isle Publishing
1000 Bishop St., Suite 806
Honolulu, Hawai'i 96813
www.legacyislepublishing.net
info@legacyislepublishing.net

10 9 8 7 6 5 4 3 2 1

Printed in the United States of America

*Dedicated to the mothers of the twenty-one
Japanese-American Medal of Honor recipients
and all the twenty thousand Nisei soldiers
who served their country in World War II*

❧ Acknowledgments ❧

So many people to thank. Noted historical novelist Bill Martin leads the list. Attending his address at the Maui Writers Conference, I realized my next attempt at writing a novel would have to be a historical one, given my reading habits. An after-the-speech conversation with Bill eventually led him to helping me bring *Picture Bride* to term. As he critiqued my early "tell instead of show" efforts, he often began, "If you want approbation, ask your family for a review. If you want to learn how to write … ?" Then his bold red notes mandated cuts, consolidations, commands to keep to the theme, etc.

A special thanks to Mariko Miho who, when I met and told her of my book project, gushed, "You must meet my father." Kats Miho, a spotter for the 522nd artillery during WWII, became my surrogate father. At our weekly lunches, Kats reminisced about not only his fighting days but also growing up in Maui and attending the University of Hawaii prior to Pearl Harbor. Mariko opened so many doors to me. I lunched with Sue Isonaga who shared her prewar days living with the FBI director and his wife as an au pair. Kats and Sue have passed on but continue to live in *Picture Bride* as Kenta and Sachiko. My appreciation to 442nd historian Ted Tsukiyama who pointed me in the research direction early in the project.

A super thank you to Lester Kaneta who gave me permission to use the wedding picture of his mother for the cover of *Picture Bride*.

I drove my Japanese wife crazy interrupting her days with incessant questions about Japanese culture. Mary Ann Berry who grew up in the Hawaiian-Japanese culture helped me use words from both languages correctly. She was merciless in catching grammar and word usage errors.

Four professional editors helped clarify, trim, and alter *Picture Bride*'s early drafts. A new novelist needs all the help one can muster. Without editors Vicki McCown, John Nelson, Julie Scandora, and Dawn Sakamoto, *Picture Bride* would be a thousand pages of rambling, disjointed scenes. Novelists are lucky if special readers of the almost-finished product will read and deliver feedback. Thus, my thanks go to Hiroko Falkenstein and Shelby Kariya who caught many cultural and grammatical errors.

A special thanks to long-passed Fred Makino who inaugurated the *Hochi*. Not only does its English language newspaper still enjoy a wide readership, but also its editor, Karleen Chinen, has been serializing *Picture Bride*.

Despite all this help, no doubt mistakes remain. The author takes full responsibility for such errors and welcomes reader corrections for future editions. You can email me at mgm@malaghan.net.

⊙ CONTENTS ⊙

PART I

FLIGHT

◌ CHAPTER 1 ◌

Amakusa Island, Kyushu, Japan – October 1904

THE YOUNG GIRL TEETERED ATOP THE GRASSY CLIFF towering over the rapid currents ripping through the Nagashima Straits. Directly across from her, Mount Unzen smoldered, a fiery god beckoning. Nickel-plated clouds waltzed low in the sky. Damp winds made her shiver, or maybe it was fear. The girl rocked back and forth on the rain-drenched edge.

Ash-black mud oozed through her *zoris*, sandals she had woven from rice straw. Drizzle dripped from her *minogasa*, a broad, cone-shaped hat, plaited from the same material. A tabby-furred cat nuzzled her ankles.

She stared down at the white-capped waves. Haru closed her eyes. *Better this*, she thought, *than a life as a* karayuki *in Borneo*. Her name meant "spring," but she called herself "*Uso*-Haru"—false spring. She thought back to yesterday when she discovered the true meaning of karayuki and her parents' deception. She had been walking along the dirt path that ran parallel to the trickling Machiyamaguchi Kawa.

"*Yaaaack-eee eee-mo!*" The sweet potato vendor's falsetto voice banked off the homes lining the river. He pushed his wooden-wheeled oven to the middle of the weathered Gion granite bridge. The wind blew the lush aroma toward Haru. She felt lightheaded. *If only I had ten sen*, she silently lamented, *just one tenth of a yen, I could …*

"Haru-*chan*!"

Over the bridge, Haru spied a woman clad in a green silk kimono wiggling a turquoise parasol painted with yellow chrysanthemums.

Behind her stood the village's only two-story building, the redbrick Gion Jinja, or Shinto shrine.

Haru knew Natsu, the karayuki recently returned from Sandakan, the British lumber port in northern Borneo. Natsu's getas clack-clacked to the *yakiimo* vendor where she plucked a coin from her blue drawstring purse and exchanged it for two sweet potatoes wrapped in newspaper. Natsu waved the sweet potatoes in Haru's direction.

Haru hurried to the bridge's midpoint.

Natsu held out a sweet potato. "Here."

At first bite, Haru's saliva flooded her cottony mouth. She bowed toward the hilltop Buddhist temple dedicated to Odaishi-sama, the legendary eighth-century monk who had devoted his life to working among the poor.

"Yes, Haru-chan, give thanks to Odaishi-sama and pray that your saint tells you to accept my advice. I saw you talking to your father."

"Yes, it's time I joined you."

Craning her neck so her face nearly touched Haru's, Natsu hissed, "No, child, it's time you ran away."

Haru stepped back, shaken, her eyes transfixed on Natsu's. Whatever those eyes had seen had robbed Natsu of her soul.

"I was only nine when my parents sold me as a … " she spat out the word, "maid. In Sandakan, I washed linen in a brothel from the moment I awoke until I fell asleep, more exhausted than your child's mind can imagine. When I became a woman and knew my true kara-yuki time had arrived, I ran away. But they caught me." Natsu's bitter eyes bored into Haru's. "I can still taste the blood, feel the bruises."

Haru's potato lost its sweetness.

"With your beauty, you are not going to Sandakan to clean rooms; you will spread your legs so men will shove their spear between them within days after your first bleeding."

Haru blushed, averted her eyes.

"Oh, child. Already?"

"Last week," she whispered.

"When ships are in port, men will stand at your door waiting their turn. You will wash yourself with antiseptic so strong you burn your private parts, never knowing when you might catch the itching disease."

Haru stood speechless, her face desolate. She grabbed the stone railing.

"Yes, go to Sandakan. On the first day, Mori will march you to the Japanese consulate where a leering official will register you as a prostitute."

"It would have been better if my parents had practiced *mabiki*," said Haru. Though the word once meant the thinning of rice stalks, it now referred to the practice of parents leaving a newborn child on the side of the mountain.

Two blocks away, a heartbroken woman had stopped pedaling her Singer sewing machine as she watched the scene from her window. Fumiyo Osawa, the wife of the Buddhist temple priest, could not hear the exchange between the innocent girl and the karayuki. But she knew. If only she could save one, she told herself.

Until recently, Haru had attended Fumiyo's reading and writing classes for a nominal fee of five yen a month, a fraction of the grammar school tuition her parents could not afford. When Haru's army brother tasted Hiroshima's port vices, the money he had sent home stopped, and so did Haru's schooling.

Fumiyo wanted to allow her brightest student to continue, but her husband forbade it.

"The lessons are tolerated only because the government no longer subsidizes Buddhist priests' salaries," he told her. "Giving girls free lessons would be viewed as currying favor for our temple. With the rise of Shintoism, it is best to avoid the attention of the authorities."

Fumiyo watched a slump-shouldered Haru walk from the bridge. Assuming Haru was going home, she returned to her sewing and missed Haru's turn at the goat trail.

∞ Chapter 2 ∞

STILL STARING DOWN AT THE ROILING ABYSS, Haru swiveled her head right for a last look at a thatched-roofed hovel near the water's edge. Her home since birth. She caught some movement there. A man wearing a Western jacket walked into her home as if it were his own. She envisioned Mori paying the procurement money to her parents.

Haru flashed back to three days ago. Her mother, preparing her for Mori's visit to negotiate her contract price, had piled her hair high and then applied beeswax to add sheen and hold the strands in place. Inspecting the process, her father glowed, "You are special. A maid's job is easier work than your sisters' spinning Niigata's silk looms."

She stopped her rocking. Her hopeless plight was her parents' hope. They had raised her, fed her. What would happen to them without the payment for selling her? She had *giri*, an obligation.

Haru stepped backwards, picked up her meowing cat, and scratched under its chin. Once feral, the animal had adopted Haru after she had left out scraps for many months. Now Susano curled up to Haru nightly. Occasionally, the proud cat would present Haru with a kill. The mice were discarded, the birds a welcome addition to the family pot.

Haru plodded down the goat path to her home and fate. When Susano squirmed out of Haru's arms, she took off her minogasa, flipped the straw hat upside down, and gathered wet twigs. She wouldn't be there to spread the sprigs to dry, but her mother would.

Upon reaching level ground with her hat full of brushwood, Haru turned left and followed the river home. She thought of her father's tales of Amakusa's golden age and its subsequent fall.

∽ ∾

"Haru-chan," her father said, "you wouldn't believe all the Portuguese ships bringing silk and spices from Macau in exchange for Kyushu's bone china. Shortly after, the great Lord Nobunaga became shogun, ending the civil wars. And who do you think helped him?"

"Soldiers and rifles from Amakusa," Haru answered by rote.

"When the second shogun died," her father continued, "a great battle took place between those favoring the family of the second shogun and those loyal to his best general, Tokugawa Ieyasu."

"Sekigahara," said Haru, knowing the battle in 1600 settled the fate of Japan for the next two and half centuries. "Then the bad days began. We backed the losing side."

"Yes. Taxes were unbearable. When grumbling peasants whined about how the unpredictable weather and poor soil left them with no rice bags to pay the exorbitant tariffs, the tax collector showed no sympathy. 'Sell whatever assets you have,' he would say, 'but pay your taxes.'"

Haru asked, "Why didn't our islanders become fishermen to pay the taxes?"

"Few fish come close to shore. If we go to where the fish are, the tides and currents are dangerous. You are never sure of coming back."

Haru's father skipped telling her that brothel procurers followed the tax collectors, ready to pay cash for daughters. Nor did he understand why the peasants' hopes for reduced taxes were not realized when the 1868 Meiji Restoration replaced the Tokugawa shogunate with the emperor as effective head of state. The high taxes, now to be paid in cash instead of rice, not only funded military modernization but had the added benefit of forcing peasants off their postage-stamp-sized farms into factories. Parents discovered a new option for the centuries-old practice of selling their daughters into the pillow trade.

Their daughters could become a karayuki-san, originally meaning "going to China" because the first women leaving Japan went there. Twelve-year-old Haru knew the word but not the consequences. By her time, karayuki-san meant a Japanese prostitute from Shimabara and Amakusa who filled the brothels of Sandakan, Singapore, Penang, and Manila.

☜ ☞

Haru's assumption that Mori had paid her contract money was confirmed even before she entered her dirt-floor home. Nearing the entrance, she smelled the aromas of Nagasaki *chanpon*—deep-fried noodles topped with a thick vegetable sauce. Upon entering, her mother offered Haru green tea made from fresh leaves instead of market leftovers. Her father smiled while drawing on a pungent, cheap Sunrise Tengu cigarette—with a filter yet—and not the usual discarded butts he scrounged.

"This month, the emperor has a new tax," he complained, waving his cigarette. "The shopkeeper said it is only a temporary tax to pay for the war with Russia. We both laughed." Still smiling, he said, "Tonight the emperor's most trusted advisor is giving a speech at the shrine. It will be a wonderful memory for your last night in Amakusa … for a few years, that is."

⤷ CHAPTER 3 ⤶

FROM ALL OVER AMAKUSA, they came and jammed the Gion Jinja to hear octogenarian Fukuzawa Yukichi, the sage of modernization and founder of Keio University, speak. Landowners and tradesmen sat cross-legged in Western suits, the new fashion promoted by the emperor's edict. Their wives, wearing their best kimono, each brought a *zabuton*—a small cushion to protect their knees as they knelt, as was proper for women.

The awed Shinto priest finished reading his fawning introduction. "We are humbled to listen to Japan's greatest living scholar review his successful advocacy of Japan's leap to Asia's strongest nation and to be equal to the world's great powers."

Fukuzawa bowed deeply. He soon got to his favorite theme.

"Japan must continue to break ties with our so-called Asian brothers. As we have seen from our victories in China, Korea, and the new war with Russia, our success requires we align ourselves with the other colonial powers. We must treat Asia the same way Westerners do."

Most of what he was saying meant nothing to Haru. She looked at her father, enthralled at every word, and began daydreaming she would be saved from a karayuki life in Borneo. Instead, at the last minute, he would change his mind and send her to the looms of Niigata to join her sisters. Her attention snapped back when Fukuzawa pounded his cane and raised his voice.

"Japan has a grand destiny."

The next statement told Haru all she needed to know about Japan's new role in the world and reminded her that "hope" was a word not meant for the likes of her.

"Our 'rich nation, strong army' policy needs foreign money. Young men, you must leave for the plantations of Brazil, Hawaii, and Malaysia. Fathers, send your daughters to Siberia, Shanghai, and Sandakan. Young girls, the money you send feeds your family and builds your nation."

Any childish fantasy she harbored evaporated. How could her father resist paying off his debts with the body of his daughter when told it was his patriotic duty? She dropped her head.

Five minutes into their walk home, Haru's mother stopped suddenly. "My leg cramped. Go ahead," she told Haru in a tone demanding obedience.

After Haru moved down the path, her mother tugged her husband's *hapi* sleeve. "Come," she said. She stepped toward the river to let the homeward-bound crowd pass. She squared herself in front of her wary-faced husband. "I cannot bear to send Haru to Sandakan."

Her husband sucked air through his gapped teeth. Angry and shamed, he kept his eyes down.

"Our niece, Fuyu, stopped sending letters and money to my sister three months ago. You know what that means."

"It can mean anything, *Okasan*. She is just busy." Even as he said the words, they sounded false to him. Selling his daughter to pay his gambling debts tore at his soul more than his wife knew. He had rationalized such bondage was an ancient Amakusan custom.

A furtive glance by his wife revealed no one was watching. She stomped her foot and edged a half step closer. She felt his quickened breath on her forehead. "You stone head! For three years, Fuyu never failed to have the scribe send a weekly letter home. The next letter won't be *from* her. It will be *about* her."

"It's too late, Okasan," said Haru's father, anger rising in his voice. "You know I already used the money to pay back the money lender."

"And then what?" She spit on the ground. "In a year, we will be in debt again with no more daughters to sell."

Withered by her gaze, he stepped back closer to the river. He heard the water tumble over the rocks. "You think I take pleasure in selling my last daughter? Do you think I don't worry about living the rest of our lives with empty stomachs?"

"Then listen!"

He did. His wife was right. After Haru left, what future would they have? He looked into the desperate eyes of the loyal woman who had stuck by him throughout his blemished life.

"Let's visit the temple."

∞ CHAPTER 4 ∞

AT HER HOME'S ENTRANCE, Haru watched the flickering of the village's oil lamps die into blackness. Where were her parents? She was about to return to town when she saw them striding down the path with a purpose she had seldom seen. But what really caught her attention was the woman walking beside her parents, Fumiyo Osawa.

When Haru heard what the three adults had to say, she stared uncomprehendingly. "Can this really happen?"

"I will give the contract man his money back when he comes for you in the morning," her father said with a feigned assurance.

"But the contract man will want Haru, not the money back," said Fumiyo firmly to forestall any thought Haru might harbor that somehow she could still stay.

Haru broke into tears.

"There is no time for crying, Haru-chan," said Fumiyo sternly. "We must make it to port before dawn."

Haru took but a few minutes to wrap all she owned in a scarf. She bowed to her parents and followed Fumiyo out the open door. At the bend in the river, she turned around. The crescent moon broke through the clouds, illuminating her parents bent by age and circumstance like sculptured tree trunks in an outdoor museum. She felt a tug on her elbow.

"We must hurry, child," said Fumiyo in an urgent whisper.

Haru and Fumiyo trekked throughout the night to reach the other side of Amakusa. Susano followed. The first cock crowed when an exhausted Fumiyo rapped on a heavy wooden door of a brick house fronted with a Japanese rock garden.

Although surprised by the predawn visit, the young man welcomed the weary hikers. Itagaki Shigenobu made tea and listened.

Fumiyo's nephew managed a coal mine for Mitsubishi. He shipped the coal to Hiroshima, the homeport of the Japanese navy since the Russian war began. One look at the frightened girl told him why the procurers coveted her. He abhorred the Amakusa tradition of selling their children.

He told Fumiyo, "My coaling ship has been loading all night for an early morning departure. I will see that Haru is on that ship."

Fumiyo gave Haru fifty yen and a letter of introduction to her sister, the wife of another Buddhist priest living in Hiroshima. "I must trek back now so I won't be missed." Fumiyo's pitted face glowed. She had saved one.

∞ CHAPTER 5 ∞

HARU'S PARENTS HAD MUCH TO DO. They scoured the few pots they owned. They beat their tattered futon in the moonlight and then rolled it neatly into the corner of their hut. They bathed in the river together. Haru's mother stooped to whisk the dirt floor while her father fidgeted outside. They left the door open for the contract man to enter at sunrise.

As they hurried under the shifting moonlight, they reminisced— the relentless taxes, the poor soil, the typhoons that brought too much rain at the wrong time.

Haru's father apologized for his gambling.

His wife gave him a gift. "Do you remember the night you came home with five hundred yen? A fortune. You took me to the hot springs. The only time we slept outside our home—if you don't count the typhoons when we stayed in the temple." She didn't remind her husband he had promised to buy cement to make a real floor but lost his brief stake the next sake-drenched evening.

"That's the night we made Haru," the husband said, allowing a rare smile.

Then they did something they had never done in their thirty-three-year marriage. They held hands. They recalled their other daughters' last visit during the August Obon festival. They shared worries over their misguided son.

"Do you think Haru has reached the port?" her mother asked.

While the father did not know, he returned his wife's gift. "I am certain of it. Did you not listen to Osawa-san? By this time tomorrow, Haru will be arriving in Hiroshima. Think of it … our daughter living in a big temple in Hiroshima. Going to school."

"We did the right thing," Haru's mother said, uncertainty tinge-ing her voice.

Her husband squeezed her hand. "*Arigato*, Okasan."

"Thank you?"

"Yes, Okasan, for giving me a last chance to be a good father."

They walked silently to the edge of the cliff. The wind lulled. Tiny white caps winked five hundred feet below them. Above, the clouds had cleared. The sky sparkled. They sat down back to back. Haru's mother reached behind her and intertwined her hair to her husband's.

"It is done, *Otosan*."

They wiggled up. Once standing, they reached behind to clutch the other's hands and sidestepped to the edge.

They did not flinch.

∞ CHAPTER 6 ∞

SHIGENOBU AND HARU STOOD AT THE DOOR, watching Fumiyo disappear into the predawn glow. Shigenobu's stomach tightened. What a muddle his aunt had dumped on him. A dangerous one at that. Sure, he hated the Amakusan trade, but it wasn't his job to stop it. What would happen to him if the gangsters learned he helped this girl escape? He imagined a beating and then scrambling for money to pay back Haru's contract with interest. And his career. If Mitsubishi—

Clop. Clop. Clop.

Shigenobu and Haru turned toward the approaching hoofs.

"There's my carriage. Let's go!" snapped Shigenobu. "We must board the ship before anyone sees you."

As he closed the door with one hand, Shigenobu snatched a cap and his leather jacket off a peg with the other. He hustled down the walk, tugging Haru behind him. Shigenobu tapped his driver on the shoulder. "Straight to the wharf."

He gave Haru a rough boost into the carriage and climbed in after her. He picked up a thin wool blanket from the carriage seat. "Wrap this around you." He shrugged into his jacket and then thrust the cap at her. "Put this on and pull it down … no, like this," he said, jerking the cap's bill over her eyebrows. "No one must know you are a woman." By the time they had reached the corner, Haru's heavy lids had closed, and she slumped against the man's hunched shoulder.

Shigenobu folded his arms tight against his chest and peered out the carriage window, relieved the morning mist blotted out the hints of dawn. He thought of how he would have to grovel at the feet of his coal bunker's captain as he half ordered, half begged him to stow away Haru. He then recalled how the Imperial Japanese Navy's torpedoing of Russian battleships at Port Arthur the previous February had put him into this predicament. If not for the war, he would not be in Amakusa. He remembered how he had yelled a triumphant "Banzai!" when the surprise attack caught the tsar's unsuspecting ships napping. A day later, Japan declared war. The navy's appetite for Amakusa's coal had exploded. Of course, if not for the war, he would not be a chief engineer.

Red lanterns hung along the pier, their oil-wicked halos outlining the shadows of men disconnecting wide chutes from empty railcar hoppers attached to the ship's side. Other darkened shadows scurried to shovel spilled lumps of coal back into the chutes. At the end of the pier, Shigenobu dropped from his carriage and raced up the ship's gangplank two steps at a time. On deck, he lifted his eyes and spied the captain behind the bridge's glass window. He climbed the steel steps and entered the warm cabin.

The captain listened to Shigenobu's hurried plea with studied concern. He squinted his eyes. "How will I get a girl on and off the boat without the company knowing?" The captain sucked a stream of air through his teeth like a rickshaw driver who had been asked to take a courtesan up a steep hill on a rainy night. "A crew member might report me."

Shigenobu recognized the shakedown. Cargo ships often took on passengers. No one complained as long as the coal arrived on time. But this was different. He had asked the captain to hide Haru. Last month, he had self-righteously turned aside his captain's hints to take advantage of a thriving black market by under-reporting the amount of coal loaded on the ships. Shigenobu was trapped. He had to get rid of the girl.

"As it happens, Captain, coal production has exceeded quota. I am worried the company will expect too much in the future. We could deliver three railcars off the books."

The captain's smile exposed crooked teeth stained a blackish red from a lifetime of chewing betel nut. He spit a stream of juice to the side. Several drops splattered on Shigenobu's shoes. The captain offered a *gomennasai* apology so perfunctory as to be insulting. His breath reeked of *shochu*, a Kyushu alcohol made from sweet potato.

"Bring up the girl. I will put her in a supply room near my cabin."

Below, Haru sat motionless, willing herself invisible while keeping a furtive eye on the bridge. It looked as if the captain and Shigenobu were arguing. Would she be able to board? The creeping dawn switched her imagination to images of her home. Mori would be arriving now. Did her father really have all the money to give back? She thought of the cigarettes, the fresh tea, and the sweet chanpon.

Shigenobu took a white handkerchief from his pocket. The signal. Clutching the small swath of cloth that held her life's possessions, Haru alighted. Her knees wobbled as she walked up the gangplank. At the top rung, Shigenobu took her empty hand. He led her to the bridge. The sight of the short, stocky man dressed in a black uniform and a naval cap, his face unshaven and stern, didn't reassure her.

"This is the captain."

Haru bowed low, her knees still trembling.

"He will take you to Hiroshima." Shigenobu turned and retreated out the door.

"Follow me," said the captain. His putrid breath enveloped her. She backed away and bowed low, unable to still her shaking knees. Haru would be forever reminded of his breath whenever she used an ill-kept public toilet. Her pleading eyes softened the captain's voice.

"You will have a small room to yourself. Someone will bring you food and change your slop bucket twice a day." The captain gave her a set of work clothes. "You can walk on the deck after dark. If anyone is about, he will think you are a boy. Don't talk to anyone."

∞ ∞

Haru vomited her way through her first day at sea, unprepared for the twenty-foot swells as the ship pitched its way north past Nagasaki. She clenched her fists at each deep tilt, frightened that the ship would fail to right itself and would sink. She envisioned water pouring into the corridor.

She thanked Buddha the second day when the ship turned east and passed Fukuoka into the calmer Shimonoseki Straits. Haru was able to keep down the rice and bits of fish. That night she cried. As bad as her life had been, she had slept every night protected by her parents. What if Fumiyo's sister refused to take her in and sent her away? Where could she go?

Feeling better the second night, Haru paced along the railing. A troop transport ship passed. Brown-uniformed soldiers strolled on the decks. Some waved at her. Pulling her cap down, she waved back. She wondered if her brother might be on the ship. A battleship passed with gun turrets so big that men could sleep in them. This was, Haru thought, the Japan that Fukuzawa Yukichi had boasted of, what the karayuki-san were paying for.

∞ CHAPTER 7 ∞

ROLLING SEAS WOKE HER CLOSE TO DAWN on the third day. She guessed they had left the straits. Hiroshima must be close. She rushed to the deck. Lights radiated from grey warships at anchor. Loaded barges lumbered to and fro. Tugboats blew horns demanding the right of way. The stench of garbage and oily smoke brought up bile from Haru's empty stomach. At the sound of heavy steps behind her, she turned. With relief, she recognized the captain.

"I have arranged for a tender to take you to shore."

The first pink of dawn glowed behind Haru as the tender weaved toward a pier pronged with bustling jetties. The sights amazed her. Smartly painted schooners covered in dripping nets jammed wharfs. Spidery-legged men pushed tubs of fish to the auction house. Fishmongers lugging carts traipsed down piers to ply the morning catch along their neighborhood routes of waiting housewives.

Drawing near the pier, Haru reviewed Fumiyo's note. "Go to a public bath and clean yourself. When you meet my sister, say, 'I am happy to do any work to make your life easier.'"

"How will I find her house?" Haru had asked.

"The Fudoin Temple is well-known," Fumiyo had said. "It's an hour walk along the Ota River to the township of Ushita. Anyone can point you in the right direction."

The grumpy tender operator tied his boat, jumped off, and held out his hand to Haru, who grabbed and hopped onto the wet pier. Bewildered by the unfamiliar commotion, she meandered into the adjacent farmers' market, dripping in swaying lightbulbs. Cone-hatted farmers carried cabbage, eggplant, and tomatoes in baskets balanced on poles strung across their shoulders. Headbanded day laborers pushed rickety handcarts jammed with potatoes, oranges, and daikon. Civilian buyers made way for uniformed men at vendor stalls. The navy buyers demanded the cheapest prices for the emperor's ships. Haru bumped her way through the market in a daze, afraid to stop and ask anyone where she could find a public bath.

The spicy smells from sidewalk canteens reminded Haru she needed to eat. Looking for a vendor with an empty stool and a kind face, she spied an old *obasan*, squatting while stirring a steaming vat of fish.

Sensing this child was out of her element, the obasan said, "Twenty sen, child. Sit down." The stooped woman handed Haru a bowl of rice topped with hot chunks of fried fish.

"Obasan, where is a bathhouse?"

The woman pointed. "Walk down this road until you reach Yokuji Temple. Plenty of bathhouses nearby and no sailors or soldiers."

Minutes later, a revived Haru sauntered toward the temple. She passed teenagers dressed in neat uniforms, laughing and holding books and bento boxes. Almost half of them were girls! Haru spied a bathhouse down a street so narrow that two donkey carts could not pass each other. She gave the wizened proprietor one of her precious one-yen coins. She waited, not knowing if she would have to pay more or receive change. The man's shaky hands fumbled until he found a fifty-sen coin and slapped it on the counter.

"Do you need a towel?"

When Haru nodded yes, the man took back the coin, reached beneath the counter, and placed a small white towel on top. She picked it up and entered the changing room through the hanging curtain marked "women." The damp sulfur smells seeping in from the bath area reminded her of Mount Unzen's volcanic odors. She placed her clothes in a wicker handbasket on the bottom shelf. Holding the tiny towel over her pubic patch, she drew back the shoji door and entered the steaming bath area.

The middle-aged bathers gave Haru a cursory glance without interrupting a noisy debate on the rising price of rice. Spotting stubby stools along the wall, she sat down and, taking a caramel-colored bar of soap from the ledge, lathered and scrubbed her body with the towel. She filled a shallow wooden bucket with water, hoisted it over her shoulders, and let the water cascade over her soapy body. Upon stepping into the green concrete bath, she squatted until steaming water met her chin. How wonderful, she thought, as the thermal sensation soothed her body.

She eavesdropped on the circle of women complaining about their husbands, a new sake tax to support the war, and the influx of women from the "floating world" to service sailors. The oldest carped about the ungratefulness of her children. So enthralled with the entertainment offered by these city women, Haru let time and worry slip away in the steamy bath.

A bell rang. Haru's face registered a question mark. One of the bathers noticed.

"It's time to leave. Each day the bath is drained and cleaned at eleven."

Haru climbed out. While she squeezed the water from her towel and dried herself with the damp cloth, she asked for directions to the Fudoin Temple.

"Oh, the Fudoin Temple," said the woman who had earlier complained about her children. "The home of our treasured *kondo*, our great golden hall. Five hundred years old, but so well kept, even after the government stopped the temple funding. And still with a Shinto shrine inside—" She stopped abruptly as if she had spoken amiss. Regaining her composure, she gave directions.

Refreshed and once again clothed, Haru hurried along the narrow, well-swept cobblestone streets. She envied the flat-terraced rice fields hugging the riverbanks, so different from Amakusa's mountainous terraces. Far in the distance, an arched roof breeched the sky. Haru strutted faster. The distant structure morphed into a three-story temple. As she neared, tall, whitewashed stone walls, enveloping the castle-sized structure and grounds, materialized. Her heart raced. In just moments, she would know her destiny. She stopped at the temple gatehouse tower. Granite gargoyles leaned over layers of flared roofs. Their fierce gaze seemed to dare her to enter where she knew she did not belong. *Turn around and run. Go back to town. Go back to Amakusa.* She bit her lip. Images of Sandakan and her bowing parents watching her leave toughened her resolve.

∞ CHAPTER 8 ∞

HARU REACHED INTO THE FOLD OF HER *YUKATA*, clutched Fumiyo's letter, and stepped through the gate into the silence of the compound. Her wary eyes fluttered left and right. Weather-beaten stone stupas of the many Buddha manifestations and dollhouse-sized wooden shrines fronted with offerings of rice wrapped in seaweed and clay thimbles of sake shaped the pebble path. Copses of well-trimmed azalea bushes, squat bonsai trees, and deer-sized granite boulders enhanced the garden's tranquility, but not for a girl only moments away from hearing her fate.

Twisted white prayer papers flowered the drooping branches of a *sakaki* evergreen tree beside a small Shinto shrine set back in an alcove. Haru recalled what the woman from the bath had said.

Still, Haru was baffled since most Shinto shrines had long abandoned Buddhist temples.

Ignoring a baby-faced monk whisking leaves to corner piles, Haru took in the ancient temple, glorying in its broad timber the color of old leather. It looked every bit a religious testimony that had withstood five centuries of earthquakes and the devastating fires that often followed. This must be the golden hall, the kondo. Even in her distressed state, Haru felt a sense of calming awe.

A little to the right, recessed and separated by three rows of cherry trees, stood a two-story house. Haru presumed this must be her destination. She turned to the soft crunching sounds of zoris approaching her from behind and found a young man holding a whisk broom.

"Are you lost?" he asked.

Haru handed him Fumiyo's letter. He studied the addressee's name and bowed low. Haru jerked a quick bow. No one had ever bowed to her.

"Follow me," said the monk, who led Haru up wooden steps and across a wide porch to a shoji door whose stained paper panels showed signs of aging. The monk hoisted a brass mallet off a wooden peg and struck the side of a long tubular bell, creating a sharp musical clang whose reverberation lingered.

A short woman wearing a grey cotton kimono slid the door open. Her black hair, laced with grey strands, hung straight to her shoulders. Shallow wrinkles lined a narrow face. Her stern eyes softened when she spotted the waif in front of her. She smiled without opening her mouth. She took the letter from the monk and, after reading the first page, asked, "Are you Haru?"

"*Hai.*" Haru bowed low three times.

"I am Midori, Fumiyo's sister. Come in."

Haru shed her zoris. Her eyes widened as she glanced inside. Wood everywhere. Polished mahogany floors. On the room's far side, open shoji panels revealed a stout clay oven crowned with a rice pot. Moving her eyes left, she admired the series of closed shoji screens the color of wheat thistle. To her right, built-in cabinets filled an entire wall from floor to ceiling.

Haru's eyes set on the *irori*, the sunken, square, earthen hearth in the middle of the room. Overhead, an iron kettle hung from a pot-hook attached to an iron rod, encased in a hollow bamboo tube stopping an arm's length above simmering coals. Red cushions squared the hearth.

Haru savored the sweet air. Whereas she had spent most of her life breathing soot in her low-roofed home without a chimney, here a slit in the lofty thatched roof kept the air pleasant. *Oh, to live in a home like THIS!*

"Haru-san," said Midori, a little louder the second time to catch the enthralled girl. She gestured to the irori hearth. "Let's have some tea."

Haru padded across the floor and knelt down across from her hostess. By habit, she leaned over and added twigs, stacked on the side, to the fire.

Midori tried to calm the nervous girl with polite questions on Haru's passage while she poured tea and offered a small plate of rice crackers.

"The boat made me sick," admitted Haru and then devoured a cracker in a single bite.

Midori returned her gaze to the letter. Her eyes moistened. "Wait here." She rose and walked over to the shoji panel nearest the front of the house, pushed it aside, and disappeared.

Alone, Haru realized she had left her sad bundle at the front door. She tiptoed across the floor to retrieve it. The sounds of an argument floated from behind the closed shoji door as she neared the front door. Haru hung back at the sound of her name and then clutched her chest when she heard a harsh male voice.

"Yes, let her stay for a day or two. But even the Buddha did not adopt young girls."

"But she needs a home," Midori pleaded. "We have room. All our sons have left. Let her stay for a month and then decide."

The gruff voice answered, "Okasan, our temple supports an orphanage. Send her there."

Haru fought back a wave of nausea. She backpedaled to the smoldering hearth, resumed her crouched position on the cushion, and closed her eyes. She imagined holding Susano and listening to the

Machiyamaguchi River slipping into the sea. She did not hear the soft steps enter the room nor smell the gentle odors of fresh green tea.

"*Daijoubu desu*, child," a caressing voiced whispered. "Join my husband in his study."

Haru followed Midori into an adjoining room. A stern-faced, brown-robed priest sat behind a lacquered, short-legged table glistening in the early-afternoon sun streaking through open shutters. Haru bowed low, kneeled, and bowed again until the tip of her forehead touched the tatami mat. She sat back on her haunches and kept her eyes down. Haru tensed in the silence. From the corner of her eye, she watched the priest scan Fumiyo's letter. She sensed his deepening frown meant he wished the letter contained a better message on a second reading. He broke the silence with questions about her family, her schooling, and the details of her last day in Amakusa—gently to be sure, but Haru imagined this was how police interrogations worked.

When the questions ended, Haru looked at Midori. "I am thankful for your sister, who helped me escape, and your nephew Shigenobu-san, who surely risked his career protecting me and arranging passage to Hiroshima." She shuddered. "This would have been my first day in Sandakan."

"You can stay in my oldest son's room until we settle your final arrangements," said Kiyoshi.

Relieved nothing had been said about an orphanage, Haru asked, "Your oldest son?"

Rather than answer, Kiyoshi excused himself. Left alone with Midori, Haru relaxed.

"You must be hungry. Let's talk in the *daidokoro*," said Midori. "I have some udon soup. Hiroshima has the best noodles in Japan."

At the kitchen entrance, Haru fitted her feet into a pair of getas and stepped down onto the hard dirt floor, the *doma*. Haru's day of amazement continued as she examined the kitchen as big as her former home. Three side-by-side clay ovens, a wooden sink, and a large bucket of water fronted the back wall. On the left side, she spotted the only other wood item in the fire-resistant kitchen, the Mizuya *tansu*—the food and condiment chest featuring varied-sized compartments behind sliding panels. A half-empty rice bag leaned against the cabinet.

At the middle oven, Midori lifted the lid off a percolating iron pot filling the kitchen with rich, savory odors. Then she ladled a thick and steaming noodle soup into a generous-sized china bowl. "Take this to the irori," she coaxed.

A minute later, Midori grabbed a photo album from the living room cabinet and joined Haru at the hearth. She turned the heavy pages until she found a picture of an unsmiling soldier. "Our oldest son serves the emperor as a chaplain in Manchuria."

Haru wondered why no one, not even wedding brides, ever smiled in photographs. She slurped her soup to express her appreciation for the tasty lunch. "I have a brother whose last letter promised he was joining the army to serve in Manchuria."

Midori turned the page. "This is Kenji, our second son."

A handsome face, thought Haru, as she studied the full-length picture of a young man in a brown robe—standing next to a palm tree! She looked at Midori in surprise.

"Our second son is in Hawaii. The bishop wrote my otosan asking for a priest. Kenji volunteered. He has the spirit of adventure."

Haru's eyes dropped back to the picture. Straight back hair. Thick eyebrows, one slightly higher than the other. Wide-set eyes. The chin a little pointed. Almost a smile.

"Is it true the weather is always good?"

"Kenji writes that the tropical weather fables are true. Few typhoons or earthquakes," she added, referring to the bane of all Japanese.

Haru waited to hear more about this strange place called Hawaii. Instead, Midori said, "I had two daughters. Both died shortly after childbirth." Such a big house and no children to fill it, thought Haru. "Come," said Midori. "I will take you to your room." Haru marveled. A room used only for sleeping. Midori unfolded a futon. "Take a rest, child," she said and left.

Haru took off her yukata and lay on her futon. Restless, she replayed the welcome interview, searching for clues that might reveal her future. What little Haru knew about an orphanage frightened her. Bad food and not much of it. Mean house mistresses. Children her age rented to factories for twelve-hour workdays. She tried distracting herself from this speculation and lulled herself to sleep by replaying her father's favorite bedtime story of how Hideyoshi, a poor commoner, rose to become Japan's second shogun.

Hideyoshi had been a sewing-needle peddler when the first shogun, Nobunaga, invited him to join his retinue. The next morning, a chilly one at that, Hideyoshi spotted his lord's sandals outside his sleeping quarters. He picked them up and warmed them inside his yukata. When the shogun stepped outside, Hideyoshi ran to give him the sandals. Soon the shogun was assigning him dirty jobs no one else wanted. Eventually, the shogun gave him soldiers to command. When Nobunaga was killed, Hideyoshi caught the murderer and became the next shogun.

A thought struck Haru. What would Hideyoshi be doing in her circumstances? He would not be taking a nap!

⨍ CHAPTER 9 ⨍

HARU OVERCAME HER FATIGUE, rose from her futon, folded it, and shoved it into the cabinet. She bounded out of the bedroom and scurried to the kitchen.

It was empty.

Haru dropped fresh charcoal on the cooking fire and washed the vegetables on the wooden side counter. She hauled the almost empty water bucket outside, found the well, and pumped until water sloshed over the bucket's rim. Back in the house, she spotted a wicker basket of dirty clothes, carried it outside, and washed the laundry next to the well. She cleaned the kitchen as though it had always been her job.

At sunset, she returned to her room and fell into an exhausted sleep. When around midnight she was stirred by the need to relieve herself and stepped out from her room, she found a tray of rice, vegetables, and fish outside her door. She devoured the food and fell back to a more restful sleep.

Haru awoke early and prepared the morning rice and boiled the water for tea. A surprised Midori entered the kitchen. After the exchange of greetings, Haru spoke quickly, "I hope the rice is soft enough."

Midori lifted the lid from the rice cooker, dipped the wooden scoop into the steaming pot, and brought a taste to her lips. She smiled. "Perfect. Your mother trained you well, Haru. Is that miso soup I smell? Let me drop in a dash of *katsuobushi,* the dried tuna shavings my husband couldn't do without."

Midori glanced at the two tables Haru had set by the hearth. "Please bring a third table to the irori."

Haru could not hold a back a grateful smile.

Kiyoshi entered just then, noticed the three low tables, grunted an "*ohayo gozaimasu*" greeting, and sat down. Midori's efforts to start a morning conversation were acknowledged with gruff responses. As he rose from the irori, he gave a slight bow and by habit recited, "*Gochisosama deshita*," the traditional Japanese expression indicating one has finished eating. He glanced at his wife. "The rice was delicious this morning, a little softer."

Midori hesitated.

Kiyoshi stared. He expected his wife to acknowledge the rare compliment with a "thank you" or, more likely, "it is nothing."

"Honorable husband, Haru woke early and prepared the rice."

When Kiyoshi looked at Haru, she felt his stare pierce though her. She wished he had said nothing about the rice.

After an unbearable pause, he said, "Maybe you cooked it a little longer." Kiyoshi stiffened his back and marched from the room.

Haru gave a prayer of thanks to Odaishi-sama that nothing was said about an orphanage. Still, neither did they say she could stay. In a home decorated with Buddhist calligraphy, Haru decided to put her trust in him and her favorite saint.

"I will clean the kitchen, Obasan," she smiled to Midori.

"Haru," said Midori during breakfast on the seventh day since the girl's arrival, "we must enroll you in school."

Haru put her hand to her mouth, backed from the table, and bowed low three times. She could not hold back a few teardrops.

Kiyoshi looked away. Midori moved over to Haru and put her hand under the young girl's chin. "We appreciate your help, Haru-chan."

Haru broke into goose bumps when she heard Midori add "chan," the term of endearment, to her name.

∞ Chapter 10 ∞

BOOM! BOOM! BOOM!

The castle cannon woke Haru. *The expected battle between the Russian and Japanese fleet must have taken place, and we won,* thought Haru. It was May 28, 1905, a date she and all Japanese would etch in their memories.

The bell. We must ring our bell first, she thought. Not bothering to change out of her nightclothes, Haru dashed out of the house, ignored her sandals at the front door, and sprinted across the pebbled compound to the bell tower. She knew the Shinto government doubted the loyalty of the Buddhist priests, whom they accused of plotting to regain the influence they had under the Tokugawa shogunate.

Inside the bell tower, Haru grabbed the thick bell rope. A maze of pulleys, chains, and sprockets were connected and powered by the rope in her hands. She squeezed the cord, took a deep breath, held tight, and pulled, simultaneously bending her knees to draw down the ropes more with her legs than her arms. Her shoulder muscles strained as the mallet drew away from the two-ton bell. She let go. The rope shot out of her hands. She heard the rustle of the spinning sprockets as the mallet rushed to impact. Hiroshima's most distinctive temple bell reverberated with authority, answering the roar of the cannon.

In seconds, other bells followed, but all of Hiroshima heard the Fudoin's bell first.

Haru dashed back to the temple. Kiyoshi stood on the front porch. His broad shoulders framed his red robes. The morning sun glinted off his shaved head and the glasses that sat low on his flat nose. He smiled as Haru trotted up the stairs two at a time.

"You have brought great honor to our temple this morning, Haru-chan."

Haru beamed at the warm smile above her. It had been months since she had last suffered his scowls. Her desire to serve and her school progress had won over Kiyoshi. Midori had long ago begun treating her like a daughter, rather than a servant. Still, the days of hunger and the fear of Sandakan were never far from Haru's mind. A walk along the Hiroshima harbor reminded her of what might have been. Girls her age, with their lipsticked mouths, dark cotton kimono, and low-hanging *tenugui* scarves to hide their eyes and shame loitered in front of shabby establishments with blinking pink signs touting their services.

Kiyoshi pointed to the gate. "Get dressed and join the celebration. Bring back the news of our victory, Haru-chan."

In minutes, she joined the rear of a crowd of university students marching toward the harbor. She joined the chants, "Long live the emperor! Long live Admiral Togo! Banzai!"

At the wharf, Haru paid five sen for the one-page newspaper. Her command of *kanji* was a work in progress, but she could read enough to understand that every one of Russia's eight battleships had been sunk at the Battle of the Tsushima Straits.

She remembered Kiyoshi's charge: "Bring back the news of our victory, Haru-chan." Kiyoshi had used "chan" after her name. Haru eased her way to the outer ring of the crowd, turned around, and sprinted back home. She found Kiyoshi sipping green tea and reading an ancient Buddhist scroll in his library. She handed him the *Yomiuri Shimbun*'s one-page extra. Kiyoshi glanced up at her with a sadness Haru had never seen. She was surprised by the low tone of his voice.

"For the first time since Genghis Khan, the yellow race has defeated the white race."

Haru nodded. Despite being disturbed by the anxious face, she said, *"Ah so desuka."* Tomorrow at school, she would ask her teacher who Genghis Khan was. She looked into Kiyoshi's sad eyes. "You look so sad on such a glorious day, *Ojisan*."

"Come. Let's go to the irori. In all the excitement, we have not eaten."

As Haru and Kiyoshi entered the irori, they discovered Midori had already placed rice bowls, miso soup, and broiled fish on the small tables.

Kiyoshi sat down. When Haru joined them, he said, "If you remember … you had asked me if our oldest son serving as chaplain in Manchuria could find your brother." Kiyoshi took a white envelope from the inside of his yukata. The oblong block in the upper corner was black, the symbol of death.

Haru took in a sharp breath. "No!"

"Your brother died a hero's death at the Battle of the Yalu River. My son's letter arrived after you left for the harbor. Inside, there was a smaller envelope from your brother's commanding officer. It's addressed to you."

Haru put her hand to her mouth. "I hardly knew my brother. He left when I was so young."

"But if he survived the war and returned to Hiroshima, you would have had a family," said Midori.

"I would have had a brother, but my family is here."

Haru's reading of the exchanged glances between Midori and Kiyoshi suggested something more amiss.

Midori's eyes dropped to the unopened envelope addressed to Haru from her brother's commanding officer.

Haru studied the envelope. Her gut tightened. "This letter … why is it not addressed to my parents? Don't soldiers have to show their family registration card when entering the army?"

Kiyoshi cleared his throat again. "Haru, we should have told you sooner. Shortly after you arrived, I received a letter from Midori's sister. The bodies of your parents were found floating in the sea. A fishing boat had gone missing a few days before. The authorities believe your parents … perhaps borrowed the boat and had an accident."

Haru had never displayed anger in her patrons' home. Until now. "Obasan, I have gone to bed each night talking to my parents! I have been writing them letters. Now I know why they did not answer!"

"It is my fault," said Kiyoshi. "You had just escaped the brothel and been smuggled away from the only home you knew. We were worried what you would do if we told you your parents had died. You might have blamed yourself."

"It *is* my fault. My father feared—no, hated the sea. Only the greatest hunger would have driven them to try fishing. If I had gone to Sandakan, they would have had money to eat." Haru rose abruptly, threw the unopened letter on the floor, and fled to her room.

Midori got up to follow, but Kiyoshi said, "Give her time alone."

"Only a few minutes, Otosan," she said. "If we were worried about her killing herself before, we should be even more worried now. Suppose she finds out her parents did not go fishing?"

"Who would tell her? No one knows for sure. They were found floating. No one saw them enter the ocean."

Midori fidgeted, waiting as long as she could. "I'd better go to her room." As Midori rose, she heard the soft shuffle of footsteps drawing closer.

Haru entered the library and prostrated herself three times. "You gave me shelter when you have could have sent me away. The great Buddha's kindness shows through your actions. I apologize for my anger. You did what you thought was best."

With glistening eyes, Midori slid over to Haru, who leaned into her shoulder. Midori put an arm around her head and gave it a slight hug. "The great Buddha has sent us the daughter we never had."

Kiyoshi picked up the smaller white envelope from Haru's brother's commanding officer, opened it, scanned the few lines of beautifully written calligraphy, and then handed it to her. "Read the letter, Haru. The emperor has invited you to Tokyo."

∞ CHAPTER 11 ∞

ON THIS DRIZZLING JUNE MORNING IN 1905, Haru gazed in awe at Japan's largest Shinto entrance gate, Yasukuni Shrine's Daiichi Torii. Its thick, red columns, cradling an imposing crossbeam of similar color and size, soared into the charcoal heavens. This majestic icon of bushido Shintoism was but a ten-minute horse ride from Tokyo's Imperial Palace where the warrior deity resided.

In 1869, the Meiji emperor ordered the Yasukuni (Peaceful Nation) Shrine built to honor his soldiers who died in the Boshin War toppling the Tokugawa shogunate and restoring him to power the year earlier. Ten years later, the Office of State Shintoism (Shinto Kokkyo Shugi) decreed Yasukuni would be the national shrine immortalizing all the the souls who sacrificed their lives for the emperor.

The emperor's invitation allowed two family members of each martyr to enter. Kiyoshi insisted that Midori accompany Haru. Twenty-six thousand family members crowded the shrine's grounds honoring the latest thirteen thousand combatants of the eighty thousand men who would sacrifice their lives to expand the empire.

The *Yomiuri Shimbun's* headlines that day screamed, "Russia Sues for Peace." Admiral Togo's sinking of their Baltic fleet led to the tsar's acceptance of President Theodore Roosevelt's offer of mediation. Both countries were sending a diplomatic mission to Portsmouth, New Hampshire, to negotiate how much Siberian land the tsar would cede to the emperor and the likely transfer of Russia's Manchurian rights to Japan. With Russia "a spent force in Asia," *Yomiuri* editorials predicted Japan would have a free hand in Korea.

Although the price of admission was the death of a loved one, Haru soon picked up the celebratory mood of the crowd. A frenzied mourner, blessed with a booming voice, started reciting the Imperial Rescript on Education that every schoolchild had to memorize in the second grade from 1890 onwards. Haru joined in the growing chorus.

> Know ye, Our Subjects,
> Our Imperial ancestors have founded our Empire on a basis broad and everlasting … Our subjects ever united in loyalty and filial piety have from generations illustrated the beauty thereof. This is the glory of the fundamental character of Our Empire, and therein also lies the source of Our education. Ye, Our subject, be filial to your parents, affectionate to your brothers and sisters; as husbands and wives be harmonious, as friends true; bear yourselves in modesty and moderation; extend your benevolence to all; pursue learning and cultivate arts, and thereby develop intellectual faculties and perfect moral powers; furthermore, advance public good and promote common interests;

always respect the constitution and observe the laws, should emergency arise, offer yourselves courageously to the State; and thus guard and maintain the prosperity of Our Imperial Throne coequal with heaven and earth. So shall be not only ye Our good and faithful subject, but render illustrious the best traditions of your forefathers.

The way here set forth is indeed the teaching bequeathed by Our Imperial Ancestors, to be observed alike by the Their Descendants and the subjects, infallible for all ages and true in all places. It is Our wish to lay it to heart in all reverence, in common with you, Our subjects, that we may all attain the same virtue.

When five minutes later the recitation came to close, a woman wearing a green silk kimono adorned with cherry blossoms shouted, "I have given one son to our emperor; I have two more to give."

A wall of murmurs rose from outside the shrine and grew into a deafening cadence of "Banzai! Banzai! Banzai!" The crowd pulsed with energy. Haru's faced glowed with rapture.

The emperor rode straight in the saddle astride a white horse. The deep furrows, wide penetrating eyes, and unsmiling lips revealed the driving character that had transformed a feudal nation into a world power. His long face, framed by a black beard flecked with grey, reassured worshipers of his godly status. His nose had turned red and his girth had widened by his fifty-third year. A deep-midnight-blue, German-style admiral's waist jacket, crossed by a silver-trimmed red sash, dazzled the eye with its medallions. His stone-white trousers reached into gleaming, black boots. His stallion high-stepped at a practiced parade gait.

As one, the crowd bowed low at the waist and were careful to avoid eye contact. Generals and admirals followed on horseback. Hundreds of priests walked on the edges of the pathway, keeping the crowd at bay. The throng fell silent. Some fainted.

Haru mourned for the brother she hardly knew, one who had brought much grief to her parents. But she also realized the way of the gods is mysterious. Her brother had died a glorious death serving the emperor. She prayed that someday she would produce sons for the emperor.

∞ ∞

The family had agreed to meet after the Yasukuni ceremony at the Zojoji Temple. Haru and Midori walked the hour journey under clearing skies to Shiba's ancient Buddhist temple, once the favorite of the Tokugawa family. At the entrance, Haru spotted Kiyoshi sitting under an oak tree and waved. He picked up a bento box and wiggled it.

"Our temple is more beautiful," said Haru as she took the lunch box from Kiyoshi.

Kiyoshi smiled. He rested his chopsticks on the bento box. "When Zojoji Temple was the Tokugawa family's favorite, pilgrims came from all Japan to honor the Buddha."

"We don't like Tokugawa in Amakusa," said Haru.

Kiyoshi laughed. "The shogunate was never popular in Hiroshima either. We welcomed the emperor's restoration. Our Dai Fudoin bet on the wrong side of the Battle of Sekigahara, and for ten generations the shogun's bakufu bureaucrats never let us forget it."

"Our teachers have told us that Shinto is the way of the gods," Haru said, her voice registering a hint of skepticism. She missed the nervous look her adopted parents exchanged.

"The Meiji emperor has made Japan a glorious country," said Kiyoshi. "He encourages Buddhism. Anyone can donate money to the temple without restriction."

Haru heard the words, thinking they were telling her something she did not understand. Having saved the pickled cherry in her box lunch, she now put it in her mouth and sucked on it, savoring its tart juices. She spit out the pit from her puckered cheeks.

"Ojisan, how did our emperor become a god?"

The blood drained from Kiyoshi's face that morphed from fatherly affection to fear.

⋒ CHAPTER 12 ⋒

K O WAS HARU'S BEST FRIEND until the day she wasn't.
Haru met Ko in early April 1909, the first day of her senior
year. Walking past a group of girls looking smart in their new striped
beige-on-brown cotton kimono uniforms, Haru, as usual, ignored the
"gang of three" clique but stopped upon overhearing them mimicking
someone's Shimabara dialect, an accent very similar to Amakusan.
The three taunters had corralled a tall, dark-complexioned new student. Haru remembered how, four years earlier, the other students
had laughed at her country dialect, and now she charged into the
mean circle, ignored the tormenters, and beamed at the newcomer as
if greeting a long-lost relative.

"Good morning! I thought I heard a friendly accent. I'm Haru," she
said in the Amakusan dialect. The clique retreated. The newcomer smiled.

Haru claimed Ko as another wounded bird to care for. When she
felt the pain of lesser creatures, she took action. She repaired the wings
of sparrows, could not resist saving abandoned puppies, and fed stray
cats until she found them a proper home—unless the cat wore tabby
fur. In that case, Haru named it Susano and adopted the feline.

Unlike Haru, Ko made little effort to lose her country accent.
Teachers took exception to Ko's lackadaisical approach to learning the Hiroshima dialect and ignored the hazing. Free to continue,
the meanest of her tormentors added a new pejorative—*ainoko-san*,
or crossbreed—mocking Ko for her dark-copper complexion. Ko
smothered her rage and never complained to her teachers. Like her
favorite animal, the fox, she used stealth to strike back. Homework
assignments disappeared from lockers; coins were pilfered from en-
abling teachers' handbags; a nail would find its way into a bully's bicycle tire. When others pointed to Ko, Haru assured them it was not
in her nature to be so evil.

The first student who had called Ko "ainoko" owned a Chihuahua.
One day, the dog disappeared. A week later, Ko shared her teriyaki
chicken lunch with her tormentor. Ko wondered if the girl would ever
make the connection. She hoped so.

The event that decided Haru's destiny started in the secret attic.

The temple's attic was not actually a secret. Occasionally, Kiyoshi pulled the ceiling ladder down and climbed the stairs to fetch or store some religious scroll, vestment, or other ecclesiastical paraphernalia. If not for Ko's first-visit remark—"What's in the attic?"—Haru might not have bothered to look at what she dismissed as an uninteresting storage area.

"Let's find out," said Haru.

The barefoot girls tiptoed over the floor's creaky timbers like naughty ninjas. Haru held an oil lamp at eye level. Dusty chests flanked the slanting rafters. Bold kanji specified the contents: robes for wedding rites, ancient scrolls, or personal effects of departed priests. The girls' hair snared dangling spiderwebs. Ko labeled the pungent musk emanating from scrolls layered with centuries of grime and pimpled by rat droppings "attic perfume." The lantern's dancing light, the wind whistling through the rafters, and the pungent odors created the perfect dank atmosphere to draw out their most intimate secrets.

At a previous séance, Ko had told Haru that her mother had been a Penang karayuki and her father a Malay prince. Haru had reciprocated by confiding how she had escaped Ko's mother's fate. Haru had hardly heard Ko mutter, "You got off with a few years of an empty stomach; my mother didn't."

Now, months later, the day's heavy rain shelved whatever adventures Haru and Ko fancied; there would be no sampan excursion on the Ota River or horse-drawn trolley downtown to window-shop or rickshaw ride to the tearooms lining the harbor.

After Saturday morning classes, Ko leaned into Haru. "I have a secret," she said, her voice throaty, conspiratorial.

Haru grabbed her hand and quickened her pace. "Let's go." She didn't need to add "to the attic." It was understood.

When the girls pranced into the Fudoin compound, several monks, engaged in landscaping duties, greeted the cheerful pair. Haru, increasingly aware of her maturing beauty and being of marriageable age, had begun to notice and enjoy a different look in the eyes of the younger bachelors.

One monk, Maki-san, who often lingered when Haru passed, told her, "The sensei and Midori-san went to town."

Of course, thought Haru. *They do every Saturday.* But feeling especially charitable, she gave Maki-san a smile and slight bow and said, "*Domo arigato gozaimashita,*" the politest thank you.

Once inside, Haru told Ko, "I'll heat the tea and grab some sweet bean cakes. Why don't you go to my room, get the lantern and incense, and prepare our tearoom."

When Haru carried the teapot into the attic, Ko was waiting and sitting cross-legged, her tawny face radiating in the lantern's glow. She fingered a picture's white edge, careful not to smudge a serious-faced soldier's photo.

Haru took the photo and held it over the lantern. "Oh, he is so handsome," she said, ignoring the scar on the right side of his forehead. "Does this mean—"

"Yes," said Ko. "He is stationed in Mukden."

"A soldier? You don't seem the army wife type, Ko."

"Not a real soldier, Haru. He is a lieutenant with our Manchurian Railroad, which controls land in Manchuria larger than Kyushu," said Ko, referring to the slice of sparsely populated territory Russia lost in the war. "He's retiring to take a grant of one million *tsubos* [830 acres] to grow soybeans. A million tsubos, Haru! The railroad is loaning him money to build a house and hire Chinese laborers and former soldiers as overseers."

"I'm so happy for you, Ko, but … " Haru faltered, puzzled. "I thought your *nakodo* did matchmaking only for Hawaii."

"She does. But since that gentlemen's agreement where our government agreed to stop sending laborers to America, the greater demand for wives is Manchuria."

Haru gave a small shake of her head. "I would never leave Japan."

"You don't have to. You have the perfect complexion. You're the daughter of an important priest." Ko's eyes narrowed. "You will live the life of a woman of leisure."

As was her habit, Haru ignored Ko's worn-out comparisons between their two lives. Instead, she clapped her hands and bounced on her cushion. "Let's play *shiritori!*"

Shiritori was a popular word game. The first person said a word. The next person had to say a word starting with last syllable of the previous word; the next player did the same, and so on. Today, the girls made it tougher. Each word had to be a living thing—like an animal or plant—and once one girl said her word, she started counting to five. If the other girl could not come up with a word in time, she lost. Words ending in the "n" sound, the most common in the Japanese language, were not allowed.

The girls had been shouting words over whistling wind and pelting rain for half an hour when Haru said, "*Usagi*," the Japanese word for rabbit and started counting. When she reached five and Ko had not countered, Haru playfully poked her friend.

That was when Ko blurted out the question that would change Haru's life forever. "In Tokugawa times, the emperor was kept in a gilded cage; now his son is a god. How is that possible?"

Haru's chest tightened. She grabbed the edge of the table. The correct answer, the safe answer, was to either giggle and say, "What a silly question," or be serious and say, "How can anyone doubt it could be otherwise?" Either response would shut down this path to jeopardy.

Ko kept silent as if to say, "Take your time. I know this is a shocking question."

Haru was transported back four years to the Zojoji Temple grounds the day she had startled Kiyoshi with the same question. It had been raining that day too, but not like the bullets pinging the attic roof today.

∞ ∞

As the blood drained from Kiyoshi's face, a frightened expression seized Midori's serene features. Haru jerked back, cupping her hand over her open mouth.

Kiyoshi set aside his bento box. His troubled eyes pierced into Haru's. His measured voice dropped an octave. "The Buddha became a god for his good works; the emperor for being the living embodiment of the Japanese nation." He paused.

Haru gave the expected "hai," normally meaning "yes" but in this context meaning "I understand."

"Our emperor was eighteen years old at the time of the 1868 Restoration, only a year older than you. He rose to a godly force because he performed acts that only a god could—transforming our backward nation into a modern country, winning wars against China and Russia, making Korea our colony."

Kiyoshi then did something he had never done before and never did since. He put his hands firmly on both sides of Haru's face and tilted her head back. His eyes bore down like a lion holding its prey. Haru's jaws hurt, and she tried to move her head away, but Kiyoshi increased the pressure. "You must never say ANYTHING that shows any doubt of our Tenno Heika's status among the gods. The police and the Shinto priesthood do not tolerate the slightest sign—even just a hint—of such unpatriotic feelings. DO YOU UNDERSTAND?"

Kiyoshi released his hands. Haru stood and bowed low.

"*Wakarimashita*. Gomennasai."

Midori clutched Haru's arm; her fingernails dug into the girl's soft skin. "You must never again ask such a question, Haru-chan. No one can doubt the emperor's divinity, or harm will come not only to that person but also to her whole family."

∞ ∞

Since that day, Haru had never said anything or heard anyone else utter a word questioning the emperor's deity status.

Until today.

Since the Zojoji Temple drama, Haru threw herself into demonstrating her reverence to the Emperor Meiji. She practiced reciting the Imperial Rescript on Education until she was perfect. Haru led the school rescript recitals when VIPs visited. She wrote award-winning school essays extolling the superiority of the Japanese over other nations and races.

Despite this public display, more unspoken questions nagged her. Even though she never doubted the emperor's greatness, she asked herself, how could a human be a god? One question tore at her soul. If Tenno Heika was a god, why did his ministers allow karayuki to be sent to the brothels of Asia?

Something else about Ko's question troubled Haru. Ko's uncle was a part-time Shinto priest who performed the *jinja* rites at his neighborhood shrine. He covered the walls of his home with the emperor's picture. She never suspected that Ko doubted. Then again, no one knew Haru herself held doubts.

Now her best friend was asking the forbidden question in their mysterious sanctuary. Haru had shared complaints about teachers, knowing Ko would never tell another soul. Except for her adopted parents, only Ko knew she had been sold as a karayuki. Haru loved Ko and trusted her, even though she borrowed clothes without asking and small coins disappeared from their home after her visits. Haru remembered the days when she went hungry and overlooked these small transgressions.

"Ko," she said, and then repeated Kiyoshi's words explaining how the emperor had become a deity.

"Yes," said Ko, "our Tenno Heika is Japan's greatest god, but how come his father was not?"

"I think all the emperors were gods, Ko-chan. For many years, the emperors trusted the Tokugawa shoguns to keep peace. But when the bakufu lost the people's trust, our great emperor answered the call of his citizens." Haru refilled their teacups with the tepid dregs. "He is a god, but not like the great Buddha, rather a god who is our wise father. We Japanese need a god to make sure we obey the laws of the country."

Ko leaned forward. The candle caught the refection of her widening eyes. "You mean you don't believe our Tenno Heika is a real god?"

A jolt of alarm pierced the inner sinews of Haru's chest. She realized she had crossed a line that might endanger her surrogate parents. "No!" she hastened to explain. "We all know Meiji IS a god. How else could he make so many wise decisions and win every war?"

Ko stood and looked out the window. "The rain's stopped, Haru-chan. Let's walk to the harbor."

"Okay," agreed Haru. *Anything to stop talking about the emperor.* "Let's go to the *shibai-goya*. A scene from *Chushingura* is playing. I will pay for both of us. Maki-san will go with us to make sure we are proper ladies. He likes the samurai plays."

"Oh," said Ko in a lilted voice. "That seminarian has eyes for you."

"Don't be silly. He's like a brother chaperoning his sister."

Ko raised her eyebrows and shot an impish smile.

The girls wrapped the tea set, opened the hatch, dropped the ladder, and descended to the second floor of the temple home. The three Susanos meowed and rubbed against the girls' legs. As Haru skipped toward her room, she half-turned to Ko. "I'll meet you on the steps." She was too polite to say she was retrieving the ticket money.

Haru entered her room, went straight to her study desk, and reached for her porcelain coin bank—a hollow statue of Lady Murasaki, the author of *The Tale of Genji*. She picked it up. The statue's featherweight drained the blood from her face. She dropped the empty statue. It bounced on the tatami mat floor but did not break. Haru tore down the hall to the front porch to confront Ko.

She was gone.

∞ CHAPTER 13 ∞

STILL BAREFOOT, Haru sprinted out of the temple grounds. She looked both ways. At the sight of a fleeing school uniform disappearing around the corner, Haru dashed after the culprit, unmindful of the woman she bumped, scattering a sack of vegetables and eggs. Haru spun around the corner and again caught sight of Ko. The geta-shod Ko was no match for the well-conditioned, barefooted Haru.

"Ko!"

Ko stopped, pivoted, and flashed a vicious look Haru would never have suspected on that face. "You have everything, Haru. You don't need the money, and I do. Besides, I was going to pay you back."

Haru charged her friend and yanked the cord on Ko's neck holding her *kinchaku* tucked inside her kimono. The purse popped out. Haru let go of the cord and grabbed at the dangling purse. Ko shoved Haru, who would not let go of the purse. They both fell to the ground. A crowd gathered.

Ko screamed, "Help! She's stealing my purse!"

A strong pair of arms hauled Haru to her feet.

Ko jumped up and spurted down the street without a backward glance.

Haru yelled, "Don't let her get away! She's the thief! That's my purse!" She tried to wiggle out of the arms of the man holding her.

From the crowd's confused murmurs, one voice emerged. "Haru, what happened?"

Another woman's voice rose. "That's Kiyoshi-sensei's daughter."

The man holding Haru dropped his hands in embarrassment. He bowed low and apologized, "Gomennasai. Gomennasai."

Haru glanced down the street where Ko had escaped. Her shoulders slumped. She had saved that money for two years. Ko had been her best friend. Now Haru had lost both.

The crowd parted allowing Kiyoshi to step forward. "Haru-chan, are you all right?"

Haru bowed. "Hai. Please, take me home, Otosan."

Around the irori, Kiyoshi and Midori listened to Haru's story. "What can I do, Otosan?"

"Let's do nothing now. Let Ko think about what she did. If she and her surrogate parents do not come here tonight to return the money, I will visit them tomorrow."

At that moment, Ko was stoking her uncle's hatred. "Uncle, Haru told me to take some money to buy movie tickets. That's why I ran ahead." He stared at her, but before he could question her further, Ko appealed to her uncle's prejudices. Too often, she had suffered through his impassioned stories about the indignities Shinto priests had suffered under state-supported Buddhism before the Restoration.

"Haru asked me if I believed Tenno Heika is really a god."

"What?" he asked impatiently.

Ko flaunted her best indignant expression. "She said the government made it all up to control the people."

"Blasphemy. I told you to stay away from that girl. Her father has poisoned her. That Buddhist apostate has never accepted the Tenno Heika as a deity. He must be made an example."

"You are right, Honorable Uncle," said Ko feigning contrition. "I should have listened."

There was no more talk about movie money. Ko held back a smirk.

At nine that evening, the porch bell clanged. Kiyoshi found two stern-faced men on his doorstep. He knew them both. Hondo-san, from the Ministry of Interior's Divine Office, wore his Shinto robes. He was a tall, narrow-faced man with his chrome hair plastered straight back. His official role restricted him to the education and assignment of Shinto priests, as well as the payment of their salaries from the state's coffers. However, the Shinto priesthood used this proscribed mandate to anoint themselves the spiritual protectors of the empire.

The other man, short and stocky, looking less forbidding in his rumpled Western apparel, was Fujita-san, the local chief of police. At Kiyoshi's surprised expression, he took off his fedora, revealing a bald head rimmed by short-cropped white hair. He bowed. "Excuse the late hour, Takayama-san."

"Daijoubu, Fujita-san. Please come in." Kiyoshi bowed in return, stepped aside, and directed them to the irori. The robed men exchanged icy smiles.

At the back of the living room, Haru stood in front of an open kitchen door panel ready to serve tea and biscuits. Kiyoshi's shake of the head warned her off. The two visitors, wiggling off their shoes, missed this exchange.

The three men sat around the irori. Kiyoshi feigned a calm he did not feel. "What brings such distinguished visitors to my home at this hour?" He surmised it must have something to do with the Haru-Ko incident and worried why the Divine Office would have an interest in an altercation between teenagers.

Fujita cleared his throat. "It seems we have a delicate police matter as a result of this afternoon's confrontation between Haru and her classmate."

"Surely you don't believe Haru's a thief." Kiyoshi's chest tightened as he caught the Shinto priest's lips curve upward. It was not quite a smirk, more like a cat waiting for the mouse to poke its head out of the hole.

"We are not here tonight to deal with the mix-up over a few coins," said Hondo harshly. Then he leaned forward and slapped the floor. "Your servant blasphemed the emperor."

Kiyoshi froze. He resisted the urge to order the priest to leave. He sensed the man had just raised the stakes in a dangerous game. "You are twice mistaken, Hondo-sama. My *daughter* Haru loves the emperor. She has won many awards in rescript recitation contests. Her brother gave his life in the Russian war."

"Merely a subterfuge to hide her true beliefs." Hondo withdrew a sheet of parchment with a set of seals pressed in wax at the bottom. "This is Ko's official statement." The Shinto priest read parts of the girl's twisted version of the attic conversation incriminating Haru who had attacked the emperor's divinity.

Kiyoshi never attempted to interrupt. When his adversary thumped the statement on the floor like a lawyer in a trial, he let the silence linger a moment and then asked, "Is that all? Some girl pilfers money, gets caught, and then accuses the victim of slandering the emperor? Surely you have something better to do with your time."

"I told the esteemed minister the same thing, Takayama-san. That's why I insisted we visit your home this very night to talk to Haru—before rumors start. She can deny it, and the story ends."

Kiyoshi trusted the police captain. They had known each other for years. But neither he nor Fujita appreciated Ko's cunningness; she knew Haru believed Buddha would not approve of her telling anything but the whole truth under any circumstances, leaving enough truth to validate Ko's embellishment.

Kiyoshi summoned Haru, who lived up to Ko's expectations. She repeated what she had said. Her recapitulation was innocent enough, but the retelling confirmed much of what Ko had accused, including the damning remark that Japan needs a god to make people obey its laws. She ended by saying, "You see, I love the Tenno Heika and was only trying to help Ko understand—"

Hondo slapped the floor again. "Enough!" He looked at the police captain. "She admits everything but tries to twist it to her advantage. How many more student minds has she tried to poison?" He turned to Kiyoshi. "This challenge to the state—coming from the Fudoin Temple as it does—undermines the empire."

Kiyoshi's face lost its color, but his Buddhist discipline maintained his equanimity.

"Thank you, Haru. Please go to your room."

"This is a very serious matter, Takayama-san," said the police captain. He turned to the Shinto priest. "You did right bringing this to my attention, Hondo-sama. Now I must investigate this charge … starting with the interrogation of Takayama-san. You may leave knowing the police will take the appropriate action."

The priest tightened his jaws.

Fujita waited.

The priest stood up. Kiyoshi started to stand, but the priest waved him away. "You needn't bother to see me out."

Kiyoshi watched his adversary walk in measured steps, slip into his shoes, and enter the night. He turned to Fujita. "I think we need something stronger than tea, Takayama-san," said Fujita.

Kiyoshi clapped his hands. Midori fluttered in from the kitchen with a bottle of Akadama port wine, a gift from one of the parishioners, and two glasses. She had anticipated their request. These two old friends had taken up this new Western-style drinking shortly after the war. She knelt down and poured two drinks and left the men to conduct their business.

"These Shinto priests," murmured Kiyoshi in a voice dripping in exasperation. "You would have thought our victory over Russia gave enough boost to the divinity question, to put all this witch-hunting behind them. Their knee-jerk reaction to invented slights is so … brutal, so … unnecessary, so … counterproductive."

"Victory over Russia?" Fujita raised his eyebrows. "Yes, we won the war, sank the tsar's fleet. But then, Roosevelt snatched the victory from us. We *withdrew* from half of Sakhalin. We settled without receiving even a yen of reparations. What kind of victory was that?"

Kiyoshi opened his mouth to object. Fujita raised his right hand in the stop position. "Yes. Yes. You and I have discussed how the Russians had moved four fresh divisions into Manchuria. That our army was exhausted. Replenishment of equipment insufficient for another major campaign. The public's resistance to more loss of life. But to those ever-vigilant Shinto right-wingers, it was our negotiators capitulating to Roosevelt protecting a fellow white nation. Those religious police are angry. Lashing out."

"*Muzukashii,*" said Kiyoshi, his furrowed forehead pinched deep.

"More than difficult, Takayama-san. If I don't show enough vigor in this case, I might find myself the police captain in some fishing village in the Kurile Islands."

"Haru is clearly innocent of any wrongdoing."

Fujita took a deep swallow of his *mizuwari*. "Most likely, but she should have never said *anything*, Takayama-san. Ko is a troublemaker from a family of troublemakers. She is under suspicion at her school for pilfering. We know her guardians all too well. They love to accuse neighbors of unpatriotic behavior."

Kiyoshi freshened up both drinks. "Stealing is the crime in this case, Fujita-san, not girlish gossip."

"Ko's guardians have arranged for her to marry one of our pioneers in Manchuria. What about Haru? She is beautiful, respectful, and the daughter of a famous priest. This little scandal might be a deterrent to arranging a marriage in Hiroshima but not overseas."

Kiyoshi twirled his glass. "Send her away? To Manchuria?"

"Manchuria, Brazil, Hawaii. Our Japanese men need wives. The empire needs sons. She's the age. You and Midori-san took in an orphan. You made her your daughter. Surely, you didn't expect to keep her much past eighteen."

Kiyoshi drank slowly. "Wakarimashita."

Fujita put his hands on the table and pushed himself up. His smile revealed embarrassment. "I am not as nimble as I once was, old friend." He gave Kiyoshi a hard stare. "You say you understand. It is important you do, Takayama-san. It is best to end this quickly. I will come by in the morning before I report to work and must confront that nasty fart, Hondo."

∞ CHAPTER 14 ∞

WHEN MIDORI HEARD THE FRONT DOOR SHUT, she glided down the hallway.

Kiyoshi's grim face increased her anxiety. "Let's take a walk."

They each grabbed a *tanzen*, a short wool jacket, off the peg and stepped into the brisk night air. As they meandered along the temple's paths, Kiyoshi narrated his conversation with Fujita.

Midori withdrew a letter from her yukata fold. "Maybe the great Buddha is sending a message. For weeks, we have discussed Kenji's letter." She pointed to the letter, worn from many readings. She recited a passage seared in her memory. "'Life on the plantations is tough. The workers look to me to ease their pain.' You see, Otosan?" She waved the letter. "The great Buddha has granted our Kenji a purpose, to build a mission in Hawaii."

Kiyoshi strode ahead, his quickened steps betraying his frustration.

"Slow down," begged Midori. "You walk too fast when you are angry."

"As though there is nothing to be angry about. I will never see my son again. Our adopted daughter must leave Hiroshima, or our temple will be hounded by those Shinto zealots."

Midori grabbed Kiyoshi's sleeve. "We must talk to Haru, Otosan."

"But … do you think Kenji will accept her?"

Midori sucked her teeth. "Kenji asked me to send a 'Hiroshima wife' and underlined 'Hiroshima.'"

"It is his way of rebuffing Haru, Okasan."

"Maybe. But he didn't say, 'Don't send Haru,' either. And he finished his letter saying, 'I trust you, Okasan.' Go pray in the temple. I will bring Haru. In the presence of the Buddha, we will make the right decision."

Inside the Golden Pavilion, the image of the ancient wooden Yakushi Buddha, the Physician of Souls, smiled from an elevated altar smudged from a millennium of fumes. Hundreds of candles flickered. In the comforting womb of their faith, the three discussed, dissected, and discarded their options all night. At dawn, they acknowledged their predicament dictated but one choice. Haru must leave, or she would be charged with defaming the emperor, and the Fudoin Temple would come under the severest scrutiny. The letter from Kenji offered an escape.

A decision made, Kiyoshi took charge. "Okasan, go to the train station and buy two first-class tickets to Yokohama for the noon departure; then send a telegram to Kenji. Haru, prepare breakfast. Empty two wicker chests from the attic and pack while the rice is cooking. I need to ask one of the monks to take Kenji's place in the ceremony."

Spotting Maki sweeping as he walked down the path, Kiyoshi stopped and, after the usual greetings, said, "Maki-san, we are conducting a wedding ceremony for Haru. I want you to stand in for Kenji. Come by in about an hour dressed in your best robes. You can have breakfast with us." Quickly turning back toward the house, he failed to see the slumping shoulders and look of dismay on his young disciple's face.

Back in the house, Kiyoshi busied himself getting vestments ready and looking at scrolls to choose the right quotes. This was only the second wedding he had conducted. By custom, Shinto priests performed the rights of celebration, like weddings and house blessings, leaving the Buddhist priests the afterlife rites of funerals and honoring one's ancestors during Obon season. However, Buddhist priests' families married with Buddhist rites.

Almost an hour passed when he heard a familiar "*tadaima*" from Midori, announcing she was back. He joined her at the irori where Haru had laid out rice, boiled eggs, and broiled fish.

Midori showed Kiyoshi the tickets and placed them on the tatami mat. "Only eight and a half hours to Kobe and then another seventeen hours to Yokohama. Unbelievable."

Kiyoshi thanked Haru for freshening his tea and said, "Maki will stand in for Kenji."

Midori put her hand to her mouth.

Haru blushed.

"Well, what's wrong? Has Maki done something?"

"Worse, Otosan," said Midori. "He is sweet on Haru. He is shy, but anyone with two eyes could see he hoped that one day … "

"Nobody tells me anything. Whom do you suggest?"

At that moment, Maki announced himself and entered wearing dress robes and a sad smile. He dropped to his knees, looked at Haru, and bowed to the floor. "Congratulations, Haru-san. You will make a wonderful missionary's wife."

At eight thirty, Haru married Kenji Takayama by proxy.

∞ ∞

Police Chief Fujita, dropping by to hear of Kiyoshi's decision, arrived in time to celebrate the solution to his problem. As soon as Kiyoshi finished the exchange of vows, a very relieved Fujita accompanied him and Haru to the city hall's registry office to update the family *koseki*.

Kiyoshi entered the marriage details on behalf of Kenji below the last entry, Haru's adoption. He then reached into his kimono and withdrew his son's *inkan* case holding Kenji's *hanko,* the circular rubber stamp the size of a small coin used to enter contracts, validate wills, and, in this case, register a marriage. Kiyoshi chopped the Hiroshima city hall's koseki on behalf of his son and then motioned Haru to press down her hanko next to Kenji's. She held it in place to punctuate her commitment. At that instant, the government of Japan recognized her marriage.

Next, the trio scurried over to the passport window in the same records office. The normal waiting period for a picture bride's passport had been increased to cut down on the number of prostitutes posing as brides. The same government clerk who happily witnessed the hanko stamping turned unsmilingly bureaucratic. "You must wait six months, Takayama-san."

Taken aback by the use of her married name, Haru hesitated in her protest. Kiyoshi stepped forward. Before he could speak, the clerk, giving an eye-check to the chief of police, said in his firmest voice, "I am sorry, Takayama-sensei, but even the daughter of such a distinguished personage—"

"*Sumimasen!*" Fujita pressed into the tiny group.

Startled by the sharp tone, the clerk swung his attention to the police chief.

Fujita pressed his face to the grill separating the clerk from the public. "The reason I am here is not to check on your diligence but to tell you it is in the national interest of Japan to issue Haru-san a passport NOW."

The clerk's demeanor melted to subservience. He pulled open a drawer and withdrew a blank passport.

"We will wait." Fujita turned to Haru. "Give him your school picture."

Midori joined them, having walked over from the nearby telegram office. "An amazing world, Otosan," she said. "The telegram clerk promised me Kenji would receive the good news by morning that his prayer for a wife had been answered."

Minutes later, the clerk handed Haru her passport.

Fujita bestowed a fatherly smile on a fatigued Haru and then locked his eyes onto Kiyoshi's. "I will handle Hondo. I wish you could be there to see the expression on his face when I tell him the case has been resolved."

They bowed their goodbyes.

∞ CHAPTER 15 ∞

MIDORI'S TELEGRAM REACHED HONOLULU'S Hongwanji Mission as she and Haru boarded their train.

The Fort Street temple occupied prime downtown real estate due to the foresight of Bishop Imamura. The two-acre temple compound looked like a no-nonsense college, with its utilitarian white, two-story buildings arced around a field used for sports and festivals. Only the vaulted roof of the central building revealed the compound's identity.

The bishop had proven to be adept at matching construction projects with the needs of his congregation. Japanese immigrant workers needed to learn English: construct a classroom building. Battered picture brides needed a refuge: buy lumber, hire contractors, and erect apartments. Abandoned children needed a home: raise money for side-by-side, two-story dormitories.

At age thirty-three, the scholar, appointed bishop, Imamura had arrived in Hawaii in 1899, a year after Hawaii's annexation, to oversee the Buddhist Honpa Hongwanji Mission of Hawaii. His straight posture and long neck added imaginary inches to his frame. The handles of his rimless glasses drew unwelcome attention to his oversized ears, while his close-cropped hair gave him a military bearing.

Imamura had been in America a month when an article written by a lanky young reporter changed the direction of his mission. Andy Pafko created a sensation when quoting the territory's chief immigration officer: "Japan is yet a pagan nation. They are morally mad. There is apparently no sense of responsibility to society or to Deity."

While the small Buddhist mission was appalled by the article, Imamura saw it as a challenge to be addressed. He began a process to Americanize the Buddhist mission by emphasizing how the philosophy of the Buddha had much in common with Christianity, and the Japanese family values of honesty, respect of one's elders, and hard work shared the same ethics as Washington and Franklin.

Imamura even found common ground with Pafko. Both agreed that the cane workers had descended into a life of gambling, drinking, and whoring as a consequence of outnumbering their women ten to one. Both berated alcoholism, wife-swapping, and dice games. When, in his second month off the boat, Imamura entered a gambling den and asked the Japanese roughnecks to come back to their Buddhist traditions of discipline and honor, they threatened to kill him. Goro Sato, editor of the conservative *Hinode Shimbun* and dependent on advertising from the low-life establishments, demanded Imamura be sent back to Japan for agitating the workers. In a contest of wills, the *Hinode* had attacked the wrong man. Sato had given Imamura a chance to show his mettle, and the new bishop was quick to seize the advantage. Imamura established his strength of character reputation by continuing his visits to the dens of iniquity.

Imamura helped new immigrants adjust to Hawaiian life. He offered free English classes and founded the Young Men's Buddhist Association, modeled after the YMCA. Deposed queen Liliuokalani encouraged Imamura's efforts. In May 1902, she engendered an outpouring of goodwill from the non-Japanese community by attending the 730th anniversary celebration of St. Shinran, the founder of Imamura's Jodo Shinshu sect.

This year, plantation owners started providing land for Buddhist missions after Imamura coaxed strikers back to work by preaching the importance of nonviolence.

While Pafko grudgingly admired Imamura's attempts at Americanizing Buddhism, he wrote:

> Yes, crime is down; yes, the Buddhist clergy speaks out against labor strikes; and yes, their Nisei children are speaking English in our public schools. But afterwards they attend cultural indoctrination at their Japanese language schools. And why do they send their children on to high school when such an education is bound to be wasted in the cane fields? It defies common sense.
>
> Behind this veneer of Buddhist civilizing, many peasants keep up their belief in ghosts, fireballs, and devil-gods. Their shamans communicate with the dead, conduct fortune-telling, practice magic, and exorcise demons. Look at their women. They dress like they are still in Edo, wrapped in their kimono accentuating their apartness. You hear the *taiko* drums at their Fort Street temple pounding in loyalty to THEIR country. They worship a foreign living emperor as a god. If war were ever to break out, which side do you think they will be on?

Imamura understood Pafko spoke for many of the ruling class. He simply resolved to stay on course to harmonize the Japanese into the American culture. Thus, he was pleased with the news from his clerk that one of his favorite priests had found a good wife.

Kenji was at the shelter helping a woman with two black eyes and three children—one crying baby in her arms and two scared, snot-nosed toddlers clutching the hem of her kimono—when a messenger told him a telegram had arrived. Kenji made his excuses and hustled to the office, another two-story white building. He asked himself why the woman hadn't left the brute earlier. He would try to place the abused woman with a new husband on a different island.

Kenji expected that the telegram was from his mother sending a positive response to his letter. After a year of anxiety and internal debate—"Shall I stay or shall I return home?"—he had made a decision. He was happy with it and wondered why it had taken him so long to decide.

"Congratulations, Kenji," said the office clerk, flashing a smile displaying a rack of misshapen teeth. He handed a telegram to the barely five-foot-tall Kenji. The Fort Street temple received a dozen telegrams a month, mostly death notices since the new cable service brought Hawaii closer to Japan.

Kenji read the telegram.

And very nearly wished it had delivered news of a death.

The blood drained from his round face, made rounder by the extra serving of rice he enjoyed with each meal and the lack of exercise. His black ambitious eyes migrated from shock to anger. How could his mother do this!

"Are you all right, Kenji?"

Kenji had forgotten the lingering clerk. "Yes." Kenji brushed his thick black hair back from his sloping forehead. "I just need a few moments alone."

How could his mother ignore his letter? He had underlined "a Hiroshima wife." For a year, he could read between his mother's lines as she exalted the virtues of "sweet" Haru—so charming, so good with animals, and doing so well in school. Didn't his mother realize that he was a priest, a leader in the community, and a man for whom the slightest scandal would undermine his usefulness and opportunity for advancement? No matter how she described Haru, the fact remained that she was from Amakusa, the island of the karayuki. No, he could not accept his mother's judgment. He started to compose a telegram response to head off this impending disaster.

"Kenji." A low, commanding voice pierced the troubled missionary's reverie. "Your mother has chosen well."

Kenji turned to face the imposing Yemyo Imamura. *How did he know? Before me! That big-mouthed clerk.* Fighting to maintain his composure, Kenji fixed a stoic smile on the man who had exchanged letters with his mother since his arrival in Hawaii five years earlier.

"Yes, Imamura-*socho*. It's just that … this news surprised me. My mother's letters gave me the impression that Haru was not the type to risk an adventure in a foreign land."

Imamura answered with a knowing smile beneath his short mustache. Kenji had grown soft in administrative duties and needed a wife to share the burdens of establishing a new parish. Imamura ignored Kenji's apparent unease with his mother's selection. "Splendid news, Kenji. We need married priests on the Big Island. The priests in Hilo never even visit half the plantations under their care. As we discussed when you first wrote your mother, Waimea cries out for a priest with your organizing skills. When is your wife arriving?"

"The telegram says only on the next available ship."

"I would like to meet … " Imamura left the sentence hanging, his neck stretching forward in silent query.

"Haru, socho." Kenji hid a flash of anger. He was uncertain whether his bishop knew of the girl's origins. While he admired his mother's compassion, he had not approved of the adoption of the runaway girl sold into prostitution. And now years later, his mother was sending him this, this … He could not complete the thought. The bishop's piercing eyes were staring straight through him.

"Your mother wrote well of her. What an excellent choice. A woman raised in the temple." Imamura gave the slightest nod of the head and strolled off, his purposeful stride leaving no doubt the issue was settled.

Kenji was just as certain it was not settled. He would need some time to work out a plan to avoid a lifetime fate of being whispered about as "the husband of an Amakusan woman."

∞ CHAPTER 16 ∞

THE MORNING SUN HAD SNATCHED THE FROST FROM THE AIR by the time the Takayama family reached the Hiroshima train station. At this time yesterday, Haru and her best friend, Ko, were strolling hand in hand up the temple path, giggling, anticipating a secret-sharing séance—never dreaming of the horrors lurking there.

Leave Japan? Never, Haru had vowed. Yet, a spark of curiosity had been ignited. Over the past years, she had come to eagerly anticipate Kenji's chatty letters to his parents but not just his depiction of endless summers, salty ocean breezes, and the warmth of the Hawaiian people. Kenji wrote of lonely men who saved too little and had to pass their final days in squalid dormitories, of women who gave birth in dusty cane fields, of harassed plantation workers enduring the misfortune of working for mean overseers, the *lunas*. For a girl who tended wounded animals, the idea of helping a priest minister to his parishioners sang invitingly.

Kiyoshi broke the girl's reverie. "Let's find your seats."

After boarding, Kiyoshi lifted their luggage onto the grated steel shelf over their seat. Earlier, he had supervised the loading of their wicker chests. Then turning to Midori who was still standing, he dug into his robe's sleeve and withdrew a red envelope.

Midori's eyes questioned Kiyoshi.

"It's a surprise." A small smile played on his thin lips. "Open it in Kyoto." He handed her a folded sheet. "I have a friend at the Enmei-in Temple who offers picture-bride courses. Most likely you can stay in the temple guesthouse until Haru leaves. The sea trunks will be shipped directly from there."

He presented another red envelope to Haru. He swallowed hard. His Adam's apple hurt. "Have a safe trip. Write often."

Haru bowed low. "Arigato, Otosan."

The train whistle shrieked.

Haru watched Kiyoshi trudge down the aisle and turn to the exit. She fingernailed the envelope and pulled out a photograph. She gazed at her latest Susano perched on her favorite stone. She snapped down the train window, poked her head out, and watched her father drop down from the carriage steps onto the platform.

"I will write every week, Otosan." Her eyes glistened.

The train jerked forward.

As she watched her father standing alongside the carriage, Haru could tell that Kiyoshi's stoic demeanor veiled his emotions as always. She wondered if his son would also hide his emotions.

Midori joined Haru and waved through the open window.

Kiyoshi bowed low and kept the position.

Haru and Midori slept most of the way to Kyoto where they switched trains to the Tokaido-sen line that ran parallel to the Tokaido Road. Fifty-three *shukuba* (post stations) offered lodging and entertainment at one-day walking intervals. Haru knew Amakusan courtesans, possible former playmates, could be found among the stations' "floating worlds," catering to life's transient pleasures. She said a silent prayer of thanks to Odaishi-sama.

She wondered what her life with Kenji would be like. Haru had heard about Kenji and his work in Hawaii for years. Yet, she did not really know him. She turned to Midori. "Tell me about Kenji," she said, then flushed slightly, and gently tapped her heart. "What kind of person is he here … inside?"

Midori had been deep into her own thoughts regarding her son. Had she been rash in overlooking Kenji's underlined request for "a Hiroshima bride"? Should she tell Haru about the dilemma? She smiled motherly. "He will love you, Haru-chan, although he may never tell you. Such is the way of men. He may start off uncertain. You might even worry that he is rejecting you. Do not be discouraged. My son will recognize the good wife you will become, the loving wife who will bear him many children." Midori paused, thinking how to approach the most delicate subject.

Haru anticipated the conversation's needed progression. "How do you satisfy the needs of men?"

Relieved at Haru's opening, Midori widened her smile. "That's our secret weapon. An enjoyable one too, once you train your husband." She leaned over. "I hope Kenji is a quicker learner than Kiyoshi." Midori finished the intimate conversation with a sly grin. "Don't worry about what to do on your wedding night. After your bath, walk into the bedroom, and drop your yukata. I trust my son's confidence will rise in more ways than one with your offering."

∽ ∽

The sun had sunk deep into the horizon when the Tokaido train pulled into Yokohama, the pride of the Japanese railroad system. No less a personage than the Meiji emperor had made the first round-trip between Tokyo's Shinbashi Station and Yokohama in 1872. Midori slid the window open, enjoying November's blast of cool air. Then she remembered—the red envelope. She was to open it at Kobe. A jolt of fear shot through her. What was she supposed to have done in Kobe? She tore it open. She read a note from Kiyoshi penned in elegant calligraphy. "A special treat for a lasting memory." The note was pinned to a telegram confirming two nights at the famed Grand Hotel in Yokohama along with a bank draft made out to the hotel.

Midori leaned out the window and hollered at the green-uniformed porters, each adorned with a twisted red bandana. A porter hopped into the carriage and collected the luggage. Haru shivered and quickly donned her *haori*, a wide-sleeved cotton jacket extending to her waist. The porter strapped the three pieces of luggage together with twine that hung from his waist cinch, hoisted them upon his head, and adjusted his cushioned head covering. "Follow me."

Excited vendors walked alongside, hawking gloves, handkerchiefs, and umbrellas, even though it wasn't raining. Touts promising "best prices" jammed photos of hotels in front of their faces. Rickshaw drivers lined the exit.

"To which hotel?" the porter asked and then called over a rickshaw driver. Midori's sharp eye caught the rickshaw driver giving the porter a coin.

The spindle-legged rickshaw driver's gold front teeth glinted in the late afternoon sun. Wrinkles lined his leathery face. Twinkling eyes peered out among the folds. "The gods have surely blessed your arrival." He gave a polite bow. "Three days of rain stopped this morning. I can take you directly to the Grand Hotel, or we can watch the sunset overlooking the harbor."

A tired Midori ordered, "Straight to the hotel, driver-san."

The grizzled rickshaw driver set off briskly. He crossed the Oebashi Bridge, turned right, crossed another bridge, stopped, and pointed. "The red-brick buildings are mostly silk trading companies."

The word "silk" felt like a slap in Haru's face. She had not thought of her older sisters working in the Niigata silk factories in months. It had been a year since they had exchanged letters. In all the turmoil, she had not thought about never seeing them again.

The driver paused. "My father was a Yokohama fisherman when Perry's 'black ships' arrived. The shogun chose our tiny village as the foreigner's port. The shogun didn't want *gaijin* close to the capital. He designated the Kannai district as their exclusive living quarters, like Dejima near Nagasaki. I remember as a child I could not enter this area, and even the big-nosed gaijin had to pass a checkpoint to get in or out."

The driver maintained a tour guide's pitter-patter until he reached the hotel. While porters grabbed the ladies' luggage, Midori handed the driver a five-yen coin. The rickshaw driver bowed profusely with a string of "domo arigatos" and pedaled off.

The long reach of Kiyoshi exhibited itself again at check-in. While Haru was dazzled by the sturdy examples of huge Western-style furniture, the arched marble reception desk, and the lobby's soaring ceiling, Midori opened a large beige envelope the tuxedo-clad receptionist handed her. Inside she found a pamphlet, *The New Hawaii*, to which a seamstress's pin attached a note. "Haru-chan, this is for your bride's class." The signature read "Judith Hamilton," written in katakana, a special Japanese-designed phonetic alphabet used exclusively for foreign words.

The next morning, Midori directed a rickshaw driver to take them to the customs house footing the Osanbashi Pier, where they were directed to the NYK shipping office. Walking inside, they discovered a middle-aged man with a receding hairline reading the *Tokyo Asahi Shimbun* in a small office uncluttered by clients. He glanced up from his newspaper, appraised the women's clothing, and managed a weak smile.

Midori was glad she had prepared for the typical petty bureaucrat's attitude toward women. She wore a sky-blue kimono made of silk with a green sash, or obi, tied decoratively in the back and had made sure Haru looked her demure best in a darker-blue kimono cut from a more modest cotton cloth with matching obi. Both women had their hair pinned and styled high, thanks to the hotel's beauty salon. Midori took care to choose her words and pronounce them without her regional dialect as she explained her need to book her daughter to Hawaii.

The agent sucked his teeth, tilted his head askew, and looked at a passenger list. "Your choices are few. Most of our ships ply the China trade this time of the year. Passengers to Hawaii avoid the rough seas the winter months bring. The only ship sailing in November, the *Yamashiro Maru*, leaves in a week, but it's fully booked. There is another ship with plenty of space in maybe—"

"Haru is a picture bride," Midori said cutting him off. She placed Haru's passport and marriage certificate on the table and held the man's gaze.

The agent straightened up. She could see he was calculating whether to comply with the regulation that picture brides be given first preference and suffer the confusion when he bumped an already-paid passenger to the next ship. This brides-first policy addressed Japan's Hawaiian consulate reports that the imbalance of too many men with too few wives resulted in scandalous incidents, embarrassing the empire. He sucked his teeth again. "Muzukashii."

"Haru is traveling second class," said Midori.

The booking agent's shoulders eased. "You should have told me that at the first. Steerage is fully booked, but we have another picture bride traveling second class. They can be roommates." Unsaid was that the shipping line did not book Westerners and Japanese in the same cabin. After paying for the booking, mother and daughter proceeded to the post office where Midori sent Kenji a telegram announcing Haru's estimated arrival date.

∞ CHAPTER 17 ∞

MOST PICTURE BRIDES LEFT THE SHORES OF JAPAN with scant training in language or culture. The typically teenage hopefuls exchanged glamorized pamphlets extolling Hawaii's exotic shores, read their husbands' embellishments, and listened to the village scuttlebutt to fathom their new life. Haru would always appreciate Kiyoshi's sending her to the Yokohama temple's orientation program.

On their third day in Yokohama, the temple's head priest greeted Midori and Haru at the gate, gave the usual low bow, and laughed off Midori's modest lodging expectations. "The wife and daughter of the Fudoin Temple's master staying in the monks' guest quarters? I could not bear the thought." He gave Haru an approving glance. "After lunch, you might want to go directly to our brides' class. They will be demonstrating how to wear Western clothes."

Haru put her hand over her mouth the moment the monk brought her into the classroom and she saw her instructor—a gaijin woman. Her fiery red tresses hung loose over a beautiful dress that met the floor in a wide hoop of white linen.

"*Irasshai*, Haru-san," welcomed the woman, her Japanese perfect. "My name is Judith. We use first names here to get used to the casual Hawaiian ways." Seeing the uncertainty in Haru's eyes, the woman gave her a knowing smile. "Yes, probably not what you were expecting. My parents were missionaries from Scotland, which accounts for this wild, red hair. I was born in Japan and schooled here, eventually married a British businessman, and moved to Hawaii where we lived for ten years before my husband accepted a position with the Silk Board."

Haru bowed and offered the traditional introduction greeting. "*Hajimemashite*."

Judith introduced Haru to her five classmates and fellow ship-mates. Natsu came first, the best-dressed girl. Haru recalled another Natsu. What would she be doing now if she had left on ship to Sandakan with Haru? The thought muddled her concentration. The rest of the names—those she would know for a lifetime—blurred by her.

Natsu scurried to the back of the room, poured two cups of tea, gave one to Haru, and like a sheepdog, managed to separate her from the others. She rivaled Haru in complexion and the same classical oval face but topped her in wardrobe and confidence. A famous artist had painted her silk kimono, and a talented hairdresser had coifed her hair. Well-spoken, she seemed to regard Haru as the one girl who just might be equal to her in status.

"I'm marrying a doctor." The word "doctor" lingered. "He lives in a big house in Honolulu. He visited my village near Saga last year, and the matchmaker introduced us." The pride in her eyes challenged Haru. "Whom are you marrying?"

"I am marrying a priest," said Haru softly. Taken aback by the braggadocio, she turned to join the others but was stopped by the restraining hand Natsu laid on her arm. "What class are you sailing?"

Haru raised her eyebrows and gently removed her arm. "Second class."

Natsu's face lit up. Grabbing Haru's arm with both hands, she enthused, "I knew it. You are the other girl. We are cabin mates. We must have dinner together tonight."

Wary about making an instant friend with this pushy personality, Haru demurred. "Domo arigato, but my mother has already made plans."

Judith clapped her hands and pointed to a table of lumpy contents blanketed with a sheet. With a flourish, she snapped the fabric off the table. The young women gawked at the concoction of the strangest garments they had ever seen. Judith dangled a bra. The girls giggled, guessing its purpose. Mouths opened when Judith pulled down the top of her dress. The picture brides had never seen a brassiere—nor breasts, encapsulated as they were, the size of those belonging to Judith, who ignored the gasps and turned around to show the metal clasps holding the contraption in place.

Pulling her dress back up, she explained, "Most Japanese women in Hawaii continue to wear their traditional wraparound undergarments, but some in Honolulu have started wearing Western clothing." Aiming a hand at the table, she said, "Pick items your size and try them on." The tittering girls rummaged through brassieres, chemises, girdles, and panties while Judith explained each garment's function. Assured by Judith that no one could enter the classroom, Haru joined the others parading around the display tables.

Half an hour of fun later, Judith announced. "Get dressed, ladies. Let's have tea in Chinatown."

"Hai," said Haru, eager to know her new classmates.

Natsu wrinkled her nose. Emphasizing her status, she spoke in the dialect of the upper class. "We have the hotel's early dinner booking."

The other four girls studied the thongs holding their getas in place.

"Teacher's treat," said Judith understanding the economics of her remaining charges. The girls clapped her hands. Off they marched.

⌒ CHAPTER 18 ⌒

THE GOLDEN DRAGON PROPRIETOR greeted Judith as an old friend and led her troop of five to a table overlooking the Nakamura River. Passenger ferries, coal barges, and fishing sampans floated by. The setting sun, broken clouds, and industrial haze mixed, creating a Monet moment of reds and purples. A Victor Talking Machine's phonograph played a scratchy Chinese string instrumental. Sweet bread smells wafted from the kitchen.

Judith ordered oolong tea and biscuits for everyone. "Why don't we tell each other about ourselves. Haru, perhaps you can go first."

Haru's chest tightened. She had not considered the problem of introductions. Saying "I was born in Amakusa" was as good as blurting "I'm from the island of the karayuki." Her first impulse was to state she was from Hiroshima, but her lingering accent would betray her.

Judith put her hand on Haru's arm as a mother would.

The gesture drained the fear from Haru's body, and she said, "I was born in Amakusa."

The four other girls sat up a little straighter.

Judith gave Haru's arm a gentle squeeze. Raised by a missionary family in Kobe, she knew about Amakusa's infamy.

Haru spoke so softly that her new friends leaned forward. "My parents died when I was young. The wife of our village's Buddhist priest found me a home in Hiroshima with her sister, also married to a priest." She finished her introduction with a brief history of her life in a Hiroshima temple and wondered what part of their lives her new classmates would also be keeping to themselves.

"Do you have a picture of your husband?" asked Judith.

The four girls offered a chorus of "oohs" and "ahs" when Haru showed a picture of Kenji and revealed he was a Buddhist priest. Haru's humble demeanor won over her audience, whose rough speech and poorer dress evoked memories of her childhood.

Judith turned to the short, plump girl whose smallpox-scarred face was as brown and round as the bottom of a copper pan. She had added lipstick and eye shadow with all the sophistication of a farm girl. She spoke a country dialect difficult for people outside Kyushu to understand, raising her voice to compensate.

"I'm Kame. My daddy owned a bakery shop. He made lots of money during the war. But he likes gambling as much as I like pastry. He lost his business." She paused, savoring her moment onstage. "When the matchmaker visited our village, my father could not run fast enough to offer me to whoever was willing."

Kame pulled out a picture of a weak-faced man standing in front of a poster of poorly painted palm trees. "His letter promises we can make a lot of money working in the cane fields and come back to Kurume to buy a farm." Kame glanced at Judith and hesitated.

Judith gave an encouraging nod.

"I had to tell the matchmaker I missed my period. She asked who knew and did I love the boy." Kame checked the faces of her audience. Satisfied with the attention level, she continued. "When I said, 'Nobody knows, and it wasn't a boy but my father's best friend,' she gave me some medicine."

"Thank you, Kame," said Judith in a tone that said that was enough. She nodded to the girl sitting next to Kame.

The bride's eyes did not match; one looked steady, but the other floated. Her protruding cheekbones and jutting jaw accentuated a too-long face. She seldom smiled, afraid to bare her crooked teeth. At twenty-two, she was past the marrying age.

"I'm Mayo from Nagasaki. When I approached the matchmaker, she looked at me as hopeless. You can see … I am no beauty. I cannot bear being a burden on my family." She took out her picture. The man was older, his hair was cut close, and his kindly face revealed the bronze ridges of a man who worked in the sun.

Judith glanced at the fourth girl, sitting to the right of Haru. She was as short as Kame but so slender her friends teased that she should carry a brick on a windy day to keep from blowing away. Her ears stuck out like mouse ears. Her eyes featured slits so narrow one might wonder if she were awake. Her smile rivaled Haru's with the addition of a dimple that shone at her happiest, which was often. Her hair fell to her shoulders like Western women.

"I'm Ume. I have always dreamed of going to Hawaii or some foreign land. My father and I would sit on the hillside over the Kobe harbor and watch the ships. I imagined leaving for Singapore, Brazil, Peru, California—some wonderful and strange place." She showed the picture of her husband. "He has satisfied his five-year cane laborer's contract. Now he is growing coffee on his own land in a place called Kona."

Judith shifted her weight and smiled at the girl to the left of Haru. She tended to hunch over to compensate for her five-foot-six height that left her looking down on Japanese of either sex. Her skin glowed a silky alabaster. If she had been born in better circumstances, she would have been taught to carry her height regally, and a matchmaker could have commanded a generous bride price for a face with such a light complexion. At sixteen, she was the youngest and the most scared.

"I am Saki, a farm girl from Okayama. I am the second youngest of eleven children. I don't want to leave Japan, but ... " the luminous eyes sought the ground, "what can I do? I must obey my father." She showed the girls a picture of a young man in a Western suit with hair pointing in all directions. "His letter to the matchmaker said he is a landscape artist for important people in Honolulu. I can't read or write so well. The matchmaker had to write my husband letters telling him about me. I am a simple girl, but I can work hard." Her large almond eyes darted about the group, looking for reassurance.

What a strange group, thought Haru. Kame, the tough girl from Kurume; the not so beautiful Mayo who would offer her kindness in compensation; Ume, the dreamer who actually wanted to live among gaijin; and this poor girl, a child really, who should be in school, not shipped off to a place that frightens her, far from her home and family.

∽ CHAPTER 19 ∾

THE MOON HUNG LOW WITHOUT A HINT OF DAWN when Judith's students scurried from the temple, hoping to create some body warmth on this chilly morning. They complained how the low-hanging fog was spoiling their hair. Before the appointed hour of seven, they had marched passed rude stevedores along the Osanbashi pier on their way to the same building that housed the ship's ticket office. Today, they joined a larger group of departing picture brides for what they would always refer to as the "lecture."

The attic assembly hall was as cold as the government official who greeted them. The bureaucrat, dressed in an ill-fitting Western suit whose trouser cuffs dragged behind his heels, looked disapprovingly on his twenty-seven charges filing into the hall.

Haru took a seat with her new friends on the front-row bench.

The official began by handing out three booklets to each of the girls while assuring them they were personal gifts from the emperor—although his tone suggested the emperor could have spent the money more wisely. With the enthusiasm of a stuffed animal, he spent the morning reviewing *How to Succeed in America*, *Guide Book to Different Occupations in America*, and *The New Hawaii*.

After lunch, the bureaucrat opened a ministry manual conspicuously stamped "Not for Distribution." He stood, paused, and eyed each woman.

Haru twitched and sat straighter.

In the same monotone but at a higher pitch, he read, "'You women are the ambassadors of the empire, the representatives of the emperor, and you must conduct yourselves accordingly. Even though you are leaving the authority of the emperor, it is your duty to practice *ryosai kenbo*. The path to happiness is absolute subservience to your husbands. You are traveling to a strange land to establish the foundation of a new family. Some flowers of our womanhood destroy the harmony of the family by insisting on equal and respectful treatment from their husbands. Never neglect your Japanese female virtues to pursue individual freedom. Selfish and vain mimicry of Western ways leads to misery.'"

The intimidated audience sang out "hai" at the appropriate pauses to assure the emperor's representative that every point was understood and would be obeyed unerringly and without question.

At length, the bureaucrat snapped the manual shut. "Now for your health check and visas." He added smugly, "Only because you are attending this course, your visa applications have been expedited."

The doctor greeted the women with a brief nod, his demeanor just as serious. Only Japan prescreened its citizens for tuberculosis, pinkeye, or trachoma before they left for America to avoid the shame of their being rejected on medical reasons, which happened to 20 percent of Ellis Island immigrants.

Following obtaining the stamped doctor's certificate, the girls shared rickshaws to the American embassy to process their visa applications.

After their visas were issued, Natsu stepped out of character and offered to treat her classmates to a new drink—coffee. The six young women walked to the bustling Noge Street. None would have patronized such a notorious entertainment zone if they were still in their hometown. Haru decided she would skip the name of the street when telling Midori of her outing. All the girls except Kame, who insisted on ordering a second cup, agreed such a bitter drink would never catch on with "us Japanese."

∞ ∞

The rest of the week, Judith prepared her brides for the American way of life—how to eat with knives and forks, use a Western, sit-down toilet, and wear high-heeled shoes. The girls found wearing such uncomfortable shoes as barbaric as the Chinese custom of binding women's feet. More shocking were the sit-down toilets where everyone's bottom touched the same cover, compared to the Japanese sanitary method of squatting and touching nothing. And though it went against the girls' upbringing, they claimed they would walk next to their husbands and not behind them, a custom Judith said, "We Westerners consider demeaning to women."

Judith drilled English language greetings, numbers, and basic food. Although Haru, Natsu, and Ume had taken English classes in high school, only Haru had learned the Roman alphabet well enough to sound out words. She improved her speaking skills by reading aloud from a child's edition of *Huckleberry Finn* Judith gave her the second day once she recognized Haru's affinity for language acquisition.

For their last class and lunch, Judith invited her charges to her mansion home on the Yamate Bluffs. She presented each bride with a scarf embroidered with their name in Romaji, the Roman alphabet they had struggled with all week. As her husband's driver arrived to take the girls back to the temple in one of only three Cadillacs in Japan, Judith passed a note to Haru and said, "Open this when you get to your room."

Haru opened the note with Midori. She translated the English. "Your friends look up to you. Take care of them." It was Midori who gave way to tears.

∽ CHAPTER 20 ∽

THE SUN WARMED HARU AND MIDORI as they tramped down the Osanbashi pier for the last time. Gentle winds pushed fluffy clouds, and the salty air invigorated. They looked ahead to the black-bottomed ship, trimmed at the top with a white railing crowded with passengers and loved ones saying their goodbyes. The smokestack belched a black coal fog that signaled the ship was ready to sail. The three-hundred-foot-long vessel had been built in 1884 in England just as Japan was developing its own shipbuilding capacity. The *Yamashiro Maru* was scheduled to retire the following year, although the freshly painted exterior suggested otherwise.

Haru joked about the bureaucrat's lecture as they passed through the midpoint office buildings. Midori laughed. A transformation had taken place. After the week's bride classes and Midori's buoyant vision of the future, Haru's expectation of an exciting married life to a priest in Hawaii eclipsed the calamity that had forced her departure.

"Maybe Ko did me a favor," said Haru.

Midori wasn't so sure but was grateful a forgiving Haru was looking forward to a happy life with her son. "The Buddha works in mysterious ways," she allowed.

While the picture brides booked in steerage, carrying a single straw suitcase, boarded at the far gangplank whose entry point led to the lower decks below the waterline, Midori and Haru boarded mid-ship with the first-class passengers. The mustached Swedish captain welcomed them with a strained smile. A white-uniformed seaman quickly directed them down two decks to the second-class cabins where Natsu greeted them. Her earlier arrival had allowed her to choose the upper bunk.

Haru and Midori said their dry-eyed goodbyes and renewed promises to write weekly. All their tears had been wrung out in the days preceding the sailing.

Two hours later, the *Yamashiro Maru* sailed into the November calm-watered twilight of the setting sun. It would be the last calm day until it docked in Honolulu. The ship's relatively small size made for deeper pitching and yawing on the rough winter seas.

As the ship slipped across the horizon, Midori hurried to the cable office. Before sending her message, she reread Kenji's telegram received two days earlier. "Not good time for Haru to come. Will write." She was thankful Haru had not been present when the telegram was delivered. Now that the ship had sailed, Midori telegrammed Kenji. "*Yamashiro Maru* left. ETA December 2. Be a good husband to Haru."

She had raised both these children to do the right thing. She could do no more.

Before sailing, the six students had agreed to meet on the common deck at 7:00 p.m. Only Haru and Kame made the appointment. The wind swirled their hair, salt spray flecked their cheeks, and darkness held sway as flying clouds hid the moon. In the chill, Haru wore a new, thick, maroon kimono, a gift from Midori. Kame's faded kimono evoked memories of Haru's Amakusan poverty. Each had donned sweaters underneath their outer garments.

Haru grimaced a woozy smile at her friend. "Natsu is busy emptying her stomach in a bucket. I wondered if I would be the only one on deck."

Kame leaned over the railing, spit, and wiped her chin with her kimono sleeve. "You can't believe the terrible smells and the engine noise, Haru! We have eighty people jammed together, including at least two dozen men who are thinking about their prospects when it gets dark."

By day three, the swells had dropped to a mere twelve feet. Color had returned to the girls' cheeks. Judith's students met after dinner—except for Natsu, who strolled on deck only during times reserved for first- and second-class passengers.

Saki wrinkled her nose, a habit that meant she had something to say. "Every meal the same. Rice, pickled turnips, fish soup, and red-dyed plums."

Mayo blurted out, "It is so awful down below, Haru! Especially with nothing to do."

Kame clapped her hands. "Why don't you teach us English?"

"Me? I can say only 'hello.'"

"No," said Mayo. "You are too modest. You exchanged words with Judith. You know the Roman alphabet. Your something is better than our nothing."

Haru dropped her shoulders, thinking, *This is not about me. This is about people who need help. The last time I thanked Kiyoshi for taking me in, he told me, "Child, the day will come when you can pay me back by helping others."*

"All right. We will meet tomorrow. I will come downstairs after dinner."

The following evening, Haru descended three flights of stairs. She smelled steerage before she saw it. She slowed her steps, then saw Kame at the bottom and smiled, determined not to let her nausea show.

Kame's eyes gleamed wickedly. "I notice your breaths are shallow. Don't worry; you will get used to it."

All eighty people were sitting on the tatami mat. Haru walked fast to hide her nervous legs. *What have I gotten myself into?* She stepped in front of the expectant faces, offered a warm smile, and bowed low. In a tight voice, she began. "Each day, we will write and pronounce five letters of the Roman alphabet and learn ten words." She hoped her vocabulary would last the next twelve sailing days.

Saki handed Haru a piece of folded cardboard with a chunk of coal. "This will be your chalkboard ... " she held up the coal nugget, "and your chalk!"

Haru gave Saki a grateful smile.

As her students responded enthusiastically to her lessons, Haru's confidence grew. Years later, she would look back on those impromptu English classes as a gift, revealing leadership abilities she never suspected she had nor expected she would need.

The routine was interrupted on the ninth day when an out-of-breath Saki rushed to her before class. "We have a sick girl. I think it's the lung disease. Everyone is afraid to report it."

A woman standing next to Saki introduced herself as Tazu. "I'm a nurse. It looks like tuberculosis. The woman is coughing up blood." She shook her head as her eyes locked onto Haru's. "She must be separated."

Why are they coming to me? Haru asked herself. She looked at the two women. If the disease spread, the ship would have to return to Yokohama. There was a British doctor on board whom she had seen on deck.

"Wakarimashita. I will be back."

Grabbing her dictionary, Haru sprinted to the clinic. A sign hung on the doorknob. She consulted her dictionary. "In case of emergency, go to Cabin A4."

Her knock brought a rheumy-eyed, lanky man to the door. He scowled at Haru as he cinched his robe. Haru read from her dictionary. "Tubberlockus."

The doctor's face turned ashen. "Where?"

Haru knew the word. "Steerage."

"Wait here."

Minutes later, the doctor, having changed into a white smock, emerged from the cabin and followed Haru's descent to steerage. Halfway down the final set of stairs, he put a handkerchief over his face. He examined the girl. Then looking at two men hovering, he said, "Place her in the engine room."

The men looked blank until Haru interpreted.

The doctor looked at Haru and put his finger to his lips.

"Secret," said Haru.

The doctor nodded. "She cannot leave the ship. She must go back to Japan." Everyone in steerage understood if word leaked, the ship would return to Japan. They worried who would be next.

The next day, steerage passengers enjoyed fruit and meat with their dinner.

⚭ CHAPTER 21 ⚭

KENJI'S HEART BEAT FASTER the closer the *Yamashiro Maru* approached Honolulu's harbor. He stood beneath a rustling palm tree. The winter trade winds slapped against his face, and the sun arced high in the sky behind him. An exuberant crowd of greeters waited at the quay. One expectant group could not be seen. Sweating picture-bride husbands were ensconced in the windowless Immigration Processing Hall, cooled by a single overhead fan. All picture brides would be required to enter the immigration office together, go to a private room, and strip naked to undergo a medical examination.

But not Haru. Kenji had seen to that. When he checked with the shipping line to verify the arrival time and date—never certain, given weather conditions—he discovered that Haru was traveling second class. A plan formed. He knew Imamura was already putting pressure on immigration to stop the naked exams. So when Kenji approached the chief of immigration to ask, "It would be considered a great favor if my wife and the other woman married to a doctor could clear immigration with all the other passengers," the chief agreed.

Thus, Kenji could have his planned confrontation with Haru without the other picture brides and their husbands in audience. It would be all over by the time they cleared customs.

Now, as the ship docked, Kenji walked over to the busy path running parallel to the fence that kept passengers directed toward the immigration office. From there, he could see the passengers disembark. Behind him, the tightly wound Kenji hardly noticed Chinese women in their black, shiny trousers manning food stalls or the portly Hawaiian women chatting among their lei booths.

In a low voice, Kenji rehearsed his marriage-avoidance speech to a palm tree. As an orator, he practiced placing emphasis on the right words and inserting a pause at the right places. "My parents have made *a tragic* mistake, Haru-san. As an *Amakusan* woman …

you will *never* be *accepted*. Your life here would be one of … *humiliation*, filled with great *sorrow*. It is best that you … *return* to Japan." He extracted the boat ticket from his sleeve and presented it to the tree trunk. "*Immediately.*"

He told himself to be cruel now and save both of them a life of shame and unhappiness. Certainly, the shock of rejection would compel Haru to take the ticket and leave quickly. He would still have to face his bishop, for whom he had concocted a quite different speech. He would explain how devastated he had been when his intended confessed that she regretted leaving Japan and realized she could not live among foreigners. In his agitated state, he dismissed his mother's reaction as a problem to be handled later.

The first- and second-class passengers began their descent down the gangplank. Kenji held the picture of Haru. He had to admit that the woman in the picture was beautiful. It gave him pause. Maybe he had made the wrong decision. But the thought did not hold. He spotted a young Japanese girl at the top of the gangplank holding a parasol. *Nothing like the picture. Must be the wife of the doctor.* More people descended. Then no one. No Haru. His spirits lifted. Had she changed her mind at the last minute and stayed in Yokohama, too shamed to marry a priest?

Haru's pulse pumped faster. Diamond Head rose to her right. The town in front looked more like a village compared to Hiroshima and Yokohama. She hung back while the upper class disembarked so she could leave with Mayo, Ume, Kame, and Saki. A representative from the Japanese consulate guided them through the steerage exit, almost at ground level, near the front of the ship.

Hawaii! thought Haru as her foot found land. Her face glowing, she prayed she would be a good wife to Kenji.

PART II

IMMIGRANT

CHAPTER 22

Honolulu Harbor – December 1, 1909

SHOULDERS BACK, a buoyed Kenji hustled to the immigration build-ing and trotted up the outdoor concrete steps, avoiding the wobbly handrail that presented more peril than protection. He barged into the NYK ship agent's office, strode to a floppy-haired young Cauca-sian, always referred to as a haole in Hawaii, fingering the manifest, and leaned over the clerk's desk.

"Takayama, Haru," snapped Kenji.

The man made a show of struggling to read the handwritten names as his thumb slowly edged down the manifest.

Reading upside down, Kenji found what he did not want to see. He jammed his forefinger on his wife's name that crushed any hope for an easy escape from his mother's blunder.

Perplexed, he strode downstairs into the sunlight, where he no-ticed the Japanese woman he had seen earlier engaged in conversa-tion with a Japanese doctor whom he knew, but not well.

"Ah, Takayama-san. You must meet my bride, Natsu. She shared a cabin with your Haru."

Then where is she? Kenji thought, greeting Natsu. "Hajimemashite."

After bowing, Natsu tilted her head. "Your Haru is the queen of steerage. She must be with *them*." Her emphasis on "them" left little doubt that Haru's choice of friends was suspect.

Kenji slowed his walk to the immigration hall like a man mount-ing the gallows.

Inside the reception area, his eyes roved over the anxious faces of the grooms wearing ill-fitting Western clothes. Some immediately recognized Kenji and greeted him with deep bows. Soon the room buzzed with the men identifying the celebrity from Honolulu's largest Buddhist mission. Underneath his strained joviality, Kenji agonized, *How am I going to extricate myself from my mother's foolishness?*

∞ ∞

While the sea-scented wind brushed her tightly bound hair, Kame strolled behind Haru and the Japanese consulate officer leading the picture-clutching hopefuls into the immigration holding facilities. Kame tried to ignore the phalanx of dour-faced public health officials scrutinizing the women, on guard for an uncertain gait, a cough, runny eyes, or any other out-of-sort appearance.

Kame was worried. This morning, her eye itched upon awaking. When she looked into the mirror, she spotted a reddish hue in the left corner of her eye. She shuddered, trying to convince herself that if she hadn't been looking for a stain, she wouldn't have found one.

As the line moved along, her heartbeat betrayed the self-deception. She chatted aimlessly, walking next to Ume, and looked straight ahead as if trying to read a sign at the end of the hall.

An inspector approached her. Kame kept up her nervous patter. The stern-faced man tapped her on the arm. "Follow me." She was escorted into an anteroom. The consulate officer stood next to a Caucasian wearing a white smock. A stethoscope hung from his neck.

The inspector pointed to Kame's left eye.

A tremble crept through Kame's body. The doctor peered intently into the eye. He nodded to the consulate officer. Kame bit her tongue. She envisioned herself slopping pigs for her neighbor, whose leering eyes forecast an imminent claim on his private sow.

The consulate officer's kind eyes and soothing voice delivered the verdict. "Gomennasai. You have the eye disease."

Usually a passenger diagnosed with trachoma would respond, "wakarimashita," and accepting her fate, withdraw from the room to be escorted back to the ship. But Kame stood there like a figurine.

"You can come again when—"

Kame let out a piercing shriek, followed by another and another, the pitch growing ever higher. Then she collapsed.

❧ Chapter 23 ❧

HER SCREECHING PIERCED THE IMMIGRATION HALL. An angry murmur arose. The second Japanese consul rushed to the door separating the two holding rooms. The waiting grooms coalesced around the frantic officer flapping his arms to calm the crowd.

The grooms, some only recently returned to work after the summer sugar strike, wavered as if waiting for a spark that would ignite them to break through the door. The immigration officers leaped from their tables to form a human barricade at the door with the besieged Japanese consul.

The consul squeaked, "Daijoubu. Daijoubu. It's okay." He tried to raise his voice. "No one is hurt. A bride has the eye disease."

The grooms, sweating in their starched white shirts and black woolen suits, retreated. They had been briefed on the medical exam. All but one of them hoped the distressed woman belonged to someone else.

An immigration officer opened the door just wide enough to call to the consulate officer. He nodded and faced the crowd.

"Aoki-san?"

The room quieted. All eyes belonging to anyone not named Aoki swept the room. One man directed his vacant gaze toward the doorway. He wore a bowler hat a size too small, a gimmick that made his lanky frame seem taller. His suit fitted reasonably well, suggesting tailoring. His white-knuckled hands held a sepia-tinted picture. A pitiful voice, one that would not have been heard if the room had not remained funeral-parlor quiet, uttered, "Aoki *desu*."

The consulate officer's voice softened. "I am so sorry, Aoki-san. Your wife has pinkeye."

The man removed his hat and dropped his head like someone long out of work begging for a day-labor job. "But the doctors in Yokohama always check. There must be a mistake."

"Yes. She must have picked it up just before leaving Japan. It takes five to twelve days from the time of exposure until the disease shows itself. Trachoma is very contagious and can lead to blindness."

The crowd parted, giving Aoki a wide berth as if he were a leper. Small rivulets of tears filled in the leathery wrinkles of a man who knew hard work.

Minutes later, another man's name was called out. He was told his wife refused to leave the ship. Resigned to his fate, the man whispered, "*Shikataganai*." Accepting his wife's apparent case of homesickness, he shuffled out of the room. He would find out months later that this was the woman who had tuberculosis. She would never be allowed to leave Japan.

A side door banged open. A haole with a red, bulbous nose led four khaki-attired officers across the room to what looked like ordinary pine kitchen tables. At a nod from Red Nose, the consulate officer organized the queues. Each table's officer would check one piece of the required documents: an identification issued by the Japanese consulate, a bank deposit book mandated to prove the groom could support a wife, and proof of employment or a business license for the self-employed. Because the Japanese consulate had previously screened all the documents, the process went quickly.

Kenji's practiced smile masked his inner turmoil. As he thought of the irony of joining a crowd including grooms who had attended his "How to Greet Your Bride" class, one of them, with cuffed trousers too short, approached. "Reverend, you are so busy you didn't have time to buy a lei." He handed one of his two plumeria necklaces to Kenji. "I bought two."

Kenji was sure the man's classmates had drawn straws to see who would give up his lei.

The happy groom said, "If only everyone attended your class, maybe this room wouldn't smell like an outhouse."

"Arigato," said Kenji, thanking the groom while inhaling the sweet smell. *You win, Mother.*

The crowd stirred as a middle-aged priest in black robes, a Roman collar, and a confident smile sauntered into the room. Reverend Gennosuke Motokawa, pastor of the First Japanese Methodist Church, had gained fame as Kekkon Bozu—the wedding priest specializing in picture-bride marriages.

Christianity among the Japanese immigrants gained an enormous boost in 1885 when Reverend Kanichi Miyama converted the Japanese consul general, Taro Ando. Blaming the demon sake for the Japanese laborers' descent into paganism, Ando not only set a personal example by forsaking liquor but also organized a chapter of the Temperance Society among the Issei. Reverend Miyama found it easy to win baptisms, but most workers ignored Christianity after taking the sacrament. They were too wedded to the profligate nature of their plantation kinship and their ingrained Buddhist customs. It would take the civilizing influence of the picture brides to turn men to religion.

Kenji strode over to greet his compatriot in the taming of Japan's rowdy labor force. He shook hands instead of bowing.

"Let's visit our immigration friends together. I need to verify the final number of marriages," said Motokawa.

The haole officer rose from his chair as the two men approached. He gave a nod of recognition and airily dismissed Kenji's offer to show his documents. "More convenient to have your bride with the group. You and she can join in the wedding ceremony."

Kenji was about to remind the officer that he was excused from the regulation that all brides must be married as part of the immigration process. This requirement had slowed the practice of picture brides running away from their intended. But before Kenji could respond, an authoritative knock resounded from the door, which then swung open.

Kenji watched as forty-two picture brides—adorned in their best kimono, hair piled as high as her neighbor could arrange, and each clutching a picture—entered the hall. He thought about how often he had counseled grooms for this moment. "Dress well. Smile. Take your bride shopping. Stay at a nice hotel the first night. Treat her kindly, for there are few women for many men." With a meaningful look, he would add, "We have all seen those fancy dressers prowling like hyenas for unhappy brides and sweet-talking them into living the gay life."

The brides and grooms milled about, searching for faces matching their handheld pictures. Most men were ten to fifteen years older than their brides. Some couples had not only exchanged pictures but had also described how to spot the other: a particular kimono pattern for the bride or a certain color tie for the groom. One groom promised to put a feather in his hat. His bride shrieked with delight when she spotted a bowler hat adorned with ostrich feathers brushing the ceiling. Murmurs of "Are you Tanaka?" "Would you be Saki?" "Excuse me, are you … ?" filled the room like the hum of cicadas filling the night air.

The river of hope continued to flow through the door to a new life as the first arrivals bowed to their intended, saying softly, "I will try my best to be a good wife."

Kenji began to wonder, *Have I missed her?*

Haru entered last. She spotted Kenji immediately—not just from his saffron Buddhist priest's robes but also because she had grown up with his picture staring out from the reception room wall at home. Her face glowed. She walked toward Kenji at a measured but confident pace. The room buzz softened. An aisle parted for her as she advanced. The eyes of her shipboard students focused on her as if she were royalty. The men found themselves caught up in the drama, their eyes searching the other grooms, trying to guess who would claim this prize, for no woman in the room equaled Haru in her beauty, her quiet dignity, and her natural poise.

Kenji's eyes widened. He recognized Haru, but this was not the girl in the school uniform whose picture he had received with the last greeting card for Oshogatsu, or New Year's Day.

Ume stepped into the gap beside Haru and touched her arm gently. Haru stopped.

Ume's radiant face picked out a dumbfounded Kenji near the edge of the crowd, indicated him to Haru, and addressed him. "We recognize your picture, Takayama-sama. You are most fortunate to marry Haru-sensei. She has been our English teacher. She has a kind heart." Ume bowed and retreated to the edge of the human corridor. The misty-eyed brides bowed in his direction. Then the grooms. The lazy overhead whirl of the fan was the only sound in the room.

"Welcome to Hawaii, Haru-san," said Kenji, remembering his advice to smile. He walked slowly to his bride and placed the lei over Haru as she rose from a low and prolonged bow.

"I will try my best to be a good wife, Kenji-san."

The room broke into applause and tears.

"Takayama-san," said Motokawa.

Kenji had not seen the priest amble over.

"Your parents have chosen a woman so gentle of manner. May I ask a favor? Would you say a few words in the Buddhist tradition at the wedding?"

"It would be a great honor," said Kenji.

∞ CHAPTER 24 ∞

HARU INTRODUCED HER FRIENDS FROM JUDITH'S CLASS and explained that Kame had been the screaming lady with pinkeye.

Kenji recognized Mayo's husband, John Fujimoto, a union troublemaker who interfered with Imamura's quiet negotiations with the sugarcane barons. Kenji hoped this new wife would settle John down. He had married a Portuguese woman fifteen years ago who had given him three sons. She and two of the sons had died in the bubonic plague that had infested Honolulu's Chinatown in 1899. The surviving boy had been one of the first children taken in by the orphanage built by Bishop Imamura.

Fujimoto bowed and in a perfunctory voice said, "Good morning, Reverend."

Kenji returned the bow and looked over to Mayo. "Congratulations."

"Arigato," said Fujimoto, a look of subdued anger in his eyes. "You know that despite our best efforts, we still lost the strike. Now that I have a wife ... " He cast a quick look at Mayo. "I will save my money to buy a small piece of land and grow vegetables. I almost had enough money before the strike to do so."

Ume and her husband drifted over.

After the formal greetings, Ume gushed, "Irie-san has leased land in Kona to grow coffee."

Measles scars dotted Irie's broad, flat face, but his eyes were intelligent and full of purpose.

Haru's eyes roamed, searching for Saki, and then stopped. Along the far wall, Saki was bobbing her head and waving a picture in front of her husband's face. Haru guessed that the picture and face did not match. The groom's attire was shabby, certainly not the look of a man who had bragged, "I am a landscape artist for rich people."

Haru turned back to Kenji and pointed out Saki and speculated on the situation.

"I suspect you are right. I've seen this before," said Kenji. He started to walk over to the couple.

Haru followed.

A teary-eyed Saki thrust a picture in Kenji's face. "Look at this picture and look at him." The picture showed a young, handsome man standing on the beach, the dramatic Diamond Head in the background.

Having learned not to mince words in these picture-swapping dramas, Kenji gave the distressed wife the only choice she had. "After the group wedding ceremony, you will come with me, and I will make the arrangements for you to return to Japan."

"Back to Japan?" Saki's voice trembled. "My father would never take me back."

Saki's intended husband looked up, his eyes flickering with hope. "I am sorry. I was so desperate for a wife that I sent you a picture of my brother. But … I will take care of you."

The room had emptied except for the sad drama and the bulbous-nosed immigration officer waiting at the exit.

Haru took her shipmate's hand. "What do you want to do, Saki?"

"What choice do I have?" She dropped the picture on the floor and looked at her husband. "Let's go." She did not bother to wipe her tears.

An hour later, the twice-married couples paraded from their pier-side wedding ceremony to rickshaws taking some lucky brides to honeymoon hotels. The not-so-lucky boarded trains or ships to their plantations.

Bishop Imamura waved at Kenji walking along with the newly-wed battalion. Once he caught up with the couple, the bishop placed yet another lei over Haru's neck. "Welcome, Haru." He beamed at the couple. "Congratulations on your American marriage."

Unconsciously, Imamura's gaze traveled over Kenji's shoulder. He didn't like what he saw.

∽ Chapter 25 ∽

A BEANPOLE OF A MAN WAS STRIDING TOWARD IMAMURA like someone desperate to catch a trolley. A Panama hat cuffed with a black band barely touched the pencil wedged above his right ear. His bony fingers clutched a notebook. Behind him, a chest-heaving man of sizable girth, his own planter's hat pulled down to his eyebrows, struggled to keep pace. Imamura knew the first man all too well, his nemesis, Andy Pafko, who invariably brought to mind those words spoken by Marc Antony in *Julius Caesar*: "Yond Cassius has a lean and hungry look." Pafko's anti-Japanese rant had only grown more strident since Imamura's arrival when both were alarmed at the cane workers' gambling and drinking. During the strike, Pafko had demonized the strikers. "Yield to his demands, and he thinks he is the master and makes new demands; use the strong hand, and he recognizes the power to which, from time immemorial, he has abjectly bowed. There is one word that holds the lower classes of a nation in check, and that word is 'authority.'"

A week later, Pafko coined the word *repaganization* of Hawaii in an editorial attack.

> A little more than eighty years have passed since the missionaries replaced the Hawaiian false idols and taboo system with the Kingdom of Christ. Now we have a recrudescence of paganism, with so many immigrants steeped in Buddhist habits of thought and loyal to the demands of Shinto. Is Hawaii a Christian land, or is it semi-Christian and semi-pagan?

That gem assured him a front-page career with the *Pacific Commercial Advertiser*.

Under his breath, Imamura said to Kenji, "You don't need to be bothered with Pafko on your wedding day. Why don't you take your bride shopping? I will suffer him by myself."

"Arigato," said Kenji.

Too late.

As he and Haru turned to leave, Pafko's sharp voice rose. "Reverend Takayama, wait."

Kenji, a puzzled frown on his face, stopped.

"This is Joshua Bilkerton," said Pafko, "the owner of Waimea's finest sugar plantation. I just told him who you are." Pafko's toothy smile turned smirky. "The gentleman is under the impression that your opening a Buddhist mission in his town provides a great benefit."

Imamura reached out his hand to Bilkerton. "Ah, Mr. Bilkerton, we have exchanged letters."

Bilkerton shook Imamura's hand. "Your telegram telling me Reverend Takayama would be coming was welcome news, welcome news indeed."

Then Bilkerton offered his hand to Kenji, who reciprocated as per Imamura's instructions to offer a firm handshake when meeting haoles.

"Don't mind him," said Bilkerton, looking at Pafko. "We need a Buddhist priest. All we have is a crazy Shinto shaman stirring up all sorts of trouble." Bilkerton dropped his voice. "But I am disappointed you plan to build your temple near our town square ... far away from your flock ... when I have generously offered land on my plantation for that purpose."

Imamura spoke before Kenji could respond. "You are a generous man, Mr. Bilkerton. But we had already accepted the land from the Parker Ranch in town to serve all of Waimea."

Before Bilkerton could respond, Pafko addressed Imamura. "Are you aware that the sheriff recently arrested five actors for putting on a play inciting workers?" Pafko pulled the pencil from his ear and opened his notebook. "Would you care to comment?"

Imamura smiled graciously. "Ah, the play with two side-by-side stage sets: one revealing the plantation owner's luxurious living room and the other displaying the squalor of the workers' quarters. As a reporter, you certainly must cherish that the American Constitution guarantees freedom of speech."

Pafko snapped his notebook shut. "Always the clever one, Reverend Imamura. You have half the haole population fooled with your Americanization of Buddhism."

"If you gentlemen will excuse us," said Imamura, forcing a smile. He turned and walked away with Kenji and a very confused Haru following.

But Pafko was not finished. "Your real design—to take over Hawaii with your Nisei—does not escape me!"

Haru caught only a few words of English, but the reporter's body language made the point. "Why is he so angry … " she hesitated, not used to talking to a husband, "Kenji-san?"

"The plantation owners need our labor but fear us."

"Why?"

"We are their most productive workers, but they are afraid we will never go back to Japan and our American children will vote away their privilege. They wish our children to follow their parents into the fields and fear we are educating them beyond what the haoles think is necessary to cut cane."

Imamura nodded supportively. Encouraged, Kenji concluded, "They take Christianity very seriously and look at all other religions as primitive threats to their belief in one true God."

"But Bilkerton-san thanked you for opening a mission for his workers."

"He understands Buddhism is a calming religion. Once I am in Waimea, he will expect me to help him mediate labor strife, as we have done on Oahu."

A little simplistic, thought Imamura, *but enough politics for today.* He called over a carriage.

Haru's eyes swiveled back and forth, as they rode up Nuuanu Street, beset with warehouses, pubs, and ship chandlers. They trotted past the Hawaiian Stockyard Livery and Boarding Stables, offering sightseeing tours of Waikiki and Moanalua Gardens for a dollar. A streetcar tooted and passed them from behind.

∞ CHAPTER 26 ∞

A BLOCK ONWARD, the street morphed into a retail valley flanked by two-story buildings. Balconies overhung wooden sidewalks hosting well-fed, wrinkled-faced, Hawaiian wahines weaving fragrant *pikake* leis, in front of pharmacies, millinery shops, hardware stores, and jewelers.

Imamura asked Haru about her health inspection during the immigration process. She replied, "We were led into a room in groups of six, where a doctor and a woman from the Japanese consulate waited. We were told to disrobe except for our bottom undergarment and then turn around slowly. The doctor listened to our chest with a stethoscope. Then we left."

"This is an improvement," said the bishop. "A complete naked exam has been required for Japanese only. We have vigorously protested for years. Yours is the first group allowed the dignity of partial clothing."

"A good friend failed the health inspection," said Haru. She explained Kame's pinkeye rejection. Imamura asked her a few questions about the condition of Kame's eyes, but Haru could offer little information.

Their carriage started up Nuuanu Street.

Further up the block in a honky-tonk bar, Andy Pafko was pouring whiskey into two tumblers painted with topless hula dancers. Near the entrance, a silver-haired Hawaiian plucked soft chords on his ukulele and crooned Hawaiian love songs with a sad voice, rasped by cheap cigarettes and cheaper rum. Lazy ceiling fans swirled the smells of fresh popcorn and stale beer. Two decades of cigar burns scarred the tops of the sturdy mahogany tables. While a Chinese cook could rally up a steak crowned with over-easy eggs, he was mainly for show. This was a drinking man's bar.

Pafko bragged he knew his limit. The bar's clientele was all men, all white, and all much too talkative—a dream haunt for a reporter. He pushed a tumbler to Bilkerton. "The Brits know how to drink whiskey. You don't ruin it with water and ice." He took a generous swallow, swirled the liquor with his tongue like mouthwash, and let it slide down his throat. "You wait to feel the warmth in your gut. Then drink a glass of water so you don't burn a hole."

Bilkerton tilted his glass and swallowed. He skipped the side of water.

"Joshua," said Pafko, "you got this Buddhist stabilization all backward. You didn't learn a goddamn thing from the strike."

"My Japs didn't strike," said Bilkerton. "I listened to their complaints, painted a few houses, and halved the interest on the loans when they buy from company stores ahead of payday."

"It wasn't about you, Joshua. All the workers on the outer islands were told not to strike. The Oahu strikers needed the money your workers sent them. All your shack painting did was to tell your workers you were running scared. We are in a war, Joshua—a war between two cultures, two nations. It's not just about cutting cane and picking pineapples."

"My Japs are hard workers. Weekend drinking and gambling are the main problems. That's why I offered to pay the steerage fee for the picture brides and welcome the priest."

"Picture brides for stability. Stop the gambling. Just calm the men down." Pafko sneered. "That's all horseshit promoted by those Jap priests. Look at all the kimono-clad women here dropping babies like coconuts from a palm tree in a typhoon. Those people are almost half the population. If we don't stop them, they will be three-quarters strong and voting."

Pafko emptied his half-full glass in a single gulp and refilled it.

"If we hadn't overthrown the queen, you'd be selling your plantation to some retired samurai."

"That's a bit of an exaggeration," Bilkerton slurred.

"You are not seeing the picture. The big picture, the long picture. Let me paint it for you. In 1885, King Kalakaua goes to Japan and offers his kingdom to the emperor and proposes a marriage between his five-year-old niece and some Jap prince. The emperor declines but agrees to send workers. In 1893," he continued, oblivious to his bar-patron eavesdroppers, "the sugar boys get the Marines to land and send Queen Liliuokalani packing and set up a republic, Texas-style, but Presidents Cleveland and McKinley refuse your bogus republic's pleas to be annexed. In 1897, Secretary of the Navy Roosevelt wants to annex Hawaii. Japan sends a warship to Hawaii to protest, and McKinley backs off! Are you seeing what's happening, Joshua?"

Pafko grabbed the bottle and filled both glasses nearly to the brim. Bilkerton nodded his head unsteadily and mumbled, "Yeah, yeah, I see."

"Then in 1898, some crazy Spaniard blows up the *Maine* in Havana's harbor." Suddenly noticing he had drawn an audience, Pafko made his listeners wait as he took a gentle sip of whiskey. He put his hand on Joshua's arm. "If not for that little prank, Hawaii might have been part of Japan's Pacific empire like Okinawa or Korea. Instead, the American navy sinks the Spanish fleet in Manila."

Pafko released Bilkerton's arm, swirled the liquid in his glass but didn't drink from it. "Thankfully, McKinley finally recognizes that Hawaii must be secure and annexes the republic. The sugar barons and Dole keep importing more Japanese labor like it's just another crop—gotta keep those new pineapple fields going. Do you know how many Japanese landed here the first year after Hawaii's annexation?"

Through the fog of his whiskey, Bilkerton managed a proud, "Twenty-six thousand!"

"But even though the Jap workers got a lot more rights with America, you still kept bringing boatloads of them here. Boatloads! Another sixty-eight thousand between 1900 and 1907 when that Gentlemen's Agreement finally stopped the invasion."

Pafko was on a roll. He stood, looked around at his audience as if he was William Jennings Bryan about to deliver his "Cross of Gold" speech. "More picture brides. More kids. More Buddhist temples. More Japanese afternoon schools where kids are taught loyalty to their god, the emperor. Someday, Japan's growing empire will bump into America. Whose side will these people fight on?"

Hoisting his drink as if to make a toast, Pafko took his time to empty the glass down his throat, eyeballed Bilkerton, and lowered his voice. "Think about that, Joshua—while riding the boat back with your picture brides."

Pafko turned his glass upside down, slammed it on the table, and called over to the bar. "Put it on my tab, Mori." His blurry eyes surveyed his audience. "School's out." He swayed and wobbled his way to the door but imagined he marched out like a victorious attorney after a contentious courtroom battle.

∞ CHAPTER 27 ∞

THE CARRIAGE NEARED THE NUUANU-BERETANIA CROSSROADS where Japanese working girls trolled the notorious intersection in white clinging holoku dresses draping from their shoulders to ankles. Kenji made a show of squinting at the sun and tugged down his fedora. He did not see the woman he hoped he would never encounter again. Had she left the trade? Would she attend a temple ceremony some day with children in tow? Would she remember him?

The incident had happened two years ago. He had accompanied Imamura on a regular foray into River Street's dens of iniquity, preaching a return to Japanese values among the gangsters, pimps, and prostitutes. After each incursion, however, he returned to his room aroused. One restless evening after they had returned from a brothel trying to shame the women to forsake their trade, Kenji had slipped out of the Hongwanji dressed in his garden clothes and beat-up straw hat. He was strolling side streets toward the river when he spotted her standing on a Nuuanu corner.

She did not see him.

Fearful of approaching her on a public street or calling out to her, he dropped a coin on the cobblestone road. Then two coins. She turned, spotted him, switched on her professional come-hither smile, and sauntered forward. She was older than he had first thought but still in the bloom of life. He vacillated—he was a priest pledged to end vice—and thought of retreating.

Kenji froze in place.

"I'm Cindy," she hushed, using her contrived English name. She grabbed his hand gently. Massaged it. "I can make you happy, either for a short time or until morning."

Kenji noticed tiny wrinkles had etched themselves in the corners of her eyes. He put his hand in his pocket and fingered his money. "I have a dollar for a short time."

Still holding his hand, she led him down a narrow dirt path and guided him inside a one-room wooden shack, roofed with corrugated steel. Lighting three scented candles, she said, "You can put the dollar on the table."

She faced him. With a practiced hand, she reached behind her neck, and eased the single button loose of its confinement and shrugged her shoulders. The single-piece holoku dropped in a heap at her feet revealing a body unconfined by any other garment. In the flickering light of the candles, Kenji saw that her breasts sagged and stretch marks streaked her belly. He wondered who was taking care of her child.

Kenji had not moved. Sensing he was new to the game, Cindy stepped forward and began unbuttoning his shirt. Next, she loosened the knot on the drawstring holding up his trousers and let them fall to join her holoku on the thin carpet. Smiling seductively, she slid her hand down his chest and under his shorts. He had gone flaccid. She tried massaging it back to life. He did not respond. His knees trembled.

She looked up at him. "What's wrong?"

Guilt had triumphed over desire, morphed to embarrassment, and settled on righteousness. "Nothing. I … I just wanted to talk for the time I paid." He willed his eyes to stay focused on hers. "Why do you do this? You could marry, get a job, build a future."

A flash of anger crossed her face. "I *am* married, although my husband may have divorced me as a runaway wife. He wrote me claiming he owned a farm. I was only hours off the ship when he admitted he was just a laborer working for a Chinese duck farmer in Waikiki. I tried to live with him for a month. He beat me for complaining that he had lied. I ran away."

"You could find a new husband. A life with dignity."

"Dignity! I send a fifty dollars a month to Japan for my parents to buy land. Where is the dignity in getting paid fourteen dollars a month on a plantation for the privilege of getting up before the roosters and looking like a hag before my thirtieth birthday? You feel shame for coming here. I feel proud. I broke the shackles of an evil man and will be one of the few who return from these islands with money."

Kenji had not moved during this exchange despite the absurdity of his standing in his undershorts with his trousers bunched at his feet. The discussion had calmed his nerves. Cindy noticed he was beginning to get hard. Her smile came back. This time he responded to her touch. With her other arm on his shoulder, she pushed him gently onto her bed, where she straddled his thighs, all the while maintaining a coy smile. She sensed this was his first experience. She knew that her face and this act would be etched into his memory forever. She wanted to perform for him and for herself … not for physical satisfaction that she never felt but because a great experience meant a return visit or maybe a regular customer. She placed his hands on her breasts and then reached over to her nightstand and dipped her fingers into a cup of coconut oil. She lubricated herself, then raised her body, and slid down on him. It did not take Kenji long to complete his mission. He tried to roll out from under her, but she leaned over. "Stay," she whispered. "Let's go a second round so I, too, can feel the clouds and thunder," while she thought, *Oh, how men love to hear those words.*

Kenji shook his head. Spent, a resurgent guilt rushed over him. He forced himself up. Cindy rolled off him.

"Wait. I need to clean you." She dipped a small towel into a basin and wiped him. She helped him dress, returned with him to the street, and as he turned to walk in the direction opposite from his destination, she said, "Good evening, Reverend."

All this flashed before Kenji as the carriage continued to their hotel. Imamura pointed out landmarks to Haru, but Kenji had not heard a word.

"Isn't that right, Kenji?" said Imamura.

The daydreaming Kenji replied, "You are usually right, Your Excellency."

"Well, in this case I am. We need wives for our ministers for both to act in partnership in this mission. Your parents are great role models."

A horn blasted as a car was about to ram their carriage. Haru looked up and grabbed Kenji's hand. Her body jerked at their horse's sudden stop. The animal rose on his hind legs, and the Packard stopped under the horse's hoofs.

The Chinese driver jumped from their carriage's perch. "So sorry! So sorry!" he pleaded as he approached the furious-faced white driver who shrieked, "Forget the sorrys, coolie! Get your hack out of the way!"

Kenji reassured the driver, "It wasn't your fault. You had the right of way."

"No want police, all haole. Better to apologize."

The carriage stopped at the Honolulu Hotel. Although Kenji and Haru would be living at the nearby Hongwanji Temple complex, Imamura suggested Kenji treat Haru as a typical picture bride on her first day in Hawaii. He had booked one of the two bridal suites despite his intention to send Haru back to Japan at the docks.

A Hawaiian ukulele band strumming "My Waikiki Mermaid" welcomed the couple ascending the stairs. The bellman grabbed Haru's luggage. Although Judith had told the girls about the American habit of tipping, she was still surprised by how casually Kenji handed the Japanese porter a quarter and how perfunctory the bellhop said "thank you." What a strange custom, she concluded: people expecting extra money to do their job and a Japanese tipping a Japanese!

The hotel manager, a Nisei born from one of the earliest 1880s immigrants, recognized Kenji and escorted the honeymooners to their room. Haru stepped into the room with the same reverence as entering her kondo's Golden Pavilion. Sweet flower fragrances that she did not recognize rode rays of sunlight streaming through open shutters. "So gorgeous," she said softly.

Kenji turned to Haru. "Let's take the Rapid Transport streetcar to Liliha to buy a set of Western clothes for you."

Haru's heartbeat spiked. She had hoped Kenji would be such a husband, one who started their marriage with this special wedding gift. Judith had told her that such a trousseau would be worn only their wedding day and then placed in a trunk as a memory. When not wearing work garments in the fields, most Japanese women continued to wear their kimono in Hawaii as they did in Japan.

Her eyes brightened. "Oh, how delightful!"

∞ Chapter 28 ∞

Electric streetcars, introduced only eight years before to replace horse-drawn carriages, had revolutionized Oahu's housing and employment markets. Workers no longer had to be tethered to their factories or offices. Manoa and Kaimuki became Honolulu's first bedroom communities.

The mustard-yellow streetcar arrived just as Kenji and Haru reached its appointed stop. They boarded the open carriage. Haru's eyes widened, reading the "NO SPITTING" sign posted over the coin box, while Kenji gave two nickels to the conductor. *What kind of people have to be told not to spit in a tram?*

The streetcar trundled along its narrow-gauge tracks two blocks up, took a gentle left onto Beretania Street, and then crossed through Chinatown. Haru put a handkerchief over her nose when it crossed the slow-moving Nuuanu River, covered with blotches of green scum. From the tram stop on Liliha Street, Kenji led Haru to the New Brides Shop, famous for outfitting picture brides in Western clothes. As they entered the store, Haru immediately spotted Mayo.

"Mayo, how lucky to find you here!" Haru said. "We can do this together."

Seeing the unhappy face of a man trying to explain a bra to his wife, Haru looked at Mayo who demurely nodded.

"We can help your wife," said Haru to a weather-beaten face. "We are familiar with the strange garments of Western women." Haru peeked at Kenji and saw him smile in gratitude.

Kenji joined Fujimoto, Mayo's husband, at the tea shop next door to wait for their wives. The tension between Kenji and Fujimoto that had surfaced in the immigration building over the recently settled sugar worker's strike still hovered over the two men. They found a table, ordered tea, and ignored the other husbands discussing the recent American Thanksgiving picnic at the Fort Street temple, which had served turkey along with sushi. Long minutes dragged into the longest hour in Kenji's memory.

Finally, Haru and Mayo entered the tea shop, each walking hesitantly in their laced-up, high-heeled boots, the current fashion favored by the younger planters' wives.

Kenji's eyes widened.

She had untied her piled hair, letting it cascade down to her shoulders, and crowned her head with a snow-white bonnet, rimmed with a pink sash, which harmonized with her tulip-red dress, hinting at inviting curves.

All eyes in the tea shop turned to Haru. She bowed to Kenji, and although she kept her eyes down as custom dictated, she felt a tingle as she peeked at his approving look.

His throat had gone tight. He swallowed hard and finally managed to say, "You … uh … look good in that dress."

Fujimoto mumbled a "you look nice" to Mayo.

After both ladies sat down, the Chinese waitress poured oolong tea for them. Haru asked a polite question to start the conversation—one she would soon regret. "How is work on the Aiea plantation, Fujimoto-san? Mayo is very proud you are a foreman."

The man's hard-edged voice jolted Haru with its reply. "The strike leaders were fired, Haru-san. I am working at the McCully taro fields behind a duck farm at Waikiki."

Kenji raised an eyebrow. "But didn't the strike settlement guarantee everyone would get his job back?"

Fujimoto's face twisted into an angry mask. He pointed a finger. "Name one strike leader who got his job back. You, Imamura-san, and the Japanese consul—all of you sold us out. How could you support haole plantation owners instead of your fellow Japanese? Do you think it's right we are paid eighteen dollars a month, but the Puerto Ricans and Filipinos get twenty-two dollars?" Fujimoto slammed his teacup on the table. "For the same work?"

Haru winced. *Poor Mayo is married to a rude, angry man who insults a priest in front of his wife.*

Fujimoto stood up and leaned over the table, his own face just three inches from Kenji's. "We could have won the strike."

"But this week," said Kenji, "the plantation owners raised the pay almost equal to that of the Puerto Ricans and Filipinos."

"ALMOST! Are we *almost* as good as the Puerto Ricans?" Fujimoto caught the shocked look on the faces of Mayo and Haru. He sat down. "Gomennasai," he apologized with a slight head and shoulder bow. "Even in the face of injustice, I should control my emotions."

"Daijoubu," said Haru, saying it was all right but thinking it wasn't.

Regaining his composure, Fujimoto spied the hostess and was about to wave her over for the check when a passing carriage caught his eye. "That's strange ... Bishop Imamura with a young woman."

Haru and Mayo turned around. In stunned disbelief, they both shouted one word. "Kame!"

Kame turned at the sound of her name being screeched across the street.

⬤ Chapter 29 ⬤

"**H**ARU! MAYO!"

From the buckboard, the normally reticent Bishop Imamura smiled widely, flashing uneven teeth. Haru and Mayo hobbled down the teahouse steps in their toe-pinching boots. Unaccustomed to high heels, their ankles gave way, and both tumbled onto the wooden sidewalk where they broke into laughter. On the other side of the street, Kame dropped from the carriage and dodged between two water buffalos driven by a mandarin-capped Chinese boy. As she reached her fallen friends, Kame put out both hands and yanked them up.

"We thought—" started Mayo.

"Me too. I was sure I would never see you again. I even thought of committing—"

"Don't say it," cut in Haru, hugging her friend. "What happened?"

Kame pointed at Imamura entering the teahouse. "He did it."

Inside, the waitress pulled over another table and brought a fresh teapot with extra cups. Kenji told her, "Let's introduce our brides to *saimin*," referring to a plantation-inspired concoction of Japanese udon, Chinese chow mein, Filipino *pancit*, and depending on the chef, maybe some Portuguese sausage.

Haru and Mayo bubbled over with questions for Kame. "So, tell us, what happened? How did you escape? How did the bishop do it? Does your husband know you are free?"

Bishop Imamura silenced the chattering with a clearing of his throat. "For some months, we have been asking for a review of the trachoma diagnosis. The chief inspector has shown a willingness to consider quarantine rather than send passengers back. Today, I asked him to use Kame as a test case. He agreed. But first, he wanted to look at her eye. When he did, he spotted something in the eye and removed it."

"Buddha must love you," said Haru gazing at Kame. She turned to Imamura. "What about Kame's husband?"

"He should be at his hotel, a few blocks from yours," said Imamura. "I talked to the Japanese consulate officer. He will track him down and then contact Reverend Motokawa to perform a wedding ceremony."

"You'd better leave for the hotel now, Kame," said Haru.

Kame's eyes fell on the waiter, balancing bowls of steaming saimin on each arm as he approached. The trade winds carried the enticing new smell across the table. "I'll eat fast!"

Imamura slurped his udon soup and then used his chopsticks to pick up the thick noodles. He wiped some dribble from his chin with a paper napkin. He gave Kenji the serious smile signifying an imminent pronouncement: "I understand there is something called 'Judith's set'—a few young women who have grown quite fond of each other. Why don't we hold a reception for the five couples?"

The three brides clapped their hands and let out little squeals of delight, betraying their teenage enthusiasm. They huddled to make their own plans.

"Haru," asked Kenji, as everyone got up to leave, "how would you like to take the tram to Waikiki to see our famous beach?"

Haru clapped her hands. "Oh, yes. The royal family's beach. You see, I did read your letters."

∽ ∾

As the tram rumbled along the way to Waikiki, a conflicted Kenji realized he had only minutes to salvage his reputation. *She must go back on her own accord.* Speaking to Haru, he painted a life of horrors that awaited a missionary wife … so unlike the life in refined Hiroshima.

After hearing Kenji's warning about the primitive bath and toilet facilities in rural postings, Haru just laughed. "The bigger the challenge, the greater the glory."

Shoulders slumped, Kenji managed the smile of one bested at mahjong. "Yes, that is what my mother always said." He looked at Haru. The sun illuminated her smile. *Have I been the foolish one?*

Haru caught his glimpse at her breasts, which the Western dress emphasized. She felt an unfamiliar warmth surge through her body.

Kenji pointed out the beach cottages of the rich and famous—grand weekend retreats belonging to the Doles, Campbells, Castles, and other sugar or pineapple barons that had replaced the humbler thatched cabanas of the Hawaiian royalty. The architectural smorgasbord delighted Haru's eye. Doric-columned mansions neighbored Victorian gingerbread castles and four-story colonial replicas. Kenji nodded toward one huge banyan tree whose mighty limbs arched over a Greek-styled portico.

"There is a story where whiskey-loving James Castle at his housewarming is telling the pineapple king, James Dole, 'My plantation is so big it takes me all day to ride my horse across it.' Dole thinks a minute, scratches his chin, and says, 'Yes, I had an old nag like that once.'"

As Haru laughed, the tram stopped at the terminus adjacent to the Honolulu Aquarium. They walked across to a boat rental dock on the swamp that was Kapiolani Park, procured a rowboat, and rowed among the scenic network of lakes. "Normally, Haru, by this time of the year, we would have to duck when crossing under the bridges," Kenji explained. "But the trade winds that bring the rain are late this year." He pointed to the bandstand on Makee Island in the middle of the lake. "Next Sunday, we can return for a concert."

The boat bumped ashore at the edge of what looked like a racetrack.

"Now for a sunset ride on horseback," said Kenji. He tied up the boat and helped Haru onto dry land. At the look of uncertainty on Haru's face, Kenji added, "The horses are gentle, used to first-time riders."

By the time Haru and Kenji rode on the beach, few bathers, dressed in their head-to-toe bathing garments, remained. Haru gazed at the orange and red horizon, awed by the sunset. And from the back of a horse! So many first-time experiences in a single day. And tonight, there would be another first.

Kenji stopped at Waikiki's only beach structure. "This is the Moana Hotel. Rooms are three dollars a night. There's talk about another hotel. Most of us hope this will be the only one so the beach won't be spoiled."

The couple returned their horses to the mild rebuke from the man at the rental stable for being late. Haru's apologetic smile cut short the complaint.

"Such a beautiful island, Kenji." Thinking of Pafko and Fujimoto, she thought to herself, *But a discontented paradise.*

∞ CHAPTER 30 ∞

THE SKYLINE WAS DYING PURPLE when Kenji and Haru returned to the hotel. Ascending the hotel's steps, Haru smiled at other honeymooners watching them from the porch's rocking chairs. She looked for Mayo, Kame, and Ume, but didn't see them. As soon as she entered the foyer, those from the porch rose and traipsed into the dining room.

"Were they waiting for us?" whispered Haru.

"I suspect they were," Kenji whispered back.

When they entered the dining room, the maître d' led them to a table full of Judith's brides and their grooms, except for Kame. "There you are," said a happy Haru.

"I hope you don't mind the presumption," said Fujimoto, who had replaced his acerbic tone with the cordiality of a sometimes orator. "But all I hear about is 'Haru this' and 'Haru that' from this little gang." He smiled disarmingly at the word "gang."

"Haru is our teacher, Takayama-san," Mayo added.

As soon as the group chorused "*itadakimasu*," the before-meal greeting, Haru's eyes savored the dishes before her—thinly sliced mahimahi, tuna, red snapper sashimi, lightly battered shrimp, and mixed vegetable tempura.

"Well, ladies," said Haru, "does this look as good as the food on the ship?" Easy conversation followed the laughter.

Irie, Ume's husband, was the first to raise his hot sake cup with a "*kampai*," wishing everyone good health. "This is Nihei sake from the new Honolulu Sake Brewery, Hawaii's first Japanese winery," he added.

"Except for the moonshine on every plantation," deadpanned Fujimoto.

"Saki, is your hotel room beautiful?"

The woman forced a smile and a stoic "hai." Her so-called-artist husband, Toshi, kept eyes cast down.

Clearly, thought Haru, *they have not reconciled to a life together.* She was grateful when Fujimoto picked up the conversation but was not prepared for his shocking revelation.

"Reverend, I understand you had two wives attending a funeral last week who both claimed they were married to the deceased."

The alcohol, along with the suddenly silent and expectant audience, loosened Kenji's usually conservative tongue. "The Mori funeral." He emptied his sake cup. "Mori arrived just after the haoles deposed the queen in ninety-three. A blacksmith by trade. After a few years, he started his own shop and wrote his mother to send a bride. She was slow to respond, and in the meantime, he met a runaway wife with a child, helped her get a divorce, and married her. Before he got around to writing his mother, she sent a letter saying his bride was on the way. He went to meet the girl, planning to find another husband for her. But she was beautiful, so he married her as well. He was a clever fellow. Moved into the auto repair business as soon as the first cars arrived, and then started a boat-engine repair business on Sand Island. Neither wife had a clue about the other until he had a boating accident and drowned."

"How did he keep his secret from them?"

"He had two brothers. Both knew, but he socialized with wife number one with the older brother and wife number two with the younger brother."

The ladies expressed feigned shock while Haru started ladling rice onto the plates.

Picking up the cue, Kenji said, "In the end, it all worked out. Each wife inherited one of the businesses, and all the children found out they had half-brothers and half-sisters."

"I hope my husband doesn't tell me he has two missions to tend to," said Haru to everyone's laughter.

The men told stories from work until Fujimoto surprised Haru by asking, "Why don't you ladies tell us about your crossing?" The animated chatter lasted through a dessert of fresh pineapple when, as if a theater curtain had dropped, a collected hush fell upon the group.

Kenji broke the silence. "If you will excuse us, gochisosama deshita."

The four women glanced at each other.

Haru knew they were all anxious. She remembered Midori's advice: "Young men are too self-indulgent to worry about your performance, dear. All they require is acquiescence. Years may pass before they consider the other person has her own needs." Haru's eyes darted right and peeked at Kenji. His face stared ahead expressionless, but his hand twitching almost made her laugh. *Why, he is as nervous as I am!*

As soon as she entered their hotel room, Haru started filling the bathtub with hot water. The idea of stepping into a tub before soaping away the stench and grime of one's body bothered her, but Judith had explained that this seemingly barbaric behavior was the way of Western people. She placed a towel and bar of soap on a small stool and moved it next to the claw-footed tub. She checked the sash of Kenji's cotton yukata to see if it had been placed through all the robe's hoops. She dipped her finger in the water, cut off the cold-water faucet, waited another minute for more hot water, and tested once more. Satisfied with the temperature, she closed the tap. Haru opened the door and bowed.

"Your bath is ready, *danna-sama*," said Haru using a most polite form for a wife addressing her husband (or a courtesan addressing her sponsor).

Haru exchanged nervous smiles with Kenji as he entered the bathroom. She expected him to relax in the tub as was Kiyoshi's habit and thus was surprised when he came out after just enough time to lather and rinse himself. Perhaps she too should show eagerness and prepare quickly.

Haru left the door ajar. As she sat in the water, savoring the last warm moments with her womanhood intact, she studied the greying porcelain sink with its water-stained copper faucets, the vanity mirror with a ceiling lightbulb directly overhead, and the white towels embossed with the name of the hotel hanging from a wooden rack next to the tub. She wanted to remember everything about this special night. She washed her private area a little longer than necessary, enjoying the sensation. Upon alighting from the tub, she donned her yukata and then reached into her toiletry kit for the cologne Judith had given her and dabbed the back of her ears.

Silhouetted by the bathroom's amber glow, Haru floated into the shadowy bedchamber. As her eyes adjusted to the dim streak of light covering the upper half of the bed, she beheld an inert Kenji, covered from the neck down with a white sheet. His eyes shone like tiny pools of quicksilver. Haru stepped forward, remembered Midori's suggestion, and, emboldened by the sake, let her yukata drop to the floor.

Kenji let out a gasp.

Standing still, she caught Kenji's hungry gaze staring at her moon-shaped breasts. Warmth surged through her body. Her confidence rose. She felt honored offering herself to the man with whom she would share her life, raise children, and build a mission together. She stepped forward to crawl under the sheet. From an impish smile, her vocal cords tightened as throaty words escaped. "Good evening, Reverend."

Twisted anger rose on Kenji's face like a cat surprised by a pit bull. "Karayuki!" he hissed.

Haru fell back, ashamed of her nakedness. She snatched her yukata and fled to the bathroom.

☜ Chapter 31 ☞

Before Haru could put her arm through the yukata's sleeve, fists banged on the door to the room as if to warn that a fire was consuming the hotel.

"Haru! Open the door. PLEASE!"

"Kame?" asked Haru as she cinched her yukata and hurried into the room.

Kenji sprang from the bed, grabbed his own yukata, and dashed into the vacated bathroom.

"Hurry! They are chasing me!"

Haru sprinted to the door and yanked it open.

Kame flew inside.

"Stop!" a rough masculine voice yelled from down the hallway. The sound of heavy steps drew close.

Kame pivoted, slammed the door, pressed her shoulder against it, and twisted the lock.

Haru flipped the light switch. Her eyes registered horror as she stared at the purple bruise around Kame's swollen-shut eye and a nose dripping blood. She sucked in a deep breath and wrapped her arms around the trembling girl. "Oh, Kame."

Kenji stepped into the bedroom. Kame's frightened stare locked on Kenji. He gaped at her mangled face. "What happened?"

"My husband beat me." Her grey yukata hung loose, the sash tied haphazardly. She was barefoot. One foot was bleeding, although she did not seem to notice.

Angry fists assaulted the door. "Kame, come out, or I will break the door down!"

Kenji strode to the door, drew himself upright, and opened it.

A wide-eyed man with his face twisted in anger put his shoulder down and took a half step forward. Kenji, his feet firmly planted at the doorway, folded his arms and leaned into the man. "I am Reverend Takayama of the Hongwanji Temple. Step back!"

Sounds of turning door handles and opening doors filled the corridor, followed by shouts of "What's going on?" and "Call the police." A half-dozen new grooms tightened the cinches on their blue hotel yukatas and quickly formed a loose circle around the would-be intruder.

The man spun angrily toward the voices behind him. The veins in his neck pulsated. "Yes, call the police. My wife is trying to run away."

Peering at the gathering ring of grooms behind her husband, Kame stepped into the doorway and pointed to her face. "Look what he did to me!"

Faces behind the wife-beater switched from shock to anger.

"Out of my way, priest." The man lunged for Kame. Simultaneously, two grooms grabbed him from behind. The assailant spun around, pulled his fist back ready to swing, and glared at the determined crowd. Then he dropped his hand.

At that moment, the hotel manager, accompanied by two assistants, came trotting down the hall and quickly took control. "Sir, you must leave now." Turning to his employees, he said, "Escort this man out of the hotel. If he gives you trouble, call the police."

The angry man stepped back from the door in one movement. He snarled at the hotel manager. "I am leaving." Backpedaling and shaking his fist, his eyes full of malice, he sneered at Kame. "This is not the end. I paid for your passage, paid the matchmaker. You are mine."

"Come in," said Kenji to the hotel manager.

Haru led Kame to the vanity table. "Sit. Let me get a wet towel."

The manager hurried over, dropped to one knee, and studied Kame's closed eye. "I'll get some ice." As he opened the door to leave, Kenji said, "We will need an extra bed."

"What happened, Kame?" asked Haru.

Inconsolable for a long while, Kame had almost finished her sobbing when a knock on the door turned all three heads. The manager called out, "I have the ice and spare bed."

Kenji opened the door. The man handed him a chunk of ice wrapped in a towel, along with some linens. He stepped aside as the bell captain rolled in the bed. As soon as the two men left, Haru repeated her question.

Kame's words gushed out. "The bishop dropped me at the hotel and introduced me to Aoki-san, my husband. As soon as he left, Aoki told me our hotel was nearby. We walked a long time; I had to carry my heavy bag. Our hotel was horrible. Smelly. He didn't wait. He took off his clothes and yelled at me to do the same. I did what he told me. He watched me like a fox in a chicken yard." She started crying. "He was rough. It hurt so much."

"He hit you after that?" asked Haru.

Kame's sobs increased. "Oh, Haru. You would not believe." Kame dropped her head, covered her face with her hands. "He told me two of his friends were waiting downstairs and they wanted a short-time wife. They would pay him a dollar each. He said, 'This is how we can buy our own land.'"

Haru's eyes sought Kenji's. "This can happen in Hawaii?"

"It's disgusting, but yes, it is done," said Kenji. "Almost every shipload of picture brides has a tragic story. Certain men force or try to force their wives into prostitution. A few beat them for the slightest infraction. That is why we have set up a dormitory for such women at our temple."

"Kame's my friend. We must take care of her."

"I will get her into our shelter, Haru," said Kenji.

Haru stamped her foot. "She is my FRIEND, Kenji-san."

Kenji's eyes locked onto his wife's, angry black pools. To have his authority as a husband challenged! He unconsciously clenched his own fist and then caught sight of Kame's frightened eyes and battered face. *What am I doing?* He flashed back to his cruel epithet just before Kame knocked. *How much different were my vicious words,* he thought, *than the physical beating Kame just endured?*

Kenji's taut face relaxed. He smiled at Kame with priestly warmth. "Of course, you can stay with us until we sort things out." Kenji glanced at the folded bed. "I will sleep on this."

He studied Haru's relieved but wary face. He wanted to whisper, "I'm sorry." Instead, he gave a slight bow, turned, and began preparing the rollaway.

Kame retold the horrible story again before sobbing herself to sleep next to Haru.

Mortified, Kenji lay on his side facing the wall. He feigned the slow and deep rhythm of sound sleep. Every part of him was alert.

He thought of his mother. He thought of his admonishments given to grooms attending his marriage classes. He had demeaned himself and his religious vocation with his ugly outburst and then had not the courage to offer a "gomennasai"—"I'm sorry." How could he tell her that the words "good evening, Reverend" were knives of shame emanating from his own weakness and wickedness? All his anger toward his mother for sending him an "Amakusan karayuki" had nothing to do with her or Haru. The word Amakusa reminded him of his own betrayal of the values his parents had taught him. Values he preached. Values he believed in.

Kenji stayed awake wallowing in a series of "if only" rationalizations for his hair-trigger outburst. If only he had told Haru to take her bath first so she would be waiting for him in bed; if only she had kept her yukata on when standing before him; if only she hadn't said, "Good evening, Reverend"; if only the carriage driver had taken any street other than Nuuanu; if only his false pride hadn't dwelled on her being from that ill-fated island famed for its karayuki. Haru was more than he deserved. She was a brave young girl who had fled from the karayuki life and been raised by his mother to be a model wife. He fell into a fitful sleep, dreading the morning. How could he explain his anger without confessing the reasons for it?

Haru listened to Kenji's rhythmic breathing. She lay prone, watching him from the edge of the bed. She felt dirty, like the karayuki Natsu from Amakusa, even though she had never known a man or even touched herself in the way Ko once described. Haru had long ago put aside her Amakusan heritage. At school and on the ship, she was the daughter of a kind priest and his caring wife, someone whose appreciation for her good fortune drove her to help others. She thought her bearing was anything but a karayuki, but somehow her demeanor had led her husband to accuse her otherwise.

Haru reviewed the day like a movie short in a continuous loop, each time asking herself, "What did I do wrong?" The day had started so wonderfully. She thought back to her walk across the immigration hall to the applause of her shipmates. She recalled Kenji's adoring eyes when he saw her in the red dress, paddling among the lakes at

Kapiolani Park, and the horse ride on the beach. She relived the happy dinner with her Judith classmates.

Mostly, she replayed over and over the last seconds before Kame's interruption. Standing naked. Midori had told her to drop her yukata. Why? Did that trigger Kenji's angry denunciation? But why? And what would have happened to Kenji and her if Kame had not banged on the door? Would they have exchanged angry words, reconciled, or would she have fled in humiliation from the room and booked passage back to Japan? No, the last option was not open. Like Hideyoshi, the humble commoner who became a shogun, she was determined that somehow she would persevere. She would not give up.

A shiver ran up her spine. Their marriage had been sudden. Had she been forced on a reluctant husband? With that thought, Haru drifted into a fitful sleep, waking several times after dreaming of dropping her yukata as Kenji's eyes turned from lust to anger. She finally fell into a deep sleep as the city of Honolulu began to awaken to the sounds of roosters and church bells.

∽ CHAPTER 32 ∽

KENJI WOKE UP ASHAMED.

The first rays of the morning sun crept around the edges of the drawn window shades. He sat up slowly, hesitating each time the bedsprings squeaked. Gazing at Haru lying on her back, he studied her deep breathing. He wanted to step over to the double bed, reach out, and caress her face with the back of his hand. His counsel to husbands plagued him: "Swallow your pride, say you are sorry, and you will have a happy wife, eager to please." He never understood why so many men just could not humble themselves with those few words.

Now he knew.

So much easier to give advice than to provide a saintly example.

Stealthily, Kenji eased his feet onto the worn grey carpet and stood up. He switched his gaze to the young girl sleeping like a cherub next to his wife. *You stopped me from whatever marriage-ending outburst I was about to let loose,* he thought, *but your problem is bigger than your innocent face can imagine. Most wives go back to their husband. If you do that, you will live a life planning how not to upset your husband, making excuses for your bruises, and worrying that one day he will beat you to death.*

A horrible thought dove into his musing. Will his wife wonder when he will hiss his next cruel words? *Even if I have the courage to say I am sorry, it will not be enough.* It was the wife-beaters who were the best at apologies. Some sobbed promises of "never again." *I am not like those men,* thought Kenji. *Yet I acted like one.*

He tiptoed over to the dull mahogany wardrobe cabinet, drew out his clothes, entered the bathroom, and spun the water spigots for his morning bath. He turned his attention to what he liked to do best: solve practical problems. Kame's case was riddled with complications. Normally, he would encourage her to press charges. Such were usually hard to prove, but there were witnesses aplenty to last night's altercation. Only Kame was not a wife. She was an illegal immigrant. As a consequence of the health inspectors' holding her back, Kame had not been married in Honolulu as required by immigration regulations. Motokawa had not been available when Kame had been released. He agreed to officiate prior to the reception of new brides at the Hongwanji Temple later today. Since Kame was not married, pressing charges would end up with her deportation and her intended husband going free since his victim would be on a ship sailing back to Japan when the case would come to court.

All these thoughts whirled around as Kenji bent over to leave a note under a geta outside the bathroom door. He tiptoed out of the room, hurried past the breakfast buffet on the ground floor, and strode straight to the Fort Street Hongwanji Temple to discuss Kame's case with Imamura.

∞ ∞

Freshly brewed oolong tea scented the bishop's office. The trade winds whistled gently through half-opened shutters. Kenji sat on the edge of the hardback chair facing Imamura across his desk.

The bishop rubbed his chin as he listened. He nodded his head when Kenji paused in his recitation. "Yes, the stout girl with the eye problem. Since we now know what type of fellow her intended husband is, she was lucky she missed Motokawa's marriage ceremony."

"But she is here illegally," said Kenji. "She will be deported unless—"

"Unless we find her a husband," said the bishop, finishing Kenji's thought. The hint of a smile on the bishop's lips told Kenji a solution was simmering.

Imamura picked up a letter off his desk. "This was delivered by a Parker Ranch cowboy, a *paniolo* as they are called, who escorted their Big Island cattle ship to Honolulu. Read it."

The letter, written on Parker Ranch stationery, reminded the bishop of his promise to establish a mission in Waimea. Kenji lingered over the last paragraph.

> Labor agitation at nearby cane fields could be greatly ameliorated by sending over a priest as early as possible. For too long, an unscrupulous shaman passing himself off as a Shinto priest has preyed on the rural superstitions of the plantation workers. My Japanese cowboys would surely welcome the attention of a priest. As I promised earlier, a house for the priest will be provided.
>
> Wellington Carter
> Manager, Parker Ranch

A PS was scribbled on the bottom of the typewritten note. "Our ranch would be honored if your priest brought us a few picture brides."

"My spring arrival will be most welcomed."

"Spring? Are we reading the same letter Takayama-san?"

"Well, yes ... I could leave earlier. What do you have in mind?"

Kenji's heart hammered as Imamura outlined his "suggested" a way to solve the Kame problem and take advantage of the Parker Ranch opportunity.

⚘ Chapter 33 ⚘

After a late breakfast, Haru and Kame strolled the short distance from the hotel to the Fort Street Hongwanji to join the reception for the picture brides. At the entrance, Haru looked up at the white-painted temple set on two acres of land. Under a canopy of umbrella-shaped monkey pod trees, jacaranda, and coconut-bearing palm trees, the midmorning sun filtered down on the trampled grass of the courtyard filled with hopeful brides and their grateful grooms. From the top of the temple steps, an anxious Kenji had been on the lookout and hurried down to meet them. He greeted Haru casually as if nothing amiss between them had happened and then said, "Come with me."

Kame excused herself. "I'm going to take a look inside the temple."

Haru followed Kenji into a large office.

A grinning Bishop Imamura greeted her and asked, "What do you think of your new assignment?"

"It will be like coming home, Imamura-san." Haru enjoyed the bishop's puzzled looks. "I was born near Mount Unzen. My husband tells me we will be living in the shadow of Hawaii's highest volcano."

So focused was she on her pitter-patter with the bishop, Haru did not notice Kenji's expression go from excited to stoic. Despite his self-incrimination over his behavior, the idea that Haru would so casually refer to her Amakusan origins shocked him.

"Yes, yes. Mauna Kea. Almost twice as high as Mount Unzen and many times more violent." The bishop noticed Kenji's discomfort. He remembered the earlier lack of enthusiasm when told his mother was sending Haru. He had guessed that his priest worried too much about what people thought. "You're quite a remarkable young woman, Haru-san. Kame told me how your bravery in fleeing Amakusa has made you a hero among your shipmates." He turned to Kenji and laughed. "And you have the challenge of a determined woman. Such women are needed in our missions."

Kenji's demeanor brightened. He was marrying a hero. The thought flickered, *How foolish I have been imagining a loss of face over her notorious birthplace.* "My mother has indeed nurtured a great gift, Your Excellency."

"What about Kame?" asked Haru, blushing from the compliments.

"We are working on finding a husband for her in Waimea," said Kenji, relieved to switch to practical matters. "We'll be leaving at midnight on the cattle ship owned by the Parker Ranch, Hawaii's largest ranch."

Haru almost leaped out of her chair in excitement.

"*America's* largest ranch," corrected the bishop, holding the Wellington Carter letter in his hand. "The ranch manager has asked us for pictures brides. If Kame were to leave with you tonight, I am sure your husband's first project would be to help your friend."

Haru's face changed from excitement to furrowed worry. "What about that horrible man who said he paid for her?"

"You remember that reporter claiming I had half the haole community fooled?"

Haru nodded her head.

"I have nobody fooled, but I have friends among the police who have noticed the sharp decrease in crime among Japanese workers since we started bringing in wives. I will make a call to a senior police officer this morning. I'm sure that evil man will sign off on his claim on Kame in exchange for the police not pressing assault charges."

Haru nodded her head.

Moving to the edge of her chair, Haru asked, "Can I go tell her the good news?"

"Go ahead. I need to talk to your husband about some boring administrative details."

Haru rose, bowed, turned, and hurried toward the door.

She flew out the door and bumped into a man about to enter. She was momentarily startled, not only by their collision but also by his strange hat.

After the necessary gomennasai apologies, Haru took a longer look at him. His leather-brown face stretched taut over the hills and gullies of chin, nose, and cheekbones. A cowboy, she guessed, although nothing like the cowboys from her favorite movie, *The Great Train Robbery*. He wore a sombrero instead of the ten-gallon hat of the American West. The faded blue shirt fit tight. The black belt, displaying a saucer-sized buckle with the image of a man on a horse, held up trousers baggy at the hips and thighs, but worn tight from the knee down and tucked into scuffed boots riding halfway up his calves.

The cowboy bowed deferentially. "Are you Haru-sensei, the English teacher and wife of the priest starting a mission in Waimea?"

Haru returned the bow. She liked him at once—his clear eyes suggested intelligence, his soft-spoken greeting was polite, and his creviced face told of someone who knew hard work.

"I am Haru."

"I'm Sam Akiyama, a foreman at the Parker Ranch. I'm escorting you and your husband on our cattle ship. If you would like, I can tell you about Waimea. There is a tea shop across the street favored by many from the temple."

"Arigato. Do you mind if I bring two of my friends who are waiting for me?"

Sam paused, and Haru wondered why this simple request would make him hesitate.

Sam cleared his throat, smiled, and nodded. "Of course not."

Haru rushed off to gather Mayo and Kame. The words "you are going with me to Waimea, and Kenji will find you a husband" were hardly out of Haru's mouth when Kame jumped up and screeched.

The three animated girls traipsed behind Sam, crossing the gravel avenue to the bamboo teahouse. They looked askance at his awkward gait and bowed legs, holding back their laughter.

Sam placed his sombrero on an empty wicker chair. A deep hat-brim indent circled his flowing black hair. He ordered green tea and then clasped his hands on the table and rotated his thumbs as he began.

"The history of Waimea and the Parker Ranch go hand in hand. In 1788, the British explorer George Vancouver gifted King Kamehameha five cows. The king let them roam and declared them *kapu*, off limits. A hundred years ago, John Parker jumped a whaling ship in Honolulu. He made friends with the king, who gave him the royal franchise to wrangle the cattle that had now grown to thousands. No horses in those days. You had to catch the cattle by running after them," Sam laughed. "But that humble beginning led to the

Parker Ranch and Waimea." Sam took a sip of tea. The twirling of the cup replaced the rotation of his thumbs.

The ladies waited for Sam to continue. And waited.

Sam studied the sloshing tea like a Greek priest contemplating an oracle. He lifted his head and stared at Kame's face.

She blushed and turned her head aside.

"You are the woman with a bad husband?"

"He's not my husband," Kame bristled. "We didn't marry."

"I'm sorry," Sam said. "You see, the news of your situation has come to my ears, and ... " Sam's deep-set eyes turned to Haru. He stammered, "She is the reason I-I wanted to talk to you."

Haru understood now and leaned forward. "Whoever marries this wonderful person will be the luckiest man in the world."

"Before you say anything more," said Sam earnestly, "I must tell you about myself, for my story is well-known in Waimea, and it is better to hear it from me."

Haru topped off the teacups and signaled the waitress for a fresh pot.

"I was born Fumio Tanaka. At age twelve, both my parents died within days of each other from the lung disease. I survived, often working just for food and shelter. A few months swabbing a fish market. A season planting rice. During the China war, I cleaned horse stables for a Hiroshima army base. When the war ended, a recruiter from the Kingdom of Hawaii visited the base. Free passage to paradise. My own bed, free food, and a salary. Me without a job. What was there to think over? I signed a seven-year contract.

"It didn't take me long to figure out why my plantation near Hilo recruited someone so young with no references. My luna ... " Sam stopped, watching a question mark drop over Haru's face. "'Luna' is the Hawaiian word for the boss man, usually a Portuguese overseer who rides his horse with a whip in his hand." Sam took a deep breath and then blew it out in resignation. "Our luna feasted on the pain of others. He stole half our salaries by levying fines over the smallest infractions. We cane cutters were jammed up eight to a small room. We all thought of running away. One tried. The dogs caught up with him trying to escape over Mauna Kea. The judge sentenced him to five months of hard labor. When he returned to work off his contract, the luna beat him so senseless that he lost sight in one eye. The beating was meant to kill the dream of freedom for the rest of us, but it made me more determined to escape."

Sam waved over the waitress and ordered bean cake pastry.

"I didn't gamble, had no one to send money to in Japan. So even with the luna cheating me, I saved money. On Sundays, I'd go to Hilo and make friends with the fishermen. For twenty dollars, one dropped me around the other side of the island at Kawaihae, a coastal village near Waimea where ... " Sam's voice quickened. "I hadn't walked ten yards down the beach when this giant Hawaiian, holding a string of grouper, came over and said something to me in English. I understood only the words 'you' and 'runner.' I'm sure all the blood drained from my face. Then he laughed and pointed to a group of cowboys—Japanese cowboys!"

Sam's face relaxed.

Kame picked up a bean cake and bit greedily. "*Oishii desu ne!*"

Sam paused while everyone tasted and agreed the bean cake was delicious.

"The cowboys welcomed me. Many had luna stories of their own. I introduced myself as Sam Akiyama and exaggerated my experience with horses when I learned the ranch was closing down their cane fields and expanding their herds. That's why there were so many Japanese cowboys. A foreman hired me to clean stables. Three meals. Meat every day."

Sam and Haru each took another bite of their bean cake.

"The Parker Ranch was like a fairy tale. The workers liked their bosses. I found I had a way with horses. Soon, the cowboys taught me how to ride and use a lasso to catch cows. So, I became a paniolo, the Hawaiian word used for cowboys that Parker brought in from California, part of Mexico in those days."

Sam sat back. Tiny sweat beads bubbled on his forehead hovering over a hopeful smile. "Now I am a foreman, a lonely foreman who dreams of a family."

Kame's eyes sparkled; warmth enveloped her smile.

"Let me tell you more about Kame." Haru emphasized Kame's hard-working virtues and joked how her blunt talk had made her popular.

"Cowboys are no strangers to blunt talk," said Sam.

The two of them exchanged looks and smiled.

"But," said Kame, "look at my face. I can't be wed today in front of all those people. I can't bear the shame."

Sam took this reservation as a yes to his proposal. "Let's visit the Puerto Rican bridal shop. I'm sure we can find a dress with what they call a mantilla." Kame nodded her head excitedly. Sam stood up and strutted to the counter to settle the bill.

"Thank you for giving me a life," said Kame to Haru. "For the second time in twenty-four hours, I was thinking of jumping off a cliff. Now I am talking to my husband about horses and cattle."

"I'm lucky too, Kame." Haru grabbed her friend's hands. "With you, Waimea won't be lonely."

As she watched Sam and Kame walk toward town, Haru remembered Kiyoshi's admonishment: to pay him back by helping others. As one of the few high school graduates among these immigrants, she understood the power an educated person had in a land where few of her own people were so privileged. She realized that Sam's deferential treatment was a consequence of her being the wife of a priest. A wife of a priest who had the power to arrange marriages. She vowed not to waste those advantages.

PART III

HOME

❧ CHAPTER 34 ❧

Waimea, Hawaii (The Big Island) - December 1909

THE SALT SPRAY STUNG HARU, standing at the bow of the SS *Humuula*. Her fingers curled around the railing in front of one of a dozen empty cow pens crowding the cattle transport's upper deck. The ship pitched forward toward a shadowy protrusion rising from the moonlit sea.

As tired as she was, she welcomed the chance to be by herself after a night holding a sick bucket for Kenji in between changing the cold-water compress to soothe the back of his neck. Haru admitted she had welcomed the opportunity to nursemaid her new husband, to prove early on her devotion to him. While tending to him, she realized that she had fallen in love with Kenji before she even considered marriage. She had read every letter he had written home, listened to Midori's stories of his childhood, and held imaginary discussions with him as a distant brother. Tears welled up in her eyes as she thought how quickly her sisterly affection had shifted to a vision of a shared life, raising children, and building missions for the overseas Japanese.

Another jolt of spray bounced high over the bow. Haru pulled back, and through mist-covered eyes, she caught a hint of dawn slipping over a majestic mountain.

But why had Kenji spit out that word at her? If only Midori was here to counsel her, she thought. She could not reach out to Kame who needed Haru's illusion of strength and not a sobbing older sister. Haru was utterly alone. Being a student had been so simple.

Now as the wife of the priest, she would be expected to dispense advice and comfort wives. Whom could she approach for support and guidance?

And then she lifted her chin, gritted her teeth, and flicked away a teardrop. "Enough of such thoughts," she whispered fiercely. Thousands of picture brides had preceded her without the advantages of an education or a priest for a husband, and here she was feeling sorry for herself. She would show Kenji she was a worthy wife and wait for him to approach her.

Haru's tiny fists gripped the railing harder. She would never display her body to him again.

"Haru!"

Haru recognized Kame's excited voice from above, donned a smile, turned, and waved to her. Kame stood next to Sam and the captain. She was holding the wheel and wearing an impish smile under a purple eye. She pointed ahead of the bow.

Mauna Kea. The glow of the sunrise formed a golden halo over the majestic mountain. Early winter snows glazed the dormant volcano rising thirty-three thousand feet from the bottom of the ocean—13,796 feet from sea level. Mt. Unzen, and even Mt. Fuji, seemed like hills in comparison.

"The best view of Poliahu is from the sea," said the voice behind her in a courteous tone.

She turned to see Sam striding over to the railing. "What is Poliahu?" Was it her imagination, or was there more of a spring in his step this morning?

"According to Hawaiian legend, Poliahu is the snow goddess who protects Mauna Kea from Pele, the goddess of fire and volcanoes."

"Ah so desuka," said Haru as the first rays of the sun now revealed a ship anchored offshore. "That looks like a twin of our ship."

"That's the SS *Mauna Kea*, built at the same time," said Sam, taking out a tobacco pouch and cigarette paper. He stooped to avoid the wind, twisted the pouch into a funnel shape, and jiggled the tobacco over the paper. Licking the gummed edge, he rolled the cigarette and brought it to his lips. Then he pulled out a matchstick from his shirt pocket, struck it against a timber beam, and lit his cigarette behind a cupped hand. As he inhaled deeply, he stood up. Smoke drifted from his nostrils. "Look toward the beach and then to the right."

Haru set her eyes on horses, their sombrero-topped riders driving cattle along a wide, black lava beach.

Clacking getas on the deck announced Kame was joining them. Her cocky smile told Haru Kame had had a better first night experience with Sam than Haru had had with Kenji.

Taking another deep drag on his cigarette, Sam pointed to horned steers hoofing right to left along the beach. "The day before the cattle board the ship, we drive them from Waimea to the Puuiki holding pens a few miles from here. At midnight, we grab coffee, saddle our mounts, and drive the herd to the beach."

The cattle ship's engines throttled down. The ship edged closer to the anchored SS *Mauna Kea*.

"How are you going to get them on the ship?" asked Kame.

Sam let out a soft laugh. "Watch and you will see how we load them."

While they stared at the paniolos prodding cattle into holding pens, a pallid-faced Kenji shuffled over to Haru's side.

Sam drew a final drag on his cigarette and flicked it overboard. "Reverend, your color looks a bit better this morning."

"Yes, I'm feeling … steadier," Kenji replied, trying to smile.

Voices drifted from the shore. As the last Hereford was corralled into the beachside pens, a cowboy raised another pen's gate fronting the water's edge. A horned beast bolted into the surf. Two paniolos rode along each side of the steer to keep it from turning. A collie barked at its hind legs. As the water rose and then splashed over the rust-colored back of the steer, a paniolo dropped a lariat over its snout, tightened the cord around the jaw, and then in one fluid motion looped the rope round the steer's neck to keep the animal's nose above water.

"A steer's huge lungs keep it buoyant," said Sam. "But unlike horses and dogs, cattle are not natural swimmers."

A second lasso from another paniolo dropped over the struggling animal's neck.

"I bet those long boats are going to drag the cattle to the mother boat," said Kame.

Sam raised his eyebrows in appreciation. "Those are whaleboats. We've adopted them for our surf roundups."

The paniolo and his horse, harmonized, working as one, delivered the struggling steer to the waiting longboat.

"The boys have it easy today," said Sam. "It's trickier in rough seas."

Five paniolos stood in the whaleboat, their hips swaying and knees bending to maintain equilibrium, and attached steers along the hull until six snouts were strung on both sides. Four cowboys picked up oars, sat two to a bench, and began rowing. Muscles on their shirtless arms, shoulders, and backs strained as their boat dragged a dozen unhappy, half-ton beasts two hundred yards to the cattle ship.

A blur and a splash drew Haru's eyes from the whaleboat to the *Mauna Kea*'s waterline. Attracted by shouts on the deck across from hers, she lifted her eyes just in time to catch a barefoot man in skivvies dive from the deck. She followed his descent into the sea where he pierced the surface near another long-haired diver bobbing in the gentle waves.

"I was a diver in my early years," said Sam standing between Haru and Kame. "Most paniolos can't swim. Being a diver is dangerous work, but it was better than shoveling dung in the stable."

"Why dangerous?" asked Kame.

"Horns and back feet," said Sam pointing to the longboat. "Watch."

Haru gazed down as the tethered cattle closed on the *Mauna Kea*. Inside the whaleboat, a bronze-backed paniolo leaned over the side and untied the rope holding a horned steer to his whaleboat. He held on to the chin lasso and raised his arms to keep the treading Hereford's nose above water.

Haru's line of vision caught a sling device being lowered over the side of the ship. She turned to Sam and pointed. "What's that?"

Sam straightened his back. "That's a belly sling. It has four parts. The big piece of leather you see dropping—the apron—has to go under the steer's belly. A metal bar is sewn at each end of the apron. If you saw it up close, it'd look like the hem of your dress. A metal triangle is attached to the ends of each metal bar."

"Hai, wakarimashita," said Haru, nodding. *How different this man is in his own element—nothing like the humble supplicant at the teahouse yesterday.*

"I bet the fourth part is the rope," said Kame.

"Right," said Sam, his smile applauding her quick comprehension. "The rope is strung through an iron loop the size of a fist that is welded to the tips of the four triangles."

Haru leaned over the railing. The belly sling hit the water next to a kicking steer. A second swimmer grabbed one of the metal triangles and began pulling. Haru could see him spreading the leather apron, which was sinking. Without hesitating, he dunked his head under the rolling swells, kicked his feet into the air, and disappeared.

Haru's eyes scanned the rolling surface near the steer. "How long does he stay down?"

"As long as it takes to get the sling between the front and back legs of the steer. He has the lungs of your famous Hiroshima pearl divers," said Sam with pride.

Haru's eyes returned to the water as the submerged diver popped up on the other side of the steer. He leaned his head back and raised both hands, thumbs up.

Haru followed his gaze to the boom operator, who was whirling his arms in a confusion of pulleys. Her eyes did not linger but dropped back to the sea. The slack in the rope disappeared; the taut leather apron hugged the sides of the steer. Haru expected the animal to thrash. Instead, the creature hung as limp as her cat had when draped over her arm. She followed the steer's ascent until an outstretched hand caught the animal's front foot to help guide the swinging boom. The steer descended slowly until all four feet met the deck, where men armed with cattle prods nudged the beast into a deck pen.

"*Sugoi!*" said Haru turning to Sam. "That's more complicated than a kabuki dance."

"Eleven more to go," said Sam, looking back at the whaleboat. "We're shipping sixty Herefords today. When the last steer is boarded, one of the whaleboats will take us to shore."

Shrieks erupting from the cattle-loading ship brought Haru's eyes to shouting men peering down. She followed their gaze to a thrashing steer that had broken loose. She sucked in her breath upon spotting the panicked faces of the two divers flailing their feet and arms while trying to avoid the animal's kicking legs and swirling horns.

One of the men cried out. In seconds, purplish water swirled around his pained face. The other diver was trying to jerk an ensnared leg free from the sling caught around the bucking steer's back legs.

Haru raised her head and sent an anguished glance to Kenji and then Sam. "Why isn't anyone jumping into the water?"

"There are no swimmers on board," said Sam, shucking his boots and dropping his jeans. He raised one foot to the deck railing and in a single fluid motion rose to the top and dove into the water.

Haru turned around just in time to see Kenji toss off his yukata and jump into the water.

By the time Kenji's head bobbed up, Sam had pulled the sling off the steer's leg. The gasping diver flipped onto the sling. The boom operator reeled him safely over the rescue drama and held the position ready to drop the sling back in the water to rescue the three remaining men.

Haru turned her attention to the bleeding diver whose arms moved too slowly. The struggling steer floated closer to him. Kenji was swimming over; Sam not far behind.

"Shark!" a voice bellowed.

∽ CHAPTER 35 ∾

HARU GAZED OUT TO SEA.

Kame saw it first. "To the right, maybe thirty *jō* (about thirty feet) away."

Haru's eyes saw the moving fin and looked back at Kenji and Sam within a dozen strokes of reaching the bleeding diver. She could tell by the expression on their faces they had no idea of the new danger. Her screams of "shark!" were lost amidst their frantic strokes and kicks.

As they drew within feet of the steer and diver, Sam shouted something to Kenji who nodded his head. He swam to the wounded man who had begun to go under. Sam moved in front of the animal like a matador.

Passengers on both ships were shouting, "Shark!"

Haru's terrified eyes stared at the shark's zigzagging course as it stalked its human prey. Finally, Sam spotted the incoming grey fin.

She watched him look up to the waving men on the cattle ship deck and slice the side of his hand across his throat.

Deckhands dropped a half-dozen machetes. The long wooden-handled knives hit the water and bobbed up. Sam grabbed the nearest one and kicked toward the thrashing steer.

Haru looked for Kenji. He had disappeared, and so had the diver. Then Sam was gone too. A grey fin sped in a straight line toward the discolored spot in the water. Haru shuddered as the shark's mouth opened wide, displaying two vicious racks of teeth. Kenji was going to die. Haru wanted to turn her head from the impending horror but could not take her eyes off the shark's teeth.

Sam rose out of the water in front of the steer, machete in hand, sliced the steer's neck, and pushed off from the beast. He had traveled the distance of two backstrokes when the frenzied shark bumped past Kenji and tore into the richer source of blood.

Haru shifted her eyes from the bloody collision to the sea. The empty sea. Sam had distracted the shark. The flaying sea foamed purple and red.

"Look!" shouted Kame.

Kenji's head bobbed in the water; one of his hands held the wounded diver by his hair. Kenji flipped on his back. Haru watched his chest heave convulsively as he gulped in air while kicking toward the ship where he grabbed the harness, rolled onto the sling, and pulled the rescued diver after him. Right behind him was Sam who slithered onto the sling and gave a thumbs up. The leather apron rose out of the water twenty yards from where the shark was tearing the steer to savory pieces.

Haru sagged in relief. "The Lord Buddha has saved Kenji for a purpose. I will help him find it."

"What kind of land have we found?" asked Kame.

Haru lifted her eyes to the opposite ship. A sailor was grabbing the end of the sling and helping the boom operator guide it to the deck, where Kenji and Sam stepped off. She turned to Kame. "What kind of husbands have we found?"

∞ CHAPTER 36 ∞

THE HARNESS FOR HARU AND KAME worked on the same principle as that for the cattle, except, instead of riding a belly sling, they settled themselves side by side into a leather seat bucket smoothed by thousands of bottoms over the years. The boom lifted them off the deck and lowered them toward the outstretched arms of their husbands balancing in a whaleboat.

"We like to give new arrivals a show," said Sam, once both Kame and Haru were sitting on a damp bench near the bow. "Getting that shark to show up on time is the hardest part."

His audience laughed, perhaps at the humor, but more likely with relief.

Two muscle-rippling Hawaiians began paddling the whaleboat toward shore. As they broke into an ancient Hawaiian melody in rhythm with their oar strokes, Sam won wide smiles by singing along with the refrain.

When the song finished, Kame pointed to crystal-laden pools in the mudflats at the far end of the beach. "Those look like the salt ponds we have in Okinawa."

"We need the salt for the cattle," said Sam. "And sell the surplus to other ranches."

Kawaihae's shanties, strung haphazardly along the black lava beach, reminded Haru of her family's lean-to in Funanoo-machi. Laundry flapped in the wind in sync with swaying saw grass blanketing dunes at the back of the beach. Drying nets covered the scrawny *kiawe* trees. Underneath, children in short pants played dodgeball.

To the right, trotting horses caught her attention. A pair of paniolos drew up their mounts in front of a tall Caucasian man. His commanding presence held Haru's attention. As the boat drew closer, she saw sandy hair flaring from under his white Stetson, piercing eyes accented by high cheekbones, and a bushy mustache that lorded over a protruding jaw. Haru's thoughts jumped to the day she had watched the emperor enter the Yasukuni Shrine.

As if he could read her mind, Sam interrupted her speculation. "That's the man who saved Parker Ranch."

"What do you mean 'saved?'" she asked.

"Five years ago, the ranch was down to the sorriest five thousand head of cattle the world has ever seen. Now we're up to fifteen thousand well-bred Herefords feeding on good grass."

While Sam spoke, the tall man turned toward their approaching boat. His wide smile exuded warmth as he raised a hand in greeting.

As Haru started to wave back, the whaleboat scraped the sand, and she lurched forward. Regaining her balance, she raised her yukata with one hand and her getas with the other, stepped out of the boat, and walked through the ankle-high surf onto the land of her new home. Her eyes caught a sudden movement on a granite overhang commanding the beach.

A solitary figure dressed in a purple robe stomped to the edge. His hairless head appeared too small for his short, slender body. He planted his feet wide apart and folded his arms like Genghis Khan surveying his troops. His malignant eyes locked on Haru's. He stared like a fox gazing at a rabbit.

A shiver ran up Haru's spine, but she refused to lower her eyes. She remembered overhearing Kiyoshi lecturing his young monks: "Never look away from a man challenging you." As a woman, she never thought such advice would ever apply to her. Now as the wife of the new Buddhist priest, she was sure it did.

"That's the Shinto priest, the one man who does not welcome your arrival, Haru-sensei," said Sam, walking barefoot in the last trickle of a surf surge.

"He looks like one of those village shamans," said Kenji.

"I doubt you have met anyone like him on Oahu. He's been here twenty years and considers Waimea his fiefdom. He's another reason we need a real priest, Reverend."

"Why's that?" asked Kenji.

"He organizes *fujinkai* groups among the women to collect and send the workers' savings to Japan for its wars in China and Russia. He recruits young women as so-called acolytes. He serves *awa* at occasional services that are more like sorcery. They start and end with everyone bowing to Japan while reciting allegiance to the emperor. He feeds the haoles' fears about Japan adding Hawaii to their empire."

When the shaman shifted his angry gaze to Sam, the cowboy ignored him. Haru dropped her eyes and turned back to the imposing man in the Stetson. He was walking beside the wounded diver being carried from the longboat. Another Caucasian ran up to the procession and began pressing a folded white cloth on the injured man's abdomen.

"That's the vet," said Sam. "If he cleans the wound right, and if the horns didn't go too deep, the diver will recover in a week or so."

"ALOOO-HA!"

Haru turned to four barefoot Hawaiian women in flowing muumuu holding out ginger-flowered lei. Haru awarded the girl opposite her a warm smile and said her second Hawaiian word, "*Mahalo*," as the girl placed a lei over her neck.

"*Irasshai*," said the woman, her smile wider on seeing Haru's cheerful face.

A small contingent of Japanese paniolos and fishermen ambled over, bowed, and exchanged introductions. Two of the Hawaiian women carried Japanese last names.

"We have waited years for you, Takayama-san," said a wiry bare-chested man, a sentiment supported by a chorus of hais from the others.

A buoyant Haru looked at Sam. "It seems so strange—these Japanese men with giant wives."

Scratching a mosquito bite under his chin, Sam said, "Hawaiian women have land." Sam paused as if he were about to add something else, and then his bearing changed from poised to humble. "Here comes Mr. Carter."

The crowd gave way and hovered. Whatever Carter said would dominate the evening's dinner conversation. Kenji proffered his hand. The broad-faced Carter shook it gently, as was his custom with the Japanese and Hawaiians. "You can't imagine how delighted I was to hear Sam was bringing a priest back with him and that the priest would be you," he said in his usual soft tone. Kenji leaned forward to hear him and the crowd became silent. More than one of his peers swore Carter spoke in low tones for effect—to make others give him their full attention.

A quizzical-faced Kenji asked, "How did you know we were coming today?"

Carter pointed to Mauna Kea. "Hawaii's mountaintops make it easy for telephone relay stations to connect our islands." He turned back to Sam. "You'll need to get started if you're going to reach Waimea by nightfall."

∞ CHAPTER 37 ∞

THE SHAMAN STRODE OFF INTO THE UNDERBRUSH with a worried expression. The priest's wife bothered him. She had not turned her eyes away from his stare. A strong, confident type. The type he feared other women would gather around. A danger. He also made note of that meddling paniolo Sam and the short, fat woman, most likely a picture bride. Would there be more of them recruited by this new Buddhist mission? Another threat.

As an angry Uno tramped through the shrubbery, he recalled his own arrival in Hawaii in 1885 with the first wave of Japanese immigrants following King Kalakaua's visit to Japan.

Unintentionally, his journey to Waimea began when his village priest had picked him, then a pious farm boy, for seminary training in Hiroshima. Uno soon discovered the unsavory side of the Meiji commitment to make Hiroshima a major port. He squandered his student allowance on gambling. He dropped out of school and joined a yakuza gang to pay off his gambling debts but could not keep away from the bones. When he met a labor recruiter from Hawaii, he signed up. Worried the yakuza would discover his whereabouts, he volunteered for the remotest plantation available: Waimea.

Uno left the bush trail to find his horse grazing where he had left him tethered. It would take him two hours of hard riding to reach Waimea. He had much to remember and to prepare. As the horse broke into a trot, Uno retreated to his first cane-working days. His back was soon crisscrossed with welts from the luna's whip. Each night, he went to sleep fantasizing cruel ways to kill his Portuguese overseer.

Then the dream. He was rolling the dice at his favorite gambling house in Hiroshima but, strangely, with Shika, the wife of one of his fellow cane workers, who looked over his shoulder like a yakuza moll. A man of superstitions, Uno interpreted his dream as a life-changing force. That morning, he reached under his bed for some awa root, the Polynesian stimulant the missionaries thought they had eradicated. He bit off a large chunk, chewed it into paste, spit the wad into a bowl, added a little water, and drank the potion all in one gulp. His face had turned ashen by the time he reported at first bell.

"What's wrong with you?" the luna demanded.

Uno swayed unsteadily; his words slurred. "I vomited most of the night. But ... I can still go to the fields."

The luna spat. "You'll be worthless. Stay here, but you lose two days' pay."

Uno watched the luna mount his horse while the field hands piled onto mule-hauled carts.

Except for Shika.

She steadfastly refused to join her husband as a nine-dollar-a-month field hand. Instead, she laundered clothes for bachelors. Despite the hard work, she had kept her beauty. More than once, Uno was convinced she favored him with a sly smile, and when he dropped off or picked up his laundry, their banter bordered on the risqué.

Within an hour, the awa nausea turned to a buzz, raising Uno's confidence. He strode down to the stream where Shika was washing clothes. Looking up at the sound of his footsteps, she gave him a saucy smile. "So much work for ten cents a bundle," said Uno, rattling coins in his hand. "And you, such a pretty woman."

Shika did not take much persuading to accept his offer of twenty cents for a tumble along a secluded riverside copse. After sharing a cigarette, Uno said, "I've seen how the luna watches you. I could arrange a pillow session where you would earn fifty cents."

Shika's raunchy smile was all the answer Uno needed.

That evening, he told the luna, "I am well," waited out the verbal abuse, and then explained Shika's availability for a dollar. The luna's licentious grin sealed the arrangement. Then Uno explained how vigorous enforcement of the no-gambling rule was not only bad for morale but was missing a profit opportunity. After settling on his cut for allowing dice, the overseer gave Uno the easy jobs—feeding the mules, counting inventory, passing out the new tools. Uno ingratiated himself with his coworkers. He covered when someone needed a rest, smoothed over sick time with the luna, and advanced a worker's salary at the rate of a dime a week for each dollar advanced. He supplied awa cheaply to avoid charges of gouging and inviting competition.

A plantation worker's death launched Uno's life vocation. When mourners bemoaned the lack of a priest, one worker said, "Why not Uno? He has seminary training." Uno accepted the charge in the humblest manner he could contrive.

While Japanese tradition favored Buddhism for funerals, leaving marriages and house blessings for the Shinto priests, Uno remembered enough prayers to satisfy the mourners. A week later, he conducted "marriages" for three Japanese men who had taken Hawaiian women. Uno was soon performing priestly functions for all plantations with a Japanese workforce within a day's ride of Waimea. By the time his labor contract had been satisfied, he was well ensconced as the *odaisan*, the revered comforter who used incantations to the spirit world along with rare herbs to heal the sick. Shika had long left her husband to support Uno's ministry as his consort.

He found commonality between Shinto animism and Hawaii's ancient polytheism, which was still clandestinely practiced, despite Christian ministers' boasts that they had expunged heathen practices. He borrowed superstitions from the latter when it suited his ecclesiastic machinations.

Mimicking his village's Shinto tradition, Uno dedicated his Waimea shrine to Inari, the kami, or god, of rice who relied on *kitsune* messengers—shape-shifting foxes—to communicate with the faithful. Worshipers deposited sake, rice, or soybean curd at the base of fox statues to improve the odds of having their prayers vigorously pressed. Uno's favorite manifestation of the kitsune was Shouko, the White Fox Princess (Byakko no Himezama Shouko), who like all magic foxes, Uno claimed, could fly and grew nine additional tails. Uno became obsessed with obtaining a white fox. He imagined his followers prostrating themselves to the kitsune. Uno promised three hundred dollars to a trading ship's bursar if he could bring back a white fox. In nine months, he had his fox.

The arrival of this exotic creature created a sensation. Within weeks, pilgrims as far away as Hilo visited Uno's shrine. They dropped quarters at the offering table, bought overpriced incense, and paid to sleep near the caged white fox. His local followers tripled.

At age fifty, Uno reveled in the fear and respect he engendered. Now all was at risk.

Uno's horse broke into a run the last mile. Turning off the main road, it galloped down the path lined with life-sized wooden foxes carved by Uno over the decades and slowed to a trot as it passed under the faded cherry-painted torii—the traditional Shinto gate of two columns bridged with a double set of horizontal rails. Uno surveyed his compound and was not pleased. His thatched Hawaiian-style hale pyramiding to the sky cried out for new reeds on the roof. Earlier, he had ridden past the home for the Buddhist priest, which was large, Western, and brand-new—a gift from that Parker haole and an insult to Uno's decades of dedication.

The ever-faithful Shika stepped forward as Uno dismounted and without a word handed him a bowl of awa.

Uno brought the calabash to his lips and slowly allowed the brown bitter juice to slide down his throat.

"They have arrived?"

Uno's face twisted into an angry gargoyle. "Yes."

He ambled over to the wooden and wire-mesh cage, the home of his aging white fox. He dropped to his haunches, picking up a cane stalk and knife from a basket next to the cage. He whittled away the green bark, then opened the cage door and held out the stalk. When the fox came forward, he grabbed the animal's neck and gently pulled him out of his cage. Uno placed the fox on his lap and watched him suck on the stalk.

"Sit," said Uno to Shika, who had brought him a refilled calabash. "Share the awa with me." Uno closed his eyes and drifted into a private world of memories. Hours later, the thudding of taikos awoke him. A welcome party in the central park tonight, he guessed.

While petting the white fox sleeping on his lap, Uno leaned over and whispered into a tattered furry ear. "You have served me well, *ko-gitsune*. You have one more mission before you meet your ancestors."

Shika opened her eyes.

"The gods have spoken to me," said Uno. "They have told me what to do." His words bespoke purpose and menace. He finished by saying, "When night falls, go to the park, float like a butterfly, and spread the message."

✷ Chapter 38 ✷

WHILE UNO RODE AND PLOTTED, Haru beach-walked to the wagon loaded with her trunks. The wood-spindled wheels reminded her of buckboards she had seen in Western movies. She gave a worried look at two replacement wheels tied to the under-belly with rawhide.

Sam moseyed over. He fed the two mules carrots and talked to them like a father coaxing a toddler to ride a bicycle. As Kame nuzzled the under chin of the animal on his left, he smiled approvingly.

When all four were squeezed together on the front seat, Sam grabbed the reins, hollered, "Duke, Prince, *ikimasho!*" and snapped the leather straps. The mules strained their harnesses and began the seventeen-mile trek that would rise twenty-six hundred feet and deliver them to Waimea under the cloud-shrouded shadow of Mauna Kea.

At the top of the first plateau, Haru gazed at the rivers bubbling down black lava hills overlooking lush valleys. This black and green canvas, not the crowded chaos of Honolulu, was the wild Hawaii of her imagination.

Pointing to a terraced valley, Sam explained, "We can thank the Chinese for our rice. They arrived a generation before us, served their time, and bought land or opened shops."

"Sugarcane!" shouted Kame, gazing far ahead. "The fields are so big, not at all like my village's small plots." As they got closer, she pointed to several empty rows of dried yellow leaves.

Sam said, "Those stalks were cut weeks ago, but next to them you have mature cane ready for cutting." He gestured to his right. "You can see seedlings starting their eight-month cycle. With our never-changing tropical weather, there's always a planting, always a harvest."

"So much open land," said Haru. "Was it always like this?"

Sam yanked the reins. When the mules settled down, he swung his arm in an expansive arc. "When Captain Cook landed, sandal-wood trees covered this land like bees on a honeycomb. By the time Parker jumped ship, most had been cut and sold to China traders. Parker asked Kamehameha, 'What happens when the trees are gone?' The king saw his point. That's how Parker received the royal concession to shoot cows and sell smoked beef to the whaling ships."

From over the next hill, Haru heard singing—as if the cane stalks had found their voice. As the buckboard stumbled along, the high-pitched sounds became Japanese lyrics. Then among the towering cane, she saw conical-hatted women, covered in head-to-toe ging-ham, swing hoes in rhythm to the singing. Further up, stooped wom-en were pulling weeds from freshly broken earth and stuffing them into jute bags. Two women carried infants on their backs.

She turned to Sam. "I thought there was a shortage of women."

"This is the Kell plantation. Like most, their bachelors outnum-ber the married two to one."

Listening to Sam use varied languages when speaking to the pas-sengers of passing wagons, Haru said, "You are a man of many tongues."

"Well, three if you include my broken Hawaiian," laughed Sam. "But I can greet the Puerto Ricans in Spanish, the Azoreans in Portuguese, and the Chinese in Cantonese."

When the mules picked up the pace even as they were climbing another hill, Haru said, "It looks as if the mules know something."

"They do," said Sam. "We're approaching our way station. The steep part of our travel is behind us. Our paniolos will change the mules to horses."

As he said it, the stubborn hill reached its zenith and smoothed into a green table fading far away onto the slopes of Mauna Kea. Ahead, a small building broke the horizon. Behind it, Haru saw mules and horses separated into two corrals.

Minutes later, Sam pulled on the reins and stopped the wagon.

Behind the shack, paniolos were brushing down and feeding the animals. Sam waved at the cowboys and then pulled their wagon up for the exchange. It took only a few minutes, and they were back on the road and headed down the hill.

The orange sun, morphing to red, slid behind white-capped Mauna Kea as the wagon bounced the newlyweds into the township of Waimea. The thudding beat of taikos brought smiles to the four travelers. Torchlights flickered in the distance.

"Smells like pig," said a grinning Kame. "I feel as if I'm back in Okinawa."

"Must be a welcome luau," said Kenji.

A tall horseback rider wearing a Stetson trotted toward them. Sam pulled on the reins. Wellington Carter brought his steed to a halt in front of the buckboard and addressed Kenji. "You can hear Waimea is eager to give you a warm welcome, Takayama-san." Carter then eyed Sam, and as was his custom, he suggested instead of ordered. "But before we introduce the preacher to the townsfolk, you might want to show Kenji and Haru their new home, let them freshen up a bit. I sent Oba Ualani ahead with some food stock."

Sam snapped his wrists on the reins and the horses resumed their steady gait.

"Oba Ualani?" asked Kame. "What kind of Japanese name is that? And shouldn't it be Ualani Oba?"

"She's our first *hapa*," said Sam.

"Hapa? You're confusing me with these strange words," said Kame.

"Hapa is a Hawaiian word originally meaning a part or fraction of something. Now hapa means people of mixed race," explained Kenji.

Sam tugged the reins right to turn the horses down a tree-canopied road. "Ualani's father came with the first Japanese contract workers in 1868. A year later, most returned to Japan because of ill treatment. Her father stuck it out, joined the Parker Ranch after fulfilling his contract, and married a Hawaiian woman, who died giving birth to Ualani."

Sam slowed the horses. "She has not had an easy life. A two-time widow—both husbands paniolos. None of her children survived two years. Carter gives her an allowance and a one-room cabin in exchange for her doing housekeeping chores."

"Here we are," said Sam, halting the horses. To the right, a freshly painted wooden structure glowed golden in the last light of the sun. Newly planted ferns rimmed the house set on wooden pillars, raising the structure an arm's length off the ground. Flickering light glimmered through the windowpanes.

Haru swept her hand over her mouth, gave a tentative look at Sam, and spoke barely above a whisper. "This gorgeous house can't be ours."

"Mr. Carter wanted you comfortable."

Sam led Haru and Kenji up the stairs to a porch just big enough for the four wicker chairs to overlook a spacious scrub grass yard.

"I wonder how they found that so fast," said Sam, pointing to a Buddhist bell the size of a pineapple that hung at eye level just left of the front door. Kame stuck her hand inside the bell and slapped the clapper. She tittered at Haru and then tried the doorknob, which turned without resistance. Kame pulled the door open and was about to step inside but remembered at the last moment to step back and allow Kenji and Haru to enter their home first.

Taking her shoes off, Haru stepped into the living room. Looking at the Western dining table and hardback chairs, she wondered how long it would take to get used to Western furniture. "Fully furnished. This is too much," she said in a voice that betrayed no disappointment.

Sam pointed outside through the dining room window. "Not ten steps from the back door you can see the top of the well pump sticking out from a wooden enclosure so you can bathe. Mr. Carter ordered an ofuro bath to be built next to it." Sam wagged his forefinger at a tall shed outlined in the sun's dying light. "Further back, you can see your outhouse."

A moving silhouette the size of a fattened calf emerged from the shadows behind the house and converged on the back door. All eyes riveted on the adjoining kitchen. A wicker lamp glowed on a utility bench next to the back entrance. The door banged open.

"Irasshaimase," a voice squeaked from a toothless smile in an accent anything but Japanese. A woman, impossibly short and wide, stepped into the yellow glow of the oil lamp. Eyes twinkled from a face the color and texture of a walnut. Grey hairs sprouted from under a blue-checkered scarf. A shapeless muumuu, ruffled at the neck and hem, gave her the appearance of a stuffed animal.

"Irasshaimase," she greeted again and waddled into the room moving her legs sideways as much as forward. She sniffed the air, shook her head in resigned sadness. "I told that Carter," she said in rough Japanese, "you would stink like three-day-old fish. It's a good thing I told the carpenters to build a proper ofuro today. You will have to bring hot water from the kitchen until we can plate the bottom of the ofuro with tin and place it on top of bricks so we can heat the water with wood underneath."

"You will have to excuse Oba Ualani's manners," said Sam, mirth enveloping his voice. "She's not use to genteel people."

"Which of you is the preacher's wife?" asked Ualani.

Haru nodded. "This is Kame, Sam's wife. I'm Haru."

"It's about time," said Ualani. She looked approvingly at Kame's hips. "Our land is lonely for wives and children. Don't wait to start a family." To Haru she said, "Better show you the kitchen. And then you can bathe." She turned her gaze back to Sam. "Well, don't just stand there. Get a move on. Bring in the baggage."

Haru held back a laugh as she watched Kenji follow Sam to the buckboard. Ualani led her and Kame into the narrow kitchen. Haru's eyes radiated worry as she took in the strange, nickel-colored iron stove resting on squat legs.

Ualani took no notice. "This is the new cast-iron Bridge Beach stove. Only Mr. Carter has one like it. Four burners."

"Same idea as in Japan, except we use clay instead of iron," said Haru.

Ualani pulled down on the handle, releasing the latch, and opened the iron door under the burners.

"That's where you put the wood?" said Haru, half statement, half question.

"Yes, and see the slanted vents on all sides? Those let air in but keep embers from escaping," said Ualani.

"Come here!" shouted Kame whose curiosity had led her to check the bedroom.

Sam and Kenji were entering the front door, each carrying a side of Haru's chest. They eased it down and followed the parade to Kame's voice. She was lying on a quilt-covered wooden-frame bed whose stubby legs drew the mattress close to the ground.

"Can you believe this? A gaijin bed!" She sat up and bounced twice on the spring mattress.

"Our ranch cottage will have a Western bed too," said Sam, "but not as fancy."

"Do you mean we will have a house with a room just for sleeping?" asked Kame.

Sam nodded, allowing a little pride to sneak into his smile.

"Maybe we should start bathing while our husbands finish unloading so we can join our welcome luau," said Haru, hoping she pronounced the word correctly.

"Listen to those taikos," said Kame. "There must be dancing. Yes, let's take a bath."

An immovable ninja shadow in black field clothes blended in among the koa, palm, and bamboo trunks behind the house. She listened to Haru and Kame bathe. The more they laughed, the more tightly the woman's face twisted. The evil in her eyes would have sent children crying to their mother's skirt. Only after the two couples pulled away on their buckboard did she slither into the night.

⧼ CHAPTER 39 ⧽

HARU GRABBED THE SEAT OF THE CARRIAGE with both hands, as Sam turned the horses sharply onto the main thoroughfare. The aroma of roasted pig rode the trade winds to the buckboard. As they approached the town square, Haru's eyes locked on the bandstand tower higher than the swaying trees surrounding the park. A string of dangling Japanese lanterns outlined a pair of headbanded men, shoulder-strapped to drums resting on their bellies, whirling their arms to pound out a steady beat.

As Sam slowed the coach, Haru clapped in rhythm to the drums and feasted her eyes on three concentric circles of dancers, the middle circle dancing in the opposite direction of the outer and inner. They two-stepped to the beat while pantomiming the planting, weeding, and harvesting of rice. The men wore blue cotton hapi jackets and white cotton breeches; the women's indigo yukatas featured competing white patterns. Those not dancing crowded the sake barrels and food kiosks offering *yaki soba* noodles and *yakitori*—thin wooden skewers of chicken, onions, and green peppers smothered with sweet-sauced teppanyaki beef.

At the first shouts of "irasshaimase," some dancers broke ranks to surround the carriage while others gestured the new arrivals to join them.

Caught in the moment, Haru elbowed Kenji, "Can you feel the music?"

He surprised her by saying, "Let's dance with our new parishioners."

Kame tugged Sam's arm.

"I'll do my best," said Sam, his voice betraying uncertainty.

The crowd buzzed as the honeymooners oscillated toward the band tower. A pair of rough hands handed Kenji a square wooden cup spilling over with sake that he quickly downed. After dancing around the taiko tower twice, Kenji and Haru ambled over to the food stalls.

A short, wrinkle-faced woman in a frayed yukata shoved a small plate of gyoza into Haru's hands. She bit into the thinly rolled piece of dough crimped at the top. "Pork?" she asked, not sure if it might be chicken. Haru got a toothless hai.

Carter, who had changed into a tawny leather shirt, clean trousers, and dress cowboy boots, strolled over to Kenji and offered him another cup of sake.

The only other white person at the festival, dressed in a black Geneva gown similar to a judge's robe over a white cassock, made his way over to Kenji. He bowed. "Hajimemashite."

"Good evening, Father John," said Carter. He turned to Kenji. "Reverend Adams is the Presbyterian minister, the pastor of our only church in Waimea."

Kenji offered his hand. He remembered Imamura's instructions: "Don't shake hands with a haole as you would with an Asian. Grab firmly as an equal, not a supplicant."

Adams paused a microsecond, then shook it, and winced slightly from Kenji's grip.

"And his lovely wife, Haru," Carter added. The reverend gave a slight bow, and Haru returned the courtesy with a deeper respectful bow.

"Welcome to Waimea," said Adams focusing on Kenji. "I have been looking after your community. I must say it has been a challenge." He let the words linger and then added, "Or at least those your shaman hasn't seduced."

"Arigato, Reverend Adams," said Kenji deciding to ignore the shaman goad. "You are right; it is time we share the burden. Let's be partners with the goal of nurturing the good character of our flocks. Is it not true, we Buddhists and Christians share the same values?"

Adams drew his shoulders back, raised his eyebrows. Kenji kept quiet, thinking haoles had a tough time with silence and would keep talking to fill the void.

"We Christians offer eternal salvation. You Buddhists offer rebirth."

"While our understanding of what happens after death differ," said Kenji, who did not correct Adams's misconception that all Buddhists believed in rebirth or even an afterlife but, rather, are focused on enlightenment in this life, "our means are the same—to treat others as you would like to be treated."

Carter widened his grin. "You both have it right. What's important is to help those in our community lead lives of honor."

"Kampai," said Kenji, lifting his sake cup in a toast. Carter and Adams joined in but then simultaneously spied a woman in black in the crowd. A frown creased each man's face.

Shika, still in her ninja-impersonating, all-black attire, ignored the disapproving glances from Carter and Adams as she walked over to another group of sake drinkers. She had taken measure of the new Buddhist priest, tipsy with sake, and his young, no doubt pitiably naïve wife. She could hardly wait to tell Uno his worries about the Buddhist mission were for nothing.

She had worked the crowd for an hour. Time to go, but she spotted a group of mostly men making space for her. She crouched down on her heels and accepted a cup of sake. After polite greetings, she motioned them closer. "Tomorrow is the night of the Inari." She held their knowing gaze, then stood up, and sashayed into the night. Slowly. Satisfied. She could feel the eyes on her. Yes, the crowd had come to welcome the new priest, but she knew the night belonged to her. Tomorrow night, the Buddhist mission would end before it had begun.

∞ ∞

As the last of buckboards pulled away taking revelers, including Kame and Sam, home, Haru and Kenji strolled to theirs. While not matching Kenji's sake intake, Haru had imbibed too much herself. Her eyes glowed.

"Did I hear a few people call you Haru-sensei?"

"Yes," she sighed. "That Kame must have talked to everyone about the English classes."

"I am very proud of what you did."

Haru blushed at the compliment. "Almost everyone I talked to ended the conversation with 'send us picture brides,' as if I could order a dozen from the Shirokiya Department Store."

A dog barked in the distance.

Kenji stopped, turned toward Haru. "Maybe you can." He raised his eyebrows.

"Midori?

"You're getting close," said Kenji.

"Me?"

"Think about it."

Because her eyes were on Kenji's face and not the path, Haru tripped over an unseen broken branch. Kenji caught her, drawing her close. They shared a laugh, their faces flushed. Kenji released his grip, and they resumed walking. But as they strode side by side, the back of his hand brushed Haru's, and she said, "I wonder who that ninja lady was?"

"I asked Sam, but he just said, 'Enjoy the evening,' and changed the subject."

Haru's eyes narrowed; a furrow between them ran halfway up her forehead. "Every time I got close to her, she would somehow manage to keep her distance as if she was watching me."

"Ah so desuka," said Kenji offering a polite "is that right." They had reached the front of the house. He touched Haru's elbow. "A new life, Haru."

Upon entering their home, inside, Kenji lit a lamp while Haru said, "I will heat some water for the bath."

⚭ CHAPTER 40 ⚭

As soon as Haru entered the kitchen, she stooped in front of the stove, opened the metal grating, and blew softly on the glowing embers left over from Ualani's visit. Satisfied with a small flame, she tossed in dry twigs and brushwood. Thinking of the frequent house fires in Amakusa and Hiroshima, she checked the side vents for escaping embers, not quite believing Ualani's claim that a stove inside a kitchen with wooden cabinets and wood walls could be safe. She breathed easier noticing only thin whiffs of smoke escaping.

So engrossed was she in the minutiae of her task, Haru at first failed to notice her audience. She did now.

Kenji stood transfixed.

Haru managed a guileless smile. Then, before Kenji could see the blush rising from her neck, she grabbed the two empty pails to fetch water to heat for the bath. So did Kenji. Their fingers brushed. Haru's knees weakened; her heartbeat galloped. With a throaty voice, Kenji said, "Let me get the water while you prepare the tea." Without waiting for an answer, he picked up the tin pails and hurried out the kitchen door.

Haru opened a tin of fresh green tea leaves and scooped a measure into the teapot's mesh strainer. *Oh, Odaishi-sama,* she thought, *don't let this be a repeat of our first night.*

Kenji returned with his back straining under the weight of two pails of water.

Haru hovered over the teakettle. Silver sweat beads gathered strength on her forehead. Kenji's hips bumped Haru's while he placed the water pails on the roaring stove. The teakettle shrieked. Kenji snatched the teakettle off the grating. "Are you signaling the coyotes to visit?" he laughed as he handed the kettle to his wife.

"Hai," Haru said, regretting she could not return a clever rejoinder. Too nervous to wait for the water to cool a bit, she gripped the kettle handle, tilted it over the teapot, and let the water cascade slowly through the tea leaves so the water would leech the full flavors. She worried Kenji would notice her trembling as she handed him his cup.

Kenji led her into the dining room where he sat down at the table. At his nod, Haru did the same. He looked over his teacup into the adjoining room. "I'm thinking we could convert the living room into a tatami mat room. Our parishioners would be more comfortable."

"Could we find a *chabu-dai*?" Haru asked, referring to the short Japanese table. Relieved to have a mundane subject to discuss, she added, "And cushions to sit on?"

"Given that we Japanese are almost half of Waimea's population, I am sure we can find one at the trading post Ualani mentioned," said Kenji.

Haru raised the cup to her lips and enjoyed the aroma before sipping. "Go ahead and bathe while the water is warm, Kenji. I'll prepare our bed. Call me when it's my turn."

"Why don't you join me and scrub my back?" said Kenji.

A hot flush washed over Haru, this one more intense than anything she had ever experienced or imagined. She spoke barely above a whisper. "Hai." Struggling to hold onto her composure, she added, "Let me fetch fresh towels and our *nemakis*," referring to the cotton sleeping robe used for pajamas.

Haru's smile brightened Kenji's eager eyes. He rose and walked toward the kitchen. "I'll carry the water to the ofuro."

Haru scurried to the bedroom. Her mind reignited the fantasy that had been building prior to that horrible honeymoon night. One of her ship's students had presented her a copy of Japan's nine-centuries-old romance novel, *The Tale of Genji*. She had savored the amorous passages between Prince Genji and his favorite concubine, Kiritsubo. She thought of Kiritsubo's rendition of their first pillow time.

Minutes later, wearing her nemaki and carrying Kenji's over her arm, Haru rushed to the back door where she slipped her big toes into a pair of getas. A sharp breeze rustled the eucalyptus trees like a whisk swishing a cymbal complimenting the drumbeat of her heart.

As Haru entered the open-air ofuro, she relaxed at seeing Kenji sitting on an *isu,* a fist-high stubby legged stool, modestly facing the koa wood wall. "Irrashai," he greeted while sloshing water over his shoulders from one of the pails. She reached up and draped the towels and Kenji's nemaki over the five-foot-high side where the roof would be if this were Japan instead of the tropics. Her shaky hands unfastened her sash. She took a deep breath and watched Kenji, still facing away from her, soaping his chest and underarms. She let her yukata fall down to her elbows, exposing the front of her torso to the open door breeze, accentuating the feeling of nakedness. The full moon gave her a chance to examine her figure. She liked what she saw. No blemishes. *Did Kiritsubo have a body as flawless as mine?* Her expectations heightened as she marveled at her nipples crinkling into diminutive rose-colored buds. Her silky hair fluttered in the draft. Haru had not realized she was holding her breath until she had to let it out. She took off her robe, prolonged the moment by folding it neatly, and placed it atop Kenji's nemaki.

She squatted behind her husband. He reached behind and handed her a soaking-wet tenugui, a paper-thin cotton washcloth. She lathered the cloth and scrubbed Kenji's back. She had never seen a man's "thing" and was too embarrassed to even consider a peek or to lather Kenji's stomach and let her fingers slither down.

"*Domo,*" said Kenji in a voice suggesting she could stop.

Haru blushed, worrying he might turn around quickly, exposing their nakedness to each other. But he did not move. Still crouched down, she turned 180 degrees and splashed warm water from the bucket over her body and began soaping. She resolved to buy an *oke,* a shallow bowl used to scoop water from a bucket to pour over the body. Trickling water bouncing on her back interrupted her thoughts.

An electric arc swept over her body at the touch of soft fingertips squeezing a sudsy tenugui that began to slowly stroke her back.

"Domo arigato," she murmured in a soft, constricted voice. She forgot about her shopping list.

"We have a lot of work to do," said Kenji. "Bishop Imamura has given us a roadmap with his example."

As Kenji's hand rubbed her shoulders with the soapy cloth, Haru found it difficult to think about Bishop Imamura's roadmap but managed a "hai, wakarimashita."

Seconds after Kenji rinsed her back, he stood up. "It's chilly," he murmured as he briskly worked the towel, after first squeezing as much water out of it as he could, on his body. Donning his nemaki, he said, "I will be inside."

Haru breathed easier as she heard Kenji's getas plop on the soft grass, followed by the kitchen door opening and closing. She took care in washing every crevice of her body. She laughed aloud at the trees, thinking of the amusing first encounter Genji had with a general's daughter.

༄ ༄

Kenji walked into the bedroom hardening, lost in images of Haru's generous breasts he had peeked at while sudsing her back. He felt tense even as his confidence rose, certain her mood meant she had forgiven him for his first-night miscue. He twisted the metal knob of the oil lamps until the wicks gave off only the slightest glimmer. Pulling the quilt off the bed, he slipped under the cotton sheet. His heart accelerated at the sound of the back door shutting. When Haru's moonlit silhouette crossed the bedroom threshold, he searched for the right words to let her know tonight would be different. "Let us hope the great Buddha blesses us with a child tonight."

Haru sat down on the vacant side of the bed, let her nemaki drop to her waist, sloughed it off, slid under the covers, and rested her head on the pillow.

Kenji turned toward her. His tentative hand slipped around her waist.

Haru brushed his hand lightly as it slipped up along her belly. "Surely, he will."

∞ Chapter 41 ∞

THE BACK DOOR SLAMMED.

Haru bolted upright. The sheet dropped to her lap. Pale streams of dawn's first light slashed through the shutters. Two pails clanged together. "Someone's in the kitchen," said Haru, looking at Kenji's sleepy stare at her exposed breasts. Haru blushed and raised the sheet.

Kenji's eyes widened. He pinched his forehead with his right thumb and index finger. "Oh, my head." He fumbled for his nemaki on the floor. As he stood up, wincing from the pain from last night's sake, he offered Haru a sheepish smile and hurried out of the bedroom.

Haru, slipping on her nemaki, traipsed behind him.

They heard a whish on reaching the kitchen. Ualani was bent over, holding a flaming match in front of the oven's open door. She lit the kindling grass under the dried twigs. Satisfied, she stood up, looked at Kenji's disheveled hair, and shook her head sadly. "Mr. Carter said to look after you. It's a good thing I came by. You might have slept through the whole day."

"Ualani?" said Haru, her tone more a question than a greeting.

"And good morning to you, too. It's a Western breakfast this morning," said Ualani, grabbing two eggs with her stubby fingers and cracking the shells together over a coconut calabash. She picked up two more with her other hand and repeated the process. Yellow yolk dripped from the shells without touching her fingers.

Her mouth half open, Haru stared at the woman. She had wanted to cook this first breakfast for her husband. Unsure of what to say to this wacky granny who had taken over her kitchen, the eighteen-year-old bride was dumbfounded and remained silent.

An imperial-faced Ualani wiped the bottom tips of the broken shells on the edge of the calabash and tossed them into a straw basket three feet away with the assurance of a tobacco-chewing paniolo who never misses a spittoon. Next, she picked up a cleaver and lifted it over clumps of onions, tomatoes, and mushrooms. Holding it at its apex, she stared at Kenji.

"Are you going to stand there all morning or take a bath? And don't think about waiting for hot water. You look like you need a cold slap in the face. When you get back, we'll eat, and I will tell you about that crazy Uno and his night of the Inari." Expecting no argument and getting none, Ualani began chopping the vegetables in rhythm to music only she could hear.

Kenji would have been more amused if he weren't so hungover. He reached for a water jug and poured himself a glass of relief.

"Let's take our bath," said Haru, grabbing two empty pails. Once out the door, she could hardly wait. "I like that old lady, but she's doing my job."

"Her words are sharp, but her toothless smile and twinkling eyes tell me another story. Ualani is playing a country character auditioning for a new purpose in life."

"*Wakarimasen*," said Haru, a question mark on her face.

"You heard Sam say that Ualani has a hut on the ranch and does a few household chores from time to time. Her predawn arrival tells me that instead living out her days on Carter's charity, she sees us as her last chance to contribute, to be important to someone." Kenji paused at the ofuro. "I need to make a stop first," he said nodding to the outhouse. "Think about it."

Haru carried the two pails to the water pump, thinking more about her first lovemaking than Ualani. Whatever demons had grabbed Kenji that horrible first evening had been exorcised, she thought. *Last night was like a chapter from* The Tale of Genji.

Lost in thought, she finished a quick bath and didn't hear Kenji's footsteps until he entered the ofuro's small confines. Putting on her nemaki as Kenji sat on the stool to bathe, Haru's thoughts returned to Ualani. *Yes, I can see Kenji's point. More important, I don't want to start our third day of marriage with an argument.* She tied the sash to her nemaki. "I can use cooking and laundry time to start English classes."

"And you would have more time to write letters recruiting picture brides," said Kenji obviously pleased he had prevailed. "I believe we have adopted a mother."

"More as if she has adopted us," said Haru, thinking Kenji had his heart in the right place. She thought back to last night. Children. No Midori to help her. *Maybe Ualani is a gift from Buddha.*

As they shook off their getas at the back door, Kenji put his hand on Haru's shoulder for balance. She turned and smiled. His throat thickening with each measured word, Kenji said, "My mother made a good choice." He opened the screened door and walked in. Ahead of Haru.

The aroma of fresh coffee beckoned from the living room table. While Haru had taken a liking to the drink in Yokohama, she would have appreciated Ualani asking if they preferred tea, but she smiled and dropped in two teaspoons of sugar.

"Delicious, Obasan," said Kenji, shoving a forkful of omelet into his mouth.

Ualani dropped her entertainment persona. Her face turned serious; her eyes locked onto Kenji's. "You have a big problem: the odaisan. That self-appointed priest means to run you out of Waimea."

"You mean the little man with the face of a mongoose?" said Haru. "We saw him when we landed. Sam told us about him."

"Humph," grunted Ualani. "Did Sam tell you Uno drives out evil spirits, tricks mothers to give him his young daughters as a-ko-lites, and has a wicked hold on his followers?" Ualani nodded at her perplexed breakfast companions. "I didn't think so. Uno's the king around here. An evil king. Now you come along to steal his little kingdom. I'm not so good at reading and writing. I speak three languages, none of them good. But I know what's going on. People talk in front of me as if I'm a tree stump. You didn't even notice me last night."

Haru and Kenji exchanged guilty looks.

"I was that bundle of rags under the big eucalyptus tree. I saw Uno's whore dressed like a ninja. Some ninja. I was the invisible one. She buzzed around whispering to people. I listened. Here's what those two shamans are planning tonight." Ualani gave her two bewildered hosts a rundown on the planned "festivities." She ended by saying, "The poor girl who's supposed to be possessed by the devil fox is Sachi. She's always been a strange one with odd parents. They live by themselves outside of town with their pigs. She's only about thirteen years old. If you ask me, she is just having a difficult time becoming a woman, if you know what I mean."

By the time Ualani finished her cautionary tale, the coffee had turned tepid.

"What can we do?" asked Haru.

"What do I know? I can make an omelet, skin a rabbit, and use a charcoal iron without spilling ashes. Your husband's the priest."

"That's right," said Kenji. "However, I have no fear. He's only an uneducated shaman."

Haru was not so sanguine. Only weeks ago, Ko's uncle had raised such a fuss that she had to leave the country. She put her fingers under her chin and leaned forward. "Obasan," she said, her voice turning soft and conspiratorial, "can anyone go to Uno's … " she paused to search for the right word, "shaman show?"

Ualani nodded.

"Tell me more about Uno's animals and how he manages them." An idea started ricocheting around her head.

Kenji rose. "Don't worry yourself about Uno. I'm getting dressed."

When Haru pressed Ualani to tell her about Uno's white fox, the talk soon digressed to pets. When they found common ground on their love of cats, Haru decided to broach an earlier subject that nagged at her, even though she had given in to Kenji. She mentally took a deep breath. "Breakfast was wonderful," she said, pointing to her empty plate. "Lunch is my turn. I hope you like it as much as I enjoyed your breakfast." When Ualani's compliant hai passed Haru's test, she said, "Why don't you take one of the children's rooms for your bedroom."

For the first time in years, the old woman was at a loss for words. After a long pause, she rose. "We need more firewood." Ualani U-turned uncertainly, waddled through the kitchen, and banged the back door on the way out.

Catching the emotive moment, Haru stood up to follow. But Kenji, entering the dining room dressed in a suit, placed a gentle hand on her shoulder. "She needs to be alone. Ualani wouldn't want you to see her tears of relief and joy. You will not forget this day."

"Nor last night."

∞ CHAPTER 42 ∞

AFTER A MORNING OF GROCERY SHOPPING at Oda's Trading
Post, Haru prepared udon soup with noodles, spices, chopped
chicken, eggs, firm tofu, and vegetables as Midori had taught her. At
the first taste of the steaming soup, Kenji delivered his oishii compliments. Haru changed his expression from smile to worry as she
revealed her plan to "know thy enemy" between noisy slurps.

"It's out of the question," said Kenji. "You are the wife of a
Buddhist priest."

"It's out of the question for a Buddhist priest, not for a curious
eighteen-year-old newcomer," said Haru, forgetting her morning
resolution to an avoid arguments "Wasn't it you who wrote how you
and Bishop Imamura walked into Chinatown's gambling dens?"

Kenji put his spoon down and sat upright. "You just arrived in
Hawaii. We have been in Waimea for a day! We don't start our mission by kicking the hornet's nest." The more he talked, the more the
anger rose in his voice. "It's been decided."

Kenji's stinging rebuke would have shut down most brides' attempts at assertiveness. Japanese women were brought up to be sub-
missive. While this was true in the majority of marriages, Haru had
witnessed the interplay of partnership of Midori and Kiyoshi and
knew an early no did not always mean no forever. She was a woman
who had looked fate in the eye twice and successfully escaped. Her
peers had asked her to teach them. In a crisis, whether facing tuberculosis on the ship or explaining Kame's plight to Imamura, she
acted decisively and made a difference.

Haru looked at Ualani. "How many times a year does Uno drive
out evil spirits?"

"Not even once a year. It's not like everyone is running around
shouting, 'The devil's got me!'"

Haru turned back to Kenji. "So, if I don't see this exorcism tonight, not only will it be a long time before I can see this, but ... "
Haru paused and started over, speaking softly to Kenji. "This Uno
is very clever. Do you think it's by chance that he is showing off his
power the day after we arrive? He is sending a message. 'I am the

one to come to for marriages and funerals. My shrine is the place for festival celebrations.'"

Like most people in an argument, Kenji was formulating his rebuttal as Haru spoke. But her words began to make sense. He hesitated but caught himself growing angry. Why couldn't he control his temper? It was Uno who was the problem, not his wife.

Haru interpreted Kenji's hesitation as meaning "My no is not as firm as a few minutes ago." She almost reached for the teapot to offer Kenji a refill but held back, worried her hand might shake. Instead, she said, "Gochisosama deshita," excusing herself from the table.

After lunch, Haru and Ualani cleaned the kitchen. This time Ualani prepared green tea. Sitting at the dining room table, she regaled Haru with Waimea's history, its recent scandals, and piled on advice on everything from buying food to how to handle rude haoles.

Laughing at Ualani's rendition of mix-ups over the Japanese problem of pronouncing Rs, Haru suddenly turned serious. "How am I going to visit Uno's exorcism? I don't even know where his shrine is."

Ualani didn't understand the word "exorcism" but got the drift. "I wondered when you would get around to that."

"You know where it is, Obasan. We could go together."

"Ha! I'm too old for that. But I have a suggestion."

Haru agreed.

Ualani walked over to the Parker Ranch offices in Waimea and made a phone call.

∞ CHAPTER 43 ∞

IN THE LATE CLOUDY AFTERNOON, plantation workers, who yesterday had greeted Kenji and Haru, now began the pilgrimage to the Shinto shrine. As their centuries-old tradition ordained, they revered both Shintoism and Buddhism. While Uno's concocted rituals might not pass muster in Tokyo, after his two-decade Waimea religious monopoly, his twisted interpretations were accepted as authentic by workers recruited from unsophisticated villages in Okayama, Kyushu, and Okinawa.

Skeptical Parker paniolos debated the entertainment prospects of the promised exorcism versus the usual thrill of gambling and drinking. Many mounted up to give it a look-see. They could roll the dice near the entrance where surely sake would be served until the shaman began his show.

Earlier, a reluctant Kenji had acquiesced to Haru's plan of "harmless reconnaissance" once she told him Sam and Kame would accompany her and then promised, "No one will notice me."

∞ ∞

Under threatening clouds, an impatient Haru descended from her porch steps as Sam pulled up in his buggy. A grinning Kame sat next to him. Before Haru reached the carriage, thunderous drumbeats sounded. Haru had to raise her voice. "What's that?"

"Uno uses a big war drum to call his flock," said Sam. He paused and gave Haru and his ebullient wife an amused look. "I told Kame this may be the year's best entertainment." He looked up at the sky. "Let's hope the rain holds off."

As soon as Haru boarded, Sam snapped his whip over the head of his horse that soon broke into a trot. At the corner entering the main road, Sam slowed the horse but not quickly enough. As he turned right, the buckboard's back right wheel toppled into the culvert. While no one was hurt, the wheel had cracked. The crowd heading toward the shrine stopped to gawk. Several volunteers grunted while lifting the tilted buckboard as Sam, fronting the horses, pulled their harnesses forward. He ignored the few drops of rain hitting his face.

Sam studied the cracked wheel. "Useless. But I have a spare underneath the carriage."

The same Samaritans hoisted the back of the buckboard as Sam dislodged the broken wheel and replaced it with the new one.

The drumbeating stopped. They would arrive late.

∞ CHAPTER 44 ∞

UNO STOOD ON THE GRANITE OUTCROP overlooking the fox cage's pine-planked roof. The drum's reverberations echoed deep inside his body. He aimed his awa-glazed eyes at the black angry clouds roiling around Mauna Kea. Kona winds buffeted his cheeks and bent the surrounding palm trees. He turned to savor the sight of his four, white-smocked female drummers. Two awa-entranced acolytes on each side of a six-foot-high war drum faced each other. They swung their fur-tipped mallets in rhythmic sequence. Sweat-drenched cotton-cloth smocks hugged their curves. Their oiled calves glistened. Uno crossed his arms in a violent downward movement.

The pounding ceased. The girls snapped their drumsticks across their chests like rifles at parade rest.

A crack of lightning split the sky, illuminating Mauna Kea and brightening the two larger-than-life stone gargoyles guarding the entrance to Uno's shrine.

A sign.

Seconds later, thunder bounced off the mountainside, and more Pele-type lightning bolts flashed overhead, threatening a heavy downpour that would drench the shrine. Then, as if Uno ordered it, the incessant trade winds chased away the storm. The setting sun shot golden arrows between rifts in the clouds, brightening the moist air with a fleeting rainbow. Soon, only a purple ribbon on the horizon remained from the sunset. Crystal-clear skies showed off a full moon blooming in the twilight. Thousands of admiring stars twinkled. Surely, the sky's rage was a message from the gods. Uno nodded at his drummers. They resumed their drumming at a slow, commanding cadence.

Uno wrapped his spiny arms around his body as if suddenly cold. In an hour, no one in Waimea would doubt his power. Tonight, he would emasculate the Buddhist intruder before he could establish his ministry. He wondered how many months would pass before the slumped-shouldered priest would return to Oahu.

Uno's eyes dropped, searching for his companion of many years. The patchy-furred fox caught his gaze and whimpered. Uno crawled down from the boulder. Shika handed him a cup of tawny liquid. He entered the cage and cradled Fushimi in his arms. Tilting the cup, he fed him milk laced with awa. Uno's voice soothed, "You have served me well, old friend. But you must make one last sacrifice tonight. You have lived a long life. Your blood will serve a great purpose. This evening, I will become an *ikibotoke*, a living saint, the most powerful form of the odaisan—the one who challenges the spirit of the fox, the one who controls good and evil."

Fushimi fell asleep in his master's arms.

Uno's eyes moistened as he set the fox down on a bed of tired straw. He duck-walked out of the cage, straightened up, and filed past the row of sculptured foxes, stopping short of the torii gate. He liked what he saw. Food sellers were firing caldrons, hanging strips of beef jerky, chopping vegetables at their booths that flanked the entrance pathway to the shrine. Volunteers dug fresh latrine ditches in the woods and then cut long branches and stuck them in the ground fronting the ditches to provide a modicum of privacy. Shouts sprung from two groups of dice-tossing men squatting in circles. A few toddlers scampered about like swirling snowflakes. Three of their mothers played *kitsune ken,* similar to the fist-pumping game of rock-paper-scissors—only the players acted out symbols for fox, hunter, and headman.

Amidst this gathering, a child pointed to the watchful Uno. Others turned. A hush descended on the crowd as the early arrivals spotted the shaman. The food sellers put down their ladles. The gamblers picked up their dice. Toddlers scampered behind their mothers' kimono.

A crooked-smiling Uno looked at no one. Admiration is comforting, but fear works wonders. With that thought, he retreated to Fushimi's replacement, an all-white terrier except for one eye looped in black fur. The breed excelled at vermin control by killing raccoons, opossums, and, most important to Uno, the red fox that was a constant nuisance to plantations.

Uno looked around searching for Shika, who stepped out from behind the cage. She was there, always as faithful as the fox. "Get the girl."

Uno did not tell Shika why he had bought the terrier. But she had guessed, and now she knew. The white fox had served its purpose. *Same as me*, Shika worried, as she cut across the compound to the acolytes' sleeping quarters where the possessed girl waited.

This morning, she had stared into the mirror and studied the tight wrinkles around her eyes, the furrows in her forehead, the slackness in her neck's skin, the droop of her nose. Once she had boasted firm, apple-round breasts like the acolytes. Now, hers drooped.

She had whispered to selected men the night before that the acolytes were going to be given as brides tonight. For years, the girls came to stay for a year or two and then moved on to matrimony. They had relieved her of Uno's rough advances. Yet now she dreaded that one of the comely acolytes would be asked to stay.

Tonight's ceremony would end the career of the white fox in stunning fashion, foretelling her own future, she speculated. Shika pushed this foreboding thought out of her mind as she spotted the girl's parents hovering in front of their daughter's door. She heard moaning like a wounded animal coming from inside the room. The disheveled parents glanced up at her, their eyes frightened. Shika nodded. The parents bowed and, as if commanded, quickly turned to the door.

Sachi's father knocked on her door.

The girl barked.

∞ CHAPTER 45 ∞

SACHI HAD SPENT MOST OF THE DAY GROWLING in her upstairs bedroom over her family's butcher shop. Having grown up in this room, she was immune to the stench of butchered pigs and their offal emanating from the Big Island's first concrete-floored pens behind the house.

Only the experienced hands of a midwife had saved Sachi from strangulation during a breech birth. The buttocks-first delivery was a bloody affair. When the sac broke, the umbilical cord twisted around the baby's neck and compressed. The midwife squeezed her hands deep inside and maneuvered the baby's arms and head to extract it. The baby's head was misshapen, the skin tinted bluish grey. The midwife spanked the infant to no avail. She then breathed gently into the newborn's mouth. On the third and last attempt to force air into the baby's lungs, it squawked shallowly.

Sachi's head almost recovered its normal shape within a few weeks, as most babies' heads do, but not quite. She never showed a sparkle in her eyes. She spoke slowly, often dropping Ds, Ts, and Ks in a word's last syllable. She could not keep up in school, and classmates often mocked her, as children will.

Sachi's mother initially hoped her love would bring her slow-witted firstborn to functional normalcy. But when the disparity between Sachi and other children increased, the mother grew to resent her burden. When Sachi wandered off into the lava fields, her mother fanaticized how much better life would be if Sachi fell down into a gorge. And now this kitsune possession absurdity was making her the object of ghoulish curiosity.

Sachi's father treasured his daughter. While not given to hugging his wife, he showered embraces on Sachi, pinched her cheeks playfully, ruffled her hair, and rewarded her smiles with bits of rock candy. Sachi shadowed him everywhere. He appreciated the company and her help feeding the pigs. As she grew older, her intelligence was sufficient to work the cash register. Customers grew fond of her gentle demeanor. Knowing her love of animals, some brought her a kitten or puppy— animals to care for that would never be subject to the hiss of a cleaver.

No one had told Sachi about the bloody event that announces womanhood. She refused to leave her room during the three-day ordeal. Her mother placed rice outside the door, and only when she left would Sachi take the rice inside. She sang over and over the few songs she remembered from her brief but humiliating school days.

When her period ended, she left her room, went to the water pump, and washed herself until her groin was raw. And then she began walking on all fours, stopped talking, and started grunting. After a few days, her parents recognized that certain grunts had meaning. They deciphered some as "yes," "no," and "I'm hungry," but could not

understand others, which frustrated the child who barked or whimpered in response.

Her parents asked Uno for help.

At the shrine, the steady drumbeats stopped. The crowd buzz at the
entrance silenced. Then, a single, four-mallet drum strike boomed,
signaling permission to enter the tree-shrouded path leading to the
shrine. The believers hustled, eager for front-row seats. The curious
ambled, hoping for circus-type entertainment. Holding up the rear,
the tipsy paniolos shuffled and wisecracked. The parade queued at the
front of the shrine where each climbed six steps to the outside portico, pulled the bell rope, listened to the clang, bowed, and clapped
hands in the proscribed manner. Shika presented each worshiper
with a thimble-sized sake cup filled to the brim.

The congregation sat down, forming a semicircle around the
fox cage and adjacent shrine too small to hold tonight's crowd.
Between the audience and shrine, six male volunteers, adorned in
ceremonial yukatas and displaying headbands inked with Shinto
phrases, sat cross-legged on a raised bamboo platform. Each stirred
an awa vat. A stack of coconut calabashes lay next to each man. A
pair of waist-high taikos flanked the stage. Shortly, four freshly oiled
acolytes marched in, holding their drumsticks high like swords
ready to attack, and froze into striking positions next to the drums.
Immediately, the awa stirrers rose to light a phalanx of Hawaiian-
style torches planted between the drummers and platform. Then
under the torches' wind-driven dancing lights, the white-smocked
girls struck their drums in a slow soft cadence.

Uno watched it all through the glass eyes of a larger-than-life fox
mask, implanted into the shrine's frontage at just the right height for
him to stand and gaze. The crowd must wait, build expectation; but
the trick was to have them wait just before they became angry. *Now,*
he thought. He shook his brown robes and sidestepped to the dangling bead-strung entrance. Taking a deep breath, he parted the beads
and stuck out his shaven head. As if prompted, the crowd gasped. The
stern-faced Uno waited for the congregation to quiet, fully parted the

beads, stepped outside, and raised his hands to the stars. The drum strokes quickened.

Directly below, the men stopped stirring the awa. In choreographed unison, they each grabbed a calabash, arched it above their heads, held the position for a heartbeat, and then dipped the gourd into the awa bowls. The tallest server rose and, holding his calabash reverently, ascended in slow, measured steps to Uno. Simultaneously, another male attendant drew a giant conch to his mouth and stirred the air with a haunting timbre eclipsing softened drumbeats. The ascending attendant stopped in front of Uno and bowed at the waist with outstretched arms, presenting the awa chalice to his master.

Uno raised the calabash to the sky, tilted it backwards, and let the thick brown liquid cascade into his mouth until the awa dripped over the corners of his lips. He closed his mouth and swallowed in small gulps. Then, to the last chords of the conch trumpeter, he swept his arms toward the crowd like Moses delivering the commandants.

At the ritual cue, his flock rose and stepped forward like Catholics approaching the altar to take the Eucharist. While the drummers maintained their soft cadence, each communicant took a generous swallow and then handed the calabash to his neighbor. When the last person in line drank the awa, Uno eased into the shadows.

Entering from the same shadows, adorned in a neck-to-toe white muumuu, came Shika with the terrier in tow. She held tightly to its leash, restraining the dog's effort to rush the fox cage. Murmurs rose from the stunned crowd. Dogs, the enemy of the kitsune, were never allowed near an Inari shrine. The excited crowd hadn't time to digest the shock when Uno reappeared with Sachi on all fours. He had outfitted her in a blue blouse and trousers like a cane-field worker. He led the crawling girl up on to the platform.

The terrier barked. Sachi howled. The fox whimpered from his cage. Uno raised his hands to the stars. The wind billowed his wide sleeves. His eyes roamed his audience until they quieted. Feeling his power swell, he opened his mouth to speak.

Then his face froze, morphed from glowing bronze to tarnished silver. His eyes, widening in dismay, riveted on three stragglers poised underneath the torii.

The congregation's bodies twisted. Their awa-buzzing heads swiveled, and their eyes labored to follow Uno's stunned gaze.

∞ Chapter 46 ∞

WITH SAM AND KAME IN HER WAKE, Haru had stepped inside the torii gate, her smile angelic. Two flanking torches gave her copper skin a golden glow and her formal, yellow kimono a noon-day brilliance. Her gaze rippled over the crowd until at the front she met Uno's shocked eyes. What fates, she wondered, had conspired to break that wheel and bring her to this moment. Not only had she violated her "no one will notice me" pledge, but she realized her kimono, chosen to show respect for the Shinto service, as she did when visiting a Hiroshima shrine, had been a mistake. She was a kimono-adorned peacock in a sea of casual yukata-clad hens.

If Haru thought she had dressed inappropriately, her future congregation did not. Accustomed to attending both Shinto and Buddhist services in their home villages, they were proud that the wife of their first local Buddhist priest was elegant. They had no idea of their expected role in Uno's scheme to harass Haru and Kenji back to Honolulu. Rotating their heads back and forth between Haru and Uno, they murmured, "Haru-sensei" and "The priest's wife."

Barely controlling his rage, Uno nodded his head in acknowledgement as a senior official might to an underling. That was when Haru saw the growling spectacle behind Uno. While Ualani had warned Haru, her gentle mind was unprepared for watching a barking child crawling on all fours. She knew of milder exorcisms from Kiyoshi's telling but never grasped the enormity of a possessed spirit until now, if that was what had happened. Tears welled in the corner of her eyes. Haru held back the urge to run forward and embrace the child. She must maintain her composure, she thought.

Haru smiled at Uno as if he were a favorite uncle she had not seen for some time. She bowed at the waist in deepest respect. Then, she short-stepped—a gait forced by her kimono and getas—down a narrow aisle shaped by the crowd shimmying aside.

Sam and Kame hung back, their faces registering something between wariness and fear.

Uno watched her promenade toward the front as his fists balled in anger at himself. His own wide-eyed hesitation had given this abomination a grand entrance. At the front, a body's length from Uno, Haru bowed a second time in acknowledgement of the elder Uno's priestly status. Her eyes scouted for a place to sit; two couples scooted sideways to make room for her.

An awa server brought Haru a sloshing calabash. She hesitated. At the entrance, she had spotted the last of the communicants lifting a calabash to their lips. Determined to pass this test, she lifted the gourd to her mouth. Despite the added cinnamon and honey, she wrinkled her nose but took two shallow sips. A slight numbing of the tip of her tongue justified her caution.

Regaining his composure, Uno's hard eyes fell on Haru's. What had he to fear? All the better she was here. *She's nothing more than a foolish girl. Oh, how she will soon regret her arrogant intrusion.*

The terrier's snarling at the cage brought Uno and the crowd back to the main event. Fushimi, perhaps remembering a time he had instilled fear in dogs, growled in defiance of the terrier's challenge and waddled to the front of the cage. Sachi, still on all fours, yelped in alarm.

Uno raised his face and howled at the moon, holding his cry as long as any mezzo-soprano. His wailing set off the fox, the terrier, and Sachi into a barking cacophony. He let out his breath, lowered his head, and heaved his chest to take in big gulps of air.

"EVIL!" bellowed Uno, whose booming voice, emanating from such a small body, never failed to awe his audience.

"EVIL!" Taut neck muscles flanked Uno's thorax like chopsticks.

"EVIL!"

The congregation sat as still as a terracotta army.

Uno stretched his neck forward like a cobra. His eyes burned from deep sockets. Keeping his torso and legs as still as sculptured granite, he swiveled his head regally. He savored the fearful, expectant effect his searing eyes had on his close-to-the-front flock—each of whom, he was certain, held the illusion that he not only had made personal eye contact with them but also had peered into their very souls. Even those disrespectful paniolos quieted in anticipation. He owned these people.

Uno gave Haru a quick glance. He resisted a smug smile, even as he relished her awed expression and the teary edges of her eyes. He refocused on the crowd, his crowd. This night of the Inari would never be forgotten.

Uno had misread Haru. Disgust, not awe, rankled her senses. The evil that Uno spoke of resided within the man, thought Haru. She had a way with animals—Kiyoshi had called her his "little zookeeper"—and she had learned what sounds placated fright. As she had when coaxing a scared dog from the bushes, she now whistled soothingly. No one noticed except the terrier whose ears fluttered, and its snarling lowered an octave.

"Look at Fushimi," commanded Uno pointing to the cage. "His fox spirit of the kitsune has possessed this simpleton, Sachi."

At the sound of her name, Sachi bobbed her head and growled.

Uno roared, "The fox demon will never leave her."

As Haru whistled at a pitch only the dog heard through the din of the crowd's murmurs, Uno returned his gaze to his audience and let his hands drop to his sides, palms out and shoulders slumped like a doctor who has arrived too late to save his patient. He paused for effect and then pumped his fist into the air. "Only the stronger spirit of the dog can save this child now."

The crowd burst alive, shouting or whispering as their nature dictated.

Uno swiveled to the waiting Shika. "Bring Fushimi."

Shika passed off the terrier's leash to Uno. He glanced down at the dog. *Why isn't the dog trying to rush the cage?* The thought passed as he caught Haru's hand covering her mouth in shock. *Wait till the dog goes for the throat, little one.*

Shika strode solemnly to the fox's cage. She unhitched the door and swung it open. Fushimi wobbled the few steps into familiar arms. Shika carried the trembling animal to the platform.

Uno raised his free hand. A sudden rush of wind ripped through the treetops. He waited for the rustling leaves to subside. His voice boomed. "Now! Now is the time for the dog and fox to face each other, and when the dog kills the fox, its evil spirit will flee from the girl like a frightened rabbit."

The crowd buzzed with excitement like Romans at the Coliseum. Three men in the crowd popped up as if watching racehorses reaching the finish line. Then five more. In seconds, the entire congregation was standing. Rising, Haru maintained a soothing whistle, louder now to compensate for the stirring crowd.

Uno turned the dog loose. The terrier's eyes flashed at the fox. Haru whistled. The terrier's ears twitched, and then he crouched down and began stalking the fox. He growled low.

The fox's cloudy eyes stared at the shadow of the dog. His legs trembled. His tongue hung.

Sachi snuggled next to the fox. She spoke her first word in months. "Water."

An awa server rushed to fill a calabash with water from a jug kept outside the fox cage.

No one noticed Haru's puckered lips.

The terrier sniffed the fox.

KILL IT! raged Uno internally. *Why didn't I move the child away from the fox? Why is this idiot server rushing to bring water at another idiot's command?*

The server handed Sachi, now sitting on her haunches and petting the fox, the calabash of water. She held the offering to Fushimi's mouth. The fox lapped the water while the dog barked menacingly.

Haru switched to a command whistle. The terrier quit growling, stood up, and looked Haru's way. Like his audience, Uno followed the dog's eyes. Adrenaline surged. He wanted to scream "**STOP!**" His mind rumbled on, struggling as to how to regain the initiative. Haru whistled again. Uno felt the urge to rush and strangle the girl but stood dumbstruck.

The woman on Haru's left handed her a bento box of leftover chicken and rice. Haru held up a well-chewed drumstick. The dog, which Uno had purposely not fed that day, jumped off the platform and walked over to Haru who let the terrier take the bone from her outstretched fingers.

A calm Sachi picked up the fox and began walking normally.

The standing crowd pushed closer to the unfolding miracle. A hushed commentary washed over the drama.

"She walked."

Sachi dropped to her knees and hand-fed the fox bits of rice. Sitting back on legs, her lopsided smile lingered on Haru. "I'm Sachi."

Behind her, Haru heard more murmurs. "She's talking to the new priest's wife like a normal person. The spirit of the fox has fled."

The fox wobbled back toward its cage.

In the back, Sam was one of the few who noted the fury in Uno's eyes.

Having eaten all the chicken from the bone, the terrier turned his attention to Sachi's fingers and started licking off the remnants of sticky rice. Sachi picked up the dog in her arms, stood up, and in a clear voice said, "I want this doggie."

Haru rose, positioned herself alongside Sachi, bowed to Uno, and turned to face the crowd. "Uno-san has driven out the evil spirit from Sachi without any killing. He is truly a great odaisan. The dog will go with Sachi to her home."

Someone farther back in the tightly packed circle of humanity shouted, "Banzai!" A second "Banzai!" rang, setting off a chorus of frenzied men and women bellowing, "Banzai!" in cadence.

Wide-eyed, Uno watched the crowd stand and bow to Haru strolling toward the exit like a princess with her attendants. This up-start sorceress would not be leaving Waimea, he thought. He realized that theirs would be a war of attrition.

Haru turned to bow to Uno one last time, but when she saw the force of evil in his eyes, she could not bend in supplication. In an instant, she knew her victory had birthed a vengeful enemy. She felt a tug on her kimono. Thinking an angry devotee of Uno was about assault her, she jumped back and turned.

A man holding a fedora, the full moon illuminating pleading eyes on a weathered face, said, "Send us wives." He bowed and retreated, stepping backwards into a crowd of men dressed in plantation shirts and trousers.

An older couple approached and bowed.

"Daddy, I am better."

Haru noticed Sachi made only fleeting eye contact with her mother.

The father's eyes misted when he bowed to Haru. "Our town has long needed a real priest," he said, skipping over the fact that he had asked Uno to intervene.

"It is late," said the mother who also bowed but in a hurried manner. "I trust this is the end of … " She let the thought drop.

Before Haru could contemplate the future of this sad family, Sam caught up with her.

"You have won the hearts of Waimea but not without danger. Tomorrow I will visit Uno with other paniolos and tell him you are under our protection."

Haru said, "Arigato," but wondered what type of life she was facing in her new country if she needed protection within forty-eight hours of her arrival.

⊂∞ ∞⊃

Uno did not notice Shika approaching him.

She put her mouth to his ear. "You have conquered the great spirit of the Inari, sensei. You have used the newcomer as your tool to expel the evil."

Uno stepped into the shrine, knowing she would follow him. Assured he was out of sight, he whirled and cuffed her face with the back of his hand. "You stupid cow. The purpose of tonight was not to exorcise the fox spirit from the dumb child but to exorcise the Buddhist priest and his arrogant wife from this island."

Shika, who had been pummeled many times, had learned to fall down at the first hit. Cowering, she gasped. "Remember, the humble man wins."

Uno spat in front of Shika's prone face. "A platitude for cowards."

⊙ CHAPTER 47 ⊙

AS THE CLIP-CLOP OF HORSES pulling wagons back to plantations and the cantering hooves of paniolos riding to their bunkhouses faded into the night, Sam guided his carriage down Haru's street. Her smile widened as she saw the glow from her home's windows grow brighter. She speculated that Kenji must have lit every candle and oil lamp.

Kenji was standing at the roadside by the time Sam reined in his horses, his face pinched with worry. Sam took one look and let out a low chuckle. "Reverend, your wife is now a legend; your mission in Waimea is assured of success."

Kame did him one better. "Haru is a hero."

"You better come in then," said Kenji. Once inside he added, "I have never been so worried. The loud drums, the conch wailing, and the banzai roars."

"Wait till you hear what happened," said Kame.

"Better to listen with bean cake and tea," said Ualani who stormed in from the kitchen carrying a loaded tray to the dining room table. She immediately joined the others sitting down as if to state, "I am not the new maid. I am the new member of the family who will help with the cooking and laundry." Haru confirmed the unspoken accord by picking up the teapot and started pouring with Ualani's cup being the first.

"I laid out the futons for your guests," said Ualani.

"What futons?" Haru asked.

"Do you think Mr. Carter would let me set up your house without bedding for guests?" Ualani said as more of a challenge than a question.

"Thank you," said Kame, looking at Haru as if she had insisted on her and Sam staying for the night. Knowing Haru would play down her role in the evening events, Kame kept the floor. "Let me tell you what happened tonight."

At the end of Kame's telling, Haru said, "Kenji, Kame told you what happened, but I want to tell you what I think we should do." Then she told him of the sad-eyed man who said, "Send us wives."

"You could tell the men in the back had decided among themselves who would approach Haru," said Kame.

Ignoring this interruption, Haru gazed deep into Kenji's eyes. "I remember what you wrote about how wives help civilize plantation life in Oahu." She turned her attention to Kame. "We can help." She was about to say, "We can write letters," and then realized Kame's education might not be up to the task. "Kame, you and I will work on a list of all the girls we know."

"Start with your mother," said Kenji.

"I will ask her to visit temples in the rural areas surrounding Hiroshima. Now that I think about it, my schoolmates won't be attracted to the rigors of plantation life, but farm families will find new hope in Hawaii."

An almost dozing Ualani perked up. "You are not the only educated girl we need. The Parker Ranch has a bachelor Japanese veterinarian. Waimea has a single lawyer, and you will want that too-lonely Dr. Goto to deliver your baby."

Before Haru could say, "Of course," Kame replied, "I heard a lot of my Okinawa dialect tonight, and I know lots of farm girls," she said, acknowledging the custom that Okinawans married their own, as did the men from Kyushu, Hiroshima, and Okayama.

Soft snores came from Ualani still sitting, but with her head dropped down.

"I believe that's a signal," laughed Sam.

Kenji stood up in agreement.

Haru looked at Kame's eager eyes and then to Kenji.

"We're too excited to go to bed just yet. I want to work with Kame on the letter to wives and write your mother before I go to bed."

Heading for the bedroom, Kenji managed a sleepy, "Hai."

At the scraping of the dining room chairs, Ualani woke. Too tired for a spiffy remark, she said goodnight and waddled off to her room.

When alone, Kame said, "If you can write a sample letter, I can copy." The finally sleepy Kame joined Sam on their futon in what Haru hoped would be the baby's room by late summer.

Haru stared at the blank sheet. She had never written a real letter. She had so much to say, so much to ask. She had kept a sometimes diary, and she followed that example. As her thoughts crystallized into introspection, the words flowed. She discovered that what she loved most about Hawaii was not the weather or even Kenji's assignment as a pastor for Waimea that she described but, rather, her excitement on finding a purpose in life. Haru related the evening's events in a fashion that revealed her coming-of-age moment. "Since I arrived at your door, you and Otosan have been preparing me to help others, as you helped me. I will do my best not to let you down. But I need some help, Okasan." Then she wrote of the need for picture brides.

Finished, she was surprised at the number of pages she had written. Haru looked out the window, and her spirits were warmed by the first glow of morning that gave an increased definition of the majesty of Mauna Kea.

Feeling guilty about missing her evening bath, she folded her letter, placed it in an envelope, and tiptoed into the bedroom. She looked at Kenji and wanted to tell him life was good. Instead, she silently slipped into bed and quickly drifted off to sleep.

PART IV

ALLEGIANCE

∞ CHAPTER 48 ∞

Waimea, Hawaii – November 11, 1918

H ARU LAID HER COFFEE CUP DOWN on the dining room table, un-suspecting that her already-tense day was about to turn awful and end worse. Ualani was washing the last of the breakfast dishes. Kenji was next door at his mission office, writing a letter to Bishop Imamura. Sachi, who had moved in with them when her parents died of pneumonia, was reading stories to the nursery school children that included Haru's five-year-old boy, Yoshio. Her oldest, Takeshi, had ridden his bicycle to his third-grade class an hour earlier. She looked down at eighteen-month-old Tommy, so-called because Yoshio mis-pronounced "Tomio," suckling her breast. Honolulu's *Pacific Commercial Advertiser*, already three days old by the time the delivery boy tossed it on her porch, lay innocently next to the saucer, still rolled and folded tight.

She rubbed her stomach knowingly. She had been lucky: three healthy sons, only one miscarriage. She remembered watching the emperor ride into the Yasukuni Shrine and how she had pledged to breed sons to serve in his wars. The longer she lived in America, the more she appreciated a country that sent its sons to combat reluctantly.

Haru's nerves tingled. This was not an ordinary day. She had accepted Mrs. Roberts's invitation to speak at her "soiree," as she called her weekly ladies' luncheon. Mrs. Roberts was an ardent women's suffrage advocate. With President Wilson changing his tune to support the Nineteenth Amendment and the House of Representatives passing it, it seemed just a matter of time before women's right to vote became law. And with states rapidly passing the Eighteenth Amendment prohibiting the sale of alcohol, Mrs. Roberts was in search of an issue. She settled on education. She had invited Haru to her home "to help us understand these language schools you people conduct."

Haru picked up the newspaper, admired its tight fold, and carefully unhooked the bottom tuck. Then instead of opening it, she mused about another haole invitation during her early days in Waimea. Her name had been included on the RSVP card Wellington Carter had sent Kenji, inviting him to a welcome dinner to meet plantation owners and their wives. Kenji had not bothered to tell her she had been invited. He did not hide the letter. Why would he? Japanese wives do not accompany their husbands to business socials. So when Haru was cleaning his office, she saw her name on the invite. When she asked why he had not told her, her husband shrugged. "It's not our custom."

Knowing Kenji's obsession with what people thought of him and recalling her "living in Hawaii" classes with Judith, Haru said, "Kenji, in America you will lose face if you leave your wife at home." So she began attending these types of events. The haole women were always polite but condescending.

In an era when non-English-speaking Japanese parents struggled to communicate with their children who spoke limited Japanese, Haru took pride in her self-taught English fluency. She listened to American music on the Victrola and for years had read the English newspaper aloud with a faded, spine-split dictionary at her side, but she remained hesitant to speak English with the haole wives. They did not know she understood their conversations and spoke in front of her as if she were a potted plant.

She opened the newspaper. While the headline exclaimed, "Armistice Close at Hand," it was the front page bannered editorial that thumped her heart: "After-Hours Japanese Schools Hinder the Americanization of its Child Citizens."

Under Andy Pafko's byline, she began reading.

> While the haole children walk home after school, ten thousand Japanese children march to one of two hundred Japanese language schools for their second school

day. And what are they learning? These so-called language schools are teaching AMERICAN children to worship a foreign emperor as a god. In ten years, these mostly pagan children will begin using their suffrage to turn Hawaii into a heathen land loyal to a foreign power. Military leaders have warned, "War between America and Japan is inevitable." Whose side will the children attending these Jap schools fight for? If war broke out, who could sleep at night wondering, if at a signal from Tokyo, men armed with machetes invaded your home?

Haru stared into space. She had wondered how long it would take the *Advertiser* to renew its attack on the Japanese language schools once the war ended. They couldn't even wait for the guns to go silent to continue their attack. But why did it have to start on this of all days? She imagined today's luncheon attendees reading Pafko's rant. *At least one of those pinched-faced matrons will shove the paper in front of me with an insincere "Have you seen this?"—with the humiliating assurance that I, an ignorant Japanese housewife, would not have seen it, let alone have the ability to read it.* Her eyes returned to the paper.

These schools are but a part of Imperial designs to rule all of Asia and the Pacific. We in Hawaii must not forget how at the outbreak of the current war, Japan, a pretend ally of the democratic powers, attempted to make China a de facto protectorate with their "Twenty-One Demands" that would have stripped China's sovereignty. While Japan retreated in the face of America's steadfast opposition, the world saw the true intentions of the Imperial Army.

This is the same Japan that only months after the start of the Great War sent its agents combing Hawaii's plantations to raise funds for the Emperor's soldiers fighting in China to take over the German concessions under the guise as an ally of England.

Haru remembered. Those agents' success had broken her heart. Many Japanese who had labored long, sun-drenched hours for years, saving so they could return to their village and buy a farm, donated their life savings to those agents. Yet, she acknowledged, for some, the donations allowed them a face-saving way of postponing their fading homecoming dream, rather than admitting they were never going back.

> How ironic that Japanese Christian ministers inaugurated these schools in the 1890s to provide daycare for plantation children with the hope that their parents would convert to the "one true faith." Fearing the loss of adherents, the Buddhist missions counterattacked and opened Japanese language schools shortly afterward with non-English-speaking teachers recruited from the homeland using textbooks provided by the Japanese Ministry of Education.

> More irony. In the early years, the plantation owners supported the schools since they kept more mothers working and contributed to plantation tranquility. Too late, they realized the sinister influence by a foreign power. Now, the owners fear labor unrest if they close down the facilities.

> The *Advertiser* demands that the legislature outlaw these un-American abominations.

Strange, Haru thought. After the night of the Inari, she was certain her greatest challenge would be the shaman, Uno. The evil in his eyes foreshadowed retribution for his humiliation at her hand. She remembered Kiyoshi's stories of the early Meiji Shinto fanatics burning Buddhist temples across Japan. She had been mistaken. Nothing happened. She never knew why. Maybe because of the paniolo warning or the sudden rush of the Japanese welcoming a real mission or the education programs she and Kenji started to help their parishioners. Or just maybe because Uno didn't have the stomach to sustain a battle.

Whatever, the threat never materialized. Haru had come to believe the real threat to her community came from within it. *Our schools frighten the haoles and make them imagine conspiracies that don't exist. Our children, all Japanese children, were being raised as loyal Americans. But our schools give the opposite impression.* While it was easy to blame the haoles and men like Pafko for enflaming passions, Haru saw their point of view. She decided she must address this issue with Kenji. Again. Tonight.

Haru rose from the table as Ualani entered to clear the dishes.

"A big day to tell those haole ladies our schools are making better Americans than their children," Ualani said.

Haru smiled. "Maybe I will take you with me so you can tell them."

Ualani popped her hand to her mouth in mock horror. Haru grinned and then pointed at the tabletop. "Leave the paper on the table, Obasan. There's an article I would like Kenji to read."

∽ CHAPTER 49 ∽

Haru had debated whether to follow her usual custom of wearing a Japanese kimono or debut herself in Western dress. A Mary Pickford fan, she noted that America's favorite actress's wardrobe was always appropriate for her part. So, given that today's subject was the Americanization of Japanese children, she had bought a pattern and three yards of material at the Parker Ranch Trading Store and sewn a calf-length, olive-hued dress with a scooped neck. She had practiced wearing high heels on the porch every day for a week. Kenji had planned his day so Haru could have the Model T, which she had learned to drive the previous year. She knew Mrs. Roberts was one of few women, haole or Asian, who drove in Waimea. *Give the ladies a bit to prattle on that wasn't school-related,* Haru thought, as she took a final check of her appearance in front of the bedroom's half-length mirror. She grew angry at herself at the uptick in heartbeats. She was no longer an eighteen-year-old bride. She managed a preschool, women in the congregation consulted her on marriage problems, and her garden supplied vegetables to the Oda Trading Post. Despite all their talk about women's suffrage, what had any of these haole ladies actually done, other than go to meetings? Still, perspiration ringed her forehead. No matter what she did, in Hawaii, she was not equal to the haoles.

Haru's mood brightened as she walked steadily down the porch steps toward the Model T. Rich plumeria scents hung in the air. Alternating ribbons of marigolds and violets ringed the porch. At the car, she stopped and gazed at the Takayama compound, home to three more buildings since her arrival, as well as a thriving garden.

The temple, running parallel to the left of her home, resembled a small-town Protestant church, a design instigated by Imamura to persuade the haoles that "our beliefs are like yours." The warm amber paint of both buildings infused a sense of harmony.

Following the birth of their second child, Kenji surprised Haru by building a cottage behind the main family house. He told Ualani, "This will give you a little privacy." Haru caught the quick wink from Kenji when Ualani had bowed in appreciation. Haru had never complained about their increasingly crowded quarters, especially since their home was a palace compared to cramped plantation housing. She treasured Kenji's thoughtfulness.

On the other side of the house, Haru had built a daycare nursery to look after the babies of the picture brides she and Kame had recruited through their letter-writing campaigns.

Except for the tangerine trees she planted between the house and nursery, Haru's home setting could pass for early summer in rural New England.

Then she glanced at her groomed rows of ripe tomato plants held straight by split bamboo supports and lime-green corn shoots looking over stubby leafy canopies hiding radish bulbs and eggplant. Her face glowed as she recalled how, two years ago, Kenji had arrived home before lunch one day with surprising news. "Mr. Carter has offered to sell us our homestead at a very generous price."

Haru had stared at him too astonished to speak.

"He wants to tidy up all the temporary land grants the Parker Ranch has issued over the years." Kenji walked toward the large window overlooking the porch. "We can own all this."

She remembered her response as if it had taken place this morning. "Accept the offer, and tell Carter we would also like to buy the lots on either side of us at market price." Like most Japanese wives, Haru controlled the family finances. "We have enough money to pay half in cash. I am sure Mr. Carter would finance the rest over ten years."

"But … what would we do with all that land?"

Haru had two dreams but thought one big idea at a time was all Kenji would consider. "I need more space to grow vegetables, Kenji. Oda-san told me if I could grow more, her store would buy them." Haru had a second vision, a secret vision. Next to her home—but not too close—would stand a hotel where Japanese travelers, such as the medicine man from Hiroshima or the food wholesalers from Honolulu, would find comfortable lodging.

Breaking her reverie, a nene, whose ancestors had been Canada geese but were now indigenous, honked. Haru looked up and watched the ebony-crowned bird roost on one of the silk oak trees lording over her jungle. *A good sign,* she thought.

As she opened the Model T's door, her eyes drifted to the cherry trees that she and Ualani had planted in front of the outhouse, just days after the night of the Inari. Each March, their pink blossoms reminded her of that event and its lessons in courage.

She would need some of that courage today.

The moment Haru drove up Mrs. Roberts's driveway, she knew the ladies had had a pre-meeting. Seven seated women looked up from two burgundy cloth-covered tables on the right lanai overlooking squat bougainvillea vines blooming in purple, red, and orange rows. Haru's thoughts raced back to another grand entrance—the night she had walked through a torch-lit crowd of her own people facing a man on stage determined to crush her. Today's lanai group was different. They were afraid. A group of people, not at all like them in race or culture, outnumbered these people. *In a generation, their children will be minority voters when my children are of age.* Haru knew that people expressed fears in different ways. Anger. Hate. Suspicion. She had no illusions about changing anyone's mind today. She would settle for just a few of the gawking women understanding the purpose of the language schools well enough to let fear ebb over a period of time. This was a talking point with their husbands. If she could not break down the wall of suspicion, perhaps she could leave behind a ladder to climb over it.

Opening the car door, Haru's heart raced. Everyone had stopped talking as if the earth had shaken in the first second of an earthquake. *Whatever the women expect*, thought Haru, *it's not a Japanese lady dressed in the latest fashion stepping out of a car she's driven herself.*

Haru smiled, recognizing a young lady in a lace-fringed uniform carrying a teapot and entering the lanai. The Japanese maid, Michi, attended Haru's English classes. The girl smiled at her and gave a hint of a bow. Haru had listened to haole ladies discussing their maids, almost always Japanese, with admiration. She wondered if they ever made the connection between honest and fastidious domestic help with the likely good citizenship of their children.

Mrs. Roberts, dressed in a yellow dress with a collared neck and only a hint of a sleeve at the shoulders, greeted Haru from the top step of the lanai. Haru's seamstress's eye approved the double-stitched hem just below the calf. Having met the still-seated women at various community events, Haru intoned "nice to see you again" salutations. She detected a new look in their eyes. Another type of fear. Haru was the youngest on the lanai and the only woman with hair hanging below the nape of the neck. Her face was unblemished and wrinkle-free. Despite Haru's pod of children, the ladies saw a girl's hourglass figure, previously hidden under a kimono, now revealed in Western dress. Haru knew rumors of haole husbands and their maids had an occasional basis in fact. She made a note to continue to wear her Japanese attire at events with husbands.

Mrs. Kinder, Takeshi's third grade teacher, started the conversation by asking Haru about her other two children. Haru understood this ploy deflected the conversation to the children of the other mothers. She did so in her usual limited vocabulary.

Haru was relieved when Mrs. Roberts moved the conversation to today's topic. In a soothing voice she asked, "Mrs. Takayama, can we afford to have future American citizens brought up in the belief that the ruler of a foreign land is superior to the government of this country?"

"And that's not all," said the never-smiling Mrs. Adams, wife of the Presbyterian minister. In her squeaky New England pitch, she added, "The use of their plantation pidgin on the playground is spreading to white children attending public schools!"

Another woman interposed in slow prim English. "Let me say this in simpler words—"

"Thank you, Mrs. Thompson," Haru interrupted. "I understand." Like a good politician, Haru chose not to argue about pidgin English, which was an amalgam of the five island languages. Hawaiian, Portuguese, and Chinese children all added to the plantation jargon, but given that Japanese made up half the students in grammar school, it was easy to pin the blame on this group. Haru addressed her audience in perfect but softly accented English. "You are fortunate. You are at home when your children return from school. Our women must work to make ends meet. Should children be allowed to run free without supervision?"

Haru smiled demurely at the women's startled reaction. She had long thought of the right moment to reveal she could understand and speak proper English. In the short silence, she imagined them inventorying all their past conversations in her presence, trying to remember what they had said that they now wished they hadn't. The pause allowed Haru to make her case.

"The primary purpose of our schools is to emphasize the Japanese values of obeying one's parents and respecting teachers. Our parents want their children taught the hierarchy of the five personal obligations: *fu-shi*, between father and child; *fu-fu*, between husband and wife; *cho-ya*, between elder and junior; *shi-tei*, between teacher and student; and *ken-shin*, between emperor and his subject. Of course, here in Hawaii, the last admonishment also emphasizes respect for the American president. While our children revere the emperor as a symbol of our culture, our schools and parents teach loyalty to America."

"A clever syrup masquerading heathen words and heathen ideas," snapped Mrs. Adams. "Your pagan festivals tell us where your loyalty lies."

Over the years, Haru had noted that the haole ladies kept their distance from the reverend's wife, who lived by the dictates of her joyless interpretation of the Bible. Attired in a gingham dress tight at the neck and long at the arms and legs, she gloried in the coming passage of the Eighteenth Amendment. Haru was not about to say anything that would garner sympathy for this woman so unlike her tolerant husband.

"Those proverbs come from a man born around the time of Moses. But our fu-shi sounds like the Fourth Commandment he brought down from the mountain, 'Honor your father and mother.' I believe Mrs. Kinder appreciates our language schools advocating shi-tei, respect for teachers."

Haru looked at Takeshi's teacher. "Mrs. Kinder, which group of students has the highest homework completion rate, fewest discipline problems, and knows their American history the best?" The red-faced reaction of everyone else in the room answered her questions. Haru didn't wait for a response. "I understand certain … people have asked you to stop encouraging your Japanese students to apply to the University of Hawaii." Haru knew that two of the women in the room, Mrs. Adams and Mrs. Bilkerton, wife of the planter, had made remarks about "Jap children going beyond their station."

"Everyone expects the children of plantation workers to cut cane. But their parents dedicate their long working lives so their children can have a better life." Her eyes swept her small audience. "I believe you would call that 'the American dream.' We are inspired that a man born in a one-room log cabin and whose farming father could not write rose to become president of the United States."

Haru worried just how far she could go with this track. Noting the silence, she lowered her voice as though revealing a secret to a best friend. "I love America, and if your government treated me like German and Italian immigrants, I would be a citizen of this country by now. I am proud my children are Americans. Could any other country in the world have something called the Statue of Liberty greeting its visitors and immigrants? Imagine the men and women huddled on ships approaching New York Harbor. No one has to tell them what the lady with a torch means. You stare at it, even at a picture, and you understand that whatever you hope for, in America, you have a chance to find it. All the children attending my husband's classes believe in the American dream."

"Thank you, Mrs. Takayama," said Mrs. Roberts after a long silence. "But can you answer our main concern? Most of the Japanese are never going back home. So why do these schools keep teaching their children how to become good Japanese using Japanese textbooks and non-English speaking Japanese educators recruited from Tokyo?"

"Our school is now using textbooks published in Honolulu. We still—"

Mrs. Adams clanged her teacup down on the saucer. "We have heard this story before. You people promised to change the textbooks before we entered the war. And all you changed were a few words and to have them published in Honolulu instead of sent directly to the schools from Japan."

"You are right, Mrs. Adams. Those textbooks need further changes. But we can't change them by ourselves." Haru switched her gaze. "Mrs. Roberts, you and women like you all over America are winning the war for the right to vote. I wonder if we ladies could quietly work together on helping our schools take another step toward Americanization."

Mrs. Roberts stared back warily and then stood up. "Ladies, I believe we can retire to the dining room for lunch. Perhaps Haru would be kind enough to tell us how she makes her home look like a botanical garden." She flicked an eye to Mrs. Adams to make sure she got the point that the discussion on schools was over.

Haru relaxed. She had been heard. She had not convinced anyone, including herself. Her defense of the language schools confirmed in her own mind how necessary it was to Americanize them. She rose and smiled at Mrs. Roberts. "I'd love to tell you about my garden, but first promise me you will give me some cuttings from your bougainvillea." *Tonight*, thought Haru. *Tonight, I will convince Kenji the only way to save our schools is to change them.*

Haru always remembered this lunch with Mrs. Roberts's group for another reason. Halfway through the meal, the telephone rang. Seconds later, Michi ran into the dining room. "It's Mr. Roberts."

Mrs. Roberts frowned. "Tell him I am having lunch."

"He said you might say that," said Michi. "The war is over."

Mrs. Roberts bolted from her chair to take the phone call.

∞ CHAPTER 50 ∞

THE SUN WAS SETTING as Haru laid out her best tableware. Tonight, she would serve Kenji's favorite fish, *unagi*—grilled eel marinated in soy sauce, sake, and sugar. She peeked inside her ceramic rice cooker simmering atop the oven and tasted the last of the Niigata rice she had been saving for a special occasion. She smiled. The softness was just right. She mentally rehearsed her "we need to change our school" plea she planned for tonight's dinner. Haru had begun converting Pafko's newspaper rant and the luncheon encounter into a reasoned proposition for curriculum change.

Earlier, she had strolled to the park to join the spontaneous end-of-war celebration with her extended family. She put today's only postal delivery, a letter from Ume, into her sleeve pocket. A few hours later, Haru pointed to impromptu food kiosks firing up their grills and told Ualani and Sachi, "Here's some money for food. I'm going home, but you can stay with Yoshi and Takeshi to watch the fireworks. Tonight, Kenji and I will dine alone."

Ualani grinned. "I understand."

She didn't, but Haru gave her a conspiratorial wink. "Nothing gets past you." She glanced over at Kenji talking to Kawaihae fishermen. "If Kenji hasn't left the park by six, remind him to come home."

Walking back home, Haru opened Ume's letter. Expecting the usually chatty family gossip, she halted, reading the short note. "Urgent. Please visit as soon as possible." Haru's years as the parish's women counselor taught her that money or the bedroom were the source of most married women's distress. But Ume? Haru had little time to speculate. Kenji would be home soon, and she still hadn't given the purpose of tonight's dinner enough preparation. Maybe she should do this another night. No! That would play into Kenji's "tomorrow is always the better day" ploy to avoid prickly topics. And what better day? The Pafko editorial and luncheon had given her the resolve to convince Kenji that to save their schools they must change those schools. Speculating on Ume's plight must wait until tomorrow. She would drive the ninety-minute journey to Ume's Kona coffee farm in the morning.

Satisfied with the rice, Haru picked up wood pieces from the tin pail and shoved them into the stove's belly. Once Kenji understood it was not the language schools per se but a matter of switching the emphasis from preparing children to return to Japan to showing how Japanese values fit in with America, they could discuss the necessary changes. Deciding she and Kenji needed to be able to read each other's facial expressions, Haru lit extra candles and set them on the dining room table.

She looked at her watch. Time to take the pan of boiling water containing a flask of sake off the stove. Drinking sake with dinner was a once-or-twice-a-month event. She knew a little sake engendered a good mood, but she had learned too much sake brought out Kenji's dark streak. Holding the flask with a towel, she heard Kenji's footsteps coming up the porch. She set the flask on the table.

"Tadaima," greeted Kenji, taking his shoes off at the front door.

"*Okaerinasai*," welcomed Haru in her most endearing voice. She returned to the kitchen and dropped the cut vegetables into a sizzling saucepan filmed with a water solution of soy and sugar. Kenji inhaled the sweet waft and looked at the covered lacquered box foretelling that inside unagi strips covered a bed of rice. He looked at the meal appreciatively, sat down, and wiped his face and hands with the hot *oshibori*. Haru brought in the vegetables on two small Imari porcelain dishes and placed them next to the lacquered box. Her eyes roamed the table. Satisfied nothing was missing, she sat down, lifted the flask, and filled Kenji's sake cup. He returned the courtesy.

"Kampai." He took a sip and offered, "My favorite meal. Arigato."

Haru could tell by the glint in Kenji's eyes that he thought tonight's private dinner was a prelude to dessert in the bedroom. If her appeal to his common sense worked as designed, his expectations would have a happy ending.

Haru lifted the top off the lacquered boxes, releasing a whiff of fragrant steam. Picking up her chopsticks, she began asking Kenji about his favorite subject: his opinion on anything. "Tell me about your thoughts on the war ending." She leaned forward on main points and, in between bites of food, alternated such attentive phrases as "hai" and "*honto ni*." She kept refilling his sake cup half full. She knew the imbibing-limiting ruse came up short when Kenji shook the empty flask with an expression that demanded a refill.

Haru rose. "I'll heat the water."

"Not necessary. Room temperature is fine."

Haru smiled and in a contrived warm voice said, "Hai," and retreated to kitchen to refill the flask. A minute later, under his watchful eye, she filled Kenji's cup to the brim.

At the end of the meal, she served green tea ice cream Sachi had churned the day before.

Then she began.

∞ CHAPTER 51 ∞

"THE WAR ENDING is bringing back the questions of our loyalty." Haru pushed the half-folded *Advertiser* from the side of the table, opened it, and pointed to Pafko's headline.

Kenji lifted a spoon of ice cream to his lips. "That again," he sighed. "The war proved our loyalty. America and Japan are allies. Our navies exchange visits. Thousands of us volunteered for the American army. Our schoolchildren bought more war savings stamps than the haole children. My plantation schoolteachers led Liberty Bond drives."

"Yes, but that's not the point. Here is what I heard at lunch." Haru's narrative closed with a Mrs. Adams quote. "'Your teachers are recruited from Japan and can't speak English. They teach loyalty to the emperor, not the president.'" Haru's voice ticked up an octave. "Otosan, your students memorize the same education rescript I recited, promising fidelity to the emperor, but they can't recite the Bill of Rights. The haoles believe America and Japan will go to war someday. They are asking whose side will we be on?"

Kenji left the spoon sticking upright in the ice cream. "Don't waste time listening to Mrs. Adams."

In a calm voice masking her rage, Haru replied, "That's always your answer when I try to discuss the schools. It's not just the Adamses' and Bilkertons' loud mouths. All the women are worried about our schools. That's why they invited me. It means their husbands are worried. Read this." She pointed to the editorial underneath the headline she had shown him earlier.

Kenji read the first few paragraphs and looked up. "This is an old song and not well played." Not waiting for Haru to refill his sake cup, Kenji proceeded to serve himself. "You read an editorial by that racist Pafko and listen to bigoted women attack our schools. You know the children attending our schools. Do you see any future Japanese soldiers amongst them? Stick to running your nursery school and stay out of my language school."

Haru's shoulders tightened. It was her turn to sip sake. This was more than she was used to drinking. "Wakarimashita, Otosan. So why make it easy for them to pressure the legislature to pass a bill outlawing our schools? Just because Mrs. Adams and that Bilkerton woman are bigots doesn't mean the haoles lack *real* reasons to question our loyalty."

Kenji opened his mouth.

Haru lifted her right hand, chin high, forefinger extended. "Let me finish, Otosan. Think how the Americans look at our schools. The Filipinos, Portuguese, and Puerto Ricans don't have schools—only the Japanese." The middle finger shot out joining the index finger. "You register the births, deaths, and marriages with the Japanese consul like a government official." Another finger out. "Our temple organizes half a dozen festivals celebrating Japanese holidays." The pinkie joined the digital phalanx. "Our children skip school on the emperor's birthday, forcing Waimea to close the public schools because more than half the students don't show up."

Haru dropped her hand back on the table. "The haoles visit your school, and what do they see? Pictures of the emperor and Japanese war heroes. Your textbooks don't have a single paragraph on American heroes except George Washington and his famous cherry tree."

Kenji shook his head. "Nonsense. They spend all day at haole schools studying American history. Spending a couple hours learning their Japanese language, history, and family values doesn't turn our children into disloyal Americans." In a calmer voice, he added, "Haru, don't forget that some of our children will be going back to Japan."

Haru's sake-fueled frustration swelled, spilling over her carefully laid boundaries. "Some?" She rolled her eyes. "Few. No, *very* few. Hawaii is their home, our home. We aren't going back, and neither are they." Haru pulled out a letter from her yukata's sleeve flap like an attorney addressing the jury with a surprise piece of evidence. "Here's a letter from Keiko Nakamura."

"The family who returned to Okayama?" asked Kenji.

"Hai." She read from the letter. "'Ta-chan is bullied at school because he can't speak proper Japanese or read his textbooks.'" Haru put down the letter. "You issue certificates to your students for learning a hundred kanji characters. Even a primary school child in Hiroshima knows seven hundred." Her voice rose despite her resolve to keep calm. "You've been selling a false promise. You make the whites angry and don't even prepare the few children who do return. What have you gained?"

Kenji's eyes narrowed. "Look at the Hawaiians. The missionaries took away their gods, their language, and most of their land. In Honolulu, lots of Hawaiians speak only English. Are they accepted? They are paraded at festivals like clowns and treated like second-class citizens in their own land. We Japanese need to maintain our culture, our respect."

Haru leaned over and slapped the table. "You just made the case for the haters. We need to teach standard English. Your students, our children, speak Japanese or pidgin. All the Americans want is for our children to assimilate like the Italians and the Germans."

Kenji stood up and leaned over the table. "Haole schools want our children to forget who they are, where they came from. World history? Hah! All about Columbus, Pilgrims, and Europe. Half the children attending school are Japanese, but the education board ignores us." Kenji wagged his finger in Haru's face. "That's why all our Japanese parents pay tuition money from their meager earnings. You are the big American in our family. The Constitution guarantees religious freedom. We have a *right* to our schools. We are Buddhists committed to passing on our values to our children. Good values make good citizens." Kenji's face flushed. "That's why we're here!"

Haru stood up. "Then use that right to help your son assimilate. Concentrate on those values. Show how they fit in with American values." Her voice rose to soprano level. "Take down those sword-carrying pictures of Togo and Nogi and replace them with Washington and Wilson!"

Kenji swept his hand across the table, sending dishes crashing to the floor. "Where is the polite, soft-spoken wife my mother sent me? Once an Amakusan, always an Amakusan!"

Haru grabbed the sake flask and raised her hand like a baseball pitcher. She caught herself and with exaggerated deliberation, returned the flask to the table. In a melancholy voice she asked, "Where is the man of God who came to Waimea to protect his family and congregation? What will happen to our children with your stone-headed thinking about the schools?"

Kenji stood silent, fists balled.

Haru dropped her voice. "I received a letter from Ume. She asked me to visit her. Something horrible happened, but she won't tell me what. I'm taking the car. I'm leaving tonight."

"Tonight! Are you crazy?"

"I'll be in Kona by midnight." Haru took three steps towards the bedroom to pack. Then, she stopped short. Her face showed uncommon anger. "I visited the doctor yesterday. I am pregnant." She stomped off to the bedroom.

⚭ CHAPTER 52 ⚭

A S SOON AS HARU STARTED TO PACK, she regretted her outburst, but not enough to back down. She had had enough of Kenji's "I don't tell you how to tend to your nursery" jibes every time she broached his school curriculum. Closing her overnight case, Haru realized that if she hadn't received Ume's letter, she would have just walked off her anger and then strolled to the park to join her children. She still could. Instead, to the sounds of fireworks, she grabbed the keys to the Ford, marched pass a still-sitting, shock-eyed Kenji, and stomped out the front door.

Haru laid her overnight bag on the backseat. She glanced up at the cloudless night and decided to leave the Ford's canvas cover rolled up and tied over the ridge of the backseat. She picked up the crank handle from the floor, walked to the front of the car, and stuck it into the grill's mouth, connecting into the engine block's crankshaft. Planting her feet solidly on the ground, Haru arm-muscled a vigorous twirl. The engine coughed to life on its first wind-up. She jumped back into the car, flipped on the headlights, and looked back at the house. Kenji stood on the porch. *Please say, "I'm sorry," and ask me to stay.*

"I'll call Irie," Kenji yelled.

Stone-headed to the end, Haru thought, as she shoved the gear-stick into first gear.

Inhaling the salty perfume of the Kona coast, Haru kept her foot on the brake as the plateau's descent sharpened. Lucky Kona, she thought, as trees and brush began replacing the stark lava fields. Ancient lava produced fertile growth; new lava sealed the earth. The great lava flows of 1801 had laid barren much of the volcano plateau south of Waimea but had stopped at Kona as if Pele knew this strip of land had potential mere humans hadn't yet discovered.

The sign for the Kona turnoff recalled the moment Ume told Judith's class about Irie. "He has satisfied his five-year cane-laborer's contract. Now he is growing coffee on his own land in a place called Kona." When the haoles' big coffee plantations began losing money at the turn of the century, the owners offered sharecropping plots to immigrants coming off their labor contracts in exchange for a third of the beans the renters produced. Some, like Irie, saved enough money to eventually buy the plots they worked.

Minutes past Marker 39, she saw a swinging light as if it was tied to the moon. In seconds, a stick figure took form. *Must be Irie,* she thought, *making sure I didn't miss the turn into his farm.* It was. As

Haru pulled into the driveway of the farm home, Ume opened the door. Haru climbed out of the car, grabbed her overnight bag, and hurried over to the ground-level porch.

The two women exchanged bows.

Ume's warm smile welcomed her friend, but her wary tone heightened Haru's misgivings. "Haru-san, you are so good to visit. But when I wrote, I didn't mean you should drive by yourself at night just to come see me."

"I've been looking for an excuse to visit, and your letter arrived just at the right time." She forced a smile. "I needed a break."

"Excuse me," said Irie. "I have to get up early." He headed to the bedroom.

Looking at Ume's questioning expression, Haru said, "Kenji and I had an argument about his school curriculum." She paused to hear the reason for her summons.

Frowning at the closed shoji doors, Ume sighed. "A Yokohama Specie Bank representative came by last week. He told Irie that the bank is eager to loan him money to buy a nearby coffee plantation. Mr. Big Shot is ready to sign."

Haru thought that while Irie might be overreaching, the news hardly qualified as a reason to send an alarmist note, so she waited for more.

Instead, Ume rose and ushered Haru to her sleeping quarters. "We'll talk in the morning."

∞ CHAPTER 53 ∞

HARU WOKE TO THE SOUNDS OF CLINKING PORCELAIN. She looked at her watch: seven thirty-three! She was embarrassed for having slept so late. Mixed aromas of warm rice and *yaki sakana*, grilled fish, whetted her appetite.

She left by the side door for the outhouse. Once in the privy, she smiled upon seeing the new Sears and Roebuck catalogue perched on a roughhewn wooden shelf. As she leafed through the children's clothing section, she wondered if the mail order company realized the importance of their relatively soft pages.

Returning to the house, she entered the dirt-floor kitchen where she found Ume bending over the open grill. "Good morning, Ume," Haru said with a smile and then offered an apology for her tardiness. "Your futon is too comfortable." Her eyes roamed around the kitchen, taking in the wall and ceiling, blackened by soot, and the dusty Coleman stove with its empty glass kerosene cylinder.

Ume caught her appraisal. "Mr. Modern insisted on buying me a kerosene stove to impress the neighbors. But with all the kindling wood from our pruned coffee trees, why would any coffee grower buy kerosene?"

Wondering about the urgent tone of Ume's note, Haru didn't think a womanizer would buy his wife the latest kitchen appliance. Or is it a guilty conscience gift? What did men who chase other women have in common besides the urge? Money, opportunity, and the time to pursue them. Dismissing the thought and a bit ashamed by the unfounded speculation, Haru concentrated on the two breakfast bentos on the table.

"Where are the children?"

"They're at a friend's house, and Irie has gone into town."

As Ume prattled on about her children, Haru wanted to snap, "Why did you ask me to come?" Speculating some great shame was holding Ume back, Haru fell in step and bragged about her boys.

Ume drained her second cup of coffee. "Let's take a walk." Beside the kitchen door, Ume retrieved a slop bucket containing tangerine peels, eggshells, and chicken bones. She added fish tidbits from their breakfast plates while Haru scraped the rice bowls into the bucket. Ume picked two floppy hats off a row of pegs, handed one to Haru, and opened the screen door.

Outside, a family of oinking pigs scattered chickens as they ran up to Ume, who held the pail high until she reached the pigs' wooden trough. She tipped the slop bucket upside down and shook out the scraps. She hung the pail on a branch.

"This way," said Ume, leading Haru through a grove of coffee trees thrice her height.

Haru followed. She looked up at the tree branches and spotted a smattering of kernels waiting to drop. Although the harvest season started in August, Haru knew the coffee berries matured at varying times throughout the fall and into the winter. She felt the pressure to break the disquieting silence. "You've come a long way since you and Irie lived in a one-room cottage." Remembering that Irie got his land at a good price because most of coffee trees in place were at the end of their twenty-five-year life cycle, she added, "You struggled digging out old trees and planting seedling replacements those early years."

Ume nodded. "When the haoles started their sharecropping scheme, Filipinos and Puerto Ricans gave it a try and quit." She gazed up at the treetops. "Only we crazy Japanese were fussy enough to grow this stubborn crop."

"At least you were working for yourselves."

"So we told ourselves each night we fell asleep exhausted. I felt guilty when I got pregnant. I knew Irie would have to do part of my work." Ume stooped to pick up two brown cherries, as coffee pods are called. "The war broke out a few months before our replacement trees' first harvest. We got a good price, and it drove us on. We'd wake before dawn, sling baskets loaded with empty burlaps bags over our shoulders, and march with our children into the fields. I carried one on my back; the other two had soup cans strung around their necks so they could pick loose cherries off the ground."

Although Haru had heard it all before, she did not interrupt.

Ume rubbed the two cherries in her hand like worry beads. "We had to harvest six times in 1914, but our quality was the best. Our extravagance that year was buying a mule to carry the burlap bags to the side of the road twice a day. Oh, what a stubborn fellow Momo was." Ume smiled at the memory. "A truck from the Captain Cook Coffee Company picked up the bags along the road at the end of each day for processing. Twice a month, we held back two bags, and I would ride with Momo to Kimura's store in Holualoa to exchange them for supplies. The trip took most of the day, but I was happy to have a break from harvesting."

Ume turned into a clearing with a matrix of sheds, some holding machinery.

Haru's eyebrows rose. "Last time I visited, this land was a garden of lumber and crates."

For the first time since her arrival, Haru saw a genuine smile on Ume's face. "This is the first year that we don't have to give away half our profits. Most coffee countries like Brazil use the easy method to process coffee. Just let the coffee cherries dry in the sun and then remove the cracked shell afterwards. The richness of the Kona coffee results from a two-step wet process. But now we process everything ourselves, except the roasting."

Ume strolled over to an open-air shed.

Haru peered at the confusion of conveyer belts, pulleys, and metal machinery. She walked to the nearest machine with a steel-strutted grater. "The handle sticking out looks like a rough version of the grill of my car."

Ume raised her hand with the coffee cherries between her thumb and forefinger. "This grinder scrapes the leathery pulp off the bean." She dropped the pair of cherries atop the grinder's wheel and gave it a spin. Two slimy, depulped white beans dropped to the bottom. Ume picked one up. "All the wet beans go up there." She pointed to a giant wooden tub. "The beans are soaked in water overnight to eat away the slime."

Ume strolled to an adjacent squat platform, covered with half of a corrugated roof on rollers. "After the tub is drained, the wet beans are released into this chute." Ume stopped to let Haru see where the chute connected the bottom of the elevated wooden tub to the platform as wide as a single-lane road and three times as long as its width. "Come on up."

All the coffee beans were covered under a rolling arched roof cover acting as a giant umbrella. Ume started pushing the sheet metal awning toward the other end to expose the beans to the morning sun. Without being asked, Haru grabbed the other side and pushed. When the cover had been rolled to the end of the drying platform, a mound of damp coffee beans was left exposed to the morning sun. Ume grabbed a wooden rake and spread them out. "Later today we will separate the beans from the chaff, grade them by size, and sack them."

Rather than being exulted by their accomplishment, Ume slumped her shoulders and then stopped abruptly. "I don't know how to tell you this, Haru-chan." Ume took off her hat with her left hand, tilted her head left, and pulled back her hair with her right hand. "Look."

✆ Chapter 54 ✆

A SPONGY, RED, KIDNEY-SHAPED BLOTCH, streaked with seams of purple, rose behind the ear and extended into the hairline at the back of Ume's neck.

Haru froze, muted.

She knew. Hansen's disease made its first Hawaiian appearance in 1848. Molokai's leper colony held nine hundred patients at its peak in 1903 and now housed around six hundred.

"I noticed this a month ago, hoping it was some insect bite." She rolled up her sleeve. Past her elbow was a red rash forming a two-inch snake. "I visited the doctor last week. He discovered spots between two of my toes and on my lower back as well."

Haru understood but could not utter the word "leprosy." "Oh, Ume," said Haru, tears forming. She thought of Irie's jaunty lamp-swinging welcome. "You haven't told anyone."

Ume shook her head slowly. "Dr. Uchida has been very kind. Once he reports my condition, I have one week to leave for Molokai. I asked him to wait until you arrived."

Haru looked at her friend. So lovely. Then the pictures of leprosy victims with their half-eaten faces flashed before her eyes. She wrapped her arms tight around Ume as if to squeeze the death sentence from her body. She raised her head, tears trickling down her face, and gazed into Ume's eyes. Haru silently resolved to visit her friend every year. The visits, not the promise, would be what mattered. "Kenji said compared to the early days, Molokai's living conditions have improved."

"Yes, I can be thankful this is not the 1860s. In those days, lepers were left on the beach with a week's ration of food." Ume rubbed the offending lump on her neck. "No doctors or nurses lived on the island back then. The inhabitants … " Ume smiled at this euphemism, "had no shelter, other than what they could build themselves. Government provided little—a shirt, a pair of pants, a sweater. And a coffin. Drinking water had to be carried from three miles away when the stream went dry. The colony descended into chaos and barbarism."

"Then Father Damien arrived," said Haru. "He shamed the government and begged business people like the Baldwins to improve conditions." Thinking of Kenji's updates, she added, "Today, there are a harbor, clean housing, and three meals a day at the village cafeteria."

"And a hospital with doctors and nurses," said Ume. "Father Damien is long gone, of course, but Mother Marianne and her Sisters of St. Francis have taken on his work." She shook her head slowly. "Why those haole nuns keep coming to the island, knowing the risks, I have no idea."

"Hasn't Irie noticed … anything different about you? That you're so … unhappy?"

"He assumes I'm angry about his plan to borrow money to buy more land. We argued about this *before* I knew I had this disease. 'You never know what might happen,' I told him."

"Let me stay a few days Ume," said Haru. "I can—"

"Haru-chan, what must be done … " She stopped, fought to keep her composure. "What must be done, must be done by me. Irie could not bear someone watching his distress when I tell him." Ume patted Haru's arm. "Even as close a friend as you."

"There's more. The real reason I needed to see you: I'm pregnant."

Haru's hand flew to her face. She stepped backwards in disbelief. "Oh, Ume."

"The baby will be born on Molokai. I want you to come and take it back to Irie." Ume showed no tears. Her voice became businesslike, the tone she used when giving the day's work assignments to her fellow housewives tending the coffee plants. "I need your help with Irie."

"Anything, Ume-chan. Anything."

Ume grabbed Haru's arm and peered deep into her eyes. "I don't want Irie or the children to visit me. Ever. Not once. They will see the others and know what will happen to me. Someday they will visit and won't recognize me. I want Irie and my children to remember me as I am."

Haru's soft voice argued, "But Irie has a mind of his own. He will say taking care of you is more important than life itself."

Ume squeezed Haru's arm tighter. "If Irie visits, I will commit *jisatsu*."

Haru felt the words were rehearsed, as if the purpose of her visit was to hear those words, to understand the conviction behind them. "Wakarimashita."

Ume released Haru's hand, rose, and strolled over to a row of coffee trees. "The spread of leprosy is uncertain. People sent to Molokai thirty years ago still live; some die within a couple years. I can still do good, Haru. I'll be a *kokua*."

"A helper?" Haru knew enough Hawaiian to understand the word, yet the way Ume said it made it sound like a vocation.

"I know Irie will give me money to build a small house. The newcomers take care of those who can't take of themselves and hope, when it's their turn, someone will see them through the last days."

Haru nodded. "I will pray for you."

"The gods have abandoned me, Haru. I'm not sure if they even exist. More important than praying for me is helping Irie find a wife. My children need a mother. The farm needs a gentle but sturdy woman who labors and sings alongside our workers. Irie is a good husband to me. He will be a good husband to another woman."

Since Buddhism did not require a belief in the afterlife, the doubting words hardly registered. What struck Haru was the Buddhist charge from Kiyoshi. "Child, the day will come when you can pay me back by helping others." Buddhism was not about after-life certainty but about living an honorable life and showing compassion for others in the present—not because of some promise of reward or threat of punishment after death but because it is the right thing to do and you want to do it. Her Amakusan parents, wretchedly poor as they were, had sacrificed their lives to give her a chance for a good life. They did it for her, not for Buddha but perhaps because of his teaching.

"I will find Irie a good woman to look after your children and farm."

Ume bowed from the waist. "Arigato, sensei." Rising she added, "And friend." Her eyes were moist. "The day is pleasant. Let's have our lunches outside before you leave for Waimea."

∞ ∞

After lunch, Haru drove off under clear, cerulean skies and traveled along the Hualalai Road lined with lush, colorful vegetation interrupted by sprays of wooden buildings bearing signs written in kanji. Each village boasted at least one Japanese cinema. Lost in thought, she saw none of this passing scenery.

The destruction of Ume's life consumed her thoughts. Neighbors would shun them. Schoolchildren would be told to avoid contact. Many children of victims stopped going to school. All three surviving families in her Waimea mission had fled to Oahu where no one knew them. Rumors sprouted that the women of afflicted husbands were driven to prostitution to support their families.

The stone marker displayed "1." One mile to home. Gentle trade winds aimed cotton-candy clouds toward home.

∞ CHAPTER 55 ∞

AT THE EDGE OF TOWN, Haru's mood improved upon catching the burgeoning sounds of trombones, tubas, flugelhorns, and snare drums pounding out the popular war song, "It's a Long Way to Tipperary." She felt pride for her adopted country's soldiers who fought the war to end wars. She knew the horrific numbers. America had one hundred thousand soldiers killed in the one year they fought. Over the four-year slaughter, Great Britain had lost eight hundred thousand, and France 1,300,000, and on it went until the totals reached sixteen million including civilians.

Entering the town center, Haru saw that the celebration filled the central park and spilled over onto the street leading to her home. Rather than beeping the horn to clear a path, she parked at the corner. As she climbed out of the car, she saw a mostly haole crowd mingling on the road leading to the town center. To her right on this street, she spied a flurry of kimono, *jinbei*, and yukata. She spotted Kenji laughing with one of the plantation owners whose labor force was Filipino. Next to him, a Hawaiian paniolo was gesturing with his hands like an Italian, explaining something to a Chinese medicine seller. Haru paused under a jacaranda tree, enjoying this moment of harmony.

Wellington Carter, his golden locks spilling out of a cowboy hat, was chewing on a yakitori meat stick as he chatted with the only Japanese lawyer in town, while Mrs. Oda from the trading post was nodding her head in conversation with the haole doctor. *One day, my children will be in the middle of the road.*

Goose bumps spread over her arms at the sight of two Issei soldiers wearing their American army khakis, clinking sake cups to a beer mug held by a haole officer.

Strolling home, Haru waved to the mothers of the children attending her day care. They were dispensing bowls of rice, stirring tubs of udon soup, and cutting fresh slabs of tofu. The paniolos had brought steaks and were digging pits alongside the temple to make grills. Sachi was helping two cowboys lay hot charcoal bricks on the bottom of a large pit next to a freshly butchered pig. Haru recognized the clerks from Oda's Trading Post filling little cups from two barrels of sake.

She heard Kame cried out, "Haru, look! Sam is back!"

Haru turned to her front porch. The man standing next to Kame was not the Sam she remembered. When the gaunt man struggled down the steps, she sucked in her breath. "Welcome home, soldier."

Behind her, she heard a familiar soft baritone voice. "Sam, it's good to have you back." Wellington Carter moved to Haru's side, thrust out both hands, and shook Sam's right arm, holding it warmly. "You still have your house at the ranch and, when you feel up to it, a job."

"I don't want to be a charity case, Mr. Carter."

Carter nodded, as though he had anticipated the response, and a small, knowing smile curved his lips. "Then you better start work soon and earn your keep."

Minutes later, Haru's enthusiasm deflated when she spotted Joshua Bilkerton and Andy Pafko together under a jacaranda tree. Haru had not forgotten their meeting the day she landed in Hawaii. She thought of Pafko's recent tirade enflaming the haole opposition to the Japanese language schools. Bilkerton was disgusting. His caneworker mothers told her how he preyed on his plantation's young teenagers. Seeing them in deep conversation, she suspected the worst.

☙ ❧

Both men took a swig out of their flasks, unaware of Haru's worried interest. Pafko's love of whiskey and mashed potatoes had added to his girth. However, next to Bilkerton's walrus-sized gut, he was a beanpole.

Pafko shook the mouth of his flask at Bilkerton. "This next legislative session is your golden opportunity," said Pafko.

"I'm tired of hearing those kids sing the Japanese anthem every day after the little buggers leave their real school, the American one," slurred Bilkerton, who had won last week's election for the state legislation.

This guy always misses the main point unless you hit him on the head, thought Pafko. "Now you can stop them." While looking at Bilkerton's floating eyes, Pafko resisted hitting him with a rapid list of points. He waited.

"Stop it. Me?"

Yes, stupid. "That's right. The same way we shut down the German newspapers when we declared war on the Kaiser."

"They squealed about the First Amendment, but we did it anyway," said Bilkerton proudly.

Good, the big oaf is following me. "Last year, nine thousand kids were born in Hawaii. Half of them Japs. That might be manageable if they were being raised American." Pafko accepted Bilkerton's nod—maybe he understood the stakes. "The solution is simple."

"Close them all down?" Bilkerton asked in alarm. "I don't want any labor problems."

"Right. So, controlling the schools ... setting standards ... that's the solution."

"How can we do that?"

Listen idiot, that's why we have something called a legislature, of which you are a member. "With legislation," said Pafko. He tilted his head forward. "We need a champion, Joshua. A man to introduce a bill that requires all teachers be certified in English."

"None of Takayama's teachers would pass that test."

Congratulations, Mr. Dunce Cap. "That's right. And the man who introduces that legislation will be recognized as a political leader to be reckoned with. Why should all the governors come from Honolulu?" Pafko stared deep into Bilkerton's eyes to gauge whether his pandering had gone too far.

"You're right. But I will need some help on the wording."

No shit. "I'm the writer. You're the action man, the hero who will Americanize those little Jap buggers."

Days earlier, John Waterhouse, the leader of the Big Five sugar barons, had invited the eager Pafko to dinner at the Pacific Club. "You can do yourself a big favor by going to Waimea and encouraging our new legislator to become a hero." Waterhouse's tone suggested he wanted nothing to do directly with Bilkerton. "It doesn't matter if the legislation is passed and, if passed, how crippling it turns out to be. What's important is to keep those people under siege. We can't allow this Bolshevik cancer to infect our islands as it has the West Coast."

∽ CHAPTER 56 ∽

WHILE THE BAND TOOK A BREAK, Haru waved at Mayo Fujimoto, shining in a bright-green kimono, and her husband. Tamatsuke, who had forsaken his baptism name, John, was standing next to her with a clenched jawline and in a black suit. Shortly before the Great War, he had swallowed his battered pride and allowed Mayo to write Haru that their taro farm had failed. Knowing Kenji's reputation as a de facto employment agent, she had asked for help finding a job for her husband. When Bilkerton's sugar mill technician lost an arm in a conveyer-belt accident—and since Tamatsuke had held a similar position at an Oahu plantation at the outbreak of the 1909 strike—Kenji recommended him to a grateful Bilkerton. Kenji had warned the former strike leader, "Don't do anything that will compromise my negotiating concessions from plantation managers."

"My union-organizing days are behind me," said a slumped-shouldered Tamatsuke.

Tamatsuke's mechanical skills earned him fifty-two dollars a month in salary, triple that of a field worker, plus a four-room cottage, double the size of their accommodations. The shoulders soon regained their confident posture. Mayo joined a sugar-sack sewing team—tedious work but better than weeding under the hot sun. Barren in Waikiki, Mayo soon produced three children.

For five years, Tamatsuke had kept his no-labor-agitation pledge, even as plantation working conditions deteriorated. Until today.

While Haru and the Fujimotos exchanged greetings, they both spotted Kenji walking into their garden with acting Japanese consul general Eichi Furuya, who had arrived that morning as part of his annual visit to the outlying Buddhist missions. Tamatsuke resisted his impulse to approach Kenji, deferring to the consul general, but then changed his mind. What he had come to say needed to reach the consul's ears as well.

"Sumimasen," said stone-faced Tamatsuke to Haru and Mayo. Shoulders arched back, he strode across the street toward Kenji and the consul whose Brylcreemed black hair reflected the sun. But as he drew close, his confidence faltered. He stopped close enough to notice the sweat ring rimming Furuya's white shirt collar.

The consul's fiery eyes locked onto Kenji's. "Now that the war has ended, relations between Japan and America are bound to change. America must stop interfering with our interests in China. We need our Japanese in Hawaii to remember the mother country."

Kenji caught Tamatsuke's presence, ignored it, and edged closer to Furuya. "Our workers don't care about imperial ambitions in Siberia and China. My time is better spent avoiding a strike by negotiating better wages. Better you spend your time assuaging the haoles about Japanese intentions in Hawaii. You can start by asking your neighbor Nakano to stop writing *Toho Jiron* editorials, calling the haoles 'villains' while defending the imperial army's strong-arm tactics in Korea."

Furuya flicked his right hand in a gesture of dismissal. That's when he realized that unwelcomed ears loitered nearby. He turned to Tamatsuke, pausing to take in the man's sunburned face and gnarled hands and then staring at him like a housewife examining a cockroach on her kitchen floor. His disdain hardened Tamatsuke's resolve.

"Please—listen to Takayama-sensei's warning about a strike." Tamatsuke's voice rose higher, and his words fell with the speed and power of a hailstorm. "If the companies could not stay alive because of low prices, we workers would understand. Before the war, sugar was sixty dollars a ton; now the owners are getting fat on two hundred dollars a ton. And while the food and clothing at the company stores have doubled, our wages remain the same. Is that fair?"

The consul stepped back from Tamatsuke and looked at Kenji in dismay.

"This is Tamatsuke Fujimoto, Consul," said Kenji. "He is the chairman of the Young Men's Buddhist Association."

"Strikes are looked upon as disloyal," said the frowning consul. "We are in a delicate situation, given all the talk about Bolsheviks and revolution."

"What about the haole telephone operators and longshoreman strikes in Honolulu?" asked Tamatsuke. "Are they Bolsheviks too?"

"Patience," said Kenji.

"Patience, Takayama-sensei? We've been patient for a decade. The more we are patient, the deeper we fall into the pit." Tamatsuke bowed, pivoted, and with his back ramrod straight, marched back to his wife. "Take the buckboard. I'll walk home. I need some time by myself."

Furuya wrinkled his nose watching Tamatsuke stomp off. "Dangerous man, Takayama-san." He lowered his voice. "I visited Hilo to check on this new agitator, Noboru Tsutsumi—"

"The language teacher who arrived last year and started the newspaper," interrupted Kenji, showing he was aware of the man.

"Yes. At first, he advocated harmony between America and Japan while protecting our culture through our own schools. But now he's writing about the so-called plight of the plantation workers. Unlike that country bumpkin," he said, nodding his head at the retreating Tamatsuke, "Tsutsumi is smart, clever with words. A strike would be disastrous to relations between our two countries. The haoles would point to this teacher turned troublemaker as proof that there is something sinister about our language schools."

"Wakarimashita," said Kenji, affirming that he understood.

The consul bowed just enough to barely pass as courteous and hurried off toward his waiting car on the main road at a pace that kept would-be supplicants at bay.

∞ ∞

While Tamatsuke had pleaded his case, Haru entered the temple to give a prayer of thanks. The same building housed the classroom used for both the Japanese language school and community programs such as Haru's English classes. The door to the classroom was open. Haru stopped short, backed up a step for a clear view. Her eyes had not tricked her. She walked inside to look at the pictures along the side of the wall. General Togo's picture had been replaced with a portrait of Woodrow Wilson standing next to a bust of Lincoln. Haru retreated to the temple wiping a tear from her cheek. Her prayer of thanks lingered.

∽ CHAPTER 57 ∾

TAKING A SHORTCUT THROUGH HARU'S BACKYARD, Tamatsuke twisted his way through fern brambles, palm trees, and koa stands. A tortured man, he replayed the consul's brush-off and Kenji's chastened "be patient." He cursed his inability to convey the severity of the workers' plight and the need to take action now.

Tamatsuke stopped, tipped his head back, and cursed the tree-tops. "Be patient!" *Why can't they see that if the price of rice doubles, but wages stay the same, families eat less? Are they blind to this injustice? Do they not see how mothers raid their savings for their children's clothes and are going into debt at the company store?* His own wages allowed him to host a Sunday picnic for the families, a trifling offset to the injustice.

As he thought how mothers skipped meals for the sake of their children, a plunging coconut skidded across his left cheek. Tamatsuke kicked it as a thin line of blood dripped off his face. The crimson splatter recalled his frantic efforts to stop blood gushing from between his screaming neighbor's legs as she gave birth—a hemorrhage that sent her on to the next world as she brought a new life into this one. The woman couldn't pay for a midwife and refused charity. The bitter memory reminded Tamatsuke of his promise: "No more union organizing for me, Kenji-san." Yet, at what point does keeping a promise become immoral if it aids injustice?

When Tamatsuke emerged from the forest shortcut onto the rutted road leading to his plantation, a car roared by, leaving swirling dust in its wake. As he drew up his cotton-sleeved arm to cover his mouth and bleeding cheek, he recognized the driver as Joshua Bilkerton. Waiting for the dust to settle, he thought how he hated Bilkerton's hypocrisy for espousing Christian values at Easter and Christmas celebrations but refusing to pay a living wage. He resumed walking while remembering how, shortly after arriving in Hawaii, he had embraced the faith of the ruling class, drenched himself in the baptism rite, and been christened "John" because he liked the story of Jesus's favorite disciple. The haoles congratulated him for leaving what they called his "Buddhist pagan ways." Since then, he had seen little of Christ's compassion evident in the treatment of workers by the plantation owners, most of them descendants of the early Christian missionaries. Angered by this duplicity, Tamatsuke returned to Buddhism and reclaimed the name his father had given him.

Dusk turned to night. The cicada choir serenaded Tamatsuke. His mind drifted back to the night he joined his plantation's Young Men's Buddhist Association (YMBA) chapter. At first, he sat in the back row at meetings, served on festival committees, and kept his mouth shut during labor issue discussions. Each meeting, he had edged closer to the first row. Now, he sat at the front table as an officer, but one who had failed his members today.

His stomach rumbled. The certainty that Mayo was keeping the rice pot simmering over a low flame comforted him. Despite the taro farming failure, she never complained. There were so many failures, so little time left to make his life right and provide more for her.

Tamatsuke would have been shocked and embarrassed if he were asked, "Do you love your wife?" He never uttered the words. But as he walked up the flowered path to his front door, his heart swelled with a feeling for which he lacked words. He thought of Mayo and admitted he was a lucky man.

He just couldn't tell her.

∞ ∞

An exhausted Haru fell into her pillows. Ume's tragedy, the fight with Kenji over the language schools, his backdoor apology replacing the Togo picture with President Wilson, and the end-of-the-war news jingled her senses. Being so busy since her return to Waimea, she hadn't had a chance to update Kenji on Ume. Cool trade winds wafting plumeria blossom scents through the screened windows calmed her nerves. An oil lamp crowding the edge of Kenji's night table provided the only light. As if yesterday's argument had never happened, Kenji had propped up his pillows against the headboard and was reading Zane Grey's *The U.P. Trail*, the previous year's best-selling novel dramatizing the building of the transcontinental railroad. Haru edged to Kenji's side of the bed. The loose sash around her nemaki exposed a breast, rosy-hued from soaking in the ofuro. Kenji put aside his book and reached out to her. She squeezed back and told him of Ume's plight and her promise to retrieve the baby in April. "I'm as strong as a goat," said Haru before Kenji could register a protest. "It's a short ride. You've gone every year."

Kenji paused before responding. "Let's talk to the midwife as your pregnancy develops, Okasan." He dimmed the oil lamp. "Did you forget what I told you after my last voyage? I was pitched about like a butterfly in a typhoon."

Not eager for a new argument, Haru put her hands under the covers. "Hai, you are right. I won't go unless I am strong and healthy." She rubbed his stomach to let him know yesterday was forgiven. The bedroom was the great healer, she thought, as she felt Kenji's strong response.

∽ ∾

"Today is Saint Nicholas Day," said Takeshi, picking up a piece of pancake. He looked at Yoshio. "December 6 is when Santa Claus was born."

"Can you help me write a letter to Santa?" asked Yoshio, chewing a piece of bacon.

Haru almost dropped a forkful of scrambled eggs when Kenji said, "Maybe we should have a Christmas tree."

"Can we? Can we?" shouted Takeshi.

Haru smiled warmly at Kenji. "I saw that trees had arrived at Oda's Trading Post. But I am not sure I could pick out the right tree."

"We can help," spouted Takeshi and Yoshio and then giggled at their synchronism.

That was this morning. Now the tree lay across the backseat of the Ford. Haru turned down her street while Takeshi explained the finer points of decorating a tree to Yoshio. In seconds, Haru sat straighter, raised her eyebrows. A woman squatted, waiting on her porch steps. Behind and to her left, two wooden lockers were pushed against the railing. Another forlorn picture bride waiting to tell her sad story? Perhaps she had been kicked out of her home or had run away in fear. Haru sighed in resignation. As she drove closer, the woman looked up. Her features came into focus.

Haru inhaled sharply; her stomach tightened. It could not be.

∽ CHAPTER 58 ∽

HARU SQUEEZED THE STEERING WHEEL. *I must be looking at a ghost,* she thought. The cheeks were thinner, the eyes not as bright, but none of these changes could eradicate the memory of that face. The last time she had seen that face, it had been twisted in anger as they had wrestled on the street while fighting for the purse of stolen coins hanging from the girl's neck.

She had not thought of Ko for years. The last time had been on her fifth wedding anniversary when after a sake-fueled retelling of her last day in Hiroshima, she told Kenji, "I can thank Ko's conniving for my unintended happiness. She brought me to you."

Ko stood and smoothed the wrinkles from the front of her yellow silk kimono, embroidered with sakura blossoms. Her hollow eyes and unkempt hair did not match her kimono's elegance.

Haru exited the car and turned to her boys, "You two go play. I have some business to take care of."

Eyes stoic, she walked toward the porch. "Ko-san? Can it really be you?"

"Hai, Haru-san. The guilty one has returned to apologize." Ko's eyes misted as if on cue. "The gods have punished me for my crime and rightly so."

"Come," said Haru, leading the way while surmising that Ko must be desperate to bet on Haru still being the girl who repaired the wings of fallen birds.

Ko's eyes tightened as she adjusted to the subdued light filtering through the lace curtains. She surveyed the room. "We have similar tastes, Haru-chan. Our house was Western in architecture, but we had Chinese furniture, more ornate but too big and uncomfortable."

Haru smiled inwardly at Ko's use of "chan," the word of endearment so easily uttered during their attic séances. "Let me prepare tea, Ko-san," said Haru more formally, thinking two can play the game of using honorifics to send a message.

Haru ushered Ko to the dining table. Sitting down, Haru reached over to her ever-ready tea set. She opened the tin of green leaves, shook some atop the teapot's strainer, unscrewed the thermos, and poured hot water slowly over the tea leaves. Silently, she filled two handleless cups and handed one to her guest. Ko lifted hers to her lips, hesitated, tightened her grip, and dropped her arms without taking a sip. "So many times, I started to write you an apology. I could never find the right words. I wanted to beg forgiveness but felt I didn't deserve it. I was so, so wrong."

Haru drank her tea without expression and let the silence linger while she replayed the images of that awful day. The missing coins from her china-doll bank, the barefoot pursuit from the temple, the public wrestling match, and then the nocturnal visit from Fujita, the police captain, and that smug Shinto priest. "So you came all the way from Manchuria to apologize?"

Ko sniffled. "Yes. No. I mean, yes. I'm here to apologize, but I came to Hawaii to escape my punishment." She took a handkerchief from her kimono sleeve and dabbed her eyes. "You remember I married a soldier. What I didn't know was that the Manchurian railroad promised extra land to our Russian war veterans with Japanese wives. Oh, what a fine house we had, servants at my call, exquisite food. But soon I found out the prettiest serving girl was what the Chinese call the '*sha tai tai*,' the minor wife. When I complained, my husband beat me." Tears fell into Ko's teacup, creating perfect little ripples of sorrow. "At first, the girl slept in the servants' quarters where my husband would visit her. After my second miscarriage, he told me, 'Since we have no use for the children's room, you can sleep there.' Eventually, all pretense was dropped. I became a tenant in my own home."

Haru sat silently, coldly evaluating her guest. Even if Ko had embellished this story, her hard face and her eyes' spiderweb lines told of tough times. For the first time since Ko's arrival, Haru's voice softened. "How is it that you came to Hawaii?"

"A year ago, my husband's manly appetites became ... more aggressive. One evening he and his concubine forced me to ... to ... " Ko cleared her throat so as not to say the unspeakable. "By that time, opium had made its way into the house. I felt certain my husband or that sha tai tai would kill me. I could see it in their calculating eyes. One night, when I saw them exchange dark glances, I knew my time was short. That night, I made the opium very strong. Whatever plans they might have had for me were lost in the haze of the pipe.

"Years earlier, I had started stashing away small bits of my household money. At midnight, I left home, pulled my trunks in a rickshaw to the railroad station, and took the early morning train to Lushin. There, I booked immediate sea passage to Yokohama, where I paid a yakuza gang to provide paperwork showing I was traveling to Honolulu on a machine-buying trip for my husband's farm. With Hawaii's shortage of Japanese women, finding a new husband seemed possible. Once in Honolulu, I visited the Hongwanji Temple. They told me where you were posted."

Before Haru could respond, the front door banged in the familiar way, announcing Kenji's arrival. As he entered the dining room, he nodded and smiled at Ko. "I heard we had a visitor, so I rushed over as soon as I finished my class."

"This is Ko, a classmate of mine from Hiroshima," said Haru.

Kenji's expression froze.

"Yes, I am *that* Ko. Whatever you heard about me is probably true. I came to beg your wife's forgiveness."

A slow smile softened Kenji's features. "Forgiveness is the path to peace," he said, his meaningful glance traveling to the small Buddhist altar at the far end of the dining room.

Ko smiled too, a bit of triumph in her eyes. "You have such a lovely home here. I hope I am not imposing."

"Not at all," said Kenji.

Haru's eyes turned to Kenji and forced an impassive expression. She had planned to send Ko on her way after their tea was finished. But now Kenji had made that impossible. Ever since the sweeping-the-plates-off-the-table argument, she had been careful to avoid conflict. Hiding her frustration under the umbrella of a gracious demeanor, she added, "Of course, you must spend the night with us, Ko. We will sort out a permanent solution to your situation in the morning."

After a cursory walk-through of her home, a closed-fisted Haru walked Ko over to the nursery. Haru fought an urge to tell her, "You understand you MUST leave in the morning." Instead, she waved to the mothers congregating under the banyan tree to wait for their children.

∞ CHAPTER 59 ∞

At dinner, Ualani, who knew the Ko story and, while getting on in years, sensed the tension in the room, solved the visitor's sleeping quarters situation. "We have plenty of space for a futon in our cottage."

Ko had the good grace to take an early bath, leaving the ofuro for Haru and Kenji's nightly family soak. Haru waited until Kenji eased himself into the wooden tub across from her. "We must find a place for Ko. She cannot stay here."

Seated on his rump, Kenji adjusted his legs around Haru's outer thighs. "How old was Ko when she stole the money and accused you of doubting the emperor?"

"We were both eighteen."

"Eighteen. So young. Such a foolish age. She gave into jealousy, stole coins, got caught, lost her temper, and struck back without considering the consequences. You both had to leave Hiroshima. It worked out well for one of you." Kenji allowed a sheepish smile. "At least I hope it has."

The water's heat soothed her ruffled emotions. "Sometimes I need to be reminded I married a Buddhist minister. I'll contact our Hilo mission to help find a husband for her." Haru didn't tell Kenji that she didn't want to look in Waimea. It wasn't necessary.

∞ ∞

Haru awoke disoriented. Light. Even with eyes shut, there was a flood of light. The plumeria tree's daily scented welcome wafting into the bedroom assured her she was in her own bed. Used to waking before the dawn, she opened her eyelids only to squint into streams of golden light streaking through half-opened shutters. Silence in a household full of children. Then she heard the distinct sound of Yoshio laughing. Outside.

Leaving Kenji still sleeping, Haru rose and, twisting the sash of her nemaki, traipsed outside where she raised the palm of her hand to her forehead to shade her eyes. Her eyes hunted for the source of the laughter. Sitting crouched on the lawn behind the tomato vines creeping up bamboo poles, Ko and Haru's three children were giggling while cradling bowls of rice. When Takeshi saw his mother, he leapt up and ran toward her. Yoshio waved his chopsticks.

"You never told us about Auntie Ko, Mommy." He looked behind him. "She has so many funny stories." He spun his head back to Haru. "Did you really have a secret room at Granddaddy's house?"

Haru smiled at her son's enthusiasm and put aside annoyance with Ko's contrivance. She studied Ko while recalling Kiyoshi's sharp words to Midori within minutes of presenting herself at their home. "Okasan, our temple supports an orphanage. Send her there." *What was my motivation the next morning when I rose early to prepare morning rice before Midori awoke?* she asked herself. *Fear. Raw fear. I wanted a place to call home. What did Kiyoshi tell me while waiting at the Hiroshima train station? "Remember, Haru-chan, the essence of Buddhism. One good deed is worth more than a thousand compassionate thoughts."*

Haru tussled Takeshi's hair. "Yes, in the attic."

Overcoming her reservations that Ko's fawning remorse was only due to falling on dire circumstances, Haru waved. "Thank you for the extra sleep, Ko-chan." Despite Ko's glib remarks about the shortage of women, unloading her quickly into a new marriage was not as easy as Ko imagined. As an educated woman, she was an unsuitable match for the largest reservoir of single men—field hands and paniolos. But ideal marriage prospects, like lawyers and doctors, preferred not only younger women than Ko without the complication of a marriage in another country but also women whose eyes revealed a less haunting history than Ko's.

She walked over to Ko and the children, thinking, *I hope you are right, honorable father, for I think this woman will be with us for a while.*

∞ CHAPTER 60 ∞

DESPITE THE LATE-JANUARY CHILL and snappy breeze, Haru was reading the *Advertiser* under the thatched roof of the recently constructed gazebo, only steps outside the kitchen door. She let her wool shawl drop to the knotty pinewood bench as she felt the rays of a midmorning sun basking on a rare cloudless midwinter day. Directly ahead, she viewed her cherry trees' pink ethereal petals dancing in full bloom. In a day or two, the petals would flutter to the ground like snowflakes but were now a perfect complement to the glistening snow-peaked Mauna Kea towering over her garden. She was enjoying her solitude when she heard the familiar tinkle of the mailman's bicycle bell. Haru didn't feel like breaking her reverie to greet Murphy, and she waited for the crunch of his retreating bicycle tires before refilling her coffee cup in the kitchen and scooping up the mail underneath the front door's mail flap. *A letter from Midori. It must be her response to my Ko letter.*

Haru had written of her appreciation of Kenji's "ofuro counsel" the night of Ko's unexpected arrival and how the next morning she had told Ko "to stay a few days until a suitable arrangement can be made," a topic not discussed since then. Without being asked, Ko had taken over most household duties the declining Ualani once performed. Haru was not sure what surprised her more—Ko's work ethic or the warmth she showed Ualani and Sachi. Within weeks, it seemed as if she had been here a long time. The crow's feet around her eyes had melted, and she was more relaxed at her new home. Haru knew battered wives needed time for their minds to heal as well.

Haru retired to her tatami room "office." While sliding the ivory letter opener along the edge of the envelope, she felt a prickle in the back of her neck as if her brain was nagging her. Ko could be playing a role, simply manipulating her. Putting aside the thought, Haru pulled out the fine stationery bordered with plum-blossom images, a reminder of Hiroshima's proud horticultural heritage. Midori's words warmed her. "Kiyoshi and I are so proud of you, Haru-chan. In such cases, a battle rages in the human heart between revenge and forgiveness. The choice you have made speaks well of your character." Yet, later in the letter, Midori cautioned, "Do not let compassion blind you. An unmarried woman living in your home is a temptation that even the Buddha avoided." This warning irritated Haru, not because of its judgment on Ko but the lack of faith in the character of Midori's own son. If there was one man who lived his life according to the ideals he preached, it was her husband. Even his school curriculum stubbornness was grounded in high principle.

The back door banged. Haru looked up. Following the sounds of hurried bare feet, a distressed-faced Sachi stood at the tatami room's entrance. Words choked out, "Okasan. It's Obasan." She couldn't say anything more and turned to run back to the cottage, assured Haru would follow.

One look at Ualani's drawn face and the bucket near her bed reeking of vomit sent a dreadful warning to Haru. Had it arrived at Waimea?

Ualani opened her eyes. She managed a weary smile. "I'm sorry for this trouble."

"Nonsense," said Haru, feigning a cheerfulness she did not feel.

Reaching over, she placed her hand on Ualani's head. *Hot, way too hot,* thought Haru.

Sachi added, "It happened very suddenly. She felt tired this morning, then got a headache, and the fever … "

Standing up and turning at the sound of footsteps, Haru watched Ko enter the room and wrinkle her nose at the smell. Ko briefly studied Ualani's grey pallor, the perspiration on her brow. "The bluish tint. The high fever. The vomit. It's the Spanish flu."

Haru put her hand to her mouth. "I feared so. Was it last week we gave thanks that Waimea has been spared the scourge sweeping the world? I will go get Dr. Tebbits."

"No," snapped Ko, before modulating her voice. "Everyone except me is exposed. I had a mild case last year. I'm immune. Quarantine is the only answer. Call the doctor. You need to close the nursery." Then, pausing, she added, "Best I stay with Ualani."

Aware the epidemic had killed more people than the Great War, Haru trotted toward the house to telephone Tebbits. Kenji had watched the running back and forth to the cottage from his mission, and he was now entering the front door. Haru brought him up to date while Doris, the switchboard operator who always had Tebbits's schedule, made three calls before locating Tebbits at the Harvey residence.

Within fifteen minutes, Tebbits rolled up to their house in his Buick. Haru was waiting on the porch. "Stay in the house," he said, carrying his black medical satchel and walking toward the cottage. Tebbits tied a handkerchief around his face like a bank robber.

Ko met him at the cottage door. "I've already had the disease in Manchuria." She led him to Ualani's bedroom.

Ualani woke up at the touch of Tebbits's hand on her forehead. She smiled weakly. "It's time. I've had a good life." She closed her eyes, breathing shallowly.

Shortly, Tebbits, followed by Ko, walked over to the home, and the two let themselves in by the kitchen door. He looked at the anxious couple. "Ko was right. It's the Spanish flu. The symptoms of normal flu and the pandemic are similar, except the Spanish flu acts faster, and its victims have the blue pallor. Ualani is frail." His next words cut into Haru's heart. "I know you want to be with her, but you must protect yourself."

Denying the diagnosis, Haru pleaded, "But I read that the healthier a person is, the more likely she will die. Half the dead were in the prime of their life, between twenty and forty years old. Ualani is ... nobody knows how old but at least sixty."

Tebbits's voice lowered. "Yes, but you said half, Haru-san. In healthy people, the disease over-stimulates the immune system, which is what normally keeps us alive. It exhausts the body until there is nothing left to fight with. In Ualani's case ... " He put his arms out slightly, palms up in the "what can we do" resignation gesture.

"We've been so lucky," said Haru. "The Spanish flu seemed to have bypassed Waimea." What she meant, however, was "my family." She felt a little feverish but kept silent, thinking what she had was something like sympathy symptoms.

"Yes, until today," said Tebbits. "With the soldiers coming back from the front, our luck has run out. This is the third case today." Hearing the children's squeals from the nursery, he said, "Let the children play outside until you can contact the mothers to pick them up."

"Why did it start in Spain?" asked Ko.

"It didn't," said Tebbits. "Because of news blackouts among the countries at war, no one knew the epidemic was killing more people than the bullets. Since Spain stayed out of the war, they reported on the virulence of this flu as it crept south across the Pyrenees Mountains into Spain."

"So it started in the trenches?" Haru asked, thinking of Sam's gruesome stories.

"Not likely," said Tebbits. "Some say Kansas, where it first appeared in America. But for sure, the troops spread it. Like a typhoon's surf, death came in waves."

They had not noticed Sachi slipping into the room. Ko saw the girl first. In a soft voice, she admonished her, "You must stay in the cottage, Sachi."

"Ualani is not breathing."

Then fear struck Haru. Sachi had spent the last twenty-four hours with Ualani. Would Sachi be next? Then herself? Maybe Kenji and then her children? Her baby?

The next day, Waimea was shut down. Wellington Carter closed off the Parker Ranch. The sugar plantations followed suit. Ko burned Ualani's sheets and mattress and bleached her bedroom.

Haru's fever was real. By the end of day, she was sleeping in Ualani's disinfected room. After Ualani's quiet funeral service, a feverish Kenji joined her. A day later, Ko announced, "The children are feverish."

∞ CHAPTER 61 ∞

SOAKING IN THE OFURO WEEKS LATER, Haru massaged her abdomen as she felt the soft kicks of her fetus, reminding her how fortunate she had been during the Spanish flu threat. Ualani, two townspeople, and three Filipino plantation workers had been the only Waimea fatalities. The flu strain had been relatively mild. While a new, more virulent strain was moving across America, Haru's entire family was now immune. Buddha had rewarded her forgiveness. Ko had been nurse, cook, and house cleaner during the two weeks of recovery. She now thought of Ko as her sister. Haru felt another kick. Although the doctor estimated she was in her seventh month, the frequent kicking and size of her belly told her it was closer to eight months.

The hot water soothed her, mitigating her worries of the upcoming birth and voyage to Molokai to retrieve Ume's baby. She switched her thoughts to her newest business notion. And that's when the tub shook, sloshing water out and bringing her reverie to an abrupt halt. Haru gripped the sides of the ofuro, held her breath, and waited for the next tremor, which never came. Her breathing eased. It hadn't been much of a temblor—just a Pele reminder that she could move the earth when it suited her, maybe a warning of a lull before the storm. *Two gathering storms*, Haru thought.

The storms had been simmering since her Armistice Day flight to visit Ume. Now, five months later and as spring rolled around, they had begun to rumble like Mauna Kea. A labor eruption and legislative attempts to ban Japanese language schools loomed ahead of them.

Plantation owners vowed publicly not to give into "Bolshevik labor demands" and hurried the harvest. Fujimoto was leading efforts to build a strike fund from field workers and soliciting the Japanese business community. He had told Kenji, "We will strike if demands for fair wages are not met."

Kenji preached patience to the workers while telling Bilkerton, "If the plantations don't raise wages a little bit, the consequences will be disastrous for everyone."

Bilkerton's standard response was, "Sure, sugar prices are high now, but that won't last. Besides, no matter what concession we make, your people will ask for more. So what's the point in giving in even a little bit?"

Peace in the Takayama home fared better. After Kenji's plate-clearing episode, Haru ceased her campaign to change his school curriculum. She had made her point. Given the compelling arguments for change, Kenji would come around to her point of view ... eventually. Tonight, she would share her newest idea for expanding their little empire.

She thought how Sam's diagnosis fit into her latest brainchild. "The doctors tell me," he had said, "I will never be able to run but eventually will breathe normally when walking." He paused to gasp, contradicting his own prognosis. "But it will be a long time before I can carry my own weight at the Parker Ranch." His eyes misted up. "I can't even sweep horseshit without stopping to take a breath every minute."

What Sam needed, thought Haru, was a real job that offered him dignity. Performing menial tasks at the Parker Ranch, surrounded by tough men riding the range, would be a constant reminder of what he had lost and who he would never be again. Kame's growing profit share from their truck garden exceeded Sam's earnings—another insult eating away at the man's pride.

Haru glanced up upon hearing the familiar plop-plop of Kenji's approaching getas. His weary eyes revealed he shared her exhaustion. He sat on the squat stool and washed himself before squeezing into the ofuro. He rubbed his wife's stomach. "Two more months, Okasan."

Realizing such talk could be an opening for Kenji to revisit his reluctant agreement to put her on a boat to Molokai in two days, Haru laid her hands on his kneecaps sticking out of the water. "I want to build a hotel, Otosan."

Kenji closed his eyes and leaned back in the ofuro. This was his usual signal for "we'll talk about it later." But this time, Kenji surprised Haru.

"Waimea needs a lodging for us Japanese," said Kenji. "I'm getting tired of the medicine vendor sleeping in our tatami room every month." He opened his eyes. "How would you do it?"

Stunned at his easy compliance, Haru hesitated for just a moment. "Sam would be the manager. He and Kame would live in the hotel. She can handle the front desk and restaurant."

Kenji nodded and rested his head on the edge of the ofuro. In seconds, he was snoring.

Haru waited a few minutes and then rose from the bath.

Suddenly, Kenji woke up, glanced at her swollen body.

"A new baby, a new hotel. It has a nice sound."

∞ CHAPTER 62 ∞

THE THREE DAYS PASSED without Kenji harping on the dangers of the coming boat ride. At midmorning, they drove off to Kona to spend the night with Irie before catching the ship to Molokai at nearby Kailua harbor. The children, standing next to Auntie Ko, shouted, "Come back soon," but Haru suspected they were looking forward to Ko's looser discipline and her easy dispersal of sweets.

Two hours later, Irie's three children squealed gleefully as they ran to meet the Ford pulling into their yard. Haru's eyes flew open, and then she snapped a hand over her mouth. She and Kenji glanced at each other in alarm. Smudges of dirt and caked food were spread over their naked bodies. One child sucked on a cane stalk; drizzle dripped from the chin of another toddler, holding a half-eaten mango.

When Kenji and Haru emerged from the car, the two older kids grabbed Haru's hand. "Auntie Haru! Auntie Haru!" cried the oldest. "We are so glad to see you!" The other child squeezed her hand and gazed at her with wide, loving eyes.

Haru peered over the car's canvas roof to Kenji. "You take care of Irie. I'm taking the children to the ofuro."

Long moments after Kenji's second knock, a disheveled Irie opened the front door. He squinted at the sunlight, combing over his unruly hair with his fingers. His mouth dropped as a wave of recognition dawned on him. He fumbled with a button halfway down the shirt that slopped over his drawstring trousers.

"Welcome to my disas'er," he said with a breath that could fumigate a room full of cockroaches and opened the door wide enough to admit Kenji.

∞ ∞

Haru washed the giggling children and then put the two oldest ones in the ofuro filled with steaming water high enough only for the kids to splash. Her anger rose as she looked across at the adjacent kitchen, its sink and counter littered with dirty dishes. Why couldn't Irie at least hire a washwoman and cook? *Oh, the injustice of leprosy! It's not just the stricken one that is ravaged.* The thought nagged at her that Ume's proscription against Irie buying a farm near the leper colony or even visiting her was having unintended consequences. Lost in thought, Haru was rubbing the older boy too hard until he cried, "Ouch!"

"Gomennasai," said Haru, angry that there wasn't a better response to the tragedy of leprosy.

As Haru walked the children to the kitchen door, she heard Kenji's angry voice. "You are not the first husband to lose a wife. You have children to live for, a business to run."

Haru practically sidestepped in. It didn't help to berate Irie for his drunken disregard of his responsibility or scold herself for not visiting Irie earlier. She began cleaning the kitchen while listening to Irie's occasional whining. Haru reminded herself that she and Kenji were in the business of helping people, no matter the circumstances. She was comforted by Kenji's first words when he joined her in the kitchen. "I'm going to visit several prospects for a housekeeper."

After the children were put to bed, a chastised Irie promised to "stop drinking and take care of my coffee farm." He had already agreed to hire the elderly widow Kenji recommended as a housekeeper. She would start tomorrow.

"Good," interrupted Haru, who understood the difference between the regret of the moment and the innate weakness of certain men. In a stern tone, she added, "But words are not enough." She pointed her finger at him. "You need to turn remorse into action.

Tears welled up in Irie's eyes, and Haru thought, *At least that's a beginning.*

Haru doused the last oil lamp in the living room and laid down next to Kenji on the futon she had spread on the floor next to the dining table. She spoke in hushed tones. "I have failed Ume, Otosan. I promised to find Irie a wife."

"Yes, but we agreed it was too soon. He wouldn't be ready. Who could have predicted he'd fall apart this way?" He looked at her thoughtfully. "Maybe you can fix two spousal problems at once?"

"Ko?" Haru asked.

"After your forgiveness set in and with her help during the flu crisis, I feel her mind has healed itself."

"I agree that she is much better, now," said Haru in a wavering tone that foretold a "but" coming.

Kenji picked up the equivocation and waited Haru out.

"It's hard to picture Ko with three unruly children, keeping house, and working in the hot sun plucking coffee pods."

Kenji suspected Haru had grown comfortable with Ko helping with the housework and tending the garden, as well as having her as a companion. However, since the plate-clearing tantrum, he had been careful not to incite an argument. "We have to get up early. Let's get some sleep."

∞ CHAPTER 63 ∞

I N THE DAWN'S MIST, Kenji drove Haru to the Honokohau-Kailua harbor. On demand, the weekly ship between Honolulu and Molokai swung around the south side of the Big Island to stop at Kailua and pick up visitors or new patients for delivery to the Kalaupapa colony.

Earlier, Irie had sent off Haru and Kenji with deep bows, muttering, "I will try my best to be a good father."

At the first curve in the road, Haru broke their silence. "When I get back, I'll talk to Ko about Irie. But I'll understand if she refuses marrying into a home touched by leprosy."

"Yes," said Kenji. He wagged a forefinger in the air. "If not Ko, perhaps we can trace the wives who fled Waimea after their husbands had been afflicted." Haru gave her forehead a gentle thump. "Why haven't I thought of this before?"

The fog had lifted, and streaks of sunshine cut through the drizzle as Kenji pulled into the Honokohau Harbor parking area. Haru spotted the approaching converted navy tugboat, its smokestack belching thick black clouds. Escorting seagulls dove into the sea for their breakfast. As she alighted from the car, Haru's eyes were drawn to a moving rock. Then she smiled at the crawling giant green turtle.

Nature was aglow this morning—not so the sad faces at the pier. This was Molokai day.

Haru riveted her eyes on a crying, barefoot girl in a sleeveless shift draped to the tip of her knees. The little girl couldn't be more than ten years old. Her tiny hands clutched at the colorful skirt of an off-white woman whose bent head was covered with a bright, red scarf suggesting a Puerto Rican or Portuguese lineage.

Standing a respectful body-length behind the clinging waif, a tall Hawaiian woman in a flowing muumuu sobbed while embracing a man of wider girth, who was holding her even tighter and mumbling words destined to be remembered for decades.

The captain stepped over. After cursory greetings to Kenji, he addressed the two other families in a firm, low-timbre voice. "Come. We want to beat the weather." His stern face told Haru that there was never a good time for his involuntary passengers to leave. Another moment was both too long and not long enough.

The captain looked up and frowned at clouds increasingly deeper in color, unusual at this time of the year normally marked by clear skies and calm waters. From Kailua, he had a 150-mile run around to the north side of Maui and then to Molokai's Kalaupapa Peninsula.

Haru couldn't keep her eyes off the child, whose wailing told the world she did not understand how just a few violet skin blotches meant never seeing her mommy, daddy, brothers, and sisters again.

The ship's horn blasted three times.

The mother's forlorn eyes locked onto the Hawaiian woman breaking her husband's embrace. Without a word spoken, the tear-faced Hawaiian lifted the crying child and crooned an ancient Polynesian lullaby into the girl's ear. Hugging the child to her shoulder, she marched, head high over the gangplank to give her husband's last vision of her as a stately woman, the memory she wanted him to hold.

Haru stepped aside to let the handsome Hawaiian woman and child pass. By now, the wearied girl's wretched cries had turned to hopeless sobs. Behind her, the ship's officer cleared his throat. Haru took the hint, collected her lunch bento and Ume's gift package from Kenji, and walked across the gangplank. Seven. She counted seven more passengers on deck who must have boarded in Honolulu. All looked normal, except for their eyes.

As the harbor disappeared, the Hawaiian woman still carrying the child, whose sobs had weakened, walked over to join Haru. "I thought I had finished all my crying last night. I hope we will become friends. I am Ipo."

"I am Haru, but I am only a visitor to the island. My friend is having a baby on Molokai, and I promised to bring the baby back."

"You are not afraid?" asked Ipo.

Haru put her hand over her stomach. "My husband worries that I am not strong enough for the trip."

Ipo's lingering gaze told Haru that "afraid" had nothing to do with traveling while pregnant.

Haru smiled. "No, I am not afraid. I know Hansen's disease does not spread through casual contact. My husband is a Buddhist priest who visits Molokai occasionally."

The two women sat on the bench that lined the deck's side railing. Ipo maneuvered the girl to her lap. She soon fell asleep. Haru and Ipo shared personal histories as if they were long-lost sisters reunited.

ᗱ ᗱ

"Whales!" Everyone jumped up, stepped over to the unencumbered bow's railing, leaned over, and feasted their eyes on an ebony humpback leaping from the sea in a majestic arch. Everyone, that is, except Haru. She started to stand, felt her stomach lurch in the undulating swells, and sat back down on her seat.

The increasingly unpleasant motion sent the butterflies-in-the-stomach Haru below deck to stretch out. At the base of the descending metal steps, she found the passenger room appointed with a single steel table, painted black and bolted to the floor, along with tattered blue sleeping mats lying about haphazardly. Two hammocks hung at one end. She pulled a cinnamon-hued shawl from her kimono sleeve and spread it over a mat. Before she could lie down, her stomach churned as bile surged into her throat. She ran for the toilet, drew down the iron door's handle, and barely made it in time. Just the rolling of the ship, she told herself, nothing more. After several minutes, she returned to the common area, reclined on the mat, and fell into a deep sleep.

Haru would often wonder how differently her life would have played out if the waves had not been twenty-feet high and if the ship had not slammed directly into one dead-on, which tossed her into the side of a bulkhead like a Chinese vase in an earthquake. She thought that she must have fallen twenty feet, which she quickly realized was impossible. She could not find anything to hold onto for what seemed like an eternity, until strong hands grabbed her and pulled her to a handrail. It was Ipo. All the passengers had descended earlier as the seas rose and were clinging to the table or handrails screwed into the metal walls. Haru tried to ignore the sudden sharp pain she felt. She prayed her baby had not been harmed.

Suddenly, the pain came from deep inside her, as if from a hot spike being hammered into her womb. *My baby!* Once more, the ship hit a swell hard. Haru lost her grip and tumbled across the room. Water came cascading down the stairs and rushed across the floor. She rose to her knees, dismayed to feel water sloshing around her kneecaps and toes. She managed to crawl back to the railing and grabbed it. She retched, her empty stomach giving up nothing. Still the boat dipped and twisted. When would it stop?

When the ship turned west along the north side of Maui into shallower waters, the high waves subsided. Relieved by the steadying ship, Haru climbed the stairs back to the deck while the crew pumped out water from the passenger area. The weather was clearing. She tried to eat a little rice but demurred after only two swallows. She slept intermittently on a dry mat laid out by the crew. The pain in her stomach sparked bloody visions of a miscarriage.

Half asleep, Haru felt hands massaging her shoulder muscles. "You can see the cliffs," purred Ipo. Haru sat up and looked to the right of the landing beach at the foliage-covered palisades, its many shades of green brightened by a sun undiminished by clouds.

"I shouldn't have come," sighed Haru. "If only I had listened to my husband. Someone else could have picked up the baby."

"Not every pain is what you think, Haru. You have been bounced and bruised. You will be okay."

A hovering little waif asked shyly, "Is the lady all right?"

Ipo lied. "She's fine but needs rest."

∽ CHAPTER 64 ∾

THE SHIP DROPPED ANCHOR IN CALM WATERS. As a welcoming procession edged down the rocky ridge leading to the beach, the ship's winch dropped Ipo and Haru into a waiting outrigger canoe. Haru kept her eyes focused on the flowing black manes of the muscled Hawaiians paddling with strong, quick strokes. For generations, the nearby villagers had volunteered to row passengers ashore.

Suddenly, Haru grabbed Ipo's arm. "The pain is back … I—" Another spasm ripped her gut—deeper, sharper than the previous one. The rites of delivery had begun. The onslaught of contractions now tore at her body.

Ipo twisted her headscarf into a sausage-size roll. "Bite down on this. I've birthed a dozen, sweetheart, most by myself. We can do this together."

The boat scraped sand. "A woman's in labor!" yelled an oarsman jumping into the calf-high surf. Onlookers surged forward. Such rare excitement was not to be missed, regardless of one's state of decay.

Gasping for breath between bolts of pain, Haru watched a centipede of human hands clawing over the sides to pull the canoe across the wet sand. Strained faces—mangled, discolored, with missing parts—leaned in. Along with the Hawaiians, they tugged the canoe beyond the lapping wave line. The Hawaiian paddlers pushed aside the onlookers, lifted a limp Haru from the canoe, and eased her onto a bed of palm leaves the women had laid out.

Prone and exhausted, Haru gazed up at the overhanging faces, some missing an eye or a nose, one with a mouth that was more like a doughnut hole. But each face held kindness. She beamed back their compassion with as much love as her own eyes could register. Then her innards revolted. Her screams silenced everyone, even the seagulls.

Ipo pushed shocked voyeurs aside. She shouted at the Hawaiians in her native tongue. "Hot water! I need hot water—now!" The giant men took off running up the beach.

Ipo whispered in Haru's ear. "Normally, I do my midwifery indoors. You won't forget this one."

Haru forced a smile. *The pain. The pain.* It was nothing like any of her other births. *Oh, God, make it quick,* she thought. She did not hear Ipo's soothing voice but felt the woman's hands on her slippery thighs. Then came a rack of even worse pain.

"Push! Push!" urged Ipo.

Haru felt hands grab her. She held tight. Her face contorted into a demonic grimace. She pushed, pushed, pushed. And then, her body surged with relief. Her face relaxed to an angelic repose. The pain stopped.

I hope it's a girl, she told herself. *Kenji has all his boys.*

∽ CHAPTER 65 ∽

L YING PRONE ATOP THE BED OF PALM LEAVES, Haru waited for her baby's first cry. Her squinting gaze locked onto Ipo lightly spanking her baby under the cloudless blue sky.

No cries.

An arc of fear streaked from her groin into her drumming heart. The baby's color was wrong—blue-greyish. Ipo breathed gently into the still, crinkled face. Haru pushed herself up on her elbows. It was a boy. Ipo breathed into the tiny mouth again and again. She shook her head, and tears rolled down her broad face. The baby's head lolled lifelessly.

Haru couldn't take her eyes off the still form. *Oh, Buddha,* she said to herself, *why didn't you take me instead? I am my baby's killer as sure as if I had dashed him against the lava rocks of Mauna Kea.*

A woman pushed her way forward. "Oh, Haru," said a shaken Ume staring at the lifeless baby. She bent over. "Why didn't you tell me? I … I killed your baby."

Haru looked in Ume's guilt-ridden eyes. "No, no, no," Haru said, thinking, *I must not allow Ume to accept the blame that is mine alone.* She grabbed her friend's hand. "All I had to say when you told me you were pregnant was 'me too,' and you would have understood."

Exhausted, Haru closed her eyes. She heard Kenji's warning voice. "It's too dangerous for a pregnant woman." *Even if he never accuses me—"Look what your stubbornness has done"— his heart will, and I will deserve his silent retribution.* Then she heard a haole voice. "You must be Haru."

Haru opened her eyes. A Caucasian nun dressed in a white habit was peering down. She pointed at two Hawaiians holding a stretcher. "They will carry you to the staff infirmary."

The nun, walking beside the stretcher bearers as they made their way up the hill, slipped a comforting hand into Haru's. Walking on the other side of the stretcher, Ume followed suit and took the other hand. Haru asked, "How is your baby, Ume?"

Struggling to keep the bitterness from her tone, Ume said, "I'm told he is fine. But I haven't seen him since birth."

Haru regretted asking her. She knew babies were taken from Hansen's-diseased mothers and given to Hawaiian wet nurses until arrangements could be made to bring the baby out of the colony. Then the thought struck her. "I have milk."

Feeling the eyes of the two women on her, the nun thought for several moments. *It would be good for this woman to have a purpose.* She tightened her grip on Haru's hand. "Thank you. That would solve the feeding problem for the baby's journey back to Kona."

Haru bit her lip, trying to stop the tears.

That night, Haru dreamt of falling overboard with her baby and trying to catch him before they both hit the water. Her nightmare of swimming after the baby, bobbing up and down in the rough seas, and never catching up to him ended only by waking up at the sound of her own voice yelling, "Help!" She shook her head, as if avoiding a wasp. Her innards ached, reminding her that no amount of denial would resurrect her baby. She blinked at the sun's last rays filtering through the shutters. When she tried to orient herself to the white-walled surroundings, she realized she was not alone.

"Your sleep is troubled, sister," said a sitting Hawaiian woman holding a baby to her open breast. She rose, lifted the baby, and handed it to Haru. "Nursing the baby should be soothing."

Haru tenderly cradled the infant in her arms and fumbled to find an opening to her nemaki. As she wondered how they had changed her clothes, she placed the baby to her breast. The tiny lips latched on easily and began to suckle. Tears trickled down Haru's copper cheeks.

The Hawaiian woman took off her lei and hung it around Haru's neck. "I lost my firstborn. A little girl. We always wonder why the Lord takes them and what their lives might have been like." She kissed Haru on her wet cheek and left, saying, "I will get the nurse."

As Haru watched the woman leave, she whispered to herself, "Yes, but you did not kill your baby."

The rays of the midmorning sun streaked through scattered angel-wing clouds to brighten rows of Kalaupapa's white crosses. A cherub-looking nun, her freckled face solemn and strands of red hair stealing out from under a white habit, pushed Haru seated in a wheelchair into the whitewashed chapel.

More than a hundred mourners crowded into the Father Damien-built church atop the cliff overlooking a marshmallow-capped sea. As a courtesy to Kenji's pastoral visits, two dozen Japanese residents, many with faces covered with blackened gauze and bearing misshapen limbs, were accorded front-row pews. At the church door, Haru insisted on walking. After reminding Haru, "You must not touch anyone," the nun held her steady as they walked to the front row. The nun positioned herself between Haru and Ume. To Haru's happy surprise, Ipo sat on the other side of Ume.

Directly across the aisle, Haru noticed a not-quite teenage girl blessed with silky hair to her waist. She wore a clean but faded blue yukata too short for her. Between two misshapen ears, her beautiful unmarred face offered a perfect-tooth smile. Haru smiled back, wondering how many suitors would have been wooing her in a few years if she were disease-free. Did she think about that too? The girl kept her hands folded into her sleeves. To hide her stumps, Haru guessed.

Haru accepted the Dutch priest's offer to deliver an ecumenical prayer. Upon closing his homily, he nodded at a middle-aged Japanese man in a black suit whose left trouser leg had been spliced to give room to his overgrown flesh. Only a few blotches, what in ordinary circumstances would have passed as sunspots, marred his handsome face. His eyes shone clear. He rose and, with surprising vigor, shuffled to the altar. Haru's chest swelled with gratitude as he chanted a Buddhist mantra in Japanese—the same one Haru had heard Kenji intone under similar circumstances.

An off-key piano started the strands of "Amazing Grace." Everyone began singing. In Kalaupapa, surmised Haru, one gets a lot of practice singing at funerals. When at the start of the third chorus the pianist pounded the keys with a drummer's intensity, the congregation recognized the cue and paraded out the side door where they marched past the white-granite slab covering the grave of Father Damien on their way to a copse of palm trees at the back of the groomed cemetery. Aided by the freckled nun and Ipo, Haru forced herself to keep pace. Six tiny crosses, placed painfully close to each other, fronted the swaying palms. Someone produced a chair, but Haru refused to sit at her son's burial.

At the end of the procession, Haru watched the man who had just delivered the mantra walk by solemnly, cradling her white-shrouded son in his arms. At the grave, partnering with the priest, they placed two wide lengths of blue silk under the body, lowered the little boy into his final resting place, and dropped the shimmering silk strips into the tiny grave. To the accompaniment of a young Hawaiian blowing mournfully into a conch shell, they shoveled the adjacent mound of damp earth over the infant.

The adolescent girl in the too-short yukata had positioned herself at the front of the grave. Haru noticed her eyes were full of purpose, anticipation. As wind stole the last notes of the melancholy wail of the conch, the girl bowed to Haru and from her blue cotton yukata sleeve withdrew a carved stone Jizo, the benignly smiling deity portrayed as a shaved-headed monk.

A fuzzy darkness clouded Haru's vision. Thinking the statue must have been a parting gift from the girl's mother, Haru grabbed Ipo to keep her balance. Jizo was the protector of a child's health. When the Jizo could not fulfill his role in this world, the statue was often placed on the tomb of babies so he could look after their soul in the nether-world. Haru was anguished and grateful when the girl squatted down and placed her prized possession at the grave's apex. Then she stood and bowed over the grave.

Haru tried to take a step toward the girl.

The nun gripped her hand like a vise. "You can thank her in the visitors' room tomorrow when you visit with Ume." She slowly walked Haru back to her wheelchair.

∞ CHAPTER 66 ∞

CUDDLING UME'S SLEEPING BABY BOY, Haru stepped into the ob-long visitors' building. *Like a prison,* she thought, as she eyed the cubicles fronting parallel steel-mesh room dividers set a foot apart to prevent touching. The condemned, in various stages of decay, sat on one side while anxious relatives and friends trudged in, casting nervous glances as they searched for their loved ones. Haru spied Ume six cubicles down, half-waving her hand.

As soon as Haru sat down, Ume looked at the wall clock. "Time is precious. Tell me what happened, but make it quick."

Haru gushed out the horrible crossing at sea and ended with tearfully telling about the moment she understood her baby was still-born. Toward the end, Ume's baby stirred and then cried. Without a pause, Haru opened her yukata to slip the baby's mouth to her breast.

Ume allowed herself a gentle, sad smile. "I never even held my baby, Haru-chan."

Unconsciously, Haru held the back of the baby's neck more snugly. "Oh, Ume-chan, I have gone on too long. You too have lost a baby and … " Haru couldn't complete the sentence and instead asked, "How do you manage?"

Ume allowed a small smile. "My new role as a kokua gives me purpose, helps me forget the life I left behind. I am practically a nurse. This is a different world with its own customs and rules. I am learning to embrace it and to forget about what cannot be reclaimed. Those who cling to the world they left behind die early, die miserably." Another glance at the wall clock. "And my children? How are they?"

Haru forced a light tone as she manufactured warmhearted stories about the children. Halfway through a story about the children picking up coffee cherries, Ume stole another furtive look at the wall clock. "Listen to me; we have only a short time left."

Haru leaned into the wire mesh.

Looking at her baby, Ume began. "After the birth, the midwife raised my baby in the air to give me a look and then took him away."

Haru looked into Ume's misty eyes. She did not know what to say and so said nothing.

Ume pressed her face against the mesh. Her fingers grabbed the laced wire like an eagle's talons. "*You* must raise my baby, Haru-chan."

Haru opened her mouth, but no words came out. She shook her head no, even as she held the baby to her breast more snugly.

"I've done nothing but worry about my three children since arriving here. Irie is not the fatherly type. He turned to drink the last week we were together. He was angry I would not let him visit me. He had these wild ideas … wanted to sell the coffee plantation and buy farmland above the colony here. He said that bringing me food and clothing would give his life a new purpose." Ume touched the purple blotch on her neck that had grown since Haru had seen her last. "But I knew better."

"Oh, you stubborn fool!" Haru wanted to scream, but her eyes encouraged Ume to continue.

"Relatives visit us lepers—monthly at first, then yearly, and then ... " She let the words hang and swiveled her head looking at the cages. "Everyone wonders if today's goodbye is the last goodbye." She took a deep breath. "You will love the baby as your own, Haru. It's not necessary to tell Irie or Kenji." Then she gave Haru a knowing look. "I listened to your stories of Irie and the children." She paused. "You know which home will give this child the better future."

Haru adjusted the baby's body. Her thoughts swirled. *Ume is giving me an escape from my recklessness. More than that, she is atoning for her unwitting role in the death of my baby. A wrongly assumed guilt that does not absolve the real guilty party—me. And it is true that Irie is raising his three children poorly. He needs a wife more than another child. This baby would thrive in my home.*

"It would be a great comfort to me if you took the baby, Haru-chan."

"If I keep the baby, Kenji will find out. He visits here."

The baby's suckling stopped. Without thinking about it, Haru lifted the infant over her shoulder and patted him on the back while she gently rocked her shoulders.

"Haru," said Ume authoritatively, "our colony holds more secrets than all the shoguns who ever ruled Japan."

Haru lowered her eyes and gave a little shake of her head. "Among the patients. But surely Kenji talks to the doctors and the sisters." She felt a soft burp on her shoulder.

"In the colony, we are one. I have already registered the burial of your baby as mine. I told the registrar he died in the night. He understood the need for this ruse."

"But the baby was not kept by you." Haru felt the infant's second burp.

"Does it matter? We buried a baby. You lost your baby for the sake of a leper. We have paid a debt. All will honor it."

A soft bell rang at the end of the building.

Haru sensed the baby had dozed off, and she gently slid him back on her bosom.

"It's the two-minute signal. You must save my baby, Haru. You are a woman of God. I am your friend. I am begging you to do this for me. Can you deny a condemned woman her only wish?"

Haru paused, frozen in time. The baby felt so much like her own. This way there would be no lifetime condemnation, silent or otherwise, from Kenji. Ume was giving her a reprieve from her own stubbornness but in exchange for a life of deceit—a secret she must take to the grave.

Another soft bell.

If only she had more time. Haru heard the murmurs of goodbyes and the scraping of chairs backing up. Her mouth, close enough to taste the wire, found strength. "I will raise him as my own. Kenji asked that his next son be named Kenta. I will tell Kenta of his brave auntie whom I was visiting the day he was born."

"Arigato."

A sharp bell ring startled Haru. Ume stood abruptly, bowed, and hurried away.

Haru hugged her baby. When the last person had left the room, she stood up and slowly walked out wondering whether she had made the right decision but knowing that there was no turning back.

⊙ CHAPTER 67 ⊙

FOUR DAYS LATER, the infirmary doctor rated Haru fit to travel. Since the next colony ship would not arrive for another week, Haru was told, "You must take the mule trail up the sea cliff. The mule ranch owner charges two dollars to drive you across Molokai to the harbor." The freckle-faced nun sent a telegram to Waimea advising Kenji of Haru's travel schedule.

Earlier telegrams had informed Kenji of the birth of his son and the death of Irie's. Haru knew that Kenji would spare her the burden of telling Irie his baby had not lived. The first of many deceits, thought Haru, who was assuaged by the fact her baby, as she now thought of Kenta, had a better future. *So does my marriage*, added Haru to herself.

With the baby bundled to her back, Haru walked with the red-haired nun to the base of the trail to meet her taxi.

"You have to love your mule," said the gentle Hawaiian who brought down visitors and supplies on the backs of his sturdy animals.

"He's so big, more like a small elephant without a trunk," said Haru.

The Hawaiian allowed himself an indulgent smile. "You'll see why we breed 'em big; they have to carry you almost straight up two thousand feet."

Haru arched her neck. *There's no space for a person on foot, let alone a mule,* she worried.

"Ikimasho," grinned the Hawaiian using the Japanese, "Let's go." After Haru was mounted, while adjusting the stirrups, he added, "As we climb, it's better you not look straight down."

Minutes later, Haru's mule was plodding upward, slow step by slow step. Gentle breezes rustled her hair. Low-hanging layers of spidery foliage protected Haru and a sleeping Kenta from the sun. Haru admired how the mule used his front feet to find purchase, pushed off his hind feet, and strained his chest and front thigh muscles to hoist himself up the next chiseled step. Then her mule paused and repeated the process. Each hundred feet or so, a heartbeat-accelerating, ninety-degree turn slowed the rhythm. The zigzag view alternated between calm azure seas to the north and a panoramic view of the colony's white buildings to the south.

Upon the ninth turn, the trail turned narrow and muddy. Haru's left leg dragged against the mountain wall. She heard a sucking sound each time the mule lifted a hoof. Curiosity overcame her guide's proscription, and she looked straight down. Haru inhaled sharply. The mule's right hoof was half on, half off the edge. Like a gambler's compulsion to keep rolling the dice, Haru could not take her eyes off the hoofs. She let out a gasp when the mule's right front leg stumbled. The mule stopped, steadied itself, and resumed its steady pace.

The Hawaiian on his mule ahead turned around grinning.

Haru let out a relieved laugh and shouted, "I LOVE my mule!"

At the top of the cliff, the Hawaiian drove Haru to Molokai's commercial harbor in time to catch the ferry to Lahaina, Maui, where after a night on shore, she would take another ship to Kailua. The boat rode gentle swells into soft breezes. The nestled baby slept, peacefully unaware of the admiring glances from his fellow passengers. Sitting on one of a dozen scattered deck chairs, Haru feigned a warm smile to the well-wishers while agonizing over why she could not have had such balmy weather sailing to Molokai. *Not only have I lost my baby, but I also have entered a life of deceit with Kenji.*

Or have I?

Except for a daily mesh-wire visit with Ume and meals with staff, Haru's recuperation had been solitary, unless you counted baby Kenta. And save for short walks to the beach to regain her strength, she spent endless self-accusing hours in bed, staring at white walls. As if viewing a film on a continuous loop, Haru kept replaying the scenes that led to her miscarriage: the angry flight to Ume's home, the next day's rash pledge to retrieve the baby, and her repeated refusals to heed Kenji's sea-passage warnings until he capitulated to avoid another family confrontation. So many times, so many times, she could have backed out of the trip.

Consumed by so many "what might have beens," Haru had failed to grasp how Ume had wrapped the gift of her baby inside an unchallenged codicil: Kenji must never know. Haru had been so relieved by the chance to escape the prospect of her good marriage collapsing into ruin that she bought into the dual conspiracy as if they were one. She could have, but had not, said, "I will raise your baby, but I must tell Kenji. *He and I* will keep it a secret." Instead, she had fixated on envisioning Kenji's wrath the moment he learned that his forewarned rough seas induced a miscarriage killing his son. She had latched onto Ume's guilt-racked "the end justifies the means" secrecy scenario not only as the right decision but also as the only one possible for both mother and child.

But was it?

Now back from Ume's haunting world, the notion burrowed into Haru that she could unbundle the two choices Ume had braided together: to take or not to take the baby and to tell or not to tell Kenji. The first choice had been made. Then she had a flash of insight. *Haven't I used the same "the ends justify the means" as a self-serving rationale to embrace Ume's pleas to take the baby as mine because he has a better future with me than Irie? A much better future.* She snuggled Kenta tighter. The first choice was settled. What about the second choice? *Shouldn't I tell Kenji the truth? He is a compassionate man who reminded me of the virtue of forgiveness when I wanted to throw out Ko. Surely, he would accept the baby and eventually forgive me.*

Or would he?

If I reveal Kenta's true parentage, would Kenji demand I give up the baby? Maybe initially, but on reflection, he would recognize that the interests of the child are paramount. Given the choice between our loving home and Irie's, what choice is there?

But would it play out that way moments after Kenji learned my stubbornness had killed our own baby?

Haru rocked Kenta while imagining variations of confessing, "Irie is Kenta's father. Our baby died on the beach." None ended well. She recalled her advice to troubled women who carried children of uncertain fatherhood. "It's not necessary to compound one problem with another. The surge of relief you imagine by confessing is not like when a dentist punctures an abscess. In one, your tooth heals; in the other, the marriage seldom recovers. Confess to Buddha. He always forgives. Seldom do husbands." Haru thought of how most who followed her advice maintained a happy marriage. Those who confessed regretted that decision.

But none of the women had hid the death of her baby and substituted it with another.

Oh, dear Buddha, let me clear my conscience and receive Kenji's approbation for my full disclosure. Despite the desperate prayer, Haru couldn't expunge the perils of confession. Her tortured mind thought how instead of only her leading a life of deceit, they both would have to put up a false front. Switching to thoughts of their comfortable lovemaking, Haru worried how an unforgiving Kenji would grow to hate that manly urge driving him to make love to a woman he regretted marrying and could no longer trust. Kenji, unforgiving? Probably not. But what if?

Haru slept little that night regurgitating the same history, rehearsing all sorts of scenarios, and envisioning all manner of repercussions of telling or not telling Kenji. On went this inner battle the next day as she dozed intermittently on the ship's passage to Kailua.

The ship's horn blast announcing its entrance to Kailua's harbor ended Haru's ruminations. She rose and looked to shore. A smiling

Kenji waved. The guilt overwhelmed her. If she didn't tell Kenji now, she would think about it, feel the urge to confess every day of her life. The burden would be too much to bear. Even if Kenji insisted they must give up the baby, that would be better than worrying that tomorrow the truth might be exposed.

∽ CHAPTER 68 ∽

HARU FLASHED HER BIGGEST SMILE and waved back to Kenji standing next to an apathetic-postured Irie—a shadow of the vibrant man she had known for years. Moments later, Kenji bounded on deck. Haru handed Kenta to his outstretched arms. "Truly the Buddha has great plans for Kenta." Cradling the baby, he added with pride singing in his voice, "This is the boy who carries my name." Looking deep into Haru's eyes, he added softly, "I was so worried about you. I heard the crossing was rough."

"You were right; I was stubborn. The trip was more dangerous than I ever expected."

"The important thing is you and the baby are safe," said Kenji, giving Kenta back to Haru. He picked up her wicker basket and headed toward the gangplank.

At the bottom, Irie placed a lei around Haru's neck.

She thought, *This is your baby, Irie, but I can't sort this out on the pier,* but said only, "Arigato." Feeling fuzzy, but not enough to faint, she couldn't say, "I am sorry for your loss," knowing that what he thought was lost had been stolen and might be given back. Kenji's fatherly pride was making the revelation difficult. "Ume is building a new life. As a healthy newcomer, she has become an active kokua."

"Let's have some tea," said Kenji, noticing his wife's reticence and excusing it as fatigue.

Looking into Irie's hungry eyes, Haru felt trapped. "Yes, there is much to tell."

Haru had to raise her voice in the crowded teahouse while she noticed that Kenji, who had insisted on carrying the baby, was beaming in response to the admiring glances aimed his way. At a break in her rendition of life in Kalaupapa, Kenji spoke, "Tell me about the delivery." He handed a fussing Kenta back to Haru.

Slipping the baby under her yukata fold to nurse, Haru thought how all her imagined conversations telling Kenji what had really happened took place privately—in the car, around her dining table, or during a walk in her garden and never in a public place ... with the real father of the baby present.

Kenji and Irie remained silent, expectant.

An epiphany brought color to Haru's face. Yes! She seized the invading inspiration like snatching a fluttering butterfly out of the air. This setting is a sign from Buddha warning her to protect her family and the baby. She began, "I was lucky. A Hawaiian midwife was on the ship. I delivered the baby on the beach." Haru continued, knowing there was no turning back. She would live the big lie the rest of her life, but today would pass in peace. And the days after that, she hoped.

By the end of her telling, the story of Kenta's birth seemed natural. Everything about the delivery was true except the moment after delivery. There was no invented scenario that in future years might change in the telling, exposing a lie. Kenji savored every word. Irie accepted his baby's death and probably was relieved he no longer faced the prospect of raising a baby. Kenta slept at Haru's breast the whole time.

On the drive home, Haru told more about Ume's adjustment to Kalaupapa and the beach birth along with the baby's first days. Haru was surprised how she was settling into the lie.

Then at the turn to Waimea, Kenji thankfully changed the subject. "I hope you don't mind, but I have temporarily taken over your job as matchmaker. I arrived early today to talk to Irie about a ... " he paused, "a housekeeper companion."

Haru detected an awkwardness in his voice.

"A wife but not a legal wife. Regardless of Ume's wishes, I couldn't ask Irie to divorce her."

"Who?" asked Haru.

Rushing what seemed rehearsed to Haru, Kenji answered. "Ko. She's the right woman for Irie. Her health, mental and physical, is back. She can't live with us forever. And … " his eyes crinkled, "we know she can't possibly marry a man of humble means."

"But days ago, he said he would never take another woman," said Haru, doubt dripping in her voice.

"I showed him a picture of Ko in a bright-red, figure-clinging Chinese dress."

"My husband the matchmaker," said Haru. "But I can't see Ko working on a coffee plantation, even as the owner's wife. She agreed to consider a proposal from Irie?"

"She's your friend," said Kenji hesitantly.

Haru nodded. Not happy with the presumption but not wanting to make an issue of it either, she said, "I'll try my best, but I think your expectations are too high." She wondered about Kenji's sudden interest in matchmaking.

Haru got the answer an hour later.

⚭ Chapter 69 ⚭

KENJI HONKED THE HORN when he took the turn onto the gravel road fronting his home.

Alerted by the sounds, Sachi and the three boys were bounding down the porch steps to greet the car. Ko surveyed the family scene from the porch. When Haru ascended the porch steps, Ko offered the perfunctory "oohs" and "ahs" as she fussed over the new baby but avoided eye contact with Haru. She tripped over a toy on the way into the front door.

After she bathed little Kenta to the enthusiastic attention of her children, Haru carried Kenta into her bedroom to place him in the bassinet next to their bed. The room glistened, its condition pristine, a surprise, given her absence. Haru sneezed. Then she noticed her Chinese vase held cut plumeria, their blooms perfuming the room.

What was this? Kenji had placed cut flowers in their room?

She opened her valise and began unpacking. As she hung up each garment, a niggling suspicion pushed its way through her consciousness. Ko's downed eyes, her reserved demeanor. Kenji's lack of anger over the premature birth and his sudden flurry of matchmaking.

She closed the valise and stored it on the upper shelf of their closet. Then she turned and fixed her gaze on their marriage bed. She stood motionless—paralyzed with dread—for several minutes. With one bold stroke, she pulled back the comforter.

The sheets were fresh.

She picked up a pillow. The cover was also fresh. She sniffed and felt a jolt. Still, she wasn't sure. Did she really want her suspicions confirmed? Haru pulled back the pillowcase halfway and sniffed again. Still faint, but it was there. Perfume. It had been years since Haru had applied perfume.

Kenta stirred, cried at the pitch Haru recognized as "I'm hungry." She picked him up with a tenderness born of sorrow. She could not bring herself to recline on the bed, so she sat on the room's only chair, an unforgiving hardback with a cushioned seat that faced her vanity table. She opened her yukata to Kenta's eager lips and then stared at the forlorn face in the mirror.

Suddenly, the door swung open, and Taka rushed in.

"Mommy, why are you crying?" he asked, bouncing with a child's enthusiasm. His eyes turned from Haru's to his new brother feeding at her breast.

Haru offered Taka a Madonna smile. "Sometimes people are so happy they cry." She stretched out a hand to rumple his hair. "You are such a big boy now. Are you going to help me take care of baby Kenta?"

"Yes, Mommy, I will," vowed a solemn Taka. "Always."

"Go now," said Haru. "I will come out when I finish feeding. And please shut the door, Taka-chan."

As the door closed, Haru bit her tongue in a futile effort to stop the tears. *How could they?* she asked herself. Did Ko sneak to the ofuro after Sachi fell asleep with one intention? Did they bump into each other at the ofuro "by accident?" Did it happen just once? A single regretted act induced by sake and circumstance? Or had they carried on their tryst the entire time she was gone? What would have happened if Taka had woken? Or did he? What burden would this knowledge have on his young life if he saw or heard her father with "Auntie Ko"?

When Haru counseled people who had been betrayed—money taken, a spouse stepping outside the vows, a lie exposed—they would lament, "I trusted him … " "I believed her … "

"Of course," Haru would commiserate, "only the trusted can betray."

Given Ko's checkered life, Haru could understand her predatory nature. Ko would forever be the opportunist who broke into Haru's doll bank. She thought of Midori's letter warning her of another woman in the household.

But Kenji. How could he fall for a temptress? And in their own bed.

The tug of Kenta's suckling reminded her of her own role in Kenji's fall. If she had not insisted on traveling to Molokai, the coupling with Ko would never have happened. Kenta's mouth worked at a slower pace. She rested him over her shoulder and patted his back as she rocked back and forth. And when it came to trust, who was the greater breaker of marital trust—Kenji's moment of indiscretion or the replacement of a dead baby with the son of another?

Haru rose and then placed the drowsy baby in the bassinet. She splashed water on her face from the vanity basin and opened the door. Her face showed purpose.

Kenji looked up from the newspaper he was reading. His eyes caught hers for only an instant, and then his uncertain look focused on the picture of the Taisho emperor hanging on the far wall.

"Call Irie and tell him Ko has accepted his offer."

Kenji hesitated. "You don't have Ko's agreement."

"Oh, Ko will accept his offer, Otosan. She will be eager to leave this evening. Tell him Ko will work as housekeeper and look after the children. Tell him to offer Ko her own room. If they come to a different arrangement later, fine."

Kenji opened his mouth as if to offer an objection, but when he searched Haru's face, he saw strength, resolve, and a disturbing lack of emotion. "Hai, Okasan." He walked over to the telephone and pick up the handset.

"And," said Haru, loud enough that Kenji replaced the receiver, "tell Irie to meet me and Ko at the turnoff. We'll be leaving in fifteen minutes."

Haru strode to the cottage and entered without knocking. Sachi and Ko looked up from their Parcheesi board. Haru inhaled deeply to calm herself, not wanting to frighten the young girl. "Sachi, this would be a good time to pick some fresh vegetables from the garden for tonight's dinner."

As always, the compliant girl followed Haru's orders. The look on her face convinced Haru that Sachi had no idea for the cause of the drama about to take place. She hoped Taka was as innocent.

Haru leveled cold eyes at Ko. "You need to start packing, Ko. I have arranged a husband for you. Irie-san."

"Your friend's husband? The coffee farmer?" Ko gave a short laugh, cynical and dismissive. "I wouldn't be a real wife. I—"

Haru cracked her four fingers on the table with such force that the Parcheesi pieces jumped from the board. "This is not an offer, Ko. This is an order. You are lucky. You will have a home. He has no idea why you are available. You will be a housekeeper unless you want more. We will leave as soon as you can pack." Haru looked at her watch. Her eyes locked with Ko's. "And you will not enter my home again—ever."

"Haru, why are you doing this? I haven't—"

Haru slapped Ko hard. "Don't bother lying to me, Ko. I know you too well, and I know what you have done."

Ko threw her hand to her cheek, her eyes radiating a mixture of shock and fear.

"You are what you are, Ko. You can't help it."

Ko's luminous eyes grew large. "But I—"

"Your alternative is working on your back in Chinatown," said Haru. "If I have to drive to the Parker Ranch and get Sam to drive you over the mountain to Hilo and dump you in a hotel, I will."

Ko dropped her head. "I'll start packing."

⌘ ⌘

Other than giving Ko an update on Irie's situation but glossing over his drinking problem, the one-hour drive was silent, except for wind generated by pushing the car to its maximum forty miles per hour on this treacherous road.

As they approached the turnoff, Haru spotted Irie's Oldsmobile. "Let's put on a happy face." The quick-adapting Ko took out a small vial of perfume. Haru wanted to slap it away but held her temper. *In ten minutes, this woman will be out of my life.* She had promised Ume to find a substitute wife for Irie. His children needed a mother. Ko was a temptress, but she had been a terrific auntie during her stay with Haru's children.

Haru noted the sad-faced Irie spark up at the sight of Ko. Haru read the speculation in his eyes and made the introductions. Irie had the good grace to note the time. "I must not keep you from your family, Haru." Happy with the cue, Haru slipped back into her car and managed a friendly wave as she drove, thinking of the two betrayals that marked this tumultuous week.

Could she ever trust Kenji again? Forgive him? When she measured his carnal misdeed against what she had done, she faltered. What would happen if he knew the truth about his baby? His promoting Ko's beauty to Irie and the clean bedroom certainly showed regret. Best to accept the offering. She might need his dalliance as a card to play if he should ever find out the truth about Kenta. She didn't like that thought, didn't like what it said about herself. Still, the hiding of one truth and the ignoring of another told her that absolute truth was not always the better policy.

Her inner truth told her that forgiveness for a marital lapse would promote a happy marriage. She would forgive Kenji without telling him. In a week, her body would heal from the birth trauma. She would reach over to him. He would know.

⟋⟋ ⟍⟍

Kenji had waited up for Haru. He opened the front door for her and handed her a cup of hot green tea. "Tell me about your ideas on the hotel."

That was Kenji, thought Haru. He would use a dramatic change of subject to keep a dispute at bay. This time, Haru welcomed Kenji's reconciliation ploy. "I've been thinking that to free Kame to run the front desk and restaurant, Sachi will have to manage the day care center. Do you think she's up to it?"

Kenji thought for a moment. "Since you and Kame are nearby and you keep the books, all Sachi has to do is watch over the children and record attendance, which is simple enough. She loves the children. They know it. They love her. Perhaps her slowness gives her the patience many adults lack."

With this settled, they went to the ofuro where, during a quick bath and soak, they discussed the number of rooms, the size of the restaurant, and the contractors they would invite to bid on the project.

An exhausted Haru fell into a deep sleep so quickly she didn't remember Kenji's last words: "I don't think I can keep a lid on the sugar agitation forever."

∞ PART V ∞

SUGAR

∞ CHAPTER 70 ∞

Waimea, Hawaii – January 6, 1920

UNDER A TROPICAL MIDMORNING SUN, Kenji, regretting he hadn't raised the canvas convertible top, slowed coming up the dusty road approaching the Bilkerton plantation cottages. Sullen wild-cat strikers milled about in small groups, refusing eye contact with him. Spotting Tamatsuke standing in front of his white, pinewood home, Kenji stopped beside him. "It's the big-stomached overseer," said Tamatsuke. "He docked a day's pay from an almost-due pregnant woman he found resting."

"Tamatsuke, a work stoppage makes it harder for me to straighten this out."

"If this was the only incident … This luna abuses the workers at every turn and pockets our lost wages."

A minute later, Kenji pulled into Bilkerton's circular driveway. Shoulder weary, he stepped onto the raked gravel. He looked up at the all-too-familiar ionic columns buttressing the porch roof. How many times had he walked up these steps to negotiate—no, he corrected himself—plead for fair working conditions or to redress a wrong?

Thirty minutes later, Kenji stepped out of the house. Down the road, he could see strikers lingering in front of the sugar mill; they spotted him and began marching forward. Raising his hands in the stop position, Kenji bounded down the porch two steps at a time. While driving the short distance to the crowd, he spied the head luna, Angus MacFarlane, strolling toward Bilkerton's back door.

Braking at the edge of the cheerless crowd, Kenji grabbed the top of the steering wheel and stood up. "Mr. Bilkerton apologizes for docking the pregnant lady's pay. He said his luna didn't know she was pregnant." Ignoring chorused shouts of "LIE!" Kenji continued, "She will be paid her regular wages."

"What about today?" demanded Tamatsuke.

"As long as you work two hours later than usual, you will be credited a full day's pay."

Tamatsuke upped the challenge. "What about a fair day's pay for a fair day's work?"

"I understand the unfairness of your situation. I believe the owners will soon see that it is in their interest to raise wages." He ended his speech with a bromide from Buddha extolling nonviolence and patience. Kenji feigned he didn't hear "fool" hissed by a worker.

He could not feign blindness when an egg splattered on his windshield as he drove off, nor could he purge the nagging doubts that he was being played by owners like Bilkerton.

∞ CHAPTER 71 ∞

LOOKING OUT HIS BAY WINDOW, Bilkerton was watching Kenji addressing his workers when his stomach suddenly knotted at the sound of familiar boots stomping up the back door steps. The screen door banged. As usual, there was no pause to scrape feet on the bristled mat. The impertinence! He listened to boots marching across his kitchen's linoleum floor.

Bilkerton hated MacFarlane for his swagger. Not that he minded it in the fields where such an attitude was necessary—the very reason Bilkerton no longer went there—but the man brought it into his plantation house! He despised the man for his competence. Too often, fellow owners reminded him, "How things have changed since you took on that Scottish fellow!" He turned to eye his overseer as he barged into the great room.

"So what bone did you throw that sniveling little preacher?" said MacFarlane, walking over to the wet bar while looking past Bilkerton to see Kenji driving off.

Ignoring the condescending question while trying to show authority, Bilkerton snapped, "Heading off a strike because one of your uncontrolled lunas hassled a woman days away from giving birth. Boneheaded."

MacFarlane popped the top off a fifth of Glenfiddich. "You don't know the full—"

"Never mind," said Bilkerton, waving his hand. "There's a lot more in play than a work stoppage. I solved that easy enough." While walking over to a mahogany boardroom-sized table and sitting down, he summarized the deal he had made with Kenji while MacFarlane threw back a jigger of scotch. "What you and this priest don't understand is the big picture. What your luna did was stupid, but I can't manage a plantation if every little incident results in a work stoppage. That priest thinks he has won a great victory. That's exactly what I wanted him to think. It's his last victory."

Thinking Bilkerton was finally showing some gumption, the Scotsman poured himself another drink, but this time filled two tumblers and offered the other to Bilkerton, who pointed to the chair across from him.

"Look at this," said Bilkerton, picking up and waving the *Pacific Commercial Advertiser*. "'Midnight Raids Corral 4,000 Communists.'"

"I heard," said MacFarlane, taking a seat. "The Palmer raids, they're calling them," referring to US Attorney General Alexander Palmer.

"It's this guy Hoover," said Bilkerton, jabbing a front-page picture, "who actually pulled off the raids. Sixty-seven in one night. The bloody fools gave us a pass, claiming they have no jurisdiction in Hawaii, this being a territory." He slapped the paper on the table and stared at MacFarlane. "It's up to us to the handle the Bolshies in Hawaii. Any way we can."

"I'm more worried about one Bolshevik, that sneaky bastard Noboru Tsutsumi. He visited us last night."

Blood rushed to Bilkerton's face. "That … that fucking agitator! He slips into Hilo two years ago, passing himself off as just another

Jap language teacher. A year later, the little shit's scallywagging all over the island, stirring up workers like a man poking a hornet's nest. Hell, left to themselves, all our field hands want is to get steady work, attend their noisy festivals, and fornicate—grow those big families of theirs." Exhausted by his tirade, Bilkerton sat back. "Speaking of agitators, what about our own Fujimoto?"

"I'm keeping an eye on the bugger, Gov."

"Watching him isn't the answer. That's what Custer did at Little Big Horn."

MacFarlane gave his boss a questioning look.

"You see, if Custer had slaughtered the savages while they slept in their villages instead of waiting for a big battle, there'd be nothing for the cursed Indians to brag about. You catch my meaning?"

"I hear what you're saying, Gov."

"This priest, this Fujimoto, that Tsutsumi … all trouble. This wildcat strike is a warning. I gave in today to give you time to put this to an end, to send a message. Action is what I am talking about. Not your 'keeping an eye' on things."

MacFarlane held his tumbler high, thinking, *Now you're talking, you fat wimp*, but said, "Some of my boys are from Mississippi. They know how to keep people in their places."

Bilkerton returned the salute. "Spare me the details, but put enough fear in their hearts to take the starch out of all this strike talk."

"Gotcha, Gov." MacFarlane threw back his head and let the last of the Glenfiddich soothe his throat. His sneer chilled Bilkerton's spine. "You got the right man for this."

∽ CHAPTER 72 ∾

"PATIENCE!" HISSED THE IMPATIENT TAMATSUKE at one of the three men huddled among sugarcane stalks piled high next to the mill's grinding wheel, roofed but not walled. It was ten o'clock, well past the time the plantation cottages turned down their oil lamps. A Pacific storm front had moved over Waimea during the afternoon. The winter trade winds cut through the men's damp clothes.

The lean Noboru Tsutsumi raised his collar. "That wildcat strike was not smart. We're not ready. You're lucky the priest got Bilkerton to back down. We have no money to sustain a strike." He was talking to Tamatsuke, but his words were for the Filipino.

The wide-eyed Manlapit, forgoing his lawyer demeanor, stomped his feet as if trampling a rat. His voice came from deep in his throat. "All day long the kahuna, Big Mango, is laughing on his horse, cracking his whip. 'No can strike, you Filipino *hilahila*," he said, using plantation talk, meaning cowards. "'No can strike, you Filipino hilahila. No can—'"

Tamatsuke Fujimoto grabbed the shorter man's shoulders. "Brother, we understand. We are as eager as you to strike, but on our terms."

"You no understand." Manlapit shook off Tamatsuke's hands. "We are human beings, not monkeys for the entertainment of the lunas."

"Strike now and you will be monkeys forever. How many weeks can you endure empty bellies before you crawl back to the lunas, begging for jobs?" snapped Tsutsumi, his narrow eyes squinting and his sharp jaw jutting.

"My people are beyond waiting. We'll be the first to strike a dagger into the owner's heart."

"Come back tomorrow, good friend. Give me another day," said Tsutsumi.

"A day." Manlapit's sneer did not require an "only." He strutted off into the downpour like a general who had just won a battle.

No one saw a dark shadow slink off in the tempest's blurry distance.

"The fool," said Tsutsumi as he watched Manlapit disappear into the falling rain.

"A scab," said Tamatsuke, referring to Filipinos breaking the 1909 Oahu strike. He spat.

"If they strike now, they will expect us to follow and provide money and food," said Tsutsumi, shaking his head.

"I'm having trouble holding my own hawks in place. Today's strike over the pregnant woman was a gamble I won. I needed to show we are ready for action." He paused and looked Tsutsumi in the eyes. "Everyone's talking about rice strikes in Tokyo. They hear rumors of dockworkers striking for eight dollars a day in San Francisco. Is it true that even the white longshoremen in Honolulu will strike?"

"True. All true," said Tsutsumi. "It is time for the working man to rise up."

"What happens if the Filipinos walk off the fields?"

"If they strike, we will have no choice but to call a general strike. The owners can find enough scabs to field a workforce on a single plantation. The only way we can win is to shut them all down. And you, my good friend, no more wildcat strikes." With a curt nod, Tsutsumi bent over and dashed toward the cane field where his horse waited tethered to a tree.

Tamatsuke ambled home slowly. The heavy squall droplets had turned to a whispery drizzle.

Mayo had waited up for him. She massaged his neck and back muscles till he fell asleep.

∞ CHAPTER 73 ∞

EARLY THE NEXT MORNING, MacFarlane rode tall in the saddle, a whip wrapped loose around his right hand. Shaggy red hair sprouted from the rim of his beaver-felt Stetson. His roving eyes spied his hapless prey weeding. He sidled up behind him and cracked his whip over the man. He barked, "You, 2436, bring me a bucket of water."

Like all lunas, MacFarlane referred to his workers by the digits stamped on a metal badge the size of a half-dollar that cane workers were required to wear at all times. MacFarlane learned the easiest way to find a compliant field hand was to discover who gambled poorly.

To keep up with his debts, 2436 earned bonuses for ratting out union activities. When he returned with the water bucket, he brought it to the mouth of MacFarlane's horse that had drifted out of hearing range of other workers. The bent-over man kept his eyes focused on the water bucket. "Last night, I saw Tsutsumi and that Filipino troublemaker talking to Fujimoto by the grinding mill."

MacFarlane knew who the troublemaker was and what it meant. While leaning over to stroke his horse's neck, he dropped four quarters into the bucket. "Go back to work."

MacFarlane spurred his horse's flanks and took off to the two nearest plantations. The message he delivered to the lunas was the same he had given his own overseers. "I'm buying the drinks at the teahouse. Got something you will be interested in."

∞ ∞

From Kawaihae's Sandalwood Teahouse bamboo porch, MacFarlane's glazed eyes fixated on the flaming red sunset sliding into shimmering blue water as he goaded his eight whiskey-swilling tablemates to "stand up and be counted." The ramshackle hideaway, which overlooked the port's salt flats, was neither built of sandalwood nor served tea. Although Prohibition had started on January 17, you wouldn't have known it at Kawaihae's notorious bar, which, in addition to free-flowing alcohol, featured waitresses who paid the mama-san two dollars a day to work there for "tips."

Three of the nine, including MacFarlane, were ship-jumping Scots, the favored choice of owners who respected their no-nonsense approach to discipline.

Two were Portuguese lunas whose parents were among the seventeen thousand laborers recruited from Madeira or the Azores in the 1880s to replace the Chinese in the cane fields. They brought their families and a four-string guitar they originally called a "*machete*," then a "taro patch fiddle," and finally the name that stuck, the "ukulele." Most Portuguese who didn't repatriate migrated to the towns as tradesmen after fulfilling their labor contracts. Those who stayed on the plantations worked their way up to gang bosses and, then by WWI, were finally accepted as a new class of lunas. But those Portuguese showed a Mediterranean complexion, and some missionary-era Caucasian descendants questioned whether they were white enough. Perhaps this accounted for the Portuguese lunas' tendency to be tougher on their Asian workers than other lunas.

The two local haole lunas, former paniolos with little prospect of being promoted to ranch foreman, were sun-bronzed to a darker complexion than the Portuguese.

"I've been thinking how you Southern boys," said MacFarlane, turning from the sea to point his whiskey glass at the Bowman brothers, "keep your niggers in line." Sweeping his eyes next to his fellow Scotsmen sporting scraggly red beards, then the slicked-back-haired Portuguese, and finally the long-haired haoles, he pontificated, "You can learn from these men of experience."

The youngest Bowman boasted, "Time for a little attitude adjustment for these slant-eyes who don't know their place." Then he smirked, "You gonna hang that Tamat-pukee?"

"It ain't like I never thought about it," said MacFarlane. "But I got something else in mind that's more fun and won't get us into trouble." He emptied his glass, tipped the whiskey bottle until the gold liquid half filled his tumbler, and winked at one of the girls behind the bar. "The party," he said with a Cheshire grin, "will be at my plantation. Bilkerton finally got the balls to let me do something."

MacFarlane outlined the plan and then added, "This message will be for all the workers on all our plantations. Let those little buggers wonder who we're gonna visit next." He paused. His glassy eyes danced evil. "I almost forgot. Bring a torch."

∞ Chapter 74 ∞

B Y THE FOLLOWING EVENING, northern trade winds had shoved the Mexico-sized weather front out to sea. The Southern Cross and a three-quarter moon glittered. Concealed near the edge of a cane field only weeks from harvest, the mounted MacFarlane let his gargoyle eyes draw a bead on his workers' cottages. Imagining himself Rob Roy, he raised his flask in a salute to his whiskey-fueled confederates. They waved theirs back. Reining their horses steady, all brought their tin beakers to their mouths, tilted them, and took one last courage-infusing swig.

MacFarlane shoved his flask into his saddleback and with the same hand withdrew his charcoal-smudged, sugar-sack mask, which he draped over his head. Fumbling in his drunkenness, he dropped a foot-long piece of string, which he had reminded everyone to bring to tie off his sack at the throat. *Fuck it, I ain't getting off my horse*, he thought. Smart winds whipped the loosely hanging hood. MacFarlane regretted not scissoring the eye slots bigger. He steadied his horse, which was borrowed—like his attire—from the Bowman brothers so his workers wouldn't recognize him. Then he opened a sugar sack tied to his saddle horn and pulled out a trimmed cane stalk tipped with wired-wrapped strips of an old shirt soaked in a kerosene-engine oil mix. He struck a match on the butt of his rifle, snug in its sleeve fitted to his saddle. Eyes blazing more than his match, he lit his torch.

His pumped-up riders extended their own torches like knightly swords saluting a medieval gallery and trotted by to catch a light.

MacFarlane drew his Winchester from his saddle's scabbard and swirled it in the air. His adrenaline-charged marauders followed suit and knee-pressured their horses abreast to form a hooded cavalry line. Their steeds stomped their feet and neighed. MacFarlane glanced right and left in quick succession and then leaned forward like a hawk ready to strike. Hearing bagpipes in his addled brain, seeing only red-coated Brits ahead, he kicked his spurs into the flanks of his horse and yelled, "Charge!"

In less than a minute, the shrieking riders were trampling vegetable patches and flower gardens behind the cottages, all the while firing their carbines in the air, unless they saw a pig or chicken and took wild, one-armed aim at them. Barking dogs and then squealing women and children quickly choked the night air.

The plan to gallop the length of the cottages and circle back to the starting point turned mob-murderous when the oldest Bowman, reliving his KKK days, ignored MacFarlane's order to "scare the little fuckers, but don't start a fire." He threw his torch into a wooden building the size of two horse stables set back from the cottages. This was a women's co-op used to boil soybeans into tofu. The flaming torch landed on a mass of kindling brush stacked next to a kerosene can.

"What the fuck!" yelled MacFarlane at Bowman. Fire was the scourge of plantations, whose wooden buildings were surrounded by cane fields with dry stalks part of the year. Then MacFarlane's own evil impulses loosened any restraint. *Hell, the tofu house isn't near anything*, he thought. The burning would cripple the bitches' earnings. Force them to work more hours to make up the income.

Shrieks of "Fire!" rose from the cottages. Pockets of unrestrained children dashed out of the homes as the horses galloped past. Men from the homes rushed to the water tower to grab stacked buckets. While MacFarlane's maddened brain did not register that windblown cinders from a burning building could ignite the cottages, the workers did.

Inside the tofu building, searing flames from the kindling scorched the kerosene can.

Reveling in the fear they had created, the nightriders spurred their horses into the crowd running for water. A woman tried to weave out of a stallion's path, but she was not fast enough and was knocked aside by a stampeding hoof. The more frightened the screams, the more aroused the riders became.

"Otosan, Otosan, what's happening?" screamed Mayo.

Nemaki-clad Tamatsuke sprinted to the door and threw it open as the raiders reached his home. Flaring light from the torches inflamed the anger in his eyes, anger amplified by the riders' scornful laughter punctuated by sporadic gunshots. The night raiders hesitated at the sight of a child clinging to Tamatsuke's leg, but not the oldest Bowman. He grabbed a torch from an indecisive rider and swung his arm in an arc, sending its fiery malice onto the cottage roof. His younger brother's torch followed. Flames on the roof flickered.

MacFarlane's hate-glistened eyes riveted on Tamatsuke, the man who had organized the workers right under his nose and undercut his authority by getting that pregnant woman's money back. And it was maddening that Tamatsuke wasn't cowering like everyone else. His eyes blazed defiance. *Have it your way*, MacFarlane thought. He kicked his horse, driving it toward the front door.

Simultaneously, the tofu building's kerosene can exploded. Under a rain of spewing glass and flaming debris, Tamatsuke backed inside his home and slammed the door. Oblivious to the fireworks and falling fragments, MacFarlane drove his bloody spurs into his mount's flanks. The horse rose up and kicked at the flimsy door, knocking it off its hinges. MacFarlane threw his torch inside. Tamatsuke's children screamed. The crashing door pinned Tamatsuke's legs to the floor. He looked up at the rider high on his frightened horse that rose again on its back feet. The mask fluttered, revealing the eyes of malice. Eyes Tamatsuke knew well.

As the horse retreated, MacFarlane aimed his rifle at Tamatsuke and pulled the trigger.

Click. Click again. Two more infuriating misfired clicks.

Behind MacFarlane's horse, a child ran, holding her hand over a bleeding eye, yelling, "Mommy!"

The haoles and Portuguese dropped their torches and fled. They hadn't come for this.

The Bowmans dismounted, picked up the discarded torches, smashed Tamatsuke's cottage windows with their rifle butts, and threw the four torches into the home.

"Okasan, take the children outside!" yelled Tamatsuke, trying to quell the flames by throwing blankets on the torches. Too many torches, too few blankets. The curtains caught fire, then the chairs, then a wall. Smoke filled the house. Tamatsuke ran outside to join his shaking wife and three terror-stricken children. The masked horse-men circled around the Fujimoto family clinging to each other.

The fire roared. The men whooped. The horses brayed.

Leaping forward and pumping his fist, Tamatsuke shouted, "You will pay for this!"

MacFarlane slammed his rifle butt into the face of the fist-waving Fujimoto who collapsed under the blow and did not hear his nine-year-old daughter shriek, "My doggie!" nor see her dart through the skittering horses and dash back into the cottage.

Mayo screamed, "Yumi-chan!" and raced after the child.

MacFarlane reared his horse. The instant the hooves hit the ground again, his spurs cut into the horse's flanks. A vicious yank on the reins sprayed blood from the horse's bit as MacFarlane bolted toward the cane fields, followed by the hooting Bowman brothers and his fellow Scots.

On one knee, Fujimoto heard the screams from the house, rose, and tore into the flaming home. Men, women, and children threw their buckets of water inside flaming windows. High-pitched screams quickened the firefighters' water-bucket line. Seconds later, a human torch staggered out, carrying his wife. Buckets of water rained on

Tamatsuke. Flames spewed from the windows. A roof beam crackled and collapsed.

"DADDY!" pierced the air.

Fujimoto turned. He tore back toward the blazing inferno. Three men tackled him and pinned him to the ground. He heard one last shriek drowned out by the roaring fire.

At his mansion, Bilkerton had been awakened earlier by the gunshots, and as he stood at his bay window, he was horrified by the fires breaking out in the workers' housing area. This was not what he had in mind. How could MacFarlane let this get out of control? How would he explain this to the Big Five?

⚭ CHAPTER 75 ⚭

COOL MIDNIGHT BREEZES swept through half-open louvers bouncing curtains throughout the tranquil Takayama household. Baby Kenta slept peacefully in the bassinet next to Haru and Kenji's bed. The family was at peace. A golden time. The language-school quarrel triggering Haru's night flight to Ume's home, the miscarriage prompting the baby switch, and Kenji's unacknowledged fall from grace with Ko had all mysteriously fostered a more caring or, perhaps some would say, a more careful relationship. Something precious almost lost is guarded even more securely going forward. Haru convinced herself that her secret made her a better wife and mother since she worked harder to compensate for the deceit, even though she often reminded herself everyone benefited from Ume's ploy.

A week ago, Haru had watched her oldest, Takeshi, hit his first Little League home run. Sachi managed her preschool day care nursery. Tonight, three traveling businessman slept in Haru's newly built eight-room hotel on the other side of the Takayama property. Resident managers Sam and Kame had pitched in, planting, weeding, and harvesting Haru's growing garden, which was now more like a truck farm.

Deep into her third hour of sleep, Haru kicked her legs against the confining bedspread. She dreamed of horses thundering down hills, just as they had in the samurai movie she'd seen at Oda's Japanese theater two days earlier. Behind the cavalry, sword-swinging soldiers charging in sun-reflecting armor shouted, "Takayama-san!"

Haru's eyes flew open. The shouts were real.

"Takayama-san! Takayama-san! Takayama-san!"

Fists hammered the front door like hoofs. Kenji awoke and leaped from the bed. "I'm coming," he cried. His fumbling fingers tightened the sash around his nemaki as he trotted to the door. He thrust it open to find a panting Kurume, the squat, barrel-chested union vice chairman, his face gritty and sweat-streaked.

"Yumi-chan, Tamatsuke's youngest child has been killed, murdered, burned to death. He and Mayo have also been badly burned."

"Come. Come in. And slow down. Tell me what happened," said Kenji. Behind him, Haru's shaking hand was lighting an oil lamp. Kurume slumped into a chair, his head in his hands. "Nightriders with torches, guns, and evil rode into our housing." He caught his breath. "Workers are threatening to burn down the Bilkerton house."

"Kurume-san," asked Haru, "how bad is Mayo?"

"Not good. We put her and Fujimoto-san in a truck and drove them to the Tebbits clinic. Then I came here."

Haru spotted wide-eyed Sachi enter the back door while Haru's sleepy-eyed children stumbled into the living room. "We're okay," said Haru to her boys, gathering them in her safe embrace. "There's been an accident, but it happened far away from here. You need to go back to bed."

The three boys retreated to the bedroom. Without being told, Sachi began preparing tea. She spied Takeshi hiding around the corner, but she said nothing.

Kenji turned to Haru. "I need to go to the plantation."

A truck beeped its horn.

"Go, Otosan. They need you to prevent more killing, but I don't think you will be able to stop a strike."

Kenji gazed at her. "Maybe I've stopped one strike too many." Then he turned to Kurume, "Tell the driver I will be out in two minutes."

Haru added, "I'm driving to the clinic as soon as I get dressed."

"Most likely the workers will be thrown out of their homes," said Kenji as Kurume ran back to the truck.

Haru refrained from an "I told you so." Instead, she said, "I will start working on housing."

"I should have listened to you, Okasan."

Yes, you should have, thought Hara. "Otosan, you are a man of character. You did what you thought was right."

Kenji nodded silently, thankful for the undeserved pardon. The horror of this raid and the child's murder squashed a decade of illusions like a sugarcane crusher squeezing juice from the stalks. All those compromises with owners for mere crumbs off the table. He had much to answer for, much to make up. Minutes later, he flew out the door and down the steps to the idling truck where Kurume waited behind the wheel. Kenji nodded at two men sitting behind the cabin on the flatbed.

A taut-faced Dr. Bernard Tebbits, a giant at six foot four, greeted Haru at the door of Waimea's six-bed clinic, alive with hospital smells. Two years earlier, Carter had recruited Tebbits right out of medical school in San Francisco. He and his German wife and his head nurse lived upstairs. Tebbits brushed aside blond locks hanging over his right eye.

"Terrible business, Haru-san," he said. He admired Haru, who served on his public health committee. "Madness."

"Tebbits-sensei, how are they?" asked Haru.

"Follow me to their room," said Tebbits. Walking down the hall, he added, "Fujimoto's burns are mostly second degree except for parts of his face. Third degree starting near the right eye and down the cheek. When he arrived, we poured cool water over the burned area. He has been in and out of consciousness. He's strong. He's drinking water. If infection does not set in, he will live."

"But the pain ... ?"

"We've coated the burns with a mixture of paraffin wax, Vaseline, cod-liver oil, and sulfanilamide. This will ease the pain, protect the wounds from germs, and help the healing. Right now, he is sedated with morphine."

"What about Mayo?"

He stopped outside a door and shook his head slowly. "Third-degree burns over half her back, second degree over a quarter of her body." He opened the door.

Fujimoto's face was wrapped in gauze. He appeared to be sleeping. Mayo's face looked peaceful, her body wrapped in the same gauze. Haru looked at a tube in Mayo's arm, her eyes crawling up it to an open flask dripping fluid into the scorched body.

Noting Haru's worried face, Tebbits said, "We learned with cholera that the main cause of death is dehydration."

Hara looked uncertain at hearing the unfamiliar word.

"Water," said Tebbits. "The body needs water."

"Of course, the burns draw water from the body. The liver, kidneys become poisoned."

"Exactly. I'm lucky to have enough burn mixture ingredients for her and Fujimoto for three, maybe four treatments. In the morning, I will call Hilo. Maybe I can beg for more."

Haru kept her gaze on Tebbits. "You said Tamatsuke would live, but what about Mayo?"

Tebbits inhaled and then let out a long breath. "Her burns are so deep that it's likely her shoulder nerve endings are numb. The smoke damaged her lungs. So much of her body ... " He let the words trail off.

Haru took up a vigil sitting next to Mayo. Her mind flashed back to the first time they met in Judith's class, telling their life stories inside Yokohama's Chinatown teahouse, the English classes on the ship to Honolulu, buying their wedding dresses together. Eventually her head drooped, and she dozed off.

"Yumi-chan."

The hoarse words woke Haru.

"Yumi-chan," Mayo whispered again more urgently.

She doesn't know, thought Haru. "Mayo, it's me Haru." She grabbed Mayo's unburned hand. "You must live for your youngest children and Tamatsuke."

Mayo squeezed Haru's hand. "Oh, Yumi-chan, all for a dog."

A weak voice drifted over from the next bed, "Live for me, Okasan."
If Mayo heard the words, they were the last she ever heard.

∞ Chapter 76 ∞

As Kurume cornered onto the dirt road leading to the plantation, a yellow glow hovered over what Kenji speculated were the remnants of the Fujimoto home and not, he hoped, the Bilkerton mansion. Kenji's speculation missed the mark. A minute later, shadowy figures morphed into men holding torches. The stench of burnt embers shifted Kenji's eyes to a stub of smoldering timber, the Fujimoto home. Bent-over, booted searchers poked through the ruins with iron rods.

Ahead, on his mansion's porch, Bilkerton stood, hands out, shaking his head and mouthing words Kenji could not hear. As Kurume drove closer, he heard the workers chant "Killer!" He read Bilkerton's pleading lips, repeating, "I did not do this." His clearly heard denials inflamed the crowd inching forward as they itched for one man to hurl the first retaliatory torch.

"Blow your horn and head straight to Bilkerton's porch," charged Kenji. Palming the horn all the way, Kurume brought the truck to a skidding halt between the jumping-back torchbearers and Bilkerton's porch steps. Kenji leaped out.

The crowd quieted down.

Kenji turned around and looked up at Bilkerton and saw the fear in his eyes that brightened as Kenji climbed the steps. "Thank God you're here, Takayama-san. We need to calm everyone down." He stared at the torchbearers who had crept back to the edge of his steps. Bilkerton raised his voice. "I had nothing to do with what happened. I promise to rebuild the Fujimoto home."

A torchbearer shouted in broken English, "MacFarlane, he killer. I see him throw fire into house."

A rock hit Bilkerton's cheek. Blood droplets trickled down his chin.

"Stop!" hollered Kenji, who spied another man's raised arm holding a fist-sized stone in its hand. "Did anyone actually see MacFarlane's face?"

"I did," shouted a man, his voice carrying above the angry murmurs. "The wind lifted his mask when he fell back from Tamatsuke's burning house. I saw MacFarlane's face ... clear as day."

The crowd tightened. A man with a torch placed his foot on the first porch step. Two more torch-carrying men yelling "Killer!" followed behind him. Encouraged, the first man raised his flaming spear in the hatchet-throwing position.

Two rapid-fire rifle shots cracked the night.

The crowd pivoted.

Behind them, the sheriff was shoving two shells into the breach of his shotgun. A pair of Winchester-armed deputies flanked him.

Kenji spoke into the stunned silence. "MacFarlane did this, Sheriff. We have witnesses."

Shoulders back, his sake-barreled chest straining his khaki shirt buttons, the sheriff strode through the uncertain crowd that gave way to him. Followed by his eye-roving men, he stepped up on the sideboard of Kurume's truck. He leaned his weapon against the truck door while his rifle-gripping deputies deployed at each end of the truck. Raising his hands, the sheriff addressed the crowd. "I stopped at the Tebbits clinic. I spoke to Mr. Fujimoto. He confirmed what you just told me—MacFarlane did this. My deputies are setting up roadblocks to catch him."

Kenji was halfway through his translation when a woman's keening stilled him.

The crowned turned.

A man stepped forward, holding what looked like a charred animal and smelling like a roasted pig. It took seconds for the crowd to understand the man cradled Tamatsuke's child.

"Burn the Bilkerton house!" the cry rose. "Killer! Killer! Killer!" the chant rose.

Fear returned to Bilkerton's eyes. He spun around, but with his girth he wobbled erratically, tumbled against his front door, and then slid down onto the porch like a wounded elephant.

A voice shouted, "I'll get some kerosene!"

The sheriff picked up his shotgun and fired both barrels over the heads of the crowd. Barely. His deputies followed suit with rifle fire. While the gun smoke hovered, all reloaded.

The crowd stopped. Waiting.

"Stay here," the sheriff ordered his deputies. He climbed the steps and helped Bilkerton up.

Kenji hissed into Bilkerton's ear but loud enough for the sheriff to hear. "You are responsible for this death. Rebuilding the Fujimoto home is not enough. You will announce a one-thousand-dollar reward for the capture of MacFarlane, two paid days for mourning, and ... " Kenji raised the level of his voice while slowing its cadence, "whatever ... money ... is ... necessary to replace any damaged buildings, gardens, or animals."

Bilkerton's eyes widened at the affront. His labored breathing quickened into shorter, angry gasps. "Never." He looked at the sheriff. "Shoot one if you have to."

The sheriff stepped closer and growled. "Listen, you stupid fuck. The priest is giving you a way out. How long do you think my two men and me can hold off the mob?"

"This isn't right." Bilkerton looked out at swinging torches, the man holding the charred child, and then back to the sheriff. His angry eyes swept over to Kenji. "Make the announcement."

Kenji turned to the crowd, shouted Bilkerton's list of concessions, and closed by directing, "Now, let's have a meeting in the school-house." He stared down the man who had been ready to throw his torch at the Bilkerton's house. Kenji breathed a sigh of relief when the man dropped it. The crowd began to disperse.

The sheriff's steely eyes zeroed in on Bilkerton. "Inside." As soon as Bilkerton slammed the door behind them, the sheriff's no-nonsense voice continued. "Joshua, your boatload of shit troubles is bigger than you think. No question, this is the work of your over-seer. If MacFarlane is caught, how long do you think it will take until he claims he was following orders? That you gave him the cash and your car to make his getaway?" The sheriff glowered at the fat man. "Earlier, one of my deputies saw him driving it on Saddleback

Road heading toward Hilo. Strange, given the time. Now we understand why."

Bilkerton stared at the sheriff, his face blank.

"I was a deputy in West Oahu during the 1909 strike. Lots of
violence. The next one's coming soon. It will be worse. If I could have
shot MacFarlane trying to escape, I would have welcomed it. The last
thing this community needs is an ugly trial to impassion vigilante
revenge." He studied the sorry excuse for a man standing in front of
him. "So, I'm giving you a pass on MacFarlane."

Bilkerton, still expressionless, said nothing.

"Here's the story," said the sheriff, the irritation in his voice rising.
"MacFarlane doubled back after the raid, picked up money he stashed
in his cottage, and stole your car. Tomorrow … " he paused to let the
word sink into Bilkerton's thick skull, "tomorrow afternoon, I'll send
telegrams to Kailua and Hilo to check their ports for your car. Do you
get that?"

Bilkerton's dim light seemed to brighten but not by much. "Ah …
right … by then he will be on some ship out of Honolulu, probably
under a false name."

"I'll leave one of my deputies on the porch. Put your lunas there
too. But only my deputy will have a gun. Got it?"

The sheriff took Bilkerton's weary nod as a yes and stomped out.

∞ CHAPTER 77 ∞

THE STENCH OF SMOLDERING TIMBER permeated Kenji's nostrils
as he walked over to the Japanese language classroom built by
Bilkerton shortly after his arrived in Waimea. The school stood only
fifty feet behind the Fujimoto home, a smoking canker to the men
gathering inside. He scanned the room jammed with standing workers, shouting, "Bilkerton!" "MacFarlane!" "Murder!" and "Strike!"
Rank body odors fouled the air. At the front, an oil lamp topped the
teacher's desk. Kenji wiggled sideways through the crowd until he
was standing behind the wooden desk. He motioned to Kurume to
take the teacher's seat. As the men settled down, a man shouted, "The

Christians talk about an eye for an eye. I say we put on masks and march back to Bilkerton's house." Applause roared in approval.

Kenji spotted the school bell on the edge of the desk, lifted it, and rang it like a fire alarm until every man had quieted. "Do you want to hang alongside MacFarlane, Nakayama-san?" challenged Kenji, eyeing the rabble-rouser inciting the assembly. "Or do you want justice and better living standards?"

"Strike!" another voice shouted.

Better than torching the house, thought Kenji. "I need a motion." A motion was put forth, seconded, and by riotous acclamation adopted. Kenji raised his hands. The workers needed to understand the commitment they were making. He used his oratorical "ask questions" technique to temper the rush to rashness. "Who remembers the Oahu strike of '09?"

Half the hands went up.

"Did you experience the strike in Oahu or hear about it while you continued to work?"

That question sapped the crowd's energy. Only Kurume raised his hand. The strike had bypassed the Big Island plantations. Kenji knew Kurume had stood in food lines and slept rough for six months. "Let's hear from Kurume."

To a smattering of applause, Kurume stood up. "Bilkerton has given us two days of paid no work. If we strike now, he will have the sheriff evict us by noon ... " he looked at his watch, "today."

The comment sobered his audience. They had known about this from their endless strike kibitzing. But that was theory. This was reality.

"He can't do that. He promised!" shouted Nakayama.

"He can if we strike but cannot if we only negotiate."

"You know the fat prick won't give us a decent wage," Nakayama added.

Murmurs of "that's right" filled the room.

"Of course he won't," said Kurume. "The point is we get two days to prepare." Kurume took the nodding of heads as a yes and said, "Let's amend our strike resolution to say we will strike in two days if we don't receive a positive answer to our demands from Bilkerton."

"Since he knows we'll strike, he might throw us off anyway," yelled a voice from the middle.

Kurume smiled. "Who is going to tell him we voted to strike?"

He waited. Several of the men glanced sideways at each other, unable to hide their conspiratorial smiles, and he knew he had his answer. "Takayama-san and I will negotiate with Bilkerton." Without realizing it until hours later, Kurume had appointed himself union representative for the plantation. It didn't matter that there was no union. When the strike began, Tsutsumi would make the formal announcement that the plantation workers had unionized.

Kenji and Kurume organized the weary men into five strike-planning groups—to list salary and work-rule demands, to start packing, to arrange transportation to campsites, to pool money for food, and to establish a civil administration for the camps. As the eastern edge of the night sky turned pinkish yellow, determined men headed home for a few hours of sleep before attending little Yumi's funeral and begin a siege that would test their resolve.

No one noticed 2436 had slipped out just before dawn to pass water and never returned.

∞ CHAPTER 78 ∞

"WATER," RASPED TAMATSUKE.

Haru brought the standing glass of water to his lips.

Sip by sip, he emptied the glass. "My wife, my daughter must not have died in vain," said Tamatsuke. His good eye froze on Haru. "Bilkerton must learn he cannot frighten us into submission."

Tebbits rapped softly on the half-open door and entered. "My nurse has arrived. You can go home. You need rest, Haru. I can drive you."

She nodded. "Thank you, Dr. Tebbits, but can you drop me off at the Shinto shrine?"

The doctor raised an eyebrow. "At our first dinner, you told me about the night of the ... " He searched for the word.

"Inari," said Haru completing the sentence. "The night of the fox."

"Something's changed?"

"Yes, Uno attended Ualani's funeral and went out of his way to be gracious." Haru paused. "We will need all the space we can find for temporary housing."

Minutes later, Tebbits dropped Haru at the shrine's entrance. As his Oldsmobile left a trail of swirling dust in its departing wake, Haru stared down the tree-shrouded path to the shrine. The memories of that night cascaded through her mind like a movie trailer. There were the pounding drums, the dancing torchlights, the fidgety crowd, and most of all her jittery legs stepping to the front where a brown-robed incarnation of the devil was postured. Then the snarling terrier, the cringing white fox, and her stealth whistling to the dog followed. Only her naïve teenage former self could have dared that imprudence. Yet she had walked out in triumph. Her response had defined her life, assured her position in the community, and launched the success of their Buddhist mission.

She looked up at the torii's crossing beam, so red in her memory, so faded now. Haru began walking down the weed-infested trail past the phalanx of fox icons—still crouched like sentinels, their presence losing a battle to the enveloping foliage. Ahead she eyed the shrine. It was nothing like the imposing structure of her embellished memory. Next to the shrine, a hunched man sitting on a tree stump faced the dilapidated fox cage while whittling a walking cane in long, slow strokes. He did not notice her. Closing in on him, Haru coughed.

Uno turned, raised his head, and nodded nonchalantly as if Haru were a friend returning from a brief errand. He rose and pointed his knife toward the open door to his home behind the shrine. Then he laid the carving blade on the tree stump next to an oiled sharpening stone. He looked at Haru with a sad smile. "Once," he confessed, "I daydreamed of cutting your throat with that very same knife, but now I welcome you as a friend. Please come in."

The talk of cutting her throat unsettled Haru, but his eyes were kind, tired. She followed him inside his cottage.

Pouring tea, he said, "I may not have been wise in my younger years."

"You conducted a ministry in a different era."

His shoulders relaxed as if some burden had been lifted. "They say you are a good listener, Haru-san. Someday, I would like to tell you about my life story. Maybe then, I can understand why I did what I did." His eyes drifted away for a moment. Coming back from wherever he had visited, he continued. "But you are a woman of purpose. You did not come here to listen to the ramblings of an old man."

"A child and mother were murdered last night in a fire on the Bilkerton plantation. I expect this will trigger a strike within the next forty-eight hours."

After Uno listened to the details, he said, "If you include the Filipinos and children, we could be talking about a thousand displaced people in the Waimea area." He continued in a low voice, "You need places for people to stay. We have a good well, lots of space for tents." He paused and then added, "Some of the men should come soon and start building latrines." He pursed his lips. "Water's more important than food. Cholera, typhoid, and dysentery will kill strikers and their families. All we can do is keep the number of deaths as low as possible." He swept his hands at his acreage. "Looks like a lot of space until you put hundreds of people here needing clean water and places to squat."

"I have much to do," she said softly.

"I expect you do, Haru-san." He lowered his voice. "I expect you do indeed."

⚭ Chapter 79 ⚭

Fighting fatigue, Kenji drove toward Uno's shrine from the Tebbits clinic where, after learning of Mayo's passing and finding Tamatsuke sleeping, the nurse told him the doctor had dropped off Haru. His fists tightened on the steering wheel while he thought of officiating at a double funeral later that day. Mother and daughter. There was no time to dwell on the senselessness of it all. In fewer than forty-eight hours, the strike would begin. An unprepared strike. Despite the tragedy, or more likely because of it, he recalled how the 1909 strike had failed for the lack of money. He ran down the list of Japanese business owners, tradesmen, and those in the professional class he must tap for donations. So little time. He was thinking of asking Sam to solicit funds from the paniolos when he spotted Haru walking from Uno's shrine. He gave a quick squeeze to his horn's bulb. Haru smiled with relief. Kenji slowed until the car stopped beside her.

"It's already a long day," said Haru, sliding into the passenger's seat. She recounted Mayo's last minutes. "Holding her hand, I was thinking of the evil Bilkerton has let loose."

"A weak man," said Kenji. "I doubt he ordered the burning of the Fujimoto home. Not a smart thing to do. But you have it right. He let loose the evil in MacFarlane with no qualms or consideration of its consequences."

"Yet Bilkerton attends church. Calls himself a Christian."

Kenji, who admired the life of Christ and his teachings, never let a direct attack on that faith go unanswered. "I don't think Christ would have approved of Bilkerton any more than Buddha or the Shinto saints approve of Amakusan parents selling their children to brothels."

"Sometimes I forget it's man who twists the religion to evil ends in violation of the words of the founder."

Having made his point, Kenji was eager to move on. "The workers have voted to strike." After updating his wife on the strike vote, Kenji added, "We must prepare." As soon as he spoke the words, he caught himself. "Okasan, you were right all along. I have been too accommodating to the owners, too satisfied with my small victories, too confident—"

"No time for that," Haru interrupted. "Your actions now are what count." Then in a matter-of-fact tone, she reported, "Uno pledged to open his shrine to strikers."

∞ ∞

A welcoming committee stood up on Kenji and Haru's porch as the couple drove into the driveway. Three Filipinos leaped off the steps and ran toward Kenji as he stepped out of his car. The straw-hatted one talked fast. "We be with you! When we go report to work, we hear of the child's death. We angry, make strike talk. Our luna, he sit on horse and laugh. His belly shake. He say, 'No can strike, you Filipino, hilahila.' We drop our tools. We vote to strike."

"We appreciate the solidarity," said Kenji, not at all appreciative of the timing and worried as to what was coming next.

As if on cue, the face under the straw hat lost its wide-eyed enthusiasm. "We have no place to stay. We must leave our homes by noon tomorrow."

"We are working on campsites," said Kenji. "Come back after the funeral."

The Filipino mumbled a fractured "arigato." The three Filipinos retreated to a tree where they righted their bicycles and pedaled off.

Sam stepped out of the front door as if he had been lurking there. "Sachi and Kame have prepared a late breakfast. I learned in the army that you can't fight on an empty stomach."

The sound of frantic horn beeps turned everyone's attention back to the road. At the sight of Kurume speeding toward the house, Haru knew he was not delivering good news.

He wasn't. Kurume's car skidded to a stop, and he jumped out the truck and shouted, "Bilkerton kicked us out! Bilkerton kicked us out!"

"We have two days," said Kenji, his head shaking in denial.

"Bilkerton summoned me to the house an hour ago. On the porch with all his lunas holding rifles, he told me, 'I know you voted to strike. The deal is off. Get off my property by sunset.'"

Kenji puffed out his chest with a confidence he did not feel. "The funerals will be at five. Start bringing the men now. We need to start preparing the campsites."

"We'll be ready," said Sam. He was thinking of the best military officers in the war. No matter the situation, they always appeared to have it under control. "I'll start pegging camping plots. We'll get tents from Oda's. They've heard the strike rumors and have a stock." Sam stopped to let his lungs catch a breath. "Some paniolos will take families into their homes. A foreman told me that, if needed, he can lend us tents they use when camping with the cattle. Our cowboys will set them up at the park." Sam seemed unaware that he was talking as if he were still a Parker Ranch hand.

"I will visit the vicar," said Haru. "They have more than enough space for the few Filipino Protestants attending their services. Maybe they'll take in some Catholics too."

"But first, breakfast," said Sam, trying not to show exasperation in his voice.

Holding little Kenta, Sachi said, "The milk is finished," referring to the milk Haru had pumped from her breasts. Haru picked up Kenta while saying to no one in particular, "I am going to the bedroom." She strolled into the house, thinking as she did in such moments that what was abnormal about raising Kenta was the normality. The imagined marriage-destroying scenarios that had initially robbed her of sleep had ebbed like the tide after a raging storm. Ume thanked Haru for raising her baby on each of her three visits since the switch. Afterwards, Haru would stop by Irie's to update him on his wife's condition and check on his household. His matronly housekeeper, whom he hired after Ko left after only three months for California, was managing to keep up with the three children, barely. Irie was drinking, but less. His business survived, just. Each visit cut another limb off her guilty tree as she compared the home advantage Kenta had, relative to Irie's children. His other children.

After nursing Kenta, Haru joined the breakfast table. When the strike-planning meal ended, Haru said, "Kame, let's inspect our garden."

⬙ CHAPTER 80 ⬙

HARU STEPPED OUT THE BACK DOOR with Kenta riding in a sling on her back. Another strap hung over her left shoulder holding an open wicker basket. She surveyed rows of corn, carrots, radishes, lettuce, and tomato plants at the back, fronting the tree line. She frowned and turned to Kame walking behind her and carrying another basket. "Yesterday the mission grounds seemed so spacious and our garden so large. Now the space seems so small for all the displaced families and our garden too meager to feed so many."

Thunk. Thunk. Thunk.

Haru turned toward the sound. Breathing heavily, Sam was pounding a peg into the ground to start marking off eight-by-five grassy "housing plots," as he called them. Holding the mallet in his right hand, he called over, "Including the front yard, we have enough space for forty families. We can squeeze another ten into the hotel." He paused to catch his breath. "Bilkerton is as evil as any man I've known. His hands have the blood of a child and mother, and yet he evicts his families. And the law stands behind him because his workers strike over this outrage."

Thinking of Tamatsuke's early morning plea, Haru said, "We will let the sheriff chase the murderers. Our mission is to focus on what we can do—provide support for families so the workers won't crawl back to their jobs defeated. Justice means we win the strike, Sam." Looking at her basket brimming with ripe tomatoes a few minutes later, she knew she couldn't postpone her next mission any longer.

Haru walked to a house around the corner from the main road and one block over, close to the village park. She had thought of bringing fresh vegetables from her garden as an *omiyage*, but she would need every bit of food for the displaced families. Standing in front of the New England-inspired Presbyterian vicarage, Haru assured herself that as wives of ministers, she and Mrs. Adams shared the same commitment to helping people. She had passed the Adams home frequently but had never been invited inside, nor had she invited the Adamses to her home. She now regretted not taking a more active approach, but given Mrs. Adams's coolness at the occasional Wellington Carter dinner, she had feared the indignity of being rebuffed.

She knocked tentatively on the door. After a few moments, it opened to reveal a tall, thin woman. Haru took in her shabby, ankle-length gingham dress, the face devoid of makeup, and the dingy, brown hair drifting down to the shoulders. An expression of unwanted surprise crossed the woman's face.

"Why, Mrs. Taka-Taka—"

"Takayama, Mrs. Adams," said Haru, noting the woman had planted her feet as if guarding the entrance. Haru waited politely for the invitation to enter, which was not forthcoming. "Mrs. Adams, the cane workers are striking, and some of your parishioners will be without a home by the end of tomorrow. Our mission is setting up campsites, but we can't take in everyone. I hope your fellow Christians can stay here, on the church grounds."

A wave of contempt washed over the woman's face, turning its everyday pasty white to the color of uncooked trout. "I'm sorry," she said in a flinty voice devoid of remorse, "but we simply cannot be involved in labor disputes."

She gripped the doorknob as if she meant to close it. Haru took a step closer, rushed her words. "I heard your husband once say that Christ and Buddha share a compassion for the less fortunate. In this spirit, I am appealing that at least you give refuge to your parishioners. The union will help with expenses."

"Union!" said the woman, spitting out the word as if she had bitten into a red-hot pepper. "That's exactly the problem. Mrs. Taka—"

"Takayama-san," said a pleasant male voice behind her. "Please come in."

The vicar's wife shuddered. She snapped a look back at her husband, raised her chin rebelliously while lifting the hem of her skirt and stepping aside. As Haru entered, Mrs. Adams folded her arms across her shapeless chest.

Ignoring his wife's rudeness, Reverend Adams led Haru into the rectory and listened to her plea while his wife stood rigidly behind him.

"We have about twenty Japanese families in our parish."

Haru raised her eyebrows in surprise, winning a smile from Reverend Adams, who said, "We do have a few small victories."

"We must not get involved in this Bolshevik business," said Mrs. Adams with desperation tightening her vocal chords.

"Quite right," said the reverend. "And we won't." Then with a no-nonsense firmness to his voice, he added, "Neither will we turn away our homeless parishioners, Japanese or Filipino."

"Well, I never!" Mrs. Adams stomped her foot and stormed out.

Smiling forlornly, Reverend Adams said, "She'll come around."

Haru, at a loss for words, waited. Her silence was enough.

Adams rubbed his chin. "I suspect some of my plantation parishioners will be calling. My church grounds are theirs."

Haru's continued silence induced a further commitment.

"In fact, you can say that any Protestants are welcome."

Still Haru didn't reply.

"I don't think we have more room than that, but I won't be asking any Filipino if he is really a Protestant, either."

"You are right about Buddha and Christ."

It was Adams's turn to raise his eyebrows.

"I listened to your Fourth of July speech last year when you said, 'If they lived in the same neighborhood, they would have been the best of friends.'"

∽ CHAPTER 81 ∾

THE CONSTANT WINDS buffeting Mauna Kea had died down. Hushed murmurs washed over the lawn as hundreds of mourners, including many Filipinos, stood outside Waimea's Buddhist mission. Inside, another two hundred bereaved jammed pews and aisles. All eyes faced the open coffin front and center on the altar. From the altar's left window, a pillow-sized stream of the day's last sunrays shone brightly over Yumi lying on her mother's chest—both mummied in white cotton. Mayo's gauzed arms held her child one last time and forever after. No one asked why the shrouds violated custom by covering their faces.

Sweat trickling down her back, Haru sat in the front right pew next to the center aisle. Feeling fatigue for the first time today, she fought off the drowsiness by digging her nails into her palms. Sitting next to her, Mayo's surviving children looked bewildered in little black yukatas borrowed from friends. Without Haru's prompting, Auntie Sachi sitting on their other side had already told them, "You will stay with me until Daddy is better." Squeezing into the pew was Uno, whom Haru had personally escorted when told he had unexpectedly arrived.

On the pew opposite Haru, Dr. Tebbits, Wellington Carter, and Reverend Adams sat. Carter had called Tebbits and Adams. "We need to show Bilkerton does not represent us."

The soft buzz silenced as Kenji, dressed in full vestments similar to a Catholic priest, walked out of the vestibule to the center of the altar behind the raised coffin. Raising his arms, he led the congregation in Buddhist mantras for the deceased. Then dropping his arms, he paused. Listening to Taka practicing his recitation of the Gettysburg Address for his history class, Kenji had come to admire the speech for its simplicity and brevity. And given the stifling heat generated by the packed bodies, today was the right time to emulate its meaningful conciseness. In slow cadence, he began speaking in his loudest orator's voice.

"Tamatsuke asks that the death of Yumi and Mayo stand for something. We here can give their lives meaning. They died because the forces of evil wanted to frighten you."

The crowd murmured. Kenji felt their anger. He saw the worry on Carter's face. This was the defining moment.

"How will we honor Mayo and Yumi? By the burning of another home or a revenge killing?"

Kenji's eyes roamed the room while he slowly stepped around the coffin until he stood in front of it. Only a stifled cough violated the silence.

"We are about to engage in a great struggle for dignity and fairness. We shall prevail in our righteous cause because we will remain steadfast. If we grow weary … as the planters are counting on … we must think of the price Yumi paid, the price Mayo paid. While we have little and our neighbors have less … we will share. When the crowded conditions anger us … we will think of Yumi and Mayo … and know … their sacrifice … far exceeds our own discomfort. Let us bow our heads and think about how we will make Mayo and Yumi's lives stand for something."

Heads tilted in respect.

Kenji nodded to the pallbearers. They walked to the altar, raised the coffin to their shoulders, and walked down the crowded aisle. Behind them, Haru and her children followed. At the door, Mrs. Oda handed Haru a lit candle. On cue, outside mourners, who had already been given a candle, each lit their own. The flickering procession followed the pallbearers to the line of cherry trees Haru had planted a decade earlier.

The pallbearers eased the coffin into the prepared grave next to Ualani's headstone. As the candles sputtered, Kenji led the mourners in a soft Buddhist chant. In times past, the crowd would have dispersed at this point. But these were mourners who were also suddenly homeless.

"File into the mission school," said Kenji. "You will find your housing assignment." Looking at Reverend Adams, Kenji continued. "The Protestant Filipinos can camp at the vicarage. The remaining Filipinos have the park."

Quietly, a member of each family formed a slow-moving line into the mission. Sam directed the mission's assignments of families to their plots. Paniolos made arrangements with families Sam had designated for Parker Ranch homestays. Kurume helped families assigned to Uno's shrine grounds find buckboards to take personal belongings there. The normally exuberant Filipinos began walking quietly to the Presbyterian church or to the town's park.

Watching in amazement as families quietly went about the business of resettlement, Adams asked Carter, "Where is the chaos?"

∽ ∾

Haru addressed the women standing only feet from Mayo's grave. "Tomorrow we will start planting new rows of carrots, cabbage, and daikon along the tree line at the back of the yard, around the edges of the building, and in any space we can find. Kame will need teenage helpers to cook community rice *twice* a day." She emphasized the word "twice" to indicate that the time to limit meals to two a day needed to start now.

Kurume marched a half-dozen men to the back of the property to dig latrines. Cooking fires sprouted. Toddlers ran around like revelers at the beginning of a festival. Older children helped set up tents. Dogs adjusted to their new homes by holding territorial barking and snarling contests.

Sam hammered a nail into the largest tree fronting the ofuro and then hung a child's chalkboard over it after writing, "Ofuro sign-up—10 minutes per family."

"Only ten minutes?" asked a shocked passerby.

"In France," answered Sam, "we had three minutes to shower. Counting the families, we may have to cut the time. But you have given me an idea. We need a timer with an alarm. I'll see what Haru-san has in the kitchen."

"I'm scared."

Haru turned around. She didn't know the woman standing there but recognized the fear in her eyes. One child was strapped to her back; two more clung to her yukata. Their close ages told a story of a man who couldn't control his urges and a woman who submitted without regard for her health.

"Good," said Haru, boring into the woman's eyes. "I'm scared too. I'm scared people will not start a garden right away. I'm scared families will fight over whose turn it is to use the ofuro. I'm scared mothers will not take extra care using clean water to drink and bathe their children. I need your help." Haru pointed to a woman standing next to the water pump. "Yamahara-san is organizing women to fill water buckets. Can you help her?"

As the woman drifted over to Yamahara, Haru felt inspired. She could stay up another hour. People were scared and confused and needed reassurance. She approached two men watching their wives cook. "Can you go over behind the tree line? You'll find men digging latrines. I am sure they would appreciate a break." In a society where men ruled, these men didn't hesitate and hurried away.

Ten yards further down the new housing alley, Haru approached three men who greeted her, "We are going to show that Bilkerton."

"That's the spirit. Right now we need more poles for the tents." Pointing once again, Haru said, "Go to the shed. You will find saws and axes."

When she spotted a woman who made tofu on the Bilkerton plantation, Haru asked, "Were you able to save anything from your factory that exploded?"

"I kept some of the soybeans and utensils in my house, Mayor-san," the woman answered.

"Good," said Haru, smiling at the moniker. "We'll set up a soy-processing station near the water pump. Tell me what you need, and I'll send someone to Oda's to get it."

And on it went until everyone was busy. Satisfied, Haru slipped into the back door. She would take a brief nap. In her exhaustion, the squatter village's newly designated mayor didn't hear the hammering or Sam's new round of orders.

∽ Chapter 82 ∽

WHILE HARU WAS GIVING ORDERS in the fresh air of Waimea, Noboru Tsutsumi was conducting a strike committee meeting in the union's smoke-clouded upstairs office on Bishop Street, a few doors down from the Makino pharmacy. Ties and shirt collars had been loosened. Half-moon sweat stains marked their shirts' underarms. All day, facts, rumors, and proposals had been bantered back and forth. Tempers rose and fell like the tide. Sipping his coffee laced with three spoonfuls of raw sugar, Tsutsumi eyed his weary organizers.

"Everything that could be said with the facts at hand has been said. It's time to make decisions that are best for us, not play into the owners' hands. While they hope we won't call a strike, they are counting on us being unprepared so they can crush us like the last time." *When I wasn't here to lead you*, he thought. "You heard me phone Takayama-sensei. The death of the mother and child did two things." He paused. "It forced an immediate strike there … " he paused again, longer, "and it shows what happens when you strike before you are ready. The situation in Waimea is in chaos," he said, outlining the problems with shelter, food, and sanitation.

Pablo Manlapit wagged his impatient head but let Tsutsumi finish his menu of obstacles. Then, Manlapit thumped the table with his fist and stood up. "Talk, talk, talk. Do this. Do that. Always planning, planning, but no action. You would all make good lawyers." The self-deprecating remark garnered a few grudging chuckles. "The lunas have stepped up the abuse of my people. Their whips and taunts have resulted in wildcat strikes in half of the Filipino plantations. A Japanese child and mother have been murdered. What does it take for you people to stand up?"

No chuckles now.

Two burly Japanese union leaders jumped up. The younger deferred to the older. "We have been standing up against them for years, and in the last year we've been preparing. We have a strike fund. You are here only to beg because YOU people don't have the words 'planning ahead' in Tagalog."

At the head of the table, Tsutsumi sensed that despite these rash words, the weary men were ready for a compromise between the "strike now" hawks and the "don't rush" doves. He looked down at the third draft penned in his neat calligraphy. Satisfied, he clinked a spoon against his cup. "This is what I propose." The firmness in his voice stifled further bickering. He looked at the men. "The death of the child is a tragedy we must not waste. However, if we walk off all the plantations now, we miss the opportunity to focus on fair wages."

Tsutsumi let the groans die as the radical wing anticipated the opportunity to strike would be lost. "My newspaper room is waiting for our statement to make ... " he glanced down at his watch; midnight had passed, "today's edition. I think we should publish the following statement."

> We are laborers working on the sugar plantations of Hawaii. People know Hawaii as the Paradise of the Pacific and as a sugar-producing country, but they do not know that there are thousands of laborers who are suffering under the heat of the equatorial sun in field and in factory, and who are weeping with ten hours of hard labor and with a scant pay of 77 cents a day.
>
> The wages of common man laborers shall be increased to $1.25 a day and for woman laborers shall be fixed at 95 cents per day.

Tsutsumi read more specific grievances and redresses to fill up the front page of his newspaper in bold print. He did not use the word "strike" as the consequence of the federation's demands not being met. He did not have to.

"What's the deadline for the owners' response?" demanded Manlapit.

If he set the deadline, then Tsutsumi not only owned it but also would give credence to the bitching that he was a dictator. He looked at his Japanese organizers. "How long will it take you to organize shelter? How much time do we need to solicit more funds once this is published?"

He let his leaders jawbone. He noticed Manlapit wisely kept his mouth shut. He would be getting a cut without raising very much, if any, money himself. He *was* a beggar.

"Five days," said the shorter burly man.

"Then that's the deadline we give the owners."

The weary union leaders voted unanimously to release the statement. Tsutsumi opened the bottom drawer of his desk and extracted a bottle of whiskey. "I think we can relax the no-drinking rule—just this once."

⟳ Chapter 83 ⟳

Four days later, while the inhabitants of Takayama-*shi* (Takayama-city)—as the strikers called their camp—settled into a routine, Dr. Tebbits was inspecting Tamatsuke's second-degree burns covering most of his back and calves. "Still no infection, Mr. Fujimoto. You are healing nicely. You must resist the urge to scratch, no matter what."

"Arigato, sensei. I am indebted to you and your wife."

Nurse Tebbits, standing next to her husband, nodded. "I'm going to change your facial bandages." She hesitated.

Dr. Tebbits cleared his throat. "You've asked to see the damage to your face several times. It won't be pretty. But you want to think how it could look later with proper surgery."

He looked at his wife. She withdrew a postcard-sized mirror from her pocket. She handed it to Tamatsuke. "Hold still while I remove your bandages." Minutes later, she stepped back.

Tamatsuke lifted the mirror and recoiled in horror.

"Over the next weeks, scar tissue will form," said Mrs. Tebbits. She looked over to her husband who said, "There are doctors who can give your face a more normal appearance. But not here. Not in Hawaii. But I do have some good news."

On cue, at the sound of the words "good news," a contrite-looking Bilkerton walked in accompanied by Andy Pafko, who carried a notepad and wore a black fedora ringed with a white band reading "*The Advertiser.*"

"Fujimoto-san," said Bilkerton, using the honorific for the benefit of his appeal. He checked to see if Pafko, who had talked him into this approach, had pencil and notepad ready. "I'm here to apologize for what my renegade overseer did. Labor problems are no excuse for criminal acts. I have put up a thousand dollar reward for the capture of MacFarlane." Both Bilkerton and Pafko knew that MacFarlane had been seen boarding a Matson cargo ship for the Far East two days earlier.

"Let your workers go back to their homes," growled Tamatsuke.

A shadow hovered outside the door.

Bilkerton sucked in a deep breath. "I am paying all your medical bills. And you will also receive a thousand dollars for the loss you have incurred." Bilkerton turned to the doctor and gave a little nod.

"Mr. Bilkerton has agreed to send you to San Francisco to a special hospital that's done wonders for soldiers who were burned in the Great War. They can take skin from your legs to make your face look almost … " he hesitated, "to look closer to how it was before the accident."

Bilkerton reached into the inner pocket of his suit jacket and took out an envelope while a Japanese man dressed in a suit, white shirt, and a skinny black tie slipped into the room quietly. He too carried a notepad but held it discreetly at his side. A look of alarm clouded Pafko's face, but he said nothing. Bilkerton, fumbling with the envelope, did not notice the intruder behind him.

Fujimoto used his elbows to lift up his torso, his eyes squinching in pain. His raspy voice spat out unyielding words. "Look at my face, Mr. Bilkerton. What do you see? It tells the story of hate and the abuse of power. I earned this face. I will wear this face as a testimony to what happens when evil is let out of the jar. I don't want anyone to ever forget what happened. It is, as you Christians say, 'the mark of Cain.'"

Pafko put down his pencil. "Why you ungrateful—"

Bilkerton grabbed the man's arm and ushered him out of the room before he made matters worse.

The Japanese man had already hurried down the hall and out into the street, where he took a quick right and ran to the Western Union office. He had eleven minutes to file his story for this evening's edition of the *Nippon Shimbun*.

⚭ CHAPTER 84 ⚭

Edward Spalding, president of Honolulu's prestigious Pacific Club, examined his Havana cigar. He wrinkled his nose and spoke to no one in particular. "Why can't someone invent a proper cigar box, one that keeps them moist?" He cut the end and dipped it into his Armagnac. The club's senior butler, a snowy-haired Azorean, padded to Spalding's side, struck a long match, and held it steady until the cigar's tip glowed uniformly red.

The sugarcane barons were sitting in high-backed, ruby-hued, felt-upholstered chairs loosely clustered around a pair of coffee tables in the men-only smoking room. They began their own cigar-smoking rituals as if they were preparing a choreographed sacramental offering.

Staid portraits of past presidents, dating from the club's founding in 1852 when it was called the "British Club," which reflected their business dominance at that time, hung along dimly lit baroque walls. Outside the windows, where vineyards once flourished, gas-lit torches glowed underneath palm tree fronds snapping in the wind. None of the trade winds ripping up from the harbor filtered into the enclosed room, which suited the men well, for they enjoyed air rich with cigar perfume, the fragrance of power.

Except for their spokesman, the lanky John Waterhouse, the men thought of their Teddy Roosevelt girth as evidence of their success. Bilkerton, the only nervous man in the circle, dipped his cigar in his brandy without first cutting off the tip. He missed the disdain in the eyes of the other men as he said abruptly, "I believe, Eddie, you were present in this club when the decision was made to overthrow the queen."

"It's Edward, if you don't mind, Joshua." Spalding drew on his cigar and let the smoke out slowly. "Overthrow? Really, now. The queen stepped aside, realizing the time for the monarchy had passed. A wise and highly respected woman. But, yes, I was present. And, as a new member, I listened." Spalding paused to sip his Armagnac without taking his eyes off Bilkerton. His tobacco-tarred voice added, "It would be good … if you did the same."

John Waterhouse tamped his pipe in an ashtray fashioned from a conch shell and struck a match to light his pipe. Satisfied with the glow, he tilted the stem of the pipe toward Spalding. "If I may?"

Smiling indulgently, Spalding swept his left hand in the "go ahead, be my guest" gesture.

Bilkerton gulped down half his brandy even while sensing this wasn't the proper way. He felt at a loss, unable to discern the meaning of the ritual playing out here. Yet, at last, he had been invited to the club. A long overdue invite. No doubt, his strong handling of the wildcat strike had earned these men's respect. He had acted decisively, firmly. He'd hired fishermen and renegade Filipino strikebreakers to cut cane at two dollars a day. He'd showed those Japs he could get along without them. It was about time these men recognized his contribution.

"We don't want any more sideshows in Waimea," said Waterhouse, his voice low and his gaze on Bilkerton unforgiving. "The killing of the child and mother has been a distraction, Joshua." He picked up the February 2, 1920, tear sheet from the *Pacific Commercial Advertiser*, its page still damp with fresh ink. "This is an advance copy of tomorrow's front page. Read it out loud, please." He held out the sheet.

Bilkerton felt the blood rush up his neck while thinking, *This isn't right. I have stood up for you.* He leaned over to take the sheet. He didn't clasp his finger and thumb fast enough and the page fluttered to the floor. "Your brandy's too good," he apologized with a sheepish smile while bending to pick it up. He extracted a pair of reading glasses from his outside coat pocket. Bringing the sheet into focus, he read barely loud enough to be heard. "'What is Hawaii going to do about the strike? What is the government of the US going to do? Is Hawaii ruled by Tokyo? The strike is not over wages, but who controls Hawaii.'"

Before he could continue, Spalding interrupted. "Thank you." He picked up another tear sheet.

Bilkerton's sphincter tightened. His mind flashed back to school where he hated sitting in the front of the class because his name started with a B.

"I will read this one," said Waterhouse, holding the front page of the *Honolulu Star-Bulletin*. Waterhouse's voice rose in pitch to that of a lawyer addressing a jury on final summation. "'Priests of Asiatic paganism, foreign language teachers, and Japanese editors control laborers to become masters of Hawaii's destiny.'" Spalding cleared his throat. "Do you understand the strategy, Joshua?"

"There's a helluva lot more at stake than wages," he said decisively.

Spalding slammed his glass on the table. "It's *only* about wages."

Bilkerton's mouth opened like a fish reaching for a baited hook.

Westinghouse lifted his index finger, quieting Bilkerton before he uttered a word. He spoke like a teacher in front of a pupil having trouble understanding a simple math equation. "If we fight the union demands on their terms—wages and benefits—we place ourselves in a tug of war that could go either way. So this strike must be sold on our terms. Who controls the destiny of these islands? White, Christian, real Americans? Or bronze Buddhists who bow every morning to their heathen leader thousands of miles away?"

"Of course," said Bilkerton, embarrassed by his precipitous reply.

"So we fight the troublemakers on the issue of sovereignty. We cannot recognize a union controlled by foreign agitators." He smiled smugly. "Now, can we?"

"I understand," said Bilkerton, almost pleading him to stop the lesson.

Spalding spoke over the groans of his fellow barons perched like bishops at an inquisition. "You idiot! You understand nothing. The day before your nightriders stirred up the do-gooders, we had the newspapers report that America demanded Japan withdraw from Siberia, proving the Japanese can never be trusted. We reminded the readers of how those damned Jap language schools are part of the emperor's design to use his overseas workers as a stalking horse to absorb Hawaii into the Japanese empire. We printed evidence of one group of plantation workers sending a million dollars in remittances to Japan. They cry about low wages while sending money to the emperor!"

Spalding stood up. "So just as we started our campaign to cripple these Bolsheviks, what happens?" Spalding swirled his arms over his head in frustration. "A front-page story about a mother and children burned to death in a Ku Klux Klan-type night raid." He let his eyes rove over all the owners.

In a steely calm voice, Westinghouse accused, "Japanese businessmen, who were sitting this out, are throwing money at Tsutsumi."

"What do you want me to do?"

"Nothing!" rasped a voice from one of the Big Five.

"Nothing," repeated Waterhouse. "Do not negotiate. Do not hire any more strikebreakers. Do not talk to reporters. Nothing."

Sweat trickled down Bilkerton's face.

Spalding's voice intoned, "I believe we can have our strike-strategy meeting now, John."

The men waited.

It took Bilkerton a half-minute to realize he'd been dismissed. He rose and walked out of the room determined to step steadily despite the alcohol and humiliation. He thought of that priest and his wife. All these years, that Takayama fellow had pretended to help calm the workers. *All the time setting me up. He will pay for this day.*

∞ CHAPTER 85 ∞

MAYOR HARU, attired in a freshly laundered, blue-checkered yukata, greeted fellow early risers as sheepish men, women, and children made their way to latrines dug along the tree line in the back of the Takayama compound. She kept her practiced eye alert for any discarded trash along what had been a grassy corridor but was now a worn dirt path.

She waved at the polite lines of people formed at the ofuro. Her own bath was finished an hour before sunrise. She and Kenji kept to the ten-minute usage limit, although her "citizens" insisted she should not have to sign up or stand in line. "Your time is too important." Rather than argue with their kindness, she adopted the rising early routine.

The "we will show those greedy plantation owners how tough we are" euphoric bravado of January's walkout had given way to the long restless days of late February, as strikers now spoke of *gaman*—the Japanese philosophy of bearing the unbearable without complaint. Haru's "city" of four hundred persevered in a routine of forbearance.

Women worked the water pump, allowing each family a gallon per person for drinking and washing dishes. Pans were placed outside tents to collect rainwater.

At Wellington Carter's behind-the-scenes insistence, Waimea's public schools went into double shifts: the morning for students who normally attended and the afternoon for plantation children who no longer had access to the public grammar schools on the plantation. Kenji taught his Japanese school curriculum before lunch. Haru used the mission school to conduct adult English classes after lunch was served to the children. Adults skipped lunch.

The Parker Ranch cowboys planted vegetable gardens. Wellington Carter allowed that one cow per week could "go missing."

Men did what idle men have done for millennia. They gambled. Haru realized she could not put human nature on hold, but she did insist on no gambling in her "city."

The worker 2436 was the first scab to sneak off for a two-dollar-a-day wage to break the strike. Kurume, suspecting 2436 was Bilkerton's source for the secret strike vote, had fed the spy embellished stories of fund-raising. Bilkerton had a tougher time raising a scab workforce than the Honolulu plantations since the smaller local communities lacked the city's urban anonymity. The bamboo telegraph informed Tamatsuke that Bilkerton's planting was down more than 70 percent and the arduous task of weeding was haphazard at best.

∽ ∾

The following morning, Reverend Adams left his church grounds, home to a chaotic group of forty striking families, mostly Filipinos with a smattering of Japanese Christians, to stroll over to the Takayama compound. Although he was losing the battle to have latrines cleaned daily and garbage picked up, he felt certain some of the pungent smells he endured must be the result of trade winds pushing the stench from the much larger Takayama squatters' camp, only a quarter mile away, into his vicarage.

He was surprised that the foul odors decreased the further he walked. As the Takayama camp came into view, he found it difficult to believe his eyes: litter-free pathways, clean-shaven men weeding vegetable sprouts, teenage boys incinerating garbage in fifty-five-gallon drum barrels opposite Haru's house, and at the back of the compound, well-scrubbed children sat together under trees engaged in lessons. Under bright sunshine, women sat cross-legged mending clothes while others were bent over buckets washing dishes, and one skinny lady was sweeping out her tent. Then, it struck him. What didn't he see? Idleness.

As the reverend set foot on the driveway, Haru ran out to greet him. "Reverend Adams! Welcome," she said with a warm smile. "We are so grateful your church took in the Christian families." She turned and swept open her arms to encompass her little village. "I can't imagine where we could have put anyone else."

"What amazing organization you have here. How do you do it?"

"Remember, we're the crazy culture that takes our shoes off before entering a house and makes our husbands bathe twice a day," said Haru with an even broader smile.

Adams nodded his head. "I suspect Kenji's leadership had something to do with this orderly camp," said Adams. "Is Takayama-sensei available?"

Haru escorted Adams up the porch steps and into her home where Kenji greeted the reverend. He nodded his head to Haru, who left the two men to converse in private. A good hour went by before Adams took his leave. As he left the house, he spied Haru walking out of the schoolhouse.

"Madame Mayor," shouted Adams. Catching up to her, he said with an apologetic smile, "Your husband has told me of your gifted organizational skills. If it is not too much trouble, would you show me around your camp? I have much to learn."

"Of course, Reverend. But, I must say that most of the camp's discipline comes from the … plantation leaders," said Haru, thinking this euphemism had a more friendly sound than "strike leaders."

After Adams left, Haru wondered if the strike, which had divided so many, might bring Waimea's Christians, Buddhists, and Shintoists into a social harmony that survived the strike.

⚬ CHAPTER 86 ⚬

WHILE HARU AND ADAMS WERE INSPECTING HER CAMP, Sam stood in Wellington Carter's mahogany-paneled office. Photographs of his paniolos winning rodeo contests lined the walls. The giant photo behind Carter's desk showed Ikua Purdy, Eben "Rawhide Ben" Low, and Archie Kaaua sitting on their steeds in Cheyenne, Wyoming, with a roaring crowd acknowledging their victory in the 1908 World Rodeo Competition. The dimly lit room, courtesy of small windows catching only patches of the streaming sun, stank of stale cigar smoke. Sam held his shoulders back but could not hold his eyes steady on the big man. "I don't think I have ever asked you for a favor, Mr. Carter. And if this were just about me, I would not be here."

"Must be mighty important, Sam. You're not the complaining type." A sly smile crinkled his eyes. "I saw Kame yesterday. Am I right in thinking that her belly has swollen?"

Sam grinned, stood a little taller. "Yes, sir. We are hoping for an April birth." He paused, his face returned to its sober expression. "The American Legion told me we couldn't march tomorrow in the Washington Day parade." He balled his fists. "They say we are not Americans, not loyal to the American flag."

"It's this strike, Sam—a nasty business, bringing out the worst in people on both sides." He ran a hand through his blond hair streaked with grey and then narrowed his eyes. "Sam, tell your boys to clean their boots. They will be marching."

∽ ∾

An hour later, the legion commander and school superintendent, William Cox, sat across from Wellington. Streaking rays had warmed the office by midmorning, but the mood was anything but sunny. "What's with the urgent summons, Wellington?"

The stress in your voice tells me you know exactly why you are here, thought Carter. "What's this I hear about your not letting the Japanese brigade march in the parade, William?"

"Not real Americans, Wellington. Hell, you know that. They do okay as cowboys, but they worship a false god, bow to the emperor—"

Carter raised his hand to form a stop sign. "Seems you didn't mind signing them up when we declared war on the Kaiser." Carter kept his voice smooth and low as always.

"A mistake I regret. Got caught up with the urgency of the war mobilization."

"The parade is America honoring all those who wore the uniform, William."

Cox stiffened his back and fixed Wellington with an uncompromising stare. "I know where you're going with this, Wellington. If I had all those Japanese cowboys working for me, I might say the same thing. But half that brigade is cane workers. *My* men won't march with Jap strikers. With all due respect, there's nothing you can say that will change my mind."

"Those Japanese boys are no less worthy than any man who wore our khaki." Carter paused to let his next words sink in. "The school board rents their classroom buildings from me for a dollar a year. Effective next month, the rent is five hundred dollars. Payable in advance." Carter sat back in his chair, stone-eyed cold.

Cox sat up straight. His frown lines deepened. "Blackmail, that's what this is!"

"It is. So either you tell the rest of your school board your refusal to allow American veterans to march has cost them five hundred dollars a month they don't have, or you contact Sergeant Akiyama and tell him you've had a change of heart." He looked at the wall clock. "I expect to hear from the sergeant by lunch."

"I won't forget this, Wellington."

"Maybe not, William. But you will get over it. You are a good American. Just wrong on this issue. Tell your men how Akiyama was poisoned by German gas and earned the right to march."

Cox dropped his angry demeanor. This was Wellington Carter. Misplaced softness on Japs, but Waimea's most powerful person. "I'll appeal to the men's patriotism." He walked out with as much dignity as he could feign.

∞ ∞

The following morning, dressed in his sergeant's olive-drab wool uniform, Sam stood erect, reviewing his twenty-seven fellow marchers. For the umpteenth time that morning, Sam slipped the half-size ofuro towel from his pocket and buffed the new specks of dust off the toes of his knee-high boots.

Waimea's only fire truck struck up its engine, tested its siren, and pulled out of the park and into the parade behind a troop of marching Boy Scouts.

"All right, men, we're next," Sam bellowed in his sergeant's voice.

"You mean last," said a vet, adjusting a strap on his backpack.

"Like Santa Claus," laughed Sam, understanding the frustration wrapped in the complaint but refusing to let it take hold. "And we've got the biggest flag," he pointed out, referring to Carter's loan of the six-foot-high American flag that normally fronted the Parker Ranch shopping complex.

The sound of galloping hoofs turned the men around. More than a hundred paniolos, fancied up in colorful shirts, wide-brimmed leather hats, buffed chaps, two-toned engraved boots, and gleaming spurs, reined in their horses. "Sorry we're late," shouted a big Hawaiian holding an American flag—large, but not as large as Sam's. "Being we have horses, I suspect it's better marching last and not first," he laughed. Sam broke out in goose bumps as he noticed that a third of the riders were haoles. Paniolos took care of their own, regardless of the slant of their eyes or the hue of their skin.

Sam faced his men. "Right shoulder arms!" The men lifted their rifles from the parade rest position and placed them on their shoulders. Sam pivoted 180 degrees. "Forwarrrrrrd … march!"

The cheers from the Hawaiians, Puerto Ricans, Filipinos, Portuguese, and Japanese lining the sidewalks carried up the street where temporary VIP bleachers had been built for the town's leaders—mostly Caucasian but including a token smattering of Hawaiians and Japanese, including Haru and Kenji.

Haru watched in dismay as several haoles began drifting off when the Japanese vets started to pass. Directly in the row above her, beer-drinking haole onlookers made no attempt to keep their voices down. "The school board wanted those slant-eyed brats to attend our school to assimilate, learn real English. And what happens? My kids come home speaking that pidgin-shit garble."

A second voice added, "And we have to close the schools on the emperor's birthday because the heathen half of the school is a no-show."

"We all know they plan to take over Hawaii."

At that remark, a nearby Hawaiian raised his eyebrows and baritoned, "Imagine that—an alien race taking over Hawaii."

"Let's get out of here," said the first haole. "I don't need to see these make-believe soldiers." The two men clunked down the bleachers, rudely bumping Haru as they did so. They made no apology, but Haru had no time to dwell on the insult. Below, Sam's sergeant voice filled the air.

"Turn right, halt!" The unit turned as one on Sam's command.

"Present arms!" The men lowered their rifles and held them out in military respect.

"Begin drill!" This was a Sam order not found in the sergeant's drill manual. The men moved their rifles in unison in eight precision movements, slapping their rifle stocks at each fast-moving change. They ended at parade rest.

More whites strolled away.

At that moment, Sam's unit began singing "The Star Spangled Banner."

The departing whites looked confused. Some stopped. By the time the chorus got to "the twilight's last gleaming," all stood still.

"And the home of the brave."

To the background of applause and shouts, Sam shouted in sequential cadence.

"Right turn! Shoulder arms! Forward march!"

That's when Bobby Zucker and Johnny Pender, not quite teenagers whose fathers were deacons in Adams's church, leaped from behind an ice cream stand and threw tomatoes at the Japanese soldiers. A spoiled tomato hit Sam on the neck. Red juice slithered down into his collar. He never flinched. Half the haoles applauded the young boy's bravado.

Not Reverend Adams. He turned to Kenji. "This strike ... " He shook his head dolefully. "It's ripping apart the fabric of our community, Takayama-san."

"Yes, it is, but what recourse do the workers have?"

"Perhaps none, but maybe you and I do."

∞ Chapter 87 ∞

SUNNY SKIES AND THE LAUGHTER OF CHILDREN gave a lift to Haru rinsing lettuce leaves along with two other wives sitting on upturned buckets at the water pump until a breathless Sachi came running toward her. Splattered red splotches hopscotched across the front of her pale-green yukata. "Setsu Kurume is puking blood!"

Haru stared at the blood spots. She grimaced. She hoped it wasn't what she thought it was—the Spanish flu. "Change into a fresh yukata after you go to the ofuro. Then, boil the one you are wearing." Haru looked at the two distressed wives. "I'm off to see Setsu." On her second hurried step, she stopped abruptly. "Someone ask Sam to join me."

By now, Haru knew the name of each family and where each was located. While most refugees slept in tents, the Kurume family was one of eight lucky families crammed inside the temple's school annex. Not so lucky now—for them or the other seven families.

After retrieving the medical kit Dr. Tebbits had given her, Haru dashed to the school annex while recalling the doctor's admonishment when the pandemic returned to Honolulu shortly after the strike began. "If the flu attacks," he said with the resignation of one who expected it would, "set up an isolation area immediately."

"When I got sick the year the war ended, the disease left quickly," said Haru.

"I remember," said Tebbits. "It didn't seem so at the time, but you and Kenji were fortunate. Your attack was mild."

"Immunity," said Haru, letting Tebbits know she remembered an earlier talk. "Why has it come back?"

"The strike restarted the killing—just as the *Advertiser* predicted," Tebbits said, referring to a December front-page editorial demanding that owners and unions put the health of the community above their selfish interests. "The disease had pretty much run its course. But now all these strikers jammed together … " He let the thought hang.

Haru parted the hanging bedsheet entrance of the Kurume space. Ignoring the stench, she knelt beside Setsu who managed a mute smile. The dripping mucus from her nostrils, along with the damp red stains around her ear canals and the bluish tint to her face, told Haru that Setsu would most likely be the camp's first death. By instinct, Haru put her hand on Setsu's forehead, felt the dry heat, and then reached into her first aid bag for a thermometer. While she waited the required five minutes for Setsu's body temperature to register, she sponged the woman's face with a damp cloth.

When Sam arrived a few minutes later, he took one look and shook his head.

"Sam, you know what must be done."

"I will have the building cleared in an hour," said Sam. "This will be our hospital."

The nearest neighbor, overhearing the exchange, started to protest.

Sam pivoted, anger rising in his voice. "Even if you move now, it may be too late for some of you. I have seen this before. I survived my attack. Many of my comrades didn't."

The neighbor drew back as if Sam had pushed him.

Raising his voice so everyone could hear, Sam ordered, "Start packing. I will arrange for tents in the clearing behind the tree line. You will have to stay isolated for three days. We will bring food and build your own latrine."

He stepped back inside the Kurumes' draped enclosure as Haru pulled the thermometer from Setsu's mouth. She held it up to the window light. "One hundred four point eight," she said in a tone just above a whisper. Haru felt a tug on her apron and looked down to find a young boy dressed in trousers that slopped over his heels.

"Is Mommy going to die?"

Haru squatted and hugged the boy. "Can you go to the stream with a towel, soak it in the cool water, and bring it to your mommy to keep her head cool?"

The boy nodded, picked up a towel, and dashed off.

She looked at the forlorn face of Setsu's husband who had just entered.

The next evening Setsu was buried; three days later her husband followed her to the grave. Then the oldest child. A family from Setsu's village took in the surviving children, now immune.

◦ CHAPTER 88 ◦

ON THE THIRD FRIDAY OF APRIL, the strike was entering its third month. Haru's camp started each day with morning exercises to the rousing slogans of "no fair pay; no work" and "we will never give up," even as their stomachs and crying children gnawed at their resolve. Deep-pocketed owners hired scabs from California and Manila to bring sugar production to 60 percent of the pre-strike level.

At midmorning, Haru introduced a newcomer to a garden detail. "This is Abe-san. He's had a little trouble with the Honolulu police."

Not exactly inaccurate, thought the man in a tattered shirt. *The police are certainly looking for an excuse to arrest me.*

Knowing that the last thing anyone wanted was another mouth to feed, Haru added, "Abe-san has brought two fifty-pound bags of rice with him."

The scruffily dressed man wore thick-rimmed spectacles. No one noticed that the eyeglasses were clear, lacking in magnification. The rim of his tattered bowler was tilted onto his eyebrows. His four-day beard set him apart from the clean-shaven campsite squatters. No one made the connection between this beaten-down laborer and the big event scheduled for that evening. He picked up an idle hoe and began loosening the earth around tomato plants. While his defiant face had appeared frequently in the Japanese press, his photos always showed him dressed in a black suit, white shirt, and narrow black tie. The man loved his Shakespeare, particularly *Henry V.* Hoeing with the strikers, he imagined himself on the eve of the Battle of Agincourt, traipsing around his camp in a tradesman's foul attire to listen to the temper of his soldiers. He glanced at his sweat-stained, leather-band watch. "I'm hungry. When do we get lunch?"

"Are you fat guys from Honolulu still getting three meals a day?" a worker laughed in an accusative voice.

A squat man, weeding among the tomatoes, said, "My children are missing their school and sweet cakes."

"No school in this camp?" the man asked, knowing that when the pandemic struck, the school board forbade children of strikers to attend school.

"That's our school," said the squat man in a derisive tone while pointing to where kids formed little circles around the fruit trees.

A man scooping weeds into a wheelbarrow stood up. "At least you have your children." No one asked what he meant. The Spanish flu had killed eighteen camp squatters, mostly younger adults, but a few children as well. He eyed the newcomer. "We were told our fat-cat business people would support us. But we have a morsel of meat only once every two days, while our big-shot union leaders eat and drink at Honolulu's best restaurants with money meant for our stomachs."

The newcomer gripped his hoe's handle hard. He regretted the time the steering committee had eaten at Honolulu's best sushi restaurant. Someone had alerted the *Advertiser.* Pafko and a photographer had rushed to the Chiba-ken. The picture of a cigar-smoking Tsutsumi with his tie askew and bottle of whiskey in front of him made the front page. It was the only time the union committee dined well, thought Tsutsumi, but once was one time too many.

Tsutsumi moved from group to group the rest of the afternoon.

"I remember 1909. We had big dreams then. What happened? We crawled back to work, broke after winning a few minor concessions to give our union leaders face."

"How long can we hold out?"

"Ichiro Matsui left in the middle of the night yesterday. He told his younger brother he would be getting three dollars a day working in Hilo. They had a fight. His brother stayed, but I wonder if the older Matsui isn't the smart one."

Tsutsumi moseyed over to Haru's kitchen door that was shooting out heat. Inside, Haru was scooping out the last of the floured vegetables from a boiling tempura vat. "I've heard enough," said Tsutsumi brusquely. "I know what to say tonight. Can you pick me up at the Tebbits clinic in two hours?" After he explained why he needed a ride, he shuffled down the street. Once out of sight, he dropped his stumblebum character and strode with purpose.

Standing at her living room window, Haru studied Tsutsumi until he disappeared. Something about the man nagged at her. While she admired his organizational skills, she regretted that the face of the cane workers union never swung a machete, was an outsider who had arrived in the islands just three years ago. Was he a man who saw the plight of the workers and was moved to help them, or did he see a chance to make a name for himself? He had arrived as a low-paid schoolteacher and was now the owner of a thriving newspaper and the paid leader of the union. She thought of the great-grandparents of the rapacious sugar barons who had come to Hawaii in gingham broadcloth to introduce the word of their God and ended up owning the island while decimating the Hawaiian population.

Taiko drummers marching up her porch steps broke her thought. She waved when they spotted her through the window. Haru watched them set down their waist-high drums, assume their feet-apart stance, and begin their ritual. The slow cadence reminded Haru of distant drumbeats from so long ago—drumbeats from the Hiroshima harbor that could even be heard at the Takayama temple up on the hill. Their slow, steady, military tempo had signaled an arriving or departing warship.

She'd better visit the ofuro and change into a clean kimono.

∞ CHAPTER 89 ∞

BY DUSK, Haru gazed in amazement at the size of the crowd. She estimated more than two thousand people—strikers, family members, Japanese paniolos, and supporters—were jammed into the dead-end street facing the Takayama compound. She inhaled charcoal fumes infused with the odor of roasting pigs from the glowing cooking fires stoked to feed the crowd as the sun gave way to night.

Following a break, the taiko drummers returned. A string of candlelit lanterns hung on Haru's porch behind them. Now, they stood astride the drumheads, their feet at a ninety degree angle like a baseball batter facing a pitcher. They whirled their *bachi* sticks like a dervish spinner. Their relentless sixty beats a minute was once a rallying call for soldiers to charge. Today's summons, thought Haru, was not much different. She picked up the car keys.

As the tempo increased to ninety beats a minute, Haru maneuvered the slow-crawling Ford through the throngs and out onto the road. Half a mile away, she heard the drummers increase their cadence to 120 beats a minute. Fifteen minutes later, she returned to the gravel road leading to her home.

"Now," ordered Tsutsumi.

As previously coached, Haru pressed the horn in a burst of three long blasts.

The drummers accelerated the tempo to 150 beats a minute. Sweat glistened on their torsos, accentuating the definition of their rippling muscles.

The crowd gave way to the Ford. They shouted greetings as they recognized Haru and Tsutsumi, newly attired in black suit and tie. They took no notice of the man slouched in the backseat, almost hidden, his coolie hat hanging low across his forehead.

The Ford eased into the driveway and came to a stop next to the porch.

The drummers' spinning arms wheeled the pace to an incredible 210 beats per minute. Sweat beads rained on the enthralled front-row spectators. The mesmerized crowd stamped their feet and shouted encouragement.

As Haru and Tsutsumi emerged from the car, Kenji rushed over to greet them. While he opened one of the rear car doors, the crowd trained their eyes on Tsutsumi walking onto the porch. He aimed his clapping hands at the drummers.

The drummers' swirling arms gave the illusion of being four instead of just two. The tempo increased to an impossible 240 beats a minute, which they sustained for ten seconds and then stopped. The drummers, chests heaving, bowed to a frenzied, waving crowd yelling, "Banzai! Banzai! Banzai!"

Chosen men shouted, "Tsutsumi! Tsutsumi!"

The crowd picked up the chant. They clapped in rhythm to their shouts. Tsutsumi strode to where his leather, waist-high megaphone awaited. But instead of picking up his megaphone, he turned away from the crowd. He held his head rigid. The crowd followed his steely stare to Haru and Kenji leading an unsteady man with the coolie hat up the stairs.

Those jammed nearest widened their eyes as the man's facial scars came into focus.

Someone shouted, "Tamatsuke!"

A hush descended as Tamatsuke completed his torturous assent up the five steps. He forced his body to effect an erect posture behind the overhanging lanterns. He took off his hat, and when he turned his head slowly into the light, the crowd gasped in horror and then anger.

Someone in the crowd yelled, "Oki Tama, banzai!" and everyone there seemed to instantly sense that this name—*oki* meaning "big" or "giant" and *tama* "precious jewels"—fit the newly hardened, forever-scarred man. The crowd picked up the chant, "Oki Tama," and from that moment on, Fujimoto would be known by his macho moniker.

∞ Chapter 90 ∞

Oki Tama eased onto a cushioned porch armchair. Haru and Kenji sat on hardback chairs next to him. Tsutsumi, who had honed his speaking technique shouting over the pounding of Hawaii's surf, placed one hand on the back of Oki Tama's chair.

He waited for the crowd to settle and then lifted his two-foot-long brass megaphone.

"You are going to bed hungry … because you want your children to have a better life. You are sleeping on the ground … so that after years of toil under a grueling sun, you might buy a farm or fishing boat or a small shop. You have suffered disease and even the death of loved ones … because you are determined to live in Hawaii permanently. In dignity. Not as slaves tied to the company store and assigned to homes without running water."

Haru nodded her head. Tsutsumi, the outsider, had it right. She knew of only two striking families who had returned to Japan. *The strike has confirmed America is our country.*

"We are a harmonious people—however, even a dog will bite its master if ill-treated. The owners claim they will never recognize our union. But with your will power, recognize it they will!"

Tsutsumi paused, his eyes challenging the crowd. A smattering of voices responded, "Hai!"

"Even the blind can see fields are vacant."

More hais.

"Even the deaf can hear the silence of sleeping hoes and machetes."

"Hai!" half the crowd repeated.

"In a test of wills, men and women fighting for justice will outlast the money worshipers."

"Hai!" roared the crowd.

Tsutsumi stamped his feet. "The owners drink champagne in their mansions, waiting for you to give up."

"*Chigau!*" the crowd shouted. Never!

"The lunas call us by a number even as we call their dogs by name. They think they have crushed your dignity. They are waiting for you to crawl back to the same conditions you left."

"Chigau! Chigau! Chigau!"

Tsutsumi raised his hands, commanding silence. "They … do … not … know … your … character!" Tsutsumi threw his left fist in the air. "Victory belongs to the stronger will. Victory is ours!"

Shouts of "Banzai!" pierced the air.

Feeling the crowd's enthusiasm, Haru wondered if her doubts about Tsutsumi had been misplaced. She had to admit Tsutsumi was bolstering the workers' resolve in ways she and Kenji had not, could not.

"You are not alone. Our businessmen, our tradesmen, even our maids are donating for your daily bread." He stood with his feet a little wider apart. "Our mother country is sending a message supporting you. The cruiser *Yakumo* is steaming into Honolulu today."

Haru's eyebrows rose up in alarm. *Turning a routine goodwill port call into Japan's support of the strikers was just what the* Advertiser *has editorialized about,* she worried. *Now, Tsutsumi has given them proof.* She saw Oki Tama turn his face sharply. He winced in pain as he focused eyes on Tsutsumi. For a second, Haru thought he was about to jump up in protest, but his pained face resumed its stoic expression.

"We will not go back to work until our demand for a $1.25 daily wage is met." Tsutsumi's eyes blazed. "If we do not win, I will make the ultimate sacrifice." He steered his hand over his stomach in the unmistakable letter L.

The *seppuku* gesture silenced the crowd.

Tsutsumi marched off the stage.

❧ CHAPTER 91 ❧

THE STUNNED CROWD DISPERSED into smaller groups. Some of the younger men worked their way to the front, shouting, "Tsutsumi, chigau!" Paniolos and businessmen waved cash. Kenji got up and offered his hat.

"That fool," hissed Oki Tama.

Haru turned to him.

"He didn't see Pafko lurking in the back of the crowd."

Haru's eyes widened. "I didn't see him either."

"He wore a cowboy hat like a paniolo."

Minutes later, Tsutsumi, his face aglow in self-satisfaction, walked around behind Oki Tama and leaned over. "Your arrival stirred the crowd, primed them for my message."

Wearing a stoic, lopsided expression, Oki Tama stood up and turned to face Tsutsumi. "What is this nonsense about the Japanese navy supporting our strike?"

"Strikers need to know they are not alone," Tsutsumi replied dismissively.

"Those remarks make us look like we are puppets of a foreign government."

Through a harsh laugh, Tsutsumi said, "You sound like a haole." Flicking his wrist like batting away a mosquito, he added, "The words are just for our people."

"You didn't see that *Advertiser* truth-twister, Pafko?" asked Oki Tama.

Tsutsumi's face lost its styled smile for just a second. Before he could answer, Oki Tama yanked a folded newspaper from his back pocket. He snapped it open. "You have given the haoles the red meat they crave." Thumbing down Tsutsumi's *Hawaii Mainichi Shimbun*, Oki Tami pointed to the editorial. "'Parade through the towns holding a red flag saying, 'Families cannot live on seventy-seven cents a day.' And this here: 'One tiny nation in Asia has overcome the tyranny of a mighty nation. You are part of that nation, the land of the Rising Sun.'" Oki Tami dropped his hand holding the paper. "March waving *red* flags? Labeling America a tyranny? Using 'Rising Sun' imperial army slogans? Your newspaper is making us look like the Bolshevik wing of Japanese nationalism. How long will it take before the *Advertiser* quotes this as proof of an imperial conspiracy?"

Tsutsumi flicked his hand again as if swatting at a pesky fly. "The Japanese consul issued a statement claiming they have no connection with the labor union."

"Your newspaper is reporting the name of strikebreakers to the mayors of the workers' hometowns as if Hawaii is a prefecture of Japan," said Oki Tama.

Through gritted teeth, Tsutsumi's voice hissed, "I have come here as a guest to give hope to our strikers, not to be lectured to."

Seeing Tsutsumi tighten his fists around the arms of his chair, Haru decided to enter the discussion. "Excuse me, I am only a woman, but I think it is important we recognize the politics of the issue and how they can be used. Our territorial expansion in Korea, China, and Russia is a factor that preys on the haoles' fears."

"With all due respect, Haru-san," said Tsutsumi, "this is not the issue."

"For many haoles, it is," Haru countered. "That Pafko reporter never lets his readers forget about Japan's supposed 'Hawaii is next' design."

Catching inquiring stares of spectators facing the front porch, Tsutsumi forced a lighthearted smile.

"All strikes end," said Haru. "But if the harmony of our community is torn apart, we will live in a territory where the whites fear us."

"Enough politics," said Kenji who had returned with a hat full of donated Washingtons. "Let's go inside and eat."

Tsutsumi rose. "Thank you for your generous offer. I think it best I walk among the workers in your strike city and give them further encouragement. I will sleep in one of the squatter tents tonight."

∽ CHAPTER 92 ∽

HARU'S EVENING INSPECTION SAUNTER was bringing her back to the street when her ears picked up the sounds of a vehicle with a sputtering muffler. She looked up in time to see a truck brake to a rough stop. The Parker Ranch emblem—a cowboy tipping his hat mounted on a rearing horse—emblazoned the door panel. A Filipino driver wearing a wide-brimmed, tan, leather hat threw open the door. He trotted toward Haru and handed her a newspaper. "Mr. Parker said you might want this."

She looked at the *Pacific Commercial Advertiser*. Her stomach tightened as she read the headline. "Jap Rabble-Rouser Threatens Imperial Navy Strike."

"You okay, Haru-san?" asked the worried-face cowboy.

"No. I mean, yes. I'm okay. Please tell Mr. Parker thank you."

As the driver hustled back to his car, Haru read Pafko's article finishing with:

> While the Bolshevik Tsutsumi lets the cat out of the
> bag, the Japanese consul issued a weak statement

trying to wheedle out of the truth. 'The arrival of the *Yakumo* is part of the normal exchange among allies.' Imperial hypocrisy at its weakest. Why the *Yakumo*, famed for its part in sinking the Russian fleet at the Battle of Tsushima? It's insulting to think anyone with common sense wouldn't make the connection between the sugar strike attacking the economic interests of America and the arrival of an armed cruiser from a country that makes a habit of attacking its neighbors.

The patter of footsteps raised her eyes. Haru managed a smile.

"Okasan, I have seen brighter smiles," said Kenji, his voice soft. He spied the newspaper headline. "Ah. Worse than we thought and so soon."

They were interrupted by the bong, bong, bong of the Chinese gong that stood at the edge of camp. Time to queue for evening rice. "Let's get in line," said Haru, who knew that as soon as they joined the queue, someone would bring them a rice bowl.

"Look," said Kenji, pointing up the road.

Haru's spirits lifted as she spied Reverend Adams walking down the street. He looked worried. She saw he was carrying a newspaper.

"You have seen this," said Adams matter-of-factly, looking at Kenji.

"Terrible," said Kenji.

"Maybe it's time to act."

∞ CHAPTER 93 ∞

THE WHITE, HIGH-STEEPLED PRESBYTERIAN CHURCH looked as if it had been transported from a Massachusetts farm town. Snow would easily slide down its peaked roof. Inside, the straight, hardback benches would have earned Cotton Mather's approval.

Today's attendance rivaled an Easter Sunday service. Adams had spread the news: "I will be delivering the most important sermon of my life."

Adams led choir voices that began with two rousing opening hymns praising the Lord. Then, the reverend commanded, "Turn to page thirty-eight." He looked up from the altar to the gathered faithful. "Please stand and sing with us."

Everyone stood. The organist began. At the sharp cue, the congregation sang out. "Mine eyes have seen the glory of the coming of the Lord."

As the hymn neared its ending, Adams felt a joyous surge. He had never experienced such religious exuberance from his flock. It was, he thought, a Biblical moment. Had Moses or Joshua felt like this?

"Glory, glory, hallelujah! Glory, glory, hallelujah! Glory, glory, hallelujah! Our God is marching on."

Sweat dripped down Caucasian foreheads and grew rings on shirts and dresses around the congregants' armpits in a church designed to trap the heat, as a proper New England edifice should. Most did not notice a Japanese Christian vacating his place in the last pew to make room for the Buddhist priest. The rustle of the congregation sitting and settling down soothed Adams, whose confidence in today's sermon had risen during the singing. He was even more certain about the righteousness of his bold plan—the most provocative of his long ministry.

After reading Matthew 8:8 at the lectern, Adams gently closed his Bible and waited until everyone's attention was directed to the pulpit. "The apostle Matthew tells us of Jesus's first recorded encounter with a non-Jew—a Roman occupier of the Holy Land, a soldier, a centurion who no doubt had sacrificed animals to heathen gods. Yet this Roman officer risked ridicule from his compatriots and disdain from the Jewish crowd by asking Jesus to cure his servant.

"We know the centurion was a righteous man, because he worried about the well-being of a servant, most likely a slave. So great is this pagan's faith in the love and compassion of Jesus, he says, 'Lord, I am not worthy for you to come under my roof, but just say the word, and my servant shall be healed.' Christ must have thought that it was not the soldier's nationality or religion that mattered but his character. So Jesus tells the soldier, 'Go! Let it be done just as you believed it would.'"

Adams let his eyes wander over the congregation and paused. Those who normally dozed off during his sermons were wide-awake.

"Half of our community is Japanese, and in a generation their children will vote."

Women's fancy hats danced to attention. Men straightened their backs. Adams narrowed his focus on the front rows occupied by the town's leading families, including Bilkerton and his wife.

"If this emphasis on the racial character of the strikers goes much further, I ask you, what will that do to the fabric of our society in the years ahead?"

His gaze traveled to the back of the church. "In the fraternal spirit of St. Matthew, I have asked Reverend Takayama to say a few words."

The congregation twisted their necks like ducks picking up a hound's bark. Kenji, dressed in a brown cassock and white surplice tailored more like a Christian priest than his traditional Buddhist robes, walked slowly down the center aisle. He kept his eyes on Reverend Adams. Craning necks followed each step in unison as if choreographed. Murmured voices buzzed like a swarm of wasps.

At the lectern, Kenji surveyed the astonished faces. He nodded to Adams who had sat down at the side of the altar. "Thank you for the courageous words, Reverend, reminding me that when the current troubles are settled, we need to come together again as a community, each of us with our familiar roles in place."

Kenji cleared his throat, his practiced eyes roving the congregation. He stopped at Bilkerton, whose beet-red face glared back at him, despite the fact that Kenji had saved his life. Unfazed by the owner's ill will, Kenji calmly returned to addressing the entire congregation.

"I have four boys. All are Americans. I have raised them to proudly recite the Pledge of Allegiance to America and mean it. And like you who have sons, when my boys are old enough, they will be told that if called up in a war, they must be willing to die for their country. That country is America. This is the country of Washington and Lincoln. No country is more worthy of defending, more worthy of dying for, than the United States of America.

"Our Japanese and Filipino sugar workers are on strike. They are following the American example of dockworkers, autoworkers, and miners. Labor and capital may disagree on what a living wage is, but we honor America by using your traditional peaceful methods to settle this debate."

Kenji paused and let the murmuring die down. "This strike has nothing to do with international politics or the threat from a foreign power. Both diversions are trumped-up, newspaper-driven allegations. The strike is simply a disagreement over wages between the plantation owners and their workers. Nothing more. Nothing less."

Turning his face to the crucifixion, Kenji held it and then returned his gaze to the congregation. "I wonder what the man who delivered the Sermon on the Mount would have to say about the growing acrimony between our two races."

Kenji bowed and then walked back to his seat. As he passed Bilkerton, the plantation owner muttered loud enough for the front rows to hear, "Your heathen religion is an attack on America's Christian values."

Adams, too, heard Bilkerton's insult but chose to ignore it. Taking his place once again at the podium, he let his voice rise to prayer level. "In the spirit of Christ and Buddha, I suggest the following." He looked at the back rows at the Japanese in attendance, including Oki Tama.

"Laborers, abandon the strike. Union leaders, disband the unions based on ethnicity and welcome all labor—Japanese, Filipino, Korean, Puerto Rican, and Azorean—in a new organization at a later time.

"Tell your union leaders to allow a secret ballot to create a workers' committee on each plantation to amicably find common economic ground."

Adams turned his eyes to the front rows. "Employers, look inside your hearts first and then at the working conditions of your laborers."

Bilkerton blurted, "Stick to visiting hospitals and burying the dead, Reverend." Then he rose and walked out. A quarter of the haole congregation followed.

Putting his fingers under a gilded bookmark, Adams reopened the Bible. "Jesus told the centurion, 'I have not found such great faith, not even in Israel!'" Adams looked at his remaining congregation. "Go in peace."

⊙ CHAPTER 94 ⊙

"WE HAVE THE OWNERS ON THE RUN and your meddling priest goes to a haole church," said Tsutsumi, throwing back a jigger of whiskey. The no-alcohol rule had gone by the wayside as the strike dragged on. The Honolulu union headquarters had been cleaned up for the visiting union leaders, but tobacco smoke still hugged the ceiling like San Francisco fog.

"Meddling priest?" challenged Oki Tama. "The owners did not offer the new bonus program until the Honolulu churches echoed Adams's sermon. In a few face-saving months from now, we will have our wages adjusted close to what you called for in your editorials." He paused and then snorted, "On the run? Sugar production rises weekly."

"There are things you don't understand," said Tsutsumi with another irritating wave of the wrist signaling he had heard enough.

Oki Tama stood up. "Then maybe you shouldn't have brought me to Honolulu." The anger in his voice silenced side conversations. The clinking of glasses stopped. "You shouldn't have paraded me at all your meetings. I am more than a scarred face whose child and wife were murdered." He jabbed his finger into his chest. "I have EARNED my right to speak here."

Shinseki, a bull-necked Maui union leader, broke the standoff. "Let's not do the work of the sugar association." His gravelly voice created the desired calming effect. "We have enough problems. The good rains favor the owners; they don't need laborers hoeing the irrigation ditches. The Spanish flu ravaged our squatter camps. California passed a referendum forbidding Japanese citizens from owning land. Sugar prices are at an all-time high. The owners publish a daily list of our workers returning to the fields. Korean scabs, angry with us for annexing their country, are cutting cane to spite us. At least the church leaders are trying to keep our community from being torn apart."

Still standing, Oki Tama splayed his palms in a gesture of peace. "What I suggest is we give a reasoned response. Short, much short of disbanding our union, but something."

Tsutsumi's shoulders relaxed. He glanced at the hard men in the room. "Of course, we must respond. I suggest we open up our membership to all workers, not just Japanese."

Murmurs of approval rippled through the group.

"Further, I suggest we demand mediation."

The union leader from Ewa Beach gave a little snort. "The owners will never agree."

Tsutsumi smiled.

"I second the chairman's motion," said Oki Tama, understanding the face-saving gesture. He sat down slowly, picked up his whiskey glass, and lifted it in salute to Tsutsumi.

A relieved chorus of hais greeted Tama's second.

∞ CHAPTER 95 ∞

THE JAPANESE CONSUL FURUYA stood staring down through his office's second-floor picture window. A meditative frown exaggerated the furrowed lines of his pallid face, revealing too little sleep, too much sake, and too much time spent indoors. He fixed his eyes on the men walking up the consulate steps. He did not want them here any more than they wanted to come. He was not sure whom he hated more: his fractious countrymen for striking or the Big Five sugar growers who had twisted the strike into a xenophobic crusade against the so-called imperial designs of Japan.

Rubbish.

What Japan wanted was a free hand in its own backyard—Korea, China, and Eastern Russia. The emperor had no desire to challenge the United States over Hawaii. What worth did the sugarcane fields on these small isolated islands have compared to the coal mines and vacant farmland of Manchuria, the trading concessions along the China coast, or the cheap labor supplied by Korea? And have the strikers forgotten the miserable farm villages they left behind?

The stupid haoles blame the emperor's foreign ambitions for starting the strike and agitating the workers. They accuse me of directing labor unrest. How ironic. Now, here I am, about to do exactly what I have been accused of—tell my nationals what must be done—on behalf of these very same big-nosed landowners.

Furuya heard his aide open the consulate's double doors and invite the puffed-up troublemakers into the conference room. He had ordered his aide not to serve tea. He would let them fidget for fifteen minutes. *Those men. Tsutsumi, a self-aggrandizing rabble-rouser from Japan. A nothing. A nobody. He lands in Hawaii and appoints himself the savior of his Japanese countrymen. A teacher! And that cane cutter, Fujimoto. The same oaf who barged into my conversation with Takayama after the armistice parade. A tragedy, to be sure, losing his child and wife like that, but not enough cause for all this discord—* Furuya balled his fist—*and unwanted media attention to our just designs in Asia. And now my Tokyo ministry seniors at the Gaimusho demand that I settle this mess after months of ordering me to separate the Japanese government from the strike.*

He caught the reflection of the man sitting in his office. *Ah, Takayama. I almost forgot the priest.* The consul had asked Imamura to join him for this meeting. The bishop had agreed the strike was undermining his Buddhist mission and threatening his schools but had politely declined attending. "The dignity of my office requires I cannot directly involve myself." He suggested Takayama as a substitute, and Furuya had readily agreed.

∞ ∞

Fifteen minutes later, Furuya strolled into his conference room carrying a copy of the *Advertiser*. Tsutsumi and Oki Tama immediately stood in polite deference to the Japanese consul. Kenji, who had followed behind Furuya, took a seat opposite the two union delegates.

Furuya tossed the paper onto the conference table so that the copy faced the two men. In no mood to sit down, Furuya bent over and stubbed his finger on the headline: "California Bars Jap Ownership."

Tsutsumi and Oki Tama stared mutely at the two-inch-high bolded letters.

"Hawaii will be next to forbid our countrymen from owning land," said Furuya. "But not before the Territorial Legislature bans Japanese language schools."

Tsutsumi looked up, opened his mouth, and said, "Our cause—"

"Stop!"

Furuya's cold grey eyes challenged Tsutsumi. "Your strike has far more consequences than mere wages. The American Congress is threatening to prohibit immigrants from Japan. The shame of it! You have no idea how our military firebrands, all too eager to undermine civilian control of government, will respond if such a humiliation should be imposed on us."

"Our cause is just," insisted Tsutsumi, anger infusing his words.

Furuya sat down, the heat of his own fury mirrored in his eyes, but his voice dropped to an icy, calm pitch. "This is no longer about your cause, sensei." He pronounced the word with unmistakable derision. "It's time to settle."

"The workers are tired, but they will not settle for what they had before," said Oki Tama defiantly.

"They won't have to," said Furuya with a wicked smile. "But you won't get everything you want."

Tsutsumi shook his head. "We are close to winning. Two or three more weeks, maybe a month, and the owners will cave in."

Furuya craned his neck toward Tsutsumi. "Pull your head out of the sand. Go down to the harbor. Watch the Filipino workers disembark, eager to work for the wages offered, hoping to replace you permanently."

"We can take care of those scabs," said Tsutsumi.

"You have enough blood on your hands," said Furuya, referring to reported attacks on strikebreakers, including one man being beaten to death. "Your thugs might have kept a few strikebreakers in line, but you've only validated haole claims that we are a barbarian race."

Kenji cleared his throat. "Furuya-san, I believe you have found a way out."

The consul leaned back. His tense, rigid body relaxed somewhat. "I have negotiated a settlement."

"You have no right," sputtered Tsutsumi.

"Hear the man out," snapped Kenji.

"Waterhouse has the word of the sugar association that the owners will raise your wages from twenty dollars a month to twenty-three dollars a month, plus award bigger bonuses—but in three or four months, after all this has died down, and only if everyone goes back to work immediately. There will be no contract. No one declares victory. No one has to admit defeat."

"We fought six months for this?" protested Tama. "That's not even a dollar a day."

Furuya ignored the outburst. "There will be major improvements in housing and sanitation. Running water will be piped into homes. When you add in the new bonuses and the better living conditions, you can see I have negotiated a gentlemen's agreement that gets you almost all that you want."

Kenji looked at Tama. "You have honored Yumi's memory with this victory."

"So you hold a press conference brandishing your coup?" said Tsutsumi.

Furuya held his gaze on Tsutsumi and took a breath to control his emotion. He was angry that his self-interest and that of Japan's required that he not only stay in the background but also grant center stage to this Bolshevik across from him. He showed Tsutsumi his best diplomatic smile.

"No one loses face, Tsutsumi-san. As the union leader, you will order the strikers back to work … in the spirit of the minister's appeal."

"And if I refuse?"

"Then I will announce the strike is over," said Tama. "Furuya-san is right. It's not everything we want, but we should be proud we stuck together all this time. The owners have admitted defeat without actually saying they have. A very Japanese way of ending the strike."

Two days later, Tsutsumi ordered the strikers back to work—a decision made easier with record sugar prices prompting equally record monthly bonuses paid to cane workers.

∞ CHAPTER 96 ∞

"The bishop would like to see you," said the soft-spoken Yukari, Bishop Imamura's secretary.

Kenji stopped packing. He looked at his watch. It was four hours before his ship departed for the Big Island. Two weeks in Honolulu was enough. The strike had been settled. Tsutsumi had ignored Kenji and Furuya's advice to take the first ship back to Japan and had been arrested for the murder of a strikebreaker. As Kenji feared, in the aftermath of the strike and its racial slant, the legislature resolved to outlaw the Japanese language schools.

Kenji hurried toward the bishop's office, which he had frequented often over the past two weeks. He had been flattered to be the sounding board for Imamura's broadening campaign to Americanize his Buddhist mission. He entered the bishop's office as the sun pierced through the open window louvers. The harsh light deepened the wrinkles of the bishop's face, making his thinning hair look like wisps of silk and drawing attention to his sagging neck. The unguarded moment stunned him. It was difficult to imagine the bishop as anything less than what his usual imposing presence commanded. Before Kenji could dwell on the startling revelation, Imamura looked up. His eyes sparked. He slapped his side, a gesture displayed only when talking to Japanese men he considered peers.

"Vestments."

"Yes ... " said Kenji, more of a question than a statement.

"Your recommendation that we wear priestly vestments like the Catholics, Lutherans, and Episcopalians. We are going to do it."

Kenji's beaming smile hid a bit of guilt. The idea had been Haru's, and he had promised to propose it on her behalf since he did not give it much credence. But the more he understood Imamura's commitment to make Buddhism accepted as an equal religion in Hawaii, he recognized Haru's proposal was but another logical step toward this goal. Yesterday, he had let the idea drop as if a flash of insight had bolted down from the heavens.

"Not only that," said Imamura, "we also will start conducting Sunday services like the Christians. I like your ideas, Takayama-san. How many times have we discussed and debated the new Buddhism these past weeks and found our combined minds are more of a multiplication than an addition. I need someone with your imagination and courage to challenge me to ensure the future of our mission."

"Thank you, sensei. It has been very stimulating for me, working with you. I regret leaving."

"Then don't," said the bishop.

Kenji laughed self-deprecatingly. "I am not in your league, Imamura-san, but I am all my poor parishioners have."

"You are more than that, Takayama-san. You and your wife are the heroes of Waimea." Imamura swept his arm. "Sit down, good friend."

An unsettling tension wrapped Kenji. Where was this leading? He looked at his watch as he eased into the chair and immediately regretted the rude gesture.

"Don't worry about your ship. I will drive you to the dock," said Imamura.

Kenji relaxed, reassured by the bishop's warm tone.

"What I'm trying to say, Takayama-san … is that I need you in Honolulu. Permanently."

❧ PART VI ❧

REJECTION

∽ CHAPTER 97 ∽

Kailua, Hawaii – August 19, 1920

STANDING AT THE REAR RAILING of the Matson ship slipping from the Kailua pier moorings, Haru waved to the hundreds of well-wishers blinking into early rays of the sun skimming the ocean's horizon. She inhaled the rich coffee aromas rising from the ship's hold. While Kenta, strapped to her back, played with her right earlobe, Haru's eyes roved, trying to make contact with all the waving picture brides recruited by her and Kame. She recognized several husbands, once carousers and gamblers, transformed into responsible family men. How fortunate, she thought, that she had matched up most men with wives before Japan self-imposed a "Ladies Agreement" banning picture brides. The postwar nativist movement sweeping America had cited picture brides, who work alongside their husbands, as a sneaky way to circumvent the 1907 Gentlemen's Agreement banning labor immigration. Congress dropped efforts to stop all Japanese immigration once Japan preempted the legislation with its own ban.

Tommy squeezed his mother's hand. "I miss my friends," he sobbed.

Haru lifted her almost-four-year-old. "Me too, Tommy-chan." She gave a squeeze. "Let's see who's first to make a new friend." Kissing him on the forehead, she eased him down on the deck. "You're getting too big for Mommy to hold." Out of the corner of her moist eyes, she caught nine-year-old Takeshi and seven-year-old Yoshio prancing up the steel-latticed steps to the bridge. She straightened her back and resumed waving at the vanishing crowd. Haru had promised herself not to shed another tear, but diamond beads tickled her cheeks.

So many send-offs, so much packing, so little time, she thought. The drama of resolving the strike had hardly settled before she had to switch gears and prepare for a new life at the Fort Street Hongwanji compound in Honolulu, where the tantalizing conveniences of a modern city—electricity, inside toilets, public transportation, and better schools for her children—beckoned. Kenji would be working directly with Bishop Imamura, perhaps being groomed as his successor—an un-Buddhist ambition about which she fantasized but would never voice.

And herself?

She didn't know. Had she really arrived only eleven years ago as a teenage bride whose honeymoon-night rejection had left her confused and desolate? Since that frightening beginning, she had evolved into a community leader, respected by even the haoles. She had built a hotel, cultivated a garden that supplied vegetables to Oda's Trading Post, supervised a children's nursery, and been the "mayor" of her strike village. She gave Tommy's hand a reassuring tug while thinking of how by finding brides and counseling troubled souls she had been able to change people's lives and change them for the better. Would Honolulu offer such opportunities?

Haru glanced over to Kenji chatting with an excited Sam, who would soon realize a dream shared by so many Nisei—to be sworn in as a United States citizen. Congress had passed a law promising citizenship to "any alien" who served in the army during World War I. Sam was being sworn in at the Schofield Army Barracks in three days. He and Kame would continue to manage Haru's Waimea hotel.

As the harbor dissolved into an emerald skeleton of the low-slung Kona hills, Haru's memory tacked to another voyage two weeks ago. She had visited Ume who still had one good arm to feed herself. Upon entering Ume's dimly lit and rancid-smelling room, Haru had swallowed bile, stifling the reflex to retch. Black gauze cloaked Ume's face. She had fashioned a metal hook around her right arm's stump.

Haru held a Kodak photo near the window to catch the sun's narrow rays slipping through drawn curtains so Ume could see her well-scrubbed, toothy children holding a sign: "We love you,

Okasan." Haru waited before saying in a soft voice, "Irie's new wife is a good mother."

"The food is better," reported Ume in a constricted voice. "We always have a doctor now. I'm moving up the kokua chain. I might have three more years where I can take care of friends and myself. We love each other."

As the outline of Kona's hills disappeared, Taka brought his mother back to the present as he came shouting. "Okasan, Okasan, the captain wants us to steer the ship. Can we? Can we?"

Haru looked up at the face of the smiling Hawaiian captain. A glance told her that he was a happy family man who welcomed her youngsters' enthusiasm. "Well, if he needs help, you better hurry up."

Taka and Yoshio each grabbed one of Tommy's hands and half-ran toward the steps leading to the bridge. Kenji left Sam and sauntered over to join Haru at the railing. Watching his children climb the steps, he said, "The sense of loss over our departure seems to have lasted about as long as it takes to prepare dinner rice." He turned his to gaze to Haru and, for the umpteenth time over the past six weeks, said, "I wonder what Bishop Imamura has in mind for me."

Haru answered for the umpteenth time, "You have built a successful mission, Otosan. You might be assigned to help Oahu priests develop their missions as you did Waimea."

By noon, the ship was passing through the Kaiwi Channel within eyeshot of Honolulu's skyline. From their elevated position of the upper deck, Haru and Kenji watched the bustling city draw closer. At the first bump against the row of tires, Haru pointed her finger. "Look, it's Bishop Imamura." She waved her hand to get his attention as the ship settled into Berth 13. Minutes later, Kenji and his family walked down the gangplank to meet a waiting Bishop Imamura at the bottom.

"Welcome home, Takayama-san. And welcome to your new home, Haru-san."

Haru bowed deeply. "What a great honor you came to meet us."

The bishop gave a slight head bow. "It seems as if we have all done this before. But I remember a shy bride taking her first step on American soil, and now you come back to us as a model for mission wives."

"We have twenty-one cartons following us, Bishop," said Kenji. "Hopefully, they will be delivered to the Hongwanji by tomorrow."

"That's another reason I am here. Your household items need to be delivered elsewhere."

⊚ Chapter 98 ⊚

As Bishop Imamura drove the Takayama family up Bishop Street toward the Fort Street Hongwanji, they didn't notice a thin, bat-eared man strutting up a set of fire stairs on the side of the two-story granite Bishop National Bank building. Hitting each steel step with purpose, the formidable fifty-six-year-old Reverend Takie Okumura—a descendant of a long line of samurai, who had converted to Christianity during his Tokyo activist days in the 1880s—wasn't looking at passing cars and missed his chance to see his new adversaries. Okumura's baptism had soon led him to the priesthood. Imbued with the zeal of a convert, he chose Hawaii for his missionary work and arrived in Honolulu in 1894 to eradicate Buddhism in Hawaii with the same zeal as the Boston missionaries who were determined to stamp out Hawaiian paganism a century earlier.

Despite anti-Asian immigration laws dating back to 1790, Okumura never wavered in his promise to Japanese immigrants that America's prejudice would be swept aside if only they abandoned Buddhism and Shintoism and embraced Christ, stopped sending their children to the language schools, and quit labor agitating. Never mind that sugar barons like John Waterhouse and Walter Dillingham, who encouraged Okumura's Christian advocacy and were grateful for his anti-strike and anti-school stances, had never granted an Asian—Christian or otherwise—membership to the Pacific Club.

After twenty-five years of Okumura's proselytizing, most Japanese remained Buddhist. Okumura blamed the poor conversion rate, at least in part, on "the two great betrayals" of Imamura and labor agitator Fred Makino.

Okumura started Honolulu's first Japanese language school with thirty students in 1896 modeled after the *terakoya*, or temple school, of Japan's pre-1868 Tokugawa era. However, Okumura eschewed mixing religion with his teaching of Japanese writing and reading. To assure the mostly Buddhist parents of the secular nature of the school, he conducted classes at the Nikkei Community Center instead of the church's grounds. The Japanese Ministry of Education supplied his textbooks, the same ones used throughout Japan. Classes began with a pledge of loyalty to the emperor.

In the late 1890s, Okumura and Imamura joined forces in their efforts to stamp out Japanese prostitution and gambling. According to Okumura, this collaboration led to an agreement to keep any schools established by either of them as secular. Since most Japanese were Buddhists, Okumura feared that given a choice between a Christian-oriented and a Buddhist-run school, parents would flock to their own kind. When Okumura's school registration reached two hundred, the Fort Street Hongwanji started a Japanese language school on its temple grounds. Attendance at Okumura's school plummeted to seventy students.

A decade later, strike leader Fred Makino was sentenced to a jail term after the 1909 strike for "conspiring to hinder plantation operations." Okumura used his considerable influence with the haole leadership to obtain pardons for him and the three other imprisoned strike leaders after they served only four months. How did Makino appreciate this Christian gesture? He established a newspaper attacking the white ruling structure, agitated for another sugar strike, and defended the Buddhist language schools, which Okumura insisted must be abolished for Japanese assimilation into America.

∞ ∞

On this sultry early August evening, Okumura entered the building's second floor fire escape door, walked down the hall to the second office on the right, and knuckle-rapped the door. Without waiting for a response, he entered, offered a perfunctory "good evening," and sat down next to Andy Pafko on a matching straight-back chair across the desk from a slimmed-down Joshua Bilkerton in his cramped legislative office. A snappy breeze swept in from the harbor and shot though the open shutters, bringing welcome relief to the stuffy confines.

Receding grey hair cropped military-style topped Okumura's narrow, intense face. He dressed like one of Henry Ford's Model Ts: black jacket, trousers, shoes, and socks. His one exception—a bleached white shirt. Never an aloha shirt for him, as opposed to Pafko in a pineapple-printed shirt and Bilkerton, who sported palm trees on his.

Observing Bilkerton now, Okumura had to admit that since his night raiders had killed the mother and child, the plantation owner had changed. Perhaps he had heard the call of Christ, but more likely, he felt the disdain of Honolulu's Big Five planters. Another consideration was Bilkerton's teetotaler claim, which given his clear eyes and weight loss, lent credibility to his assertion.

"The fed's education report has given us the gift we asked of them," said Bilkerton. "The question now is how far do we go with this opening."

"The Buddhist indoctrination schools must be abolished," Okumura insisted. "Trying to regulate them will only lead to endless ploys to avoid regulations. We must remove the children from the daily influence of those wily priests."

Note-taker Pafko could not resist a barb. "This is quite a change from your early days, Reverend."

"You know quite well, Mr. Pafko, that a generation ago my curriculum was designed to help children fit back into Japan when their parents' contract ended," said Okumura, skipping over his school's more damaging avocation of *chukun aikoku*, or loyalty to the emperor.

"Gentlemen," said Bilkerton, irritation showing in his voice, "let's focus on the issue at hand. The attorney general warned me that we might have constitutional issues if we ban the schools while ... " he put his fingers in the air mimicking quotation marks, "regulating them will strangle the schools out of existence in a few years."

"Why did you petition the federal government to conduct a survey of Hawaii's education only to ignore its key recommendation?" Okumura railed. "No matter how we follow up on the fed's report, Makino and his gang will attack you, attack us. This is a war for the soul of Hawaii. There can be no half measures. Abolish the schools now."

Bilkerton nodded. "I take your point, Reverend. Still, if we overreach, we might get nothing. Makino has threatened to go to the federal courts and argue that these schools are protected by the First Amendment. Who knows how the courts will rule?"

Okumura bowed his head slightly in acknowledgment. "If the courts rule against us, we can always go back to regulation. But regulation is a weak first hand. You must understand: these schools cannot be reformed."

"What about parents who want their children to speak and write Japanese?" asked Bilkerton.

"Include in your bill the hiring of Japanese language teachers for the public schools. Do that, and you abolish the Buddhist priests' claims that their schools are the only choice to learn Japanese."

"Sounds good, Reverend, but it's not the real reason for these so-called language schools, is it?" challenged Pafko.

"No, it is not. Emperor worship underlies everything they teach and is why we need to be rid of them."

"That's what I wanted to hear, Reverend," said Bilkerton. "We need your support so that this legislation is not just a haole punishment for striking."

⚭ CHAPTER 99 ⚭

As HARU STROLLED DOWN FORT STREET with a snoozing Kenta secure on her back, she thought of herself as Alice in Wonderland finding herself in a strange world after falling into a rabbit hole. She marveled at the many cars on the street. But it was not just the cars jostling with the trams that made her feel so out of place but also the men wearing suits, ties, and hats of all descriptions who strode purposefully into granite-built banks and office buildings. Not just the haoles but also Asian men, Japanese men. These were not the cowboys and tradesmen of the Big Island. Japanese ladies wearing more colorful kimonos and yukatas hustled in and out of crowded shops.

After several people passed her impatiently, nearly bumping her, she changed her pace from a stroll to a walk to keep up with Honolulu's faster-moving pedestrians.

She turned right at Beretania as she wondered how Kenta managed to sleep through all the honking and shouting. The chugs and rumbles from the nearby Honolulu Iron Works filled the air with pride. She knew that the massive factory manufactured sugar refinery equipment for the Caribbean and the Philippines, as well as local plantations.

She replayed the bishop's stunning words upon entering Imamura's office an hour previously. "It had been my intention," he had said to her and Kenji, "for you to help me at our Fort Street Hongwanji until we needed a head priest at one of Oahu's missions. A sudden illness has created exactly that situation. As you know, Takayama-san, the Moiliili mission serves both our University of Hawaii students in nearby Manoa as well as the growing Japanese population in Moiliili's farming community."

But that wasn't the bishop's only request. As she turned right on Beretania, Haru recalled how his eyes had focused on her. "If you have the time, you might visit Fred Makino at his pharmacy."

Haru looked back uncertainly. "The same Fred Makino who publishes the *Hawaii Hochi*?"

"The very one," smiled Imamura. "The man who led the strike and now defends our schools."

"Why me?"

"I think a *Hochi* human interest story on the mayor of the Waimea strike camp will provide a wonderful introduction to your new parishioners."

Haru ignored the compliment, puzzled by what Imamura had said, that Makino had been the leader of the strike. "But wasn't Tsutsumi the strike leader?"

The bishop's face hardened. "Tsutsumi is a gangster. He was the worst voice we could imagine. In a day or two, he will be arrested for conspiracy in dynamiting the Sakamaki house," referring to the explosion designed to intimidate cane workers refusing to strike. "When that happened, Makino broke ranks with him."

Haru remembered the incident and had questioned the newspaper's claim of Tsutsumi's involvement. "Of course, plantation owners accuse me," he had said. "I am leading the strike." She had been skeptical of Tsutsumi's denials, but given the diabolical charges each side slung at each other, she had not pressed.

Imamura's forceful voice continued. "Without Makino's fundraising and newspaper support, the strike would have folded much earlier." Switching to a softer voice, he concluded, "He's at his pharmacy now. We can keep an eye on your boys."

Haru looked at Kenji. "You go along," he said. "I have more business to go over with the bishop."

Imamura opened a side drawer in his desk and pulled out a hand-drawn map. "I have indicated Makino's business here," he said, pointing to a red dot on the map. "It's not far, about a fifteen-minute walk."

Now at the Fort Street and Beretania corner, Haru stopped to look at the street sign. "Nuuanu." One block up just as the bishop's directions promised. Minutes later, she spotted the Makino Drug Company sign ahead at the corner of Nuuanu and Hotel Streets. Slowing her pace, Haru's eyes darted to sunbeams glaring off a polished, four-door, Model T Ford sedan—black, of course. "Hawaii Hochi" was stenciled in three-inch-high white lettering on the door. Haru's knees wobbled. *Why am I nervous?* She had met influential people before. Then she corrected herself. Who else besides Wellington Carter? He had made her feel welcome as a nineteen-year-old bride. For the most part, her township social circuit was comprised of men and women like herself, small-town people. She now stared at a Schwinn bike leaning against the wall and wished she could snatch it and ride away.

Unconsciously taking a deep breath, Haru stepped into the apothecary. A tall, thick-necked man with a rectangular face—not quite Asian, but not Caucasian either—his head crowned with a Panama hat, was tending to a haole customer. He wore a white suit, a white shirt still holding its starch, and a white silk tie. The confident face glanced up at the tinkling sound of the doorbell. His intriguing hazel eyes were set in sockets not quite round or almond and perched over a parrot-beaked nose and a wide-mouthed smile. At forty-four, Fred Makino was in the prime of his life on the day

Haru walked into his pharmacy. He was the son of an English merchant who died when Fred was only four and a Japanese mother who remarried a Japanese businessman.

Makino, the former playboy of Yoshiwara, Tokyo's famed red-light district, joined his brother's general store on the Big Island the year after annexation. Three years later, in 1901, his brother gave him the stake to start a pharmacy in downtown Honolulu.

Haru recognized him from newspaper pictures and introduced herself. "*Watashi wa Haru desu*," she said and bowed.

Makino nodded agreeably and returned his eyes to his customer. "Wes," Makino's commanding voice assured the man, "take two of these every four hours, and you will feel your old self in three days."

Haru raised her eyebrows. A Japanese addressing a haole on a first-name basis surprised her. And, Haru thought, judging by the man's tailored pinstriped suit, fedora hat the color of maple syrup, and buffed black shoes, a man of substance.

The man took the pills wrapped in cellophane, slipped them in his suit jacket pocket, and then sauntered out. Makino hollered at an assistant who was stocking shelves. "Shinzo, man the counter for a few minutes please." The college-age boy bowed his head and stepped over.

"Let's go upstairs to my law office," said Makino, whose eyes twinkled at this designation. Taking in Haru's quizzical expression, he added, "Had breakfast with the bishop this morning, and he told me about your posting. What an opportunity. The mayor of the Waimea strike village settling in Moiliili." Makino failed to mention that Imamura had asked him to mentor Haru on the issues facing the Japanese community.

Haru followed Makino up the grated steel steps of the spiral staircase that rose behind the counter. At the top, she squinted into the sunbeams streaking through the large windows facing Nuuanu Street. A strange office, thought Haru. There was no desk, only a large family dining table surrounded by sturdy chairs. A pair of four-blade ceiling fans spun languidly over the table laden with open-faced books, their pages kept in place by polished stones lodged on their edges. Floor-to-ceiling bookcases, crammed with tomes of all sizes, occupied the other two walls. More books were stacked haphazardly on the floor under the windows.

"Is this an office or a library?" asked Haru.

"Welcome to my law office," said Makino, his voice warm, rich, and inviting. "Have a seat while I prepare us tea." Makino stepped over to a Korean medical chest serving as a kitchen countertop. "When I moved to Honolulu twenty years ago, there were no Japanese lawyers." He picked up the teakettle from the electric hot plate and carefully poured hot water into a Chinese dragon-decorated teapot with one hand and wagged a forefinger with the other. "But lawyers were needed to handle marital matters, immigration processing, and run-ins with the police. While knowing nothing about the law, I started buying the collection you see here. I became a layman advocate and taught myself how to navigate the American-Hawaiian legal system while also learning, I might add, about pills and potions." Makino carried the teapot and two empty cups to the table. "At twenty-three, I felt there were no mountains too high to climb." He sat down across from Haru and poured tea. "Then, a few years later, when tensions built up between Japanese cane workers and planters, I stuck my rather long nose into the budding conflict." Makino brought his cup to his mouth, inhaled the aroma like a man preparing to drink a vintage wine, and sipped his tea. "Let's see ... 1909 ... I believe, that was when you arrived."

"Hai, just after the strike was settled," said Haru, adding "delicious" after tasting her tea.

"One futile negotiation led to another. By spring, Fred the pharmacist-lawyer had become Fred the strike leader." Makino spread his arms in a gesture that suggested, "How did that happen to me?" and continued. "The strike ended without resolution. But just like this recent strike, the owners quietly agreed to increase wages 'voluntarily' a few months later." He downed a generous swallow of tea. "Then, two years later, not knowing anything about the newspaper business, I launched the *Hawaii Hochi*, the fourth Japanese daily newspaper. Do you know why?"

Taken off guard, Haru hazarded a guess, "The other Japanese newspapers supported the plantation owners?"

"Exactly." Makino pursed his lips in surprised approval. "Our community needed a voice that fought for our rights."

Thinking of what Imamura had said earlier in the day, Haru added, "When the strikers this year needed a voice, you gave it to them again."

A little feigned humility is in order, thought Makino. "Arigato. We tried our best." His voice turned serious. "The strike is over. Now the battle for our schools has begun."

Makino watched the cloud of uncertainty envelop Haru's face.

Good, he thought. *Given her husband's sponsorship of a language school in Waimea, she is not new to the issue. She is, however, naïve to the coming struggle, the bigger arena.* "Before I describe the battle we face, tell me about your days as mayor of your strike village. I want to introduce you to my readership before we cross swords with Okumura and the legislature."

For the next hour, Makino encouraged a reluctant Haru to tell her story—the evolution of a Japanese activist-wife, a rarity in their community. Makino drew out her history: establishing the kindergarten, the migration of the family garden to a commercial enterprise, and building the hotel; then the awful episode of the nightriders who killed Mayo and her child, followed by the strike; her cooperation with the Shinto and Presbyterian priests to create tent cities; the Spanish flu outbreak; Oki Tama's scarred face and his inspirational leadership; and Tsutsumi's disturbing speech.

"This is a story worthy of a Sunday feature series," said Makino, shuffling his sheaf of notes.

"I am not sure if ... "

While Haru struggled for words, Makino said, "My job is to sell newspapers and give our readers hope. The two goals are best served together, like rice and sashimi in sushi. But there is another reason. You are a woman of accomplishment. You need an introduction. Moiliili is the home of the new Japanese." Haru nodded her head as Makino added, "The most ambitious sugarcane workers have been leaving the plantations, many to settle in Moiliili. A whole new community coexisting with the Chinese and Hawaiians. And your mission is the heart of that community."

"But there are also college students," added Haru. "I don't have that type of education."

"Our students do not need a professor at your mission; they need a mother," smiled Makino. "Let's stroll back to the Hongwanji while I fill you in on Reverend Okumura and the school battle we face."

∞ CHAPTER 100 ∞

MAKINO PATTED THE FORD outside his pharmacy. "This one's a charm. Has the new ignition system. Don't have to crank it to start."

Walking in the opposite direction of the Hongwanji, toward the harbor, he pointed to a second-story sign: Nakamura & Nakamura, Attorneys at Law. "Now we have real attorneys. The Nakamura brothers are University of California graduates. To the horror of the haoles, they are constitutional specialists, even though their daily bread comes from small business clients."

Makino pointed out restaurants, notion shops, vegetable grocers, household goods, and farm supply stores, all Japanese owned. Haru noticed a signboard in Japanese, "The Pacific Photo Shop," and made a mental note to bring Kenji and the children there. It had been years since she had sent Midori and Kiyoshi a family photo. "I'd heard we were opening businesses in Honolulu, but this is ... "

"Amazing," said Makino, breaking into her pause. "When I opened my pharmacy, I owned one of very few Japanese businesses—one of the few Asian, for that matter. The Chinese had their restaurants and laundries, but that was about it. Americans rejected us, but we didn't reject America. If you're willing to work hard, save a little money, and accept that you might fail but try anyhow, the American dream is open to all races. The banks like my money as much as the Dillinghams."

Haru struggled to attune her ears to his voice competing with trolley bells, car honks, and engine noises.

Makino laughed and then stopped suddenly, so Haru had to look back at him. "Well, that's not exactly true. The haole banks were slow to offer banking services to us early Japanese—poor folks, cane workers. They had no idea of our fanatic saving habits. So the Yokohama Specie Bank set up a branch in the 1880s." He pointed to a four-story, L-shaped, brick-and-steel façade across the street.

Makino resumed walking. "Enough about banks and lawyers. Let me tell you about Reverend Takei Okumura," he said in an animated voice. "A most dangerous person because of the absolute sincerity of his calling. He is a man of impeccable character. I wish he was on our side. I do not believe he prays every night to split our community, but that's the result of his misguided efforts. His twin pillars of assimilation—that we accept Jesus Christ as our savior and also shut down our schools—undercut our efforts to unite and press for fair wages and to retain our culture, language, and religion. He confuses assimilation with acceptance and thinks they are the same. He claims our children cannot assimilate except on his terms."

Makino's walking pace increased as if his legs were trying to match the urgency in his voice. Given her shorter stature, Haru had to almost double-step to keep up, but she tried to appear unhurried.

"We can deal directly with the Pafkos and the haole newspapers, the Bilkertons and the legislators, the sugar barons. That is, if we are united." Noticing Haru's increased breathing, he slowed down. "Okumura, however, is another story. He has made the haoles' hostile attitude toward us more acceptable."

Makino put his hand out across Haru's arm as she started to cross the street. He pointed to the policeman in the middle of the road directing traffic, indicating they should wait. "Okumura spoke out against the strike, yet almost all Japanese plantation workers struck anyway. Perhaps worse for him is that, despite twenty-five years of proselytizing, maybe 10 percent of Japanese have converted to various Christian congregations, including his Makiki church with four hundred parishioners. But I freely admit his influence far exceeds the number of attendees at his church."

The policeman dropped his hand, and Makino stepped over the curb. "Tell me, has your husband ever given a sermon attacking Christianity?"

"Never," Haru said, her tone betraying her shock at such a notion.

"Christians quote Christ as saying things like 'he who is without sin among you, let him be the first to throw a stone,' and then attack us as heathens who are destined to spend eternity in the fires of hell."

He let the thought linger and then switched subjects again. "There is a fellow named Ozawa petitioning the Supreme Court for citizenship. He was adopted and raised a Christian in a white man's home in South Dakota, is a college graduate, and fought in the trenches in the Great War. I hope he wins his case, but American law says Asian immigrants cannot become citizens. It's been that way since 1790. By birth, our Nisei are American citizens. Many angry whites clamor to take away that right."

Makino sidestepped a fishmonger balancing the day's catch in buckets on two poles. The pause gave Haru a chance to speak. "We have a friend who served in the army who will be sworn in as a citizen tomorrow."

"Yes, but will it stick?" asked Makino. "Right behind Judge Vaughn, a Justice Department lawyer will file a claim that the judge is in error." They stopped at the curb to wait for a break in passing cars at Beretania. Makino nodded at the Hongwanji ahead. "There's not much we can do about citizenship requirements and immigration. There are federal issues. But we can and must fight for our schools."

As they hurried across the street, Haru debated on whether to express her own reservations about the language school curriculum. She did not want to argue with such an important man, but he was soliciting her help. "Sometimes, I think the haoles have some legitimate … reservations about our schools. We not only teach language and values but also still glorify our military heroes and recite the Imperial Rescript on Education pledging loyalty to the emperor." She held her breath.

Makino stopped again. Looking into her eyes, he nodded his head. "You are right. We missed an opportunity to change our textbooks. The script is a habit best dropped. But I wonder if that would have changed the haoles' objections. They should be cheering the time we spend teaching our children values, the same values America holds dear. No matter how we change the curriculum or even if we closed our schools, we will still look Asian, we will still be Japanese.

We're fighting so our children can have the same pride in their heritage as the descendants of the *Mayflower* have in theirs. If we lose this fight, we lose who we are, our very soul."

They heard a burst of cheers erupting from the baseball game being played across from the Hongwanji. Realizing their chat was almost over, Haru asked, "What can I do?"

"Okumura is establishing a Christian community center in Moiliili offering English classes, providing technical training, and sponsoring a baseball team."

They stopped in front of the Fort Street Hongwanji. Haru looked across the street and strained to see if her boys were still watching the ball game and then came back to the task at hand. "Are you saying the Moiliili Hongwanji doesn't?"

"You have a lot of work to do, Haru-san." Makino bowed. "Tell the bishop hello. I'm going to enjoy writing the first article about the mayor of Waimea's mission village."

"Arigato," Haru said while bowing deeply.

Makino returned the courtesy, turned, and charged down the street.

Haru stood watching his retreat while thinking, *What have I walked into?* Then she took a long look across the street and spotted her boys. Tommy saw her first, elbowed Takeshi, and pointed. In seconds, all three came running to the street.

⌘ CHAPTER 101 ⌘

WHILE WAITING FOR HER SONS TO CROSS, Haru noticed another Model T Ford, not as fancy as Makino's but brand-new. Could this possibly be theirs? She and Kenji had originally planned to ship their current car along with the household goods until they found that the price of a new Model T was only $260—half the price of their current car bought five years ago. No wonder the streets were jammed. Had Kenji moved so fast?

Takeshi's shouted "Okasan! Okasan! Otosan bought a new car!" answered her question.

"Be careful, boys," Haru yelled back as they prepared to sprint across the road. Behind her, she heard Kenji's familiar voice. "What do you think?"

What Haru was thinking had nothing to do with cars. The sudden destination switch and Makino's warning on the developing school war crowded her thoughts, but she managed, "It's lovely."

They all climbed into the new auto, and Kenji drove the same route their honeymoon trolley had taken eleven years ago. But how the landscape had changed. Beach Boulevard, hugging Moana Beach from downtown to Waikiki, was no longer a rutted dirt road but now a paved concrete highway. At Atkinson, just before Waikiki's famed beaches, Kenji hooked a left and drove a quarter-mile up to Kapiolani where horse- and mule-drawn drays and carriages still outnumbered cars. The survey pegs sticking out of the water reminded Haru that sugar baron Walter Dillingham would soon begin dredging the marshy Ala Wai River and its swampy tributaries to convert the meandering waterway into a man-made, two-mile-long canal.

On the left of Kapiolani, she gazed at Moiliili's waterlogged rice fields, square fishponds, grazing black-and-white Holsteins, and copses of banana trees. New wood-framed homes, built of Douglas fir imported from Washington State, balanced on concrete blocks. In between them, a colorful variety of older edifices vied for Haru's attention: car repair shops hedging their bets by maintaining blacksmith forges firing horseshoes; joineries fronted with bed frames and cabinets; green grocers with street displays of strawberries, bananas, and pineapples resting on chopped ice; bicycle shops; smoky tofu processing works; and more. She noted a children's clothes shop and told herself to buy the boys back-to-school clothes. No time for sewing this year. An enclosed piggery reminded her she had read that Honolulu would ban raising pigs within the city limits by year's end.

Kenji took a left on University Avenue. "Taka, Yoshio, keep an eye out for Kuliei Street." Moments later, the raucous roar of "Kuliei Street, Otosan!" directed Kenji to turn onto the tire-crunching, crushed-coral road. Haru's heart thumped as she spied the decorative top of a pyramid roof on what had to be the Hongwanji. Her imagined quiet entry into her new home was gloriously shattered as a crowd of people suddenly appeared.

"Okasan, look at all those people," shouted Yoshio into her ear. A crowd of men in black suits, women in shimmering silk kimonos, and jumping children decked in white school uniforms spilled into the street to greet their new pastor. Haru instinctively waved back. Thoughts of Makino and Okumura and the coming struggle over the language schools faded.

"It appears we are welcomed," said Kenji, now understanding why Imamura had been insistent for the time when they expected to arrive at their new home.

Upon exiting the car, a grey-haired woman wearing a deep purple kimono with a wide, white stripe on the front fold introduced herself and presented Haru with a gold-foiled box wrapped in a blue, gossamer cloth. "Let me show you your home."

The tour of their new home, the attached mission building, and the Moiliili Japanese language school had hardly ended when greeters echoed each other. "Don't let the haoles close our schools!"

Kenji gave his stock reply. "We will try out best."

After an hour of greeting everyone, Haru breathed easier when the grey-haired lady announced, "We are leaving now so you can have private time to move in."

Haru bowed. "Arigato." As she stood up, she spied a woman next to a sturdy post somewhat turned away from her. Although Haru could not see her face well, the curve of the neck and slight hunch of the shoulders seemed familiar. Could it be? When the woman cast a furtive glance at Haru, she noticed eyes that looked as if sandpaper had rubbed the life out of them. The woman turned away as if ashamed, but Haru hurried over.

"Saki, is that you?"

Slowly the woman faced Haru, a wary smile on her lips.

"It *is* you," said Haru softly, and the forlorn look on the woman's face encouraged Haru to reach out her hands and grab Saki's in a gentle grasp. "It is so good to see you." Deep lines creased Saki's haggard face, which resembled a crumpled brown-paper bag. Haru released her hands. "The last time you wrote you had a fourth child on the way."

"Nine. I have nine children now."

"I just had my fourth," said Haru, cringing inwardly at the lie. "You have the hips for a large family."

"That's the only part of my body that seems to work right," said Saki, who at twenty-seven looked closer to forty.

Seeing Kenji saying goodbye to the last of the greeters, Haru said, "Come inside and have tea. I don't know where everything is, but we will find it."

"No. No, I can't. I need to go home. I should not burden you."

"How far is home?"

"We have a farm on the next street."

"Oh, good. I have my first friend in Moiliili," said Haru. "Why don't you show me? Kenji and the boys can start opening the boxes."

Haru made eye contact with Kenji, who apparently did not recognize Saki from the group wedding eleven years ago, but his nod told her that he understood she had found her first wounded bird.

Saki led Haru to the back of the adjacent language school compound. "Oh, I see we have a stream," said Haru, noticing a thin, meandering waterway.

"We all wash our clothes here. The water flows from the marsh on the other side of Beretania."

After crossing a makeshift bridge of boards stretched across the brook, they turned left at Hausten Street, a rutted, hard-baked lane much in need of freshly ground coral. Haru slowed her pace to match the plodding Saki. Just before Date Street, Saki stopped in front of what appeared to be a fence constructed of abandoned construction materials. The bare-planked house showed thin gaps in the wooden walls. Patches of grass, losing the battle against thistle weeds, fought to cover the tiny front yard. Limp marigolds hugged the concrete blocks holding up the house. Along both sides of the house, neat rows of scrawny vegetables struggled to be free of the earth.

Children floated into the front yard like tumbleweeds in the wind. Their hand-me-down clothes were tattered but clean. Each of the older girls held a baby, one only a month old, Haru guessed. The youthful tribe stared wide-eyed and curious.

"This is the lady who came with me on the boat," said Saki. "Her husband is our new pastor." The older children bowed, causing the held babies to bawl in unison.

From the backyard, an old man appeared, straining to both walk straight and carry a hoe. He offered a tooth-gapped smile. "Haru, it is you." He leaned on his hoe as if it were a third leg.

Haru held back her shock. She remembered Yoshi as the trickster who had sent Saki's matchmaker a picture of a younger, more handsome man. It was hard to reconcile Yoshi's swagger of that day with the man in front of her.

"Yoshi is a carpenter," said Saki. "But other than making and maintaining plantation drays, he never had any training. He wanted to go to that Christian priest's carpentry class, but I warned him to stay clear of the new community center and Okumura, the evil man who stabbed the strikers in the back."

"Does Reverend Okumura's community center make the students take religious classes?"

"No," said Yoshi quickly.

Saki spat betel nut juice on the ground. "Oh, that Okumura is a tricky one. Pretending to help us. But you just wait. As soon as people start coming, attending his bookkeeping and sewing classes, he will sneak in Bible lessons. He wants to make haoles out of all of us."

"I don't want to be a Christian, just a carpenter who can make a chest people will buy," said Yoshi more plaintively this time.

"I understand," Haru said and looked down. "I'd better get back to help Kenji unpack. Only Buddha knows where he and the boys will put things."

As Haru walked back home, she promised herself to take a look at this community center. Okumura might have two agendas, but a class is a class. Surely, Kenji and Okumura could find some common ground to help the Japanese in Moiliili.

Exhausted as she was at the end of a long day, she welcomed Kenji's approach to consecrate their new home. Haru hoped her next child would be a girl.

∽ ∾

Two days later, Kenji drove Sam, along with Haru and the boys, to the Schofield Army Barracks where Sam and twenty-three other Asian veterans, mostly Japanese, took their Oath of Citizenship from Judge Vaughn.

District Attorney S. Hubor, who had disputed Judge Vaughn's judgment, also attended and spoiled the event by declaring he had prepared "bills of cancellation," claiming that the citizenship was wrongly granted since American law prohibited the naturalization of Asians.

"File what you will, Solicitor," said a stern Vaughn. "The law explicitly stipulates naturalization to any alien who volunteered. They did not say just those of European heritage. I am a federal judge charged by statute to determine who qualifies for citizenship."

Hubor fumed, "Congress would not have singled out Filipino volunteers as eligible for citizenship if they weren't excluding all other Asians."

"Noted," said Vaughn as he walked away.

Haru smiled, again reassured that in America, the courts, not the politicians, had the final say.

∞ CHAPTER 102 ∞

UNCONSCIOUSLY, HARU RUBBED HER SWELLING BELLY that soon would be noticeable, even under a loose-fitting yukata. She looked at the calendar: December 1. She had put off visiting the Christian community center, always finding one reason or another to postpone it—register the children for school, meet the new parishioners, chair the ladies' auxiliary meetings, etc. Yet almost every day her errands, usually on her bike, routed her past Okumura's center. She saw that their facility sported a half-court, outdoor basketball tarmac. A neatly framed signboard near the edge of the dirt road promoted classes in sewing, bookkeeping, English, and carpentry. She thought of Yoshi. Haru prayed that a little goodwill diplomacy with Okumura might ease some of the tension.

∞ ∞

Since her arrival on Oahu, the conflict over the Japanese language schools had turned vicious. Pafko, having moved over to the strident anti-Japanese *Star-Bulletin*, pounded the drums, demanding Governor William McCarthy call a special session of the legislature to prohibit Japanese language schools. "Why pay the federal government to conduct an education assessment of Hawaii and then ignore its recommendations?" wrote Pafko.

The governor, well-known for his anti-Asian views, duly called the legislature into session. McCarthy also savaged the Big Five in private conversations. "You cannot see beyond the next harvest. You have imported a labor force whose children will outnumber yours and, by their vote, eventually rule us."

In an about-face, the *Advertiser* offered a lonely voice arguing against the bill. Its writers attacked the Washington report and proposed legislation as "un-American, devoid of the spirit of freedom, and inexcusably tyrannical to make it a penal offense for a man to teach his own child his own language."

While Pafko wrote and the governor postured, Okumura and his son visited seventy plantations, preaching his version of assimilation.

The Territorial Legislature passed the Language School Bill on November 24. The regulations would force the schools out of existence, effective July of the following year.

Today is the day, thought Haru, as she biked past the Moiliili center. She had spotted Okumura's Studebaker Big Six Touring Car, donated to his ministry, according to the bamboo telegraph, by Walter Dillingham. She was dressed in her shopping yukata. Her bicycle basket brimmed over with that morning's fresh vegetables and fruits.

At home, she had pulled out her chest of kimonos. She didn't want one too gay, as if she were attending a wedding, but not funeral black either. She settled on a blue kimono with a single crane in full flight on the back, complemented by a formation of smaller cranes in front.

The stroll to Okumura's center was only twelve minutes—so short a distance for such a wide gap in outlook. Haru did not feel the nervousness she had when first meeting Makino. Her early months in

Moiliili had been heartening. The *Hochi*'s feature stories had given her credibility without overdoing it. She and Kenji were enjoying what the Americans called a "honeymoon period" within their community. The parishioners welcomed Kenji's sermons reinforcing Buddha's guide to a fulfilling life while never delivering drinking and gambling admonitions. Kenji's approach was simple: If you want folks to give up bad habits, keep them busy with good activities. He organized festivals, potluck dinners, and sumo exhibitions. Takeshi convinced him to sponsor a baseball team.

As Haru entered the foyer, the young receptionist looked up in surprise, rose, and bowed. Before the woman could utter a greeting, a male voice from an open side door spoke in deep, rich tones. "Irasshaimase, Haru-san. Welcome to our center."

Haru turned and bowed in proper Japanese form when addressing an older man of eminence. "Good morning, Reverend Okumura." She took in his unlined face and his straight-back hair more black than grey with the scent and shine of brilliantine. "I have heard so many nice things about your center. And I saw your car … "

"Let me show you around," said Okumura, a wary politeness infecting his voice.

Haru couldn't help but be impressed by what she saw: the outdoor shed featuring a vast array of carpentry tools, the classrooms, one with stacks of English textbooks, another with countless accounting and business books. When they entered the sewing room, Haru's eyes brightened at the sight of a half-dozen of the latest electric Model 99 Singer sewing machines. On impulse, she sat down in front of the nearest black Singer stenciled with its signature gold lettering. Okumura noticed her fumbling for the switch for the tiny bulb hovering over the needle. He reached down, flipped it on. The little light flooded the needle-stitching surface.

"This is astonishing," breathed Haru, thinking of her Waimea years of sewing that had been dependent on sunshine and flickering oil lamps. Her enthusiasm drained the tension between them.

"I was thinking of starting a sewing class," she said. "But I don't think I can compete with this. And why should I? Maybe it's best that we each offer something the other doesn't."

Okumura's temporary geniality turned condescending. "We welcome all students, but your regular temple attendees will not enter this building."

Haru stood up to look the man in the eye. "The strike is over, Reverend. Perhaps it is time to move on."

"Ah, if that were the only issue, Haru-san. Despite your Buddha's call for tolerance under the principle of enlightenment, not only will most of your parishioners refuse to attend our classes; they also will disapprove of those who do."

"There must be other ways we can cooperate."

"I suspect not," said Okumura, his voice hardening and his eyebrows pinching his forehead. "Your Hongwanji undermines the future of the Japanese in Hawaii and America. Only the spirit of aloha keeps the worst of California's Yellow Peril hysteria from spreading to Hawaii. The failed strike was an enemy of peace. Look what's happened since then: The plantation owners are importing Filipinos to replace Japanese workers, leaving them mostly helpless. That strike has lost us many friends here. Your schools are losing the rest. We are guests in America, Haru-san. You cannot expect America to adapt to us; we must adapt, assimilate, and become part of our new country. Your Hongwanji's so-called language school is a blight on our future."

Haru ignored the man's strident tone. This was the Okumura her parishioners called "an American dog." There had to be a middle way, as the Buddha taught. "You might be surprised to know that I share some of your reservations. Our textbooks need to be modernized." Her face brightened hopefully.

Okumura waved his hand dismissively. "You claim you teach Americanization to your students. But you do not." His next words were spoken in an ominous growl. "Those who will not embrace America should return to their mother country." Then suddenly the smile returned, a hard smile, a satisfied smile. "The governor has signed the bill regulating the schools. The people have spoken."

"Yes, they have." Haru's voice bristled, its polite tone gone. "Requiring only English-speaking teachers certified by the Department of Education. Limiting our classes to five hours a week. These and other regulations will effectively close down our schools." Haru forced a friendly tone. "But there are those, including the *Advertiser*, who say the bill is neither fair nor constitutional."

"A misguided minority. We must expunge everything that differentiates us from our hosts. Other immigrant groups keep their racial identity, but only we Japanese make a fetish of it. Who else has language schools?"

Still striving for common ground, Haru nodded. "You are right. We must respect the law of the land. However, in America, when people disagree about a law, they take their dispute to court. The court decides the correct interpretation. What makes America great is that its people accept its court rulings, not just laws passed by short-sighted legislatures."

"That's the problem with Makino and his lawyers' gang. But it is not about court decisions and who's legally right. It's about assimilation. It's about proving to Americans that we are one of them." He paused, his face twisted in righteous indignation. "Your Buddhism is the greatest obstacle to assimilation."

"Surely you cannot ask us to give up our culture, our religion."

"Yes, I am asking you do exactly that. Our forefathers built this Hawaii. They Christianized a heathen land and brought prosperity. We volunteered to work in America, not bend America to our way of life. Assimilate or leave." With an exaggerated sigh, he gave a perfunctory bow. "Please excuse me. I must get back to Honolulu."

Okumura turned and strode out the door, leaving Haru stunned at his ill manners and wrong-headed righteousness. If she had been tentative about the fight ahead, that ambivalence had vanished.

As she walked home, Haru made a point to keep her shoulders straight, her head high. She thought of additional arguments: There was a synagogue in Honolulu—Jews kept their faith while no one accused them of being un-American. As she approached her home, Haru realized that an appeal to reason would fall only on deaf ears with Okumura. With him, there was no middle way, no compromise.

Walking through the door, she found Kenji sitting in his favorite chair, reading a newspaper. He looked up at his wife. "Okasan, we must join Makino and fight this school law in the courts."

Haru replied, "Let me tell you about my visit with Okumura."

∞ CHAPTER 103 ∞

November 22, 1922

EXCEPT FOR THE WIND WHISPERING THROUGH THE SHUTTERS, the rustling of a turning newspaper page, and the clinking of a porcelain cup set on a saucer, the post-breakfast ritual silence enveloped the Takayama dining table. Four daily newspapers, which earlier had thumped down on or near the front porch, lay neatly folded as they might in a library. Haru and Kenji sat reading them one by one. Earlier, the three older, barefooted boys had traipsed off to school while four-year-old Kenta was "helping" Sachi push the stroller with Haru's long-wanted daughters—Hiromi born in spring 1921 and Sachiko, a July baby this year. After a visit to the park, Sachi would stop at the Chinese grocery store for today's vegetables and fish.

The quiet time.

Haru couldn't say when this tradition began, but she knew Sachi made it possible. Moiliili had initially unsettled her. The community was so different, so new, its bustling activity so unlike Waimea. It took several months before Haru's patience and the community's kindness bolstered Sachi's confidence to a point where she enjoyed the morning stroll with Kenta and shopping by herself.

But today, the *Star-Bulletin*'s headline soured the plumeria-scented calm of the morning: "Supreme Court Ruling – Ozawa Not a Citizen."

Haru shook her head as she read the first sentence of Pafko's front-page celebration.

"Yesterday, the Supreme Court unanimously ruled, 'Caucasians are white and Japanese are members of an inassimilable race.' That's all you need to know," gloated the reporter. Not satisfied with reviewing Ozawa's challenge and the court's ruling, he speculated on the "false citizenship" of Japanese army veterans sworn in by Judge Vaughn. No doubt, Pafko predicted, "The Supreme Court will get around to invalidating these 'mistakes.'" He reminded his readers that the Territory of Hawaii has never recognized the "Vaughn Citizens." "The court has ruled—once a Jap, always a Jap."

Pafko didn't stop there. He stepped up the tempo of his column by trumpeting the new legislation passed earlier in the month "to put some teeth in shutting down these anti-American schools." He wrote on. "Patriot Joshua Bilkerton pushed through the bill, forbidding Japanese children to attend language schools until the fourth grade, limiting school hours, and requiring their teachers to pass English language proficiency tests." But he then went on to bemoan the lack of progress on implementing those regulations. The Department of Education had claimed it needed time to prepare a brief for Makino's threat to challenge the law in court, which never happened. "Why should Makino press forward," wrote Pafko, "when government officials acted as if he already had won his case?"

Pafko paid lukewarm homage to the companion Foreign Language Press Control Bill passed in the same session. "While as a journalist I respect the Fourth Amendment on press freedom, the legislation requiring Japanese newspapers to translate articles dealing with politics, labor issues, and laws into English and to submit such articles for a censor's approval prior to publication is temporarily necessary to maintain order in our society."

Pafko closed with his usual reference to the "good Christian Japanese" led by the Reverend Okumura.

The reference to Okumura rankled Haru. He had split the Japanese community, even if it were an eighty-twenty split in favor of the Buddhists. She recalled her first meeting with Okumura. Despite his cold reception, she had encouraged the down-in-the-mouth Yoshi to register for Okumura's carpentry class. He did. Then the furor began as the smug Okumura predicted. After Yoshi attended his first class, the Moiliili Hongwanji lay committee scheduled a special meeting to ostracize Yoshi and his family from the Hongwanji unless he quit his class. While Kenji was able to have his lay committee back off, Yoshi got the message, withdrew his registration, and delivered an apology at the next Sunday services.

Haru got the message too. Hopes for any type of compromise were dashed. She had a better understanding of why nations went to war, rather than traded concessions.

Haru looked up from the paper to Kenji sitting across from her, reading Makino's *Hawaii Hochi*. "More coffee?"

"Hai, Okasan." Kenji laid down the paper. "Same story, but you would hardly know it from reading both versions of their truths," said Kenji. The two of them had started the morning as usual: Kenji reading the *Hochi* and Haru the *Star-Bulletin*, and then switching newspapers before either glanced at the *Jiji Shinpo* and the *Advertiser*.

"Makino keeps publishing without having his stories approved," smiled Haru.

"Fred-san has lost most of his haole advertising," said Kenji.

Haru's mouth switched from upturned to downturned. "I doubt if he will be able to pay back the five-hundred-dollar loan we gave him for rent and back wages, even though he's cut his staff in half."

"He may have to use money from his pharmacy to pay us back, but he will," said Kenji, who had insisted on a larger loan than Haru had wanted.

"The crisis issue is the school bill," said Haru.

"That's why I invited Makino to dinner tonight. He claims now is the time to go to court."

Haru raised an eyebrow.

Kenji noted the skepticism. "I think this time he means it."

"Will our school join any action?"

"Let's hear Makino out," said Kenji. Changing the subject, he added, "I am going into downtown Honolulu this morning. Do you need anything?"

Haru smiled ruefully and shook her head. "Well, I need some yarn, but for you to translate my description of color into the right choice is beyond my language skills."

⊙ CHAPTER 104 ⊙

As KENJI DROVE OFF, Haru padded over to her Singer. "A seamstress day," she addressed the new machine while thinking, *You are the only good outcome of my meeting with Okumura.* She sat down next to her boys' trouser pile for shortening or lengthening, depending upon which hand-me-down she was working on.

Thirty minutes into her sewing project, the sharp, short ring of the front doorbell interrupted her stitching of Tommy's cuffs. Seconds later, she heard a thunk, followed by the soft whishing of an envelope. She waited for the clunk of the wooden flap slapping the mail chute before she investigated the day's post, but already her mood had lightened. The thunk meant a catalog. Which one? Last week, she had received the Montgomery Ward winter catalog. As she entered the foyer, she was surprised to see an unfamiliar tome lying on the welcome mat and had to stop to read the spine: Spiegel.

A jolt of excitement ripped through her as she spotted an envelope bearing Admiral Togo's portrait on Japanese stamps. *Must be from Midori*, she surmised. She stooped to pick up the catalogue and letter and sauntered over to the tatami room, her favorite spot. As much as Haru embraced Western furniture with all its conveniences, she always felt soothed when entering what her family had recently started calling "Mama's retreat." The centerpiece of the sparsely furnished room was the squat, lacquered, rosewood tea table. Four *zaisu*, or floor chairs, surrounded the table. She moved one of the padded zaisu to her private tatami *tsukue*, a knee-high sandalwood desk. Haru squatted down on the back of her legs in front of the floor desk, which still gave off hints of its famous aroma. A smile softened her face as it always did when she looked up at the watercolor of a cherry tree branch in full bloom against a pink sky honoring the facing wall.

She flipped the envelope around. The return address was her Hiroshima home. She lifted her ivory letter opener. And stopped. She stared at the unfamiliar handwriting. Who besides Midori or Kiyoshi ever wrote her from the Fudoin Temple? Her heart bumped against her rib cage. Something had happened to her parents.

Haru wedged the ivory blade under the seal and withdrew two thin sheets of paper. Like all of Haru's incoming correspondence, this letter would be added to a string-tied batch, carefully sorted by sender and kept in a wobbly bamboo letter box built by Yoshio three birthdays ago. With dreaded expectations, Haru began to read.

"Dear sister" was as far as Haru read before tears drowned her eyes. It couldn't be. But it was. She managed to read the next words. "I am Kin. Gin and I are fine." Haru took a handkerchief from the cuff of her yukata to wipe the free-flowing tears. She wanted to rush out and tell Kenji, the children, someone, everyone. Ever since arriving in Hiroshima in 1905, Haru had posted a letter, first monthly, then twice a year, to her sisters at their last known address—a silk factory in Niigata. The correspondence always came back undelivered. Despite the failures, Haru continued writing the letters after arriving in Hawaii. As the years passed, she realized the returned letters constituted more of a diary than a correspondence.

She glanced left at the family portraits resting on the raised flooring that served as a knickknack shelf separating the tatami mat from the wall. *Soon I will be able to add my sisters' photos.*

Her eyes went back to the letter. "This summer, we returned to Amakusa to pay our respects to our parents who gave their lives for your freedom."

Bile rose in Haru's throat. Her left hand grabbed the low table as she tried to fight her lightheadedness. She breathed slowly and deeply. She had always wondered about her parents' sudden deaths at sea. An image of their last minutes, struggling in the icy water, arose before her. Now she fully accepted what had happened. Her father had used the procurer's money to pay off his debts before she was scheduled to depart. Had she really believed that her father was going to pay back the money to the procurer when he told her to escape? But she had honored their sacrifice. She became a cherished daughter and the wife of a good man, a gifted priest. Together, they had dedicated their lives to helping others. She looked up at the cherry blossom painting while thinking that only now did she realize the depth of her parents' love. That night, when they had sent her on her way to freedom, they knew the cost. They knew they had only hours to live.

Long moments passed before Haru could resume reading.

Amakusa's Buddhist temple told us the story of your escape, adoption, and move to Hawaii. Then I understood why the postman sent back a letter addressed to Otosan with a note, "Family deceased." After that notice, we wrote you a letter at the same address. Another note from the postman on the back of the returned envelope. "Haru ran away. No one has heard from her." Such a small matter for such a long separation. Once we learned you had gone to the Fudoin Temple, we went to Hiroshima. Kiyoshi and Midori were so kind. They insisted we stay with them until we decided what to do.

Susano padded over and snaked her furry body through Haru's legs. The calico Persian was rewarded with gentle but absentminded strokes along her arched back.

After the Russian war, our company promoted us to supervisors on the condition we move to Sendai. We were happy to leave. Our boss in Niigata was very mean. No mail was ever forwarded from that workplace, even though we left a forwarding address. In Sendai, we lived in a dorm with the young girls we managed. We often talked about going to the matchmaker but kept putting it off. Now, at thirty-four, we are too old for any man to accept us as a first wife. And we don't want to be someone's minor wife.

Haru had stopped crying by the time Sachi returned with Kenta and the groceries. Looking at Haru's red eyes, the girl asked, "Are you all right, Okasan?"

"I have found my sisters." Then she told the story to Sachi. When Haru finally finished, Sachi laid a gentle hand on the woman she so admired. "If not for your parents, who would have taken care of me? I will fix lunch. You can start writing a letter to your sisters."

Haru placed her own hand on Sachi's in thanks. "Perhaps I can write a few pages before the boys and Kenji come home. We have so much to do this afternoon."

"Yes," said Sachi, proud she had remembered that Mr. Makino and other important people were coming to dinner to talk about the school laws.

∞ CHAPTER 105 ∞

Diamond Head – Easter Sunday, 1923

"WHAT'S AT STAKE IS what type of Nisei citizens will be voting—those molded in the American tradition in public schools or those indoctrinated by the Buddhist-run, so-called language schools."

Squared-jawed Walter Dillingham was holding court with Hawaii's power elite this Easter Sunday afternoon in his library. His fawning audience ignored the clacks of mallets striking a wooden ball followed by a whistling swish across the perfectly manicured pitch. The sprinkle of raindrops pinging open bay windows drew no notice. Still wearing his riding boots and formfitting polo shirt, Dillingham paused to let his words sink in as his commanding eyes snuck a glimpse at the continuing polo exhibition. Outside, women adorned in their Easter finery held dainty umbrellas over fancy bonnets and cheered the Farrington and Dillingham polo team riders competing in an exhibition match. A rainbow stretched from the tip of Diamond Head into the far end of Dillingham's pot of gold, called "La Pietra"—a half-million-dollar Italian Renaissance villa inspired by the fabled Medici family's sixteenth-century Florence residence.

While Walter Dillingham believed in the Bible and in the prerogative of the white race to rule the planet, including the lesser races in America, he was a practical man who accomplished big tasks—erecting the dry docks at Pearl Harbor, draining the wetlands of Waikiki to create the Ala Wai Canal, building hotels, and clearing land for Oahu's largest ranches and sugar plantations. Dillingham believed that any problem simply required study—picking the best solution and making it happen, like closing these un-American schools and bringing the Japanese labor force to heel.

His father was not a missionary descendant like most of Hawaii's elite, so he married one. Seaman Benjamin Franklin Dillingham landed in Hawaii in 1864, fell sick, and his ship sailed without him. He procured work at a hardware store, soon bought it, and wooed his missionary mate. In debt most of his early life from land purchases, he made his big score founding the Oahu Railway that created the foundation of the Dillinghams' wealth and power.

Young Walter dropped out of Harvard to help run the family business when his father fell ill in 1904. While second-generation sons often dissipate the family fortune, Walter Dillingham multiplied his manyfold. Now approaching fifty, he kept fit by playing polo and moderating his eating and drinking. His still mostly blond hair, neatly trimmed and with only a hint of receding, gave him the youthful look of a man closer to forty.

Governor Wallace Farrington and a half-dozen key legislators hung on every word Dillingham uttered. Governors are appointed; legislators bought and sold. Walter Dillingham, beholden to no one, was a constant. His penetrating eyes now locked on Joshua Bilkerton, a man he had dismissed as a buffoon during the strike but who had somehow righted himself. Next to him sat the bulbous-nosed Andy Pafko, his pen hovering over a pocket-size spiral notepad. It amused Dillingham that this useful scribe considered himself an investigative reporter, instead of a puppet.

"That Makino is tying us up in court appeals," said Bilkerton, trimming the cap of his Havana cigar with a stainless-steel cutter. "Judge Banks's injunction staying the implementation of the Foreign Language School Bill still stands. The schools remain active." He put the flame of his Ronson to the tip of his cigar and took a slow, steady draw.

"Let Wallace fight the court cases, Joshua," said Dillingham, drawing on a Vuelta Abajo cigar he allowed himself at these functions. "Let's stay on the offensive. And no more press-control bills that flag themselves so obviously and make us look like King George's tea-tax parliament. Stick to the objective: It's the schools."

"What about a head tax?" said a tentative voice from several seats back. "Six bits or a dollar for each student."

"Now that's the spirit," said Dillingham, giving a warm smile to the man, who beamed at the approbation. "Yes, a tax."

"A head tax for each student to pay for the government's oversight of the schools," said Bilkerton, eager to take charge.

"A dollar a head should do it," said Dillingham.

"It's April," said Bilkerton. "We'll be in session next week. I can whip this through committee and on to the floor before the end of the month."

Dillingham took another deep draw on his cigar. "I haven't given up on my petition to Congress to let us immigrate thirty thousand Chinese laborers. As you know, last year I gave the immigration committee an earful on the military danger of all these Japs in Hawaii. They cheered me and then kowtowed to the State Department and refused to move the bill out of committee. Now this Teapot Dome scandal over oil concessions has brought Washington to a standstill; Harding's not about to push on anything big like immigration."

A skeptical-sounding voice challenged, "Congress letting in more Asians from anywhere, Walter? There's a groundswell for an immigration bill banning all Asians excepting the Flips."

"We have a friend with Harding," Dillingham pontificated. "Not like that sanctimonious, save-the-world Wilson. Last year, Harding sent his own commission to investigate those language schools. He sent me a letter expressing his concern about the future loyalty of the Nisei."

Dillingham flicked ashes over a crystal ashtray. "I think the Republican Congress will do what needs to be done to bring permanent labor peace to Hawaii. Even if they pass a bill banning future Asian immigration, they can grant a one-time exception for Hawaii to lessen our dependency on Jap laborers." He took a quick puff and pointed the cigar at Bilkerton. "Let 'em know there is a consequence to striking."

Pafko looked up at the word "striking."

"Use my words on permanent peace, Andy, but skip the part about breaking or punishing strikers."

"I know better," said Pafko.

Dillingham turned and looked out the window, watching the riders dismount and walk their horses to the stable. "It's time to get the servants cracking to set up our luau."

❦ CHAPTER 106 ❦

Kapiolani Park

A LIGHT SPRAY FLECKED THE FACES OF HARU and her young charges. The three o'clock sun painted a double rainbow arching down from the rainy Waahila Ridge and curving into the sunny Kapiolani Park a mile from the Takayama home.

"Check your backpacks," said Haru.

A dozen boys ages seven to eleven, including her Tommy and Yoshio, stood almost at attention in their starched, blue Cub Scout uniforms. Stitched merit badges peppered the upper sleeves. Unblemished yellow bandanas hung around their necks.

Haru extracted a list from her yukata sleeve and began the check-off. "Three Band-Aids?"

"Hai," the chorus shouted out.

"*Onigiri*?" said Haru, referring to plum-centered rice balls wrapped in pressed seaweed.

"Hai."

"Water canteens?"

And so the list went.

Haru and her assistant den mother, Saki, were donkey-loaded with marshmallows, hamburger meat, buns, ketchup, and mustard.

In need of another income, Saki had taken to raising rabbits, thanks to an advance from Haru.

"Better than pigs," Saki said. "They don't smell, not much poop, and they multiply like … rabbits." The line always got the laugh she'd learned to expect. Her husband's carpentry business "was starting slow." After quitting Okumura's carpentry class, Yoshi had pressured his critics to let him join their *tanomoshi* loan club and lend him money for an electric planer.

The Cub Scout idea had been birthed in Waimea by Haru as a way to Americanize her children. She had approached Wellington Carter, whose ranch sponsored scouting for his paniolos' children. Haru had served as an assistant den mother for three months with the cowboys' Cub Scout troop. She had entered her apprenticeship in order to provide her mission's children something American but quickly found she enjoyed the outings. While the Cub Scouts was an American institution, the activities of rope-tying, reading a compass, and identifying birds and animals held universal appeal to boys of any culture. Later, when Takeshi was of age, Kenji had promised to start a Boy Scout troop.

Satisfied everyone was prepared, Haru announced, "Until we get back, let's speak English only."

One voice squeaked, "Each time somebody speaks Japanese, he loses a marshmallow."

After a ragged chorus of "hai" and "yes" and then finger-pointing at the "hais," it was agreed to count the marshmallows. "Eight," said Yoshio. "There are enough for everyone to have eight."

Haru caught herself before exclaiming, "Ikimasho," and instead yelled out in her best sergeant's voice, "Let's go!" The boys set out at a trot, a pace the women hoped would soon slow.

Two hours later, the point scout on the hike yelled, "That looks like a good spot."

Haru hurried to the front and took a look. Flat ground. The remains of burnt wood settled in shallow fire pits told her others had found the spot to their liking. She glanced at Saki who nodded her head.

The boys gathered firewood. Yoshio swung his machete to trim branches to fashion poles for the tents. When Saki started to make hamburger patties, Tommy dug his fingers into the ground beef mixture and squealed, *"Orega yaruyo!"*

"You might do it," said Yoshio, "but you just lost a marshmallow." Ignoring the rebuke, Tommy looked at his mother. "To earn our merit badges, we must do everything ourselves."

Saki stepped back making way for the proud hamburger chef.

After dinner and with the clean-up finished, someone hollered, "It's time to roast the marshmallows!"

And play the presidents game, thought Haru. Could the boys name all the American presidents from Washington to Harding? As she was about to open her mouth, one of the boys pronounced, "The

Yankees will win the pennant again this year because they've got Babe Ruth, the greatest player."

"Maybe they will win," said Yoshio, "but Ty Cobb is the greatest player. Almost four thousand hits and nine hundred stolen bases."

"You are both wrong," said another boy. "The best hitter ever is Roger Hornsby. He averaged almost four hundred for the past three seasons. Nobody else ever did that."

Maybe, thought Haru, *debating America's baseball players is more important than ticking off the presidents.* The boys certainly needed no prompting to study America's favorite pastime. She and Saki retreated from the fire. If the boys noticed their departure, no one said anything. The last name Haru heard was Cy Young. Was that a name or a description? she wondered. Setting down her empty backpack off to the side, Haru pulled a light-blue aerogram letter from her yukata. "I think my parents are worried my sisters plan to stay forever," she laughed.

"Well, read it out loud," said Saki.

"Let me jump to the part about my sisters." Haru unfolded the letter, held it at an angle to catch the light from the fire, scanned toward the bottom of the front page, and began reading.

> Your sisters are settling in your old room. We welcome them to share our meals and enjoy their silk factory stories. If I were younger, maybe I would start growing mulberry trees. Gin and Kin are delightful companions, although they seem a little lost. Their initial energy looking for work has diminished. The best place for their skills is in Tohoku, but they seemed to have fallen in love with Hiroshima, my cooking, and your room.

Haru placed the letter down on her lap.

As if on cue, Saki asked, "How old are your parents?"

"Kiyoshi is almost seventy, and Midori five years younger."

"Your parents are rather elderly to take care of two middle-aged women," said Saki with a disapproving voice. "It should be the other way around."

A shout from the sweet-smelling marshmallow campfire distracted them for a moment. "Ty Cobb never had a candy bar named after him!" Haru smiled and then added, "My sisters lacked the love of parents such as Midori and Kiyoshi. They were sold off to a Niigata silk factory in their early teens. If they were younger, they could find husbands."

"Are they really too old?" said Saki with renewed interest. "Maybe too old for a man's first wife in Hiroshima. But what about a wife to a man in Hawaii who lost his first wife and is now burdened with children?"

"Before Japan stopped the picture bride program, that might have been possible," said Haru.

"Some desperate men are traveling to Japan to marry their arranged brides and bring them back as wives," said Saki.

"That loophole might not last much longer," said Haru. "The *Hochi* reports that Congress is considering passing an immigration law that will prohibit any more Japanese immigrating to America."

The thought lingered until Saki blurted, "The Miho brothers are widowers. They both lost their wives to the Spanish flu."

"Who?" asked Haru, who knew practically everyone in Moiliili.

"They work with Oki Tama at the Ala Wai dredging project. They had machinery jobs on a sugar plantation."

"Why didn't they remarry?" asked Haru. "There were plenty of widows who needed husbands."

"I don't know. That's your department," laughed Saki.

Haru nodded, looked at her watch, and began to rise. "Let's get our adventurers inside the tents."

∞ CHAPTER 107 ∞

February 1924

"OTOSAN, COACH WILLIAMS wants me to try out for the baseball team," said Takeshi. Haru heard the strain in his voice, even though he tried to sound casually enthusiastic. "He thinks I could be the starting first baseman for McKinley."

The Sunday brunch table quieted, a horse-drawn carriage crunching the crushed-seashell road outside the home the only sound. Smells of bacon, pancakes, and maple syrup hung in the air unnoticed. Tommy and Yoshi knew what was happening. So did pinched-faced Haru. Even though four-year-old Kenta did not have a clue, he picked up on the silence.

Kenji lifted his floral cotton napkin and wiped an imaginary piece of food from his lips. "That's quite a promise to a young man entering school."

Takeshi heard the skeptical wariness in his father's voice. That was better than anger. "I'm tall for a Japanese and am one of two kids who hit over four hundred last summer for our mission team."

"The time to play baseball is in the summer," said Kenji. "You played several times a week for our mission team."

"It's not the same, Otosan. Every athlete wants to play for his school."

"You have other responsibilities after school more important than practicing baseball."

"It's only a couple months during the spring. I can keep up my JLS lessons in the evening," said Taka with more forced casualness.

"Let me consider this," said Kenji.

Taka stared at the set of his father's jaw. "When you say 'consider' and wear that face, it means no. That's not fair. Why can't I be just like the haole kids, the Hawaiian boys, and everyone else at my school?"

"Your father said he would consider," admonished Haru. "That's enough for now. Let's enjoy our breakfast."

Taka picked up his plate and turned it upside down, spilling eggs, pancakes, and syrup onto the table. He pushed his chair back so fast it clanged to the ground, but he took no notice. Seconds later, they heard the front door slam and watched out the picture window as Taka sped away on his bike.

Haru broke the stunned silence. "He is a confused—"

"Silence, Okasan. No excuses for Taka." A stoic Kenji looked at his remaining children. "Please, let us finish our breakfast. We must not allow a foolish outburst to starve us." Then, Kenji jabbed his fork into his pancake as though he were thrusting a trowel digging for turnips. He was thinking not of Taka but, rather, of another night long ago when he had cleared the dishes off the table with one sweep of the hand.

Haru forced a bit of scrambled egg into her mouth. She too remembered that night and its consequences. Like father, like son. Her mind twisted in turmoil as she fought to think of what needed to be done to restore family harmony. It was time to have a mother's chat with Taka on keeping his temper and honoring his father. He must learn to find some common ground between the language schools and playing sports.

Her family sat still, forks down. Kenji finally said, "Gochisosama deshita," signaling the end of the meal. He rose and strode over the connecting bridge to the Hongwanji to conduct Sunday services. Although weekly church services were not the Buddhist tradition, Bishop Imamura insisted on regular Sunday services, as well as designing the temple's interior similar to what he had seen in Protestant churches.

Haru forced a smile. "Sachi, I will take care of the kitchen. Why don't you take Tommy and the girls outside."

"Hai," said Sachi, who started wiping eggs and syrup off Sachiko's mouth.

Haru turned on the hot water tap to fill the dish tub. There was more on her mind than the outburst between father and son. She feared the California disease.

∞ ∞

Only this morning in the *Star-Bulletin*, Andy Pafko reported on a rabid speech given to the Honolulu Rotary Club by V. S. McClatchy, president of the Japanese Exclusion League of California. He had ended his stop-Japanese-immigration rant by debunking Okumura's efforts to which he had facetiously alluded moments earlier. "It is impossible for the Japanese to assimilate, and this preacher's campaign ... is unnecessary."

But Haru was cheered when she read further. "This is not San Francisco," Rotarian Governor Bob Jefferson had challenged. "Have you had any experience with the Hawaiian attempt at Americanization?"

"No, it's not necessary," huffed McClatchy.

"No? I beg to differ. Only a fool would promote anti-Japanese sentiment with no firsthand knowledge of the campaign for Americanization."

Haru felt goose bumps rise as she read, "The Honolulu Rotary Club stood to a man and cheered their own."

Pafko ended his column by reporting, "Walter Dillingham canceled a scheduled dinner at his home with McClatchy."

Pafko's reporting confirmed what Haru believed: not every haole was a racist. *I only wish I had the answer to the dilemma of how 40 percent of Hawaii's population can maintain its culture while assuring the haoles we are neither a threat to their way of life nor a fifth column for an expanding Japanese empire.*

Haru pushed her musing aside. She needed to focus on the problems she could help alleviate. That meant her son, husband, and sisters.

Her sisters.

Shortly after the Cub Scout hike, she had visited a family friend, the Buddhist priest at the plantation where the brothers had lived until they accepted a job with the Ala Wai project.

"They were good husbands," the priest had attested.

Then, she had met the Miho brothers. They had impressed her as diligent men. "So," Haru had asked, "why haven't you remarried one of the Spanish flu widows?"

After the brothers' hemming and hawing, Haru squeezed out the excuses—wariness of a bigger family a widow would bring to the marriage plus the comfort zone the granny they had hired to mind the children, cook, and clean made it easy to put off wife-hunting. The younger brother had allowed, "If the Japanese government had not stopped bringing in picture brides, we would have written our parents to send us wives." *Like so many of our men*, thought Haru, *they don't want to be involved in the messy business of courtship.*

Given the opening, Haru asked, "If you could find a bride in Japan who is a little older than usual but unmarried, would you be interested in providing your children with a mother?"

"Mother*s*?" said the older Miho emphasizing the S. That was enough show of curiosity to encourage Haru to offer Kin and Gin as prospective brides. The men agreed.

She wrote her sisters extolling the history and virtues of the Miho brothers, closing with "The Miho brothers have done well enough, so they can afford passage back to Japan. You can be married in Hiroshima and come back to Hawaii with your husbands."

When she didn't hear from them immediately, Haru wrote again urging Kin and Gin to decide quickly. "There is a new immigration bill working its way through Congress that might break the 1907 Gentlemen's Agreement and bar all Japanese immigration." Still, the two sisters dithered, as if marriage proposals were as abundant as the stars. A frustrated Haru sent a telegram. "I promised the Miho brothers to find wives. You are the first choice. Please tell me if I should look elsewhere."

⌒ CHAPTER 108 ⌒

AS MUCH AS HARU WANTED TO HELP HER SISTERS, the most troubling issue at hand was the tension between Taka and Kenji. Taka was not the first Nisei teenager to take issue with the daily rush from public school to the language school. Advising mothers on how to address the issue of older children resenting the "boring and meaningless" lessons was much easier than handling it with her own son. As she started to rehearse key points, she saw Taka pedaling up the street.

"Let's ride over to Waikiki," shouted Haru through the back door. She untied her apron and hung it on the wooden peg next to the kitchen's vegetable cutting board, swung the screen door open, and hurried down the steps to the backyard where Taka had just pulled up on his bike, his legs on the ground straddled over his bike's chipped, red-painted, steel bar. Haru ignored her son's wary look and stepped under the kitchen overhang to grab her ladies' Schwinn. "Let's go by the way of Kalakaua and McCully. We can see how the Ala Wai dredging is progressing. I want to share a special memory with you."

Relieved that he was not being reprimanded, Taka managed an "okay."

Haru led the single-file ride—Sunday traffic made a side-by-side formation dangerous. Besides, she needed time to gather her thoughts. As they cycled, she couldn't help but notice how much Moiliili had changed in the four years since the dredging had begun. Where Kapiolani met McCully, which until the dredging had been a vast mosquito-infested marshland, "For Sale" signs now marked pegged lots on black soil pushing up lime sprouts of recently seeded grass.

Haru stopped. The canal had taken shape—a surveyor's straight line from the beach on her right and then, turning her head left, the canal's starting point far out on the edge of Kapiolani Park. "What a change," she said loudly as Taka came up beside her. She pointed to gurgling pumps on board a barge near a monster scoop, dripping mud as it rose out of the water like the head of a Tyrannosaurus rex slaking its thirst. "I wonder if Oki Tama is working today."

This respite on the canal reminded Haru of another day, another tour, a previous life. "Let's go to the park across from the Moana Hotel and find a bench." As she biked down Kalakaua, the memories flooded in. Why hadn't she done this earlier? *Four years in Moiliili, and I have never brought the children here*, she thought, *never told them the whole story of my first visit.* Her eyes lolled left and right as she glanced ahead at the sidewalks lining the avenue where the aloha-shirted men and muumuu-adorned women strolled hand in hand. On her left, youngsters in swimsuits pranced around food-laden concrete tables and blankets checkerboarding a spinach-green grass park. To her right, the mostly white sunbathers lay on the beach with a sprinkling of the new phenomena of brown-skinned native beach boys among single, Mainland women seeking to realize their island fantasies—or so the newspapers salaciously hinted.

"Over there under the palm trees," said Haru, wanting to avoid direct sunlight. She loved her copper skin but did not want it turning sunbaked and leathery. Regretting she had not brought something to sit on, she squatted while Taka sat cross-legged on the grass still damp from the morning dew. "Let me tell you about my first visit to Waikiki." For the next thirty minutes, Haru relived her honeymoon tour. Her children knew the bare-bones account of their mother's arrival, but she had never colored the details.

At fourteen, Taka was eager to hear the rendition. Soon forgetting his morning rage, he envisioned his mother's unsteady steps down the ship's gangway at Honolulu Harbor and searching the faces of the waiting crowds for his father and heard about the pinkeye crisis Haru solved for Kame and the afternoon "honeymoon" trolley to Waikiki. "We rode our horses," she said, pointing to the surf, "on the beach past the Moana Hotel. The sun was setting over Pearl Harbor like a molten ruby."

Haru looked over at Taka. He was only a year older than she had been when she had fled Amakusa. Such a different childhood. Was she angry that Taka did not appreciate the good life he enjoyed? "Your father is a protector of Japanese culture."

Taka's eyes of wonderment turned pugnacious.

"Taka-chan, you are the son of a good man."

Taka's face softened. "Of course, I know that, but even you were against the schools."

"Advocating change is not the same as being against them," Haru corrected. "When you think of Hawaii's best farmers, the best fishermen, and the best coffee growers, whom do you think of?"

"Us Japanese."

"Which group of immigrants has the highest percentage of university students?"

"Us Japanese." Taka nodded his head. "I understand, Okasan, but what has that to do with Otosan not allowing me to play baseball?"

"The spirit of being Japanese does not just happen. We have our traditions of giri—duty and always repaying a favor with a favor; of gaman—enduring without complaining, no matter the struggle; and meiyo—honor, never bringing shame on one's family—"

"I know the pillars of our nation, Okasan." Taka caught his mother's disapproving look. "Our culture, our identity that transcends nationality. It's not geography but our essence—no matter where we might be."

"Gisei?" asked Haru.

"Sacrifice. We put others, the group, ahead of our desires." His tone softened.

Haru looked at him expectantly.

"*On.* A kindness to me is a debt of gratitude that I am obligated to pay back, if not to the person granting me the favor, then something of equal value to another."

"And *chugi?*" Haru asked encouragingly.

Taka's voice firmed up. "Loyalty. Loyalty to our family. But that is like *ko*—loyalty or obedience to one's family." He caught Haru's nod. "To one's ... to my father." He paused. "But chugi to me means loyalty to my country. To America." He stared at his mother. "What does it mean to you, Okasan? I am American. I know no other country."

A beach ball bounced up and hit her shoulder. Haru looked up.

A blond girl, maybe nine years old, reached for it and said, "Sorry."

Haru smiled and tossed the ball at the girl's feet. "Have fun." She noticed that the noise had picked up as more picnickers had spread straw mats on the grass. She leaned into Taka. "America will not give us Issei citizenship. We must live and die as aliens here. Thus, we are forced to choose between America and Japan. For myself, in my heart, I am an American. I will not go back to Japan. I have made my decision. This is my country."

A more relaxed Taka said, "More like *gambari*, or persistence." And then with an impish grin, he added, "But maybe in your case ... stubbornness."

"That's why almost all Japanese parents feel *sekinin*, or responsibility, to pass on our values and sacrifices ... "

"An example of gisei," said Taka.

"Yes. You see how it comes together. When your father arrived in Honolulu, those values had slipped away from the laborers here. One's values must be reinforced, or one loses them."

"Yes, Okasan, but I think it was more due to picture brides who took the men away from the bars and gambling dens."

Haru smiled. "We humans need a social environment. But look around, Taka. All cultures have values, but whose values keep families together the best, help their neighbors the most, and bestow the highest trust among their own? We are flesh and bone like everyone else. It is the constant struggle to keep our values alive that gives us purpose, makes us persevere when the haoles attack us. Even all those little things like taking off our shoes when entering a home, bathing frequently, paying back our debts quickly contribute. These habits are not accidents."

"That's why Otosan directs our mission language school," said Taka.

"And that is why you must make peace with your father. I will talk to him and Coach Williams to see how everyone can win. Maybe you can play baseball and still attend the mission school most of the time."

"Maybe it's best that I apologize and promise to attend school ... but I'm hoping you will work on Coach Williams and Dad. I'm not the only one, Mom."

"You've learned a good lesson, not just about our values but also about losing your temper. It diminishes your negotiating ability. Your behavior, rather than your point of view, becomes the issue. The person who must apologize for bad behavior has lost half the argument. In your weakened position, the other person's position is more likely to prevail than if you had kept control of yourself."

∞ CHAPTER 109 ∞

Taka took his accustomed seat at the silent dinner table. Everyone except Haru studied his or her empty dinner plate as if some hidden script could be read on the design rimming the edges. Haru looked into Taka's eyes, willing him to follow up on their beach conversation.

"Otosan, the preservation of our Japanese culture is more important than a baseball game. I apologize for losing my temper this morning. I will accept any punishment you give me without complaint."

Furtive eyes peeked at their father and husband. Kenji's stoic face hid his hurt as he accepted his son's apology. As the family began scooping rice out of the bowl in the middle of the table, Kenji feared this was not the end of his son's rebellion. At his core, he believed that Taka's assertiveness was the downside of America culture. Kenji's self-assurance in the righteous cause of the language schools made it almost impossible for him to see his son's side, to understand his frustration. He had not played sports in school. The idea that somehow this game of baseball could be important was foreign to him.

That night as Haru pulled back the sheet to enter the bed, she asked, "Now that Taka has apologized, isn't there some way he could be excused from some of the classes for a few months?"

Kenji tightened his grip on *Babbitt*, Sinclair Lewis's book Imamura insisted he read to "get an insight into America." He avoided Haru's eyes. "Our son has done the right thing. I have accepted his unconditional apology. He promised to attend the classes without objection."

"He did, and he meant it," said Haru. "But who sponsors a mission team that allows the highly talented a chance to show how good they are and then denies them a chance to move to the next level?"

Kenji's face hardened. "Maybe at another time. But our schools are under attack. Taka is my son. We have joined with Makino to press the district court to overrule the territorial legislature. How could I let my own son skip school? What example would that set?"

"Wakarimashita," said Haru. The discussion was closed.

Haru sat in Coach Williams's office, perched uncomfortably on a folding chair across an empty desk. The locker room stench wafting into the room reminded her of the ship captain's breath when she had fled Amakusa. Basketballs, soccer balls, volleyballs, badminton nets, and scuffed-up baseball bats cluttered the cramped pigeon hole. A single wooden-louvered window let in an occasional whiff of fresh air and the shouts of a touch football game.

Haru felt humiliated at having to plead her son's case to Coach Williams. *It's not our nature to ask for something where a positive answer is doubtful,* she mused. But to not even try guaranteed failure. Perhaps if it had been only Taka, she would have let it pass. But almost half of McKinley's students were Japanese. Surely, the coach wanted to field his best team.

A mangled "ohayo gozaimasu" boomed behind her.

Haru turned and stood, craning her neck at the giant who stood two heads taller than herself. She had determined not to bow. "Oh," said a wide-smiling Haru. "You speak Japanese."

"Only 'good morning' and 'thank you,' Mrs. Takayama," said Coach Williams as he worked himself around the desk and sat down. "Your boys are natural athletes. Takeshi has what we call a sweet swing."

"That's why I am here. Taka speaks so well of you." Haru paused, thinking of how haoles like to get to the point. "Coach Williams, is there a way Taka could practice on Saturdays, during the lunch period, or during the physical education period?" She made a point of looking behind him at the football game in progress. "It's not just Taka; there are so many Japanese boys who are good players."

"Mrs. Takayama, perhaps if the legislature, the court cases ... " Williams stopped as if looking for the right words, "if the current environment was not so ... difficult. It's not the time to work around the problem. Besides, some Japanese parents have given their boys permission to take a break from your schools on practice days."

She knew he was right. Haru admitted to herself that some boys—with their parents' permission—skipped language classes to play high school football, basketball, or baseball. Not many, but enough to make the case for Coach Williams. In addition, at Okumura's urging, many Japanese Christian congregations had closed their language schools, thus freeing up close to 20 percent of Japanese children for school sports.

"Thank you, Coach Williams. This is a difficult position for you to handle. You have been very understanding."

Will this ever end? wondered Haru as she biked home.

∞ CHAPTER 110 ∞

Moiliili – May 26, 1924

"QUIET," HISSED ONE OF THE BOYS. "They are starting to vote."
A hush settled over the Takayama living room. Twenty-three of Taka's fellow Nisei McKinley students stood leaning over the breakfast table or sitting at it. Atop the table, a new Crosley radio was broadcasting the proceedings. All ears strained to hear the voice

emanating from the four-tube radio receiver, the size of a loaf of bread. Its companion battery cabinet was stacked underneath. Taka's civics class, playing hooky at the end of the school year, needed no further admonition to silence. On this auspicious Monday morning, Haru and Sachi had risen at five o'clock to steam rice, crack four dozen eggs and scramble them along with diced ham and chopped onions in a Chinese wok, and slice six loaves of bread to toast in the oven. Sachi's right hand was sore from squeezing fresh oranges for juice. The large coffee urn, normally used exclusively for mission socials, was percolating on its third refill.

KGU radio was broadcasting the coming immigration vote in the Senate on a shortwave relay from KHJ Los Angeles. Taka's class was as American as any in Kansas that might also be listening to this "democracy in action" radio coverage, but with a big difference. In an hour, they would learn if men and women of their racial ancestry would be forbidden to immigrate to America.

The news announcer intoned, "The vote will commence in five minutes due to a procedural question."

Everyone surrounding the radio began talking at once as shoulders eased and spines relaxed. "Americans complain that the Jews and Italians are diluting white America. Now Californians see the racial purity campaign as an opportunity to include us," said a male student.

"*Exclude* us," corrected Amy, who always made a point not to act Japanese.

Crew-cut neat Koichi ignored her. "What these nativists really want is an America the way it was in 1776, white and Protestant."

"The whole thing with importing African slave labor turned on them after emancipation," said Amy. "They don't want another minority race, particularly one that is educated."

"The immigration pushback started with the starving Irish Catholics who came to America by the boatload," another boy said.

"In 1848," supplied Amy.

"Yeah, but later there were all the Jews fleeing Russia and Poland after the Great War. And don't forget the Italians." Koichi pinched his fingers together, raised them to his mouth, and mimed as though he were throwing a huge, juicy kiss. "*Mama mia*! They came to America by the tens of thousands."

That got a good laugh from the group—all except Amy.

"It started with the 1922 quotas," she intoned. "Our fair-faced congressmen came up with the plan to 'keep our country very, very, VERY white' by restricting future immigration. From then on, country immigration quotas were based on the number of people from that country who were already citizens."

"That system favors Northern Europeans—the British, Irish, Swedes, and Germans," said Taka, "the so-called good Americans."

"Isn't that half a laugh," said another voice. "Only a few years ago, the Germans were our enemy, and a generation before that the, Irish were called drunken papists."

"Now the Germans and the Irish want limits on the Jews and the Meds," said Amy, pointing her nose in the air.

A girl sitting close to the Crosley waved her hands. "Alabama just voted yes."

Thirty minutes later, Senator David Reed of Pennsylvania, co-sponsor of the bill, was not satisfied with voicing a simple yes vote. The chair granted him a chance to state his views for a national radio audience.

"Let me remind you of the good words of Valentine McClatchy, president of the Oriental Exclusion League of California who appeared before our committee:

> I have a very high regard for the character and ability of the Japanese nation and the Japanese people. And I realize that it is their strong racial characteristics which make them so dangerous a factor if admitted to the country as permanent residents. Even US-born, second-generation Japanese were not assimilatory because they had been raised by Japanese parents.
>
> With great pride of race, they have no idea of assimilation. They never cease to be Japanese. They do not come to this country with any desire or any intent to lose their racial or national identity. They come here

specifically and professedly for the purpose of colonizing and establishing here permanently the proud Yamato race.

"I vote yes."

When it came time for Senator LeBaron Colt from Rhode Island, chairman of the Committee on Immigration and Naturalization, the chair allowed him also to speak. "Here is this great question of racial discrimination. Don't pass a law, which Japan said to America 'would denote our inferiority. Leave it to honor.' That was the essence of the Gentlemen's Agreement. The Japanese kept their word. Labor immigration practically stopped. We can count on their continued restrictions without the need for this act.

"I vote no."

∞ Chapter 111 ∞

HARU FIDGETED. She glimpsed at her rooster-emblazoned kitchen wall clock, her heart thudding like a taiko. Would SS *Lisbon Maru* arrive on time? On board, her sisters, now brides with their husbands, originally had been expected yesterday. As soon as the vote was finished, she and Kenji would drive to Honolulu Harbor to meet the ship's arrival. "Hopefully, no later than 9 a.m.," the YKK agent had said when Haru called. She knew it would take at least another hour for them to clear customs and immigration—maybe longer, given the ship was overcrowded with immigrants sailing to beat the possible prohibition. They had cut it close with only a day—maybe just hours—to spare.

Why, she agonized, had her sisters waited to so long to accept the Miho brothers' offer of marriage? And why had the Miho brothers taken their sweet time sailing to Tokyo to collect their brides? "The bill in Congress might stop all immigration," Haru had reminded the brothers more than once.

"Yes, yes," said the older brother. "But the consul says nothing will happen until summer, if ever. The Japanese government is really working hard to make a compromise."

"But if they don't … " said Haru, whose strained voice registered an exasperation she normally suppressed.

Wiping her hands on a kitchen towel, Haru was thinking how her premonition had been worse than right. Once the Miho brothers arrived in Japan, the bureaucracy grinded slowly, even with the urgency of America's threatened immigration bill looming. Under Japan's 1920 volunteer agreement to stop the picture bride program, her twin sisters were not allowed to apply for a passport until they were married. Finally, they had left Japan on May 19 for the five-day, northern-crossing run, which winter-like rough seas had extended to six days.

Thank Buddha they will be here in hours, thought Haru. Even if the immigration bill passed, and she was certain it would, it was not the law of the land until President Coolidge signed it. With the presidential election only five months away, she had been relieved to read the president would wait a day or two and make the signing a big Rose Garden production.

∞ ∞

Masanao Hanihara, the Japanese ambassador in Washington, was listening to the vote count in the office of Secretary of State Charles Evans Hughes. The voting had reached the states that began with the letter M.

"Mr. Secretary," said Hanihara, "I urge you to advise the president to veto this bill and promise instead to sign a bill that treats the Japanese like the Italians and Jews. Give us a quota. How many of us are here? What's two percent of two hundred thousand? So few. Japan is divided between those who support America and those who see a future war. Don't make us lose face and turn the half that supports America into an enemy."

Secretary Hughes ran long, knobby fingers through his thinning hair. "This is nativist legislation at its worst, Mr. Ambassador. You and I have fought long together to avoid this day." Hughes had the diplomatic grace not to mention that the ambassador's recent interview, warning of "grave consequences" in American-Japan relations if the bill were passed, created a frenzied media backlash. Proponents of the bill seized on his statement as "a threat from a foreign nation," and the fallout had undermined Coolidge's quiet efforts to soften the bill's anti-Asian prohibition.

"I'm afraid we won't have a chance to offer an alternative. I've been told the president will sign the bill as soon as the vote is final," Hughes said.

"Today?"

Hughes's weary head nodded. "Yes, today."

∞ ∞

"Look at the crowd," said Haru as Kenji parked the car. "Triple, maybe four times the typical crowd on the dock."

"Everyone knows this docking is the end of an era," said Kenji, his voice almost sounding forlorn. He couldn't help adding a frequent refrain. "When I arrived a quarter of a century ago, we Japanese were recruited by the thousands, tens of thousands. The growers couldn't bring enough of us over. When Bishop Imamura said the men needed wives to civilize their laborers, the owners encouraged him to bring as many as possible as soon as possible. What happened? What changed?"

"We stayed," said Haru.

∞ CHAPTER 112 ∞

"**I** THINK I SEE IT," said Kenji, pointing to a dot on the northwest horizon.

Haru shaded her eyes with her hand, strained to see what Kenji saw. Nothing. It wasn't the first time she considered she might need glasses. "Maybe ... I am not sure."

Other finger-pointing soon confirmed the appearance of the SS *Lisbon Maru.*

"They made it!" sighed Haru.

"Only barely," said Kenji.

In minutes, the outline of the ship clearly marked the horizon. The beaming sun highlighted the slow-moving vessel like a theater spotlight. The coffee and food kiosk owners who had the foresight to bring along battery-powered radios to their stalls enjoyed the lion's share of the day's snack business.

Suddenly, as if a host of bees had descended on the broadcasting kiosks, the hovering listeners appeared agitated. Then just as quickly, they seemed to freeze, their faces mirroring disbelief, horror, pain.

"Something's happening," said Kenji, who began striding to the nearest kiosk.

"I hope a plane or train hasn't crashed," said Haru, fast-stepping in Kenji's wake.

"No, it's worse," said a man at the edge of the crowded kiosk. "Coolidge signed the bill."

A plaintive voice bellowed, "The people on the boat!"

"No, don't worry, they are already on American soil," argued a man, like a teacher who enjoys correcting his charges.

"What soil?" cried out the bellower. "They are on a boat!" He didn't add "stupid," but his voice implied it.

Tugboats guided the SS *Lisbon Maru* closer to the pier.

"This really is the last group of immigrants," said a sad Haru, backing away from the agitated group and thinking that, while the passengers were not on "soil," they had passed into American territorial waters before Coolidge's signing made the bill a law.

Kenji noticed uniformed immigration officers hurrying from their own coffee-drinking kiosk. A feeling of unease swept over him. His worries increased when he watched the official car of the Japanese consulate drive up. Within seconds, the consul general exited from the backseat, hurried grim-faced toward the immigration office, and then quickly disappeared inside.

"This is not good," whispered Haru more to herself than to Kenji. Her anxious face joined an army of anxious faces.

"Good morning, Takayama-san," said the familiar voice of Bishop Imamura. Both Kenji and Haru turned around.

"Maybe not so good," said Kenji.

"The consul called me ten minutes before the radio announcement. Secretary Hughes informed our ambassador that a White House signing ceremony would take place within an hour of the Senate passing the bill."

"But surely the people on this boat … " said Haru. "I mean … they are already here in American territory." She looked at the ship edging toward the pier in slow motion. "Someone needs to call Judge Vaughn," she said, thinking of the federal judge with immigration powers and with his known sympathy for the Japanese.

"That might have worked thirty minutes ago," said Imamura, shaking his head. "The bill removed federal judges from the immigration process. Immigration is now solely under the jurisdiction of the expanded Bureau of Immigration." Pointing to the building the consul had just entered, Imamura added, "Those men inside now have full authority."

As if on cue, Hawaii's newly empowered director of immigration was striding over the tarmac toward the immigration office like a man approaching the pay window at the Kentucky Derby. His steely, self-satisfied face told everyone on which side of this unfolding drama he stood. Haru remembered him from Sam's swearing-in ceremony. As he had portended, the Supreme Court was soon expected to rule Asian veterans, except Filipinos, were not entitled to citizenship.

The ship bumped into the dock. Suitcase-carrying passengers queued at the gangway as deckhands began lowering the gangplank. Two white-uniformed immigration officers trotted out from the back of their building, arms gesturing wildly, their meaning clear. The gangplank rose back up.

Minutes later, the grim-faced Japanese consul emerged from the building. The slump of his shoulders foreboded ill tidings. He was quickly surrounded. "Immigrants will not be allowed off the ship." Glancing over at the gathering swell of stevedores hovering at the cargo bay, he said, "As soon as they unload the freight, the ship will return to Japan. You will be permitted to send packages and letters to the ship." He could see that his circling audience wanted more of an explanation. "We tried our best." He bowed and walked with as much dignity as he could muster back to his limousine.

"I must write a letter," said Haru. "Otosan, please go to the bank and bring back two hundred dollars."

"That's half of our account," protested Kenji, taking a startled step back.

"We cannot allow my sisters to return to the Hiroshima mission," said Haru in her seldom-used "this is not something we can argue about" voice. "Our parents are old. They are retiring to small quarters on the mission compound this year. The sisters must start their own lives."

"Maybe their husbands would join them in Japan?" Kenji said halfheartedly.

Haru shook her head while thinking, *How naïve my husband can be.*

Stunned by the urgency of the matter and not wanting to seem less concerned about his parents, Kenji managed a hai. While his instincts urged for more deliberation, the time allotted demanded action.

Haru maneuvered through the dismayed crowd to the roped barrier, a railroad-car length from the ship. She tilted her head to gaze at the upper deck to search for the Miho brothers among the rail-grabbing, forlorn-faced passengers looking down. Haru had a recent picture of her twin sisters but knew it would be easier to recognize their spouses. She spotted them at the front of the open deck and waved frantically, but then everyone on the pier was waving frantically. After a small eternity, the younger Miho brother spotted her. Haru and her sisters then exchanged waves. She mimicked one hand holding a pen writing over the palm of her other hand and retreated from the crowd.

Haru was angry with Congress, angry with the mean-spirited chief immigration officer who could have cleared the ship if he had wanted to, she reasoned, mostly angry with her sisters and the Miho brothers. She had warned them, told them to hurry. What had they been thinking!

Where to get paper? She should have told Kenji to bring some. Then she eyed a new crowd forming around the Chinese youngster who normally sold newspapers at the docks, now selling paper and envelopes. She paid the outrageous sum of five cents for two pieces of stationery and an envelope.

It took every ounce of her Buddhist compassion to keep her angry "why couldn't you have hurried" thoughts from spilling over onto the paper. Instead, she poured out her heart with empathy and then closed with a set of directive words that do not come easy to Japanese. "You must start a new life. With $200 you can buy land, start a small shop, even purchase a couple of apartments to rent in a small town." She resisted adding, "You must leave the mission." Even the most obtuse, she assured herself, would understand that this was the real message.

Convinced the ship had control of its passengers, immigration officers signaled the lowering of the gangplank. As soon as the steel footbridge touched the pier, half a dozen immigration officers climbed aboard, two steps at a time, to sort out, Haru surmised, returning citizens and other properly documented returnees from those who moments ago thought they were the newest immigrants. The stunned Miho brothers were among the last passengers to leave.

Haru had already handed a ship's officer her letter with the cash; he had put it into a bag with other last-minute letters and offered a sympathetic, "If it were up to me, everybody would go ashore."

"So sorry, so very sorry, Miho-san," said Haru, as she greeted the brothers exiting from customs. She resolved to keep any recriminations to herself. Then the older brother stunned her by admitting, "We have been married for two weeks. Our marriages have been consummated."

And maybe spawning fatherless children, thought Haru, understanding the implication. "Wakarimashita."

∞ CHAPTER 113 ∞

L ATER THAT DAY, Andy Pafko wrote a column that only he and his editor ever saw. Titled "Overreached," he accused Dillingham's appearance in front of Congress the previous year—stirring up the California congressional delegation by asking for a special allotment of thirty thousand Chinese laborers while warning of the dangerous Japanese immigration—for yesterday's pier-landing fiasco.

"Andy," said his editor at the *Advertiser*, "I didn't bring you back to get us both run out of town."

More sober than when he wrote the column, Pafko balled it up and tossed it into the trashcan.

"Good choice," said the editor. "We've had enough social wars over schools and immigration. It's gone on longer than the Great War. You saw the crowds yesterday. Subdued. While the racists in California held bonfire celebrations, our haoles did not. There is a sense enough is enough. It's a draw."

"A draw?"

"Yes. No more Japanese immigrants, but they get to keep their schools."

"That's not settled," said Pafko, perking up into a fighting mode.

"We never thought Makino would actually make a federal case of these school-restriction laws," said the editor. "But he did. The lower courts have called all our school acts violations of the Fourth Amendment's freedom of speech. It will eventually end up in the Supreme Court, which has been clear about freedom of speech challenges for a hundred and fifty years. "By the way," added the editor, "Okumura phoned. You might want to return the call."

∽ ∾

The next day, Pafko quoted Okumura's response to the immigration act.

> It is important to resolve to cultivate one's own destiny by oneself. ... There are two paths we can take. One, we can pack up and make a neat parting from Hawaii to return home or start anew in places like South America or Manchuria. Or two, we can patiently endure until the US awakens to justice while we show them the results of assimilation and Americans recognize that we are essential elements to a prosperous society.
>
> I am taking the second path. On this occasion, we should reflect deeply on our own conduct and become fully awakened to our circumstances in order to "do in

Rome as the Romans do." We should be as the smile of
the dandelion that blooms even when stepped upon.

That evening, Haru walked over to the Moiliili Christian Center
to hear Okumura speak. What congregants remembered was Haru
sitting in the front row and leading the applause.

"Exhaustion brings its own peace," Haru murmured to Kenji that
night as they soaked in their ofuro.

"Isn't that how the Great War ended?" said Kenji.

"Ever since we moved to Honolulu, it's been one fight after another: the strike aftermath, attacks on our schools, and dealing with immigration. As bad as the immigration law is, at least the battle is over."

"And I can quietly be more flexible with our schools," said Kenji.
"Next year, Taka can play baseball. I will add curriculum changes com-
paring Christ and Buddha." He reached for his sake cup and then realized it was empty. "In some strange way, this bill has brought our various communities together. I don't think that those who oppose us saw
where this might lead. It is as if all of sudden the haoles realize they
have to find a way to live with 40 percent of Hawaii's population."

"I am not sure Congress understands what it has unleashed," said
Haru barely above a whisper. "I only hope Japan can put this behind
itself. The radio reports mentioned riots."

⚭ Chapter 114 ⚭

As Haru read the newspaper reports from Japan in the following days, she realized her worst fears were but a tepid foretelling of the anger the immigration act had released. A shocked Japan
had turned angry and bitter. The *Japan Times and Mail* called the immigration act a "declaration of war."

A middle-aged Japanese man left a protest note in front of the
American embassy in Tokyo demanding—much like Martin Luther
nailing his edict to the All Saints Church in Wittenberg—that America

repent. But with a dramatic difference: the man sat down and slit his throat. Days later, eight hundred leading politicians and senior military officials in full uniform attended the man's funeral.

Right-wing groups marched, shouting, "National humiliation."

Cities vied with each other demonstrating their outrage. Promises to boycott American goods and calls to stop importing American cotton gained traction.

A week later, Haru read an article on page six of the newspaper that troubled her more than anything else she had read. A junior Japanese navy officer, who was part of the Japanese delegation visiting the US Naval War College in Newport, Rhode Island, when the legislation was passed, was asked by his hosts what would be the reaction of the Japanese military. Navy Captain Isoroku Yamamoto replied, "We have two militaries. I can speak only for the navy. We will wait for you to change. We do not wish war."

Haru doubted few Americans understood the nuance of Japanese phraseology and thus Yamamoto's warning. By restricting his comments to the navy, Haru knew that what the captain did not say was far more important and portentous: "The other military, the army, is eager for its next war. You have removed powerful restraints."

Haru put the newspaper down, recalling her teenage years in Hiroshima when the newspapers railed against Russia. She thought of her brother's death in Manchuria, her barefoot sprint to tell her father, "Togo sank the Russian fleet in Tsushima," and her pledge at the Yasukuni Shrine to produce "many sons for the emperor."

She feared for her four sons.

PART VII

THE TRIALS

∞ CHAPTER 115 ∞

December 6, 1931

Hawaii's cool season blew in from the North Pacific, shoving the Japan-Hawaii shipping lanes from the shorter northern route to the calmer southern waters. Blustery trade winds twisted Ala Moana Beach's palm tree leaves and snapped off coconuts padded inside with chewy pulp harboring a quart of sweet water. North Shore surfers rejoiced as the height of the waves mounted. Beach sunshine and afternoon mountain showers coupled to arch rainbows from the slopes of Punchbowl into Honolulu. Christmas tree lights decorated downtown.

On this Sunday afternoon, nervous citizens brought their children to the nativity scene across from Honolulu's courthouse. As in years past on this racially diverse island, no one seemed to notice the contrast of the swarthy complexion of the Magi kings and shepherds with the milky-white skin of the Virgin Mary and Baby Jesus. The adults weren't here for the nativity scene. Their eyes were locked on the imposing Doric-columned structure promising justice and threatening its miscarriage. When would the jury bring a verdict? It had been five days since closing arguments in Hawaii's famous Thalia Massie Trial in which five locals—two Japanese and three Hawaiian boys—were accused of raping a white naval officer's wife. Rumors abounded that the Sunday session meant a verdict was close. The waiting white minority freely mingled with the Hawaiians and Asians. The preschool children of all races giggled and played together happily, oblivious to the drama surrounding them. Their wary older siblings and parents each hoped for a verdict that was just—meaning one that validated their own verdicts they had wedded weeks ago.

Reporters grew weary staking out the courthouse. They had run out of angles predicting the outcome and demonizing or defending the accused. Minor traffic incidents between those of different races were handled either with exaggerated politeness or quick tempers. Work slowed as employees and employers hashed and rehashed the points of the case for or against. Rumors floated that the jury could not reach a verdict, that fights among jurors had broken out, and that the jurors had repeatedly asked the judge for legal clarifications and copies of testimony.

"Look!" a voice bellowed. The nativity scene gawkers followed the man's pointed arm to a haole in a Panama hat, suit, and tie running up the steps of the courthouse. Police, who had been milling around the statehouse nonchalantly, grew more alert. Two squad cars arrived, each disgorging five more police.

A car radio bellowed from a midnight-blue Cadillac parked at the curb, its passenger door left ajar. A crowd coalesced as the word "verdict" punched the air, followed by phrases such as "the judge has ordered the defendants to court" and "police are ringing the courthouse."

∞ ∞

Slanted rays from winter's early sunset streamed through half-open louvers into the high-ceilinged office. Three overhead fans lumbered at their lowest speed. Lawrence Judd, the grandson of the missionary advisor to King Kamehameha III and governor of the US Territory of Hawaii since his appointment by President Hoover in July 1929, returned his handset to its cradle. The Massie Trial judge had told him court would convene in thirty minutes. Now fourteen people knew the outcome ahead of the public. Judd had told the judge, "A fifteenth needs to know."

"Agreed," said the judge.

As he did any time when stressed, Judd pinched off his steel-rimmed spectacles, blew hot breath over the lenses, and rubbed them clean with his white handkerchief changed daily. He was about to find out whether his thin, boyish face and weak jaw masked the steel backbone needed to handle this developing crisis. Judd put his glasses back on and pushed the intercom buzzer. "Get Mr. Dillingham on the phone."

Less than a minute later, he was speaking into the tightly gripped phone. "Walter, we have a problem." After recounting his brief conversation with the judge, Judd said, "You'd better come on over." He did not add that he needed help handling the expected vicious blowback from Admiral Yates Stirling, the Southern-born commander of Hawaii's naval forces, who harbored nothing but disdain for the Japanese population—"a brutal race that shares our island but does not share our civilized values"—and who brooked no doubt about the guilt of the accused.

Taka had stayed home after Sunday brunch and his father's services. Several dorm mates had come over to play acey-deucey, where the boys bet pennies that their draw card would fall between the two face-up cards on the table. They were all tuned to the KGU broadcast sharing a local obsession Taka had named in his last UH newspaper column as "radio anxiety."

"No one turns off the home radios," Taka had written. "Every office has at least one radio on low volume just in case the judge convenes court. Lucky luxury car owners keep their engines running if they are within listening distance of their car radios."

Taka's thrice-weekly UH newspaper reports telling the Japanese side of the trial, which had been picked up by Fred Makino's *Hawaii Hochi*, had turned into a running battle with the *Advertiser* reporter Andy Pafko. His incendiary editorials had inflamed the growing percentage of the white population eager to be inflamed, eager to have an articulate voice validating their prejudices.

Taka was leaning over the table to pick up a small handful of his acey-deucey winnings when a shrill voice broke into the *Hawaiian Music Hour*. "Breaking news. Breaking news. This just in. In fifty-five minutes, the verdict for five defendants in the navy wife's assault case will be announced at the courthouse."

Taka jumped up. "I gotta go."

Reading in "Haru's refuge," the tatami mat room, Kenji rose as well. He padded into the living room, nodded to the card players, and said, "Taka, I'll start the car." Unintentionally embarrassing him, he hinted that his forgetful son needed parental reminders. "Get your notepad and press card and meet me out in front."

Taka rolled his eyes, patted his shirt pocket, and followed his father out the door.

∞ ∞

Thalia's mother, Grace Fortescue, paced the living/dining room inside her rented Manoa cottage, her fifth martini of the day nearly drained, when the radio's "breaking news" pierced her fuzzy thoughts. Wiry and elegant, she had lost eleven pounds since her arrival in Hawaii three weeks earlier, even as Honolulu's ruling class had fêted her. She often wondered how they would treat her if they knew she had to take in boarders in her Washington home to make ends meet.

She threw back what remained of her drink and then addressed the radio announcer. "At last, those savages will get what's coming to them."

Fortescue grabbed the keys to her rental car and then bustled and tottered down the twisting walkway to the waiting Whippet Sports Roadster. She dropped her keys on the floorboard twice before she fumbled them into the ignition.

∞ ∞

Walter Dillingham strutted into Judd's office. The governor, standing by his wet bar, shook his head. "A hung jury, Walter. The worst of all outcomes."

"The worst," Dillingham agreed and continued over to the large window beside the governor's desk, giving him a view of Kamehameha the Great's larger-than-life bronze statue watching over the courthouse. "I wonder what he would do," he said softly, more to himself than Judd.

Judd poured whiskey into two tumblers. "With a six-to-six vote split between conviction and acquittal, I don't see a better outcome the next time out. Most likely another hung jury or even an acquittal."

Upon hearing the clink of ice, Dillingham turned and took his drink from Judd. He swirled the amber liquid but didn't drink it. "Our right to rule, to maintain standards in a community where we are a minority, has become compromised. The *Advertiser*, the navy, and that woman have done more damage than those boys."

∞ ∞

The judge gaveled the crowded courtroom to silence. Fewer white faces than usual looked on from the lower gallery—no maids to stand in line and save places for their employers. Outfitted in a blue, calf-length skirt and white, long-sleeved blouse, Thalia Massie sat between her mother and Tommy, her husband dressed in navy whites. Admiral Stirling sat ramrod straight next to Grace Fortescue. All four haughty faces telegraphed their expected vindication. Behind them, the press gathered in the press box. Taka from the second row exchanged glances with Pafko turning into the front row. As was their custom, neither spoke to each other.

"Have you reached a verdict?" intoned the judge.

"No, Your Honor," announced the foreman.

Thalia and Grace stared at the foreman, stunned. Stirling's face twisted in disgust.

"With more time, can you reach a verdict?" pressed the judge.

"There is no hope of that, Your Honor."

Grace Fortescue shot up from her seat. "NO!" she cried and then fainted into Tommy's arms. Thalia stared at the five defendants, her dark eyes mean with venom. Stirling said not a word, stood up, and marched out of the courtroom. His combat-ready face warned he was mapping out an attack to right this absurd injustice. *A battle lost is not a war lost*, he thought.

Taka broke into a wide smile, almost giddy with exhilaration. His mother had been right. He fought the urge to jump up and shout, "Justice wins!" Instead, he pushed his way out of the press box and joined the melee of shouting reporters looking for quotes on the courthouse steps. He scribbled down a few from the beleaguered jurors and raced to the *Hochi* office, composing his column as he ran.

∞ ∞

"We need that judge to convene a second trial immediately," boomed Stirling's voice, even before he entered Judd's office. As he stepped inside, he nodded to Dillingham.

"I've already talked to the judge," snapped Judd. "He will order a second trial. But given the split decision, I wonder if we can find twelve jurors who would convict."

Stirling took a shot glass of whiskey offered by Dillingham and drank it straight down.

Dillingham's calm voice reasoned, "Those boys probably didn't do it, Lawrence, but the future of white authority is at stake here."

"The Japanese and Hawaiian community would have exploded over a guilty verdict," said Judd, giving Dillingham an icy stare. "Have you thought about that?"

"That's why you have a national guard," growled Stirling.

Dillingham ignored the admiral's interruption. "Of course there's danger. Haven't you and I discussed that enough?" He shifted his attention to Stirling. "There is no good way out of this, Admiral. But the worst outcome is for us—the pioneers who took this island from the savages and built it into an American paradise. We will lose the right to govern. We'd be back in grass shacks before you know it. God made the white race to rule and the colored to be ruled."

Stirling wondered why Dillingham, someone equal to the task, hadn't been appointed governor. He looked back at Judd and, in his command voice, warned him, "We have twenty-five thousand military on the island. If you need help to squash civil disorder, we will do it with an iron fist."

"Have them ready, Admiral," said Dillingham as if he had the authority. Turning to Judd, he added, "Best to call up the National Guard now, Lawrence. A show of force."

Judd was dumbfounded. He knew he owed his appointment to Dillingham, and it would take only a few phone calls to remove him from office, but he had kept a lid on a volatile situation so far. He tapped into reserves of political common sense and showed some backbone, giving the two men a steely look. "You're right. We need a speedy retrial. Given the verdict, I expect a quiet night." Looking at the disbelief on the other men's faces, he added, "The police are out in full force just in case. We don't need military intervention." Then, as an afterthought, he threw the two men a bone. "Yet."

Dillingham rose. "We'll see, but let's go forward with the speedy trial and be prepared to call up the guard."

Stirling put his glass on the credenza and followed Dillingham to the door. He turned back to eye Judd. "Leaders do what they have to do." His voice left no doubt that he didn't think Judd was up to the task.

∞ CHAPTER 116 ∞

AT THE *HOCHI* OFFICE, Taka quickly typed up his column and submitted it to Makino. He stood back while the editor read the hurriedly written copy.

Makino looked up and almost smiled enough to show his teeth. "Good copy, Taka. Clean up the grammar and spelling. You just made the front page of the extra. Stick around; it will be off the presses in an hour."

Justice Wins Out
By Takeshi Takayama

This morning, twelve citizens representing the ethnic blend of Hawaii validated my mother's belief in America. These honorable men would not be bullied by an intimidating prosecutor emboldened by an outrageous press that had already convicted the defendants.

The prosecution could not prove its case.

If you heard the racist taunt of a senior naval officer outside the courtroom today, you would believe the reason for the hung jury was "brown people would not convict brown people."

But what are the facts? My interviews with the exhausted jurors revealed that a Japanese Nisei led the six-jurist conviction faction while a white jurist advocated acquittal. Don't expect to find this fact reported in certain newspapers because it is at odds with the verdict they have been drumbeating since the Massie woman first claimed being raped.

In their view:

A white woman lie? Never!

A white woman accuses a brown man of rape, which, and here I quote from our biggest competitor, "is typical of his fiendish class of colored men lusting for white women." Case closed.

When the police arrested the five accused the morning after the alleged rape, they gathered their clothes, certain they would find semen stains. There weren't any. But did that raise doubts about the woman's story? NO! The white woman identified the five. Case closed.

The doctors could not find any damage to the "victim's" private parts. No matter. She said they did it. Case closed.

When Thalia Massie gave the time of the assault and the police discovered the accused could not have been there at the time she claimed, she suddenly remembered the "correct" time. A navy wife would not lie. They did it. The police said so. The newspapers said so. Case closed.

But then, twelve men heard the evidence. The strength of our Constitution's Third and Sixth Amendments requiring the accused to be judged by a jury of peers is based on the belief in the common sense of twelve ordinary citizens. Today, half of them were not convinced. Where was the proof?

There wasn't any.

Most likely, the judge will order another trial.

But then again, maybe not.

There is not just anger over this jury's failure to convict, but given the even split, there is also the fear that the prosecutor and police will not be able to prove

Mrs. Massie's rape claim at the next trial and the one after that and the one ...

A great dread hangs over a righteous community blinded by racism.

These five accused will never be convicted.

This is a terrifying prospect for the navy and certain groups of our island who have invested so much in their prejudices. Could they have been wrong? Never! Is it possible that these men did not do it? NO!

An entire segment of our community has allowed themselves to buy into the woman's unsubstantiated story. She has unleashed an evil we thought was restricted to certain Southern states.

In a few weeks, we will celebrate Christmas. Perhaps the original message of the missionaries that visited our islands more than a century ago will prevail over the passions of the moment. When our privileged class looks into the many nativity scenes in their churches, maybe they could ask, "What would the Baby Jesus think of all this hate and suspicion?"

"A stupid miscarriage of justice" led Pafko's own front-page story. "They were let go because of their race." Then he rehashed all the venom he had spewed for two months.

Judd twirled his fourth whiskey as he put down Pafko's rant, the last extra he read under the bronze eyes of the King Kamehameha outside his office window. The every-thirty-minutes phone calls from the police chief verified Judd's take on the mood of downtown Honolulu. Stunned haoles and sullen "browns" quietly vacated the city to return to their homes. He mused how this place called "Hawaii," which only a few months ago had been synonymous with paradise, was now irreparably sullied. Pictures of brown Hawaiians and white tourists had seemed as natural as apple pie and ice cream. He agreed with Dillingham on the merits of the case. One white woman, who may have had an out-of-marriage indiscretion, accused five local boys of raping her and, in so doing, ripped asunder the harmony of our island. Of course, he belatedly admitted to himself that this could not have happened if a deep distrust between races had not been seething beneath the surface, waiting for a single tectonic shift to create an earthquake.

He picked up the *Hochi* newspaper and reread Taka's column. Judd wondered why he was not outraged. Why wasn't he on the phone demanding Makino write a retraction? Deep down, he knew why: The kid, the son of that Buddhist priest and his activist wife, had it right.

⤔ CHAPTER 117 ⤕

WHILE JUDD MUSED ON THE LOCAL REACTION to the trial, his island was about to be assaulted from another direction. A manic Admiral Stirling was firing off an incendiary report to Washington. "Hawaii is not safe for white women. Hundreds of rapes remain unsolved by an inept police force. Recommend you cancel Pacific fleet's annual visit to Hawaii." If that was not enough of an attention-grabber, he concluded, "The civilian government is incapable of providing the basics of public safety. The police are corrupt. The governor is weak. In a few years, the non-whites will have a majority and vote in their own kind, resulting in a complete breakdown of civilized society. Hawaii must be placed under navy rule until such time as public order and political maturity can be assured."

Although Stirling labeled the report "SECRET," he made sure someone in his staff leaked his invective to a *New York Times* reporter.

⤔ ⤕

Judd hated the rat-a-tat-tat staccato of the teleprinter. Even with his door closed, the machine adjacent to his secretary's desk clanked away with incoming messages at sixty noisy words a minute. Most communications were mercifully short reports from Hawaii's territorial delegate in Washington. But today, the day after the trial, the clanking was insistent. While the machine continued to bang away, his secretary ran in with the first page off the machine. "You'd better read this," she said, her face ashen. "It's from the *New York Times*."

This is war, thought Judd halfway down the page. His mind swirled as he finished reading the hatchet job on his governance. *It's not enough that Stirling's blind belief in Massie's story is fracturing the harmony of our island, but now he is determined to discredit us before the world. His Southern heritage, nurtured by those who take the law into their own hands when a colored is accused of violating a white woman, has led his raging temper to dream up a complete fabrication of civil breakdown and label it a report that demands, in so many words, that only his appointment as military ruler can save Hawaii from savagery. The nerve. This cannot stand*, Judd told himself. *Stirling! He says I'm weak. Well, let's see how I can correct that bigot's impression. Let's see how he handles the truth.*

The *Times* reporter said he had thirty minutes to offer a rebuttal. "Call this reporter," Judd told his secretary. Judd's calm-under-fire intuition told him that a direct attack on the admiral's character and mental fitness would only incite a war of words that would sell more newspapers. So, in a reasoned voice belying his outrage at the admiral, Judd assured the reporter that a hung jury merely meant "American justice was running its course and the islands were as safe as ever. When have you ever heard of crime in Hawaii before this single alleged incident?"

When he put the phone down, he looked at yesterday's newspaper extras and today's editions strewn across his desk. He reached for the *Hochi*'s four-page sheet and once again studied Taka's column.

∽ ∾

Andy Pafko loved the teleprinter. It meant hot news. An hour after Judd talked to the *Times* reporter, Pafko was standing at the *Advertiser*'s teleprinter reading the front-page *New York Times* story. "Hawaii Unsafe. Outrage boils over. A sweet society girl has been ravaged. Worse, Hawaii, an AMERICAN territory, refused to convict the perpetrators." The *Times* printed the so-called secret report in its entirety.

"Has the man gone mad?" Pafko mumbled to himself as he read the Stirling report a second time. Military rule. Breakdown of civil order. He strolled over to the coffee machine, poured the thick dregs into his mug, and added two heaping teaspoons of sugar. He imagined reporters from every major newspaper in America gathering around their teleprinter right now. He saw the many versions of "Hawaii Unsafe" screaming across mastheads in hours. A twinge of guilt wormed its way up his gut as he realized half of the report could have been lifted from his own articles. But he had not meant to instigate the collapse of Hawaii's tourist trade or a military takeover of the islands.

What remained of Pafko's conscience demanded he defend Hawaii, lambast the navy. But if he did, it would kill his favored position with the navy brass. But not to respond … He let the thought simmer. Pafko hated making either/or choices. He sipped his coffee and glanced around the *Advertiser*'s city room. With an inner flash of insight, he meandered over to his desk and stuck a fresh sheet of paper into his typewriter. Someday Stirling would be replaced, but Dillingham and the Big Five would continue in power.

Pafko hedged his bets. His feature article referred to the expected stateside hysteria over exaggerated reports of the breakdown of Hawaii's civil order and then warned of navy designs on Hawaii. He closed with "Now is the time to show the world that Hawaii is a territory of laws. We did not ask for America's spotlight. But it shines brightly on us. We have only one sure course to move ahead. A quick and speedy trial and a conviction of these brutal assailants to prove we can govern ourselves."

∞ ∞

As he entered the *Hochi* office that evening, Taka saw Makino waving him over. The editor handed him an envelope. "This came for you … from the governor's office."

A question mark falling over his face, Taka opened the envelope reverently. His face registered another surprise as he pulled out a neatly scissored page of the *Hochi*. His last column topped with a handwritten note. "Well presented. Keep up the good work. Lawrence Judd." He showed it to Makino.

"Our governor is fed up with navy interference."

"Can I use this somehow?" asked Taka.

Makino shook his head. "No. But keep it. Years from now, if you write a book on this mess, that would be the time." Makino paused, smiling like the Cheshire cat. "There's more. The governor's aide called. He would be happy to see you got access to all police records regarding rape since Hawaii's independence."

It took a few seconds for Taka to register the offer. His first inner reaction was *Why me?* But what he said was "When?"

Makino tapped his watch and handed him a scrap of paper with a telephone number.

"Right," said Taka. "Now."

At midnight, Taka returned to the *Hochi* office waving a sheaf of notes. "You won't believe this."

"You have an hour to write a column that Hawaii and America will believe. We are holding the presses."

At eleven minutes past one in the morning, Taka delivered his "Truth and Fabrication" column to Makino. He read it, scribbled a few red edits, and called in his typesetter.

☙ ❧

The next morning, Judd knew he had made the right decision when he read Taka's column.

> In Hawaii's thirty-five years of self-government, until Thalia Massie, no white woman has ever reported a rape by a man of another race. In fact, just the opposite is the stunning truth: Almost all reported interracial rapes were perpetrated by naval personnel on "native women." Having fabricated a nonexistent threat against white women and claiming civil disorder, Admiral Stirling proposes a preposterous solution: Make himself the administrator of our territory. While he recommends only that the president put the military in charge, the implication is clear. The last thing Hawaii needs is a racist ruling our multi-racial community.

Then Taka proceeded to summarize his findings reviewing decades of police sexual assault records discrediting Stirling's allegations. He finished his column like a lawyer concluding his admonition to a jury. "The number of rapes cited by the admiral was a fabrication."

∞ CHAPTER 118 ∞

"THESE LOCAL JIGABOOS will never convict one of their own," spat Grace Fortescue. "The judge will order one retrial after another until poor Thalia can't take it anymore, and those animals will get off scot-free."

While ukuleles were strummed under swaying palm trees, Grace held court in the shade of the Moana Hotel's giant banyan tree. Tommy Massie and his navy buddies, who were at the Ala Wai Inn on the night in question, drank whiskey. No sissy tourists' drinks for them. Grace sipped a gin and tonic.

"The police and prosecutor will present evidence to dispute the coloreds' timeline," Massie offered.

"And the defense will once again note her memory lapse and attack the honor of your wife. Make her out be a whore and a liar," snapped Grace in a tone of voice that questioned his manhood. "We need a confession." She looked each man in the eye, tipped her glass into her mouth, and then added with a regal air that by now had irritated most of her social class in Hawaii, "One way or another."

∞ ∞

A towel wrapped around his waist, his hair still wet, Taka barefooted down the hall from the communal shower to his dorm room. He usually timed his shower to end before 7 a.m. so he could catch the KGU morning news. But today had been a shaving day, and he was thirty seconds late.

"Queen's Hospital reports that the victim of the beating is in stable condition. 'Remarkable, given its severity,' according to the attending physician." Another horrible nightclub altercation, thought

Taka. However, the look on his roommate's face suggested otherwise. He mouthed a silent "Ida" over the continued radio report. "'The other four men in the Massie case will be given protection,' said the chief of police, 'and every effort will be made to bring the perpetrators to justice.'"

Takeshi threw on boxer shorts and slacks, grabbed a shirt, which he buttoned haphazardly while running down the stairs, and biked to Queen's Hospital in twelve heart-thumping minutes.

Taka dropped his bike on the grass next to the Queen's Hospital emergency entrance. Chaos reigned. Above the din of police officers, orderlies, newspaper reporters, and relatives, a smocked doctor stood eyeball to eyeball with the chief of police.

"What is it you don't understand? The patient is sedated. I am trying to keep him alive. You talked to him when he came in. Men beat him senseless. Get out of here and find them."

In the sudden silence, a cop murmured loud enough for the suddenly quiet reception area to hear, "If the jury had done its duty, this wouldn't have happened."

Taka spotted a smoldering Candi, Ida's sister who had attended every session of the trial. Communications between them had been limited to greetings and an occasional "Good story, Takeshi." He knew the normally glamorous woman worked as a teahouse geisha. This morning her face was drawn, her hair tangled in a ponytail, and she was wearing a house yukata. Not surprising, given it was seven thirty in the morning, and she must have been there since three.

"I'm so sorry," Taka offered, looking at the loudmouthed cop. "I wish there was something I could do."

In her throaty voice, she said, "Get the truth out. Look at these brave police." She mentally counted. "Seven brave men milling about." She eyed Pafko talking to the chastised police chief. "The chief demonizer!" She turned and burrowed her bitter eyes into his. "You want to do something? Get the truth out today. Let's go get some coffee, and I will tell you about five navy cowards who couldn't beat a false confession out of a brave young man."

When Candi had given Taka all he needed for his story, she said, "You want a real story behind the story? Maybe you should take some time to learn more about who we are, about those of us who must live in Mosquito Flats. It's easy for the haoles to drive by, see our squalor, and vilify us as a lower form of life. Let them know there is more to us than the poverty we live in."

Taka wondered if she was talking about the haoles or Nisei like him whose parents warned, "Stay away from the Flats."

"Yes. My columns could use more … context."

"Come on Friday night. See the parade." She gave him directions, adding with a knowing look. "It's the roundabout way."

He closed his notebook, said, "Thank you," and began to rise.

Candi grabbed his arm. "I know the back stairwell way to Horace's room. I want you to see what they have done to him."

☙ CHAPTER 119 ❧

BY MID-MORNING, Taka handed in his column to Makino. Taka's restrained approach to the ongoing battle of the columnists had wilted the moment he saw Ida's battered body. He would out-Pafko Pafko.

Makino skimmed quickly down the page. He nodded his approval.

Beating Proves Ida's Innocence
By Takeshi Takayama

The belt-buckle welts on his back, the missing teeth, the white-gauze-wrapped head oozing blood, the broken ribs, all have proven Horace Ida's innocence. If any one of us had suffered the beating Ida endured, we might have confessed to anything to save our lives. But Horace Ida, left for dead on the Pali, would not break. He would take any kick, punch, or flogging his cowardly attackers rained on him before besmirching his honor. This courageous young man would rather die than admit to something he did not do.

Neither he nor the others accused ever touched Thalia Massie.

Horace Ida is a hero.

Who IS guilty? Certain newspapers and writers whose unfounded accusations and evil-mongering created the atmosphere that made this beating not only possible but likely.

I talked to Horace Ida. Through a wired-jaw, he mumbled, "I was beaten because of the hysteria whipped up by the *Advertiser*."

Will our territorial government continue to turn a blind eye and watch the fabric of its community destroyed, the possibility of statehood extinguished, and turn our justice system over to navy mob rule?

Makino's extra hit the streets for the lunch crowd. Even some haoles snapped up the English version. The *Advertiser* held back its own extra to give Pafko a chance to print the navy's official response and demolish Taka's rhetoric.

Ida Was Lucky
By Andy Pafko

"He got off with a beating. It could have been worse, given the nature of his crime," says Admiral Stirling. "Of course," he continued, "the navy does not condone a forced confession, but given the fact that a fair jury cannot be impaneled, it is only natural that righteous men take action."

There are newspapers, foreign-owned newspapers bent on pandering to their non-American readership, that completely distort the facts. The prosecutor proved his case. But a native jury would not do its duty. That Horace Ida, a despicable heathen, did not admit to his heinous crime only points out the dangers of an alien culture in Hawaii so completely at odds with the ideals of American democracy, a form of government that grew from American soil and the American experience and its Christian religion. Japan has been and will forever be ruled by tyrants, be it shoguns or emperors, who create in their populace the desire to reach out and take what they want, be it a foreign land or a white woman's virtue. So it is there, so it is here.

Just look at the Japanese—their flat features, protruding teeth, and short legs mixing with other races—an abomination. This brutish element must be sent a message. Find them guilty and execute them to save our civilization.

∞ CHAPTER 120 ∞

GRACE FORTESCUE SCREAMED, "Lies! Lies! Lies!" and slammed the *Hochi* down on the sofa.

"Mama, what is it?" Thalia cried, running from the kitchen into the living room. Her mother was visiting her that afternoon. Neither woman could stand the other, which was why Grace had rented her cottage after spending just two nights with her daughter and son-in-law.

"Another newspaper story from those ... those colored people, making a hero out the rapist who got off with just a beating."

"Let me see." Thalia picked up the paper and read Taka's article. She wrung her hands. *This boy reporter is such a source of trouble,* she thought.

"Mama, I don't think I can stand going through this again."

"Of course you can," snapped Grace. "Our family honor demands it. You back out, and everyone will think you made up the whole thing." Her piercing eyes beat Thalia into submission.

"Yes, Mama."

∞ ∞

While Grace fumed, Governor Judd slapped his own *Hochi* down on his desk. Taka's "Ida is a Hero" column stared back at him. Pafko's "Ida Was Lucky" editorial lay aside. *That reporter and Stirling,* he thought, *are as much to blame for this boy's beating as if they had been on the Pali, flaying Ida with their own belt buckles. There are always violent-natured men eager to break the chains of civilization if authority and society sanction their primeval urges. And, in this case, encouraged it. What's next?* he asked himself. *A murder?* But first things first. In the matter of police corruption and incompetence, he knew Stirling was right.

The cops—his cops—were rotten to the core. If the Massie complaint had been handled professionally, the case would have never seen the light of day. That navy wife got her tit in a dalliance wringer and blamed it on the boys when the police served them up on a marriage-saving platter. How did it come to this? The question was self-incrimination rather than a search for a Paul-to-Damascus revelation. He knew the answer. Hell, everyone knew: the good ol' boy system that had evolved since early territorial days—all the top police jobs were political payoff appointees. He winced internally thinking of the incompetents granted his patronage. However, the bungling of this alleged rape was the last straw. He caught himself. Did he just say "alleged"? He knew the almost certain truth. Dillingham knew. But he had stuffed the truth in his back pocket in favor of the "bigger issue"—our right to rule must not be undermined, even if a few of society's lower class must be sacrificed. He now knew what had to be done, what was right, and what immediate action he must initiate to head off the navy's grab for control of Hawaii.

He walked over to the legislative offices and entered the door marked "President of the Territorial Legislature." After the two men exchanged their dismay at the disastrous consequences of the police incompetence, Judd stated the obvious. "We need to fix the police department, clean it up. Bring that bill on establishing a police commission out of committee. You get it passed; I'll sign it." Judd turned and strode out of the room without waiting for an answer. He knew what he would have seen on the man's face—initial shock that would surely evolve into a gloating smirk that said, "Exactly what I have been telling you for years."

The next day, the legislature passed the law separating the police from the governor's office and placing it under a commission. It was understood that Walter Dillingham would head the commission and quietly "suggest" who the other four members would be. Hawaii would act. Quickly. On its own. It was fighting to retain its sovereignty.

Back at his office, Judd ended his day by writing his boss, the president of the United States, a letter refuting Stirling's charges and had his secretary send it over the teleprinter.

⚭ ⚬

"Okasan, why do they hate us?" asked little Hiromi, holding a spoon over her ice cream Haru had just served for dessert.

Taka had brought home both the *Hochi* and *Advertiser* extras and had just finished telling everything he knew about Ida's beating. He was relieved Hiromi had directed her question to Haru. He worried about his little sister. If she, raised in a Buddhist priest's family where tolerance was fostered, harbored these dark convictions ... He left the thought dangling.

Taka wasn't the only relieved person at the table. Kenji knew Haru was better than he when admonishing his quick-to-anger daughter.

"Why do we hate the Koreans?" Haru asked, also worried about Hiromi's racial prejudice. She remembered her daughter's remark the moment she heard the five young men had been arrested. "It's crazy to think Japanese boys would rape a white lady. But it doesn't matter if they did it or not, the haoles will send them to jail."

"I don't hate the Koreans or even the Chinese. You taught me better, Okasan."

Haru did not reply. Her widened eyes and folded hands demanded a more forthcoming response.

"Okay," said Hiromi, "many of us Japanese do hate the Koreans and Chinese. But not because they are a different race. We have been at war with them for centuries."

Her mother arched her eyebrows another notch.

"Japan is modern. Korea and China are backward." She wrinkled her nose and smiled. "We bathe more often. But the whites hate us just because we look different."

Haru's eyes moved to the small Buddhist altar.

"And pray to Buddha," Hiromi added dismissively, "which wouldn't matter if we looked like haoles."

Haru refused to become sidetracked over the relative weight of race and religion. "There are always prejudices," said Haru, thinking how a veil of normalcy had cloaked relations between the Japanese and haoles since the immigration and language-school turbulence of the early 1920s. She shook her head slowly. "Now this white woman's claim of being raped has rekindled all the fears, distrust ... " she was about to add "and hate" but caught herself, "and hostility. This will pass." She took a sip of tea. "How we respond will determine how soon it will pass."

Hiromi blurted out, "I hate them! I wish they were all dead!" Seeing the look of shock and dismay on Haru's face, Hiromi said contritely, "I wish I could be like you and Daddy. But I can't. If someone hates you, you should hate them back. Double."

"Wakarimashita," said Haru, knowing that an "I understand," rather than more pushback at this emotional moment, would be the wiser response. Resistance only created entrenched attitudes. *How many more innocents*, she thought, *will we lose to hatred if this crisis doesn't end soon?*

A few hours later and five thousand miles away, President Herbert Hoover, responding to the media and congressional uproar to "do something" about the breakdown of law and order in Hawaii, convened a sunrise cabinet meeting to review the conflicting Stirling and Judd reports. "I need to find out what's happening before suspending the government of Hawaii and handing over its administration to the navy." He sent Assistant Attorney General Seth Robertson to Hawaii to assess the situation and make his recommendations.

∽ CHAPTER 121 ∾

Mosquito Flats. Taka stood next to its edge looking at the piles of garbage piled high against the unpainted back concrete wall of the Nippon Theater on the corner of Aala and Beretania Streets. So different from the movie theater's regal front entrance. A rat too big to fit into a shoebox showed its disdain by ignoring Taka's footsteps and kept chewing on something smeared red. Ketchup, Taka hoped. He glanced down at his notes detailing Candi's circuitous route to her Cunha Lane home. Looking right as Candi's drawn arrow indicated, he studied the three- and four-story faded tenement buildings streaked with industrial soot and cooking oil. From postage stamp–sized lanais, blouses, trousers, bras, and panties danced on stubby clotheslines. Underneath the balcony's bent rebars, wrinkle-faced Chinese men with long-hair queues and their aging picture brides with bound feet mingled with Japanese teenage prostitutes in high heels. The whiff of sweet opium covered the garbage stench. A shout in Tagalog caught Taka's attention just in time to see a shirtless young man toss a pair of dice hard against a wall down an alley. He shook his head thinking how Mosquito Flats families had arrived on the same boats as Moiliili families, all full of the same dreams. How did the separation happen?

Taka took a deep breath as though he were about to step into a sewer and began snaking through the narrow urine and cabbage-perfumed alleyways of Blood Town, Tin Can Alley, and Hell's Half Acre as he followed Candi's map. *So*, he thought, *this is where Horace's Kalihi gang and the neighboring School Street gang fought border skirmishes to control their turf.* "Don't worry about your safety," Candi had said. "Our streets are crime-free in the sunshine." She couldn't resist an impish smile. "Most of the time."

"See the parade," Candi had said. Taka's mental lightbulb switched on. A vanilla blur of white canvas "Dixie cup" caps, white poplin shirts, and white drill slacks prowled the grey ghetto canyons. Navy payday. Stirling's "stay on base" orders had been lifted. The flesh hunters trolled, their eyes roving like snipers choosing a target. Pouting lips and sly eyes in hip-slit dresses promised an erotic interlude without having to order a watered-down whiskey for a bar whore plying her wares in a nearby River Street speakeasy.

Taka forgot his mission momentarily when he caught a come-hither set of eyes drawing his attention to the girl's black hair draping to her narrow waist, contrasting dramatically against a red Chinese cheongsam tight at the neck. He turned away just long enough to spot a street sign nailed askew to a telephone post. Cunha Lane. He found the house number smartly painted on a sturdy wooden postbox at the edge of the road. A surprise. A real house. Tiny, but still a house—corrugated roof bent at two edges, yellow paint fading, but clean and graced with a porch just wide enough for a row of mismatched straight-backed chairs. *The royalty of slum dwellings*, thought Taka.

At his knock, Candi opened the door.

Taka caught his breath. The lady who smiled at him with soft, red lips and peacock-blue eye shadow was not the woman who had attended the trial nor the one he had shared coffee with at the hospital. She stood taller in a blue silk kimono with a white crane in flight that seemed to glide as she moved aside and back to let him in. Her hair, as silky as her kimono, hung straight to her shoulders. The smell of incense and lemon permeated the home, a welcome relief from the streets.

"Taka, hello," she said, deep throated. Seeing his startled look, she laughed. "I don't normally greet visitors so fashionably, but after we talk, I must hurry to the teahouse. Today is payday for officers too."

Inside, Taka's pupils widened, adjusting to the dimness. Narrow streaks of sunlight squeezed through four wooden louvers. The home's cleanliness that would have passed Haru's closed scrutiny impressed him. He felt a shiver of shame at this reaction, as he realized he had fallen into a Pafko-fed stereotype of scruffy expectations for anyone living in the Flats. He surveyed the cherrywood hutch with glass doors revealing its contents of cups, saucers, plates, and treasured bric-a-brac. Six hardback chairs surrounded a matching dining table with military precision. A plastic-covered couch, upholstered in a lively fabric, decorated with red hibiscus flowers, hugged the wall on the right; the opposite wall displayed an array of family pictures circling the emperor's portrait. He looked at Candi's smile, almost smug. *You wanted me to see this*, he thought. *You knew what I expected.*

He followed her eyes to an older woman and two barely teenage girls sitting on the floor around a short-legged pinewood table playing pinochle. "These are my mother and two sisters." The girls were dressed in matching, spotless, red-gingham dresses set off with high white collars. They sported identical curled hairdos in the Clara Bow style, rather than the traditional straight Japanese hair. Their mother dressed as if she was going to temple.

"You look so cute," greeted Taka, smiling at the girls, who giggled back.

"We're going to our first taxi dance," said the girl nearest the door, referring to the practice where dance halls recruited girls to dance with patrons for five cents a dance. To the chagrin of the mostly military patrons, the younger girls were chaperoned. Not every sailor spent all his time chasing working girls.

"It's time they pitched in and helped with the rent," said Candi. "We don't want to live like those people." She pointed to the back of a five-story tenement building. "More than three hundred people sharing seven bathtubs, six toilets, and five kitchens." She gestured at the dining table. "Please, sit down."

Taka took a seat and noticed the porcelain tea set. "A busman's holiday," he chuckled.

Candi flashed her teeth at the remark, sat down, and began pouring green tea. "This is not the life my father envisioned when he moved our family here from Maui. He was a fisherman, worked hard, up early every day. A good provider. We moved into a five-room cottage in Manoa a year after we arrived—not much but big enough for a garden and a swing set." She smiled at the memory. "Sundays were the best—we always had ice cream. Even today, I never buy ice cream on any other day."

Taka lifted his teacup toward Candi as though making a sake toast, "If your walking-through-a-maze directions were intended to give me a new perspective of the Flats, it worked."

"This is the neighborhood of broken dreams, or for those born here, no dreams. They think hopelessness is the norm." She sipped the steaming tea, taking time to form her next words. "I was so mad when

Horace dropped out of high school. He is the only man in our family but didn't act like it. He was smart, but the neighborhood sucked him in. Hanging out at the pool hall, he primped his wavy pompadour like a tough yakuza, Mr. Swagger in the neighborhood gang. He was handsome enough to be a beach boy but lacked the confidence to approach stateside girls looking for a brown thrill."

Candi swirled her teacup in both hands. Taka had seen his mother do this during a pause in conversation and understood that there was more to come if he stayed silent.

"He was angry," said Candi. "Angry with the haoles who control our lives. Angry with the Hawaiians, even though they're fellow gang members, because they are allocated half the government jobs. Angry with the Koreans and Chinese for being losers in wars with Japan and angry with our mother for taking in their laundry as a washerwoman. Angry with me for working as a geisha." She took a deep breath to calm herself, but still her eyes misted.

Taka realized the slapping of cards on the table and playful chatter had stopped. He didn't have to turn around to see the perked-up ears. No secrets in such cramped houses.

"But down deep, I think he is angry with himself. We live in a castle compared to our tenement neighbors. So many of the boys feel trapped seeing Japanese from most other neighborhoods work in restaurants, hire themselves out as maids or gardeners, and the smart ones like you go to the university. But this place just traps your mind. You know there is a better world out there—so close, yet so far—because you've convinced yourself that the better world is beyond your reach."

Her face turned earnest. "I gave him money to go to California to look for work. If only he had found a job, if only he had stayed a few more weeks … " Her gaze faded into the world of what could have been.

Taka waited, not sure what to say.

Then Candi suddenly remembered her guest and focused intently on Taka. "But your column cannot be just about Horace. Tell the story of this neighborhood."

Taka nodded his head. "That's why I'm here."

"None of these boys did it," said Candi with conviction. "Horace a rapist? Why? In this neighborhood, force is not necessary. Raping a white woman. Never. It's taboo."

A good word, thought Taka, and he knew he had the lead paragraph for his next column.

"Do you ever go to Waikiki on the weekends?" she asked.

"Not often. Mostly tourists."

"Think of your high school days. Native beach boys and white female tourists. You want a Coke? A beach boy was there to get it for you. Want to learn to surf? Ten copper-skinned, grinning guys eager to teach. Do you remember seeing the local boys rubbing suntan lotion on the girls' backs?"

"Sure, but what's that got to do with Horace?" Taka asked.

"Now what do you see on weekends since the navy increased their fleet stops. Hundreds of navy boys. The navy is big on recruiting good old boys from the South where niggers know their place. You can see the disgust in their eyes when they watch brown boys and white girls laugh together, sometimes walk hand in hand off the beach together."

A gust of wind from the hills blew through the open shutters. Candi refilled their teacups.

"All that anger just waiting for an incident to redress the abomination."

"I hadn't made the connection," said Taka.

I am sure you didn't, college boy, thought Candi, but she moved on. "It's not just the enlisted men, Taka. My teahouse is upscale. We cater to officers and local businessmen. The officers talk in front of me as if English was not my native language. At some point, there's usually talk of war with Japan—when and where it will start. Then someone will always have to remind the group, 'We've got to keep our eyes on our local Japs.' I smile. It's my job. I'm good at it. I hope my gracious service and impeccable English make them question their feelings about their assumptions of our disloyalty and inferiority."

"Candi, you speak so well. You would have been a good UH student." He regretted the words as soon as he spoke them.

Candi nodded. "That was my parents' dream. My father was saving money to buy his own boat. Then all the profit would be his. There would be money for college."

"Then your dad disappeared into the water," said Taka.

"Yes, they never found the boat or any bodies." Again, Candi seemed to drift somewhere else, a profound sadness in her eyes. Then she lifted her gaze and gave him a wan smile. "Shikataganai," she said, using the Japanese expression that roughly meant, "What can we do? It can't be helped. We must move on."

Across town, Haru sipped her afternoon tea as she listened to Lowell Thomas.

"American Secretary of State Stimson has declared the Stimson Doctrine proclaiming America will not recognize any Japanese government inside China. The League of Nations has passed a resolution condemning the Japanese violation of Chinese sovereignty. However, despite the international censuring, Japanese troops continue to push south into Manchuria."

As she always did when listening to reports of war, Haru gazed at the wall photos of her four boys. She tried to push out images of them in black-laced boots, green-khaki uniforms, brown-metal helmets, and carrying a rifle. But couldn't.

Over the next three days, after finishing with classes, Taka biked to Mosquito Flats to spend time with the other four rape defendants and their families. Whereas Pafko simply wrote them off as unrestrained animals, Taka humanized them. They had families, jobs, and ambitions. They were troubled young men to be sure, but nothing in their background suggested they were capable of the violence Thalia Massie accused. Taka did not sugarcoat their character but portrayed them as young men struggling to survive in a world offering them few opportunities.

☙ CHAPTER 122 ❧

THE SPIRIT OF CHRISTMAS papered over the racial tension in Hawaii. Christmas lights brightened the longer nights. Department store Santas settled children of every skin hue on their knees. The YMCA and Rotary sold Canadian evergreen firs in church lots. People belonging to different ethnic and religious communities, including the Buddhists, went out of their way to wish "the others" a Merry Christmas.

Behind Honolulu's veneer of tolerance, its worried citizens waited for the judge to set a new trial date that would certainly reignite the fire under the pressure cooker.

Grace Fortescue was tired of waiting for Hawaiian justice. Each day, she drank more and slept less. The etching around her eyes grooved deeper. She had the shoe repairman punch a new notch on her belts to cinch a thinner waist. The daily humiliation of living on charity had shorn her regal airs.

She saw another trial ending with the same result: the same people refusing to convict their own, even with the guilt of the accused staring them in the face. Nothing but a confession would save her daughter. Nothing but a conviction leading to a lifetime of hard labor would satisfy her thirst for revenge. These thugs had sullied the Fortescue name—an honorable name dating back to the American Revolution.

On the evening of January 6, 1932, Tommy Massie entered his mother-in-law's rented Manoa cottage. Grace greeted him, drink in hand, but offered him nothing. She snapped, "Why aren't you doing something to defend your wife's honor?"

Tommy had heard the taunt before—from his fellow officers. Before he could respond, Grace fired on.

"Your navy buddies beat up Ida, the strongest of the five by all accounts. But they didn't finish the job." She paused to take a long swig from her martini, but her eyes never left Tommy's. "We need a confession to end my daughter's nightmare. I am not having her humiliated on the stand again. You are her husband, for God's sake. You're the one who needs to fix this."

"What can I do?"

In the silence, Grace refreshed her drink, mixed one for Tommy, and handed it to him. "Sit down, and I will tell you."

⚬ Chapter 123 ⚬

Honor Slaying
By Andy Pafko

Joe Kahahawai, one of the notorious assailants of a navy wife, was shot dead this morning after confessing that he and his savage gang raped Thalia Massie. The distressed husband and two navy friends, using a forged document requiring Kahahawai to be driven to the judge at another location, picked him up outside the courthouse. They then took him to Mrs. Grace Fortescue's East Manoa Drive cottage where they interrogated him until, according to Mrs. Fortescue, he confessed to assaulting her daughter as charged and was then accidently shot.

After a few paragraphs suggesting that those on the hung jury were the real killers of Kahahawai and defending the honor of "that poor girl and her mother seeking justice," Pafko addressed the Mainland's call for martial law.

The attempt to interject racial warfare into this incident is deplorable. This incident is not racial. There will be no need for martial law.

Not a word of sympathy for the murdered victim. He was a rapist, after all. It was an honor killing, biblically justified.

Haru put down the newspaper with Pafko's version of the abduction and killing. She looked at the slumped shoulders of her reporter son.

"A man is murdered, and the haole newspapers call it honor," Taka said in a subdued voice. "I give up, Mama. I'm quitting the *Hochi*. Lincoln or no Lincoln, I think little Hiromi had it right from the start."

"Give up? Quit? People count on you to give them a voice, Taka. America will get this right. You know that police already have Joe's killers in custody."

"Arrested, Okasan, but not in police custody. I called Mr. Makino before I came over. He told me that they are being held in unlocked quarters on a ship at Pearl. Our local jails are not safe enough for navy murderers."

"Still, they have to go to trial."

"Not if the navy has anything to do with it," Taka said with a defeatist shake of his head.

"This is still a land of laws. Believe that, Taka. You are a journalist. You need to tell—"

"I'm a student who is falling behind in his classes thanks to all my column writing."

∞ ∞

At that moment, Admiral Stirling sat across from Lawrence Judd in the governor's office.

"A horrible thing," said the admiral halfheartedly. "This has gotten way out hand. Still, it's what happens when a court won't deliver a just verdict. Men do what they have done since time immemorial. An eye for an eye." He paused and then added, "Grace Fortescue deserves special consideration."

If Stirling was suggesting that the Fortescue woman should not be charged, Judd would have none of it. "You have killed one of my people. There *will* be a trial. A civilian trial for all involved."

"But first," said Stirling, raising his voice, "you must order your prosecutor to empanel a jury for the second rape trial for the remaining four. That ... happened first."

Judd put his elbow on his desk, leaned forward, and pointed his trigger finger at Stirling. "You, sir, are in charge of Pearl Harbor. I'm in charge of Hawaii. The *murder* trial ... will take place ... first."

Stirling's face tightened. "You have that authority. But I'm keeping my boys and Mrs. Fortescue on the navy base until the trial."

"Fine, but if they don't show up for the trial, I will send the National Guard to get them."

Stirling stood up. "They will be there." Head aligned with his ramrod-straight back, he stomped out of the office.

∞ ∞

They walked miles in their muumuus. They rode horses in their overalls. They took the buses and trolleys in their aloha shirts. They drove their cars in black suits. The nervous police, aided by the National Guard called by Judd, stood lining the roads to watch at least ten thousand white and every shade of bronze mourners climb the last mile to the cemetery hills overlooking the Pali to pay their last respects to Joe Kahahawai.

Brown Honolulu seethed with rage. White Honolulu feared reprisals. Navy personnel were restricted to their bases. All Hawaii waited for the explosion. The civil disorder. The uprising.

From his office, Judd studied the streets of Honolulu, clear of people as if a typhoon of biblical proportions was about to land. To the likely disappointment of Stirling, thought Judd, the stunned Hawaiians had quietly returned to their homes after the funeral. As did the Japanese. Shops had closed in respect. Perhaps the whites stayed away in fear. Judd hoped all reflected on the consequences of distrust leading to hate leading to beatings and murder.

∞ ∞

A week later, Assistant Attorney General Seth Robertson stepped off the gangplank in Honolulu. He spent two weeks in Hawaii to witness firsthand Stirling's expected crime wave of the colored looting shops and violating white maidens in response to the "honor" killing.

None was forthcoming.

Robertson researched the history of crime in Hawaii, looking for a persistent breakdown of law and order. He came up empty-handed. While he found evidence of police incompetence and corruption, the same could be said for New York and Chicago. Judd had already handed over his police authority to the new commission. A new police chief had been installed.

Robertson dropped by Judd's office before leaving. "I think you will be pleased with my report."

∞ CHAPTER 124 ∞

THE SUNDAY BRUNCH AT THE TAKAYAMA HOME that February was a dismal affair with no one more dismal than Haru. She believed in the promise of America. Now this.

"What did I tell you about the whites?" said Hiromi. "The killing of a non-white by four whites is an honor killing. They are demanding the murderers go unpunished."

Haru sighed, her eyes roaming over all six children. In a voice more defeatist than her family was used to she said, "I confess that I never suspected the degree of loathing haoles feel toward us, seeing us only as their racial inferiors. Buddha knows how hard I've worked to raise you all as good Americans."

"Sorry, Mommy," blurted Hiromi, "but our citizenship has only made the whites hate us even worse. We will vote. And then, good-bye, Big Five." Suddenly she flared, "Ha ha. They will *never* let that happen. You just wait and see. You don't see any colored governors in Mississippi or Alabama, do you? Well, they will make sure no Japanese will ever govern them." She waved her chopsticks in the air. "Just like a few years after I was born, they passed an immigration law. NO MORE JAPS!" Hiromi's shrill voice silenced the table.

Haru was at a loss for words. For the first time, she harbored doubts. *Have our children's scholarship, our politeness, and our reputation for hard work and fair business practices been for naught?* she wondered. *One unproven rape charge undermines all the good that we do and brings to the surface the haoles' worst fears.* She knew that the low crime rate among the Japanese was far less than those white navy boys, but it had made no difference. So engrossed was she in her thoughts, Haru hardly heard Kenji's rebuke directed at Taka. Hiromi's outburst was getting another pass, she thought, as her attention snapped to the present.

"You have disappointed many people, Taka," said Kenji. "Your words spoke your readers' thoughts. You undermined that Pafko fellow, but now ... "

"Otosan, my words are like the trade winds. They blow over. They are read by the powerless. They might make people feel good or righteously angry. But in the end, they have no impact. Pafko's words are like a banyan tree. They take root because his voice represents the people who control Hawaii, control our lives, those who decide what scraps off their table we can fight over."

Kenji raised his fork, let it hover over the scrambled eggs. "And giving voice to the voiceless is bad?"

"It's just ... " Taka shook his head like a beleaguered quarterback after throwing his fourth interception. "It's just so pointless. I write the words. I feel I have expressed the truth. But so what." It wasn't a question.

"I don't think that Joe confessed," said a bitter-voiced Hiromi. "Those navy guys lied. If he had confessed, they would have taken him to the police."

"They aren't even in jail," said thirteen-year-old Kenta, Haru's youngest son. "Get this. That mother's prison," he hammered at the word, "is the captain's quarters on the ship."

A resigned Taka looked at Kenta and Hiromi, and then focused on Tommy, now a high school sophomore. "It's about to get worse. The *Advertiser* is setting up a fund to hire an attorney for the murderers. And not just any lawyer ... Clarence Darrow."

"What?" said Haru. "The Monkey Trial lawyer?" She was referring to "the trial of the century," the 1925 Scopes Trial in which Darrow represented a teacher who taught the theory of evolution in violation of Tennessee law. Darrow lost the case, but Scopes was fined only one hundred dollars. The year before, Darrow had represented Leopold and Loeb, two teenage boys from wealthy families who confessed to kidnapping and murdering a fourteen-year-old boy. Darrow's eleventh-hour plea kept the boys from the electric chair.

"If this famous Monkey lawyer is coming to Hawaii," said ten-year-old Sachiko, "doesn't that mean those people are going to trial?"

A chorus of murmurs said, "Yes, that's right, good point," encouraging their youngest to speak up.

"So again, it comes down to twelve people," said Tommy, looking at Hiromi. "The last time, you said they would find the five boys guilty, but they didn't."

For the first time that day, Haru's face brightened. "You are both right," she said, looking at her two youngest. "Even the navy and the *Advertiser* can't fix a jury trial."

⌒ CHAPTER 125 ⌒

THE MORNING OF MARCH 24, Taka was eating a late breakfast at a brown wooden table in the student cafeteria after attending his 7:30 a.m. Asian history class. He was shaking his head like an older brother catching the much younger one with his hand in the cookie jar as he read the *Advertiser*'s fawning front-page coverage of the "great" Clarence Darrow's arrival at Honolulu's cruise ship pier. Pafko's accompanying editorial would have one believe that, at age seventy-four and with a lifetime of court victories behind him, Darrow's dazzling oratory would soon put all this unpleasant murder indictment business to bed by convincing any jury of the righteousness of bringing back a not-guilty verdict for the four defendants.

Taka's anger grew, not with Pafko but with himself. It wasn't enough just to shake his head in disapproval. He swirled the final morsel of his over-easy egg into the rice remains on his plate, lifted them to his mouth, and washed it down with the last of his coffee. Taka rose, crumbled the newspaper in his fist, walked over to the trashcan, and jammed the offending newsprint on top of napkins and paper plates. He fast-stepped to the bike rack. As he pumped his legs down Kapiolani Boulevard, he began writing his next column. A touch of arrogance, considering his predicament. He was an unemployed writer.

Twelve minutes later, an out-of-breath Taka stormed into the *Hochi* office. His father was right. He was a voice. He recalled the last time he likened his cause to Don Quixote fighting windmills. One of his pals who had heard the bromide once too often reminded him, "Don Quixote never gave up." He had also missed the buzz of the copy room and the adrenalin of pounding keys to meet a deadline. As he walked down the aisle leading to Makino's office, seasoned newspapermen looked up from their typewriters and greeted him.

He returned their smiles, straightened his back, and stepped up his pace. He belonged here!

As Taka entered his editor's office, Makino smiled wryly, not quite a smirk. "Taka, my young frustrated idealist. Have a seat."

On Makino's desk, Taka could not help but notice a press pass on which the words "Takeshi Takayama" were printed.

Taka's eyebrows rose. "You knew I'd be back?"

"Don't flatter yourself. I saw you charge in. I'm guessing you want your desk back."

"This Darrow thing—"

Makino waved him off. "If it wasn't for your mother, I would have thrown this out. You quit. You ran away from the fight. I never did."

"Yes, sir," Taka said, sinking lower in the seat. "I made a mistake."

"Listen to me. It's a good thing for the Japanese community that I did not fall prey to hopelessness during the last sugar strike, to the legislature's attempt to ban our language schools, to the immigration wars." Makino picked up the press pass and twirled it with the index fingers of each hand. "We did not win every battle, but if I hadn't fought, we would have lost them all." His eyes hardened as he handed the pass to Taka.

Taking the pass, Taka said, "I promise never to walk out like that again."

Makino folded his hands over his elbows resting on his desk. "You must live all your life knowing you quit when it got tough. Will this be a life pattern or have you learned something?"

Taka opened his mouth.

"Stop. There is nothing you can say. You have a lifetime to live out the answer." Makino pointed his fingers of both hands at Taka like two side-by-side derringers. "Taka, you are the cusp of the new Japanese in Hawaii. A Nisei. A Japanese American. A new type of citizen that Anglo-America will have to abide as it did with the Irish, Italians, and Jews. Our community needs bright young people from your Nisei crop. You have the makings of a good journalist." Makino dropped his hands to the desk and paused to let all this sink in before getting to what, for him, was the main point. "You want a meaningful life, Taka? Make things happen? Fight injustice? Be a catalyst?" Makino leaned over, his eyes intent. He lowered his voice, slowed down his cadence. "Do you want to make a difference, a real difference?"

Taka straighten his back. "Yes. Of course."

"Watch the trial, Taka. Each day ask yourself, 'Do I want to report on the events that shape people's lives, or do I want to enter the arena?'"

Taka's eyes opened wide as if to say, "I don't understand."

"If you have your mother's spirit, if your quitting in the face of adversity was an aberration you spend the rest of your life proving will never happen again, I think you would make an outstanding attorney. Watch Darrow … and Kelley," referring to the lead prosecutor in the case. "Could you do what they do? Could you represent litigants in court to fight injustice? Could you wave a sign at six in the morning on a street corner in Moiliili to ask people to vote for you as their legislator?"

Makino held Taka's gaze and was heartened the younger man did not look away.

In that instant, Taka saw another future. He saw himself standing in front of a witness stand asking a withering question that revealed a previously hidden truth. And for a fleeting second, he was dressed in black robes, sitting high on the bench, and delivering final instructions to a jury. But did he have the nerve, the intelligence, and the persona to enter this arena?

∞ CHAPTER 126 ∞

APRIL 7, 1932, the first day of the murder trial, dawned with soft breezes pushing puffs of cotton clouds over Honolulu Harbor's blue silky waters. Four blocks up from the piers, Taka signed in at the courtroom he knew well from last year's rape trial. He had arrived early, even though this first day would deal only with jury selection. He took his accustomed bench seat at the end of the press box's second row—which came with a polished mahogany post that obstructed his view. He had to move his head either right or left to see any court action. But he was the kid reporter and knew his place.

With Makino's law career suggestion still fresh in mind, Taka shifted his perspective. He put himself into the shoes of the combatants, the dueling attorneys, refereed by another attorney, the judge. By mid-morning, watching the judge chastise Darrow and Kelley for their delaying tactics in finding sympathetic jurors, Taka wondered if a Japanese lawyer would ever sit on the bench in Hawaii. Of course, there had been Japanese attorneys in Hawaii for decades. But in big cases like a murder trial, even with Japanese defendants, the lead attorneys, the prosecutors, and the judges were always haoles, as were the key police witnesses. Haole justice ruled.

Taka speculated what he would do in Darrow's place. There is only one issue. How will the great Darrow convince twelve jurors that, despite Tommy Massie's confession that he pulled the trigger, extenuating circumstances demand a verdict of not guilty? Honor killing? Sounded too biblical to Taka's Buddhist ears. It's one thing to demand such in newspaper editorials or around a bar ... but twelve men of varying backgrounds sitting in a jury room? That seemed a stretch to Taka. Temporary insanity? Taka had done his research. Recent insanity pleas to stateside juries had not gone well. Very risky. Still, it would be Darrow tugging on the jury's emotions.

∞ ∞

While Taka observed the jury selection and daydreamed about Darrow's strategy, across the street Governor Judd was reading the Seth Robertson report. The overhead fans swirled at mid-speed as he nibbled on his mid-morning pineapple jam–filled doughnut. His chewy smile broadened as he read Robertson's key summary: "Navy claims of unsafe streets and a breakdown of law and order have no basis in fact."

Judd sat back in his leather-upholstered chair, gazed through his window at the courthouse, and smiled. "Fuck Stirling," he said without the usual circumspect sensibilities of his class. Of course, his door was shut and only the wall heard him. He smiled, imagining Stirling's response to the selfsame report.

∞ ∞

At Pearl Harbor, Stirling threw the report down on his desk. *Crap. It's all crap. Robertson missed the whole point*, he said to himself. *The fucking natives are taking over the island and tearing down everything the white man has built.* Stirling punched the intercom on his desk. "Get Judd on the line."

"I take it that I owe the honor of this call to the Robertson report," said Judd, not able to hold back a note of triumph in his voice.

"This mendacious political misrepresentation of the facts needs to be sorted out before we release any info to the press," snapped Stirling.

Judd, who already had a call from Walter Dillingham asking to suppress the report because it criticized the local press coverage of events, told Stirling what he had told Dillingham. "Someone has already leaked it to the *New York Times*." He couldn't resist the next dig. "Can you imagine someone leaking an official government report to the press?"

"Damn, damn, damn!" blurted the admiral before he slammed down the phone receiver.

∞ ∞

Once the trial moved from jury selection to hearing testimony, Taka compared the battle of the old warrior Darrow against the Young Turk Kelley—with all their competing motions, clever questions, and objections—to the last World Series. Taka likened the battle-hardened, wrinkle-faced Darrow to veteran spitball-pitcher Burleigh Grimes of the St. Louis Cardinals, the last of the spitballers grandfathered in after the 1920 ban. Opposing Grimes had been the younger thirty-one-game winner for the Philadelphia Athletics, Lefty Grove, who Taka equated to the youthful prosecutor John Kelley. In their only direct matchup in the 1931 World Series, Grimes bested Grove and a few days later, Grimes won the seventh and deciding game to give the Cardinals the World Series title. Taka fanaticized calling the game unfolding in front of him as if it were from the press box in Sportsman Park. He hoped Darrow was more past his prime than Grimes.

Taka was taken aback by Darrow's opening statement. *He's going for temporary insanity*, Taka realized, *which means Tommy Massie has to be the distraught triggerman.* Taka shared Kelley's innuendo that

Darrow, violating the ethics of his profession, coached Massie's confession. Taka placed his own bet on the nasty-eyed Grace Fortescue as the shooter. She had the steel. Tommy, though a naval officer, seemed a bit of a wimp. Taka dismissed the other two defendants, enlisted men, as possible shooters. It wasn't their fight.

Taka admired how Darrow set up his proposition. He spent days in front of the jury establishing his case, including testimony from a California psychiatrist who claimed that Tommy was not in his right mind when he pulled the trigger. Darrow was the low-key professor weaving a new truth—until his four-and-a-half hour summation broadcast live to the States. Then he turned it on. He thundered, whispered, cajoled, pleaded. And finally after a pause so long that Taka thought he might be having a heart attack, Darrow finished.

"There is the great unwritten law dating back to biblical times, one that says what is right transcends the law. What would you do if these beasts raped your wife?"

Prosecutor Kelley was Darrow's opposite. During the trial, he laid out the facts. A man is dead. One of the defendants has confessed. All participated in the kidnapping, a premeditated kidnapping as evidenced by the planning required. There is no question of guilt.

Kelley saved his best words for a short counter to Darrow's Broadway performance. Facing the jury, he said, "You have the most vital duty to perform of any twelve men who ever sat in a jury box under the American flag. Do not pay any attention to what the admiral says," referring to his earlier remarks of the threat of military rule in Hawaii. "I say the hell with the admiral. If you do what is right, you will have nothing to fear. I put this case in your hands. I pray that there will be no racial lines. In Hawaii, there are no excuses for murder. You have no choice other than to bring back a guilty verdict."

Taka wanted to jump up and yell, applaud, not only because he admired Kelley's closing but also because at that moment, that exact moment, Taka knew. *Yes!* he thought. *This is what I want to do, why I was born. Let someone else write about* me.

∞ Chapter 127 ∞

Taka and Pafko saw the same trial, but their columns would have had you believe otherwise.

Prosecution Proves His Case
By Takeshi Takayama

Despite the brilliantly clever defense by renowned Clarence Darrow and tear-filled testimony by alleged assault victim Thalia Massie, the defense failed to make its case. In response to Darrow's rhetoric, Prosecutor Kelley pointed out, "If an unwritten law or temporary insanity defense can excuse murder when one's wife accuses a man of rape, where does it stop? What other injustices can excuse one for the murder of another?" Kelley presented the simple facts. They did it. And asked the simple question, "Will you let them get away with murder?" The prosecutor added, "The only compassion available is a recommendation for compassionate sentencing."

A nice touch, that ending. Kelley let the jury know they can bring back a guilty verdict while considering the mitigating emotions of the defendants. These twelve men know their duty. They will bring back a guilty verdict.

Since Biblical Times
By Andy Pafko

America is a nation of laws. Yet not every law is just, nor is every crime punishable. There are grievous acts of violence that require punishment. But what happens when one group within society gives a free pass to their own—one who committed a crime—by refusing to do their civic duty?

To claim that a not-guilty verdict invites all of us to murder those who violate our freedom, whatever our excuse, is ludicrous. If that were so, we would have such cases weekly. The crime against Thalia Massie was singularly the worst type of injustice.

Rape.

Assault.

An ignorant race having their way with the wife of a navy officer.

This case is about public safety. When the jury in November refused to convict these wanton rapists, they made the streets of Hawaii unsafe for any white woman. The four heroes who made rapist Joe Kahahawai confess made Hawaii a safer place. It was a tragedy that something UNPLANNED and unfortunate happened in the moment while he was in their custody. But that is mitigated by the fact that a rogue jury set him and his fellow thugs free.

The defendants should be commended, not convicted.

❧ CHAPTER 128 ❧

TAKA WAS AT SCHOOL, thinking about the subject of his next column, figuring that the jury would take days, maybe a week, to decide this case. He was shocked when on April 29, only forty-seven hours after the jury had retired, the radio announced Judge Davis had called the defendants back to court. He rushed to the courthouse.

Taka took his seat in the press box just in time to hear Judge Charles Davis intone: "Have you reached a verdict?"

"We have, Your Honor," said the jury foreman.

"What say you?"

"Guilty of manslaughter ... " a dramatic pause, "with a recommendation for leniency."

The courtroom's haole gallery erupted in protest.

Judge Davis banged the gavel repeatedly but to no effect and then retired to his quarters.

Across America the next morning, the Hearst papers screamed, "Gangsters run Hawaii," "Forty women had been attacked in the last year," and "Fiendish men rule the streets of paradise." William Randolph Hearst demanded, "Pardon the defendants immediately." If the governor refuses to do his duty, Hearst declared, "Then, the president should do it and put Hawaii under martial law."

One hundred twenty-one members of Congress sent Judd a message: "We, as members of Congress, are deeply concerned in the welfare of Hawaii and believe that the prompt and unconditional pardon of Lieutenant Massie and his associates will serve that welfare and the ends of substantial justice." Hawaii's non-voting delegate to Congress, Victor Houston, telegraphed Judd, "Issue a pardon at the appropriate time." Local clergymen claimed, "The jury has erred," and organized petitions asking for a pardon. As if this were not enough, Judd received a call from President Hoover urging him to "commute any sentence without any jail time."

Walter Dillingham, outraged at the conviction, called Pafko. "Write one of your usual columns. Demand a pardon but skip the brute stuff. We need to start healing the damage done by the verdicts of these two trials."

"This will not stand," said Stirling in a meeting with his officers.

Judd refused to take his calls.

Grace Fortescue's captain's cabin "prison suite" overflowed with flowers of sympathy from all America. Tommy and his convicted shipmates were treated like heroes and enjoyed steak, lobster, and a 1919 Bordeaux with the admiral.

Judd held steady. Thinking of the dilemma in which Pontius Pilate had found himself, he told everyone including Hoover, "There is nothing to pardon. The defendants have not been sentenced."

He slept little, thinking of scenarios of how Judge Davis could get him off the hook.

∞ Chapter 129 ∞

ON MAY 4, Taka made it to his seat just in time to watch Judge Davis stare the standing defendants in the eye. His own eyes roved the courtroom, silent except for four languid fans stirring the air halfheartedly. Stirling sat in the front row, his own mean eyes on the judge as if to say, "You had better do the right thing." The judge cleared his throat, more from nerves, Taka speculated, than the need to eliminate any phlegm from his vocal cords. After another studied look at his notes, the judge intoned, "You have taken the law into your own hands and murdered a fellow citizen. Either America is a nation of laws or the mob. You are each sentenced to ten years of hard labor."

Ignoring Grace's collapse, the haoles' dismayed shouts, Hawaiians applauding, and Japanese remaining seated in relieved silence, Admiral Stirling stomped out of the courthouse. Moments later, he charged into Judd's office to find the governor and Dillingham at the window looking at the crowd exiting the courthouse while the radio on the governor's desk, tuned to KGU news, broadcast live from inside the courtroom. Hawaii's two most powerful civilians turned around at the heavy-footed intrusion.

"Larry," said the admiral, "this is no longer about what is right or wrong or what is just. The judge decided that. Wrongly, but it's decided. The baboons have won their case. But I cannot control ten thousand naval personnel. And looking at the reaction in the courtroom, you won't be able to control your citizens either. We are on the verge of a civil breakdown."

Judd did not argue. *For once, we are in agreement*, he thought.

As Judd strolled over to his desk and snapped off the radio, Dillingham spoke. "Our class has taken a beating, Larry. We will never recover our authority; these trials were a benchmark. Grace and that accusing daughter have done our island irreparable harm. They are stupid and evil. But we can't let this linger any longer." He stopped to cast an accusing look at Stirling. "Our control over our community must not be allowed to disintegrate."

"We don't want civil disorder. Nor do we want to put Hawaii under martial law," said Judd. He looked outside to the reporters, including Taka, gathering around Washington Place as uniformed sheriff's deputies escorted the defendants toward his office. "Judge Davis made the right decision as a man of law. Now I have to use the powers of the governor to put in place what is the greater good for everyone." He looked at the two men and handed them a statement that he had drawn up the night before shortly after Judge Davis had called him. "I'm a judge. I must make my sentencing based on the rule of law" was all he would say. It was enough.

Dillingham and Stirling read the document. Stirling started to object. "This does not go—"

"Enough, Admiral!" Looking outside his door at the sound of booted men nearing his office, he continued in more modulated voice. "Best you leave. I have business to attend to."

Minutes later, the defendants were led into Judd's office where he read the statement commuting their sentences to one hour in the sheriff's custody. He refused to pardon them. And so the law was honored, but the defendants, now convicted felons, were set free.

Taka stood stunned as the governor's aide passed out the statement to reporters. *These four people are getting away with murder*, he thought and then sprinted to where he'd left his bike and rushed off to the *Hochi*.

"There will be no extra," said Makino. "There's been enough drama. Everyone knows they walked. No use pouring gasoline on the fire. We need your column. Don't write now while passion riles your blood. Go home. Ponder on this. Come back after supper."

Taka biked home. He found his mother there alone.

"So it's over," she said.

"There are still the four boys and a second trial," said Taka. "But the governor sanctioned murder."

Hearing the fatigue and failure in Taka's voice, Haru asked, "And if the governor had not commuted their sentences?"

She studied her son, wondering what conclusions he would reach. She knew this to be a turning point in her son's life.

"Not good, Okasan. Riots. Maybe even a Ku Klux Klan type of reaction. At some point, Japanese and Hawaiians would be driven to strike back. Martial law would likely ensue. Congress could possibly hand Hawaii over to the military, meaning Stirling and the navy."

"So the governor did what he had to do?" Haru asked.

Taka gave her a fond but wan smile. "Can I write that? Are my readers in the mood for that?"

"Taka-chan, the truth is the truth."

"What should I do?"

"That is your decision."

∞ CHAPTER 130 ∞

A FULL MOON WAS RISING into the embers of the sunset when Taka returned to the *Hochi*. He walked to his desk, rolled a sheet of paper into the typewriter, and began striking the keys.

The Governor Had No Choice
By Takeshi Takayama

Four murderers walked free today. Governor Judd did not pardon them. In fact, he validated their guilt. And yet, he commuted their sentences. It does not seem just: one hour for a killing that has torn apart the fabric of our island.

However, if I were governor, I would have made the same decision in an effort to stop the escalating trauma that is tearing apart our society and might have led, if riots ensued, to military rule of our islands. No one—haole, Hawaiian, or Oriental—wants that.

Taka continued to make his case of the likely consequences of "attempting," as he phrased it, to take the convicted killers from navy custody and place them in Hawaii's prisons.

∞ ∞

"This is your best yet, Taka," beamed Makino. "You are going out like a champ."

Taka raised his eyebrows.

"Get back to your lessons. When you graduate, you have a job here." He paused. "Did you give any thought to what I said about the law?"

"Yes, sir. Watching Kelley and Darrow convinced me your advice was good. But I'll need a year or so of work after graduation before I can think of law school."

"Don't be too sure about that. You know Hung Wai Ching?"

"Sure. The popular director at the YMCA. I've played ping-pong with him. Never beat him," smiled Taka. "I hear he's in Boston getting a divinity degree."

"He and I have a group of businessmen who look for young men with promise, young men like yourself. We help them get advanced degrees if they are willing to give back to the community."

Taka was dumbstruck, unsure of what to say.

"Keep your grades up. Wai Ching will be back in a month. This Massie thing will be behind us. Let's have a chat then." All Taka could do was nod his head. "Off with you now. Study hard and make your mother proud."

Taka left the *Hochi* pressroom with a heavy heart, but not because it was his last time there. A powerful realization struck him as he biked into the night. He had made the case for the haoles, the ruling class.

At some level, he had accepted their designation of him, a non-white Buddhist, as someone of a lesser class. He had agreed without thinking too much about it—just the way of life in Hawaii. And such a life was not all that bad. He lived in a nice home, went to the university, and now maybe was on his way to law school.

Yet no matter how hard he worked, neither he nor any Japanese American would ever be appointed governor or elected mayor. He had always accepted a certain fairness of such an arrangement without examining it. The haoles had developed Hawaii into an island paradise and an agricultural powerhouse. *Our parents never wanted to replace the whites; they came to Hawaii just hoping to better their economic lives or, like my father, to serve the people who came here for that purpose. We accepted these conditions.*

What the trial had done, he figured, was expose the fear of the white community. *We have not asked for equality, never really thought about it all that much. We were not, are not revolutionary Bolsheviks. But there are so many of us and so few of them.* He thought of the stories of how slaveholders slept with guns in their bedroom, fearing an uprising. *So many slaves; so few whites. We are not slaves, but the numbers are the same. There will be no uprising. No burning of homes. But some day, we will be the voting majority. The underclass will choose.*

That's what this trial was all about—the right to rule. This Massie woman had turned a subterranean fear into racial animosity. This woman turned what might have been a gradual change, like the frog in a pan of water set to boil, into a jarring awareness that their "God-given" right to rule might be challenged.

A good subject for a column, he thought, as he parked his bike by his dorm. *But no.* His writing days were finished. There would be plenty of others giving their own broader meaning to these trials. He would stick to spirited dorm debates and great breakfast discussions with his family.

Back to those poli-sci notes.

∞ CHAPTER 131 ∞

"WEEDS ARE SNEAKING INTO THE ROSES, Okasan," said Kenji gently as he entered "her" tatami mat room and sat down on his haunches across from Haru. The house was empty in the last of quiet mornings. School finals were in progress. Noisy mornings were only days away. Wind fluttered through open louvers.

"I just don't have that morning energy," Haru said slowly.

It had been three weeks since the four murderers had been set free. She recalled coaching Taka that the governor did what he had to do. Her son agreed and made a good case for the commuted sentence. She was proud of him. Coming from a Japanese, the column had set off a firestorm of debate. Letters to the editors of all the local newspapers, not just the *Hochi*, either attacked or supported him. At Sunday service, congregants approached Haru with a "How could he side with the haoles?" or "He did a brave thing. We need to put this behind us."

And so the island's wounds began to heal.

But not Haru's. While she agreed with Judd's decision, knowing it would forestall further conflict, it did not live up to America's high ideals about justice and equality for all. In the end, the four murderers went free. Forever. Sentence served. The minority ruling class had won. *There is no real justice for Hawaiians and Orientals*, she thought. And the Immigration Act of 1924 was put in place to keep it that way, at least for now, for her generation.

Haru knew she needed to weed the failing roses, wash the clothes in her overflowing laundry basket, scrub away the grime building up on the kitchen floor. But she couldn't. She just did not have the energy. "Maybe later, Otosan. I'm tired. After a nap, I might feel better."

"Wakarimashita," said Kenji, not at all sure he understood. "I have to go the Fort Street Hongwanji this afternoon."

∽ CHAPTER 132 ∽

WHILE HARU NAPPED, Taka's knees were unsteady as he walked up the stairs of the University of Hawaii's main administration building. His sweaty hands held a letter, more like an invitation or summons. Charles Hemenway, the president of the board of regents, had sent Taka a letter in the middle of finals. "If you can make yourself available at 2 p.m. Wednesday, June 15, at my university office, I have something I would like to discuss with you."

Taka was aware his column writing had turned him into a public figure and speculated that the summons most likely had something to do with that. But what? He was graduating. Certainly a man as important as Hemenway, who was also vice president of Alexander & Baldwin, one of the Big Five corporations, hardly had time for a newspaper reporter who no longer was writing. Still, he knew the man wasn't endeared as "Papa" Hemenway for nothing. His reputation for guiding and helping students was legendary. It had to be good news, didn't it? Taka demanded of himself. He hoped his knees would be steady.

A friendly female smile greeted him as he entered Hemenway's outer office. Looking at the clock, she said, "You must be that reporter everyone is talking about. You are a bit early, but they are all here. Let me check if they are ready for you."

They? Taka repeated in his mind as his face went flush with the compliment.

"You can go in now," said the woman a moment later.

Three men, all in white shirts and light-colored suits, rose from chairs ringing a low coffee table to the side of Hemenway's ornate desk. Taka recognized them all: Makino with a twinkle in his eye; short, well-shouldered Hung Wai Ching wearing horn-rimmed glasses; and the icon, lean Charles "Papa" Hemenway. Taka framed the picture of the three men standing, much as a photographer on Hotel Street would capture a moment in time. That held image of a haole, a Japanese immigrant, and a Chinese American would stay with Taka all his days. They were here for him. He flashed back to what Makino had said about men helping students. His knees no longer shook, but the adrenaline still pumped. Was this that moment in life when destiny strikes? He shook hands with the three men and hardly heard Hung Wai Ching's half-question–half-statement.

"You must be pleased with the governor's decision to hire the Pinkerton agency to investigate the Massie allegations?"

"Ah, yes, sir. Those of us who took the time to get all the facts know what the Pinkerton people will find. I suspect the governor does too."

"I would imagine," said Hemenway, "that the Pinkerton people will give the governor the cover he needs to drop the rape case."

Makino, never one to miss a story, went fishing. "I understand Dillingham wants to put this to rest as well."

"So it would seem," said Hemenway, sitting down. "Please, Takeshi, take a seat." He looked at the other two men and said words Taka would never forget. "You have two good friends here, Takeshi, who would like to help you. But you have helped yourself. I have read your columns; they were well written. Your schoolwork is excellent. Between what Mr. Wai Ching and Mr. Makino have raised in their communities and my own private resources, we'd like to pay your way through law school and not just any law school, but Harvard."

∽ ∾

A half-hour later Taka burst into his home.

"Hey, everybody! I'm going to Harvard!" When he received no response, he called out, "Okasan! Where are you?" He knew at least his mother must be home since the front door had been unlocked.

His shouts finally awoke the napping Haru. She walked into the living room, rubbing her eyes. At the sight of Haru's disheveled hair and drawn face, Taka toned down his news. "I'm going to law school, Mom. Harvard University.

"Okasan, I could hardly believe what these people are doing for me. It's not just tuition and board. They are paying for my transportation and even giving me a spending allowance. They want me fully engaged on campus without working a part-time job."

"A Chinaman, a haole, and one of our own did this for you?" Haru asked, amazement radiating in her eyes.

"Hai, Okasan."

Later, that afternoon, Haru weeded her roses.

PART VIII

SUSPICION

∞ CHAPTER 133 ∞

Honolulu – December 1, 1937

T HE RUMBLE OF ARTILLERY THUNDER punctuated the static-crack-ling voice from the Motorola.

"This is Lowell Thomas … reporting from Nanking, the capital of the Republic of China. Japanese troops are advancing south toward this city, drenched in rumor and despair."

Haru hurriedly rinsed the last lunch dish. She pushed back the faucet handles, shutting off the gurgling cascade competing with the one o'clock NBC News. Six time zones ahead, East Coast listeners prepared for dinner.

"Generalissimo Chiang Kai-shek, reeling from the loss of Shanghai to Japanese imperial forces, is rumored to be moving his Nanking government to Wuhan, deep inside China. This morning, the general, staying behind to defend the city, promised 'to fight to the death.'"

Haru picked up a jelly jar holding some furniture polish—her own concoction of lemon juice and mineral oil—and grabbed a rag. On the balls of her feet, she quick-stepped her way into the dining room, set the jar atop the Motorola set, bent over, and tweaked the radio dial to improve the signal quality.

"Secretary of State Cordell Hull issued another 'grave concern' statement condemning continued Japanese aggression. Senator Cabot Lodge scolded FDR, 'You must do something.'"

Resigned to the uneven reception, Haru dribbled a few drops of furniture polish onto the rag and began massaging the sides of the radio's walnut console. Susano, her latest calico cat, nuzzled up against her legs.

Lowell Thomas reminded his listeners, "Last year, Japan withdrew from the League of Nations after protesting that the Geneva-based body was interfering in its internal affairs."

Haru lifted the family photo from the top of the console with one hand and began buffing with the other.

"Earlier today in Tokyo, the foreign ministry issued a warning over congressional calls for sanctions. 'We would consider such action a declaration of war.'"

Fear snaked its way into Haru's gut. She gazed at the innocent smiles of her four young sons, now at or near military age. Haru's neck tilted up to study the faces of the two portraits hanging on the wall like sentinels guarding the radio. A vibrant Franklin Roosevelt, wearing his famously wide grin, his teeth clenching a cigarette holder, waved from the backseat of a top-down roadster. On the right, a stern, military-uniformed Hirohito sat imperially on a white stallion. Fear drove her hand down to her thumping heart as she thought of her boys, so full of the juices of life.

Storm clouds slipping over the mountains burst. The rustling wind blowing through the windows and raindrops pinging on the rooftop drowned out Thomas's voice. Haru's thoughts drifted from her living room back to another time and place. She plopped down on a dining room chair, and Susano jumped onto her lap. Haru scratched idly under the cat's chin while she recalled that fateful morning in June 1905. She had watched the Meiji emperor trot into Tokyo's Yasukuni Shrine to honor her brother and the other seventy-eight thousand men who had died fighting the Russians. The memory of her naïve vow to birth sons to fight for the emperor made her shudder. She thought about Japanese mothers of every generation since the Meiji Restoration sending their sons to fight foreign wars—against the Chinese in 1895, against the Russians in 1905, putting down the recurring Korean uprisings after the 1910 annexation, capturing the German-Chinese concession in 1914, and now pouring troops into China again. She imagined Japan and America as two mythical giants sloshing across the Pacific Ocean, each with a sword held high in one hand and chains swirling in the other—huge angry-eyed, fire-breathing warriors stomping toward one another in slow, menacing steps. She twisted her hands as she contemplated the two inevitabilities—war between Japan and America and her four, rifle-toting, khaki-clad sons marching resolutely into battle, all too ready to die proving their loyalty to the Stars and Stripes.

She looked back at the family photo and zeroed in on her oldest, Takeshi, her only son with long hair—well groomed with a part splitting at the top of his head. He had recently returned from Boston after graduating from Harvard Law School. His mentor, Hung Wai Ching, had found him a spot on Hawaii's legal team petitioning for statehood. From October 6 to 22, 1937, a joint congressional committee of seven senators and twelve House members held hearings in Hawaii to debate the issue of statehood. Haru had been sitting in the visitors' area on the last day of the hearings when one of the senators nodded to Governor Joseph Poindexter and said, "Expect a positive recommendation to Congress." Later, her chest swelled when she overheard the governor tell her son, "Be prepared to be appointed secretary to the planning committee for the referendum."

After the hearing, Takeshi had splurged by taking his mother to the Natsunoya Tea House overlooking Pearl Harbor from Alewa Heights. "My treat," he said, squeezing her hand.

Her eyes delighted at the sight of well-groomed bonsai trees and freshly raked rock gardens. Orchid plants crawled among the bigger rocks while brisk mountain breezes freshened the air. Comfortably seated at a wrought-iron table overlooking the distant battleship-filled harbor, Haru said, "I heard what Governor Poindexter said to you."

"It would be an honor to receive the appointment, but my real mission will be working with Hung Wai Ching on his committee to prevent the internment of Hawaii's Japanese community ... when war breaks out between America and Japan."

Haru felt the blood drain from her face. Despite her light-headedness, she forced a swallow. Worse than his words was her son's casual tone, as if he were discussing a certain change of weather.

As Haru drifted back from that memory, the rain erupted into a roof-hammering downpour. The wind banged a living room shutter closed. When the electricity blinked, powering off the radio, her eyes shifted to Yoshio, her second oldest, standing next to Taka in the family photo and whose close-cropped hair was military-ready. Right after Christmas, he would sail for Tokyo to attend Todai University. Until classes started in March, he would live with Midori in Hiroshima to improve his Japanese. When Kiyoshi died a year after the Massie Trial, Midori had been given a small cottage as a sinecure on the Fudoin Temple grounds.

Next, Haru smiled at Tommy's toothy grin and bushy crew cut. The family storyteller and a University of Hawaii freshman, he had embraced Christianity last year after proclaiming, "The path to acceptance is to be more American than the Americans." Haru had laughed to herself when his defiant proclamation at the dinner table had been met with a "please pass the rice" from his father. After ladling a generous scoop onto his plate, Kenji had said matter-of-factly to the tense table gathering, "Many of our young men have embraced Christianity. Christ and Buddha would approve a switch between them either way. They both preached love and tolerance above all."

Only Haru's eldest daughter, Hiromi, a high school sophomore, had given Tommy her best withering look. "Those big-nosed haoles love to spout off about Christian love. Words, nothing but words without meaning. Look how they treat us Japanese!" She had stabbed a piece of broccoli with a vengeance and glared at Tommy. "I would never accept such a hypocritical faith."

Haru's youngest son, Kenta, president of his high school senior class and lettering in three sports, had showed once again why he was the family's resident peacemaker. "We have a good life. Mother has cooked a delicious meal. Father supports both your decisions." Broadening his smile and extending the palms of his hands over his dinner plate, he had asked, "What's the problem?"

As Kenta had bobbed his head to encourage harmony, Haru could not help staring at his cowlick, just like Irie's. She noticed it often and worried that one day someone else would make the connection. She wished he favored a crew cut.

The radio sprang back to life just as Lowell Thomas shouted into his faraway microphone. "I'm looking at a single-engine Zero fighter, its sleek fuselage emblazoned with what has become the icon of terror—the blood-red rising sun."

Haru exhaled after an image flashed across her mind—a khaki-clad Takeshi aiming a rifle at the plane. She knew this image would come back to haunt her dreams. She pushed Susano off her lap and strode over to the Motorola. "Enough war news," she muttered and twisted the dial to "OFF" but not before Thomas added, "The Chinese have asked me, 'Why can't the Americans stop this?'"

She shook her head at the now-quiet radio. "I must not let this war news darken my twenty-eighth wedding anniversary." As Haru arose to prepare dinner, movement directed her attention to the rain-spotted window facing the street. Her youngest daughter, fifteen-year-old Sachiko, was skipping up the damp wooden steps without a care in the world.

∞ CHAPTER 134 ∞

ACROSS TOWN, HARU'S ELDEST SON, Takeshi, sitting quietly at the back of the Iolani Palace's throne room, scribbled notes as the Hawaiian statehood committee meeting wrapped up. Seven US Senators and twelve House Representatives were reading their final remarks after two weeks of hearings.

An hour later, Taka took his usual spot in Washington Place's cabinet room. Still armed with pad and pen, the committee's official scribe was struggling to keep up with Territorial Governor Poindexter's fiery address to his statehood delegation. "Despite their rum-tongued promises at the reception last night, the congressional committee punted. Today, the hungover, backtracking chairman pontificated, 'You have fulfilled every requirement for statehood. Conduct a referendum, and we will consider statehood.'" Poindexter spat out the word "consider." "I am too mad to *consider* ... a response to their retreat from a promised 'recommendation' for statehood."

Shigeo Yoshida—renowned orator, school principal, and son of a samurai warrior—who had spoken eloquently in support of statehood at the hearings, ran a hand over his wavy hair. "This back-stepping is all about whose side we … " he paused to look at his two fellow Japanese on the committee, "will support when war breaks out. It would be better if Japan declared war today and we settled the loyalty question once and for all."

Sitting across from Yoshida, Charles Hemenway, chairman of the University of Hawaii Regents, tilted his head. "A bit dramatic, Shigeo. But I grant you, the loyalty issue is at the heart of the matter."

"Did you watch the indignant eyes of the Southern delegates looking at us *colored folks*? Elect a Jap to Congress?" Giving a poor imitation of a Southern drawl, Yoshida continued, "No sah, we mustn't allow such an abomination."

Minutes later when Poindexter closed the meeting, Takeshi turned his gaze to his mentor. "Wai Ching, when do you want today's transcript?"

"Since your mother was good enough to invite Elsie and me to share in the celebration of your parents' wedding anniversary tonight, you can give your notes to me then."

Takeshi looked at his watch. Thinking Wai Ching had just spoiled his surfing plans, he forced a smile. "I'll have them ready by the time you arrive."

∽ CHAPTER 135 ∾

THANKS TO HIROMI PLAYING THE VICTROLA at its highest decibel level, the Takayama house rocked with Count Basie's "One O'Clock Jump," followed by the equally ear-blasting "The Lady Is a Tramp" by Sophie Tucker. Haru would have chosen a Crosby tune, but if it took jazz to motivate Hiromi and Sachiko to set the dinner table, she could stand the noise. Born only a year part and often mistaken for twins, Haru's daughters could not be more different. Pictures of Clark Gable and Errol Flynn smiled from the pastel-blue wall above Sachiko's desk. On the other side of the room, a *butsudan*—a wooden miniature Buddhist altar—rested on a shelf over Hiromi's desk.

Outside, Tommy and Kenta were carting bags of ice and salt from Kamada's corner store to the utility shed behind the house. After picking mangos from the backyard tree, they dusted off spiderwebs crisscrossing the wooden ice cream churner.

While arm-weary Tommy and Kenta were taking turns churning the thickening ice cream, Yoshio burst in the front door. He carried a brown bag stenciled "Otani Fish Market." As he slipped off his Buster Browns, Yoshio bellowed, "Matsujiro held back choice slices of toro, sake, and *ika* for us." Rather than have Matsujiro cut the slabs of raw fish into sashimi slices, Yoshio bought foot-long slabs, each finger-length wide and knuckle high. He took pride in his filleting skill with his nine-and-a-half-inch Tadafusa sashimi knife.

As the sun slipped behind Pearl Harbor, Wai Ching and his wife, Elsie, walked up the steps of the Takayama home. Takeshi, typing the last page of the statehood meeting minutes, rose to open the door. When Haru walked in from the kitchen, Wai Ching bowed and handed her a red envelope, held by fingertips from both outstretched arms. "You might want to open it now."

Haru wiped her hands on her apron and thumb-nailed the flap, careful not to tear it so she could reuse the gift envelope. She shook out a batch of movie theater tickets. When she read the top one, Haru's eyes lit up like two fireflies. "How did you know?"

"Two days ago, I told Takeshi how Elsie and I enjoyed *The Life of Emile Zola* at the Waikiki Theater. He mentioned you wanted to attend."

"Oh, I do! I have heard about Zola, how he brought back the wrongly accused Captain Dreyfus from Devil's Island and how he stood up to anti-Semitism. We Asians need a Zola." Her eyes dropped to her handful of tickets. "But eight tickets—that is too much."

"In your next life, have fewer children," laughed Wai Ching.

Later, as the daughters began clearing the table, Wai Ching said, "Can we older folks retire to the tatami room for tea? I have something interesting to share." Turning to Takeshi, he added, "You might like to join us."

Haru looked into Wai Ching's eyes, not the gay eyes that had just asked the children to share their favorite mom-and-dad memory but cold eyes. A feeling of foreboding swept over her. Still, she brightened. How distressing could the news be if she and Elsie were included?

Once Hiromi had set down a plate of pineapple chunks, poured tea for everyone, and closed the shoji doors upon leaving, Wai Ching pulled a string-tied bundle of papers from his coat jacket. As she watched Wai Ching smooth flat each sheet, Haru realized the almost gossamer sheaves were carbon copies and, by the grey, faded print, maybe fourth or fifth copies. Wai Ching turned pages upside down and laid them on the table so everyone could read the line typed in capital letters on the top sheet. The typist had obviously hammered the keys hard to give the phrase the feeling of a newspaper headline.

PLAN: INITIAL SEIZURE OF ORANGE NATIONALS
Lt. Col. George S. Patton - Head of Army's G-2

"This document was delivered to Poindexter after our meeting today. He agreed I could share it with people I trust. Colonel Patton arrived in 1935 with a mission to evaluate ... " he paused for effect, "the loyalty question."

While Wai Ching lit a Camel, Haru said, "He's a dynamic man. I met him at a social function to which Buddhist priests and their wives had been invited. He was overly polite to me, the way men are when they think they are better than you."

Wai Ching's voice took on an ominous cadence. "Patton forecasts that an alien orange race will pose a fifth column danger to its host country. He specifies how a hypothetical army must respond to a hypothetical threat, from a hypothetical disloyal race, in a hypothetical war ... against the homeland of the hypothetical resident aliens."

"In other words, don't trust the Japs," snapped Takeshi.

Wai Ching ignored the interruption, picked up the report, and started scanning the document. In between puffs, he stopped to read various points. "'In the event of a war with an Orange country, the army should arrest and intern certain persons of the Orange race. ... It would be desirable to hold as hostages leaders of the Orange race ... confiscate amateur radio sets ... close harbors to Orange race fishing vessels ... seize all Orange-owned banks in Hawaii ... close down

Orange travel agencies ... place Orange-owned hotels under military control ... remove all Orange house servants and personnel from military bases ... close all Orange language schools ... confiscate all Orange-owned cars ... strip the Orange community of its leadership ... proclaim martial law.'"

Silence chilled the room.

Haru thought of the years of internment, concentration camps, and prison rumors that had hopscotched among the Issei gossipmongers. Most conversations ended with "but this is America. They would never do that." Now here was an official army report recommending that this country of laws, not men, was planning to do exactly what she believed was impossible. Another thought brought a wave of nausea: The Americans are planning a war with Japan.

Wai Ching flipped through the report's back pages. "These are the names, addresses, and phone numbers of the Japanese to be arrested." He pointed to Kenji's name. "As a Buddhist priest, you are on the list." Wai Ching flicked ashes into a tray.

"So we just wait until the soldiers come?" asked Haru, the anger in her voice rising.

"Haru-san," said Wai Ching, his voice a blend of silk and steel, "you know me well enough. It is not my nature to wait for events to unfold, nor would I use the auspicious occasion of your wedding anniversary just to sound an alarm." His eyes turned to the two men, father and son. "Takeshi, Kenji ... I have a plan. I need both of you to help me."

The ring of the living room telephone drifted through the closed doors. Moments later, the hurried patter of feet approached the room. The shoji doors flew open.

"Irie is dead!" cried a shocked Hiromi. "Teiko's on the phone."

∞ Chapter 136 ∞

The blood drained from Haru's face. It had been five years since Ume had passed away, shortly after the Massie Trial, and three years since Haru's last visit to Irie and his three children. Teiko, the youngest, had been born less than a year before her mother had been sentenced to Molokai. Haru rose and, putting her hand over her mouth, hushed an "excuse me." In the living room, she picked up the phone left lying on the dining room table. "Teiko-chan, my child! What happened?"

"Oh, Haru-san," came the halting voice, "our lives ... they have not been good for some time. On your last visit, you did not see what our family had become. Otosan was drinking shochu again, but he sobered up for your visit. My *mamahaha*," said Teiko, referring to her stepmother that had long ago replaced Ko, who had run off to California, "hired her *cousin* to manage our coffee farm." She spat out the word "cousin" in an ugly voice, leaving no doubt the man was anything but a cousin.

"When Otosan got tuberculosis, he almost died and never really recovered. Drank and slept. I think he wanted to die. Then that cousin moved into the house, came to the ofuro when I was there and ... " Her words disintegrated into weeping that tore at Haru's heart.

Haru decided this was not the time to hear the whole story. "Where is your father now?"

"We ... we buried him ... today," Teiko said between sobs. "Haru-san, I'm afraid of that man."

"Where are your brothers?"

"Oh, they are here. They love their new daddy. He takes them fishing, teaches them baseball."

Haru held the phone, too stunned to speak. She did not ask about the stepmother. In such convoluted arrangements, it would not be the first time a stepmother overlooked her companion's interest in a teenage daughter. If only Ume had not been so stubborn and had let Irie follow her to Molokai. He and the children would have ...

"Haru-san?" Teiko's plaintiff voice drifted across the line.

"I'm here, Teiko," said Haru. She realized the girl had no one to turn to and must have agonized over calling her mother's friend from long ago who had not visited in years.

"Can you get a bus to Waimea?"

"Yes, I think so."

"Taiko-chan, pack your personal belongings and go to the Waimea mission." Haru then explained that she could stay with Sam and Kame until they arranged her passage to Honolulu. "You are a sweet child. We look forward to your staying with us."

After she called Kame, Haru returned to the living room, but her mind could no longer focus on Wai Ching's plan to cope with the implications of Patton's "Orange People" report.

∽ CHAPTER 137 ∾

HARU HARDLY RECOGNIZED THE YOUNG WOMAN walking down the wobbly gangplank in a blue dress. Too short to be appropriate, thought Haru, then her stealthy glance at the admiring Kenta, who formed the other half of the welcoming committee, confirmed her judgment. Still, Haru couldn't help remembering walking up the steps of the Fudoin Temple when she was six years younger than Teiko. Haru surmised the girl was carrying all her worldly possessions in the knotted cloth bundle.

"Teiko-chan," said Haru as the girl stepped onto the pier. "I am so happy you are here. You have a home with us."

Teiko bowed deeply. "Arigato, Haru-san,"

"Hello, sister," said Kenta, reaching out to take Teiko's free hand.

Haru gasped, and her knees buckled.

"Okasan! Are you okay?" asked Kenta, releasing Teiko's hand to support his mother.

Sister? Haru mentally repeated Kenta's greeting. Somewhere deep inside, could he know without knowing? She dismissed the thought as absurd. "I'm fine, Kenta," she said, regaining her composure. "Just a flash. Must be showing my age," she laughed.

The nervous girl bowed slightly to Kenta, a gesture seldom exchanged between Nisei. "I'm sorry to disturb your family."

"Please don't feel that way, Teiko-chan," reassured Kenta. "We were so sad when our okasan told us your father died ... and that you were not welcome in your own home." Teiko lowered her eyes. "We have plenty of room, and our family welcomes you."

Haru could not help but notice Kenta's appraisal of the girl whose snug summer dress emphasized generous curves. Her thoughts skipped to Teiko coming out of the bathroom with only a towel wrapped around her and tiptoeing to the girls' bedroom with dripping wet hair. The girl would be treated like a sister until her boys started thinking she was anything but a sibling, which, for one of her boys, she actually was.

Kenta gently grabbed Teiko's bundle and pointed past Aloha Tower. "It's just a few minutes' walk to the car. I'll drive through downtown to give you a glance at Honolulu."

Over Teiko's objections, Haru insisted, "Sit up front. You'll have a better view."

Playing the role of tour guide, Kenta pointed out all the local landmarks. Sensing Teiko was a bit overwhelmed by the hustle and bustle of a big city, he said, "Don't worry, sister. You'll get used to it all."

"Thank you, *brother*," teased Teiko.

Haru sat quietly throughout the banter. What had she expected? Kenta was doing his best to make the girl comfortable, just as Haru had requested. It was only after she had put down the phone, impulsively asking Ume's daughter to live with her, that she realized she was inviting Kenta's sister to live with them. She did not regret the invite. *Giri*, she thought. She owed Ume, who had given her a son. Ignoring the flutter in her heart over the flirtatious exchange, Haru said, "Let's do a little shopping. River Street is a good place to start," referring to the main shopping street in Chinatown.

"These days, there are more and newer shops on Bishop Street," said Kenta.

"Kenta," said Haru, disapprovingly.

Kenta understood the tone and did not want to be dressed down in front of Teiko. "Hai, Okasan." He found a parking place off River Street.

Haru smiled as they stepped out of the car and began walking down the street marked by overhanging signs in bold red Chinese characters. Her smile vanished at the first Chinese clothing store, where pictures of *Life* magazine's coverage of what was being called the "Nanking Massacre" were taped to the bottom of the store's front window. The sun-bleached photographs included a picture of a Japanese solder tightly gripping a sword poised high over a kneeling civilian. Additional photos captured a child sitting on the ground wailing and a trench of dead bodies guarded by imperial soldiers casually smoking cigarettes. Haru caught the eye of the proprietor behind a cash register who, noticing Haru's yukata, spat on the floor and turned away.

"Maybe it's better if we shop on Bishop Street after all," said Haru.

∞ ∞

Upon entering the Takayama home, carrying shopping bags with Teiko's new wardrobe, Kenta said, "Tommy can help you get registered for the university. The next semester starts in late January."

Teiko look dumbfounded.

"No rush, of course," said Kenta, sensing the girl's distress.

"I never finished high school."

It was Kenta's turn to look surprised. At McKinley High, all of his fellow Nisei had graduated.

Haru hurriedly added, "When her father got sick, Teiko had to drop out of school to take care of him."

"Wakarimashita. We can enroll you at McKinley for the spring and summer semesters to get enough credits to graduate."

The anxiety would not leave Teiko's eyes. "I don't know ... It's been so long since I've been in school. Maybe I'm not smart enough anymore."

"Don't worry about that," said Kenta. "I'll help you with your studies."

The smile that flashed across Teiko's face rewarded Kenta. Haru noticed the exchange with trepidation.

∞ CHAPTER 138 ∞

AFTER A LATE-MARCH, rain-drenching front finally moved on, the returned sun enticed Kenta's class of one to move to the backyard picnic table.

"Don't think of algebra as some kind of spooky math," said Kenta, trying to ignore the swell of his pupil's breasts. "When you see the letter A, think about cars or apples. It's just a symbol. Instead of having to write out 'one hundred apples' or 'twenty cars,' we use a letter."

"I'll never get it. Your younger sisters find it so easy. I'm just dumb," Teiko pouted.

"Don't say that!" Kenta put a consoling hand on Teiko's arm. "While my sisters have been studying, you were taking care of a family. There's a difference between not knowing how and not being able to know."

From the kitchen, Haru watched. Kenta's gesture was innocent enough. She tried to think how often he touched the arms of Hiromi and Sachiko. She couldn't recall any incidences, but then she had never bothered to record such a trivial event. Kenta often gestured as much as an Italian would ... like Irie. The thought registered like an earthquake rumbling through her mind.

Teiko had moved into her daughters' room. While at first her daughters had welcomed the girl in light of the tragedy, friction soon developed. The problems started with Teiko's skipping baths. While Haru's chat with Teiko resulted in a daily bath before bed, Haru remembered how fastidious Ume had been. How could Irie or Teiko's mamahaha have been so negligent? That girl needed—as much as her current studies—a good Japanese education.

Haru diverted her attention from the picnic table to the back row of cherry trees. The rains had stopped just as the tips of the buds split open, and now the sun was performing its magic. The first blossoms had burst, signaling her to keep the promise she had made to herself—that before the first petals dropped, she would talk to Kenta. Looking back to the picnic table, she watched Teiko's blouse brush Kenta's arm as she leaned over the table to look at an open book. Haru hoped the cherry blossoms had not come too late.

When Teiko went in for a bathroom break, Haru strolled to the picnic table. "Why don't we go to the movies today," she said. "They're showing *Stage Door*, with Katherine Hepburn and Ginger Rogers." While all the family enjoyed a good movie, she and Kenta were the cinema's biggest fans—except when Errol Flynn or other heartthrobs drew Sachiko's interest.

When Kenta asked, "Can Teiko come too?" Haru managed to keep her expression neutral. "It's been a while since just the two of us have enjoyed a movie together."

Kenta took the hint. "Hai, Okasan."

∞ ∞

"Let's have a tempura bento," said Kenta as they exited Waikiki's Seaside Avenue Cinema. He knew his suggestion meant eating at Haru's favorite Waikiki eatery, Choco House, two doors down from the theater.

During lunch, Kenta talked about his favorite subject—himself—as was the custom of all Haru's children except Sachiko and, now that he was older, Takeshi. Haru nodded as Kenta spun a web of words about spring practice for football without a word of appreciation for his father who had finally relented to allow his students to skip language school classes for school activities. Then he offered his opinion on casting Jane Wyatt in *Lost Horizon*—he would have preferred Barbara Stanwyck.

On another day, Haru would have responded to Kenta's remarks. Instead, she played with her food. She had rehearsed her pending conversation with Kenta often over the years in case the day ever came, more frequently since Teiko's arrival. She never composed it quite to her satisfaction. Now she wanted to be done with it.

"Your mind seems elsewhere, Okasan," said Kenta as they prepared to leave.

"Why don't we stroll along the beach?" Minutes later, as she and Kenta walked along where the grass meets the beach in front of the Pink Palace, she shook her head and commented, "Three hotels on Waikiki Beach."

"I don't think you have to worry about more hotels, Mom," said Kenta as they ambled past the hotel. "With only one ship arriving each week, the Waikiki hotels are complaining about empty rooms."

"And what about Pan Am's flying boats?" Haru asked, recalling the first commercial flight from the Mainland two years ago.

"Well, the China Clipper carries only thirty-six passengers," Kenta replied.

On another day, she would have countered, "The first whaling ships didn't have many more than that," but she had other things on her mind.

At that moment, the surf lapped inches from her feet. She took off her shoes. As was the custom with boys at the time, Kenta went barefoot even to school and the movies. He hooked his fingers around the straps of his mother shoes. The gesture earned him a warm smile.

Then, she took a deep breath and let it out slowly. "I need to tell you a story, Kenta. A story I never thought I would tell anyone."

Kenta stopped in time to watch a single tear slide down Haru's cheek.

"You know the story of how you were born on the beach of Molokai."

"Of course," he said, worrying where this was going. "You were picking up Ume's baby. You were keeping your promise to Ume. Giri." Watching the distress in Haru's eyes, Kenta felt compelled to keep talking. "You were tossed about in heavy seas. You weren't due for two more months. A woman … " Kenta hesitated and searched his memory.

"Ipo," helped Haru.

"Yes, a Hawaiian woman condemned to a leper's death helped you. She delivered me as people meeting the boat watched. You were lucky you made it to the beach in time."

Haru grabbed both of Kenta's hands. Her head did not move. She hardly noticed the gentle surf sweeping over her toes. "I wasn't lucky, Kenta."

Kenta felt a stirring in a stomach full of popcorn, Coca-Cola, and bonbons. "What are you saying?"

"My baby died on the beach."

Two beach boys, hurrying past, dove into the surf.

Haru held Kenta's hands tightly.

"Then … who am I?"

"You are Ume's son," she said in a low voice.

Kenta made out only the word "Ume."

Haru held his gaze, took her time. "Teiko is your sister."

Kenta bent over and retched popcorn smudged in acidic chocolate. Knees on the beach, he cupped salt water from a surf surge and wiped his mouth. He fist-pounded the sand. "No, no, no, no, no … "

Haru lowered her eyes. Her worst fears cascaded through her mind. Would Kenta run away? Condemn her for her deceit? Would he tell his father? How could Kenji bear it?

Kenta stood up, confusion but not outrage in his eyes. "I need to know everything, the whole story."

Haru stared directly at the sea. The mid-afternoon sun was descending on her right over Pearl Harbor. Fluffy clouds danced. A surfer cried out as a wave flipped him on his back.

Kenta grabbed his mother's hands. "Is any of the beach birth story true?"

"My baby was stillborn on that beach. Ipo tried to breathe life into my baby. You can't imagine the devastation, losing my baby. Kenji had begged me, *begged* me not to go. My stubbornness killed my baby."

"So you switched babies."

Haru silently thanked Kenta for the lack of an accusatory tone in his flat voice. "When I saw Ume's baby ... " Haru raised her eyes tentatively, seeking out Kenta's still disbelieving eyes, "he ... you ... were so healthy but motherless. Ume insisted I take you and raise you as my own. She wouldn't accept my protests. Told me Irie could not handle another child. I knew that better than Ume. So I put you to my breast, changed your diapers, put Band-Aids on your skinned knees, and walked you to kindergarten. You were my son in every way that counted."

"If Irie hadn't died, leaving Teiko without a family, I never would have known," Kenta said soberly.

Haru nodded.

Kenta raised his eyebrows. "Does Otosan know?"

Haru withdrew her hands from Kenta's grip. Her constricted throat squeaked, "By the Lord Buddha, no." The wind and surf drowned out the strained words, but Kenta read her lips.

"Then, this is our secret. You are my mother." Kenta wanted to add "I love you" but could not. Boys did not say such things to their mothers any more than men professed them to their wives.

They walked silently to the beachfront Elks Club. Haru wanted to freshen her face in the ladies' room but knew that, except for employees, Asians were not allowed on the premises. She settled for splashing her face over the water fountain across the street in Kapiolani Park.

∽ Chapter 139 ∾

Kenta and Haru returned to a house filled with the entire family. Unable to face the crowd, Haru made for the stairway. "I need a bath," she explained and scurried up the steps. A ball of calico fur bounced up the stairs in pursuit.

Kenta put on his best happy face and described the movie in animated detail, holding his siblings' attention. Afterwards, he said casually to Tommy, "Let's check the fruit trees and pick what's ripe."

As they left the house, Tommy said, "You could have just broadcasted 'I need to talk to you in private.' Everyone knows Dad inspects the trees every morning."

"Okay, Sherlock, I do have a problem. Teiko."

"How so, little brother? Have you fallen under the spell of those … " Tommy fluttered his eyelashes with great exaggeration, "luminous doe eyes?"

"No!" snapped Kenta, yanking a yellowing frond hanging limp from a palm tree and hurling it to the ground. "It's not what you think. Hey, I admit I have enjoyed the … hero worship. But her intentions are not the sisterly type. I need to end this before she makes me an offer I won't refuse—but will regret. I want you to take over my teaching duties."

Tommy raised his eyebrows. "Me? I'm not the type. Besides, she's not the quickest fox in the pack."

"Don't I know it. But I need this favor to wean the fox off her dependency."

"Well, you would owe me—really owe me, brother."

"Arigato," said Kenta, wondering what price he would have to pay later.

After supper, Kenta told Teiko in a "this is it" tone she had heard before from him, "I have asked Tommy to take my place as your tutor. I'm falling behind in my own lessons. And with spring football practice starting—"

"Hai, wakarimashita," she snapped, cutting him off.

The next morning, Haru found a note on the kitchen table. "I should never have come here. Teiko."

Haru rushed upstairs. She eased the door open. Teiko's bed was empty.

A sleepy-eyed Sachiko mumbled, "Okasan?"

"I was looking for Teiko. She … left a note and I … "

Sachiko looked around. "Doesn't look like her bed has been slept in." She sat up, more alert, surveying the room. "And her bag—it's gone."

Hiromi popped up.

"What's going on?" she asked, rubbing her eyes.

"Do you know where Teiko is?" asked Haru.

Hiromi looked around the room and a smile crept across her lips. "I'm beginning to think prayers really do work." *My other prayer was granted too,* she thought. *If Yoshio can study in Japan, so can I!*

∞ Chapter 140 ∞

White House – August 1939

THE SHORT, PEAR-SHAPED MAN puffed on his Havana cigar—an aide's offering from their boss's private stock. As he was escorted outside, the aroma from freshly mown grass mingled with the fragrance of his burning cigar. Under the scorching sun, sweat beads quickly trickled down from his receding hairline. The man's girth had expanded as much as his reputation, an indulgence he did not tolerate from his field agents. He wore a brown suit in a city of de rigueur grey and blue. J. Edgar Hoover, the FBI's director since 1924, found Franklin Roosevelt already seated on a white, wrought-iron chair in front of a matching glass-top table, no wheelchair in sight. Since Hitler had just signed a nonaggression pact with Russia, Hoover expected the president wanted to be briefed on German espionage in America.

He guessed wrong.

Roosevelt inhaled through his signature ceramic holder, held his breath to capture its calming effect, and upon exhaling, surprised Hoover. "Now that Hitler has protected his eastern flank, I expect England and France will be at war with Germany soon. Once that happens, it's only a matter of time before Japan goes after Europe's Asian colonies. At some point, we will be at war with Hirohito. What is happening to our plans to intern the Japanese?"

"Mr. President, we maintain extensive files on the Japanese community. Since Nanking, we have pictures not only of everyone who greets Japanese navy ships, but also of who meets their commercial ships or entertains Japanese VIPs. We know who is organizing donations to their war effort. I even have agents figuring who is yelling 'banzai' at Jap movie theaters during the war clips from China. We take pictures of people leaving the theater and match up faces."

FDR raised his eyebrows.

"After years of surveillance, we know whom to arrest the moment war begins."

Roosevelt pulled a carbon copy of a letter from under a bald-eagle paperweight and dangled it.

"Edgar, in October 1936, I directed you that the moment war begins you are to intern the Japanese. You have repeatedly made your case that the FBI can pick up all the potential saboteurs. But if you miss just one … " The president let the letter flutter to the tabletop. "When war breaks out, I want all Japanese removed from Hawaii and the West Coast."

"It's the army's—"

"Edgar, I will take care of the army. You build up the list of all the Japanese residents and visitors—so when I give the word, we know where they *all* are."

"We're doing that, Mr. President," Hoover said more respectfully.

Roosevelt took another long puff and then aimed his ivory-tipped holder at Hoover. "You don't even have a field office in Hawaii where there are 150,000 of them."

"We've been planning to reopen our territorial field office, Mr. President."

"When?" FDR held his gaze.

Holding his anger at the president's insistence on this agent-wasting internment policy, Hoover kept his eyes steady under the president's stare. "We have an exceptional man just coming off medical leave. He's arriving at my office this afternoon for his first briefing. We should have him in Honolulu … "

FDR raised his eyebrows and leaned forward in anticipation.

"Within four weeks."

"Not a day longer." Relaxing back into his chair, FDR took another puff of his cigarette.

∽ CHAPTER 141 ∽

NEARLY SIX THOUSAND MILES AWAY, Kenji had risen from bed and padded into the bathroom where he emptied a full bladder. A chill ran through him on seeing his stream flow pink. As he washed his hands, Kenji tried to recall what he had eaten at dinner last night that would have caused the pink color. Nothing came to mind. By evening, his stream had returned to its usual marigold yellow. He sighed with relief, thankful he had not alarmed Haru.

The next morning, his urine streamed rose-petal red. At breakfast, Kenji maintained his usually calm demeanor, although he drank more coffee and orange juice than normal. An hour later, he watched in dismay as a deep crimson stream rained from his body. A visit to the doctor would surely result in a simple remedy, such as taking a few sulfur tablets to control an infection. No need to alarm Haru.

Dr. Tebbits had remained in Waimea for eleven years before moving to Honolulu to satisfy his wife's desire for a more cosmopolitan life and a better education for their four children. Shortly after the Spanish Flu epidemic, he had met Gertrude, a German nurse, who had accompanied her father, a representative of the A&P grocery chain, on a cattle-buying visit to the Parker Ranch. The Takayama friendship with the Tebbitses, begun in Waimea, had continued with regular dinner exchanges in Honolulu.

Gertrude greeted a nervous Kenji warmly as he entered the Tebbitses' clinic. "What brings you to our clinic today, Kenji?"

An embarrassed Kenji paused. Even though there were no other patients in the waiting room, talking to a nurse—even a family friend—about his most private body functions made him feel uncomfortable.

Gertrude leaned forward and in her most reassuring voice said, "I've been a nurse for twenty years, Kenji."

"I passed blood in my urine." Kenji watched the unguarded alarm in Gertrude's face turn impassive as the door to the examination room opened and a very pregnant Hawaiian lady waddled out. Gertrude hooked the door with her fingers before it closed. "Bernie, you have a distinguished visitor," she said, waving Kenji inside.

"Sensei," said Tebbits. He and Kenji referred to each other as "sensei" out of respect, but the tone of voice carried an obvious professional affection. Hearing Kenji's complaint, Tebbits asked for a urine sample. When his patient returned with a half-full plastic cup, the doctor examined its reddish contents with no change of expression. "We'll let Gertrude take an X-ray."

Minutes later, Kenji's gut tightened as he watched Tebbits's frown line deepen as the doctor's eyes focused on a shadow on the film.

"Cancer?" he asked, his matter-of-fact tone camouflaging his heart flutter.

Tebbits understood the Japanese propensity to avoid hearing bad news from doctors—cancer was referred to as "stomach trouble." But, Tebbits remembered a dinner conversation where Kenji and Haru claimed they preferred being told a true diagnosis.

"Most likely," he nodded. "I can't be certain." Pointing to the shadow on the X-ray, he said, "You can see this snake-like line on your right kidney—maybe two inches long." Tebbits turned back to Kenji. "When I cut you open, I might find nothing. Or … I might find that the cancer has spread, and all I can do is sew you back up and advise you to put your affairs in order. Those are the two extremes. Unlikely extremes." Pointing back to the X-ray's shadow, Tebbits continued. "Given the location, we might be able to save half the kidney. Even if we have to take out the whole organ, you can still lead a normal life with just one—eat and drink modestly, flush yourself out with a lot of water, and you're fine."

"Where do you do this?"

"Queen's," said Tebbits, referring to the hospital Queen Emma established in 1859. "I can do this myself but would rather have Rudy Hornsby, the internist, perform the operation, with me acting as his assistant."

∞ ∞

That evening, after finishing a dessert of homegrown strawberries topped with a dollop of vanilla ice cream, Kenji forced a smile at Haru. "Let's take a walk."

Serenaded by cicadas and surrounded by flickering fireflies, Kenji revealed his condition. Back home, Kenji stopped at the bottom of the porch. "I've had a good life, Okasan. Maybe it's my time."

"Maybe *you* are ready to leave *us*," said Haru, tugging his yukata sleeve. "But *we* are not ready for you to leave. Where is the fighter who charged into the Adamses' church to preach tolerance in front of all those haoles? You have told me often that spiritual toughness extends life. Now it's time to follow your own advice."

"This is cancer."

"Yes, the forbidden word, Otosan. But Tebbits-sensei told you that kidney cancer is the one cancer that can be cut out before it spreads. How many times have you talked about the hidden blessing in tragedy? How the Great Buddha sends us tests to reveal a more enlightened path ... a change in direction."

Kenji stared at his wife. "You have something on your mind," he said warily.

The Takayama porch light caught the gleam in her eyes. "Let's return to Waimea. I am getting too old to attend all these temple meetings. Chairman of this, organizer of that. I feel like that frog in the pot of water boiling so slowly he doesn't know he's being cooked."

Haru gave Kenji's sleeve another tug as her words tumbled out faster. "Kame wrote me that Izawa-san, the Waimea priest, will be asking for a transfer. If the bishop knows you want to return to your former parish, he will grant the transfer. Most priests have retired ... " she almost added "or died" but caught herself, "by your age."

Kenji fought his first impulse to object and then caught himself. Maybe Buddha had noticed his grey hair. "Bernie said to expect a decline in energy for a while. I think he means forever." He waved away a buzzing mosquito. "But what about the children? Where will they live? Kenta is attending UH; next year Sachiko follows. And Tommy?" He let the thought hang.

Haru welcomed the question. It meant a "how" consideration, not his usual stubborn "no" to sudden changes. "Wai Ching can find Kenta dorm space at the YMCA's Atherton House. He's in charge, after all. Tommy has a job. He can move in with Takeshi and share expenses. He should be doing that anyway. And I am sure Takeshi can ask to find Sachiko a position with a haole family, helping out with chores for room and board."

"In a stranger's house?"

"Don't look so surprised. We have helped families from Waimea find haole homes for their daughters when they come to Honolulu to attend school. Their English gets better, and they pick up some spending money."

"Let's wait until after the operation," said Kenji. "If it is successful … we can consider a return to Waimea."

Haru widened her smile. "It will be successful. I'll call Kame."

Before Kenji could object, Haru had walked up the steps into the house.

⌒ CHAPTER 142 ⌒

"How's your father's recuperation?" asked Hemenway, carrying his coffee mug from his office desk to the chair facing a low, ivory-inlaid mahogany table with carved elephant legs. Sitting across from him on a matching leather-upholstered chair, Takeshi leaned over and stirred two spoons of raw sugar into his creamed coffee. He had arrived fifteen minutes early for the weekly Committee for Interracial Unity's two o'clock meeting. He hoped his anxiety didn't show.

"Actually, the operation has been postponed. Dr. Hornsby caught the flu. It's been rescheduled for Saturday." Takeshi fidgeted. He had been rehearsing his forthcoming request. "Sir, you were gracious enough to offer help … You said if there was anything you could do that I shouldn't hesitate to ask … "

Hemenway turned on his grandfatherly smile. "Yes, I remember, and I meant it, Taka." He took a sip of his coffee—black, no sugar.

Taka's nerves throttled back. "It's Sachiko. She's in her senior year at McKinley. My parents are returning to Waimea. But there's no high school there."

"Sweet girl. I remember meeting her last month when she was waiting for you after our meeting."

"I need help finding a haole family she can stay with," said Takeshi. "Mom could find her a home with one of our parishioners … " he added, his poised tone tailing off.

"But Haru wants Sachiko to Americanize her English."

Takeshi flashed a grateful smile. "With Hiromi winning the battle to study in Japan, our mother wants at least one American daughter."

"Haru is right." Hemenway paused. He had been about to add, "As a matter of fact, I have a candidate who needs to be exposed to a Japanese born and raised in America," but held back, thinking he should talk to his arriving nominee first.

A soft tap on the office door was followed by Wai Ching stepping in. He greeted everyone while walking over to the Sunbeam Coffee Master resting on a credenza. As he poured himself a cup, school administrator Shigeo Yoshida, tall and full-voiced amongst his soft-spoken and shorter compatriots, stormed through the door, eyes on fire. He snatched a sheaf of notes from his hand-tooled satchel, which he let plop to the ground before yanking back a chair, sitting down, and then retrieving and slapping the papers on the table. He leaned back and put his hands on the chair's grooved arms like a pope ready to have his ring kissed.

"You have our breathless attention," deadpanned Wai Ching, handing Shigeo a cup of black coffee and placing his own sugared and cream-laced brew on the table as he took his seat.

"What a wonderful week," said Yoshida, sarcasm ripping through his voice. "Hoover announces he is sending a G-man to reopen the FBI office, and at the Bishop Museum, Stokes gives a speech claiming the Japanese have been planning to take over Hawaii since the last days of the kingdom. If that's not enough, the same congressman who called me to testify on behalf of statehood now refuses to take the Hawaiian statehood bill out of committee for a floor vote. Some old fogey from Alabama did a body count and claimed in ten years there'd be enough of us … " Yoshida thumped his chest, "to elect a Jap to Congress."

Everybody waited for another rejoinder, but Yoshida sat back in his chair.

As if waiting for his cue offstage, a voice boomed, "My meeting with the police chief lasted longer than expected." Upon entering, John Burns turned a serious face to the Sunbeam. He took a step toward it and then stopped. "I'm coffeed out." The only permanent member of the Interracial Committee who did not carry a briefcase sat down and retrieved his spiral notepad from his ink-stained shirt pocket.

The lanky, thirty-year-old Burns had been a street-smart kid from the tough, mixed-ethnic Kalihi neighborhood on the northeast side of Honolulu. His army sergeant father abandoned his family in 1913 after being dishonorably discharged for stealing. A troubled child at sixteen, Burns was sent to live with an uncle in Kansas. Two years later, he joined the army. His drinking and refusal to buckle under military authority led to an honorable discharge after one year. He returned to Hawaii, and at the ripe old age of twenty-one graduated from St. Louis High School. He attended the University of Hawaii for a year and then bounced around a series of jobs before being accepted into the post-Massie Trial police force in 1934.

"We can stop speculating why Hoover's reopening the FBI office. This new field agent, Robert Shivers, is being sent to prepare transporting our entire Japanese community to Molokai the moment war breaks out."

Yoshida and Takeshi immediately exchanged alarmed glances at Burns's announcement. The others could almost hear the two young men thinking, *What will happen to my parents?*

"The Patton report recommended interning only Japanese leaders," blurted Takeshi, who normally kept quiet at these meetings.

Burns eyed Taka. "FDR claims the only way to make sure there is not one disloyal Jap threatening our security is to intern them all."

The news did not change Wai Ching's placid expression. "We expected this all along. Our committee's purpose has been validated. Now we must work with greater urgency." He looked to Hemenway. "Charles, is it time to bring the military into our committee?"

"Army intelligence is on board," said Hemenway. "Last Tuesday, on the golf course with the army chief, we agreed on a middle-ranking officer as a low-profile liaison. In addition, he is recommending creating a separate Nisei unit."

Shigeo sneered; his eyes narrowed. "Is this an echo or what! The army tried that two years ago, and Washington came back with 'Reduce the number of Nisei in the Territorial Guard.'"

Hemenway cleared his throat. "Within months of arrival, almost every senior army officer, regardless of his prior prejudices, comes around to the idea that a wartime Hawaii needs its Japanese citizens. Most realize that loyalty suspicions are overblown. Farrington," referring to Hawaii's non-voting Congressional delegate, "told me that Hoover argued with FDR against internment. Let's move on to … changing minds." He stopped short of looking at Yoshida and added, "Starting with our own."

Yoshida pulled a pack of Luckies from his suit pocket and tapped it on the edge of the table. "I meant no disrespect. Nevertheless, this FBI directive, the assignment of this Shivers agent … " pronouncing the name to rhyme with "givers."

"Enough for today," said Hemenway. "I'll be going to the airport tomorrow afternoon to meet Shivers." He enunciated the name with the long I slowly and stared at Shigeo. "Our mission over the next months is to make sure that Special Agent Shivers sees the real Hawaii."

∞ Chapter 143 ∞

HARU SAT IN THE TINY WAITING ROOM at Queen's Hospital, mindlessly twiddling her wedding ring. Watermarks from exposed pipes hugging the ceiling tear-dropped the faded mustard-colored walls. A lethargic overhead fan swished the antiseptic-infused air. Ukulele music from KGU's *Hawaiian Hour* filled the room. Takeshi enclosed Haru's twitching hand in his own. Tommy and Kenta sat across from them.

When the swinging door flung open, all looked up expectantly. Doctor Tebbits had predicted the surgery would take at least another hour. Haru's mind flashed. Had something gone wrong?

Instead of a man garbed in green scrubs, Sachiko rushed into the room and gushed, "How is Daddy?" Hiromi, carrying a bouquet of roses, followed her.

"We haven't heard yet," said Kenta. Getting up to offer his seat so his sisters could sit together, he asked, "Anybody want coffee?" Two hands went up, and Haru nodded. "*Kekko desu,*" chimed Sachiko and Hiromi, meaning, "It's okay," a polite Japanese no.

Minutes after Kenta left on his coffee run, Dr. Tebbits walked in. He glanced at Haru and then locked in on Takeshi and Tommy. "We need blood."

Haru stood up and grabbed Tebbits's arm. "What has happened?"

"There's been a tear in a major artery. We're sewing it up. Kenji will be okay," the strain in his voice not lending credibility to his words, "but he's lost a lot of blood." He paused. "Where's Kenta? We need him too."

"He went to get coffee," said Tommy. "Don't you need to check our blood type?"

"Both your parents are type A, so I know you will be too."

Tebbits turned his attention to Sachiko and Hiromi. "Find Kenta and tell him to go to the basement's blood bank. Stay close in case we need another pint."

Haru's face froze in suppressed terror. Her mind flashing to her lying on the beach at Kalaupapa, she said in a low tone, "What happens if the person giving blood doesn't have type A?"

"What does it matter?" replied an exasperated Tebbits. "You all have type A. We're in a hurry here." Then, embarrassed by his rude reply, he said more calmly, "I'm sorry, Haru. If you are type O, you can give blood to anyone. But if type B or AB blood were given to Kenji, his body would reject it and he would die."

⚭ ⚭

The Pan Am Clipper airboat carrying Field Agent Robert Shivers was taxiing on Pearl Harbor's lagoon. The Constellation's four whining Boeing engines ruffled the water behind them as the pilot brought the world's largest seaplane to its pier much like a Matson luxury liner. Hemenway's hair strands swirled in the wash as he ambled over to the bottom of the gangway almost parallel to the wharf. He squinted into the afternoon sun streaming over the fuselage encasing three decks.

Shivers, his usual black suit rumpled by the eighteen-hour flight from San Francisco, emerged from the doorway, followed by his wife, who stood a half a foot taller in her high heels. Her well-coiffed bangs flared under a red-brimmed black hat tilted jauntily to the left. Her neat hair and rose-colored lips suggested she had "lady-upped" before landing.

Robert Shivers's face held a sober expression in keeping with the seriousness of his mission. His wife's smile and wide-eyed wonder told Hemenway she looked forward to a good stay. A slash of wind stole her hat. She laughed as she watched it sail over the wing. A good sign, thought Hemenway. As the couple stepped onto the concrete jetty, Hemenway introduced himself and placed a lei over the heads of each.

"What an unexpected pleasure," said Corrine in her well-bred, Southern accent that widened Hemenway's smile. He had speculated on why the Shivers had no children. Taking in the woman's radiating warmth, he was convinced it was not for the lack of trying. If his instincts were right, his Sachiko proposition would land on receptive ears.

On the drive into Honolulu, Hemenway pointed out the various landmarks and sprinkled in a little local history. "We have booked you into the Pink Palace for the night," he said, referring to Waikiki's hostelry pride, the Royal Hawaiian Hotel. "If you like, I can show you a view of Honolulu from a hilltop house. It's only a few minutes out of the way."

Shivers nodded an okay, and his wife gushed, "Oh, yes, please."

Hemenway took a left off the ocean-hugging highway at the Aloha Tower, dodged the trams on Bishop Street, and worked his way up to the lower Punchbowl area. He stopped at a house graced with a wide, wraparound porch and within walking distance of downtown.

"Why, I do declare. What a delightful home," said Mrs. Shivers, stepping into the living room. "And all of downtown within view." Hemenway pointed out the federal building from the house's living room bay window. "That's your office." He then led them to the back porch. "Oh my,

Robert," said Corrine. "Look at that rainbow falling over the mountains. Have you ever seen anything so beautiful in your entire life?"

"You will see many more, Mrs. Shivers. If you are like me, you'll never tire of them."

"This isn't your home, is it, Mr. Hemenway? It doesn't look like anyone is living here. I mean, no one, not even my mama, keeps a house and furniture this clean."

"It's yours to rent if you want it," said Hemenway. Corrine turned to him openmouthed. "Your husband sent us a request for a home, and this is our best choice."

"A home within the FBI budget," Shivers added.

"The owner is living abroad and told us just to charge what you can afford. But we have other homes if you would like more choices from which to choose."

Shivers saw the sparkle in his wife's eyes. He stepped over to the railing and put an arm around her waist. In less than minute, he turned to Hemenway. "When could we move in?"

Hemenway threw out the palms of his hands. "Right now." He enjoyed their surprised look. "I arranged to stock the fridge with a few essentials like milk and eggs, just in case you fell in love with this home."

"We'll take it," said Agent Shivers.

"So much to do, so much to see!" said Corrine.

My opening, thought Hemenway. "You might like a little help around the house. Many of our female students without family in Honolulu board in homes in exchange for helping with light chores. One such girl has recently come to my attention. Sachiko Takayama. She's a senior at McKinley High School, a short bike ride from here. Her father is a Buddhist priest in Honolulu, but due to ill health, he is leaving next month for a more limited assignment on the Big Island where there's no high school. Sachiko's brother is our recording secretary for the Committee for Interracial Unity."

"Oh, I don't need a maid," said Mrs. Shivers.

Shivers's facial expression did not change, nor did his voice. "A Japanese girl?"

"Yes, many live-in students are Japanese. Families prize their neatness, polite demeanor, and willingness to help. However, the girls are not maids. They help with the dishes and laundry, but you can't expect her to iron shirts or to make your bed."

"I agree with Corrine; we don't need a … a helper."

Hemenway noticed Corrine's widened eyes.

"Well, of course," he said, "it was only a suggestion."

In a low voice, Mrs. Shivers asked, "She has no place to go?"

"I'm sure I can find her a place. This came up only yesterday. Given your arrival, I thought the timing might be fortuitous. Perhaps, I have been presumptuous by assuming you would enjoy a young person who could show you around the town and help with the shopping. I apologize for putting you on the spot. Not a good way to begin a relationship."

Shivers watched the rainbow disappear as the sun touched the top of the mountains. "Charles, you have gone out of your way to make us feel welcome." He waved his hand over the porch rail at the sun turning gold. "Tell the young lady she can stay for a week or two until you find her a permanent home."

☙ CHAPTER 144 ❧

TEBBITS HAD LEFT THE WAITING ROOM, Takeshi and Tommy on his heels.

"I'll find Kenta," said Sachiko.

Haru stood up, took one step, and stumbled. One hand grabbed a chair arm, and the other clasped Sachiko's shoulder.

"Okasan, are you all right?"

"Am I all right? I might be a widow in an hour!" Haru immediately regretted this outburst. "I'm sorry, Sachiko. I am so scared. I didn't think." She stepped back, her face flushed. "You and Hiromi stay here. I'll find Kenta." When Sachiko opened her mouth to protest, Haru said. "You two need to be here in case Dr. Tebbits needs your blood."

Without waiting for another objection, Haru walked out of the room and fast-stepped toward the cafeteria. She entered the wide space, her head twirling to survey every table. No Kenta.

"Is this the only place to get coffee?" she asked the cashier.

The woman nodded her head absently as she rang up an order for a customer holding out a dollar bill.

Haru trotted back to the waiting room. Nobody. Feeling light-headed, she sat down. In seconds she got up. *I have to stop him*, she thought. All these years a secret kept. No harm to anyone. She half ran to the nurse's station. "Have you seen Kenta?" Seeing the question mark, she said, "He'd be carrying coffee. There would be two girls with him."

"Yes. Yes. Kenta. The cute one. They were heading to the blood bank. You take the elevator, then—" Reading the panic on Haru's face, the nurse hurried around the counter. "It's easier if I just take you there."

Haru followed behind the nurse, nearly tripping over an electrical cord and wishing the strolling woman would step it up. Over the next three excruciatingly long minutes, they waited for the only elevator car, rode slowly down to the basement level, took a series of left and right turns, and finally arrived at the door labeled "Blood Bank." Haru gasped at the sight of her sons sitting in chairs, each one with an IV attached to an arm and a hanging plastic bottle filling with blood.

A young nurse technician was talking to Takeshi. "It looks as if you have a full tank," she purred and then leaned across him unnecessarily to disconnect the IV.

Haru didn't notice Takeshi's embarrassed smile, for her gaze had frozen on Kenta's arm.

At that moment, Tebbits strode in, snapping off his rubber gloves.

"Good news, Haru. We stopped all the bleeding. We've stitched him back up. The operation went very well. We got all the cancer, saved half his kidney. He should recover fully." Looking at the three boys with IVs attached, he added, "Your father's blood pressure is low, but as soon as we administer the transfusions, that will normalize."

The nurse handed him the plastic bag holding Taka's blood. "I'll bring up the other two bags to the OR in a few minutes." Holding the blood bag in both hands, Tebbits hustled out the door.

Haru stood stricken, her eyes still on Kenta, silently pleading with him to somehow extricate himself from this disaster.

"I already knew I was type A, Okasan," he said casually. "Coach Malloy takes blood samples from all the football players in case any of us gets injured and needs blood."

Relief flooded over Haru's face. Then she slid onto the floor in a dead faint.

⟡ Chapter 145 ⟡

SACHIKO'S KNEES QUIVERED as she stepped out of the Packard and looked up the path to the house on the hill. She took a few steps—slowly, hesitantly. The scent of plumeria blossoms should have reminded the girl of her Moiliili youth. Instead, all she could smell was her own fear.

Coming around from the other side of the car, Charles Hemenway spoke with calming reassurance. "It may be hard to imagine, but I was young once and can still remember what it's like to leave home for the first time." He shifted Sachiko's wicker suitcase to his left hand and gently guided the girl up the path with his right. "But I wish I had had your mission."

"Mission?" Sachiko's voice came out as an anxious squeak.

"Why, yes. Mr. Shivers might be a FBI special agent, but he is new to Hawaii. He and his wife have no children, no friends to show her around." What Hemenway did not say—but Sachiko's older brother had hinted at—was that her presence in the Shivers household would give the Japanese community a human face, even if it was just for a couple of weeks.

Hemenway and Sachiko were halfway up the porch's wooden steps when the screen door opened. Corrine Shivers stepped out, sporting a brightly colored muumuu and a toothy smile.

"You must be Sachiko," she said in her warmest Southern drawl. "It's so wonderful to meet you." She gave Sachiko a conspiratorial look and whispered, "Now, you just ignore Mr. Shivers's severe face. It took me months before I ever saw his teeth."

Sachiko's knees stopped quavering. She started to bow, caught herself, and held the awkward pose for a moment of indecision, before completing the gesture. She tried to hide her surprise when Corrine bent slightly at the waist in response.

"That's a lovely custom, sweetheart, but I think a simple hand-shake with Mr. Shivers will do."

Robert Shivers stood uncomfortably in the middle of the living room.

"Hello, Sachi … ko." He had practiced saying the unfamiliar name but still separated the third syllable.

Taking her cue from his wife, Sachiko offered her hand. The hesitant Shivers glanced at the limp offering before clasping the girl's hand and shaking it gently. "We hope you will be comfortable here … in our home … for the next few weeks."

Having completed his delivery, Hemenway said, "Sorry to rush off, but Jane and I have plans this evening at a university function."

"Thank you, Charles," smiled Corrine. Then she turned to Sachiko. "Sweetheart," she said, not realizing she skipped her Rs much like the Japanese did, so "sweetheart" came out "sweethaat," "let me show you to your room. Our bedroom is on the left side of the home … " she gesticulated vaguely and then added, "along with Robert's home office. Your room is this way."

Sachiko's face lit up as she entered the room catching the sunset's last rays. Her own private room for the first time in her life. A twin bed, a desk with a scratched top and a rack of pigeonholes at the back, and a tired grey dresser had been crammed into the cubby-sized room. She warmed at the sight of a petite Chinese vase stuffed with violets sitting atop a nightstand. No closet, but hangers dangled from a row of hooks nailed to the wall opposite the bed—more than enough for her skimpy wardrobe. A double-screened window, its shutters split open, brought the smell of cut grass to freshen the musty smells of the long-vacated room. She spotted a rocking chair on the porch outside her window that seemed ideal for reading her school assignments. A wonderful setting to find out if Hester would commit seppuku.

"I know you Japanese love fish. Maybe you can show me how to cook." A little doubt crept into Corrine's voice. "Tonight, we are having steak."

"Oh, I love steak. My parents lived next to the Parker Ranch in Waimea before they moved to Honolulu."

"Why, yes. America's biggest ranch. You simply must tell us ALL about it."

When Sachiko asked to help in the kitchen, Corrine told her, "There will be plenty of time for that over the next few weeks. Tonight you are a guest. Have a seat in the living room and entertain Robert."

Entertain Robert? Sachiko asked herself. She was relieved the living room was vacant. Wherever Mr. Shivers was, she hoped he'd stay there awhile. She noticed the *Pacific Liner*, her favorite Hollywood magazine, atop the coffee table. She picked it up and flipped to the Lana Turner feature story. As Sachiko gazed wistfully at the starlet's photo and wished she had breasts like America's "sweater girl," Mr. Shivers walked in. Flustered, she closed the magazine.

"I see you and Corrine have the same interests," said Shivers, sitting opposite her.

Wondering if she had been being caught envying Lana Turner, she couldn't find the words to respond.

Assuming the girl's reticence was a consequence of youthful nervousness in a stranger's house, Shivers asked, "Who's your favorite movie star?"

Sachiko breathed easier. "Clark Gable. But I like Errol Flynn too."

"Who is your favorite Japanese movie star?"

A perplexed expression washed across Sachiko's face. "I can't speak Japanese so well," she said, feeling a bit guilty.

"So you don't go to Japanese movies?"

"I went once with my mother when I was ten or eleven. I fell asleep."

"So your mother goes to Japanese movies?"

"Sometimes. But not so much anymore. Her favorite actor is William Powell. He's a little boring for me. But she also loves Gabby Hayes. We both like Westerns. We wish Gene Autry and Roy Rogers would sing together in a film." Remembering her mother's admonishment that a polite lady shows interest in others, Sachiko braved, "Who is your favorite movie star?"

Shivers's G-man instinct urged him to snap back that he would ask the questions, but he resisted. He could not help but smile at the names rolling off his lips. "James Cagney and Bette Davis."

As Sachiko looked at Shivers's teeth, she thought of his wife's welcoming remarks. "Have you seen *Dark Victory*? It's playing downtown right now. I like Humphrey Bogart. Mother likes Ronald Reagan and thinks he's handsome. But when he speaks, you can tell he's just memorized the lines. He's not very believable."

"Actually, Mrs. Shivers and I saw *Dark Victory* in Washington shortly before we left." Shivers found himself enjoying the light conversation and went on at some length about how he had enjoyed Bette Davis's portrayal of a vacuous socialite suffering from a malignant brain tumor. When he finished, Shivers looked into Sachiko's expectant eyes and reminded himself why he had asked Corrine to give him some time with the new houseguest before dinner.

"Did you go to a Japanese language school?"

Sachiko's lips turned down, telegraphing unhappy memories. "Yes, my father runs one of those schools. We—that is, my brothers and sisters and I—we hated it once we got to junior high school."

Trained to ignore such protests from hundreds of suspects he had interviewed, Shivers continued, "What did you learn at your father's school?"

"I can write my name in kanji and read simple signs over Japanese shops in our neighborhood. Father taught us Confucius's golden rule, 'Do not impose on others what you do not wish for yourself.' Respect the elders; take good care of them. Honor our teachers. Bathe twice a day. Wash your hands after you … " She blushed.

Shivers locked onto Sachiko's eyes. "What do you think of the emperor? Hirohito?"

"He likes horses."

Shivers's face betrayed his confusion.

Seeing his reaction, Sachiko hurried to explain. "I don't know that much about him. But we have his picture in our home. He's sitting on a white horse." Sensing that this didn't sound quite right, she rushed on. "His picture is right next to President Roosevelt's, who's sitting in a car. I think this shows America is more modern." Her voice rose at the end of this statement, making it more of a question.

"But Japan has modernized very quickly. You must be very proud to be Japanese."

Sachiko snapped her shoulders back. "I'm not Japanese!" She pressed the fingers of her right hand over her upper chest. "I'm

American." Leaning forward, she pressed her fingers harder. "I'm proud to be an American, Mr. Shivers."

Shivers felt he had overstepped some type of boundary with the naïve seventeen-year-old. He wondered how he would feel if he had a daughter of a similar age whom the FBI surreptitiously interrogated.

They were both relieved when Corrine walked in. "Dinner is ready."

In between bites of steak and forkfuls of mashed potatoes, the three discussed movies. They all agreed John Wayne was a comer and planned to see *Stagecoach* together.

The following morning, while he drove to his office, Shivers studied the many Asian faces that he passed on the street. Most were neatly dressed, walking along the sidewalks with purpose or standing at tram stops engaged in relaxed conversation with Asians, Hawaiians, and whites alike. He wondered how many Japanese Americans were like Sachiko. She was so at odds with his mission to intern her and her parents when war with Japan broke out.

∽ CHAPTER 146 ∽

SACHIKO QUICKLY FELL INTO A SET ROUTINE. From the first day, she washed the breakfast and dinner dishes without being asked. She presented herself in the kitchen every afternoon, eager to peel potatoes, wash the green beans, or shuck the cornhusks. She enjoyed learning how to cook haole food. When asked, she cooked mahimahi dressed in soy sauce. Her big success was shrimp and vegetable tempura, one of Haru's favorites. She enjoyed playing the role of a shopping guide to both downtown and Chinatown. It was easy for Sachiko to be a good listener, being too nervous to start a conversation herself.

Three weeks into Sachiko's homestay, Corrine was drying breakfast dishes that Sachiko was sudsing and rinsing. "Did I hear McKinley has a home football game next Friday?"

Sachiko's face lit up. "Yes, it's our home opener against St. Louis."

"I might like to go." Corrine stopped drying for a moment. "With your friends, of course, if you don't think they'd mind." She had already learned that Japanese parents seldom attended high school sports.

"Oh! That ... would be ... wonderful, Mrs. Shivers. I'm sure you'd like my friends. They're ... well ... " She giggled. "We're all just typical teenagers."

"There's one condition," Corrine said with an impish smile. "I think 'Mrs. Shivers' is a bit formal."

Sachiko stood still, her wet hands holding a coffee cup. She could not call Mrs. Shivers by her first name but didn't want to offend her.

"I was thinking ... You know how some of the kids in the neighborhood call me 'Mom Shivers'? How would you feel about your calling me that too?"

Sachiko almost dropped the coffee cup. Tears flooded her eyes.

Mom Shivers stepped over to Sachiko and wrapped her arms around the girl. "I guess that means 'Mom Shivers' will work. If you have not already guessed, Robert and I would like you to spend the school year with us."

Sachiko could not control her sobbing.

Neither could Mom Shivers.

∞ ∞

Kenji's recuperation dragged on. His expected three-day stay at Queen's was extended to three weeks due to the artery tear complication. Having given up their Moiliili home to the parish's new minister, Haru stayed at the Fort Street Hongwanji, bereft of children for the first time in almost three decades and worried about her husband's slow recovery. It was October before they returned to Waimea.

Five months later, Kenji was back at Queen's—this time for a hernia operation. He had been lifting a heavy item and thought he pulled a muscle so not only ignored the unknown hernia tear but also aggravated it.

Haru felt her age. More important, she was aware of Kenji's mortality. He had never regained the weight he had lost during the kidney operation nor anything close to his former vigor. He struggled to maintain the schedule his Waimea parish responsibilities required. After three decades raising children, Haru missed them more than she had anticipated. The four in Honolulu had promised to visit. While they wrote weekly letters faithfully, they had visited only once—for Kenji's birthday. She wondered, *Did we made a mistake returning to Waimea?*

Bishop Kuchiba solved her dilemma. The second successor to the legendary Bishop Imamura, who had died in 1935, had not tried to compete with the towering figure who had changed the face of Buddhism in Hawaii. Rather, Kuchiba reinforced his mentor's message with his constant refrain in speeches and on the marquee outside the Pali Highway temple: "Prove your loyalty to the Stars and Stripes through the Buddhist faith." When his parishioners complained the island's best jobs were kept for the haoles, he replied, "Buy land, farm; buy boats, fish." Many Nisei did exactly that. Only a few of the ruling class caught on that job discrimination brought about the unintended consequence of handing over Hawaii's fishing and farming industry to the territory's hardest-working, best-educated ethnic group.

A few days after Haru shared her worries about an immediate return to Waimea with Kuchiba, he told her, "Let me give you some good news to lighten your mood. When Kenji recovers, he can help me with the daunting task of compiling forty years of messy archives into a history." As uncertainty clouded Haru's face, the bishop continued, "We have found a charming cottage downtown on Queen Emma Street. There is a lovely garden, lots of rose bushes. We will pay the rent plus a stipend to Kenji."

Haru's sense of Kenji's aging was reinforced when his reaction to the news was not the expected resistance to the idea, but "perhaps it is best."

∞ CHAPTER 147 ∞

Downtown Honolulu – April 1941

ROBERT SHIVERS AND JACK BURNS waited in a smoke-filled, windowless room marked "Storage" in the basement of the Dillingham Transportation Building. The pride of downtown Honolulu's love affair with the Italian Renaissance was at the foot of Bishop Street across from the city's bustling piers. The ground-floor façade showed off bas-relief medallions displaying nineteenth-century sailing ships and steamers, an arched arcade, and Art Deco motifs. The Mediterranean design suggested a sense of tropical openness, despite the granite building's fortress-like assurance. Beneath the courtyard of glazed bricks arranged like a ship captain's compass, the two men waited in their elegant dungeon for their furtive visitors.

∞ ∞

The first time Shivers met Detective Burns, he offered him a job as his number two man.

"I'm flattered, but I just took a demotion from being captain of the detective squad to lieutenant in charge of our counter-espionage unit. I'm to liaise with the FBI—for which you should read 'head off the FBI invasion.'" Burns laughed softly and took a sip of his fourth coffee of the morning. "What's your second question?"

Not easily given to humor, even Shivers chuckled at the irony of the situation. "A welcome like that leads to the next obvious question. Would you like to help me keeps tabs on the Japanese community?"

"I thought you'd never ask," said Burns. "We know when the FBI comes to town who rules the jungle."

Between stateside transfers and local hires, Shivers built a cadre of FBI agents. Burns staffed his unit with men well connected to the Japanese community. Between them, they recruited a stable of informants. Shivers set the priorities. Burns executed the assignments.

∞ ∞

Today, in their stale-air hideaway, the two men waited to debrief two informants personally.

A sharp knuckle rap on the metal door interrupted their debate as to whether Bobby Feller threw his fastball a hundred miles an hour. Takeshi stepped into the cellar, trailed by Saki, whose pallor betrayed her nervousness. At Haru's request, Wai Ching had found her picture bride neighbor employment as a kitchen helper at the Natsunoya Tea House, which offered a stunning view of Pearl Harbor from atop Alewa Heights. When Haru told Takeshi what Saki had seen at the restaurant, he asked her to share the story with Burns and Shivers. The Japanese sense of giri, meaning "obligation," left her with no choice but to accept Takeshi's invitation. She asked the meeting be held in secret. "If my boss knew what I was doing, he'd fire me."

Saki wore her best kimono, the colorful one reserved for the emperor's birthday festival. She bowed. Shivers and Burns acknowledged her with a respectful nod of their heads. "Please, Mrs. Suyama, sit down," invited Shivers.

"Saki-san," said Burns in his modulated reassuring voice, "we appreciate your coming here today. You are a very brave woman to do so."

"Why don't you tell us in Japanese what you saw," said Takeshi, "and I'll translate."

"I work in the kitchen. Cut vegetables and wash dishes. But I am not always inside. I take out the garbage. A couple of months ago, as I took out the garbage, I saw a well-dressed Japanese man standing on the rooftop looking out at the ocean through our telescope."

After the translation, Shivers's eyebrows lifted and he repeated, "Telescope?"

"Yes. Some years ago, Mr. Fujiwara, the owner, put a telescope on the rooftop so customers could enjoy the beautiful view. So, when I saw this man, I did not think it was strange. And then a few weeks later, I saw him there again. When I mentioned it to one of my coworkers, she said she had seen him too, more than once. He would look into the telescope and then write something on a pad. We thought he was just one of those bird watchers."

Shivers, who had been briefed on the gist of Saki's tip, pushed a photo album across the table to her. Each page held four photos. "Saki-san, please look at these pictures. Tell us if you see the man."

Saki reached for the album, opened it to the first page. The room went silent. On the fourth page, Saki jabbed a finger at a picture. "That's him."

Takeshi looked at the typewritten notes under the picture. "Yoshikawa, visa clerk, Oct. 1939." He glanced up. "A nobody who is somebody."

Saki looked at Takeshi.

"Arigato," he said, indicating the meeting was finished. He rose, as did Saki. The two left the room.

Minutes later, Takeshi returned with Pug McCain, the stevedore union chief, so nicknamed because of his youthful prowess in the ring. His blue uniform of the International Longshoremen's and Warehouse Union was starched and pressed. His left hand held a burning stogie between his index and middle fingers.

After making the introductions, Takeshi excused himself. Earlier he had told Burns and Shivers, "McCain will more likely open up without a Japanese face in the room." They welcomed the suggestion, one they would have made themselves if he hadn't volunteered.

McCain offered a meaty hand to Burns and Shivers and then he sat down without being asked. He had been Burns's first recruit since his brother served on the police force. Two days ago, the cop told Burns his brother had something to report. Burns dropped his cigarette into the dregs of his paper coffee cup. After the "ssss" of the stub subsided, he said, "Why don't you tell us what you know."

"Better yet, I can tell you what I saw and heard with my own eyes and ears. No hearsay."

McCain inhaled his cigar while keeping his eyes skewed to its red-glow tip.

"It happened like this: We're down at Pearl, unloading a Matson ship full of PX supplies. A navy guy shows up and tells me, 'I'm from intelligence.' He's too good to introduce himself. But I can tell by the epaulets that he's an ensign. His name tag says 'Harding.' Like the president. He demands—not requests—that I send him all the Japs working that day. Ogawa's the only Japanese in my crew that shift. I find Ogawa, bring him back to my office. The navy guy's sitting at my desk, leafing through my files. I couldn't believe this jerk, but he just looks up at me and says, 'Intelligence,' like that gives him some kind of right. I'm pissed, but I don't want to make a scene.

"He orders Ogawa to sit down and asks whether he sends money back to Japan. Ogawa admits that he does. Like what Jap doesn't, right? So this ensign tells Ogawa to sign a form verifying he sends money to Japan. That's it, the guy leaves, and Ogawa goes back to work."

"That doesn't seem all that out of line. Hardly worth the outrage or our time here," said Shivers, reprovingly.

"I ain't finished," McCain snapped back. "The form is in duplicate, so I get a copy. It's written in English, so Ogawa didn't know what it said. But I see the words 'I support Japan' on it. I'm troubled by that, but the navy guy has left the building, so I just file it away." Seeing Shivers's impatient look, McCain adds, "Now I'm getting to the pissed-off part. Three days later, Ogawa comes to my office in tears, begging me to lend him a thousand bucks. The navy guy's running a scam. He shook down Ogawa for two thousand dollars, saying he signed a paper admitting he was a spy and would be arrested and his wife deported. His wife had managed to save a grand over the years, so he needed to find the rest somewhere to pay off this guy."

"What did you tell him?" asked Shivers.

"I'd get the money. Ogawa's a hard worker, but an actor he ain't. If I told him I was going to the FBI, there's no way he could keep his shit together when the navy guy came to collect."

"Smart," said Burns. "We'll set up a sting operation and nail the son of a bitch."

"Any suspicious activity to report?" asked Shivers.

McCain understood "suspicious activity" meant "Japanese suspicious activity."

"Naw. Most of my Nips sympathize with Japan's war against the Chinks. Spirits go up when they win a battle. But if war ever breaks out between America and Japan, they're on our side, every last one of them. They're scared. They got their homes and children here. If any of my guys ever saw a Jap spying, they'd tell me quicker than me hitting the floor in my last fight."

The next day, Shivers and Burns briefed navy intelligence on the two meetings. The confident lieutenant took perfunctory notes. "Not a big surprise," he said in response to the telescope story. "We have our chaps visit the foreigners' cemetery on the hill overlooking Yokohama. On a clear day, you can see all the way to the Yokosuka harbor. We count their ships; they count ours. Since we moved the fleet from

San Diego to Pearl, there are more ships to count. A good warning to behave themselves."

"What about the shakedown?" demanded Burns.

"Nasty business. Hard to sort out these ... situations. Nevertheless, we'll ship him out. You can have McCain tell the Jap not to worry. The case is settled."

"That's it?" The normally unflappable Burns telegraphed his exasperation across the oak table.

"We can hardly undercut the credibility of navy intelligence over an alleged incident with an alien whose country might attack us, can we?" It was not a question. The lieutenant snapped his notebook shut, rose, and marched from the room.

∞ CHAPTER 148 ∞

"I'm asking one more time, little brother," said Tommy, out of breath from running up three flights of stairs to Kenta's Atherton dorm room. He was waving his Japanese citizenship document, automatically granted to every Nisei. "It's time for us to burn this and renounce our Japanese citizenship."

"I said no last week, I said no yesterday, and I am telling you no today. No is no," said Kenta, his voice more agitated and louder with each refusal.

"You owe me a favor," said Tommy, almost begging.

"If you're trying to call in a chip on school lessons you never gave Teiko, forget it." The mention of his sister's name stirred up rueful feelings—more so since Takeshi told him, "Don't tell Mom, but I saw Teiko, dressed in a kimono, enter the Tale of Genji." He did not need to say more about the notorious Chinatown nightclub infamous for patrons paying a bar fine to escort the hostesses out of the club. Nor did he admit that since Teiko left, there had been a void in his life. She was his sister—his truest sibling, yet unacknowledged. He would like to reach out to her, but how? He let the thought flicker past and answered his brother. "If you think expatriation will make the Americans forget you're Japanese, go to the burning."

"There are thousands of us showing our loyalty to America by renouncing our Japanese citizenship. You should be there."

"Damn it," said Kenta, exasperated that he had to repeat himself over and over. "Why should I give up what is mine by birth? America and Japan have a treaty granting us Nisei dual citizenship. It's my right. Just like voting when I come of age."

"That's why this is needed."

"Then do it. Turn your back on the only country that gives Mom and Dad citizenship. Are you embracing America or getting back at Dad for making you go to language school all those years?"

Tommy's open hand cracked across Kenta's cheek.

Kenta, the younger brother but the better athlete, clenched his fist. He did not strike back. His icy stare, however, forewarned his brother against a second slap. His voice turned low, menacing. "Don't think expatriation will convince a single haole we are loyal Americans. Those who don't trust us have their minds made up. You want them to accept you? Have your slanted eyes rounded, add an inch to your nose, and bleach your skin white on the way to your bonfire."

"You are not the brother I thought you were."

Kenta rubbed his face where Tommy had slapped him. "That makes two of us."

Tommy stormed toward the door, flung it open, and then turned. "Last chance, Kenta."

Kenta turned his back on his brother and walked over to his desk to struggle over his calculus assignment. He stared at the formulas for twenty minutes before giving up and walking over to the cafeteria for a burger.

⌀ Chapter 149 ⌀

"You don't have to do this for us," said Robert Shivers, not for the first time.

Robert, Corrine, and Sachiko, now at her request called "Sue," stood in the Shiverses' living room, revisiting a discussion from three days earlier. At the time, she had surprised the Shiverses, telling them, "I want to expatriate."

"So you said," Sue reminded him. "I know … I heard you. But expatriation is for me, Papa Shivers. I know all about the treaty guaranteeing my dual citizenship forever. My brothers argued about it all the time."

Robert Shivers felt a catch in his throat and could do nothing but look at the young girl who had stolen his heart; he admired her patriotism in a way that most Americans could not appreciate. "All right, then … if you're sure." He flashed a last glance at Corrine, whose eyes shone with pride. "Let's go."

The Shivers family hiked up the granite steps of the Federal Court House, which faced the Iolani Palace. Heads no longer turned when the Shiverses showed up in public with a Japanese teenager in tow, nor did eyebrows rise anymore when Mr. Shivers introduced Sue as his daughter. When gossipers referred to "the girl with two fathers," most knew they meant the daughter of the Buddhist priest, living with the FBI family.

At the top of the stairs, an *Advertiser* reporter and photographer ambushed the threesome. Shivers fought to control his temper. The courthouse clerk, whom he had called saying they would arrive near closing time to avoid crowds, must have betrayed him. He glowered at the pair from the paper.

Sue froze in place.

Mrs. Shivers whispered in her husband's ear, "Didn't you say the Nisei need to publicize their commitment to America? Smile." She turned to the photographer and, with her inimitable Southern charm, said, "Go ahead, young man. Fire away."

"Why are you renouncing your Japanese citizenship?" asked the reporter.

"I am proud of my Japanese heritage, so I don't look at this as a renunciation of anything. But I am American. I don't need two countries."

∽ ∾

Across the street from the courthouse, sitting on a concrete bench and dressed in a voluminous Hawaiian muumuu and floppy hat, Haru watched her daughter walk up the steps to the courthouse. Earlier in the week, Sue had stopped by and told her, "You've always said, 'Embrace America,' so that's what I am doing." Although Sue had invited Haru to go with her, the tone of the invitation seemed more obligatory than sincere to Haru's ears, and she declined. Only at the last minute did she give in to the urge to watch, if from afar, her daughter renounce her Japanese citizenship.

The words "embrace America" rang in her ears. Haru had used them often over the years. So she could not explain her inner turmoil as Shivers opened the courthouse door for his wife and their "adopted" daughter. It struck her that Sachiko, now Sue, was more American than any of her children—perhaps her greatest patriotic success if she believed her own words. Yet why did she feel pain mixed with the pride? This is what she wanted.

An unpleasant twinge, like an electric arc, flashed through her heart. Did Sachiko really have to change her name too? Western names for Japanese-American children were in vogue with children born in the 1930s, as more Japanese converted to Christianity and the first Nisei bore children. When Tomio's name migrated to "Tommy," it had not bothered her. She had found it amusing at first and then just accepted it as what often happened in families when young children couldn't pronounce a sibling's name. Was the name change a personal rejection of her, given that this was the name Haru had so carefully chosen? And yet, she felt unmistakable pride watching her daughter entering the courthouse and regretted not accepting Sue's invitation.

As Sue disappeared behind the wooden doors, Haru clutched Hiromi's Tokyo letter delivered yesterday. How could two daughters be so opposite? She reread her troubled daughter's opening sentence.

> Living in Tokyo has opened my eyes, Okasan. Japan is fighting only for what the white countries took away from Asia over the last four hundred years. Why is it all right for America to go to war against Spain to grab the Philippines but not for the Japanese to develop Manchukuo? Why is it all right for the navies of America, England, and France to force the Chinese

to give them concessions but it is not for our armies to occupy Nanking? White people rule Hong Kong, Singapore, Saigon, Manila, Sandakan, Batavia.

Hiromi's letter seemed like a Ministry of Propaganda rehash. Haru knew that writing back and pointing out the difference between Western colonialism and the slaughter of Chinese civilians, with the Nanking Massacre being the worst example, would be a waste of time.

Haru rose, brushed off her muumuu's backside, and strolled to the harbor's Aloha Tower. The decades-old port symbol pulled her back to that November day three decades ago when she stood on the upper deck of the *Yamashiro Maru* drawing near Honolulu. America! And on its shores waited a husband—the son of her beloved adopted parents. Then came Kenji's cool reserve and his horrible rejection. For a long time, she had wondered what she had done to so provoke her new husband that first night and feared she might do something else to trigger another outburst. As the years passed, she came to understand it had not been a flaw in herself but some demon that had wormed its way into Kenji's psyche. Their marriage had exorcised that devil.

Whatever pre-marriage secrets Kenji kept had been trumped by her own dreadful secret. She contemplated how many marriages she had saved by advising guilt-ridden husbands and wives to keep a past transgression a secret.

Haru wandered over to the row of shops and found a wooden stool and a rickety aluminum table outside the Kona Coffee Factory. The Japanese waitress's mouth dropped opened when Haru ordered in Japanese. Dressed in her muumuu and straw sunhat, she had passed for Hawaiian. Haru smiled inwardly. While she knew the young Nisei's first language was English, she still liked to conduct her own survey to find out how many could speak Japanese—at least well enough in this case to take a coffee order.

Then she reopened Hiromi's letter, skipped more drivel summarizing Japan's right to empire building, and went to the end. "In Japan, I am treated like a human being, not the enemy. In another generation, the Japanese in Hawaii will be like the Filipinos, addressing every white person with a deferential 'sir' and 'ma'am.' You and Daddy should come back home."

Daddy, thought Haru. *Oh, how American you are, child. Do you realize that you prosper in Japan because your un-Japanese ways are a novelty? But you will soon learn that no traditional Japanese man would ever marry such an outspoken woman.* It wasn't until she put the letter down that Haru noticed a faint penciled note along the margin. "The Japanese Imperial Army has drafted Yoshio."

Her heart raced—denial, despair, anger pumping her blood at a furious pace. Like Haru's twin sisters, Yoshio floated through life. If only her sisters had moved with more urgency, they would be living in Hawaii, raising children with the good husbands she'd chosen. Yoshi, too, had not heeded her admonishment: "Get your American passport. Then the Japanese army cannot draft you."

Like many other Nisei going to school in Japan, he retorted, "I don't want to bother with all that bureaucratic paperwork. The Japanese won't draft Americans."

Haru stared at the words, hoping to glean more from them. Why hadn't Hiromi taken the time to explain this more thoroughly? Will Yoshi be allowed to finish his last year at Todai? Will he be sent to China? She bit her lip. Of course he would—that's where the fighting was.

Absentmindedly, she nodded her head when the waitress approached her table with a coffee pot asking if she would like a refill. Out of the corner of her eye, she caught a slouching man in a white linen suit walking across the café. Her stomach quivered. Pafko. Andy Pafko. That man was now penning front-page *Advertiser* columns speculating on the coming war and the need to keep an eye on the 40 percent of the island population whose loyalty lay with an emperor who claims he is a god. Dropping her head so she could peek underneath her wide-brimmed straw hat, she watched Pafko sit down at a table occupied by a man wearing a crisp, white, naval uniform—its shoulders topped off with officer epaulets. Whatever the purpose of the meeting, she was certain it would not be good for the Japanese community. Since the Massie Trial, Pafko had lost a cause and his front-page notoriety until the gathering war clouds had given his anti-Japanese rant a resurgent audience.

Haru noticed that the reporter ordered for both of them without asking the officer what he wanted. A minute later, she raised her hand to call for the check. While Haru pushed back her chair, she caught a last glance of the lieutenant pointing at the Honolulu Steel Works.

∽ CHAPTER 150 ∾

THE FINGER-IN-THE-AIR LIEUTENANT was telling Pafko, "You ought to angle a story about all the Japs working in the steel mill. Right now, they are manufacturing sugar mill equipment, selling most of their production to Cuba and the Caribbean Islands. We'll need to convert the mill to fabricating replacement machinery for damaged ships. Can we trust the little fuckers to produce war materials to shoot their relatives?"

"Good story idea, Ray."

They paused while the waitress brought coffees with side jiggers of Jameson whiskey.

"You could add some research on the Great War, showing how peacetime manufacturing switched to making ships, field artillery, and armor-plated vehicles. You could even ask those Big Five owners if they have thought ahead. They're the ones who are protecting the fifth column."

Pafko smiled. He had already figured this out but would let his navy contact's enthusiasm wax on. He got some of his best info this way. "They do need the Jap labor."

"Precisely," said Ray, slapping the table. "Putting profits ahead of national security. Why aren't they hiring tradesmen from California, training the local Chinese, turfing out Japanese nationals who will be squeezing sushi into the machinery when war breaks out?" The lieutenant paused to tip his Jameson shot into his coffee and sipped the enhanced Kona brew. In a calmer voice he added, "Do you have anything for me?"

"Shivers is sending another report to Hoover, claiming he can't find any disloyal Japanese," said Pafko.

The lieutenant nodded, knowing Pafko had cultivated a leak within the FBI, an agent who grew up in Seattle with a nativist attitude toward the Japanese. He loathed Shivers's soft-headedness about the "slant-eyed Nips." The navy and the FBI traded hard intelligence, but neither was privy to the other's reports going up the chain of command. "With that Jap girl living in his house, how hard is he looking, for God's sake?"

"You can't use this, or it'll blow my source's cover," said Pafko.

"Don't insult me, Andy. I'm in intelligence."

Pafko smirked. "Suppose the reason the FBI can't find any Jap espionage agents is because there aren't any?"

"Then, you wouldn't have much to write about, would you?" he asked, with a matching sneer.

Pafko smiled. "Mama Cherry has two new colored gals fresh from New Orleans. I suggest we mosey over to Hotel Street, have a drink, and test-drive the new talent."

The lieutenant pushed back his chair, took a generous swallow of his coffee, and stood up. "What are we doing here!"

While Pafko and the lieutenant strolled over to Hotel Street, Japanese naval intelligence officer Takeo Yoshikawa entered the Japanese consul's office overlooking the garden that was bigger and better maintained than the governor's Washington Place mansion. Flowers bloomed all year long. The koi swam through a carefully laid rock garden. Yoshikawa bowed, placed a manila file on the polished desk, and sat down. The consul outranked Yoshikawa, but with the military's ascendancy in Tokyo, neither was sure who really outranked whom. Still, Yoshikawa showed deference, knowing that in a crisis, he would assume control.

He waited as the consul read his report. Yoshikawa was a patient man.

The consul looked up. "So many ships in one place. Your report includes the number and types of planes on two carriers. How can you be so sure? Some could be below decks, others parked on Ford Island."

"I was at the teahouse when a group of beer-drinking NCOs asked the waitress to call a taxi. That's when I rose and said I had to leave and would be happy to drop them off."

"Surely they've been warned not to talk about military matters, especially to a man obviously Japanese."

"Despite any warnings they must have had, those drunken petty officers bragged how the *Yorktown* had more planes than the *Hornet*."

The consul picked up his empty cigarette holder. "Roosevelt is threatening a total embargo on oil."

"An undeclared act of war. He is pushing us to attack America so he can help Churchill in Europe," explained Yoshikawa.

The consul finessed a Chesterfield into his holder. "America. So big, so rich. We have the best ships and planes now, but if war starts, America can out-produce us. We cannot fight a long war against this giant."

Yoshikawa noted the consul's defeatist attitude. He would include it in his secret report, which would be hand-delivered by one of his couriers without the consul's knowledge. Despite his disgust, Yoshikawa picked up the silver lighter on the desk, snapped the fuse, and held the flame for the consul to light his cigarette.

The consul took a long draw and exhaled. "I remember the army promised a short war in China. A few decisive battles. And the Chinese are so much weaker than the Americans."

"The Chinese don't mind sacrificing their people. Do you think America will fight a long war for European interests in Asia?" Yoshikawa did not wait for an answer. He had met enough American sailors at the teahouse. They wouldn't stand up to men trained in bushido, men who embraced the way of the warrior. He rose, held his hands tight against his hips, bowed, and left.

∽ ∾

Later that day, Haru heard footsteps bound up the porch stairs. Either Tommy or Kenta, she guessed, listening to the thumping ascent. As the screen door opened, Kenta's voice rang out, "Can you feed one extra?" Most of the time Kenta ate on campus, but he knew Haru treasured the days when any of her children showed up for dinner.

She tried not to show anxiety upon seeing Kenta step into the kitchen wearing his ROTC green khakis and laced boots. Any time she saw him in uniform, she visualized him hunched over, holding a bayoneted rifle while charging into a hail of bullets and bursting artillery shells. While ROTC training was a requirement for freshman and sophomore male students, only Kenji had accepted the army's invitation to continue as an upper classman.

Another pair of footsteps banged up the porch. An aloha-shirted Tommy breezed into the kitchen. When he saw his brother, he waved an official-looking envelope. "Looks as if you won't be the only Takayama in uniform. They're forming two Japanese infantry reserve units at Schofield. I hope they draft me early so I can get a head start on rank."

Haru's face lost its color. From the moment Congress had passed the draft by a single vote this past year, she dreaded that one of her boys would receive such a letter. She knew Tommy, who at twenty-five had graduated and completed two years in ROTC, was the most likely son to get the call.

"Okasan! Are you all right?" asked Kenta.

The color slowly returned to Haru's face. "No, I am not all right. Three of my sons might die fighting each other."

"Three?"

"Hiromi wrote that Yoshi has been drafted." Haru retold Kenta of the day she had watched the Meiji emperor ride his horse to the Yasukuni Shrine to honor her brother who, along with seventy-eight thousand other boys, died in the Russian war.

Kenta and Tommy had heard the story often but listened as if it were the first time. Like most young men, Kenta and Tommy considered battle deaths as statistics.

∽ CHAPTER 151 ∾

IN THE WAKE OF FDR's JULY 1941 oil embargo announcement, Shivers convened an emergency meeting of the Committee of Interracial Unity at his home.

As usual, Colonel Kendall J. Fielder of army intelligence charged with internal security of Hawaii was first to arrive. Sue greeted him at the door. She wore a zebra-striped dress cinched conservatively at the waist and trimmed with white lace around the hem. She took the colonel's foldable garrison cap and slim leather briefcase and then waited for him to unlace his boots. Shivers had assured his guests that removing their shoes was not mandatory; still, the Shivers family had adopted the habit once it was introduced by Sue. Like half the haoles in Hawaii, he admitted tracking dirt into the houses made no sense.

Sue, like a family cat who was ever ubiquitous and hardly noticeable, walked over to the wet bar. She did not have to ask if or what Fielder wanted to drink. She poured Coca-Cola into a glass halfway, adding ice cubes but leaving room for a generous shot of bourbon.

Shivers and Fielder turned to the sound of footfalls approaching the front door. Wai Ching, followed by Takeshi, entered after a perfunctory knock. Behind them, Burns and Yoshida slipped through the door, their shoes already off and left on the porch. Burns ambled into the living room without a word, satisfied with a nod and a two-fingered salute.

Shigeo Yoshida opened with one of his usual zingers. "My mom's best friend just got the sack by a navy captain. He told her Japs couldn't be trusted with his children."

"He actually said that?" asked Fielder, incredulously.

"Well, not in those exact words," said Shigeo, grabbing a highball glass from the bar setup. He used the bamboo tongs to drop ice cubes into it. "But that's what he meant. The embargo news breaks; he comes home and finds *this woman* playing in the backyard with his two kids, and says, 'In the current circumstances, you might be more comfortable not working on an American navy base.'" He poured a shot of Johnny Walker Black over the crackling ice, added a dash of club soda, and tossed a glance at Wai Ching. "You're going to tell me you can find her an off-base job. Maybe you can for one person. But what about all the others?"

Wai Ching accepted a cup of oolong tea from Sue. "Yes, most likely I can find your mother's friend a job. More important, my ladies' committee made phone calls this afternoon. There have been very few firings. Most military wives are reassuring their Japanese maids that rumors of war will not affect their jobs. And except for one egg-throwing incident, the Korean and Chinese communities are calm."

The thunking of boots racing up the front steps and across the porch turned everyone's attention to the door. The screen door smacked open, and the navy intelligence officer marched into the living room. Sue stood in front of him, ready to take his cap.

The officer glared at Sue who resisted putting her hand over her nose to deflect his alcohol breath. His body wobbled, and in the same motion, he swept his hands out like Marc Antony about to address the mob at Caesar's funeral. In doing so, his arm whacked the waiting Sue across her chest. She stumbled backwards until her head hit a portrait hanging on the wall. The Shiverses' wedding picture crashed. Glass shattered on the floor.

Takeshi quickly rose from the table and rushed to his sister's side.

The intelligence officer slurred, "This wouldn't have happened if you didn't have a spy living here."

"We'll handle this," said Wai Ching, watching Takeshi balling his fists and taking a step forward. With his pulse pounding and his face flushed, Takeshi muttered, "Wakarimashita."

"Are you all right?" asked Shivers, grabbing Sue by both hands and helping her up.

Sue shook glass off the back of her dress. "Hai ... yes, Papa Shivers. I'm okay."

Shivers put his arms around her.

The intelligence officer studied the embrace. "Your *daughter*! No wonder you've gone soft on them and defied the president's orders. I will send an official report regarding this breach of security to Admiral Kimmel."

Burns smelled alcohol on the officer's breath and then caught a whiff of something else—perfume and the scent of sex? Hotel Street, thought Burns, saying in an iron voice, "You might be doing it from a prison cell. You just assaulted a woman in front of a police officer and the FBI."

Having walked Sue to a chair, Shivers strode over to the telephone atop his radio console. "I will save you time." He started dialing. "I am sure the admiral would like to hear of your little … raid."

"You can fool the admirals," hissed the intelligence officer. "But *we*," throwing his shoulders back, "know what you are doing here." He teetered backward on his heels, almost lost his balance, steadied himself against the wall, and then stomped out of the house.

Shivers dropped the phone handle into its carriage.

"Are you okay?" Takeshi asked.

"He didn't actually hit me, just knocked me off balance." Sue smiled. "Mom Shivers bought some fresh strawberries," she said in a tone suggesting nothing had happened. "Maybe now is a good time to bring out a bowl."

Wai Ching nodded his head. "Ah, how very Japanese of you, young Sue." This drew laughter from the men that eased the tension in the room. Everyone knew she would return with a bowl of cleaned and cut strawberries snowed with powdered sugar.

"If there was any doubt about the critical nature of our work, this navy officer gave us our marching orders," said Shigeo. "What's he going to do? What are we going to do?"

"Nothing and nothing," said Shivers. "He won't report anything, fearful of assault and battery charges, and we won't do anything that distracts us from our mission. As we know, the admiral is not the typical anti-Japanese scourge of his predecessors. He has met Sue at my home and has been the epitome of graciousness. He's very much aware of the critical nature of the Japanese community to the economy and to the maintenance of his ships. With war drawing closer, I will recommend he assign a more senior officer to our future meetings."

Fielder snapped his valise open. All eyes watched him extract a beige envelope marked "TOP SECRET." While he unwrapped the figure-eight string spun around the two buttons on the envelope, he spoke in a voice permanently hoarse from his three-pack-a-day habit. "I have a copy of Grew's telegram sent to State," he said, referring to the long-serving American ambassador to Japan, Joseph Grew. Fielder fingered a yellow sheet from the envelope and held it in front of his face. "Japan will do whatever is necessary to secure oil. If we wanted to give Tojo an excuse to completely take over the government, the embargo has done it."

Fielder put the telegram copy on the table. "Unless Roosevelt rescinds the oil embargo, Japan will attack American interests. Our forces in the Philippines and Guam cannot stop an invasion, and there is no way we can supply MacArthur's limited troops."

"This makes our purpose all the more urgent," said Wai Ching, never missing an opportunity to focus everyone on the committee's mission—to prevent internment.

"I just got back from Tokyo High," said Shigeo, using the common nickname for McKinley High School because of the predominance of Japanese students. "I asked a community gathering there what worried them the most if war breaks out. Their biggest fear is the police. There are more prongs on a fork than Japanese on the police force. They want you," Shigeo eyeballed Burns, "to recruit more Japanese into the force."

"If it were up to me, I would," said Burns. "But I can tell you with certainty … it's not an option."

Shigeo stood up. "Then why have these public meetings, supposedly to reassure the Japanese and elicit their input if their recommendations are just dumped in the trash?"

"Rein in your horses, Shigeo. You know recruiting more Japanese for the police force is not a possibility. Let's not start trouble with the Hawaiians. The police force is one of the few decent jobs reserved for them. But maybe there is another approach, something less dramatic than your do-or-die ultimatum."

"A liaison group?" asked Wai Ching.

"Something like that," said Burns. "I would call it a 'contact group.' Ask neighborhoods to choose a few guardians—or whatever we want to call them—to act as the contact officers with police. I think we could get them some type of badge. Make it official."

"Jack, we've all heard you say the Issei should have the right of citizenship. Why not go on public record?"

Burns looked around the room. Facial expression and nods were affirmative. "Maybe the *Star-Bulletin* would let me write an editorial in response to all the theatrics from the *Advertiser*."

"They would, Jack," said Wai Ching.

"And speaking of the *Advertiser*," said Shigeo, "no doubt you all saw how Pafko claims that since the Japanese grow half of Hawaii's vegetables, we are all at risk of food poisoning once Tojo gives the word."

Ignoring Shigeo's distraction, Wai Ching looked at Fielder and then Shivers. "What's the latest from Washington?" The oft-asked question was shorthand for "What is the likelihood that the army or FBI will be ordered to intern all Japanese in Hawaii?"

Fielder said, "The army is satisfied that our Japanese will do little or nothing to support Japan if hostilities begin." He paused for effect. "Any threat to Hawaii will come from a Japanese invasion force. Highly unlikely, but if they landed, we would be hard-pressed to defend the island. Washington vetoing our latest request to recruit a local Nisei battalion is a mistake."

Shivers waited until he swallowed a strawberry. "Hoover is satisfied with the list of approximately two thousand names of outspoken imperialist sympathizers and community leaders." His eyes involuntarily darted to Takeshi, and he instantly regretted this indiscretion. Since everyone caught the look, he acknowledged what it had conveyed. "That includes your father, Takeshi. He is not one of the four hundred nationalists, but—"

"It's okay, Mr. Shivers, no offense taken," Takeshi said quickly. "If you are not seen making a large number of arrests quickly, the call for mass internment will raise its hysterical hydra head. My father understands. All the priests, language schoolteachers, and union organizers expect to be arrested if war breaks out. My dad has been interviewed twice. He realizes the few might save the whole."

∽ CHAPTER 152 ∾

A COUGH FROM THE BEDROOM sent a shiver down Haru's spine. Kenji's latest flu bout had dragged on for weeks. Ignoring the sound of a car rumbling to a halt in front of the house, she stood up from her Singer to check on Kenji. But when two car doors slammed shut, sounding like gunshots, followed by the fast clip of two pairs of shoes smartly hitting the concrete stones leading to her porch, Haru turned her attention to the front door.

She peeked out the tiny gap between the curtains. FBI. She recognized the "uniform." Dressed just like in the movies, each man sported a black suit and black fedora, which they now removed from their heads in tandem. Takeshi had warned her to be prepared for another visit. All Buddhist priests were being interviewed again.

"Interrogated, you mean," Haru had snapped back at him. She padded to the door, opened it, and bowed. "The FBI is always welcome in our humble home."

As the men stepped in, she laid out two pairs of slippers aside the shoebox. The men paused. When the first one bent to untie his shoelaces, the other followed.

Haru smiled inwardly. She had mentally rehearsed this moment many times, wondering whether she would ever have the courage to actually follow through with it. On earlier FBI visits, she had allowed agents to simply walk in, fully shod. She couldn't help judging them as uncouth for lacking the courtesy to remove their shoes when visiting a Japanese home.

"Who's there?" a weak voice rasped from the bedroom.

Haru understood Kenji's use of English meant he must have seen the men come up the steps. "Mr. Shivers's men," said Haru.

As soon as the special agents entered the living room, their eyes riveted on Hirohito's picture. As in Haru and Kenji's former Moiliili residence, the portraits of the emperor and FDR dominated the wall space above the Motorola. As Haru had anticipated, both men squinted at the embroidered quilt plaque she had stitched after the second FBI visit. If they visited again, and she assumed they would, she knew they would not be able to resist seeing what it said. As if a magnet drew the men, they both stepped closer to read it.

"You have two mothers. Japan who gave you birth, America who nurtured you. You must give your loyalty to the one who nurtured you." The men dropped their eyes to photos of her four sons atop the polished Motorola. Tommy and Kenta in American army uniforms, Takeshi in Harvard cap and gown, and Yoshio in a McKinley High School football uniform.

The soft shuffle of slippers whispered from the hallway connecting the bedroom to the living room. Kenji walked in slowly, slightly bent. "Gentlemen, we have been expecting you. Has my honorable wife presented you with tea?"

Haru bowed. "Sumimasen," she said and hurried to the kitchen.

Kenji pointed to a desk. "All my papers are stacked there in a pile. Of course, you are welcome to check under the bed and inside the garden shed. But, you must open the door slowly, or a rake might drop on your head." He sat down and swept his hand toward his desk in a gesture commanding the men to begin.

Haru brought out tea and a tin of Lorna Doone cookies.

"What state are you young men from?" asked Haru.

"Missouri," said the taller agent.

The other agent, his chin sticking down like a shovel, ignored her question. Instead, he intoned in his official voice, "Do you send money to buy kits for Japanese soldiers?"

Haru spoke to the tall agent in her warmest tone. "Why, that's Mark Twain's home state. My favorite author. Do you know he visited and wrote about Hawaii?"

Kenji addressed the second man's question. "Of course," said Kenji. "These young men fighting in China have no choice. Sending food and sweaters does not mean we approve of the war. My Chinese friends send kits to the Chinese soldiers. We all take care of our brothers."

"Ah, I did not know that," said the tall agent, smiling at Haru. "All I managed was *Huckleberry Finn*."

"My favorite Twain character," said Haru.

"Do you believe your emperor is a god?" said the shovel-chinned agent.

"No," said Kenji. "That's a Shinto belief. I am Buddhist. And we don't use the word 'god' as Christians do. The emperor is like the father of the nation, like King George VI in England." Kenji coughed. "The emperor is the embodiment, the soul of Japan."

The taller agent turned his attention to Kenji. "What will you do if war breaks out between America and Japan?"

"I hope I have enough time to remind my boys to fight for America before you come and arrest me."

"Your tea," said Haru.

The Missouri man looked at his partner. "We have two more stops to make."

Shovel-chin took the hint. "We are finished here."

The men moved to the front door. An awkward silence ensued as they put on their shoes; then with a quick nod, they marched out the front door.

Haru and Kenji drank the tea and ate the cookies. They remarked how polite the men had been, but neither said what was on their mind: their sons might die in the coming war.

∞ CHAPTER 153 ∞

HARU'S CONCERN FOR YOSHIO was misplaced. Miserable as he was, that son would never see a battlefield. He wore the emperor's uniform at a Mitsubishi coal mine in Manchukuo, far from the frontline battles, supposedly protecting Chinese miners from Mao's Red guerillas. In reality, Yoshio was a prison guard preventing conscripted Chinese coal miners from escaping their slave-like working conditions.

"Hey, you Yank," bellowed his sake-besotted sergeant.

The sergeant called Okinawans "pig eaters" and "sugar suckers," and his Tokyo-born underlings "city wimps." He had a derogatory handle for everyone. Underlying his mean streak was the Japanese military system's abuse of its enlisted men, the sergeant's anger at being relegated to guard duty far away from the frontline, and his own failed resolve to stop drinking each morning when he awoke to a screaming headache. An hour after rising, his morning sake eased the pain and mellowed him. But by midday, steady nipping had turned mellow to nasty and by evening to vicious.

"Hey, you Yank!" shouted the sergeant a second time, louder, angrier.

Yoshio shivered at the sound of the rough voice. It was late in the day, the time when the uglies got worse. He pretended not to hear the man. A mistake. The sergeant stomped over to Yoshio, lifted his rifle butt, and struck the conscript in the mouth.

Yoshio's head snapped back, his knees buckled, but he stood his ground.

"You Yanks are stupid, disloyal, and lazy, but not deaf!"

Yoshio spit out a tooth.

The sergeant, who had lost more than one tooth in his early army days, grinned maliciously. "Count the workers coming out. If the number is short, send them back for half a shift."

"What about their supper?"

The sergeant poked the rifle butt into Yoshio's gut.

Yoshio bent over.

"Go outside the gate and sell it, stupid. Keep 10 percent commission and give me the rest." He fixed his malevolent eyes on Yoshio. "And don't try to cheat me."

Yoshio nodded his head in compliance. As he watched his nemesis march back to the NCO barracks, he turned his anger onto himself—for what seemed like the millionth time. Why hadn't he heeded his mother's pleas to obtain an American passport? To save a few hours of time filing paperwork and obtaining a passport picture, he would be spending years in Manchuria distrusted and abused as a Yank.

In Tokyo, Hiromi watched the angry demonstrators parade through the Ginza from her tenth-floor cubicle. Some held pictures of Roosevelt turned upside down, with an evil grin on his face. Little pockets of protesters stopped to burn American flags. She could not make out the words of the parade leader's chants, but the crowd's angry "Banzai!" refrain carried stridently through her open window. She turned back to her desk and resumed translating a *Collier's* magazine advertising copy for Dial soap into Japanese. As a copywriter for the American products section of the Sumitomo Daibutsu, or trading company, she spent her days enticing the Japanese into coveting the American lifestyle. She feared for her job. How could the stupid American government impose an oil embargo? The *Yomiuri Shimbun*, Japan's most read national newspaper, had called for a boycott of all things American, which, until recently, had been popular status symbols.

As if reading her mind, her boss, a squat, beefy man who spoke enough broken English to garner his *bucho* management title for Sumitomo's international section, stepped into her cubicle. "You are very lucky, Hiromi," he said in Japanese, which she spoke almost perfectly, if with a Hiroshima dialect. "The Ministry of Foreign Affairs has a job for you as a translator."

"I don't want to work for the government. I am happy here."

The bucho smirked. "You don't read newspapers, listen to street demonstrations outside the window? The American products section is being closed down. Today."

"I don't want to work for the government," she repeated, more urgently this time. "I can stay here at half-pay and just teach the English classes."

The bucho leaned over her desk and hissed through his clenched teeth, "There will be no more classes teaching the language of the enemy."

Hiromi thought of two *kibei* friends who had been "invited" to work at the Ministry of Trade and Industry. The one who had resisted had been questioned all night at the Tokyo police headquarters about her spying activities. The next morning, she had reported to work.

"Let me clear my personal items from my desk."

The bucho smiled in triumph.

∞ CHAPTER 154 ∞

WONDERING ABOUT THE URGENCY of the summons, Jack Burns walked into Shivers's office the first Monday of December. Shivers motioned him to close the door. At the sound of the click of the latch, he announced, "This is for your ears only. We're going to be attacked before the week is out."

Burns's facial expression didn't change. They had prepared for this day. "What makes you so sure?" He took his accustomed seat fronting Shivers's desk.

Shivers fished a cigarette out of a pack lying on his desk. "J. Edgar called. Japan's carrier fleet has left Yokosuka. Maybe eight hundred planes and who knows how many marines. Washington-Tokyo talks have stalled." He lit his cigarette, inhaled, tilted his head upward, and blew out a pillar of smoke.

"Is Hawaii under threat?"

"No, no," said Shivers, dismissively. "Even if Yamamoto headed this way, we would know before he got here since we have planes going out hundreds of miles every day. No doubt, our teahouse spy has wired our preparedness. What our spy doesn't know is that the navy has that radar apparatus we talked about in place on the North Shore."

Burns said, "I'd bet on Singapore, but you said *we're* going to be attacked."

Shivers remained poker-faced. He said nothing. His silence said it all.

"That means the Philippines," said Burns.

Shivers crushed the half-smoked cigarette into his seashell ashtray. "Take the pulse of the Japanese community." Shivers ran a forefinger across his lips. "And Jack, not a word about this to anyone else."

Burns looked out at the Aloha Tower. "We've bet the farm that navy intelligence's fear-mongering about our Japanese is ill-founded."

Shivers turned his eyes up. "No doubts about your community at this minute, Jack?"

Burns's eyes turned back to Shivers. "None."

"But we're prepared just in case we're wrong."

"Yes, we are." Burns stood up and nodded his head. "I'll call with a daily pulse reading."

Once Burns left his office, Shivers stared at the photos on his desk. The picture on the left memorialized a smiling couple on their wedding day, the middle photograph featured a serious Sue in her high school cap and gown, and on the right, he let his eyes linger on the "family" portrait taken Easter Sunday of him in his best suit flanked by Corrine and Sue in ribboned bonnets and white dresses. The picture caught Sue's warmth and sense of security. He had never told Sue he loved her. When he introduced her as his daughter, he assumed she understood his fatherly affection. How much was he betting on this one teenager's representation of a whole race?

He and Burns had vetted the Japanese community for two years. They had not found a single piece of evidence to support any local Japanese plan to sabotage a military response to aggression. Yet, with a population of 140,000, the Japanese—who still clung to an alien culture and religion while looking so different from most Americans—understandably aroused suspicion. It would not take many saboteurs to blow up a few power transformers, cut key telephone lines, or poison the reservoirs. A dozen dedicated men could wreak havoc.

Until today, all had been theory and rhetoric. Now they were embarking on a great gamble: no mass internment—the decision made. He and Jack were almost certain that the Japanese community was not harboring saboteurs.

Almost certain.

Almost.

He kept his eyes focused on Sue's picture. Had his love for this girl led him to the right decision or blinded him to his duty? More than anyone else on the Interracial Committee, he was responsible for Hawaii's internal security. He had been charged with preparing the Japanese for internment. He had not done so. Instead, he worked with the local community leaders to make sure that it would not happen.

He did not worry about a ruined career if he were wrong or even a criminal charge for neglect of duty. But what would be the effect on America if he were wrong?

"So much is resting on your unsuspecting shoulders," he said to the young woman smiling back at him from the picture.

Burns returned to his office and called a meeting with his staff. "Boys, I am worried we've become a little complacent." He tried to strike a tone of dispassionate resolve, hoping to motivate his men to swim among the Japanese community with renewed diligence—without raising the alarm that there was a special reason for his urgency. Seeing no raised eyebrows, he continued, "Let's do a 'listen-in' over the next couple days. Look for signs that the Japanese are expecting something ... runs on nonperishables at the grocery store, stocking up on water, things like that."

Each day, the reports confirmed what previous intelligence had assessed: No one was acting suspiciously, nor were there any signs of preparation. However, one detective noted all the airplanes at Hickam Field and Pearl were lined up in the middle of the runway. "I guess the military doesn't believe the reports we and the FBI are sending. They're thinking some Japanese fanatic is going to sabotage the planes through the fences."

"At least we know they don't expect an attack, or they wouldn't leave all the planes lined up like ducks in a shooting gallery," said another detective.

I hope you are right, thought Burns.

❧ Chapter 155 ❧

The Re-Paganization of Hawaii
By Andy Pafko

Don't be fooled by the Buddhist temples looking like your friendly garden-variety Methodist church. The more these heathen outposts look like our places of worship, the more the threat to our Christian heritage. Don't be fooled by Roman Catholic-style robes. ...

Haru tossed down the paper. The *Advertiser* had sunk to a new low. *All rubbish*, she thought, using an old word she had recently picked up with new meaning. How could the newspaper allow Pafko to roll out such old, worn-out drivel? But she knew why. By pandering to racist haole readership, the *Advertiser* sold not only newspapers but also advertising. While Haru considered only a minority of haoles to be racist, she feared that if the white community were fed a daily barrage of biased muck, some of it would stick.

If war broke out, she knew the Interracial Committee's fight for the evenhanded treatment of the Japanese rested on the goodwill of white men and women who were watching from the sidelines of this polarized fight. *They want to believe in us.* But one undermining incident, and all the wary trust would evaporate like the first raindrop on a hot tin roof of public opinion.

Lowell Thomas, reporting from Washington, assured his listeners, "Japan and America are still talking." He postulated, "Each week Japan does not attack America increases the odds that cooler heads are prevailing in Tokyo. New prime minister General Tojo must realize that with his army stalemated in China, striking America would be the last thing a prudent military leader would do."

Haru picked up Hiromi's last letter that rejected the latest plea to return home. Her daughter tried to soothe the worst of her mother's anxieties: Japan was adapting to the embargo. The street marching had stopped. The raucous neon cacophony in the Ginza, Tokyo's "Times Square," had dimmed. Army officials spun assurance that their scientists were developing a new technology for converting coal into gas.

"Somehow," Hiromi wrote, "Japan's clever engineers will wiggle through this crisis without war." She ended, pledging to "jump on the next ship to Hawaii if war is imminent."

Haru could not remember a happier start to a day than this balmy Saturday morning. The University of Hawaii football team would be playing its season's last game that afternoon. Four of her children and a host of friends would enjoy a pre-game buffet at the Takayama home. She looked around her living room, only basic furniture still in place. She glowed. Yesterday, the movers finished packing the better cutlery and china along with most of their clothes and personal treasures. The forty-some packing boxes should be miles out of the harbor by now, on their way toward the Big Island. This time, there was no talk of taking back the mission Kenji had started. They were retiring. An annex had been added to the hotel for their living quarters.

Tonight, she would sleep in her Queen Emma Street home for the last time. Tomorrow, she and Kenji would take the noon ferry for Kawaihae. *No more cattle boats*, thought Haru, *but a real passenger ship with a restaurant and snug cabin with bunk beds for the twenty-six-hour journey—provided the seas remained calm.*

She was going home to Waimea. Her children had seen the first light of day when the sun peeked over Mauna Kea. She had come to Waimea an expectant teenage bride and left as a mother, an advisor to many of her husband's parishioners, and a businesswoman who had built and managed a hotel—a valued member of the community she loved.

Haru looked out the window at her husband dozing in his backyard rocker. The last two years in Honolulu had not been kind to Kenji. He had left Waimea a robust, vigorous man but would not return as one.

And she was needed in Waimea. Sam's health had deteriorated too. His WWI gas-attacked lungs were giving out. He could not help around the hotel as he had in the past. Kame confessed she had a difficult time keeping up with the workload.

Waimea was calling them home. But, like her sisters' procrastination that had stranded them in Japan, Haru hoped she had not waited too long.

⨊ CHAPTER 156 ⨊

THE SCREAM OF THE AIR-RAID SIREN ripped through Honolulu as it did the first Saturday of every month, and as always, it made her shudder. Haru glanced up at the clock that hung next to the calendar: December 6, twelve noon. Exactly on time. Dutifully, Haru grabbed her gas mask, went to the fridge, stuffed a half-dozen rice balls wrapped in seaweed into her apron pockets, strolled out of the house, and headed for the designated air-raid shelter inside the River Street Methodist Church's basement.

At the next block, she heard a familiar voice call out to her. "Haru-san!"

Haru turned toward her young neighbor. "Dr. Danny," she shouted, teasing the high school senior who had dreamed of becoming a doctor ever since anyone could remember. "How's your father?"

⨊ ⨊

Danny Inouye's father was somewhat of a community legend. When Danny was born in 1924, his father was expected to register his new-born son at the Japanese consulate. Instead, he had marched into the consulate to announce that he, his wife, and Danny were Americans and demanded they not be listed on his village's records henceforth.

The declaration had infuriated the consulate officer. His face had turned scarlet as he had hissed and hollered about Mr. Inouye's pa-triotic responsibilities. Most Japanese would have buckled under the assault of this authority. But Danny's father was no cane worker and had stood his ground.

He did enroll Danny in a Japanese language school at age six, as was the custom. But a few years later when Danny came home from school early one afternoon with welts on his back from a whipping, his father strode into the language school and administered a beating to the teacher. Danny never returned.

When Kenta challenged his father about the incident, Kenji's first swear word stopped the dinner conversation. "The little shit of a teacher deserved the beating. If you had come home with welts, I hope I would have done the same thing." While not voicing approval of the vulgar language, especially at the dinner table, Haru was proud of her husband's answer.

Haru noticed Danny's dancing eyes. She waited for the siren blast to pause. "So what's the good news, Dan-chan?"

"Double good news," he spouted out, hurrying his cadence and trying to beat the next siren warning. Danny failed, and so he raised his voice. "I received my letter of acceptance to UH in the morning mail. And I just finished my advanced first aid course."

At 12:30 p.m., the third and last siren blare faded out, signaling the end of the exercise and leaving Haru's ears ringing.

She strolled by Chen's fruit and vegetable shop. She waved. Mr. Chen, with a wide smile and his eyes sparkling, wedged himself be-tween rows of carrots, celery, and fat eggplants. He bowed.

"We will miss you, Haru-san." This warm goodbye reminded her that, as much as she looked forward to returning to Waimea, she would miss the friendly shopkeepers and the conveniences of Honolulu. She paused to look at the row of multi-lingual signage jutting over the sidewalk from the second-story floors where most shop owners lived: a shoe shop, dry cleaners, radio repairs, and Tang the butcher. She convinced herself she would quickly adjust to the limited access to electricity in Waimea and the resulting lack of modern appliances. After enjoying the electrical conveniences of Honolulu, Kenji had insisted on shipping a generator for their apartment annex.

∞ ∞

By one o'clock, boisterous UH students stuffed Haru's home. Sue presided as hostess of the affair. Kenta and Tommy, the latter who had a weekend pass, were the official greeters of fellow fans who walked in without knocking, as had become the custom after the first pre-game party.

A couple of haole boys, friends of Kenta from his ROTC regiment, whose fathers served at Pearl, popped in with their dates. A Chinese and a Portuguese student arrived together, and a Filipino from the neighborhood joined the gathering. The youngsters identified themselves as the Queen Emma Street Gang, rather than by their ethnic groups.

Haru and Kenji mingled with their young guests for a short time and then retired to chairs in their snug backyard. They played gin rummy, a game they had picked up from Takeshi. Haru made sure she never won more than half the games. She savored the cool trade winds mixing a cocktail of ocean smells with the kitchen aromas of sweet bread and saimin—the pungent plantation-inspired concoction of Japanese udon, Chinese chow mein, and Filipino pancit.

Around one-thirty, Tommy ducked his head out the back door. "We're off to catch the bus." Haru and Kenji rose and walked into the house. Everyone was scurrying around picking things up, washing out glasses, and sweeping the floors.

Life was good. Her children were happy, healthy, and well mannered and had friends of good character. She and Kenji were going back to Waimea for a quiet life. They owned a hotel. All her children had graduated from or were attending college. They were living the

American dream. In Japan, the equivalent would not have been possible. She tried to push away any negative talk of war or thoughts of Yoshio in Manchuria, but they lurked beneath the placid surface of the day's carefree diversions.

After the students left for the three o'clock game, Haru and Kenji continued their gin rummy while listening to the football game on the radio. The colored All-American halfback and co-captain of the team, Nolle Smith, ran the Willamette University Bearcats ragged, gaining 166 yards and leading UH to a 20-6 victory.

After the game, they strolled hand in hand around the neighborhood for one last look, then stopped at a shop, and bought some Chinese takeout, which they ate on the porch, watching the light slowly leak out of the day.

They went to bed early, and when Haru said, "This is the last time we will spend a night in this home or in Honolulu for a long time," Kenji took the rare hint and moved his hands under Haru's yukata to gently rub her breast. They made love slowly, languidly. Right after the moment of joyful release, she noticed the two boat tickets resting on her vanity table. She drifted off to sleep savoring the happiness that awaited them.

⚭ Author's Notes ⚭

Tom Coffman's *The First Battle* documentary premier set me off on a course I did not fully imagine. After the lights came on, I watched a frail eighty-five-year-old on stage play down her role in saving 140,000 Japanese living in Hawaii from internment during World War II. At that moment, I knew I had found not only the book I wanted to write but also the purpose of my so-called retirement years.

Anyone living in Hawaii for any length of time knows the valor of the 442nd Japanese regiment that produced twenty-one Medal of Honor recipients who fought the Nazis and earned the respect of their fellow Americans.

My lead character, Haru, and her husband, Kenji, are the products of my imagination. Her two oldest children are inventions. The two youngest boys and the sisters are modeled on Miho family Nisei. Kenta, an artillery spotter for the Nisei 442nd regiment and the next book's main character, was modeled on Kats Miho. Sachiko is a stand-in for Sue Isonaga who changed the course of history simply by being an ordinary American teenager and, by chance, living with a family brought to Hawaii to intern her and her family. Most of her major scenes, such as Shivers's surreptitious interrogation of her views on the emperor, although sometimes embellished by me, are based on Sue's recollections at a luncheon we had at our home and various videos she recorded.

But where to begin this story? Originally, I began the novel the day Pearl Harbor was bombed with the idea of following the young men whose bravery is well chronicled but seldom dramatized in novel form. But soon, I asked myself, "Where did these exceptional men come from?" And why were only 2,000 of 140,000 Japanese in Hawaii imprisoned or interned, rather than all of them as in California, located 3,000 miles further east from Japan. The story's ambition grew. What was happening inside Japan in the early twentieth century that led to war with America, even as thousands of its citizens were immigrating to work on Hawaii's cane fields and California's farms?

Allow me to digress. Years before I even thought of writing this book, my wife and I visited Sandakan, Malaysia, to see the orangutans. Hearing there was a nearby Japanese cemetery, Tomoko wanted to pay her respects. Rather than a cemetery of WWII soldiers, as I anticipated, the little gravestones were etched with the first names of Japanese women. Most had died in their twenties, a few in their late teens. These were the karayuki, sold by their parents to the brothels of Sandakan, a vibrant British lumber port in the late nineteenth century. A Japanese writer used the proceeds of her book, *Sandakan 8*, the story of karayuki, to restore the once-tattered cemetery to the well-maintained memorial we had discovered. Little did I know that the specter of those karayuki would inspire the beginning of a novel I had not even thought about writing at the time of my visit.

So once I knew where the story must begin, Tomoko and I visited Amakusa, a land of ancient churches courtesy of Saint Francis Xavier, modern hot springs, soaring mountain peaks, and a buried karayuki past. Climbing the tallest peak overlooking a fast-moving channel across from smoldering Mount Unzen volcano, I knew I had the opening scene for *Picture Bride*. As I walked the stone bridge over the Funanoo-machi's trickling river, I imagined Haru's youth and could see and hear Natsu reveal her fate as she bit into the sweet potato. Above, looking at the second floor of Gion Jinja, I could see the priest's wife look forlornly on Haru.

A novelist is given license to move characters and places and even extend the life of historical characters a life insurance actuary would envy to fit the story. So it was with Fukuzawa's Amakusa speech, gleaned from words he had earlier written, revealing Japan's ambitions and how sending karayuki overseas was necessary to pay for those ambitions.

All the Shinto shrines and Buddhist temples in Amakusa, Hiroshima, Tokyo, and Honolulu existed in the era the book lives and were visited by me. The temple in Hiroshima where Haru spends her teenage years was chosen with care. I needed a structure outside the atomic bomb's destruction area because in a future book Haru's oldest son will attend the wounded at the Gion temple, converted in August 1945 to a temporary hospital.

Both pairs of Haru's parents—her Amakusan biological parents and her Hiroshima surrogate parents—bear no resemblance to anyone living or dead. The same is true for her husband, Kenji, and all the characters in Hiroshima, including her best friend, Ko, who exposes the tension between the emperor—worshiping Shintoism that is carrying Japan's military to its ascendancy and Buddhism that had been the state religion until the1868 Meiji Restoration.

Reporter Andy Pafko is an invention. Most of what he wrote is not, though it has been embellished and amalgamated by me. I started by using real reporters and their names spanning the three decades of the novel. But they became too many characters for either the reader or the novelist to keep track of. Pafko represents them all.

Historical characters Bishop Imamura and Reverend Okumura were giants of their era, each deserving a novel of his life, so I trust readers who attend either the temple or church they founded and still stands will forgive me for focusing mainly on one issue that divided the men—the Japanese language schools.

Except for Fujimoto, who went through three first-name changes, and his assistant, Kurume, all the main characters introduced in the sugarcane strike chapters not only existed but also said and did most of what the story states, although not always in the time frame imposed.

The Massie Trial was one of the several trials of the twentieth century. All the characters appearing in the courtroom scenes, except for Taka and Pafko, existed. Their editorial combats were inspired by the newspaper reports during the trial. Horace Ida's sister Candi existed only in my imagination. She proved a very useful invention to show Haru's cub reporter son how the other half lived. Unhappily, that nasty piece of work, Admiral Stirling, existed, and much of what I have him saying was lifted from speeches or interviews he gave.

As a postscript, I can report Thalia Massie divorced her husband two years after the trial and committed suicide in 1963. In 1966, Albert Jones, one of the navy men who helped Grace Fortescue kidnap Kahahawai, admitted he pulled the killing trigger.

Colonel Patton's recipe for arresting all leaders of the "Orange People" in the advent of war is presented exactly as he wrote it. Roosevelt's advocacy of internment over Hoover's strong objections, Shivers's conversion from "intern them all" to a minimalist approach, and Jack Burns's assurance of Japanese loyalty all happened as reported. Burns, with the backing of Japanese voters, won the governorship after the war. Robert Shivers gave away his "daughter," Sue Isonaga, in marriage in 1949 to a 442nd veteran introduced by Wai Ching. A year later, Shivers passed away.

Hung Wai Ching did all I claim he did. Readers of the sequel, *A Question of Loyalty*, will see how he followed up his role as a catalyst to avoid internment by playing a critical role in bringing the famed Nisei regiment into being. He later founded Aloha Airlines. Charles Hemenway used his enormous prestige to encourage Japanese scholarship and assure admirals and generals they had nothing to fear from Hawaii's Japanese residents. Shigeo Yoshida made such an impression on the Congressional Statehood Committee in Hawaii in 1937 that the delegates promised they would recommend statehood. As *Picture Bride* dramatizes, once the congressmen returned to the anti-Japanese environment of Washington, DC, they reneged. I took much license inventing quotes for Yoshida. I needed someone to reveal the frustration of trying so hard to earn full acceptance as an American citizen. Yoshida did well in practice and in my book.

The characters continue their story in *A Question of Loyalty*.

⤳ Glossary ⤲

ah so – "Is that so?"; "I see" (short form of *ah so desuka*)

ah so desuka – "Is that so?"; "I see"

ainoko – crossbreed, used as a slur

arigato – "Thank you" (a short form of *domo arigato*)

awa – Hawaiian for kava, a root sometimes used for sacramental and/or sedative brew

bachi – in music, a drumstick for taiko

bakufu – Japan's feudal government

banzai – "Hurray!"

bento – a boxed meal, most common for lunch, but can be any meal

bonsai – ornamental miniature trees or shrubs

bucho – senior department head or manager

bushido – code of the samurai warrior

butsudan – a wooden miniature Buddhist altar

chabu-dai – tea table, low collapsible table

chan – endearing ending for first names for children or female sweethearts

chanpon – deep-fried noodles with a vegetable sauce

chigau – "That's wrong!" or "Never!"

cho-ya – personal obligation between elder and junior

chow mein – sautéed Chinese noodles

chugi – loyalty

chukun aikoku – loyalty and patriotism

daidokoro – kitchen

daikon – radish

daijoubu desu – "It's all right"

danna-sama – an honoric a wife might call her husband; a patron of a geisha

deshita – pass tense with a verb

desu – present tense with verbs

desuka – used at end of sentences that are questions

doma – hard dirt floor, usually a kitchen area meant to prevent fires

domo – "Thank you" (a short form of *domo arigato*)

domo arigato gozaimashita – polite form of "Thank you very much"

fu-fu – personal obligation being between a husband and wife

fujinkai – women's club

fu-shi – personal obligation between a father and child

futon – Japanese bedding

gaijin – foreigner

Gaimusho – ministry of foreign affairs

gaman – persevere

gambari – persistence

geta – wooden sandal, clogs

giri – obligation

gisei – sacrifice

gochisosama deshita – polite ending of a meal; "I'm finished. Thank you for the good food."

gomennasai – "I'm sorry"

gumi – suffix meaning "group"; often used in Yukusa groups, as in Yamaguchi-gumi

gyoza – meat dumplings, steamed or fried

hai – "Yes"

hajimemashite – salutation used when meeting a person for the first time; "How do you do?"

hale – house, in Hawaiian

hanko – person's rubber-tipped seal used to "sign" casual documents

haole – Hawaiian for non-native; in Haru's time, a white person

haori – thigh-length, light jacket worn open

hapa – Hawaiian slang for mixed race

hapi – short, tradional cotton coat, like a casual half-kimono

hilahila – Hawaiian for cowardly, used in sugarcane patois

holoku – neck-to-ankle, close-fitting, usually white, Hawaiian dress; popular wedding attire

honto ni – "That's true," or "That's right"; can also be a question, "Is that right?"

ika – squid

ikibotoke – an incarnation of Buddha

ikimasho – "Let's go"

Inari – Shinto fox spirit with many lives; fox statues often guard entrance to shrines

inkan – a more polite form of hanko, the signature stamp (chop) used to "sign" documents

irasshai – greeting when entering a home or shop

irasshaimase – more polite form of *irasshai*

irori – sunken, square hearth

Issei – first-generation Japanese immigrant

isu – chair or sofa

itadakimasu – before-meal greeting

jinbei – a pajama-like garment worn by men, women and children

jinja – Shinto shrine

jisatsu – suicide

jō –Japanese traditional measurement; almost ten feet

kabuki – stylized theater performance

kahuna – Hawaiian: a wise man, important man

kami – god or spirit

kampai – "Cheers!"; a toast

kanji – Japanese character writing borrowed from the Chinese

kapu – Hawaiian for forbidden

karayuki – a woman sent overseas, usually for prostitution

katakana – phonetic alphabet for foreign words written in block characters

katsuobushi – dried tuna shavings

kiawe – spreading bush or short tree

kekko desu – "It's okay," as in "It doesn't matter," or "Don't bother"

ken-shin - obligations between the emperor and a subject

kibei – a Japanese American who has returned to the United States after living in Japan

kimono – traditional robe-like Japanese garment

kinchaku – traditional lady's cotton purse

kitsune - a mythical fox with magical powers

kitsune ken - a hand game similar to rock-paper-scissors with hand positions portraying a fox, hunter and headman

ko – loyalty or obedience to one's family

kogitsune – a male shapeshifter that can transform into a human or fox

kokua – Hawaiian for help or relief; in Kalaupapa, used as a noun to designate a nurse-like helper

kondo – main temple in Fudoin Temple complex in Hiroshima

koseki - family registration

lei – Hawaiian for a garland of flowers

luau – Hawaiian for a feast

luna – Hawaiian for boss or overseer; during Hawaii's sugarcane era, many lunas were Portuguese

mabiki - In the Edo period, the practice of parents leaving a newborn on a mountainside to die

machete – Portuguese for a ukulele (not to be confused with "machete" meaning a large knife)

mahalo – Hawaiian for thanks, respect

mamahaha – stepmother

meiyo – honor, prestige

miso - soybean paste

minogasa - straw hat

mizuwari – liquor diluted with water

muumuu – Hawaiian for a loose-fitting dress

muzukashii - "That's strange," or "That's difficult"

nakodo – go-between or matchmaker

ne – used at end of Japanese sentences meaning "Right," or "Isn't that so?"

nemaki – pajamas, nightclothes

ninja – spy or stealth warrior

Nisei – second-generation Japanese

obasan – aunt

obi – sash

Obon festival – festival honoring the dead

odaisan – a shaman who could invoke the power of the spirits

ofuro – bath or bath house; sometimes also called "furo"

ohayo gozaimasu – "Good morning"

oishii – delicious

ojisan – uncle

okaerinasai – "Welcome home"

okasan – mother or wife

oke – a wooden bowl or bucket

oki – big

omiyage – a small gift or souvenir

on – a serious burden of obligation (more than *giri*)

onigiri – packed rice wrapped in seaweed

orega yaruyo – "I'll do it"

oshibori – wet cloth to clean hands and/or freshen one's face

Oshogatsu – New Year's Day; may also refer to new year celebrations

otosan – father or husband

pancit – Filipino noodle dish mixed with veggies and maybe bits of meat

paniolo – cowboy in Hawaii

pikake – white flower often used in making an expensive lei

ryosai kenbo – a good wife and wise mother

saimin – a noodle soup

sakaki – evergreen tree found in Shinto shrines for people to attatch paper prayers

sake – rice wine or salmon

sakura – flowering cherry trees

sama – honorific ending for an important person

sampan – Chinese stubby boat used throughout Asia

samurai – warrior

san – honorific ending for surnames

sashimi – raw fish

sekinin – responsibility

sen – one hundredth of a yen

sensei – teacher, or honorific after a name

seppuku – ritual suicide by slitting of the abdomen

sha tai tai – Chinese for a minor wife or concubine

shi – city

shibai-goya – town theater for kabuki plays

shikataganai – "It can't be helped"

shiritori – a word game

shi-tei – obligation between a teacher and student

shochu – distilled beverage with 25 percent alcohol from rice, barley, or most popular, sweet potatoes

shoji – wood-framed paper doors

shogun – hereditary commander-in-chief; real leader of Japan 1600–1867

shukuba – a way station along the Tokaido Road

socho – president or director

sugoi – awesome or extraordinary

sumimasen – "Excuse me"

sumo – Japanese form of wrestling

sushi – seasoned rice topped with, usually, raw fish

Tadafusa – Japanese kitchen knife

tadaima – a form of greeting one says when entering the home, similar to "I'm home"

taiko – Japanese drum

tama – precious jewels

tanomoshi – money club

tansu – Japanese chest of drawers

tanzen - a heavy jacket

tatami - mat made of woven straw

tempura - batter-dipped, deep-fried food

Tenno Heika - the emperor of Japan; literally "from heaven"

tenugui - handkerchief or small towel

teppanyaki – meat and/or fish fried with vegetables

terakoya - temple schools common during the Edo period

teriyaki - food broiled or grilled with a glaze of soy sauce, mirin, and sugar

tofu - soybean curd

torii – gateway of a Japanese shrine

toro - prime tuna

tsubo – Japanese measurement of area, equal to almost four square yards

tsukue – desk

udon - thick noodles

ukulele - a small four-stringed guitar played in Hawaii

unagi – freshwater eel

usagi - rabbit

wahine – Hawaiian for woman

wakarimasen – "I don't understand"

wakarimashita - "I understand"

watashi – I

yakiimo - roasted sweet potato

yaki sakana - grilled fish

yaki soba – sautéed noodles

yakitori - grilled chicken on a stick

yakuza - gangster, Japanese mafia

yen - Japanese coin, worth about a penny

yukata - robe or dressing gown

zabuton - cushion

zaisu - a chair without legs

zori - slippers

CHARACTERS AND HISTORICAL REFERENCES

∞ CHARACTERS, FICTIONAL AND HISTORICAL ∞

FICTIONAL CHARACTERS are noted with an asterisk (*) before the name. All are arranged alphabetically by last name or, when no last name is given, by first name.

* Adams, John - Presbyterian minister in Waimea
* Adams, Mrs. - unhappy wife of John Adams
* Akiyama, Sam - cowboy at historical Parker Ranch; replacement husband for Kame; one of the few Issei volunteers who saw combat service in France
* Amy – student in Takeshi's history class listening to immigration vote
* Aoki – husband of picture bride Kame
  Baldwins – Big plantation owners on Maui
* Bilkerton, Joshua - owner of the Bilkerton plantation
* Bilkerton, Mrs. - wife of Joshua
* Bowman brothers - MacFarlane's thug friends from another plantation
  Burns, John – police liaison officer to Morale Committee and army intelligence
* Candi – see "Ida, Candi"
  Carter, Wellington - trustee of Parker Ranch and then general manager; turned around the moribund ranch
  Castle, James - one of the Big Five businessmen who controlled Hawaii
  Chiang Kai-Shek – leader of China from 1928 to 1949 and then Taiwan until 1975
* Cindy - Nuuanu prostitute, former picture bride, and cane worker

Colt, LeBaron – Rhode Island senator who opposed legislation banning Japanese immigration

Coolidge, Calvin – US president in 1924

* Cox, William – Waimea's American Legion commander and school superintendent

Damien, Father – Catholic priest who dedicated his life to lepers on Molokai; died in 1889

Darrow, Clarence – Scopes Monkey Trial lawyer; defense lawyer in Massie Trial

Dillingham, Walter – one of the Big Five businessmen that fought strikers

Dole, James – pineapple king; one of the Big Five

* Doris – switchboard operator at Tebbits's clinic

Farrington, Wallace – governor of Hawaii, 1921-1929

Fielder, Colonel Kendall J. – director of army intelligence; liaison with Wai Ching's Morale Committee

Fortescue, Grace – mother of Thalia Massie

* Fujimoto, John – husband of Mayo; active in 1909 sugar strike; first wife died in 1899 from the plague; took back his Japanese name, Tamatsuke Fujimoto; known after the sugar strike as "Oki Tama" meaning "big balls"

* Fujimoto, Mayo – picture bride from Nagasaki; married John Fujimoto

* Fujimoto, Tamatsuke – see "Fujimoto, John"

* Fujita – chief of police in Hiroshima

Fukuzawa, Yukichi – founder of Keio University; writer; promoted Japanese expansion in Asia. Died in 1901, but his life was "extended" for the story. The words attributed to him in the story are his.

Furuya, Eichi – acting Japanese consul general during sugarcane strike

* Fushimi – rare white fox bought by Uno as a sacred symbol

* Goto, Dr. – Waimea doctor who, at Haru's urging, helped flu victims

* Gin – twin sister of Kin, older sister of Haru; working in Niigata silk factory; name means "silver"

Grew, Joseph – US ambassador to Japan

* Hamilton, Judith – British subject; taught picture brides Western ways

Hanihara, Masanao – Japanese ambassador lobbied Congress not to ban Japanese immigration

* Harding – navy intelligence ensign

* Haru – see "Takayama, Haru"

* Haru's brother – in army fighting Russians in Manchuria

Hemenway, Charles "Papa" – chairman of the University of Hawaii Board of Regents

Hideyoshi – shogun in the 1590s who rose from humble status; an inspiration to Haru

* Hondo – Shinto priest in charge of Ministry of Interior's Divine Office

Hoover, Herbert – US president during 1931-32 Massie Trials

Hoover, J. Edgar – director of the FBI

* Hornsby, Rudy – internist at Queen's Hospital

Huber, S. – district attorney

Hughes, Charles Evans – US secretary of state

Hull, Cordell – secretary of state under FDR

* Ida, Candi – fictional sister of historical Horace Ida

Ida, Horace – man accused of rape by Thalia Massie

Ieyasu, Tokugawa – shogun who began Tokugawa Shogunate in 1600, which lasted to 1867

Imamura, Yemyo – bishop of Fort Street, Honpa Hongwanji Mission, Jodo Shinshu sect

Inouye, Danny – high school student in 1941; later US senator

* Itagaki, Shigenobu – coal mine engineer

* Ipo – Hawaiian woman who met Haru on dramatic boat scene

* Irie – Ume's husband

Jefferson, Bob – Rotarian who gave an important speech

Judd, Lawrence – governor of Hawaii, 1929-1934

Kahahawai, Joe – man accused of rape by Thalia Massie

Kalakaua, David – king of Hawaii, 1874-1891

* Kame – picture bride from Okinawa

Kamehameha I – Hawaii's first king (1810-1821); also called Kamehameha the Great

Kamehameha III – king of Hawaii, 1825-1854

Kekkon Bozu – nickname for a priest who performed many marriages

Kelley, John – state prosecutor in the second Massie Trial

Kimmel, Admiral – appointed commander-in-chief, US Pacific Fleet, in February 1941

* Kin – twin sister of Gin, older sister of Haru; name means "gold"

* Kinder, Mrs. – third grade teacher for Takeshi

* Kiritsubo – commoner and Genji's main love interest in *The Tale of Genji*

* Ko – classmate and friend of Haru

* Koichi – student in Takeshi's history class listening to immigration vote

Kuchiba, Bishop – bishop of Fort Street Hongwanji after Imamura

* Kurume – Plantation worker on Bilkerton plantation

* Kurume, Setsu – wife of plantation worker on Bilkerton plantation

Liliuokalani – deposed queen of Kingdom of Hawaii

Lodge, Cabot, Jr. – Massachusetts senator, elected in 1936

* MacFarlane, Angus – luna on Bilkerton plantation

* Maki – Fudoin monk novice

Makino, Fred – founder of *Hawaii Hochi* newspaper

Manlapit, Pablo – leader of Philippine Sugar Union

Massie, Thalia – woman who accused two Japanese and three Hawaiians of rape

Massie, Tommy – navy lieutenant married to Thalia Massie

* Matsui, Ichiro – strikebreaker who left Haru's camp to work in Hilo

* Mayo – see "Fujimoto, Mayo"

* McCain, Pug – longshoreman crew boss

McCarthy, William – governor of Hawaii, 1918-1921

McClatchy, Valentine – president of the Japanese Exclusion League

McKinley, William - US president who annexed Hawaii in 1898

Meiji - Japanese emperor who replaced 267-year Tokugawa shogunate in 1867

* Michi - Mrs. Roberts's Japanese maid

* Miho brothers - shop owners

Miyama, Rev. Kanichi - first Japanese-American Christian missionary

Motokawa, Gennosuke - pastor of Methodist church; "Kekkon Bozu," or the "wedding priest"

* Nakamura, Keiko - a mother who returned to Japan

* Nakayama - cane worker on Bilkerton planation

* Natsu - Sandakan, Borneo, prostitute

* Natsu - in Judith Hamilton's class and shipmate with Haru

Nogi - general leading Japan's army in 1905 Russo-Japanese War

Odaishi-sama - great teacher of Buddhism, Buddhist saint/deity

* Ogawa - longshoreman

Okumura, Reverend Takie - founder of Makiki Christian Church in 1904

* Osawa, Fumiyo - wife of Buddhist priest in Haru's hometown

Otani, Matsujiro - founder of Otani Fish Market

Ozawa, Takao - born in Japan, raised in America

* Pafko, Andy - reporter in Honolulu for the *Pacific Commercial Advertiser*

Palmer, Alexander - attorney general associated with Palmer Raids arresting leftist radicals

Parker, John - founder of Parker Ranch

Patton, George S. - army lieutenant colonel

* Pender, Johnny - twelve-year-old boy

Poindexter, Joseph - appointed eighth governor of Hawaii in 1934

Reed, David - Pennsylvania senator, 1924

* Roberts, Mrs. - Waimea socialite; wife of legislator

Robertson, Seth - assistant attorney general

Roosevelt, Franklin D. - US president

Roosevelt, Theodore – US president who negotiated the end of 1905 Russo-Japanese War

* Sachi – mentally challenged girl possessed by evil spirit

* Saki – see "Suyama, Saki"

Sato, Goro – editor of the *Hinode Shimbun*

* Shika – cane worker's wife under Uno's influence

Shivers, Corrine – wife of Robert Shivers

Shivers, Robert – special FBI agent; opened Honolulu office in 1939

Shouko – the White Fox Princess (*Byakko no Himezama Shouko*)

Smith, Nolle – UH black football hero and captain in ROTC

Spalding, Edward – president of the Pacific Club, the most prestigious club in Honolulu

Stirling, Yates, Jr. – rear admiral during Massie Trial

* Susano – feral cats Haru adopted (all had the same name)

* Suyama, Saki – picture bride from Okayama farm; wife of Toshi Suyama

* Suyama, Toshi – Saki's husband

* Takayama, Haru – born in 1892 in Amakusa; adopted by Takayamas; picture bride to their son, Kenji, in Hawaii

* Takayama, Hiromi – next to last child of Haru and Kenji, the first of their two daughters

* Takayama, Kenji – born in 1876 to Midori and Kiyoshi; Buddhist priest in Hawaii; husband of Haru

* Takayama, Kenta – born in 1919 and raised as the fourth son of Haru and Kenji

* Takayama, Kiyoshi – born in 1855; Fudoin Temple priest; adoptive father to Haru

* Takayama, Midori – born in 1860; wife of Fudoin Temple priest; mother of Kenji; adoptive mother to Haru

* Takayama, Sachiko – Haru's youngest daughter; character is based on Sue Isonaga

* Takayama, Takeshi "Taka" – born in 1910; oldest son of Haru and Kenji

* Takayama, Tomio "Tommy" – born in 1916; third son of Haru and Kenji

* Takayama, Yoshio "Yoshi" – born in 1913; second son of Haru and Kenji

* Tazu – Japanese picture bride and a nurse on the ship with Haru
* Tebbits, Bernard – doctor at Waimea clinic
* Tebbits, Gertrude – clinic nurse; wife of Bernard Tebbits
* Teiko – Ume and Irie's youngest child
  Thomas, Lowell – famous radio newscaster for NBC
* Thompson, Mrs. – member of Mrs. Roberts's women's group
  Togo – admiral leading Japan's navy in 1905 Russo-Japanese War
  Tsutsumi, Noboru – Japanese language schoolteacher
* Ualani – first hapa (mixed race); Haru's housekeeper
* Uchida, Dr. – Kona doctor
* Ume – picture bride from Kobe; wife of Irie
* Uno – the odaisan, Shinto shaman
  Vancouver, George – British explorer; introduced cattle to Hawaii
  Vaughn, Judge – federal judge
  Wai Ching, Elsie – wife of Hung Wai Ching
  Wai Ching, Hung – YMCA executive, businessman, and civic leader
  Waterhouse, John – manager of Alexander & Baldwin
* Williams, Coach – baseball coach at McKinley High School
  Wilson, Woodrow – US president
  Yakushi Buddha – the medicine Buddha
* Yamahara – caneworker
  Yamamoto, Isoroku – Japanese naval captain
  Yoshida, Shigeo – statehood and Morale Committee leader
  Yoshikawa, Takeo – Japanese consulate officer
* Yumi – Tama and Mayo's daughter
* Zucker, Bobby – twelve-year-old boy
* 2436 – Bilkerton plantation laborer, McFarlane's informant

❧ Historical References ❧

Ala Wai – canal defining Waikiki as a peninsula

Amakusa – Japanese island south of Nagasaki

Atherton House – YMCA dorm near the University of Hawaii's Manoa campus

Azores – tropical Atlantic Portuguese chain of islands west of Portugal and Morocco

Big Five – the five scions of Honolulu's powerful families; most were missionary descendants

Captain Cook Coffee Company – company that bought coffee from farmers

China Clipper – one of Pan Am's fleets of clippers, flying boats landing on pontoons

Chinatown – Chinese restaurant and nightclub area next to downtown Fort Street in Honolulu

Committee of Interracial Unity – committee formed to prevent Japanese internment

Dai Fudoin – grand hall of the Fudoin Temple

Daiichi Torii – huge red beams at the entrance to the Yasukuni Shrine

Dejima – a special, designated foreign residential district in Nagasaki

Dillingham Transportation Building – downtown Honolulu structure built for Walter Dillingham

Enmei-in Temple – Buddhist temple in Yokohama, near the Grand Hotel

Fudoin Temple – Buddhist temple in Hiroshima

Funanoo-machi – tiny seacoast village on Amakusa

Gentlemen's Agreement - agreement between the United States and
	Japan in 1907 whereby Japan stopped labor migration and
	California kept schools integrated

Gion Jinja - Shinto shrine in Funanoo-machi

Golden Pavilion - Hiroshima's Fudoin Temple's kondo (main building)

Grand Hotel - prestigious hotel on Yokohama's waterfront bund; still
	operating

Hawaii Hochi – newspaper founded by Fred Makino in 1912; still
	published bi-monthly today

Hawaii Mainichi Shimbun - daily newspaper published by Tsutsumi

Honolulu Hotel - downtown Honolulu's renowned hotel in the early
	twentieth century

Honolulu Star-Bulletin - Hawaii's second-largest English newspaper

Hongwanji Mission - Buddhist temple on upper Fort Street,
	Honolulu, until 1918 and then moved to the Pali Highway;
	center of Hawaii Buddhism in Hawaii and bishop's residence

Hotel Street - downtown Honolulu's bar and brothel street

Immigration Act of 1924 – May 1924 legislation banning Japanese
	immigration and setting quotas for Europeans

Imperial Rescript on Education - filial pledge to the Japanese
	emperor recited in all schools until WWII ended

Japan Times and Mail – Japan's leading English-language newspaper

Kalaupapa, Molokai - leper colony in Hawaii in existence from
	1850s to today

Kannai - unofficial name for a district in Yokohama, originally the
	foreign settlement district

Kawaihae - port for Waimea

KGU – Hawaii's first and most popular radio station

King Kamehameha statue – larger-than-life statue of Hawaii's first
	king; located in Honolulu in front of Aliiolani Hale, the state
	supreme courthouse

Kona - Big Island's coastal district, famous for its coffee; an hour's
	drive from Waimea

La Pietra – Walter Dillingham Italian Renaissance villa

Makiki Christian Church – founded by Takie Okumura in 1904

Makino Drug Company – Honolulu business established by Fred Makino in 1901

Massie Trials – name for two 1931–32 rape and murder trials featuring Thalia Massie

Mauna Kea – mountain, 13,796 feet high, overlooking Waimea, Hawaii; protected from Pele by goddess Poliahu

Meiji Restoration – overthrow of Tokugawa shogunate in 1868 began Japan's modernization

McKinley High School – Honolulu school nicknamed "Tokyo High"

Moiliili Hongwanji – Buddhist parish near the University of Hawaii in Honolulu

Mosquito Flats – mixed-race slum near downtown Honolulu

Mount Unzen – active volcano near Nagasaki on Kyushu, Japan

Nanking Massacre – Japanese slaughter of hundreds of thousands of Chinese in late 1937

Natsunoya Tea House – teahouse overlooking Pearl Harbor with telescope on roof

Nippon Shimbun – *Japan News*, a Japanese-language newspaper

Noge Street – famous entertainment street in Yokohama

Oda Trading Post – biggest Japanese store in Waimea

Osanbashi Pier – main pier in Yokohama; most picture brides left from here

Otani Fish Market – famous River Street fish market

Pacific Club – prestigious all-white male club for power elite; now more than half Asian

Pacific Commercial Advertiser – leading English newspaper published in Honolulu from 1885 to 1921 when renamed *Honolulu Advertiser*; still published today as *Honolulu Star-Advertiser*

Parker Ranch – huge ranch granted to John Palmer Parker by King Kamehameha about 1840 picture bride – early twentieth century practice of immigrants selecting brides from their native countries via a matchmaker, who paired bride and groom using only photographs and family recommendations of the possible candidates

Pink Palace – nickname for the Royal Hawaiian Hotel painted pink, opened February 1927

Queen's Hospital – downtown Honolulu's hospital founded by Queen Emma in 1859

Rapid Transport - streetcar company in Honolulu

Sandakan - British lumber port in Borneo

Sekigahara, Battle of - 1600 battle that established Tokugawa shogunate lasting until 1867

Shinto Kokkyo Shugi - Office of State Shintoism

Stimson Doctrine – American 1932 refusal to recognize Japan's seizure of Chinese territory

Spanish flu - 1918 influenza pandemic that killed fifty million to one hundred million

SS *Humuula* - Parker Ranch cattle boat

SS *Lisbon Maru* – Japanese transport ship

Sumitomo Daibutsu – Japanese trading company

Tale of Genji, The - Japan's first and most famous novel, written in the eleventh century

Todai University – the Harvard of Japan

Tokaido Road - eastern road linking Osaka to Tokyo

Tokaido-sen - railroad along the eastern sea in Japan

Tsushima Straits, Battle of - 1905 battle where Japan sank the Russian fleet between Kyushu and Korea

Waimea - small town at the foot of Mauna Kea; main entrance to the Parker Ranch

Washington Place – Hawaii's governor's mansion and office in Honolulu

Yakumo - Japanese naval ship that paid a courtesy call in Honolulu during sugarcane strike

Yamashiro Maru - passenger/cargo steamship

Yamate Bluffs – foreign housing area in Yokohama

Yasukuni Shrine – Shinto shrine built in 1869 to honor and host souls of war dead

Yomiuri Shimbun – The Reader's Newspaper, Japan's largest newspaper by circulation

Young Men's Buddhist Association (YMBA) – Buddhist version of YMCA

Zojoji Temple – Tokugawa Buddhist temple in Shiba, Tokyo

∞ About the Author ∞

Following a decades-long career as a businessman in Asia, Mike Malaghan turned his passion for history into writing. He and his wife, Tomoko, live in Hawaii. Their visits to all the locations featured in *Picture Bride* inspired some of the best scenes. He is now working on *A Question of Loyalty*, the sequel honoring the twenty-one Nisei Medal of Honor recipients.

Mike Malaghan welcomes your comments about *Picture Bride*. Please contact him at mgm@malaghan.net.

www.mikemalaghan.com